"The large cast is handled adroitly, the tension level is high, the big ideas make you think, and I was kept up all night!"

—S. M. Stirling

"Government cover-ups, ecoterrorism, nanotechnologies, blind obedience to mass destruction; what if it was all true? *Directive 51* reveals in vast fictional detail the terrifying possibility. John Barnes makes it conceivable with his knowledge of interior government strategies and terroristic mentality. He portrays relatable, unaware Americans, the deeply diminished mental thinking of terrorists, and our nation's current process for dealing with heightened government threats with political savvy.

"Barnes's ability to intricately weave a complex story line with multiple characters adds credence to the plausibility of something this devastating happening to our country and our government . . . He aptly plants the seed of doubt and allows the reader to become engrossed in this terrifying story."

—*Sacramento Book Review*

"Does indeed contemplate [the consequences of collapse or disruption], much as in the 1950s Nevil Shute imagined the world after nuclear war in *On the Beach*. Barnes's view of the collapse of financial life, the halt of most manufacturing systems, the evaporation of the technical knowledge that now exists mainly in the cloud, and other consequences is so alarming that the book could draw attention in a way no official report can."

—*The Atlantic*

"A fascinating near-future thriller that looks deep into what would happen if modern-day technology . . . suddenly stopped working and reverted back to the early nineteenth century . . . Fans will enjoy this cautionary tale that proclaims that sometimes you get what you wish for." —*Alternative Worlds*

continued . . .

"On one level, this novel can be read as a sort of end-of-the-world, apocalyptic story. On another level, it's very much a political thriller. The cast of characters is quite large, and the author managed to write a character-driven story fueled by Big Ideas . . . Following each set of characters gives the breakdown of technology and the effects on groups and individuals a real immediacy."
—*CA Reviews*

. . . AND FOR JOHN BARNES

"A master of the genre."
—Arthur C. Clarke

"Welcome this writer to the front ranks of contemporary science fiction."
—*The New York Times*

"John Barnes knows how to make readers care."
—*Los Angeles Reader*

"John Barnes carries us away."
—Orson Scott Card

"Barnes excels at combining the tension of the chase with the elements of science fiction."
—*Rocky Mountain News*

"One of Heinlein's spiritual descendants." —*Science Fiction Age*

"[Barnes's] characters both live and fascinate."
—Steven Brust

"Barnes is concerned with the grand struggle between individuality and the survival of society . . . A lesser writer would have cast the contest in pure black and white. Barnes—like Twain, like Heinlein—discerns much finer gradations of good and evil."
—Paul Di Filippo, *Asimov's Science Fiction*

"The very best writers are those who can think through a concept, work out a set of logical consequences, and wrap a briskly paced plot around the path from idea to fully developed execution. John Barnes is in that group."
—*Amazing Stories*

Ace Books by John Barnes

DIRECTIVE 51
DAYBREAK ZERO

DIRECTIVE 51

JOHN BARNES

ACE BOOKS, NEW YORK

THE BERKLEY PUBLISHING GROUP
Published by the Penguin Group
Penguin Group (USA) Inc.
375 Hudson Street, New York, New York 10014, USA
Penguin Group (Canada), 90 Eglinton Avenue East, Suite 700, Toronto, Ontario M4P 2Y3, Canada
(a division of Pearson Penguin Canada Inc.)
Penguin Books Ltd., 80 Strand, London WC2R 0RL, England
Penguin Group Ireland, 25 St. Stephen's Green, Dublin 2, Ireland (a division of Penguin Books Ltd.)
Penguin Group (Australia), 250 Camberwell Road, Camberwell, Victoria 3124, Australia
(a division of Pearson Australia Group Pty. Ltd.)
Penguin Books India Pvt. Ltd., 11 Community Centre, Panchsheel Park, New Delhi—110 017, India
Penguin Group (NZ), 67 Apollo Drive, Rosedale, North Shore 0632, New Zealand
(a division of Pearson New Zealand Ltd.)
Penguin Books (South Africa) (Pty.) Ltd., 24 Sturdee Avenue, Rosebank, Johannesburg 2196,
South Africa

Penguin Books Ltd., Registered Offices: 80 Strand, London WC2R 0RL, England

This is a work of fiction. Names, characters, places, and incidents either are the product of the author's imagination or are used fictitiously, and any resemblance to actual persons, living or dead, business establishments, events, or locales is entirely coincidental. The publisher does not have any control over and does not assume any responsibility for author or third-party websites or their content.

DIRECTIVE 51

An Ace Book / published by arrangement with the author

PRINTING HISTORY
Ace hardcover edition / April 2010
Ace mass-market edition / March 2011

Copyright © 2010 by John Barnes.
Cover art by Craig White.
Cover design by Judith Lagerman.
Interior text design by Laura K. Corless.

ISBN: 978-0-441-02041-6

ACE
Ace Books are published by The Berkley Publishing Group,
a division of Penguin Group (USA) Inc.,
375 Hudson Street, New York, New York 10014.
ACE and the "A" design are trademarks of Penguin Group (USA) Inc.

PRINTED IN THE UNITED STATES OF AMERICA

10 9 8 7 6 5 4 3 2 1

For Diane Talbot

PART 1

ONE DAY

DAYBREAK

All the days of the modern world begin at the International Date Line, in the middle of the Pacific. When it is midnight on the Date Line, the midnight that ended yesterday touches the midnight that begins tomorrow, and the whole world is in a single day.

October 28th was a date that would be known everywhere, forever; bigger than July 4th or 14th or 20th, bigger than December 7th or even 25th. As 12:00 A.M., October 28th, entered at the Date Line, nothing had happened yet, though many thousands of people, millions of machines, and billions of messages and ideas were already moving. When 11:59 P.M., October 28th, exited through the other side of the Date Line, the world had just tipped and begun to fall over into its new shape.

The Earth turned, rotating lands and seas in and out of shadow. October 28th was already old in northern New Guinea as it was just being born in Washington.

SENTANI INTERNATIONAL AIRPORT, NEAR JAYAPURA, PAPUA PROVINCE, INDONESIA. 6:20 P.M. LOCAL TIME. OCTOBER 28.

Across the bay, darkness rushed into Jayapura. Vice President John Samuelson sighed and tried not to see that as a metaphor. From the window of the unmarked 787, where he had lived for more than a week, Jayapura was a tumble of white and gray below the craggy green mountains still lit by the setting sun. Lights were flickering on; he liked that metaphor better.

He hadn't so much as dipped a toe in the bay, set a boot

on the hills, or shaken a hand in the town. Not that it would have been better if he had. Jayapura was maybe the size of Akron, Ohio, but as a provincial capital in a Muslim country, it was never going to be known for its night life. He had been there, once, thirty years ago, when he was demonstrating his backpack-to-anywhere skills to Kim, during the wildly romantic couple of years when he worked his way up to proposing to her.

To be here today, he'd sacrificed twelve days of campaigning in the last month before the election. Might as well just have taken Kim to the Caribbean for swimming and sun.

No one even knew he was here.

"Mr. Vice President?" Carol Tattinger, his State Department minder, said, "The communications techs say that if you have a message for the President, we should record and send now; once we're airborne, we're under radio silence."

The mission had been thrown together so suddenly that a replacement satellite uplink hadn't been available for this plane; they were stuck with tight-beam microwave to the American consulate across the bay. Typical, Samuelson thought: The budget for peace was just never there.

Samuelson stood up, his head almost touching the ceiling, and said, "All right, let me wash my face and put on a jacket and tie. I guess we'll have to do this."

Tattinger nodded; as he had so many times in the last few days, Samuelson watched her for any trace of sympathy or understanding, and saw none. With her hair in a tight bun, and her slightly large, beaky nose, she reminded Samuelson of a cartoon witch.

A few minutes later, he took his seat in front of the camera. "Roger, you and I have been friends a long time and I'm going to be blunt. The mission is a failure. I think that's ninety percent them, ten percent us. We've spent the past eight days in an impasse, and now we're at the deadline you set. I'd ask for more time but it wouldn't help.

"Per your orders, and monitored by your people from State, Defense, and Homeland Security, I have repeated our offer without modifications. They still have not responded."

Specifically, he thought, they had said neither yes nor no, but talked endlessly of general principles, mixed with hints about what might be possible.

He did try to keep the reproach out of his voice. "In my opinion, if *someone* could hold a more open-ended conversation with them, a deal might be within reach; but per your orders, I was only able to repeat our basic offer, and thus I can do absolutely nothing. Sorry, Roger, but I just don't have a deal for us. We'll be taking off in less than an hour, and I'll see you when we get in. Good night, Mr. President."

That was awfully brusque. He decided against re-recording. Unlike most presidents and vice presidents, they were friends, and had been friends long before they took their present jobs. If this message pissed Pendano off, well, Samuelson had always been able to get Rog's forgiveness. *Hell, give me a little more time, and probably* I'll *forgive* Rog.

Martin Reeve, the Defense liaison, looked in. "Sir, I thought I'd let you know I'm sending a message concurring with you. I think we just didn't have enough flex to have a dialog."

Samuelson made a face. "Thanks for the support. I don't suppose Tattinger agreed with you."

Reeve lowered his voice. "Everyone at State frets about whether they're firm enough. I wouldn't read anything personal into it, any more than I would into your following Pendano's orders, sir."

"I suppose not. Well, anyway, this was a lot of time in the plane I'd rather not have spent."

"I'll be happy to get off the Batplane myself, sir."

Samuelson felt childish pleasure in that nickname, which made him feel like one of the guys. The design of the 787, with so many curves, made it look sissy to military eyes, so it had a million nicknames like "the Batplane," "the Deco-Wrecko," and "the Melted Boomerang." Men's planes should look like darts or spears; grace was for girls.

Technically this Covert High Level Missions plane was Air Force Two, like any plane carrying the Vice President; the Boeing 787 Dreamliner that was usually Air Force Two was back in Washington, parked in plain sight. "You know," Samuelson said, "I never heard our cover story for this plane's being here at Sentani."

Reeve had no expression. "There's a rumor that this plane is carrying the mistress of the Sultan of Brunei, and those men who visit are setting up a deal to make her his heir."

"Well, no wonder you couldn't let me get off the plane. I'd look like shit in a wig and a dress."

Reeve grinned. "I'm glad you understand the necessity, sir."

"There's something else I still don't get." *Another full day before I can just talk to Kim—I wonder . . .* "Once we're in the air, we have long-range radio even though we don't have satellite uplink; wouldn't it still be encrypted?"

"Sure, but you don't need to be able to read the messages to use a direction finder to track the plane. And because this mission is covert and they kept the allies out of it, we don't have escort fighters till they can come out and meet us from Guam. Till then . . . well, till we have the escorts, shit could happen, sir, if you'll pardon the expression."

Samuelson smiled. "I'm acutely aware that shit can happen, Mr. Reeve."

Reeve grimaced. "Once we have escorts, chances are it'll be okay to call home if you need to."

"Understood." *Maybe I can talk to Kim in a couple hours. I'd sure feel better.*

Reeve looked over Samuelson's shoulder. "What's *that* about? We've already refueled and resupplied."

A panel van was pulling up alongside the plane; they could hear the pilot talking to the tower.

Over the intercom, the pilot said, "Sir, it's representatives from the opposite organization. They're requesting permission to come aboard; they say their principals are offering to give you much of what you've asked for."

Carol Tattinger and DeGrante, the usually silent man from Homeland Security, came in.

Samuelson said, "All right, instant input?"

Tattinger folded her arms across her chest and nodded. "When you negotiate with Middle Easterners, oftentimes they won't reach for what's on the table until you go to take it off. And doing it in the way that causes maximum hassle and inconvenience is very much in character. So this very well *could* be legit."

Reeve said, "It's up to you, sir."

Usually DeGrante would just nod or say "Concur," but this time he said, "I don't like it. When I was a bodyguard, anything that moved suddenly in my peripheral vision was bad.

That's what this feels like. Maybe it's just what Ms. Tattinger says, negotiating the way they do in their culture. But I want to say 'Don't.' "

"Noted," Samuelson said, "and thank you for your candor. I'll count that as a two-to-one vote unless you want to exercise your veto?"

"Not on just a hunch, sir. But since we couldn't do a pat-down at the gate, would you let me frisk them at the door?"

"Yeah. There should be *some* penalty for this dumb last-second stunt. Frisk them at the door, and be *thorough*, and *not* excessively gentle. If you piss them off, I'll square it up. Just let me change pants, and we'll get this thing going."

"I'll cue you when we're ready," Tattinger said. She and DeGrante went forward to talk to the pilot.

In his private compartment, Samuelson appreciated the last streaks of deep red sun over the rugged mountains to the west, then shuttered his windows; *mustn't have any maintenance workers catching a glimpse of the Second Most Important Boxer Shorts In The Free World.* Red sky at night, supposed to be a good omen.

He sighed happily as he stripped from his sneakers and jeans and pulled out slacks and wingtips. He felt it—this would work out.

Just like old times. As a mayor, John Samuelson had walked into a Crips and Bloods summit, armed with nothing but his confidence, and worn them down with round-the-clock talking and listening. As a governor, he'd hung on for five nearly sleepless days for a peaceful end to a prison hostage situation; just this June, he'd brokered a deal between UFCW and hotels to save the DNC.

Give Samuelson space to improvise, and you got a deal. This time—

Bang.

Sharp, flat, loud.

Two more bangs. Shouting. A cascade of bangs, thumps, screams—

Not bangs. Shots.

Samuelson froze, his fresh pants draped over his hand.

The door broke inward at him.

Man with a sledgehammer.

Two men beside him. Not Samuelson's people. Not the

other side's negotiators. They pointed guns at him. For a stupefied instant, he thought of asking them to let him finish dressing.

One of them lunged, throwing something over Samuelson's head. They pinned his arms behind him, punched him, kicked him, and grabbed his genitals and twisted. He puked.

His screams made no difference. Even with his head in a vomit-soaked coffee sack, sobbing for breath, he still understood the implications when he felt the big jet begin to move.

ABOUT THE SAME TIME. JAYAPURA, INDONESIA. 6:30 P.M. MONDAY, OCTOBER 28.

Armand Cooper was reflecting that if people actually make their own luck, he would give himself about a B- for what he was making. *That* was something to taste with an icy rum and Coke from his personal fridge in his office; as the American consul in Jayapura, he was the highest ranking, as well as the only, State Department official stationed here. And anyway it was out of regular hours—Abang and the other Indonesian clerks were never in here.

In a smallish city in the backwoods of one of the biggest Muslim countries in the world, you really appreciate your liquor. And your ice.

He'd had the tight-beam microwave antenna up, synched in, and checked out for an hour; he liked to be ready early for everything. One of those areas where making your own luck gets you an A.

Pointing the soles of the feet toward anyone was disrespectful, even through a third-floor window, so when he dragged his office chair around to give him a view of the street, he carefully placed the hassock to hide his feet from view. *Good thing they can't see what's in my glass, the old hands say it wasn't always this way, but this country has gotten pretty tight about everything.*

Pluses, he thought, and savored the rum on his tongue: one of the youngest consuls in the Foreign Service. Especially hard when the younger ranks are so dominated nowadays by Asian-Americans; an African-American male rising so fast, well, hell that it's a cliché, I sure did give Moms some bragging material.

Minuses, boondocky town in a Muslim country, near the equator.

Pluses, nothing to do except try to keep American tourists and businessmen out of trouble, or rescue them from it, and this far into the back of beyond, most of the people who get here are pretty savvy.

Minuses, social life consists of the Australian consul (nice old guy who likes to play chess), French consul (middle-aged lesbian couple), and the aging drunk that runs the Amex office downstairs.

More minuses, ever since they expanded the consular corps so much, consulates aren't the dignified old Gothic or Victorian fortresses they used to be—*I'm in an office over a bank, and security is the bank guard downstairs.*

Come to think of it, the crowd outside—streets in Jayapura were crowded except during prayer—looked kind of odd, like they were waiting for something; maybe a popular preacher or an outdoor concert in the park nearby? All right, *bigger* minus, as hard as I work at it, I never really feel like I know what's going on.

Biggest minus, being in charge this early in the career meant being in charge of something so small he had to be here all by himself after hours. He tasted the sourness and bite of his drink before he laughed at himself.

Armand, you are going to whine yourself to death someday, his mother had said to him, more than once, and his father had called him Mr. Glass Half Empty. And now not only was he grumbling about being in a tropical paradise with virtually no supervision, he was also on the fast track for promotion, he'd been doing well here, and the simple, easy task he had to do was part of a vital mission at the highest security level; all he had to do was not screw up and there was a great big plum of cred on his resumé.

He swirled the rum and Coke to make sure the ice was doing its job, and swallowed the rest. Maybe his next post—

His cell buzzed in his pocket. "Cooper, US Consul."

"Cooper, it's Seagull. Routine op in ten seconds, are you ready?"

He glanced at the computer screen, which said his antenna was aligned. "Ready . . . send the test . . ."

"Sending."

The screen said **confirmed clear.**

"Good here."

"And good here. Sending one main message."

The screen said **msg rec'd 48 mgb, relaying.**

"Just the one this time?" Cooper asked.

"Just the one."

Successful relay, wiping msg.

"Relayed and erased," he said.

"That's it for tonight. Unofficially, thanks for everything and bye."

"Bye."

So they were leaving. He'd thought they would be, soon; he'd been fielding more and more odd requests from the big white plane that he could just see through binoculars, across the bay at Sentani airport.

Well, time to bag it and head home. He might give himself a few days off sometime soon, maybe hop over to Oz or Tahiti for some nightlife and just to feel like nobody was watching his ass all the time. He rinsed his glass thoroughly—wouldn't do to have it smelling of liquor when the Indonesian help came in—and locked the fridge after making sure he had returned everything to it. He started the sequence that would do a secure memory wipe on the satellite uplink server's disk, and did some straightening up and putting away while he waited for it to finish.

The crowd outside was shouting and chanting; his Bahasa wasn't terribly good and rumbling AC and armored windows made it hard to hear, so he went to the window.

The first brick bounced off right in front of his face, and he ducked away and crouched as a dozen more thudded against the window. *Thought I heard "America" in that chant. And the uplink will be down for another five while it finishes—*

Slams and scraping noises overhead. Ropes passing by the windows, flying up or spiraling down. Then a groaning and creaking overhead, a loud bang as bolts gave, and he saw the satellite uplink antenna plunge past the window to the ground. *Make that the uplink is* down.

Cooper crawled to the opposite wall, where the light switch

was, but before he quite reached it, the power went out. He made sure his door was locked, sat up behind his heavy desk, and dialed the emergency desks at the Embassy in Jakarta, the Consular Service in Washington, and the local police department, leaving voice mail each time. Probably the person on duty at State was in the bathroom, the one in Jakarta was napping, and as for the local police, they might be out there with the mob or gone fishing for the month.

He was glad he had a prerecorded native-speaker message on the phone, and gladder still he'd made Abang stop giggling and record it perfectly straight. Minuses, he thought, I'm in a place where a prepared guy like me has LOCAL POLICE FOR VIOLENT MOB in his prerecorded speed phone list. Double minuses, voice mail all around.

He called Seagull to let them know there was trouble in the city; no voice mail picked up while he let the phone ring fifty times after he started counting. The stones and bricks had stopped after that first flurry, but so far three shots had caromed off the armored glass and screamed off into the dark.

ABOUT HALF AN HOUR LATER. 151°6'E 11°23'N; ABOUT 450 NAUTICAL MILES EAST-SOUTHEAST OF GUAM, IN THE PACIFIC. THE NEAREST LAND IS GUAM. 9:10 P.M. GUAM TIME (8:10 P.M. JAYAPURA, 6:10 A.M. EST). MONDAY, OCTOBER 28.

Seagull Watchdog One, the flight of three F-35s, arrived on the dot—literally, because the rendezvous point, 151°6'E 11°23'N, was just a dot on the map of the Pacific. The nearest land was Guam, which they had left about forty-five minutes ago, taking off from Andersen AFB. As agreed, they fanned out in the Touch Hands formation, a slowly rotating equilateral triangle in which each plane was at its highest cruising altitude and just close enough to the others to put them three degrees above the horizon. In Touch Hands, they maximized their chances of detecting the white, unmarked Dreamliner that they had been told was designated Seagull; the mission itself was SCI, Sensitive Compartmented Information, a designation above Top Secret.

The F-35, after a rocky start, had been thoroughly shaken

down and its bugs worked out once and for all during the Second Iranian War. Its electronics suite had been redesigned and refined by the ten years of anti-terror patrol since the suicide attack on the carrier *Franklin Roosevelt*. The same routine anti-terror, anti-drug, and border patrols had trained the Air Force pilots to execute Touch Hands flawlessly. If the Dreamliner named Seagull was coming to its rendezvous at 151°6'E 11°23'N, Seagull Watchdog One would find it; the dark was no barrier. A typhoon would have been no more than a nuisance, but the sea was calm tonight.

With their large drop tanks, Seagull Watchdog One could circle the rendezvous point in Touch Hands for more than an hour and still have plenty of fuel to complete the escort mission before turning the Dreamliner over to fresh escorts out of Hawaii.

They had been warned that the Dreamliner might be as much as twenty minutes late; unofficially, the flight leader had been told they were coming out of some bush-league Third World airport to the south and west, the kind of place where delays were routine and anything could happen. When they picked up a plane on radar, they were to hail it via secure transponder code; once they had positive ID, they would close in to fly a protective formation around the Dreamliner. Until contact, or unless there were problems, they were to minimize radio contact with the controllers back at Andersen.

At twenty minutes after arrival, the flight leader radioed in that there had been no trace, and called for a radar and satellite confirmation that they were in the right place. They were. Twenty minutes later he requested and received permission to try to raise the transponder buoy that Seagull would have released if it had gone down. There was nothing. At about 10:35 P.M., with safety margins for completing the mission running thin, they were relieved by another flight, Seagull Watchdog Two, and headed back to base.

They went in for immediate debriefing by more high-ranking officers than any of them had ever seen in the same room, but they had nothing to report except that they had flown out to the rendezvous point, waited, and encountered nothing.

"Was there anything that *could* have been a trace of Air Force Two?" a man in a civilian suit asked, and only then did they know what their mission had been and what was lost.

ABOUT THE SAME TIME. WASHINGTON, DC. 6:54 A.M. EST. MONDAY, OCTOBER 28.

In Washington, DC, wherever great hordes of Federal workers pour in and out of big, blocky office buildings all day long, there are more small coffee shops, cafés, and grills per block than in any artists' quarter or bohemian enclave anywhere. They are nearly as essential to government operations as the Pentagon, the White House, or the Executive Office Building.

People in private industry hold meetings to coordinate what people are doing, decide issues in which several people have a say, and gratify some boss's ego, not necessarily in that order. Only the third purpose is the same in Washington.

Decades of sunshine laws and open-government policies guarantee that anything discussed at any official meeting is eventually going to be public, so the most important rule for any meeting is to have nothing said that might ever attract any attention. Rather than coordinating or deciding, *official* government meetings ratify pre-made decisions and avoid ever saying anything unexpected.

To achieve such perfect official meetings, there has to be a "meeting before the meeting," where the people involved caucus about what is going to be said. Disclosure laws and media scrutiny force any bureaucrats who need to think freely to do it in a place and time that is not official in any way—and thus those coffee shops and hole-in-the-wall cafés are vital.

Heather O'Grainne knew all that as well as birds know breezes; as she rounded the corner, finishing her morning run around the Capitol area, it compressed to *time for the meeting that can't be a meeting.* This year marked a milestone: At age thirty-nine, she had now been a desk bureaucrat for eight years, one more than she had been an active Fed cop in her younger days. It tasted sour that she knew these bureaucratic games better, now, than she knew current procedure for arresting a suspect or obtaining a warrant.

This was bound to be a big, messy, uncomfortable meeting-before-the-meeting. As Chief of Staff, Allison Sok Banh was one of the few people in the Department of the Future who could make Heather jump on command. She had "invited" Heather to an "early breakfast" to "talk things over" at the Angkor Coffee Shop, which happened to be owned by Allie's Uncle Sam, and had a convenient back eating area that wasn't open during the mornings. Translated from bureaucratese, Allie had summoned Heather to an urgent emergency meeting, and whatever was up, Allie *really* didn't want it to leak.

Sam, in his seventies, stooped, face deeply lined, had to be a foot and a half shorter than Heather's six feet. He greeted her with a bow and a grin. "You're here to assess my cooking?"

"Only if it's a threat." It was their inside joke, ever since Allie had explained that Heather headed up the Office of Future Threat Assessment.

"Allison is already here, in back. Your usual order?"

"Yes, Sam, thanks."

The food here is so good I even eat here when we're not skulking around on some piece of intrigue and politics, Heather thought. *I guess that enhances the cover for days like today.* The thought seemed slightly paranoid, but *Remember, paranoia is one of the leading signs of having secret, all-powerful enemies.*

She found Allie at the sunny table by the window; the curtains were drawn. Arnie Yang was with her, and that was more bad news. First of all, Arnie was *Heather's* senior analyst in OFTA's communications-monitoring program, and Heather should have been the one to bring him if he were needed. But coincidentally, he was also Allie's boyfriend, *and maybe her spy.* And worse yet, his area of investigation was the last thing Heather wanted to talk about.

Allie and Arnie were eating already. Heather had barely sat down when Sam served her a Cambodian Breakfast Number One—chili-flavored pork, rice, and pickles, plus a big mug of chicory coffee with condensed milk. He vanished, carefully closing the door before Heather quite finished saying "Thank you," and in the outer, public room, the music was abruptly much louder.

Heather relished her first swallow of the sweet, thick coffee. "You're gonna make me fat with these meetings here."

Arnie smirked. "I know you're mostly muscle, boss. Bet your dad had to buy a tractor when you left the potato farm."

"Do they farm potatoes with tractors? I'm an LA city chickie." She sipped again at the rich brown coffee and then dug into the pork and rice; once Allie started into business,

Heather knew from past experience, there wouldn't be much time to eat.

When they had all finished wolfing down the food, Allie put her iScribe on the table.

"You're *recording* this?" Heather said, shocked.

"Thought I'd better. CYA for all of us."

"So, as soon as I saw you here, Arnie, I knew it had to be about Daybreak."

"Heather," Arnie said, "I haven't said one word to Allie about—"

"You don't have a leak in your organization," Allie said, smoothly, heading off accusations and arguments. "But we do need to do something, soon. This comes down from Secretary Weisbrod, Heather, he says we've *got* to crack this open and let everyone else into the playpen."

"Damn," Heather said. *Hunh, Secretary Weisbrod, not "Graham," like Allie and I always call him. A little reminder that he's the boss. Better give up before I get stomped.* "I just hadn't wanted to share it around the department because it sounds so crazy—"

"Too crazy for DoF? That's *got* to be crazy."

Heather returned the lopsided smile. The Department of the Future had a rep for madness; it had come into existence because Roger Pendano, who was about to be re-elected president, had once been a student of Graham Weisbrod, and some people—Heather and Allie were two—just never recovered from that experience, remaining "Weisbrodites" for decades no matter what else they did. As America's most public futurologist, Weisbrod had made his slogan, *We can't afford just any old future*, the title of a best-selling book, and now national policy.

DoF was the smallest, newest, and least significant department, but with Weisbrod at the helm, the Department of the Future had bombarded the public, the media, the Congress, and every government department with an endless stream of reports, studies, and scenarios. When a columnist at NYT-Blog described them as "useful, sometimes necessary, lunatics," Weisbrod threatened to make that the Department motto.

"Yeah, I think it's crazy even for us," Heather said.

Allie said, "You've been stalling on reporting this out of

your office for months, Heather. Are you just afraid you'll sound like Chicken Little?"

"Kind of. Look, every time I've ever made the news, it was because something blew up or went south. Daybreak might be nothing, and then I'll look like a fool. It's sort of like an asteroid strike; so highly unlikely that it seems irresponsible to waste time talking about it, but . . . but it could be so serious that . . . has Arnie told you anything?"

"Nothing," Arnie said, flatly, obviously annoyed. "I said that already. I don't game you behind your back, boss."

Heather looked into his eyes and nodded; his lips tensed, barely acknowledging that they understood each other.

Allie had been watching them as if she expected one of them to pull a knife. "It's not a security breach, Heather," she said. "As far as we can know, Daybreak is still dark, tight, and close in your office. It's just that you've been watching this for months, it hasn't gone away, it keeps getting scarier, and it's time to involve the rest of the government, that's all. I haven't gotten a word out of Arnie on the subject."

If there's a subject you can't get a word out of Arnie about, Heather thought, *that would be a first.* But she said, "Well, maybe he *should* give you some words. It's been his research baby."

Allie said, "However you want to do it. But the Secretary wants us to roll this out, first to the other branches of the Department of the Future, then immediately to other Federal agencies. He's assuming full responsibility if it turns out we're crying wolf. Now, lay it out. In two hours we're meeting with Browder and Crittenden—"

"Christ, Allie, they'll tear us apart!"

"Not with me sitting in the room and Graham nodding along with you—and especially not if you practice first. Now tell me about Daybreak, just as if I didn't know anything at all. What it is and why it's important. And then after we rehearse you, we rehearse Arnie, because when you bring him in, your two asshat colleagues will be ten times as hard on him."

Heather drew a deep breath and began an impromptu revision of the speech she'd been making to her bathroom mirror three or four times a day for many weeks:

"Daybreak looks sort of like the formation of an international terrorist movement, sort of like a philosophic discussion, sort of like an artists' movement, sort of like a college fad, and sort of like a shared-world online game. It's a complex of closely related ideas that strongly attract maybe five million people worldwide, with a hard core of about a hundred thousand, of which maybe thirty thousand are in this country. Daybreak people identify with Daybreak the way communists identify with the Revolution, funjadelicals identify with the Rapture, or technogeeks identify with the Singularity. But Daybreak seems to involve many thousands of people doing widespread sabotage and wrecking all at once—it could change overnight to self-organizing, spontaneous, widespread terrorism, maybe."

She could see Allie was trying not to make it a reprimand. "That's supposed to be your office's job—to look for long-range implausible threats and *alert other Federal*—"

"But DoF has been burned so often about—"

"OFTA's job is to cry wolf," Allie said, very firmly. "Whenever you think you might see one. It's in the hands of others to see whether there's a real wolf or not. So is *that* the wolf? Thirty thousand Americans might start wrecking stuff at random?"

Heather glanced at Arnie Yang and said, "Okay, giving you fair coverage, you've been saying for a month that it's time to tell her how bad it could be."

To her surprise, Arnie was nodding, not popping up with some version of *Told you so* or *Well, duh*. He said to Allie, "Maybe I just have contagious paranoia. That's what Heather's really worried about, that it sounds like such a scary wolf that everyone will go berserk about it. But the thing is, the bottleneck for being able to assess it accurately is cryptography. We're reading their coded traffic, but we're reading it three to five weeks late, because that's as much as Lenny Plekhanov is able to do for us."

"Who's Lenny Plekhanov? Other than the nice guy in the wheelchair that Heather goes out with now and then, I mean?" Now that it was clear Allie was going to get everything she wanted, without a fight, she was back to her sweet, pleasant, teasing self.

Heather flushed slightly and said, "Well, that's the main way you've met him, I know. But we met because over at No

Such Agency, there's an amateur crypto section—ever since secrecy collapsed, computers became so cheap, and the economy produced a mathematician surplus, it's been pretty cheap and easy for anybody—drug gangs, animal liberators, little political outfits, computer-crime outfits, *anybody*—to create codes as hard to break as only governments used to be able to do. So any Fed agency with an amateur-crypto problem goes to Lenny, and he gets them whatever analysts he can. It's not timely or efficient, but we don't have the resources—"

"Then you are going to go into that meeting, say 'thirty thousand saboteurs could attack any minute,' and I'll find you the resources, Heather." Allie didn't sound as happy. "Arnie, how fast could you be up to date with a dedicated crypto operation?"

"Almost overnight."

Allie looked at both of them. "You know I adore you both, and there's no one I value more around DoF, aside from the personal side of things. But this is dumb, guys. Now tell me how you're going to flatten Browder and Crittenden."

Heather hated these moments with Allie; never a second to think of what you were going to do. But before she could start to stammer and temporize, Arnie handed Heather a pill drive, and said, "She's going to use this, and then I'll come in and be the brilliant explainer if they still have questions."

"What is it?" Heather asked.

"I've scripted a slideshow on the subject—suitable for presentation by you, and with some stuff that ought to shut Browder and Crittenden up—and it's only a few minutes long. Plenty of time between now and the morning meeting to go over it and rehearse. And no, I didn't show it to Allie first."

"Thank you. Great idea." Heather's relief was tempered by her realization that Arnie was, "Managing your boss, Doctor Yang?"

"Somebody has to," he pointed out.

Heather really didn't like the way Allie nodded at that.

**ABOUT THE SAME TIME. GILLETTE, WYOMING.
5:12 A.M. MST. MONDAY, OCTOBER 28.**

DarwinsActor reminded Zach of the jackass science students back in college, but he still had to listen to the weird little turd of a man explain how they were going to break into the holding bin at the Gillette Municipal Plastics Recycling Facility.

They'd already been over it a few dozen times; this particular Daybreak AG should probably have called itself Team Obsessive Compulsive. *Especially me,* Zach added to himself. *Thank you, Jesus, for letting me see the beam in my own eye, even if it makes me struggle with seeing the mote in his.*

DarwinsActor had a hooked nose, one of those vague East Coast accents, a slim, too-hairy little body that made you think maybe *he* was evolved from a monkey, anyway, and a dab hand at genetically modifying bacteria. He wore an old military-style coat over a torn sweater, a paint-spattered black watch cap, and ripped jeans; all six men in the AG were in bum outfits, sitting in the dark interior of the RV in the freezing predawn of Wyoming October.

Bugs—the other biologist in the team—finally said, "Dar, it's time, and we all know our parts. Let's just do it."

Zach disliked Bugs much less than he disliked DarwinsActor, even though both of them were always trying to put in all that unnecessary evolution crap about how their part of Daybreak would work. DarwinsActor himself had said that they had targeted this facility exactly because it was so badly run that it was practically *designed* for Daybreak; somehow that never made those bioweenies like DarwinsActor and Bugs realize there had to be an Operator for the universe, too—one Who had designed it for what needed to be done. It was funny how these science guys never thought of anything important; that would need fixing, some day.

But not right now, Zach reminded himself sternly. *That's the beauty of Daybreak. First Daybreak, then everything else.*

Zach cleared his throat. "Bugs is right, let's just get it done."

ChemEWalker said, "I'm with Bugs and WalksWDLord. That's a majority. No more talk. Let's go now."

Took me a moment to remember WalksWDLord is me, Zach thought. *I've only seen it typed, mostly.*

The six men slipped out of the RV. It made Zach nervous to carry his end of a big plastic tub filled with two-liter pop bottles of black powder. He and ChemEWalker were carrying the first tub; as a precaution, the others gave them a hundred-yard head start. Zach didn't like thinking about what it was a precaution against. He had plenty of faith in the little microprocessor/RC detonators buried in the black powder in each bottle because he'd built them himself, but he was edgy about the stability of the black powder, even though ChemEWalker was a chemical engineer and a fellow Stewardship Christian.

Lord, help me trust my fellow workers in this great endeavor. Lord, also, steady our hands, and don't let us trip.

Bugs had said black-powder explosions were cool enough and low pressure enough not to hurt the biotes on their way to their destiny. *We all have to trust each other,* Zach reminded himself. *No AG works without that. No doubt they're all worried about the radio detonators because WalksWDLord is a crazy Christian.*

They stayed on the smooth concrete path; SirWalksALot had scouted it in daylight, and they knew there were no stairs and usually no obstructions. The operator here was too cheap to hire a guard, relying on the distance from town to keep the bums out of the recyclables.

At the holding bin, Zach and ChemEWalker gently set down their tubs in the deep shadow. Surrounded by a chest-high chain-link fence, the concrete tub, the size of a semi trailer, yawned empty; tomorrow it would receive a fresh load of plastic from the city, filling it almost to the top.

The two Christians bowed their heads and held hands. "Lord Jesus," Zach prayed, "let this be the first step in cleansing Your Earth. Bring off Daybreak and bring us a world fit for our children to grow up in. Let what we do be done according to Your will. Amen."

ChemEWalker echoed, "Amen."

Zach pulled out his bolt cutters, took the lock neatly off the chain-link gate, opened it, and descended the short iron ladder into the bin. ChemEWalker began handing him down the two-liter bombs, and Zach placed them using an equilateral triangle of PVC pipe twenty centimeters on a side, to space them roughly an equal distance apart. When he had placed about twenty, the others returned, and after that, the swift, silent work, in all but total darkness except for the pinprick stars above the bin, went very swiftly.

It was still night-dark when Zach, GreenCop, and Sir-WalksALot climbed out of the concrete pit, whose bottom was now covered with evenly spaced bombs. DarwinsActor handed him the laptop, and Zach logged into his secret account, clicked a couple of buttons, and said, "The weather stations are all reporting; the bottles are all reporting; they've confirmed messages between each other. We're good to go. Arming now."

He realized all six men were holding their breath, and he wanted to grumble that he had trusted the biologists to make the organisms, ChemEWalker to make the black powder, and everyone else to carry the tubs and not drop them. But he supposed they were entitled to nervousness too.

The list scrolled by. "They're all armed and talking to each other. Let's go."

He started the computer's hard drive reformatting on the laptop as they walked back, and left it under the front tire of the RV; when they pulled out, the brief, grinding crushing sound under the tire meant that nobody, ever, could retrieve the codes to disarm the system. "The sweet crunch of commitment," DarwinsActor said, and for once, Zach didn't find him irritating at all. *Thank you, Lord,* he thought, and almost jumped at the coincidence when Bugs said, "Amen."

ABOUT THE SAME TIME. JAYAPURA, PAPUA PROVINCE, INDONESIA. 9:25 P.M. MONDAY, OCTOBER 28.

The local police called back in about two hours, and Armand Cooper thought that had to be a good sign; if they were in on the riot or had instigated it, they'd have pretended he'd never called them. "We would like you to stay down very low behind furniture," the police captain said; his English was excellent, with a mild Delhi accent. "We are going to try to put a perimeter between your building and the crowd. We do not think they are serious because, you know, if they were, they would have broken down your door by now, but accidents can happen with such a crowd, you know, and we'd like to make sure it doesn't."

"I agree completely," Cooper said.

The captain laughed. "Good, you are in good spirits. Have you been hurt?"

"No."

"And you can reach food and water, without showing your-self through the window? We need to make sure you have no snipers before you stand up."

"It's dark in here, and shots have been bouncing off the windows," he said. "I can chance it if there's a reason, but I don't think there's much of one yet."

"Well, the infrared scopes are cheap and standard now, and a shot upward from a handgun in the street might bounce off, but I would not want to bet the same thing would happen if it were to be a high-powered rifle coming straight through the glass."

"I'll trust your expertise."

Another laugh. "Stay low. Wait for us. Don't get hurt. We'll be there soon. And sometime you and I will have lunch and talk about all this and laugh very much."

"I'll enjoy that."

After they rang off, Cooper stretched and smiled. Police service this good could only mean one thing—the captain needed some favor an American consul could do. Maybe a visa to spend a year visiting a sister in LA, maybe a cousin in immigration trouble in New York, it didn't matter much. Cooper's father had been on the Board of Public Works in Terre Haute, and he'd often thought that was great preparation for the way things got done in Jayapura. *Whatever he wants, he's getting it.*

Shortly, there were a few shots and some angry shouting, followed by some general uproar. Cooper crept over to the window and peeked through, looking down, and saw the cops with their helmets, batons, and shields shoving the crowd back. It was noisy but halfhearted somehow, the mark of a mostly-paid mob. *Hunh. More projects for the next week. Find out who paid them and why. Yes indeed, that captain is getting whatever he wants.*

ABOUT THE SAME TIME. EAGLE, COLORADO. 5:30 A.M. MST. MONDAY, OCTOBER 28.

Jason had slept well when he hadn't expected to, and that made him hate Super 8 even more. Last night he had expected to be awake all night: too soft a bed, sheets that smelled totally chemical, no sound of wildlife, the couple in the next room watching TV and quarreling. No friendly snores from his buds. No Beth cuddled against him. But here he was, well-rested, seduced by comfort.

He opened the curtains on the big west-facing window, sat cross-legged on the bed, breathed, and meditated. Across the dark parking lot . . . why should there be so many cars? So many ripping-outs of the guts of the mother. So many people who didn't *need* to go *any*where going *every*where. So many scars on the planet. His gaze rose steadily upward from the rows of shiny metal and plastic earth-trashers to the dark mountains against the just-lightening sky.

Dawn among the bones of the Earth, he thought, then tried:

Truth comes at dawn.

No, too Hemingway.

Creation begins in my inner unfogged eyes.

Oh, yeah, needed to remember that. *Might be my first line.* No! *Whoa*—prewriting the poem; monkey mind. He watched the slow forming of the light in the air and on the stone and pines, and let it be in his mind, without words.

You had it right there, the statement of everything:

the mountains and the parking lot.

Title, or first line? Let it be whichever it would be. Let it be like the Earth, let it be, just accept. He breathed it all in pairs,

mountains and parking lot,
trees and cars,
plastic and wood,
metal and stone
free elk and cheap plaztatic doublewides
beautiful bears and ugly wires
brave mountain goats and chickenshit tourists in buses
asshole sales directors like my dumb-ass father—

No. Corny, personal, not dichotomous. Besides, Dad sometimes googled Jason, read his poetry, and wrote annoying little notes about how talented he thought Jason was and how happy he was that Jason was keeping up with his writing.

Like I need support from an asshole sales director.

Damn monkey mind.

Shut up, brain, or I'll stab you with a Q-tip. Not original, joking with himself. Congratulating himself on the jokes. *Damn monkey. Damn monkey.*

Supposedly you could eliminate monkey mind by paying it some extra attention, rewarding it even; *ook ook ook, anybody want a banana with barbiturate?*

His felt his mind dash about, demanding his attention, until once again, as lightly as a soap bubble, it rested in the V of indigo between the black mountains, balancing the seductive warmth of the hotel room and the humanity and spirit of the cold hillsides. The crystal of a first line—insistent, an elegant angel of truth, banishing the monkey—started to form in his mind.

Carefully, watching the stacked cardboard boxes in the corner as if they could leap out and attack, he pulled his laptop from his pack. It was in a double Ziploc with a scattering of Drano crystals in the bottom. He held the bag up to the light; the crystals were all still well formed, and the litmus paper was reassuringly blue.

He plugged his laptop in and set it on the little fakewood circular table facing the big window. He breathed reverently and slowly. The disk zummed to life. Software booted up, offered him menus, connected to the wi-fi, faithfully went about its work.

"I'm going to pull kind of a dirty trick on you," he whispered to his laptop, "but it's for a good cause and it has to be done. Just the same, I know I'll miss you, little buddy."

Silent mighty strength of the eternal mountains.

Little town of Eagle—little settlement, really, use a colonialist word for a colonialist thing, or pocket of people, nothing you could dignify with a grand word like *village*.

Pointless neon. Vulgar little fakey business fronts. People who ate too much and thought too little.

The blank document was ready. He spoke softly into the microphone, let himself flow into his words, his singing glorious words against the Big System, full of love for all the beautiful good in the world and rage for the fat bastards keeping all the good and gentle people away from it.

When he finished, he read through it twice, treasuring the way it fit so neatly into the sunlight now caressing the tips of the mountains. "Command, post document, anon poet channel," he said. The screen glowed back with **posted**. Through Super 8's wi-fi, words of magic and power found their way from him to the mighty stream of Daybreak.

He pulled on heavy-duty gloves, dampened a rag with Liquid-Plumr, and wiped all over the laptop and the table around it. Then he blasted through all the laptop's ports with a can of compressed air and wiped its surfaces again. The rag went into a plastic bread bag, which he dropped in the wastebasket. Each glove went back into its own Ziploc; he'd be needing them all day, so he put them in his "dirty" bag—an old laptop case—with his Drano, Liquid-Plumr, pliers, screwdrivers, and tubes of glue.

He wiped his computer with distilled water, then propped up the laptop to dry. He dipped the ends of the power cord into some Liquid-Plumr in a cup, rinsed them in the sink, dried them with toilet paper, and stowed the power cord in a plastic bread bag with more Drano crystals. By then the laptop was dry enough to go into its special home among the Drano crystals in the Ziploc.

With everything he was keeping closed up tight in the pack, he took it down to set it into a closed plastic trash can in the passenger seat's foot well. He pulled out his Drano, Liquid-Plumr, duct tape, and protective gloves, set them on the passenger seat, and sealed on the can's lid with duct tape.

Wearing the gloves, he hauled down his boxes of egg cartons. His clothes from the day before, and the contents of all the wastebaskets, went into a garbage bag, which he discreetly emptied into the open bed of an old pickup in the parking lot, adding it to the heap of construction junk, rusty tools, and old pop cans. He turned the bag inside out and left it blowing around in the parking lot.

After checkout, he plunged right into the Big System's comfort trap, just this once: the free Continental breakfast of plaztatic corporate bagels, probably-made-from-petroleum cream cheese, grease-and-sugar doughnuts, and the inexcusably transported, chilled, and probably-crawling-with-pesticides orange juice, and plenty of corporate coffee. *What the hell, it came with the room.*

All around him were loser biz guys: goopy bags of lard and fascism, empty heads poking out above neckties, men like his dad and brother, eyes dead and shoulders drooping, stuffing in plaztatic petroleum pastry, engrossed in little grunty conversations over their *USA Today*s, about Game Seven of the World Series, about the upcoming election, about ten billion reasons to rape the mountains and scar the land.

Daybreak begins today.

Wake-up call for all the fat bastards of the world.

He got on the road half an hour late, but what the hell, it was a freedom mission, and there might as well be a little freedom in it. The old truck had a stereo thing that Elton had set up, along with a special flash drive just for this trip, one to be left somewhere and picked up by some poor stupid fuck when Jason was done. The flash held hours of awesome coustajam and ambvo, to keep Jason feeling good all day, and if it died, that would warn him that the nanospawn was beginning to eat into the truck itself.

He had another poetic flash; that little flash drive was like the canary in the coal mine. You could enjoy the music, but its real purpose was to let him know what was really going on, by when it died. "Silicon Canary"—definitely a poem title. Maybe a band name—some of the coustajam bands were pretty aware, maybe one of them should call itself that.

The mountains in the early-morning light were glorious. The truck's heater worked well enough to keep him warm in the crisp morning, Marty Beelman's amazing "Mount Elbert Jam"—Aaron Copland beatjected onto acoustic guitar and spirit drums—boomed from the speakers, and the sky was that deep blue that he was sure they did not have anywhere else in the world anymore. *But you will,* he thought. *You will.*

ABOUT THE SAME TIME. OVER THE WESTERN PACIFIC, JUST NORTH OF THE EQUATOR, ABOUT 650 KILOMETERS SOUTH OF THE ISLAND OF KUSAIE. JUST PAST THE MIDNIGHT TERMINATOR, SO IT IS 12:40 A.M. LOCAL TIME. TUESDAY, OCTOBER 29.

They had taken the bag off Samuelson's head and roughly scrubbed him with a wet towel, so he only stank slightly of vomit; he was in a T-shirt and a pair of underwear, tied by the ankles to his bed in the private cabin, sitting upright.

After an interminable time, the door opened. Two of the

young men came in. They dragged in a man in a suit; Samuelson recognized Taylor, one of the Secret Service special agents, more by his build than by his bruised and battered face.

"This man can do you no harm," Samuelson said. "Let me clean him up. We cannot escape, and—"

One of the men backhanded him across his face. Then they turned to Taylor; he was breathing but seemed unconscious. One of the men drew a box cutter and slit the Secret Service man's throat, an arc of arterial blood spraying onto the walls of the compartment, staining the American flag and the pictures of past presidents.

Samuelson could do nothing but watch the man die, *and at that, he's probably lucky.* Yet he had to ask. "Why? Why did you do this?"

He had not expected an answer, but in perfect, almost-accentless English, the leader of the group said, "Because we can, and because we want you to know we can."

They left Samuelson with the corpse, propped up so that he seemed to be looking at Samuelson from the depths of sleep or stupor. The vice president thought about looking away, curling up, doing something not to see, but he would still smell the blood no matter what, he would still know the broken body was there; he preferred to know with his eyes open.

Silently, he thought to Taylor, *I'm sorry you were here for this. I'll try to find something I can do, however petty or invisible, for you and me and the country.*

He remembered that Taylor's wife was named Beth, that they had one child, a boy that Taylor thought the world of. Taylor's first name had been Charles and he'd endured teasing from the other Secret Service special agents about being named after a shoe. He'd been a quiet type who spent his breaks reading, and had always preferred to go home late in the afternoon when he could enjoy his family.

I remember you. That's about all I can do right now.

Now that he was used to Taylor's shocking appearance, the corpse was almost company, *someone to talk to, anyway, and what politician doesn't always need* that?

Taylor, he thought, *I hiked and camped and visited the back country all over the planet when I was younger, and I was the most traveled vice president in history, and I had*

*more than enough experience so that I should have been able
to see what these assholes were up to, but I just didn't, and
look what it's done to you, buddy. I sure as hell wish I could
promise I'd avenge you, but I don't think that's in the cards.*

*I guess I'll be making my apology in person pretty soon,
anyway.*

**ABOUT HALF AN HOUR LATER. JUST WEST OF SANTA ROSA
ISLAND, ABOUT FIFTY MILES FROM THE CALIFORNIA
MAINLAND. A LITTLE BEFORE 6:00 A.M. PST. MONDAY,
OCTOBER 28.**

Grady Barbour wasn't used to being up this early, though he
was sometimes up this late; and he wasn't at all used to being
sober when he was up this late. But here he was, three days
without a drink because Daybreak mattered, and after a long,
lingering morning twilight, the sun was finally looking like it
might decide to come up. That would bring on the land breeze
that would make the rest of the day's sail down the California
coast a lot easier; they'd had to use the engine to get out here
early this morning, and somehow that seemed wrong, just as it
seemed entirely appropriate that *Mad Caprice* was a wooden
boat that he'd re-rigged with hemp.

It was cold, but he had a nice big lidded mug filled with
coffee, and the wind was light but steady. He kept a hand on
the wheel, drank the coffee, and thought about Daybreak and
what life together with Tracy would be like after this.

Tracy was taking her turn at launching, working as clean
as possible because their electronics needed to work for a
couple more weeks.

Normally, just watching Tracy could get him horny; to
Grady, she pretty much defined "trophy wife." But in the
baggy jacket, rubber gloves, hairnet, and rubber boots, she
didn't look like much just now. Also, he was feeling unchar-
acteristically clearheaded because they'd agreed not to drink
until Daybreak was actually delivered.

Yet he didn't feel grumpy, tired, or sad at all, as he usually
would, cold sober and up too early. With just enough breeze
to fill the sails, the day promised to be warm but not hot, and
they were on their way to a new world.

Tracy scooped out a cup of the little gelatin capsules and dumped them into a flaccid black balloon, as big as her own torso. Really, the longest and hardest part of the job had been building the glove box that let them load the gelatin capsules without spreading any of the various nanoswarm and tailored biotes around, but Grady had always been good with his hands. Tracy was always saying that he looked like a sculptor, with his craggy, weather- and gin-beaten features.

Tracy poured a cup of seawater into the balloon, enough to get the biotes going once the sun warmed it. She squirted the sealant on the surface inside the mouth of the balloon, then fitted it over the special adapter built by a Daybreaker in Seattle, sort of a friendly hippie machinist who usually made stuff for drug labs. She cranked down the gasket, opened the valve to the cylinder of welding hydrogen, and filled the balloon to its full two-meter diameter, bigger across than she was tall, enough to lift the water and capsules plus itself. She tightened the tie around the neck and released the adapter, letting the balloon rise away from the bow, carried well downwind before it was at mast height. It climbed slowly but steadily.

Grady visualized the rest of the story; in an hour or so, the seawater would dissolve a capsule containing a biote that would begin to grow and eat the balloon; while that continued, the other capsules would dissolve, leaving a gray, active breeding sludge of mixed nanoswarm and biotes, floating above the Big System inland, invisible to radar, and drifting on the breeze.

Sometime between two and five hours later, depending on whether the sun was out and how well each particular strain of biotes did, the balloon would rupture. Probably it would happen at the bottom of the puddled seawater, where exposure had been greatest. Then the escaping hydrogen would spray the solution and nanospawn into the air as the balloon whipped madly around, and a rain of ending would fall gently on the Big System below, perhaps in drips and spots across several square miles. Two hours later, the balloon itself would be gooey sludge on the ground somewhere—and another source of infection.

"Yeee-hah!" he yelled, as the balloon rose higher and caught the bright morning sun.

"Thank you for your applause," Tracy said. "That was

sixty-seven seconds, but I bet I can get it under forty before the day is out. Which will leave me the world record holder since we'll never need to do this again."

"I'll brag endlessly of your record," he said. "Just one of many things to brag about."

She came back and insisted on a kiss before getting back to work, and that was lovely too. Daybreak was honestly the best idea Grady had ever encountered. Even being up in the morning sober would be all right if he had to do more of it, which he might, because they had already discussed that until things settled down after Daybreak, they might have to do some fishing or cargo-hauling to conceal the existence of the half ton of gold beneath the false lowest deck.

Contemplating a world where he had nothing to complain about, he grinned, and shouted, "Yeee-hah!" again.

ABOUT THE SAME TIME. ALONG COLORADO STATE HIGHWAY 13. 7:10 A.M. MST. MONDAY, OCTOBER 28.

The long, winding two-lane road that snaked up into and over the mountains into Wyoming was nearly empty and Jason drove through deep tunnels of evergreens, burst into sunny meadows, and descended around the edges of wide, sunny valleys.

This road would become a track for wagons, then just a trail with the occasional traveler with a leather or canvas (never nylon again!) pack. Elk would graze on whatever popped up between the old cracked asphalt. The neat metal buildings of the ranches would fall into rusty piles. Stupid ranch houses, made of bricks hauled up here from a thousand miles away, would be dens of bears and roosts of crows. Great idea, too late to be a poem, probably. Maybe after.

Jason had taken this job because someone had to lay down the Daybreak seeds in the far back country so that, if the Big System tried to retreat from its deadly, miserable cities and spread its ecocidal madness to the clean wilderness, the nano-swarm and biotes would be here already, dug in and ready to stop the Big System from doing anything other than what it needed to do—stay in place, and die.

It was an honor to be trusted with such a vital assignment,

when so many others were just out throwing biotes and nano-swarm any old place in the cities and along the highways. Besides, Jason admitted to himself, he had always loved driving in the mountains, especially in the fall, and this would probably be his last chance ever to do that.

He made his first stop in a broad meadow, about two miles across, at one of those solar-powered signs that talked to the satellites or the distant cell towers and displayed messages from the Highway Patrol: DRY & CLR THRU RIO BLANCO. During the winter it probably had more important things to say.

Nobody coming in either direction, not even a distant rooster-tail of autumn dust. He pulled on his gloves, leaving the engine running despite the added pollution and waste of gas, taking no more chances than he had to with his starter.

Jason reached in among the egg-packing cardboard and pulled out an object about the size and shape of an egg, the color of polished obsidian with a thick coating of clear varnish, except for one flat side, where a ring of white plastic surrounded a silvery spot the size of his thumbprint. From the toolbox in the back, he pulled out a caulking gun loaded with Liquid Nails, and applied a neat ribbon of the brownish glue to the white plastic, careful not to lap over onto the metal. He didn't need the stepladder; the sign wasn't much taller than he was.

The sign was double-sided, and the other side said, OPN RNGE—CATTLE ON RD. The solar collector faced south, on an eight-foot pole, and its cable ran down to a black box that joined the two sign faces. Jason considered for a moment; put it on a south-facing surface to be able to collect the maximum heat? Put it on the black box to be less conspicuous and have the maximum immediate effect?

Compromise and do both, he decided, and slapped the black egg high up onto the face of the solar collector. He went back to the truck for another black egg, squirted that with Liquid Nails, and stuck it to the black box, low on the south surface, where he hoped the sun would touch it for at least a couple of hours every day.

He pushed the capping sixpenny nail into the nozzle of the caulking gun and tossed that into the toolbox. Then he sprinkled Liquid-Plumr on his gloves and wiped them over each other as if washing his hands, peeled them off inside the Ziplocs, and set the bags on the front seat. In seconds, he was rolling again, the coustajam playing loud enough to shake the inside of the truck, like an anthem of victory.

ABOUT FIFTEEN MINUTES LATER. JAYAPURA, PAPUA PROVINCE, INDONESIA. 11:12 P.M. LOCAL TIME. MONDAY, OCTOBER 28.

"Armand," Captain Tuti said, "I do apologize that we'll probably have to wait until morning to turn your power back on. We could do it, but if your lights come on, it's apt to draw more unfavorable attention."

"I don't much like unfavorable attention myself," Cooper said, gesturing at the bullet hole in the window, which had been created by "the only sniper who knew his business," as Tuti explained. "My men were right on him, saw his muzzle flash from the roof, but he was quicker than we were and gone by the time we got up there. I'm afraid I don't quite have my A Team on this, you know; most of them are out trying to liberate the airport. Or rather dug in twenty kilometers from the airport, because someone shot at them, and they are afraid to go on in the dark."

"I don't much like being shot at, myself," Cooper pointed out. "Another?"

"Gladly, Armand, gladly." Tuti had found a way to gently hint that if there happened to be liquor around, he had no religious objection to it; considering how many favors he was in a position to do Cooper, Armand had figured that most of a bottle of Captain Morgan was a perfectly reasonable price.

An hour after Tuti had come up to tell Cooper he was reasonably safe but couldn't leave until the mob did, Cooper had established that the captain had a son with some minor, high-spirited events in his police record, who had a full scholarship to Tufts and needed a student visa. They'd be taking care of that in a day or so.

With business taken care of, there was little to do except establish their mutual experience that being bureaucrats here was not easy but also not dull, and that they had a similar sense of humor. Cooper remembered what his father had told him—*It's always nice to have one of the friends you need turn into a friend you want.*

The phone rang. "Cooper, US Consul, Jayapura."

"Hi, this is Jasmine at State in Washington. I just came on shift and found your voice mails. I have no idea what the person who was supposed to have the desk was doing, but I'm here now. First thing, are you safe?"

He sketched out the situation: that he was holed up but secure, that Captain Tuti was there, that the airport was in the hands of rebels who had previously not shown enough competence to seize a city bus stop. "Definitely some ringers on the team," he explained to Jasmine.

"All right, we appreciate the report. And just this minute Secret Service asked if Seagull got away before the airport was taken."

Secret Service? Who the hell was on that plane? Half an instant later, Armand Cooper realized what prominent politician had been unexpectedly missing from public appearances. *Oh, shit. Here I am in the middle of history.* But he held his voice even. "The consulate was attacked while they were still on the ground, and the assault on the airport was half an hour after that. Maybe, maybe not. Let me get the binoculars and see if they're still on the ground there. I'll call you right back."

The big white unmarked 787 Dreamliner was not anywhere he could see; he explained the problem, without saying why he was looking, to Tuti, who borrowed the binoculars. "I can tell you for certain it is not there."

"How do you know—"

"Because there is just one large repair hangar at Sentani, the only place where a plane that size could be concealed, and it has room for only one plane at a time. And I see the rebels are towing a Lion Airlines 737 into it right now. So since there is nowhere for it to be, it isn't there." Tuti lowered the binoculars. "They teach us these clever tricks, you know, in police school."

Bad as the situation was, Cooper laughed, but then he called Jasmine back and told her, and she transferred his call to an Air Force general who brought in an admiral and a Secret Service liaison in conference, and Cooper went over things with them a few times. By the end of that he figured there just wasn't going to be much to laugh about for quite a while.

**ABOUT HALF AN HOUR LATER. WASHINGTON, DC. 9:40 A.M.
EST. MONDAY, OCTOBER 28.**

The Department of the Future contained three "Offices-of,"
each headed by an assistant secretary. Besides Heather's Office of Future Threat Assessment, Jim Browder's Office of
Technology Forecasting watched the science and technology possibilities from the perspective of an old grouch of
an engineer–science writer who was quite certain that most
things wouldn't work most of the time, and that if they did,
it would make things worse. In theory, Noel Crittenden's Office of Political Futurology tried to understand developing
situations around the world, focusing partly on what governments were doing but mainly on trends in the political class
and nascent mass movements. In practice, Crittenden was a
broad-but-not-deep historian who could easily call to mind
six other times when something had happened but couldn't
seem to reach a conclusion if his life depended on it.

Normally, Heather ignored her two colleagues, with
Graham and Allie's tacit encouragement. Allie liked to say
Browder was mad about a girl getting hold of the boy toys
like guns and money, and Crittenden's office was actually the
Office of Whatever a Retired History Prof Remembers; she
made it abundantly clear that in the battle for funds and attention, she thought Heather's office was the department's only
real star.

More than once, Graham Weisbrod had given Allie and
Heather a stern lecture about everyone's being on the same
team. Heather wondered if he'd ever said the same thing to
the two men.

So far, the meeting had gone exactly as Heather had anticipated: Browder was vocally, and Crittenden was sullenly, impossible. Browder, with malicious sarcastic glee, had forced
Heather to explain and defend each slide, turning aside all
suggestions that he wait and ask Arnie in a few minutes.

Meanwhile, Crittenden looked every stuffy ounce of his
Cambridge doctorate. His ancient three-piece suits and the
slash of his gray mustache against his dark skin made him
look like some old-time big-city mayor of 1990 or so. He sat
with his arms folded, his good ear pointed toward Heather,
watching each new slide with the same sour glare.

Crittenden's the reserve force that'll come in to loot the dead and shoot the wounded after Browder finishes his massacre. And where's all the support Allie and Graham told me I'd have? They're both sitting there like lumps. Allie isn't even looking up from her laptop.

Heather drew a deep breath before tackling Browder's latest hostile question. "That's why Dr. Yang's statistical semiotics research is housed in our office of our department. It's not about intuition or recognizing patterns. It's about the mathematics that finds things that *would* be recognizable or recurring patterns—if anyone had ever seen them before. And Daybreak's signprint—"

"What's a signprint?"

Heather suspected that Browder already knew. *At least I know this one, and I won't give him a forty-minute version like Arnie would.* "In the noosphere—the overall total environment of all the communications going in all directions at any one time—"

"I know what a noosphere is, Yang wore the subject out for me once."

"Oh, good. Well, in the noosphere, we only detect signs when they move—we only know a word exists when someone speaks or writes it into a message, we only know an image exists when someone includes it in a bigger image, we only know a mistake is there when it's spotted and corrected, all that. The signprint is the pathway in the noosphere that a group of signs, uh, flying in formation, I guess you could call it, they're separate, but they stick together—it's the pattern they leave—"

"Like a wake in the sea of meaning," Crittenden suggested.

Hunh. That was almost friendly.

"Good enough! Well, different kinds of organized populations of signs leave different kinds of signprints. In fact, from a historian's perspective, a signprint and the thing it's a signprint of are really just the same thing, one's what you see and one's the thing that's there, is the way Arnie puts it."

"That's a very old idea," Crittenden said, "with considerable merit."

I feel so blessed, she thought sarcastically, and said, "Good, all right, then the thing that Arnie's kind of math has going for it is that it doesn't look for signprints by looking for structures that are like preexisting signprints. It just finds things that stick together and move together. Another way Arnie says it is that the pattern-recog guys sit and stare at the screen and look for clouds that look like a horse or a ship. Arnie's stat methods just look for clouds—which is what you want if you want to know the weather. It means his way of doing things can see the 'clouds' in the noosphere that no one else can and then try to understand them. Because in the noosphere, unlike in the atmosphere, there are often storms of a kind no one has ever seen before, and being able to see them the second or third time they show up is not good enough if we're trying to foresee what messes might hit us in the near future.

"So—the signprint of Daybreak. Clearly there. Jumps out of the numbers like a sore thumb, according to Arnie." She clicked to the slide.

Browder, to her surprise, nodded. "If I read that right, the variances are tiny, and the connectedness is huge. That's not a cloud, that's a boulder."

"That's right," she said. *Both of them reasonable within a minute of each other. Who'd've thunk?* "That graph measures basically how distinct Daybreak is from everything else in the noosphere, and you can see it's very distinct. So since it's definitely there, the next question is, what is it? And the answer is, to quote my favorite book when I was a kid, 'Something very much like something no one has ever seen before.' Daybreak has some of the aspects of a religious cult, an artistic movement, a blogweave, a terror network more like the old al-Qaeda or the Japanese Red Army than like the modern il'Alb il-Jihado network, and some unique features all its own."

"But that's just how they communicate, right?" Browder asked. "What *are* they?"

"What are they, like—"

"Engineers or Catholics, old people, women, I guess I'm asking who, what do they have in common other than Daybreak?"

"Well, it's a bunch of people who only agree that they hate the Big System, but they literally spend two to four hours a day making and consuming messages of one kind or another to each other about that. You could think of it as a mutual-hypnosis hate-the-Big-System club, maybe. No central office keeps them on message, either, it sort of runs by local consensus. They seem to have no permanent organization any bigger than three-to-twenty-person AGs."

"AGs?" Browder asked.

Crittenden said, "Affinity group. Anarchist idea, goes back to the mid 1970s, sort of like a self-organized exec committee; team of people who are doing something or other they all think is the most important thing to do."

"Uh, yeah." Jim's resemblance to the Incredible Hulk, gone old and soft with drinking, was especially noticeable when he raised one side of his single, massive brow. "And the Big System is what, the Trilateral Commission? The Catholic Church? The Elders of Zion? The Man?"

"The totality of plastic and computers, advertising and pornography, pop music and space travel, nuclear power and celebrities, everything that makes money, attracts attention in the media, or just originated after the Civil War. To Daybreakers, the whole freakin' modern world is all just an avatar of the Big System."

Browder's tone sprayed mockery over them all. "And a pack of romantic loons like that is a *threat*?"

Stand your ground, Heather, he's just a big bully, and you could drop him with one punch. She made a point of sighing. "*Future* threat—maybe. That's our territory; if they were trouble right now, we'd be handing them off to the NDI or the FBI."

"Which is what I favor doing," Allie put in, making Browder jump. *He tends to forget where the real authority is in the room,* Heather thought.

He was softer but just as sarcastic when he asked, "And—repeating my question—who *are* these scary-talking weird people?"

"Well, here in the States, it's some of everything: greenie granola hippies with windmills on their goat sheds, wannabe mountain-man racist tax resisters, dope-farmer computer hackers, oddball fundamentalists who think bar codes are the Mark of the Beast, ex–Special Forces snake-eating back-to-Jefferson types."

Noel Crittenden coughed and tented his hands. "That does *not* mean they aren't dangerous, Browder. Who'd've thought the Nation of Islam could have worked with the Panthers *and* the SCLC? Or that de Gaulle could put together the French Resistance out of a dozen factions ranging from royalists to commies? Don't underrate the power of a common enemy. If I may ask—what do they mean by Daybreak?"

Heather said, "The event that breaks the Big System, causes it to go down so it never comes up again. They almost always capitalize *Daybreak*, like *the Revolution* or *the Rapture*."

Crittenden nodded seriously. "And it's international?"

"Dr. Yang reports that over seventy percent of the messages with identifiable locations are outside the US. There's one mostly Asian cult, geeky engineers in Tokyo and Seoul, who read a lot of Tolkien and think that once the iron all rusts, the elves will come back. They might be the scariest of all; those guys are burned-out, frustrated engineers and technicians—single men in their forties with great salaries whose lives have gone by with no prospect of starting a family, sitting in concrete boxes full of pricey toys in Osaka or Seoul, figuring out where the modern industrial system is vulnerable.

"And plenty of others—young Islamic fundamentalist men, stuck sitting on their asses in perpetual unemployment, who want the good stuff they'd have had in 1400. Hindu fundamentalists, ditto except they mean 1400 B.C.

"What scares me the most is that they're *not* all loser-nuts; far from it, there are a lot more dissatisfied successes. People with serious tech skills who aren't finding happiness in a big paycheck, who sit in comfortable apartments beating off to American porn on the web and insisting that life should have a meaning."

Crittenden made a face. "'Whenever some damn idiot starts wanting life to have meaning, he finishes by helping other people to meaningless deaths.'"

Graham grinned. "Source?"

"Me, of course. In my first textbook. Out of print now." Crittenden's smile stayed on when he turned from Graham's not-at-all-subtle flattery back to Heather.

Thanks, Graham! This could be worse. She explained, "Meaning-of-life stuff accounts for the usual-suspects component of Daybreak, too. French poets who think any words that resonate must be true. German performance artists who want to overthrow the tyranny of words and live in a world of pure action. Popomos looking for something to replace the Revolution. Back-to-peasantry long-bearded Tolstoy wannabes.

"The really big innovation with the 'Daybreak' crowd is that they don't talk about purpose, plan, or program anymore. It's Daybreak for Daybreak's sake. They often say, 'The point is, there's no point.'"

"Why do it if there's no point?" Browder snarled, now more angry than amused.

"The Daybreakers would say, 'Why do it if there *is* a point?' The idea is that they'd all like to blow up all the Wal-Marts, so why worry about which reason—"

The door opened, and Arnie came in. "Heather," he said, "something big."

"Um, Arnie, I'll call you when it's time to—"

"Lenny Plekhanov had some extra time and people this morning and they got a breakthrough on the keys for Daybreak, so we caught up with one—"

"Arnie, we're—"

Arnie stopped leaning forward, stopped gesticulating, and stood as still as if he were at attention; that stopped Heather when nothing else would have. In a perfectly normal conversational voice, not moving a muscle, he said, "Heather. Secretary Weisbrod. I'm sorry, but it's urgent. Daybreak started today, at midnight, GMT. There are at least nine hundred AGs reporting they've started their actions, which means maybe seven thousand people doing some kind of sabotage or other for Daybreak just here in the States, right now. That's just what I've been able to attach an ID to. I'm guessing there are maybe as many as twenty thousand. Probably three or four times that overseas. Up to a hundred thousand participants worldwide."

They all sat, stunned, and it was Crittenden who broke the silence. He stared out the window at the trees, red and gold in the autumn morning sun, as if somewhere in the wild colors, there were a puzzle to be solved. "A group of saboteurs the size of a medium-sized national army—"

Browder snorted. "With no point and no plan. And many of them seem to be people who couldn't get a job delivering Domino's."

Crittenden speared Browder with his over-the-reading-glasses stare. The heavy, rumpled man sat back, as if startled; Heather thought, *I'm glad I never had a late paper with that guy.*

The old professor's mouth crooked sardonically. "You *haven't* been listening. Engineers, technicians, applied scientists—*dissatisfied successes*, in Heather's useful phrase. And if that's ten percent of their movement, that's all they need; a pizza-delivery boy can carry a bomb if someone builds it for him." He glanced back at Heather. "You had me once you said they were leaderless and programless. Daybreak sounds far too much like nihilism or futurism, back around 1900."

Browder shrugged ostentatiously. "The world lived through that."

Crittenden shook his head as if Browder were trying to BS through an oral quiz and not convincing anyone. "Better a high card you know in another man's hand than a joker loose in the deck. The nihilists' thirty years of bombings and assassinations smoothed the road for Lenin and communism in a dozen different ways. The Futurists . . . well, Marinetti, their founder, was among the first intellectuals to support Mussolini. So before Dr. Yang entered, I was about to say, Heather was absolutely right to bring this to our attention." He favored Heather with a sardonic smile. "But Dr. Yang's news has convinced me that we should not be worried. We should be *scared*. Heather, if there's anything my office can do to help you determine what we're dealing with, please call me at once."

"I know I can count on all of you," Heather said.

Graham was beaming at her, leaning back against the wall just below the poster Heather had given him. She'd found an old magazine in the library with a perfect article title—and the facing page for the article had depicted a robot taking dictation on an old-fashioned steno pad, a typist in a space helmet, and a woman doing her nails in front of what appeared to be some sort of gigantic computer console—all those images surrounding the caption THE SECRETARY OF THE FUTURE!

She'd had it blown up to poster size as a gag gift; Graham had insisted on hanging it in the conference room to remind everyone how silly it was to spend your life trying to predict the unpredictable.

Her old teacher dropped her a wink; in that instant, it was like he'd seated her on the couch by his fireplace, handed her a drink, and heard her troubles out—something he'd done often enough in reality.

Browder was still sitting where Crittenden's glare had frozen him; with a grudging nod, he said, "Let me see how many resources I can shift to cover the technical side of Daybreak."

Allie looked up from her notes and grinned; Graham was already smiling at her; and it was left to Arnie to spoil the mood by saying, "Well, by the way, it's nice that everyone agrees, but we probably *are* under attack."

ABOUT THE SAME TIME. WYOMING STATE HIGHWAY 789, NEAR BAGGS, WYOMING. 7:50 A.M. MST. MONDAY, OCTOBER 28.

Jason had placed sixteen eggs; the most entertaining one was right on the crotch of the smiling cowgirl on a neon sign over the gate of a roadhouse. *Wish I could've jumped higher, I could've put black-egg nipples on her neon-tube boobs.*

The two-lane road had climbed up into the park-and-pass country, where whenever a car came the other way, both drivers would raise a hand off the wheel in salute, kind of an *I know we are both here* that always made him feel like he was finally out among the real people. Most of the other cars were SUVs, but after all, he was driving a big old F-150 himself, the only thing they'd been able to find that was cheap, untraceable, and old enough not to rely on as much electronics, so that it stood a chance of finishing the trip.

Anyway, up here, where you could be coping with ground blizzards, deer and cattle on the road, snowdrifts, washouts, all kinds of whatnot, Jason saw no problem with pickups or even the old SUVs.

Emily back at the commune said people used their SUVs for evil things like hunting and going to logging jobs. He'd had a lot of good arguments with Emily about that.

The coolest thing about Daybreak: Almost everyone thought something about the Big System was all right, even positive. But when you put everyone together, you could compromise and agree, hey, we'll get rid of the thing you hate, if

I can get rid of the thing that I hate, and when you were all done, there'd be no Big System left.

A solar sign in the middle of an old clear cut announced to the saplings and brush that there was NO MESSAGE—DRIVE SAFE. He needed the stepladder this time to leave two more little black eggs.

He rolled on, glorious coustajam cranked to rattle the windows, the F-150 tracing the edges of gulches and crossing steep-sided creeks on high truss bridges—almost like flying, with the land coming up and falling away.

In the last low hills, the small, stunted trees thinned out. The park was all rich browns and grays, dried out and ready for winter, with just streaks of green, gold, and yellow where aspens and cottonwoods revealed creeks. About a dozen pronghorns ran away from the road as the old truck roared by. "Soon, guys," Jason said. "Soon. Your grandchildren won't have any idea what an engine means."

ABOUT THE SAME TIME. SENTANI INTERNATIONAL AIRPORT, JAYAPURA, PAPUA, INDONESIA. MIDNIGHT, LOCAL TIME. OCTOBER 28 JUST BECOMING OCTOBER 29.

The ground crew weren't happy. Guns pointed at them made their unhappiness irrelevant. One or two of them had tried to explain that you couldn't use auto body paint on an airplane and expect it to look like anything, but the small man with the big mustache and the rage in his eyes had caressed the pistol on his hip, and now they were working fast, painting out the Lion Airways insignia on the 737.

They worked from ladders and scissor lifts, using mops, long-handled brushes, even brooms. The drums of white paint stood open all over the hangar, emitting clouds of strong fumes, enough to make men sick. The mustached man said to vomit if they had to but keep working.

He walked over to look at the three captured Americans; the dark-skinned, short man was dead or unconscious, not surprising after the beating they'd given him. He flipped the motionless man over with his boot toe; the open eyes were dried and dull.

The tall white man and the skinny woman lay huddled

against each other. *In one of your stupid movies,* he thought, *you would fall in love, overpower all of us, and escape to save the world, but here in reality, you cling to each other like a refugee child clings to a stuffed animal. It is pleasant to see that expression in an American's eyes instead of a refugee child's.*

He could see no gain in separating the man and the woman, so he returned to shouting at the impromptu paint crew. Already, the Lion Airways insignia was more than half covered; they were at least a half hour ahead of schedule.

ABOUT AN HOUR LATER. GILLETTE, WYOMING. JUST BEFORE 9:00 A.M. MST. OCTOBER 28.

Zach coasted up to the next recycling cart on his mud-spattered single-speed pink girl's bicycle. He still rode awkwardly with his large bags of plastic bottles; he hoped people would think it was because he was drunk. He threw the lid back and glanced around. The first ten seconds was the highest risk—it wouldn't look like a real bum stealing plastic. One more look around; surely it looked realistic for a bum stealing recyclable plastic to be paranoid?

Zach didn't know much about being homeless, and even less about being a drunk. The cheap whiskey he'd poured all over his clothes was all the liquor he'd ever bought in his life.

His heart was pounding. Oh, well . . . *Step One, here we go.* Zach dumped his front left bag into the recycling cart—whoever heard of a bum putting plastic bottles *into* the trash? He mixed them thoroughly with the bottles that were already there, stirring with the yardstick he carried. *Wonder if this looks like I'm looking for something?*

Step Two was less conspicuous. He scrounged in the recycling cart, looking like any other bum as he filled up his bag, not worrying about happening to take back a few of the bottles he had just deposited there.

He hoped Step Three would look weird enough. He pulled out a Dad's Root Beer two-liter bottle with a wadded paper napkin inside and uncapped it, retching at the smell. No question, Bugs and DarwinsActor had known their stuff; the inside of the bottle smelled like a fart from a sick cat, and the clear surface was already spotted with cloudy slime. From his coat pocket, he drew a whiskey bottle filled with a mix of beef broth, molasses, and fine-chopped plastic bottles, swirled it, and splashed about a teaspoon into the plastic bottle, taking care to soak the infected napkin.

He carefully left the Dad's bottle on the top of the heap in the recycling cart; holes would form within an hour, and the solution would drizzle down through the cart.

If anyone in authority asked about the care he took of that special Dad's bottle, he would explain that it was demonic and he had to sacrifice his whiskey to it and send it away before it destroyed all his plastic.

That made him laugh to himself in a convincingly weird way. So close to the truth, no one would believe it.

"Hey, *shithead*!"

Zach turned around slowly. Scrawny, red-skinned old white man. Bad leg, visible cataract, about six flannel shirts. "This here block is mine," the man said. "You don't take no plastic from it."

"I'm sorry, I didn't know it was your territory. In fact, let me give you a couple bottles from my bag." Zach handed him two seed bottles; he had more than he would need and was supposed to improvise with some of them.

"That's real nice a-you," the man said, "'Preciate it." As he went to tuck the bottle into the huge bag he carried, he caught a whiff, and said, "These smell awful, where'd you get them?"

"Some kids' party house I think. Think they maybe pissed in 'em. They're still money."

"Yeah." The old man reached out and tapped his shoulder in what was probably intended as a friendly gesture. "Got any money? Want to come in and drink or something?"

"Gotta get me to some more carts," Zach said. "Any more of these blocks yours?"

"Naw. I ain't got no block that's mine. Just people shouldn't fuck with me, you know?" The old man scratched and squirmed, as if he'd had about as much human contact as he was prepared for. "My name's Peter. You come by anytime."

"My name's Paul," Zach said. *After all,* he thought, *we're two guys spreading the stuff that's going to make the whole world better.*

**ABOUT THE SAME TIME. OVER THE WESTERN PACIFIC.
AROUND SUNRISE LOCALLY. TUESDAY, OCTOBER 29.**

With his face against the window, Samuelson could just see the rising sun. The point of what they'd done to poor Taylor, and of leaving Samuelson with the corpse for so long, and the beating that followed, could only be to make him despair; since that was what they wanted, he'd have to hope.

But not hope to live. He knew in his bones that he wouldn't live. Whether they killed him or not beforehand, they meant to die themselves. They'd left the door open while they beat him, and he'd seen the big gray metal box, with two of them fussing over it, and the array of fifty-five-gallon drums, in the lounge. He was quite sure that whatever the box and the barrels held, it wasn't supplies or documents, and their destination—no, their *target*—was a big crowd, a famous building, or both.

The three strong young men who had beaten Samuelson had left bruises everywhere, and now his back and gut ached, and his whole face was sore and puffy.

They'll demand that I make a statement for broadcast before we hit, he thought. *Almost for sure. That's got to be why they care about what I'm feeling. I wonder if I can say the whole phrase "Mohammed is sucking Satan's dick in hell" before they kill me on camera?* He was surprised at himself, but only a bit. *"New situations call for new insights,"* he thought, quoting some of his speechwriter's best work. *Maybe I'm just getting in touch with my inner hawk. Some things are hard not to take personally, you know.*

He lay sideways on his bed, chained to a furniture bracket, with two guards always watching him.

He really missed Kim.

He wished he'd been more suspicious, more paranoid—maybe just more angry—back when it could do some good, but had to admit that the too-trusting, too-open way he had walked into this had always been his whole approach to life.

He could see now what Rog had been trying so hard to tell him. If your biggest worry was that the other side might stop talking to you . . . . well, sooner or later, if there was one genuinely malicious force in the world, you'd meet it, and something like this would happen. *Once I made myself into* John Samuelson, The Man Who Can Always Get a Deal, *I was doomed to come out and meet these guys, even though Rog and everybody who really knew anything told me that it smelled bad and they didn't want to do it.*

He hated feeling like a fool, but it was still no excuse for despair. *I've done my best, even if I was wrong. Somebody had to take the chance that they were telling the truth when they said they wanted to talk, and they wanted to make peace. You don't make peace with people who aren't dangerous in the first place; that's not peacemaking, that's just negotiation.*

And now that it turns out it didn't work, I guess someone else will have to make the lying, treacherous fuckers pay for that. Wish I could be there to see that.

Wish I could help.

They had kicked him for looking too closely at his handcuffs, and for looking around the room, and for wiping his face with his sleeve, and for sitting up. Since those were the rules, he'd purposely made a couple of fiddling, fumbling gropes at his cuffs and at the brackets they were attached to, taken the kicks, and let himself subside on his bunk, against the wall, face resting on the window, and pretended to cry uncontrollably—it hadn't taken much pretending.

With his face on the window, he tried to look like he was finally without hope, overwhelmed by the shock.

"Hang on to your advantage," he'd been told, over and over, way back when he took the classes in negotiation. "Whatever they don't know about you, that's an advantage." Right now his one advantage, and it wasn't much of one, was that they didn't know he was still looking for something he could do.

The water below was featureless. Time hunched, lurched, and hobbled, mocking him with its slowness; if any sort of chance came along, he didn't want to have to jump into it with stiff and unmoving muscles. He did what he could to ease the muscles without visibly moving. He whimpered and blubbered whenever he had to move a larger muscle, hoping that would make him look broken.

He was hungry and thirsty and really needed to take a crap, but he was afraid that if he asked for anything, they'd decide he was conscious enough to worry about, and they would move him away from this little airliner window, the only real source of hope in his life. *Actually, there's not much life left; weird that I still want hope.*

Christ, as long as I'm asking for the impossible, I'd like one more time to hold Kim. Thirty-one years together, and I won't be able to say good-bye.

HALF AN HOUR LATER. CRESTON, WYOMING. ABOUT 10:00 A.M. MST. OCTOBER 28.

Thinking the word *eggs* all morning made Jason remember that if there was one thing they did well here in the high country, it was breakfast.

The old F-150 roared over the rise; a few miles ahead, he could see a town. Obviously the powers in the universe were trying to help out.

At a truck stop with four semis in the parking lot, Jason backed the old pickup in against the building, putting the expired plate toward a blank wall where it was unlikely anyone would look, right in the shadow of a big Fruehauf trailer. He got out, stretched, yawned. Ugly little dump of a gravel parking lot and concrete-block building, a human zit on the face of the mountains—*not* a poem idea, he decided.

Inside: country music, Fox on the television, dead animals on the wall. But the eggs, fried potatoes, and French toast were as great as Jason had expected, and as in anyplace that does a busy morning trade, the coffee was this-minute fresh.

The truckers were all at a table together, and Jason figured out, listening to them casually, that two of them had regular routes through here, and the other two passed through now and then and preferred to convoy with friends who knew where the treacherous downgrades, blind curves, and intolerant deputies were.

It was weird, Jason thought. Out here, people worked outside in all weather, and you'd think that would put them in touch with the Earth. Yet they all lived at the end of a long line of trucks and roads, everything dependent on petroleum and metal from thousands of miles away, and their loyalty went to the trucks and the roads. The Big System had a hook into everything.

The Fox yakkers on the television made the point, over and over, that the World Series was the most exciting in a decade and the election was the dullest since '96. *Last time people were this bored at an election,* Jason thought, *my parents were barely old enough to vote.*

The Pirates underdog miracle team was tied three games to three against the ever-loathsome Angels. The Bucs had come fighting back after being down three to one. Game Seven tonight in Anaheim was going to be a *game.* Jason smiled to himself. *Also the last night baseball game, ever, and the last one televised.*

The election *was* dull in comparison. The truckers were all agreeing with the talking heads on Fox that Roger Pendano was going to be re-elected, and Will Norcross didn't have a prayer (or rather prayers were all he had).

Four years ago, Jason had taken a semester off to ring doorbells for Pendano, and later he'd met Beth at a Pendano for President rally. He still liked the corrupt old oily preppy, even though he was just as much a part of the Big System as that right-wing Jesus-boy Norcross.

Still, even with a landslide in the making, Roger Pendano had apparently not wanted to jeopardize his massive victory and had really fastened the muzzle on John Samuelson, his much-more-liberal vice president. Now, *that* was a shame; Samuelson sometimes said something that needed saying. But Samuelson hadn't even been seen in public for almost two weeks—whoever heard of a disappearing vice president just before an election?

Maybe Daybreak would make enough difference so that Samuelson could be president next time—without all the Big-System media and technobullshit distortion, it might be *worth* electing a president again.

The right-wing hairdos were now working up a harrumphing rage because some people wouldn't vote for Norcross because he was openly Pentecostal. Jason shook his head; since when was it unusual for anyone in Congress to gibber like a nut in public at the direction of unseen forces?

The waitress topped up Jason's coffee, following his glance to the TV. "Politics. Gah."

"Yeah," Jason said.

Back in the parking lot, he opened his passenger-side door, pulled his gloves on, extracted a few eggs from a box in the back, and considered where he might plant a few before moving on. Truckers were protective and observant about their rigs, but maybe on that yellow illuminated—

"Hey, there, hippie-dude, what'ja got there?"

He looked up to see the truckers; the question came from a slim little man with protruding ears, a mop of black curly hair sticking out from around his strap cap, giant sideburns, and big brown eyes, who resembled a leprechaun going to a costume party as a trucker.

Jason gave Leprechaun the warm grin that had gotten him through a lot of college classes when he hadn't done the reading. "Well, it's pretty dumb, and I don't really know how to explain it," he temporized. Then his eye fell on the deer whistle on the hood of the nearest cab. *Hah!* "I was just going to go inside and ask you whether you wanted one of these," he said, holding two eggs out so they could see. "Don't touch them, they'll give your fingers the itch the way fiberglass will. My stupid dad thinks he's an inventor, and he's created this wind-resistance cutter. Supposedly you put it on your hood and it sends, like, radio waves forward that harmonize the sound vibrations in the wind stream and make the air flow real smooth over the car, which reduces wind resistance so much, supposedly, you get some extra miles to the gallon. I think. I gotta admit, I don't understand Dad three-quarters of the time even when he's *not* talking about physics."

He caressed one of the little eggs with a gloved finger and let himself sound as if he were trying to hide his pride. *There's the ticket. Good old Dad. Genius inventor. I'm his amiable dimwit hippie son. Got it.* "It's solar-powered, so it has to be somewhere the sun gets to, but that way it doesn't draw any power from the rest of the vehicle. Dad says it's an idea from Nikola Tesla, who was this scientist dude that, like, studied air and electricity. So he sent me out to give away a bunch of them 'cause he can't get the big companies interested. The one on the hood of my truck doesn't do much for my gas mileage, though."

"On the hood of your truck?" another guy, a square-built older type, asked.

Jason looked at the hood, and said, "Dammit. *Third* one that's fallen off. I *told* Dad they wouldn't stay on with Liquid Nails."

Leprechaun-trucker snorted. "D'you think your dad's really a genius with no common sense? Or is he just a guy who's got so little common sense he don't realize he ain't a genius?"

Jason let himself grin broadly. "Well, we lived on his patent money most of the time I was growing up, but the company that paid him didn't *make* any of his gadgets; it was some oil company that said 'the market wasn't right yet' for energy-saving gadgets."

"Damn," the big beefy older trucker said. "Of course they said that; why would an oil company want anyone to save energy?"

"Yeah, I guess. So the patents ran out, the money dried up, and we had to move out to the boondocks to find a place cheap enough for Dad to keep working on his gadgets. Nowadays, the little bit he makes just lets him buy more parts for the next gadget. Doesn't sound like a lot of common sense, does it?"

Leprechaun said, "No, it don't sound like common sense, but I been following Tesla stuff for twenty years on the web, and your dad *might* just be a genius. Even if he don't know that Liquid Nails won't stick a piece of slick glass to a rusty old truck hood."

"Well," Jason said, "I'm supposed to offer one to anyone with a vehicle, and Dad said the bigger the vehicle, the more fuel it would save. They're solar-powered, they work anywhere on the front of the vehicle where the sun gets in enough to charge it. Maybe we could put one on your grille? I'd hate to screw up the paint job on your hood."

Leprechaun-trucker was beaming. "Let's give it a try. If it don't work, it weighs what, a couple ounces? And you can't beat free for a price. I'll even spring for some of that Superstick High-Temp they sell inside; that keeps trim on a truck, oughta keep one of these on the grille."

After he'd equipped all four trucks with an egg on each grille, Jason also gave an egg carton with six more in it for his new Tesla-freak buddy Leprechaun to give to other truckers. "Handle them with gloves only," he said. "You can trust me that you don't want to know how much you're gonna itch—or how much it will spread to anything you touch with your hands—if you don't. And remember, whether it works or not, we'd sure appreciate a note at three w's dot tesla hyphen waveflow, dot org, about whatever you observe."

"Will do," the short trucker said, pulling out a ballpoint pen to write it on his hand. Jason spelled it out carefully; there was no such site as far as he knew, but well before Leprechaun might try it, there'd be no web.

To keep it convincing, Jason was visibly at work, scraping at the rust on the hood of the F-150 to better attach a black egg, as the truckers pulled out. The moment the last truck vanished over the rise, he tossed the egg up onto the flat roof of the little diner, figuring there'd be plenty of sun, and with things like the air-conditioning, satellite antenna, and gadgets inside, there ought to be enough stray electromagnetic fields around as well.

Then he sloshed Liquid-Plumr over the place on the hood where the black egg had briefly rested. The truck had to make another 250 miles, even a POS this old had an electronic distributor and fuel injection, and with so much ground to cover, Jason couldn't afford excessive irony.

ABOUT AN HOUR LATER. WASHINGTON, DC. JUST AFTER 1:00 P.M. EST. OCTOBER 28.

Edwards, the liaison from FBI, looked around the DoF's main meeting room, as if seeking support from his dozen other law-enforcement, security, and military colleagues, folded his arms, and asked, "And you didn't have crypto resources to find out about this sooner?"

Arnie looked as embarrassed as Heather felt. She said, "The only thing we could get was assistance from the Amateur Crypto Section at NSA."

Susan Adler from NSA nodded. "It's as much our neglect as yours. OFTA asked for more help all the time, and Dr. Plekhanov several times told us that you needed it badly."

Edwards, a tall, thin, bald man with a crooked nose, who tended to look like Popeye on a bad day, said, "Well, that's probably enough recrimination right there. Just another case of you can't watch everything. But . . . *thousands* of people doing minor sabotage?"

Arnie nodded. "Maybe not minor. The tech analysts from Dr. Browder's office gave us a preliminary opinion that what we're looking at is at least weaponized nanoreplicators, which the Daybreakers call *nanospawn*, and a mix of genetically modified organisms they call *biotes*. Coordinated release not just across the country but around the world."

"We've had to run on borrowed resources," Heather said. "I've had a request in for two full years for a cryptologist, longer than that for more science and engineering staff—"

Edwards made a sour face. "I said this is no time for recriminations. Now, when they weaponize a nanoreplicator, what do they make it do? I thought in the most sophisticated labs they've got, right now, they're barely making nanotech do anything."

Jim Browder rubbed his porcine jowls, shoving so much flesh up toward his ears it looked as if he were about to peel his face off like a bag. "*Non*-replicating nanotech works just fine in industry, everywhere, these days, and has since the late twenty-teens. Replicating nanotech is a stunt that hobbyists do. It's not hard to make nanos that make copies of themselves, and it's not hard to make nanos that do something useful, but so far it's hard to get them to do both because for any useful, creative purpose, they'd have to communicate and work with each other, and that's *very* hard. But if all you want a nanobot to do is make nitric acid whenever it senses that it's near an electric circuit—that's what our weapons guys were looking at. They thought it was too unreliable, it would attack our own gear, and you'd never get rid of it once you released it. But if *all* electric machines are the enemy, forever, I guess that's an advantage."

"Why nitric acid?"

"Just an example," Browder said. "Because you could theoretically synthesize it from air and wouldn't have to have any other material available. But depending on what they intend to attack, and what they can expect to find near it, there's at least a hundred other possibilities: fluorine gas, or hydroxide or peroxide ions, or a bimetallic strip that works like a battery. For sabotage, you only need nanoreplicators to reproduce in clusters around something valuable, and excrete a substance that attacks it. Achieving that is down at the college sophomore lab level these days."

Hannah Bledsoe, from DHS, tall, handsome, dignified, with a deep red dress and pearls that seemed as much a part of her as her soft curly gray hair, looked up from her laptop. "And what are the biotes? Disease organisms?"

Browder grunted. "Sort of, but not against people as much as against artificial materials. The Daybreakers' genetic-modification stuff that we've decrypted so far is all devoted to modifying ordinary decay bacteria, molds, funguses, any bug that eats dead stuff, to make engineered enzymes to break down long chains of carbon."

Edwards said, "Pretend that some of us skipped chemistry class."

"A lot of artificial materials—most plastics, for example—and the common fuels like gasoline and kerosene—have molecules that are built around a long, branching string of carbon atoms, with various other atoms attached on the side. The reason they usually don't decay is because the carbon-carbon bond is fairly strong, and where there's a long string of them, there's not much—at least not much that a living thing *naturally* makes—that will attack the chain and break it into pieces small enough to digest. Basically the biotes are molds or yeasts, bacteria or maybe viruses, that turn synthetic materials and liquid fuels into sugars, fats, proteins—*food* that rots and spoils."

"My god," Bledsoe said, "and that's what's loose out there? But how did they get the technical expertise?"

"They don't have to be tech wizards," Arnie Yang put in. "Nowadays a process is no sooner understood than it's automated. The guys who wrote the first computer viruses back in the eighties were pretty smart, but they created scripts for them, and now any eleven-year-old script-kiddie with a boot-leg kit can write a virus that will steal your password, e-mail him your credit-card numbers, and fill your hard drive with porn.

"Once they had computers big enough to do molecular simulations and cheap enough for the public—like about the time the ApplePi came out a few years ago—it was really more just a matter of who *wanted* to do genetic engineering. Sure, it seems like it's big news, and true, even ten years ago, biohacking was still all guesswork. But that's just because people don't keep track. Last year a kid biohacked a completely synthetic RNA prion for his Science Talent Search project—and only got second place because there was something more innovative going on."

"I know Agent Edwards said no recriminations," Susan Adler said, stroking her forehead as if it hurt, "but how the hell did we let something like that get loose to the general public?"

Browder shrugged and looked at Heather; he was right, it was her department more than his. "By the time anyone paid attention, it was making too much money to get rid of. It's the basic technology of biohacking," she said. "All those booming industrial plants around Baton Rouge and Portland, where they create cows with human blood, and that erosion-control ivy they use in burned-over areas, and those gasoline-from-saltwater-algae farms that they're just starting around San Diego. Biohacking was making too many people rich. No one wanted to squash it."

Hannah Bledsoe sighed. "So you're saying your umpty thousand saboteurs—or more—might be spraying this stuff around the country—"

"*Definitely* spraying it around the *world*," Arnie said.

Edwards cocked his head to the side and squinted hard, as if trying to see. "Uh, right. So bottom line, what's it going to do?"

Everyone looked at Heather, and she said, "Well, it looks like what they were trying to do with the biotes was make plastic rot like soft cheese on a hot day and gasoline spoil like milk."

"Any reason to think it won't work?" Edwards asked, softly, breaking the grim silence.

"I don't think Daybreak would have initiated itself until they had it working," Arnie said.

Edwards nodded. "I get it. So the nanoswarm must be working too. I understood what you said it did inside the machines, but what does it do to things as a whole?"

"As a whole, you mean—?"

"Well, Dr. Browder told me the biotes cut up molecules into little pieces, and I understood that, but it took me a moment to understand that that makes plastic rot. What does something that drips corrosive acid inside microchips do?"

"Hell if I know. Something big," Arnie said.

Browder added, "Probably many things. None of them good."

"Well," Edwards said, "I've heard enough. Dr. Yang, do you have any kind of list of the leadership of Daybreak?"

Arnie sighed. "That's why I said Daybreak initiated itself. It's a concept and a process that some people devote themselves to; there's no leadership except within tiny little affinity groups. Daybreak has no leaders, no theoreticians, nobody who runs it or made it up. In fact it probably had no creator, or no one creator. It's more . . . improvisational, like that improv comedy stuff that was popular when I was a kid? But more so. Nobody said, *Okay, we're ready for Daybreak, roll it.* Nobody gave an order, prepared a report, made a decision, voted, or took an assignment in committee. What happened was . . . more, um . . . more like a flock of geese taking off to fly south in the fall."

"I thought the goose out front was the leader."

Browder and Arnie were both looking nervously at Heather because she'd been pretty harsh with them in the meeting over coffee before this meeting. But she nodded at Arnie; it wouldn't look good to evade the question.

He said, "No, there's not really a leader as such. It's what's called flocking behavior. Some of them honk *I'm leaving* and take off, then more of them honk *I'm coming too*, and they circle and maneuver to line up in each other's slipstreams, and that forms them up into Vs, and the goose that finds itself at the head of the V heads south. That goose out front is not the leader; it's just the goose that happens to have a clear idea of south at the moment. Shoot or confuse the goose at the tip of the V, and a couple will peel off to take care of the damaged goose, and the rest will just form up behind some other goose. You can't decapitate it because it doesn't have a head."

"But . . ." Edwards didn't look at all happy. "But then how do they stay on the program?"

"The program is whatever they happen to stay on," Crittenden said, from the back of the room. "Which is taking down the Big System."

Heather wanted to hug him; she'd been afraid that Arnie would say the words that made everyone resist what he was saying—*pure system artifact*—and she wanted people committed by action before they heard that, because it was more frightening than what they'd already heard—and worse yet, probably true. "If there are no questions," she said, "let's take five minutes for bathroom and coffee, and start self-organizing, ourselves." Much as she liked Lenny Plekhanov, she was glad he hadn't been able to come on such short notice; he'd have suggested that they get all flocked up.

ABOUT FIFTEEN MINUTES LATER. GILLETTE, WYOMING. 11:30 A.M. MST. OCTOBER 28.

When Zach had loaded every recycling cart he was supposed to, he had a good twenty seed bottles left; he was supposed to improvise until late afternoon, when a guy he was giving a ride to would be calling him.

For the moment, he was just enjoying pedaling along a deserted residential street—nice houses, suburban styles from the eighties and nineties, back when they really built for the family that only went out as a unit to Chuck E. Cheese's, church, and youth activities, the way Zach remembered when he was a kid, when they'd understood that a Christian dad *needed* a home that was a fortress. *You can't bake a good cake if other people can throw in any old ingredients they want, and you can't raise a good kid if you don't make sure that everything he hears and sees is good,* Zach thought. This was the kind of street where, after Daybreak, there'd be big, healthy families, with lots of healthy, clean kids and dogs, and moms to stay home and raise them, and dads with time to play ball and go fishing and just plain hang out. Maybe Zach could move Tiff and the boys here, once Christian families had a fighting chance, and help fill the town back up.

For now, though, what to do with twenty seed bottles? Empty houses had empty yards and empty garages, which attracted bums, kids looking for party spots, and the remaining neighbors' heavy trash. All of that meant a lot of stray plastic in piles sitting out in the open, exposed to the wind. *Watch them try to put* that *toothpaste back in the tube.* By the third empty house, he had seeding a back yard down to a science.

ABOUT THE SAME TIME. LAMONT, WYOMING. 11:30 A.M. MST. OCTOBER 28.

So far Jason had reveled in miles and miles of gorgeous scenery and great music, punctuated with the amusing challenge of putting a black egg somewhere vulnerable.

Lamont, Wyoming's computer store had a going-out-of-business sign and a south-facing window. Jason walked in with faked-up questions to confuse the clerks; while they were in the back trying to figure out whether they could sell him anything, he slipped behind the counter. He left two black eggs on top of two old tower servers, right where they'd get a few hours of sunlight through the dusty front windows in the morning.

Judging by the dust on the servers, the clerks probably wouldn't see the black eggs till it was far too late; meanwhile, probably people having computer troubles—there would be a lot of those by tomorrow—would bring them in here. Jason was happier than Typhoid Mary at an all-you-can-eat salad bar.

ABOUT THE SAME TIME. GILLETTE, WYOMING. 11:30 A.M. MST. OCTOBER 28.

Howard and Isaac liked to say that trash was their life, and vice versa. Twin brothers, they liked driving the city trash truck, happily taking turns driving or loading, just as they took turns buying rounds at Mary's Retreat, buying breakfast at Perkins, doing the driving on fishing trips, and in pretty much everything else. Their joint motto was, "Me too, on everything."

Coworkers who knew the twins well often said that was why they'd reached forty years old unmarried; they couldn't find a girl who wanted them to take turns. Those friends would have been very upset to know how close to the truth they were.

This morning, they were discussing the smell of some recycling carts; Howard thought it was more like a backed-up sewer line, and Isaac thought maybe more like a diaper pail—just something to talk about as an alternative to Game Seven of the Series.

As usual, their truck was the first to the holding bin. Isaac found the lock cut off and lying on the ground; then they discovered the too-neat array of bottles in the bottom of the bin. Howard called Davidson.

"So you're calling me," Davidson said, his voice slurred from his usual four beers at lunch, "because someone put plastic bottles in the bin where we keep plastic bottles, and they cut off the lock to do it."

"Well, yeah," Howard said. "And they put them in like a pattern, like they're kind of evenly spaced over the floor of the bin, and that's pretty weird. And I climbed down and looked at one bottle—"

"I don't pay you to *look* at the bottles," Davidson said. "I pay you to bring 'em in and get us all paid. Dump your load and clock out, like you're supposed to. Don't bother me with petty weird crap. I'll put on a new lock in a few days; it's just there 'cause the Feds say I have to lock my holding bin."

"Okay, Mr. Davidson, sorry to bother you."

As they went back to the truck, Isaac said, "Should we maybe take one or two bottles to the police?"

Howard considered. "Couldn't hurt to take one or two of them and hang on to them, maybe, as evidence, in the back of the truck. Just for a couple weeks, till we knew it wasn't going to mean nothing."

"Sounds good," Isaac said. He dropped down the ladder and retrieved two bottles. "Full of some black crud. And these smell *terrible*."

"Yeah, it's weird all right," Howard agreed, swinging up into the cab of the recycling truck. "Let's get this fella dumped so we can get to the Tokyo Spa."

Howard backed the truck in (this week was his turn), and Isaac worked the hopper-gadget to send the load of plastic into the holding bin.

A moment later, he vomited, and when Howard came out to see what the strange sound was, he did too. They backed away, eyes streaming, miserable with retching and the vile smell.

"Like somebody shit a pile of strong cheese," Isaac said. "That's what it's like. It got a lot worse while it was in the truck."

Howard lit cigarettes for both of them to clear the smell,

and after bracing themselves, they moved the truck to the washing barn.

From the upwind side, the piled plastic in the holding bin looked strangely dingy, smeared with gray and brown slime. They climbed into their own pickup; Isaac put the two mystery bottles they had saved into the back, among a tangle of old rope, tools, and fishing gear.

"Whether they offer it free or not," Howard said, "at that Tokyo Spa, I think I want that full wash. Might stop off at home and pick up some clean clothes to change into, for after, too."

"Me too," Isaac said, "On everything. Might even want to shower and change before we go to the Toke. No reason those ladies should have to deal with guys that smell like we do."

Howard nodded. "Me too, on everything."

ABOUT AN HOUR LATER. WASHINGTON, DC. 2:50 P.M. EST. MONDAY, OCTOBER 28.

"So," Heather said, "before you take all this back to your home agencies, do—"

Graham walked in, looking over the three knots of diligently chattering bureaucrats with a wry little smile of approval, and shoving his wayward glasses back up his nose as always. "Heather. Something vital. Step into the hall a second."

"Sure."

Outside, he lowered his voice and said, "A limo is going to take you straight to a special meeting at Homeland Security. It will pull up outside the building in five minutes. They said to have your laptop and your current files with you. They told me what it's about but I'm not supposed to tell you—they said they'll tell you when you get there."

"Got it," she said. "Pill drive's in one pocket, cell phone's in the other, I'll snag my laptop."

"Three quick other things, Heather. One, can you deal with it if they go past midnight? This is one of those things that might."

"Bad?"

"The worst. Do you need emergency toiletries?"

"All the purse crap—and I don't need much—is in the side pockets of my laptop case. I'm good. Two?"

"Two, I don't know if there's a connection to Daybreak, but there could be, so I'm going to take our DoF part of the Daybreak team and keep them together on standby; when they go home, they'll all be on call, so if you need the Daybreak team for anything, you already have it. For that matter, if you need your boss, you know I don't have a life anyway, but I'll be extra available tonight."

She felt her breath drawing in and her shoulders squaring, the way they had in her late twenties when she was kicking down doors and busting bad guys. Usually she didn't notice how much she towered over Graham, who was only five-foot-seven, but at times like this it was hard to miss. "So *something's* in the soup."

"That brings me to number three. Cameron Nguyen-Peters is convening it. We both know what kinds of thing *he* deals with."

"Uh-huh. Bound to be interesting. 'Kay, I'll grab my stuff and tell the troops something; Nellie can handle the wrap." Truth to tell, her administrative assistant always did handle things like this, and a good thing too.

She cleared her throat at the door; they all looked up. "Everyone, I've been called to an emergency meeting. They won't tell me what it's about until I'm in the secure room, but it may be something to do with Daybreak. Nellie?"

"Ready." Her assistant's fingers poised above her laptop keyboard.

"Contact list from this meeting, available for all of us ASAP. See about a tentative meeting two days from now; DoF folks, Graham wants to talk to you right after this meeting. Sorry to run but I have to."

Everyone stared at her. She didn't blame them; she'd have been staring too. She folded her laptop, dropped it into its case, and was out the door.

Cell, pill drive, laptop, survival stuff, good till next morning if I have to be. Ready to go, just the same as the old days. There's a dance in the old dame yet, she thought smugly. *Hey, if I'm not entitled to be arrogant, who is?*

She had just time enough to notice what a beautiful fall day it was, with the leaves a wild uproar of bright colors in damp golden sunlight, before the limo shot up the main drive and braked in front of her.

Man, this is big *and someone is* worried, *for real.* The driver seemed military; as she climbed into the front seat and got a better look, she saw it was a Secret Service ERT in light-duty uniform, no external armor, but a telltale holster-buckle bump on his left shoulder. "You'll want to buckle up."

"Always do," she said. As her belt clicked closed, he whipped the big car out into the mid-day traffic, letting tires squeal and horns honk as they would, and gunned it across three lanes of traffic.

"Isn't Homeland Security in the Nebraska Complex?" Heather asked, since they were going the other way.

"Most of it still is. Secretary Ferein and some key offices have already moved to the new complex at St. Elizabeth's." He took another turn fast and tight. "Escort should pick us up next block, then we can go faster."

A DC police cruiser with siren and lights going cut in front of them, and the driver gunned the engine, apparently trying to park the limo on the cop car's bumper. They roared up an entrance ramp to the parkway, zagged across to the left lanes, and headed south at what the speedometer said was just over eighty miles an hour, the regular traffic fleeing to the right in front of them and re-merging behind them.

Heather had never realized that St. Elizabeth's was this close; usually, she supposed, it wasn't. The driver turned off with a wave to the cop, drove without touching the brake through four gates that opened inches in front of his grille, and followed a short driveway to a side door on a big, old mock castle of a building.

"Let me guess," Heather said, as he pulled the car around the little circular drive. "They just said deliver Heather O'Grainne to this door, as fast as you can?"

"That's all they told me."

The limo halted and Heather opened her door. "Thanks for keeping it down to terrifying."

He grinned at her in a not-quite-professional way and departed at a much more sedate pace.

A slim young woman, discreetly armed and overtly capable, led Heather to an elevator, which must have descended at least eight floors.

St. Elizabeth's had originally been built as the first national insane asylum, before the Civil War, and over the decades had been used for many things that needed to be hidden from the public: advanced weapons, cryptology, off-the-record briefings on black ops, meetings with outlaw governments, meetings to make decisions no one wanted to own—like a toxic dump for unspeakable secrets, as if the madness and violence at its foundation had drawn every dirty, secret thing to the old fake-feudal brickpile.

The elevator door opened, and Cameron Nguyen-Peters was waiting for her. "Hey, there, buddy," she said, grinning and throwing an arm over his shoulder, a half hug that she knew would simultaneously please him (he'd had a crush on her for fifteen years) and offend him (he'd grown steadily stuffier in his dignity with time, and he hadn't exactly started off as an egalitarian hippie, anyway). "How the hell are you?"

"Life's been better. We have one big mess on our hands." He seemed to be looking at something through the wall, twenty miles away.

"Well, if *you're* holding this meeting on the day of Game Seven, I know it's nothing small."

"Exactly." He glanced around. "Gotta say the Pirates appear to be getting a very unfair level of divine intervention. Anyway, thanks again for coming right—".

"Mr. Nguyen-Peters," a female voice said from a speaker somewhere, "the DoDDUSP"—she pronounced it daw-dusspee—"and the liaison from Deep Black are here."

Dude, Heather thought. *This is* big.

Deep Black was the satellite reconnaissance office. They didn't show up for many meetings because the breach of security in talking to or about them was so often worse than any situation that might have come up.

But if "Deep Black" was a red flag, DoDDUSP was a shrieking siren—the painfully long abbreviation for Department of Defense Deputy Under Secretary for Policy, which could be roughly defined as the guy in charge of having at his fingertips all the plans for all the wars the United States seemed likely to get into, in case the President should say, "occupy Sudan," or "seal the Mexican border," or ask "How long would it take us, starting from right now, to seize Abu Dhabi?" For forty years and more, DoDDUSPs had planned Grenada, Haiti, Kosovo,

Somalia, Afghanistan, Iraq, Pakistan, Eritrea, Jordan, the Second Korean War, the Taiwan defense, both Iranian wars, and the Myanmar Relief in Force—and a few more things the public had never heard about.

If DoDDUSP was here, it was because Cam thought there might need to be a war.

Cameron was nodding slightly, his lips pressed together, signaling her, *Yes, that's right, it's that bad.* "I have to confer with—"

The voice over the speaker said, "Mr. Nguyen-Peters, the President is just now coming in through the ultrasecure entrance."

"We should talk some time when there is time to talk. Meanwhile I have bigwigs to prep for the ops room. I know *you* can be ready on your own. Down that way, then left, someone'll set you up."

"Thanks." She hurried down the hall. *He* did *say the ops room, didn't he?* A real working space for things that were truly bad.

At the door, she was retina-scanned by an apologetic young man. Inside, no one looked up as she came in. A map of the West Coast and the Eastern Pacific dominated the big central screen, with tables and graphs scrolling by in adjoining windows. Grim-faced people in headsets, some military, some civilian, many that radiated "cop," a handful of geeks, a few who had the spy's trick of giving off nothing, were all staring into screens and tapping the keys on their desks.

Lights were low so everyone could read screens easily, and to keep voices low; it felt like two minutes to midnight. A hundred feet up it was a nice fall afternoon with the trees bursting with color, and the people didn't know this place was here. For a fleeting moment, Heather envied them, and then she strode to the station where a slim, olive-skinned young woman was beckoning her.

God, she's young—surely they're not using interns in here? Damn. No, I've just reached an age where some real live adults look young to me.

A transparent screen wrapped the far edge of Heather's desk like an armor plate, so that she could look through the screen to see everyone else, or opaque it to concentrate.

A small shelf with indentations for cups slid out of the desk to her left. The young woman set four containers into the nearest ones. "Water, Gatorade, and coffee; the last container has squeeze bottles of half and half, vanilla extract, and honey, is that right?"

"Perfect." *Oh, good, the end of the world will be comfortably to my taste.*

"Just hit the space bar when you're ready to read the briefing. Anything else I can do for you?"

"I'm good, I've been through these before." *Too many of these,* Heather thought, fixing her coffee. She sipped, pressed the space bar and looked.

Her gaze froze onto the screen. So *that* was where Samuelson had been while the media were lathering about whether he'd been muzzled or had a breakdown. Jayapura was not exactly where you'd think to look—a place most Americans hadn't thought about since MacArthur invaded there.

She scrolled down, and as she read more, her belly seemed to hold a ball of solid ice. *What the hell had everyone been doing for all this time?* How had they let the VP be in that isolated town halfway round the world in the first place without proper security? *Dammit! Samuelson thinks agreeing is more important than what you agree about, and they strung him along forever, then rushed him, and because he didn't want "small details"*—like proper security!—*to be in the way, all the normal security just got peeled off like a guy trying to finish a dogsled race and throwing off his camping stuff, then his spare food, then his water, then his coat—and now the blizzard hits.*

So the whole time, as they sacrificed all his security, our brave good-hearted goddam fucking naïve Samuelson kept reassuring everyone that he wasn't afraid, and nobody said, "But, sir, it's not just the danger to you, and the reason you're not afraid is that you're a fool."

Radio silence; going out without the direct-to-satellite transmitters, when it turned out they didn't have one on short notice; not flying one out ASAP because another plane landing at Sentani might have drawn attention; who the hell's brilliant idea had *that* been?

Three real stupid temporary solutions. Or *were* they *stupid*? Did they all come from the same place?

Shit. All three from one Samuelson advisor, Atela Pawhan,

formerly Mary Davis. Back when she was Davis, she'd been briefly married to a guy who was now identified as a sometime stringer on the edge of the il'Alb il-Jihado network. Pawhan had a cousin, Lorenzo Bell, who worked in the secured storage where they kept the encrypted direct-to-satellite boxes—

She had almost posted **round those people up, now**, before she saw the screen title: **BELL GROUP, IDENTIFIED MEMBERS AND DISPOSITIONS**.

Duh.

The reason it was all there on one screen for her to find was that the FBI had already tried to arrest Pawhan and Bell about an hour ago. They found Pawhan dead in her apartment, which had been trashed in a way that fit the script for "surprised an intruder." Bell had extensive gambling debts, and a suicide note, to go with being found hanging from his showerhead. The feebs didn't believe either, of course, and were searching their apartments to see if they could find some clue to their controllers.

An IM glowed in the corner of her screen: **L. Plekhanov, NSA.**

Lenny! Aside from being her source for cryptology, and the only reason Arnie Yang could read Daybreak's messages, Leonardo Plekhanov was also responsible for the last three dates she'd had—each about a month apart. She looked around for his wheelchair, and then spotted the thick, wraparound glasses surrounding Lenny's outsized square head above his tiny shoulders; she waved, and he raised his small, twisted left arm at her, smiling.

His message said, **shitload more relevant stuff 2 read B4 strt. back 2 wrk, Beautiful. Bell Org prolly=no clues.**

Okay, this is seriously weird. **how U know?**

clenched fists, rubbing back of neck, uncanny analyst ability, sherlock holmes-like attn 2 detail! He turned his wheelchair to give her the full effect of his big grin. **also i can read the files backward on yr screen cuz not opaqued.**

Addressing me as Beautiful is not exactly opaque either. She took the time to type that one all the way out. *Hunh. Assuming the whole world didn't blow apart, wonder if he's got anywhere to watch the Series tonight, and if he likes brats baked with sauerkraut? And the Angels, of course.*

She put her mind back on the briefing; sheesh, her old tai

chi coach would be all over her for the bad case of monkey mind she was developing today. Center, breathe, be in the flow . . .

Heather felt a twinge of guilt for enjoying good coffee in a comfortable chair, reading about Our Man In Jayapura trapped in that office over a bank. The supplementary data noted that he was twenty-seven years old and on his third assignment with the Foreign Service. *At least someone else somewhere had an early career experience that actually sucked worse than mine.*

The report noted that he'd destroyed the confidential documents and erased all computer files, standard practice for a consul in his situation, and that his morale was assessed as "good to very good" in the circumstances. *There's a relief,* Heather thought, *some people might think being surrounded by an angry mob in a foreign country might excuse negative thinking.* An attachment to the document said that overtime had been authorized since he couldn't get back to his apartment. *Not only is his morale good, he's getting* paid; *can't do better than that!* He had been strongly advised to take all necessary measures for his personal safety. *I'm sure he wouldn't have thought of that on his own.*

Indonesian authorities in Jayapura, after much polite demurral and reassurance, had finally admitted that Sentani International Airport had been seized just at twilight, when Islamist rebels had come out of the low hills above the airport and overwhelmed the small security force. A "reinforced national police battalion"—internal security troops with a few light machine guns—had gone out from Jayapura to try to retake the airport, but they had been ambushed and thrown back on the only road around the bay. Unequipped for night fighting, the Indonesian soldiers had dug in for the night and would wait for dawn, when, "if God wills it," a raider battalion would arrive. There were two links to raider battalion, so she clicked on them; the first explained that raiders were what Indonesia called special forces, and the second that the military attaché at the Embassy in Jakarta thought that an Indonesian raider battalion, assuming one arrived, could probably succeed in retaking the airport, unless of course there were more rebels than he had been told or "other unforeseen circumstances."

In other words, the government forces will win unless they don't. Nobody said anything about how the raiders would be getting there, with the airport closed. "Naval units" (but the communiqué didn't say which ones) were "on their way," and "we expect a satisfactory resolution within a short time" according to an Indonesian defense spokesman, also in Jakarta—farther from Jayapura than DC is from LA.

Heather scanned the FAQ window (*and just how can any question about* this *situation be asked "frequently" yet? Illiterates!*). She found **timetable**.

Two hours before anyone knew that Air Force Two was missing.

Almost five hours before anyone American realized it was probably in hostile hands.

Modified Boeing 787 Dreamliner, cruised at Mach 0.9, fully fueled. Still seven hours flying time left at normal cruise; could reach the opposite side of the planet without refueling.

They had been unable to turn on the secure transponders via satellite, which probably meant Bell had told the other side how to find and destroy them.

Satellite and air reconnaissance revealed no trace of the big white plane on the ground or in the air anywhere near Jayapura. The "Air Force Two Possible Area" now extended nearly from pole to pole, and along the equator from the 135 West meridian (about two-thirds of the way from the mainland to Hawaii) all the way to the 55 East meridian (just short of Madagascar and running north through the Persian Gulf and Iran).

A light touch on her shoulder made her look up at Cameron. "I just wanted to say," he said, "I'm glad you're here."

"Big mess, eh?"

"Just wanted to say hi to a friendly face before I got into this."

"Best of luck," she said, "and I mean that." At the FBI, she'd been the closest thing he'd had to a friend; that had always made her feel sorry for him.

President Roger Pendano entered, flanked by DoDDUSP Mark Garren. Both men looked tired, shocked, and old. "Here we go," Cam said, and hurried to the rostrum by the big screen.

"By now you are all aware of the basic situation, but more

bad news, just confirmed, will update your timelines on your screens in a couple of minutes. Here it is in brief:

"About forty-five minutes ago, three bodies fell into a large town square in Nakhon Ratchasima, Thailand, apparently dropped from a large unmarked white plane, with twin engines, which was flying low over the town—no positive identification, so far, by anyone we can trust to definitely identify a 787. Local air traffic control confirms that they had a big plane that didn't answer any radio hail and continued on its way to the northwest.

"The American Embassy has claimed the bodies for an autopsy, but they fell more than a mile and landed on pavement. A Navy doctor from the *Franklin Roosevelt* is still on her way to do the positive identification. Tentatively, we believe them to be Carol Tattinger, the State Department liaison for Vice President Samuelson's mission; Martin Reeve, the Defense liaison; and William DeGrante, the Homeland Security liaison. A great circle route from Jayapura through Nakhon Ratchasima extends along a line that skirts the Burma-China border, and then across the very northern edge of India—which is to say one that more or less walks the line between Indian and Chinese airspace. Those are the two competent air forces in that region, and they don't get along with each other, so if that is Air Force Two, the hijackers may be hoping to be able to dodge across the border if either side tries to intercept.

"That great circle line would take the plane up into wild country in Central Asia, where various Islamist warlords and criminal gangs hold actual power.

"We've lofted minis—short-term satellites—using the Raptor augmented system, out of Germany, and Global Hawks have already taken off from Bagram, so if it stays in the air, we should be able to find that white plane within the hour. India has been completely cooperative—they've offered us landing rights as needed and some of their own planes are out searching even as we speak. When you ask China for help, of course, you never know what the answer is going to be until they give it."

That caused State and Defense reps to interrupt and argue; Heather had time to access the spreadsheets that had generated the graphics on the main board.

Cameron was going on. "—well be a diversion or a part of

some larger plan, or there may be something we are not seeing. This is not a usual sort of—"

That's it. Heather typed the numbers in frantically, saw the result, scrolled back, found what she wanted, and highlighted it. She tagged it **Inconsistent data / possible ruse** and hit SEND.

Cam was saying, "So if there are no more questions—wait. Ms. O'Grainne?"

Heather said, "Based on flight time since Air Force Two left Jayapura, and the time the bodies fell in Thailand, that great circle arc is only about half as long as it should be. On that course at cruising speed, they ought to actually be in the 'Stans by now. And why throw three bodies from a plane over a city, let alone fly low over inhabited areas, when you could have gotten rid of the bodies for literally hours over the sea, or just left them behind in the first place? Especially when their best hope of success has to be in going undetected?

"Look at the consul's report. They towed a Lion Airways plane into the hangar early that night; I just Goo-22ed photos of Lion Airways planes. They're mostly white already, and they fly some 737s, which is a twin-engine airliner even if it's an old one. You'd just need a few hours to repaint the tail and the markings and refuel, then drop bodies somewhere very public. They couldn't make the timing come out right, and someone who knew something might recognize it was an old 737 and not a new 787, but they probably thought it was worth gambling that we wouldn't be thinking clearly because we'd be too angry about what they did to our people."

Cameron froze, which was a good sign; his first instinct, when things didn't make sense, was always to stop moving until they did.

"It still might have been Air Force Two; those things could be explained," Mark Garren, the DoDDUSP, pointed out. "Why would they run a whole second operation just as a ruse?"

"Mr. Plekhanov of NSA has a comment," Cameron said.

Lenny's good hand trembled as he adjusted his headset. "*Timing.* There must be something we could do that would make a difference if we don't waste any time. So the target is only partly the Vice President, since they already have him. They're going to do something with him and that 787, and they want us to dither before we act. Meanwhile, Air Force Two is going somewhere to deliver the main blow. Look at the edge of the possible area."

On the big board, slowly, just barely visibly, the curve of the places Air Force Two could have gotten to continued to widen.

"Not Hawaii. Not Australia or anywhere in Asia," Cameron Nguyen-Peters said softly. "They'd have hit them hours ago if it was a target there. Anchorage just came within reach, Juneau will soon—Marshall, can you do us a geometric, focus on the next areas to become vulnerable in say the next two hours—show us when each part of the West Coast comes in range?"

"Already working on it, sir, coming up—" a voice said over the speakers.

The screen popped and adjusted, revealing a severely distorted map of the west coast of North America. The familiar coastline had been bent and twisted till it looked like claws reaching into the Pacific. "Nearest targets south of Alaska," Marshall said, his voice calm and dispassionate over the speakers, "on the great circle routes. First the area around Coos Bay, then Puget Sound, and then gradually down to south California, with a lot of hops and skips because the coast bows out a long way toward New Guinea around the California-Oregon line, and again down by LA."

Garren drew a breath. "Mr. President, I recommend you activate Forward Sentry West."

Pendano looked like he was going to throw up, but he turned to the quiet little man carrying the case beside him, and said, "Hand me the football. I certify that I am sane and there is a National Defense Emergency."

"Authentication: Nineteen," Garren said, and the football-carrier stepped forward and handed the little black case to the President.

Pendano opened it, placed his hand flat on a reader plate, brought a microphone to his mouth, and said, "Authenticate."

"Authenticated," the football said.

"Authorize Forward Sentry West. Not a drill. Mu Nu Brave Walker. Repeat not a drill. Mu Nu Brave Walker. Verify."

"Authorize Forward Sentry West," the football said. "Authorization begins in one minute unless intervention—"

"Accelerate. Gamma Omicron Dominant Eagle."

"Forward Sentry West commenced."

Pendano handed the football back to the carrier and sank into his chair, rubbing his eyes.

Garren looked around. "You should all know. Plan Forward Sentry West is a joint American-Canadian-Mexican total aerial blockade of the West Coast. All incoming flights will be diverted to quarantined landing fields, if they obey orders; if they don't, they'll be shot down." He looked around and said, "Forward Sentry West will be run out of the Pentagon and NORAD at Cheyenne Mountain. So officially Secretary of Defense Kimura will be taking over. I'm going to request that they leave me here; it's a mature plan and once a warplan is settled on, as DoDDUSP, I don't have much to do; forgive my arrogance, Mr. Nguyen-Peters, but I think I'll be more useful here, where we don't know what we're doing yet."

"You'll certainly be welcome." Cam was normally all but expressionless, but even more so now; Heather wondered whether he was displeased to have a backseat driver or relieved that this wouldn't be his affair much longer.

Garren nodded politely. "Given that this is the room where people will be cleaning up the domestic damage, it seems only reasonable for me to answer any questions you may have."

"Hernandez, Agriculture." The heavyset woman's arms were folded on her chest, and she was glaring over her bifocals. "Are there any limits on the blockade? If it doesn't comply, they shoot it down, no matter where or what or how?"

"Pilots are allowed some judgment," Garren said. "If the legendary man in a lawn chair with balloons is out there, they'll look at him before they shoot. But discretion cuts both ways. They don't have to ask permission, just exercise judgment, to use tactical nuclear weapons in the interceptions."

Cameron said, "Ms. Nakayara, FAA?"

The petite woman looked up from her desk. "Why would you use a nuke?"

"Gas, germs, or another nuke could be on that plane," Garren said, quietly. "And airbursts of tactical nukes don't produce much fallout. So the safest thing we can do in the circumstances is to, um, sterilize it thoroughly, if it's someplace where collateral damage is tolerable. For example, if we'd been following Plan Forward Sentry back on Septem-

ber 11, 2001, we would have shot down but not nuked the
planes once they were over DC and New York; but we'd have
used a nuke on the one over rural Pennsylvania."

"Good Christ," Nakayara said, very quietly.

Heather thought she'd never heard anything put better.

**ABOUT HALF AN HOUR LATER. JUST EAST OF BUFFALO,
WYOMING. 2:20 P.M. MST. MONDAY, OCTOBER 28.**

Jason's parking spot at the truck stop at the junction with I-90
was a jackpot. To one side of the F-150, he tossed a black egg
through a rolled-down window into an open bag of electri-
cian's tools in the back of a rusty Subaru. El Slobbo Electrico
would spread nanoswarm everywhere he went, and if Daybreak was working, he'd be going a lot of places soon.

On the other side of the F-150, there was an elderly Prius
that looked like it had last been washed when Bush was president, with junk-food wrappers, parking tickets, unopened
mail, eviction orders, and court notices scattered across the
back seat, an ode in debris to a freshman year ending at fall
midterms.

Hunh. Massachusetts plate, new U of Montana bumper
sticker. Probably on her way home. No doubt Little Muffin
Dropout was all liberal, going to vote for Pendano, always did
her community service at school with a smile, all that shit,
and thought all her spiritual talk was making a difference in
the world. *Muffy, you are about to make the biggest difference you are ever going to make.*

"Hey, you like my ride?"

Jason turned. The plump girl with thick glasses and a
dozen band buttons on her jacket held a giant mug of coffee
and a big container of chicken nuggets.

"Just looking and thinking you were probably cool."

"If you have some weed, we could chill."

"We're both out of luck," he said, "but I was just thinking,
this car needs some serious help, and like, I'd hate to have a
cool person get all stranded and stuff." *Jesus, I hope I'm being
inarticulate enough to sound trustworthy.*

About cars, Jason only knew what he'd picked up from being a gofer and light-holder for Carrie, the girl who kept the

commune's three old beaters running, but he was sure Miss Little Lost Muffin knew even less.

"Oh, man, that would suck to get stuck someplace. Once I got stuck when I was out with this guy drinking at UM, up at Lolo Hot Springs? and it turned out I was just out of gas and the battery was dead? but I like had to call my dad so he could call Triple A to tow the car the next day? but I like didn't know that like at the time? So we needed to stay warm for the night, and the guy—"

Jason turned and fished in the toolbox for a few wrenches and screwdrivers, and shuffled four black eggs into his hands under the tools. "Well, let's make sure you don't get stuck this time. Pop your hood."

He poked around and hmmed until she became bored and asked if she could turn on the stereo. That took about three minutes.

While she sat in the driver seat, eating her chicken, on the other side of the raised hood, Jason planted two eggs down low on the rear surface of the main generator—ambient heat wasn't as good as solar, but it would work as long as one side of the egg was about 25 C warmer than the other. It looked like the cooling fan motor would blow the nanoswarm backward and down so that it didn't build up and stop the engine too soon; he wanted Muffin here to keep rolling for a good long way, because I-90 would take her all the way back to Massachusetts, with bright sun on the south side the whole way, and if he could make this old prehistoric hybrid car scatter nanoswarm all along that highway, he could infect tens of thousands of cars. She was a perfect Patient Zero, and he didn't want to squander the opportunity.

If I wanted to spread the clap, I'd give it to a slut who was following a band for the summer, he thought. *If I wanted to spread flu, I'd cough on a flight attendant with a compromised immune system. And to spread nanoswarm . . . bright sunlight, badly shielded electrical system with lots of old-fashioned strong electric fields, on a platform traveling along one of the busiest roads on the continent.*

He loudly said, "Just want to see what's up on one passenger-side motor, looks seriously weird," and crouched down beside the car, cheerfully putting two black eggs above the rear passenger-side wheel, where they would have plenty of sun if she was driving the way he'd guessed, and whirling electromagnetic fields from the motors no matter what, and thus produce a snow of nanoswarm as it ate her fender from inside, not destroying her car, but dropping nanoswarm onto the highway for hundreds of miles.

Then he closed it up, told her to get it looked at in "B-town," and declined again the offer to get wasted and listen to some tunes before he went. She insisted on giving him something in trade, which turned out to be a plastic sandwich bag of weed. He waved at her as she drove away.

Once she was gone, he added a black egg to the baggie and left it in the sun on top of a transformer box by a lamppost. *I don't really care who picks that up or why, as long as they put it in their car.*

He checked his cheapo plaztatic Wal-Mart watch; it showed a series of upside-down u's, and when he pushed the reset button, it died completely. He dropped it in the back of the nearest pickup.

Backing out, he thought:

> *Little Muffin had a car*
> *I gave it nanospawn.*
> *And everywhere that Muffin drove,*
> *The Big System was gone.*

ABOUT HALF AN HOUR LATER. YUMA, ARIZONA. ABOUT 3:00 P.M. MST. MONDAY, OCTOBER 28.

Ysabel Roth's parents had been service-oriented pacifists, raising her in a dozen countries while they bounced all over the world working for justice and development. She'd just kind of naturally gravitated into taking care of the world, doing two years' service in Mexico right after college. Last year waiting tables at The Green Mother had been less dramatic, but she'd still seen a lot of life.

She yawned, stretched, and rubbed her face. *Not nearly as much life as I'm about to see; life never involved a Stinger missile before.*

The TV-control thing, linked to the launcher on the roof, showed a big white blimp, which Aaron had said was technically not a blimp but an aerostat. He had nice eyes and such a comforting, technically competent manner that she listened to him explaining tech stuff just to enjoy the sound of his voice. Apparently a blimp had a motor and went somewhere, and an aerostat was just tied to the ground by a long rope. But this aerostat did have a motor, Aaron had made a point of that, and she had nodded and liked the way he pushed his hair back off his face, and the motor put out infrared radiation. It made her sick that people would put radiation into the sky like that, but it would allow the Stinger to home in on it.

It was kind of like a video game, right down to little red letters she couldn't read because she'd never picked up much Farsi.

Aaron had driven off that morning in a beat-up old Ford Hybridstar, loaded with all her stuff. He'd promised to set it into her room so it was all there when she arrived at the commune in Mexico. To stay here for two days, Ysabel had picked up an air mattress, two cups, a tea ball, and an old teakettle at the Salvation Army, and liberated a few sandwiches and some tea from The Green Mother.

She felt ashamed; Miriam always had been nice to her, even advancing her her first month's rent for this place.

Well, after Daybreak, things would be better for local businesses, anyway. Meanwhile, Ysabel really needed the tea.

Other than her tea, all she had left was her purse and the cell phone she'd bought at a convenience store three weeks ago, to allow time for them to overwrite the surveillance video.

The kettle whistled; she made her tea; while it steeped, she contemplated the screen. She put the crosshairs on the motor, which turned a generator, which powered a radar thing, which shot radiation into Mexico to keep Mexicans out of the United States.

The idea that someone would keep out peasants, especially with radiation, made her sick. Ysabel loved peasants; she had learned wisdom and truth from peasants everywhere. One supercilious snot-chick at school had said that Ysabel had never met a peasant who wasn't a great person in wonderful harmony with the whole Earth.

The thing was, it was *true*. Che had loved peasants, and so had all the great Latin American poets and writers, and for that matter fucking Jesus had loved peasants. Peasants were just, you know, lovable.

Aaron had that Che-Jesus-Latin-American-poet look about him, big wet brown eyes, curly black beard and hair in a mad scraggle, soft sensitive lips and expressive eyebrows . . .

Ysabel wanted to just talk with Aaron about her love for peasants. She loved faces with real character shaped by troubles, and simple faith in simple stories, and everything about the peasants. She loved their work ethic. She loved their gentle way with children—even when they hit them, it was totally different from some dad in the suburbs mindlessly pouring out rage on a little kid; you could feel the love. She liked the blunt, open sense of humor and the earthiness of the peasant women.

Daybreak was, really, truly, just the beginning of an America with acoustic folk and no country, deep faith and no religion, peasants and no rednecks.

Surely, for that, one little Stinger fired at military property was okay. You had to be practical, ends and means, omelets and eggs, all that stuff she'd had in college.

She smiled. Dad had once told her that instead of playing violent video games, she should be learning something practical.

ABOUT THE SAME TIME. OFF SAN NICOLAS ISLAND, CALIFORNIA. ABOUT 2:00 P.M. PST. MONDAY, OCTOBER 28.

"Forty-eight seconds," Tracy Barbour said, as the black balloon tumbled upward and away, rising quickly and disappearing into the bright blue afternoon sky. "Beat that."

"If you'll take the helm."

"Just what I was hoping you'd say. And how 'bout a beer for each of us? We're down to our last two tanks of hydrogen; only about a hundred balloons to go. We won't be drunk before we finish launching."

Grady made his way to the cooler, his mind already on the next few months of loafing from port to port while they saw what shape the new world would take.

They always had been very green, from their long vacations spent hiking, to the natural fibers they wore, to the family land they'd put in conservation trusts, and of course their wooden boat, so when Tracy had been IMing with a few interesting people some years ago, they had immediately understood the promise of Daybreak, and a world without industry, because of the stories they had heard as children: Tracy's grandmother had told her about life in a really big, comfortable house with abundant servants; Grady's great-grandfather had described, in loving detail, how it was to own the whole estuary of a small river and maintain it for waterfowl and fish.

Rich was always better than poor, of course, but after Daybreak, Tracy liked to say, there would just be more *point* to being rich. Today's twenty-first-century squalid, poor industrial world, where even the best of family and school meant only that you could afford a nanny and a cleaning service, a world where there was plenty of stuff but the stuff was all crap, and every damn body that wanted it could go anywhere whether they properly appreciated it or not . . . *faugh*!

Daybreak would bring back the world where people had a place, and filled it well, and knew they belonged there.

Grady and Tracy had about half a ton of gold in the concealed second hold, but until there was a safe way and place to spend it, they planned to fish and do small trading; hard work, but climbing mountains and sailing long distances *is* hard work, so it would be nothing they couldn't handle.

Grady handed her a beer. "Hard work is overrated."

"Where did that come from?"

"The cooler."

"No, silly boy, what you just said."

"Oh, I was just thinking, the trouble with people who do hard work is that they think it entitles them to whatever they want. Every damn rice farmer in Asia wants to be able to buy all the cheap plastic crap his shack can hold—"

"Do they call them shacks?"

"They call them something in Chinese or some language, hon, it's just an example."

"I mean, is it something we'd call a shack or is it more like a hut?" That little smile he had loved madly since St. Albans quirked up the corner of her mouth.

He gulped some icy beer and said, "I did have sort of a point."

"Okay." She squirmed to sit up straighter and did her best to look very, very serious.

God, he thought, *it's good to be this in love with my wife after fifteen years.* "Oh, just that Asian rice farmer—let's call him Wong—"

"Fong." The challenging twinkle in her eye meant *You are so getting laid tonight.*

"Fong it is. Anyway, Fong's an example of someone who really overrates hard work. See, because he works like a sonofabitch farming rice, and his kids work hard and long making cheap plastic crap in the factory, he thinks he's entitled to buy all the cheap plastic crap he can stuff into his shack. He doesn't get that *life* is hard work, whether it's picking rice or climbing Everest or managing a company. Hard work doesn't have anything to do with it; you should work hard wherever you are and shut the fuck up. You see what I mean?"

"No," she said. "Six minutes."

"What?"

"Six minutes since you took over launching balloons, and you haven't launched even one. You're not even close to beating me."

He laughed and said, "Now time me on this next one."

"Go," she barked.

He lunged for the next balloon and jar. One hundred four more tries, and he never beat her best time, but he was pretty bombed for the last thirty. "What a grand day," he said, watching the last one sail off toward the California coast. "What a goddam well grand day, with a grand life to follow."

ABOUT HALF AN HOUR LATER. ON I-90 EAST BETWEEN GILLETTE AND SHERIDAN, WYOMING. ABOUT 3:30 P.M. MST. MONDAY, OCTOBER 28.

Probably that nice hippie mechanic guy just didn't realize that some younger girls like interesting older guys, Marshalene decided. He was a good mechanic, though, no question. According to the graphics on the dash, the gas engine had settled right on the peak of the power curve and was purring away in easy perfection, despite being an antique 2012 model, spinning power out to the wheel motors and filling up the batteries. Or maybe it always did that, but she preferred to think hippie mechanic guy did it. *Especially if he was thinking about me while he did.*

She had finished the chicken from the bucket and was well into the Doritos, her coustajam hookmix cranked up to the top, buzzing the two car windows that weren't quite tight. Well, it was sad college hadn't worked out, but right now she had food and tunes and open road ahead of her, and she was good at accepting what was good and not worrying much.

To her left, in the other lane, she saw a column of trucks drafting; the IBIS wireless system on the interstates, one of Prez Pendano's big deals that her dad was always complaining about the cost of, let a whole big huge row of trucks work their brakes all together, so they could be almost on each other's asses, taking turns breaking the wind for each other. It meant sometimes you'd have like five gazillion trucks passing you on the highway.

No worry about passing *them* because when they were drafting, they were doing like a hundred or better; that didn't seem fair to Marshalene, but shit, life wasn't fair. She'd just barely found her groove, living in Missoula, when they threw her out of her apartment and made her go home. The whole world was full of mean people, and like the sticker said, they sucked.

. . .

Behind the rear passenger-side motor, where Jason had planted them, the two black eggs were getting steady sunlight from the south, warmth from the motor, and a steady flux of alternating magnetic fields; as programmed, each of them kept resetting and streaming out slightly different versions of nanoswarm every hundred thousand copies or so, which was about every four seconds.

Almost all of the nanoswarm were caught in the slipstream as the air rushed around the spinning wheels, scattered into the wake in the air behind the Prius. The strong southwest wind off the mountains blew them in a thick cloud across the wide median; some landed in the dirt, many on the small, scrawny pine trees or in the brush, but millions of nanoswarm were sucked into the six-mile-long cyberlinked truck convoy, lighting in the engines and on grilles, finding energy sources and metal and beginning to feed and reproduce.

By the time Marshalene's Prius had passed—only about two minutes, since they were going in opposite directions—all 562 trucks in the locked chain were infected, and for the next few hours, they covered Wyoming, Montana, and Idaho's lifeline highway with tens of billions of nanoswarm, till a few peeled off the convoy; till their engines, electronics, and motors failed and stranded a few more; and till the rest piled at the foot of a cliff in Lookout Pass where IBIS had gone dead and so had the warning system.

ABOUT THE SAME TIME. GILLETTE, WYOMING. ABOUT 3:30 P.M. MST. MONDAY, OCTOBER 28.

Behind a boarded-up apartment building, Zach stripped off his coat, and with it the cheap whiskey smell; his dirty, ragged outer shirt; and his filthy dreadlocked wig and knit cap. He left the clothes on the old bicycle, to be stolen and carry the bug farther. The wig might look suspicious, so he threw it under the old, rotting deck—anyone who saw it would think it was a dead animal.

At the mall, Zach squatted in the stall till the men's room was empty, then climbed at once onto the sink, pushed up the ceiling tile, and pulled down the white plastic bag. He jumped down and scrubbed the brownish blotchy makeup off his face, hands, and neck in the sink.

In the stall, he took clean shoes, shirt, pants, and a light jacket from the bag. He dug out the hotel keys and car keys from the pocket of his bum pants, and put his bum clothes into the bag. As he emerged from the stall, carrying the white bag discreetly by his side, a high-pitched voice declared, "I'm going to poop right *in here*," and an indulgent adult male voice said, "That's right, Malachai, that's what we come here for."

Zach nodded at the little boy and his harried father; the kid looked a lot like his firstborn, Noah, at that same age. *Enjoy indoor pooping while you can, Malachai.*

He emptied the bag while unobserved in a toy store (plenty of plastic there).

At the opposite end of the mall, he caught the shuttle bus to the Holiday Inn, where his car, regular-person clothes, razor, and tub were waiting for him. On the shuttle bus, he bowed his head to pray gratefully. His phone vibrated; he put it to his ear. "Hey."

"Hi, I'm looking for Laura Haxson."

"Nobody by that name at this phone." Zach hung up.

In his hotel room, he hit the dialback.

■ ■ ■

The view from Jason's picnic table at the roadside rest, just outside Gillette, was very Hollywood: water towers and steeples above the blaze of fall colors from the old trees. No doubt it would turn out to be seedy and run-down.

His cell phone vibrated; the call was from UNAVAILABLE. "Yeah?"

"Did you want to buy a snowmobile?"

"Yeah."

"What do you have to trade?"

"Real old F-150."

"Okay, meet me at a rental property I own, it's real run-down and doesn't look good, just bring the truck all the way up the driveway."

Sounded like WalksWDLord had found a good concealed spot, just as they'd agreed. Jason scribbled directions in ballpoint on his hand. "Got it."

"I've got a shower here." WalksWDLord explained how to walk to the Holiday Inn. "I'm in Room 215. You can clean up here and then we'll grab some dinner and be on the road."

"Very cool."

Jason prayed that the truck had one more start left in it. He didn't think the nanospawn would be able to knock out the alternator quite this fast, but shorting out the battery or eating the electronic distributor was well within their reach, to judge by the way the music had gone dead half an hour ago.

He thought about peeking under the hood, but there'd be time enough for that once he got to his destination, and meanwhile it would be better not to let in light, or more nanospawn.

The house with the FOR RENT sign was right where it was supposed to be, and Jason followed the driveway around to the garage in the back.

Jason stripped off coat, hat, gloves, and sweater, and tossed them onto the back porch. Maybe some homeless dude would find them and spread the nanospawn. He erased the cell phone's recent calls, turned it off, and tossed it over the alley into a toy-crowded back yard to spread more nanospawn.

Jason took out his second pair of clean chem-proof gloves (sprinkled with Drano crystals, inside tied-off condoms) and slipped them on, walked back to the truck, opened the passenger-side door, poured Liquid-Plumr over the top of his pack, rinsed with a bottle of distilled water. He shrugged the pack on.

He left both doors hanging open and the keys in the ignition. On a whim, he raised the hood too, and looked inside by the bright afternoon sunlight.

The battery top had been clean the night before, but now it was covered with fluffy white crystals. The ends of wires everywhere were clotted with colored metal salts, and corrosion mixed with too-bright spots to speckle the whole surface of the engine. *Definitely working—good. I'd sure feel like a damn idiot if it wasn't.*

ABOUT THE SAME TIME. WASHINGTON, DC. 5:54 P.M. EST. MONDAY, OCTOBER 28.

Heather was huddled with Working Group Jayapura Ground, going over how the supposedly secure TBMW signal had probably been tapped. "A guy in Jim Browder's Tech Assessment Office, Paulton Shapiro, has cataloged the ways to steal tight-beam microwave signals. The one I think happened here is called phased-interference edge-diffracted scattering, PIEDS, because it's best adapted to a situation where a beam has to go between very precisely known locations and pass through an aperture surrounded by a conductor, like say the aluminum frame of a window."

"Is that off-the-shelf tech?" Khang from CIA asked.

"You can't buy it in a store, but DARPA's labs have been trying to build them since way back in the Obama administration. Probably fifty countries have experimented with it. Somebody was bound to make PIEDS work in field conditions, sooner or later. It's not intrinsically expensive, just needs very fast processors and some work-arounds on a couple physics issues. And it makes sense. To take the plane by subterfuge, intact, they needed to go the instant the plane went into radio silence. They knew the right time because the Pawhan/Bell cell set them up so that they were vulnerable to PIEDS. So—"

Cameron tapped her shoulder. "I know I've taken you through three working groups in an hour, Heather, but I need you in another one. Please come with me."

At first she thought she was going to be in Working Group Pawhan Bell because he led her to the conference room where they were, but he just stuck his head in and said, "Dr. Edwards."

"Coming."

It was Edwards from the FBI, the one who looked like Popeye and had been at the Daybreak presentation. He nodded politely, and said, "Here we are again."

"Yeah." Heather was trying to think of how to ask what was going on, but Cameron hurried on, and the two of them hurried to catch up; he gestured them into a conference room but didn't go in himself. Lenny Plekhanov was the only person in there. "Hi, do you guys have any idea what Cam's doing?"

"None at all," Heather said. "Lenny Plekhanov, this is Agent Edwards—Dr. Edwards, I guess, from what Cam—"

"The doctorate's in social psych," Edwards said, "and Lenny and I know each other, we worked on—"

The door opened and an assistant brought in five more people; the four Heather recognized were Reynolds, who was another FBI agent; Robbins, the CIA analyst from the Daybreak meeting; Nancy Telabanian, a quiet woman in a dark suit, who was Lenny Plekhanov's boss from NSA; and the guy from Deep Black. The one Heather didn't know was an African-American woman in a colonel's uniform with the Army's Cyber Command patch. They had barely sat down and begun shaking hands and getting acquainted when Cam came in and closed the door.

He walked to the end of the table and stood resting his hands on it, as if he might need to lunge out the door at any moment. "Heather, I have to ask right away, bluntly. Hannah Bledsoe told me about your presentation regarding the Daybreak movement this morning, and that whatever Daybreak is, it is apparently already active. Can you assure me that it has nothing to do with this present situation? And whether it does or not, do you see an impact on what's going on?"

Heather felt the implicit criticism—as Cam had doubtless known she would—in the pit of her stomach. She could feel herself being fitted with the tag that read FAMOUS UNKNOWN IDIOT, the tag that adhered to the officer at Pearl Harbor who saw planes on the new experimental radar and thought they must be a much smaller flight of American planes he was expecting, the intelligence officers who ignored aerial photos of all that Russian construction gear moving into Berlin in 1961, and the FBI administrator who didn't see anything urgent in so many Saudi men with al-Qaeda links taking flying lessons; she could imagine headlines on a billion screens: DOF COP COULD HAVE PREVENTED DISASTER.

Edwards gazed at her like the eyepits of a skull. "Well, if—"

Cameron silenced him with a glare. *At least he understands that I'm thinking.*

If the seizure of the Vice President wasn't connected to Daybreak, it had to be history's most amazing accidental—

Timing.

The thing their unknown enemy was best at.

"I think," she said, "that there *has* to be a connection, even though it's so improbable that it didn't even occur to me." She looked around the room. "Those of you who weren't at the briefing, how much do you know about Daybreak?"

"I only heard about it fifteen minutes ago," Cameron said. He managed not to sound as if he *should have* heard about it sooner, one more thing Heather owed him for.

"I read through the liaison's notes earlier this afternoon," the colonel from Cyber Command said. She shrugged. "Not with the attention I should have; I thought it was interesting, not urgent for me."

Heather sketched it out in a few brief sentences—a leaderless, directionless-on-purpose anti-movement, built around the idea that with enough small, self-replicating bio- and nano- sabotage carried out simultaneously, the Big System—the modern world, really—could be taken down so that it never arose again. She took full blame for not alerting people earlier. "Just this morning, Graham Weisbrod himself had to corner me and tell me that we needed to talk to the rest of DoF, and while we were doing that my chief researcher on the project discovered that Daybreak had started."

Nancy Telabanian from NSA, said, "Lenny, I'm guessing you didn't see how vital this was going to be."

"I gave Heather as much support as I could out of the amateur section," Lenny said. "But Daybreak uses continuously modulated one-time keys for their ciphers—the same basic tech that spy agencies and armies use nowadays all over the world—and what they were using was good enough to keep us weeks, sometimes months, behind Daybreak's key changes. We usually read their traffic five to nine weeks behind, till just this week when we identified what they were using as their modulator key." He pushed his big, soft flop of black hair off his forehead, distracting Heather for an instant. "I'm afraid I was every bit as blind as Heather—"

Edwards glanced around the room. "I am quite certain my office would have done no better with this, Mr. Nguyen-Peters. We all claim to expect the unexpected, but it's a lie we tell to protect our budgets. We don't need to analyze how we missed Daybreak. I don't think that's productive. I do think Ms. O'Grainne almost certainly has to be right—Daybreak and this attack on the Vice President are linked, or it is the greatest coincidence in history."

"Does everyone agree?" Cameron asked.

Nods all around the room.

Cameron leaned forward, resting his hands on the table. "Unless someone dissents, Heather O'Grainne is now the head of Working Group Daybreak, and you're all members. Your mission is to find the Daybreak link to the seizure of Air Force Two; no action plan just yet, we'll decide what to do once we know what we're looking at. Heather, bring over whoever you need from OFTA and DoF for the duration of the crisis; I'll message Graham Weisbrod and square that. Are there any crypto resources that NSA can spare for getting caught up on Daybreak's communications?"

"I'll get them for you, Lenny," Telabanian said.

"Good." Cameron stood back up and said, "You've got this room any time you need it, but I imagine you'll want to work mostly from your desks in the main room. Any objections to anything I've just decided?"

Edwards said, "I'm very glad we're finally giving Assistant Secretary O'Grainne what she needs to do the job right and quickly."

Heather realized then that Cam had more or less forced a buy-in on everyone in the room, especially Edwards. *Now they're on record that whatever I did wrong about Daybreak before, it was because I didn't have the resources. Now that I do have the resources, the price of keeping my job is that I really have to do it. The only way Cameron could throw me a line was to give me enough rope to hang myself. That's the nature of friendship in this town.*

ABOUT TWENTY MINUTES LATER. GILLETTE, WYOMING. 4:38 P.M. MST. MONDAY, OCTOBER 28.

It looked like a weather station. An anemometer on a waist-high tripod turned slowly around in the light breeze; a wire from its base went to a telephone-sized aluminum box, connected by a short wire to a black box the size of a matchbox—a cellular wireless server.

Inside the aluminum box, a computer continually compared the time and the windspeed. Decisions about time took priority, and up until recently had been very simple: The program said do nothing until 4:00 P.M. or later, so every second, right on cue, the computer woke up, saw it wasn't 4:00 P.M. yet, set a timer to tick off another second, and went back to sleep, like a child on Christmas morning who checks every five minutes to see if it is time to get up yet, and then dutifully goes back to bed before checking in another five minutes. At the speeds at which computers operated, that was less than a billionth of its working time.

After 4:00 P.M., the computer began to consult its rolling record of the windspeed across the last twenty minutes. This was more complicated. On the plains close to the Rockies, a strong west wind tends to rise in late afternoon, almost every day, as the shadowed east faces of the mountains cool and pour a torrent of cold, dense air down to where air warmed by a whole day of sunshine is still rising off the ground. The wind blows strong and flows across hundreds of miles; it's a perfect medium for dispersing anything in the air.

Zach had written the program to detect the point when the strong evening wind was well-established; it took windspeed readings every second and kept a back file of 1200 of them, twenty minutes' worth. Each second after 4:00 P.M., it averaged the list; when the average windspeed across the last twenty minutes was more than thirty-five kilometers per hour, it reviewed the list to make sure that there had been no more than ten consecutive seconds below 25 kph, Zach's test to make sure that this was the real, strong mountain breeze, not just a stray gust.

At 4:42 P.M., those conditions were all met. The computer sent 750 phone numbers to the server, which dialed the triggers in all 750 of the bottles filled with black powder. As each came online the computer told it to arm and check; all were armed and checked in less than four seconds. The computer sent a signal to fire; a hundredth of a second later, when the 750th call dropped, the computer fired a small charge to destroy itself. People on the street thought it was a gunshot, looked around, and concluded it was something else.

. . .

Davidson resented like hell the way he had to be out there on collection days from fucking three thirty till goddam well six fucking o'clock sometimes, because although he had a great team with Howard and Isaac, and a tolerable one with Dorothy and Juan, the team of Fred and Annie was just absolutely not to be trusted at all. Sure enough, they came in late because they'd stopped to check on their kid in the day care, and they gave him some routine about how it smelled so bad they had to take showers, because it would never've occurred to numbnuts Fred or his fat slobby wife that maybe they should wait till they were done to shower instead of just getting all stunk up again.

Now they were busy telling Davidson their whole fucking life story, which was something they often did on the clock. He could have told it for them: Fred used to drink and party, and Annie did too. They got Jesus after their firstborn baby died, and he must have been sent from heaven to straighten them out. *I'm sure that comforted the shit out of the little fucker, drowning in the bathtub while you idiots got stoned.* But Davidson didn't say that; people who would at least show up weren't all that easy to find.

So he let them ramble on about how bad it stunk, and take him to the bin to show him. It was about three-quarters full of plastic bottles, a good week, but son of a *bitch*, this was like putting your head up a constipated cheesemaker's butthole, and the slimy look of the plastic was weird too. And—hadn't it been in the middle of lunch? Erin had just been doing the red lingerie number—Howard *had* called him, something about—

Wham-boom.

The biggest boom since the IED in Iraq, when he'd gone there for Bush twenty years ago. This one knocked all three of them flat on their asses. Lying on his back, he was perfectly positioned to see the sky fill instantly with a great cloud of dirty blue smoke, which tumbled to the east almost before it fully formed. From the cloud fell a rain of plastic bottles, a few into his plant, most over the fence, and quite a lot of them, caught in the strong mountain breeze, tumbling and blowing off far to the east. Some of them were going to be in fucking South Dakota before they came down, he thought, and then he realized that one whole day of recycling had just blown off into the sky, with all the trucks and workers already paid for, and he screamed and beat the ground with his fists like a two-year-old having a tantrum, until he realized that Fred and Annie, with their bleeding ears, couldn't hear it, his hands were getting sore, and his ears hurt horribly. He couldn't hear anything, though bits of plastic bottles were crashing down all around him and on the steel roofs of his buildings, and it should have been a terrible din.

* * *

Howard was stroking Michiko's breasts and hair, real soft and gentle the way she said she liked. She was handling Isaac, who was breathing like he was about to finish.

Something went off like a cannon. Isaac, sitting up, bumped heads with Michiko; they were both still apologizing when Lenya, the Russian lady that owned the place, knocked on the door and said, "Howard, Isaac, so so sorry, something happen to your truck, dress and come out, okay?"

A few minutes later, hastily stuffed into their clothes, barefoot on the sunny parking lot, they stood stupefied in awe by the burned and scarred truck bed and the shattered windows. One other car, nearby, had taken a big crack in the rear window, but Reverend Nickleson had already driven it off to the auto-glass place, saying he didn't want to involve his insurance company.

The cop who came out, unfortunately, was Matt Storey, who had enough trouble figuring out how to fill out speeding tickets, so no matter how much they tried to tell him about the two mystery bottles they'd been carrying in the back, he just kept shaking his head and saying it was probably kids. It was dark before he left to write his report, which would say something blew up in the pickup truck bed and it was probably kids.

After they swept the glass off the seat, Howard tried starting the truck. It was drivable, though it stank like a firecracker, and most of the gauges weren't working.

"Probably leaking everything everywhere, too," Isaac said, shining his flashlight under it. "Got oil and radiator, at least, dripping, and a couple things I ain't sure of. But if we top up the oil and drive it home slow and careful, we can probably get it there. Think we got gas leaking?"

Howard sniffed. "I don't smell any—just the sulfur from those bombs."

Lenya told them no charge, rain check, and she'd take care of paying Michiko. "Reminds me when I'm still one of the girls, back in Brooklyn," she said. "I had me a real good customer, one day he goes out, turns on his car, boom, he's not a good customer no more. I even gone to his funeral and cried, especially when I seen he had a pretty wife and a bunch of kids. Never did heard what that was all about. You boys ain't have no enemies?"

"Just bums going after the recyclables," Isaac said.

"There's a bum in my recycling cart this afternoon. I chase him away. He tells me God loved me anyway."

"I doubt it was him," Howard said.

As they drove through town, keeping it to about fifteen miles per hour from fear of the gas tank and because of the shattered windshield, Isaac said, "You know, old Lenya will still be feeling generous about that rain check tonight, but she might not in a week. It's only about three miles, we could walk back in an hour. I say we park this thing, walk on in, let Lenya spoil us, and maybe catch the last of Game Seven and have us a steak at Mary's. Hitch a ride or take a cab after. It's been a day."

"Me too, on everything," Howard said.

**ABOUT THE SAME TIME. NEAR THE BOUNDARY OF JAMMU
WITH AKSAI CHIN. DISPUTED TERRITORY CLAIMED BY
CHINA, INDIA, PAKISTAN, AND KASHMIRI SEPARATISTS.
JUST BEFORE DAWN, LOCALLY. TUESDAY, OCTOBER 29.**

"Green Leader, Green Flight is authorized to cross over into
Aksai Chin. The American satellites have laid you an intercept course at 321 degrees 9 minutes; we're relaying it to your
computer now—"

The flight leader passed orders to the other three planes in
his flight. "Looks like we're cleared to go get them."

"How was it authorized so quickly?" Green Two, the pilot
of one of the two fighters in the flight, asked.

Normally the flight leader would have reprimanded the excess chatter, but he was excited and nervous himself. "They
told *me* the Americans told—not asked—Beijing and Islam-
abad to let us do this."

The four Sukhoi jets of Green Flight flew on, high above
the spectacular, deadly wastelands: the Aksai Chin, a flat, featureless saline desert surrounded by the high Himalayas. It
could be reached by road for less than half the year, was more
than three miles high with almost no rainfall, and offered
death by thirst, starvation, or exposure at all times of year;
three nations and one liberation movement claimed it, but not
one of them would have expended a single life to maintain
the claim.

China patrolled there more often than the other nations,
but today India was there first with the requested flight of
two fighters and two fast reconnaissance planes to the target.
Swift agreement by all parties that this was strictly a favor to
the Americans and reflected nothing else had been enabled by
their shared perception that the United States was about to go
utterly berserk.

Dawn overtook Green Flight. The old silver Sukhois
glinted with steely fire in the abrupt daylight, and the missile
pods on two of them, camera package on the third, and radar/
communications boom on the leader stood out like diagrams
of themselves.

"I have it on radar," the flight leader reported. "Confirming orders: We are to secure as many photographs as feasible,
while repeatedly warning them; if we are defied, or not an-

swered, we are to shoot them down at the last feasible prudent time."

"Those orders are confirmed, Green Leader."

Feasible prudent time. I suppose it wouldn't be prudent if it weren't feasible, and maybe vice versa. Green Leader shrugged the thought off; the phrase was obviously just cover for his superiors if anything went wrong.

The high peaks off to their east dazzled them like monster flashbulbs as the morning sun found angles from glaciers and snowfields into the pilots' eyes. Long, deep shadows extended across the salt plain below, crawling visibly back toward the mountains in the first moment of dawn. In late October, the mountains were piled high and deep with snow; they would have been snowcapped even in July, but for practical purposes that inaccessible, high, far land below them had been in winter for more than a month.

Coordinating with an American satellite operator, two of their own radar operators, and what must be an American observer relaying information from a Chinese or Pakistani radar, they moved in on the target. "Green Leader, this is Green Three." That was the camera plane. "I have him on visual, Green Leader, proceeding to close with him."

They turned to follow Three and then they all saw it: a white 737 flying at what must be about its max cruising altitude, gleaming white in the morning sun. In moments they had closed with the white plane and were circling it in the air like American Indians around a covered wagon in one of their old Westerns. The 737 neither deviated from its course nor answered any radio hails, though there was a soft hiss in one distress channel.

"Green Three, do you have a clear photo of that tail?"

"Several. Yes, and in close, you can clearly see that it used to display a red Lion Airways logo, under that runny, patchy paint. I'm going in close to see if I can see anyone in the cockpit and perhaps photograph them."

"I'll follow you in for a look, myself."

After two passes, and with just thirty kilometers left in authorized airspace, Green One and Three had seen no evidence of life; the 737 continued to fly on a constant heading and altitude. Nothing moved in any window. The recon planes backed off to observe.

"Green Two and Green Four, we're clear now. You are authorized to close in and fire at will."

Two and Four accelerated past them, taking up positions at an angle behind the white airliner. R-73s lashed out in long white streaks. Two's rocket blew the port engine to fiery bits, and the wing fell away; as the airliner tipped, the second R-73 tailpiped the remaining engine, stripping off the starboard wing. The airliner's fuselage tumbled wildly downward, end over end; the rest of Green Flight circled while Green Three descended for better pictures of the impact.

The fuselage slammed into the gray-white, stony ground and vanished in a great blob of white-hot flame. Green Three peeled away; a collision with wreckage thrown into the sky might have doomed him to crash into the nightmare void of the desert below.

"Did you get spectroscopy, Green Three?" Green Leader asked.

"The instruments say we've got everything we're supposed to get. That was quite an explosion. I wonder what they had on board?"

"They'll know when they analyze your recordings, but you know they'll never tell *us*. All right, let's head for home, we have a storm coming, and I don't want to be here when it hits." They wheeled and headed for home, four contrails tipped with silver spearheads; with nothing but itself to burn, the wreckage burned briefly, smoldered a little longer, and was as bitter cold as everything around it before noon.

ABOUT THE SAME TIME. GILLETTE, WYOMING. 5:09 P.M. MST. MONDAY, OCTOBER 28.

When Jason reached to knock on the door of Room 215, it opened. *Suburban dad-type, knit polo shirt, cheapie chinos, penny-for-the-love-of-god loafers.* "Hi, I'm Zach. I'd rather not be too close to what you have there, so I'm going to prop this door open"—he did—"and walk over to the Denny's across the street. I'll be having coffee at the counter. My stuff's already in the car so here's the key to the room." He tossed the card onto the bed. "Are you carrying anything plastic you need to keep?"

"Yeah."

"Okay, my stuff ferments flexible plastic, loves beverage bottles but really any plastic, semiaerobic so you kill it with bleach or peroxide. There's three gallon jugs of peroxide on the table—pour it over any surface you need to touch before you handle any of your plastic."

"My stuff makes nitric acid wherever there's a fluctuating electromagnetic field, and powers off a temperature gradient," Jason said. "Strong alkali, like lye, shuts it down temporarily and neutralizes the acid."

"Thanks! Why don't you walk out, and then I'll walk in?"

"It's a deal." Jason stepped back to let Zach walk past the door and out into the sunlight. He was obviously careful not to step anywhere near where Jason had stood.

Not worrying about the Holiday Inn's carpets since they'd never have time to bill Zach before Daybreak took hold, Jason poured peroxide over a big patch of the carpet, and followed up by sprinkling Liquid-Plumr there. He set his pack in the center, disinfected it, and gave it some more Liquid-Plumr, splashed more of the nasty chemicals onto his gloved hands and onto the plastic bags that had held his laptop and change of clothes.

With water from the faucet in a glass he had just removed from the hotel paper wrapper (SEALED FOR YOUR PROTECTION), Jason rinsed his sealed plastic bags, including the one with the laptop. He stripped and threw his clothes and shoes on the bed, helping the maid to scatter more of his nanospawn and Zach's biotes.

After the long day, he took longer in the hot shower than he'd meant to—might as well enjoy the Big System one last time.

When at last Jason walked across the parking lot to Denny's, the air tasted sweet and clean. *Still an hour of daylight left?* He reached for his watch before he remembered it had already died. *Good fucking riddance.* He was whistling "Natural Mountain Man" as he sprinted across the street.

"So the Indian Air Force had good remote sensing?" Cameron asked.

The Air Force liaison said, "As good as ours—it's the same gear, we sold it to them, and they know what to do with it. So yeah, we can count on this result. The spectroscope was consistent with light hydrocarbons—at a guess, that would be a largish tank of propane in the plane's body, maybe juiced with a few cylinders of aviation oxygen. We think the pilot and crew probably parachuted somewhere over wild country not long after they dropped the bodies in Thailand; jumping into a jungle would be a lot better than riding the plane through the operation."

"How did they know we'd get it together fast enough to shoot down the 737?"

"They didn't have to. A big white airliner with two engines crashing anywhere in that part of the world would just have been one more good decoy." Nancy Telabanian sat back, folding her arms around herself. "Because the Indian pilots are good and know their business, we can be pretty sure about three important facts: It's almost certainly the Lion Airways plane stolen from Sentani, with its tail repainted; it's consistent with being the plane that dropped the bodies of Samuelson's three key liaisons into the market square in Thailand; and it was unmanned by the time we shot it down. And it couldn't possibly have been a Dreamliner. So Air Force Two is still somewhere, and the blow is going to fall . . . somewhere."

Marshall—whoever or whatever his official job and title were, he seemed to be the one in charge of getting useful graphics up in a short period of time—spoke over the loudspeaker. "Per your request, Mr. Nguyen-Peters, we've got a graph to show estimated arrival times on the West Coast and other locations. Shall I put it up on the main screen?"

"Yes," Cam said, "I think you'd better."

The map of the eastern Pacific, and western North America, could not have been clearer; it showed the ocean as black, areas where the 787 could already have hit as red, and areas still safe as aqua. Hawaii and coastal Alaska from the Bering Sea almost to the panhandle were red. So far the West Coast was aqua. But a tongue of red crept down toward Juneau, inexorably south, like a glacier of fire and blood, widening as it went.

ABOUT THE SAME TIME. RAPID CITY, SOUTH DAKOTA. 5:04 P.M. MST. MONDAY, OCTOBER 28.

Marshalene still had half a tank and a full charge, but she'd had way too much liquid, and besides, she was bored. She liked truck stops because they always had a lot of silly junk that she could buy, and show to people to show them how she was kind of above it all, but not like being all superior, just she knew this stuff was junk and some people bought it for real.

It was dinner time and the café smelled good with all the white-trash cookin', and she decided she could stand country music for some good meatloaf and pie. Besides, the lot had been so crowded, she teased herself, that she'd had to walk all the way here from where she'd parked, almost back by the highway.

The booth felt good and there were three cheesy bobbleheads and a couple cool T-shirts to linger about buying, so it was almost an hour before she got back on the road. Meanwhile, the wind under the Prius shifted, and nanoswarm blew across the parking lot and on into Rapid City itself; more than a hundred more trucks, bound all over the northern United States, were infected, along with four big transporters hauling wind-generator blades to Fort Collins, a Gray Liner bound for Winnipeg, and seven diesel-electric locomotives, three headed into the DME system and four for the old Great Northern. Within twenty-four hours, nanoswarm from Marshalene's Prius would spread from Manitoba to northern California and Vancouver to Little Rock. It so happened that Jason's eggs were among the most efficient ones out there, producing some of the fastest-reproducing nanoswarm, and Jason had been right all along; Marshalene's car was perfect for the job. In any evolutionary system, tiny advantages become gigantic population shifts; it was nothing more than that.

Well, I guess I'm seeing the World Series, after all, Greg Redmond thought, circling Anaheim at forty-three thousand feet, all the higher the old A-10 could go. What he'd been told back in Arizona, while the ground crews ran around madly, was enough to scare the shit out of any sensible man with a wife and three small kids—phrases like *get there ASAP, you're already late, vitally important to obey all orders at once,* and the single scariest phrase in the military lexicon: *This is not a drill.*

The Navy had the front line. Somewhere far out over the horizon, F-18 Super Hornets out of North Island NAS and LeMoore were scouting up and down the coast, using the hastily-given tactical callsign "Noseguard." They were highly capable planes, each carrying more-than-good radar and a full array of long-range and visual-range missiles, but there weren't many of them. Still, if the enemy designated "Bad Dreamliner" happened to come in through any of the territory the Super Hornets were covering, they had the tools for the job.

That was the scariest part. The CO had told them that there was *"Unlimited authorization to destroy that plane."*

Greg's buddy Nate had said, "Sir, I'm not clear. Unlimited authorization means—"

"Unlimited authorization means unlimited. Nothing is off-limits as long as that 787 gets destroyed before it can get to where it's going. Use the Sidewinders, use the big gun, hell, use the Mavericks or ram the sonofabitch if you have to." Greg had swallowed hard; the Mavericks were used to take out tanks, and it did not sound like the CO was kidding about ramming, either. "Everybody who is out on this mission—and they have called out *everybody*—is carrying the full suite of weapons. They are there for you to use. Of course, avoid collateral damage if you can, but if you can't—destroy Bad Dreamliner. There's no such thing as exceeding this order. Clear?"

And all the Hog Drivers on the bench had nodded, and said, yes, yes, sir, clear.

Greg wondered if everyone remembered what he did. Not about his own plane, but about some of the others. *Some Super Hornets, on a stop-at-all-cost mission, might be carrying* nukes. *Whatever was on that thing had to be a nightmare.*

Behind the Noseguards, in the middle range, from just over the horizon to perhaps eighty miles out at sea, were the Tackles—the main interception force, still being gathered from a dozen air bases. Land-based Navy and Marine F-35s out of North Island, with their extra fuel and longer patrol times, were already flying search patterns up and down the coast; Air Force F-35s and F-22s out of Holloman AFB in New Mexico were arriving and joining them. The fence was getting thicker, but it still had holes.

Along the coast, where the public could see them, the Halfbacks were just getting organized. So far the Arizona Air National Guard had just come in, flying F-22s and even old F-16s that Redmond's grandfather might have flown in one of Reagan's little wars. Redmond laughed privately; most of the F-16s were younger than his own A-10, but "old" in a fighter was different from old in an attack bomber, kind of like a gymnast versus a golfer. The Halfback part of the defense would grow thicker as more ANG fighters arrived from New Mexico, and extend farther north as the California Air Guard's fighters, up in Fresno, got into the air and spread out.

The colonel had said, unofficially, that the A-10s almost weren't invited to the party. They were a close-air-support plane, intended to attack targets on the ground, and slower than the Dreamliner. But with the whole West Coast littered with potential good targets for attack, and minimal prep time, they needed Fullbacks, planes patrolling around any likely target—such as Game Seven of the World Series here in Anaheim—and the A-10 was meant to loiter: circle a battlefield slowly, waiting to be called into action.

It wasn't yet dark down below, but they were turning the stadium lights on. He took another slow wide turn over Anaheim, nursing the fuel, and wished he'd hear that the Bad Dreamliner had been picked up and nailed. It would be nice to be headed home.

As he made a turn, he saw something out of the corner of his eye; in the setting sun, there was a black dot. He talked to his controller, got cleared to investigate, and came around, descending gently and dropping down almost to stall speed for a better look. The low late-afternoon sun made the black sphere much more visible; a stray radiosonde balloon, floating along at about twenty-two thousand feet, one of the two-meter ones that you could buy from any scientific supply house, but with no instrument package.

Redmond made a report; it gave him something to do. In return, the controller informed him that the Pirates had just finished batting without having gotten a man on base.

He banked around and saw that the stadium lights were clearly visible; potentially a great target for the terrorists.

Against the red glow of sunset, he spotted three more dots, and called it in. "I think we've got somebody out there launching balloons for fun," he said. "Anybody in Japan who doesn't know the war's over?"

"I'll kick it upstairs," his controller said. "You never know what's significant. Thanks for the word on the balloons, Fullback Fourteen."

Out of the corner of his eye, Greg thought he might have seen a dot move abruptly, but when he looked it was gone. *Probably just popped. Lord, let that be the most violent thing I see on this trip.*

ABOUT THE SAME TIME. WASHINGTON, DC. 7:55 P.M. EST. MONDAY, OCTOBER 28.

Visualized as a fan of great circle trajectories, the West Coast reached toward Jayapura like a vast splayed hand, with parts of the coast as much as forty minutes closer than others. But which extended finger would the viper strike?

Alaska continued to glow red; nothing happened there. A new red blob popped up in Coos Bay, Oregon, but no blow fell.

The red cancer had spread out from Coos Bay for a few minutes until Vancouver, BC, had become another possible center of attack; in a few minutes the two red blotches had joined and begun to sweep down the coast and inland. Nothing hit; probably the enemy was not aiming at Seattle or Portland. In the Northwest, the red area moved inland in a sharp curve. A long red finger from the northwest blob reached down the coast, nearing San Francisco.

No 787 appeared on any radar, on any ship, plane, or ground station. High-altitude satellites might have seen something, but if so, it had not yet emerged from the analysis; even the NSA's quantum computers couldn't instantly scan the imaging from so many millions of square miles for something that would fit into one city block. A couple of low-altitude satellites would pass over soon; maybe they'd have better luck.

No calls came in about explosions, planes crashing, planes where there should be no planes; nothing. Perhaps they were taking some longer way round, had found a hole in the defenses or were planning to make one?

The big red patch in the Northwest grew, and its finger slid down over the Bay Area and thickened into a wedge, and nothing happened.

In the safe aqua zone, Newport Beach, California, well down the south coast, blossomed red, another victim of geometry that made it stick out from a great circle perspective centered on Jayapura.

The new red blotch spread rapidly, engulfing Irvine, reaching toward San Diego, as the older, bigger malignancy crawled into the northern suburbs of LA. The whole American/Canadian coast would be solid red in another minute.

There were down spots in the Mexican radar fence, but the holes were temporary problem spots, not where anyone—

Check that assumption. Heather typed a quick note and posted it in general discussion: **Some radars down in Mexico. NE1 chkd Y? &when?**

About five seconds later she saw MISO from Cam—his personal abbreviation for "make it so." Shortly after that, a note came in from someone at Homeland Security, saying DoD was getting an answer through their liaison with the *ministerio del ejército* in Ciudad de México.

Ejército, the Army? Why not Defense? Heather clicked up a footnote. Technically Mexico has no Defense Department: Army and Navy are separate, the Air Force is part of the Army, and so the Mexican official with the most defense radars under his control is the Minister for the Army. *Pretty much the same setup as we had in the United States around 1940; but unlike us, the Mexicans haven't had a lot of wars lately. Mostly because we've been behaving our asses, sorta, comparatively anyway.*

Heather looked up. The West Coast was bright red from Bellingham to San Diego. Red was now spilling down Baja, spreading east over the deserts and mountains, and racing around the northern head of the Gulf of California. She was holding her breath, as if somehow she could hear a shot or an explosion from here.

A note popped up on her screen to say that the Mexican Army should soon have a complete report on the radars that were down. So far all reports were of people not getting the word to defer scheduled downtime; more pale green curves popped up along the west side of Baja.

ABOUT THE SAME TIME. NEAR GUERRERO NEGRO, OFF THE PACIFIC COAST OF BAJA CALIFORNIA. 5:15 P.M. PST. MONDAY, OCTOBER 28.

At first, Samuelson hadn't even been sure that the dark area coming over the horizon was land, but now below him, it was not just land, but a place he knew. From the air, the Bay of Sebastian Vizcaino has a distinct hooked-curve shape that is easy to pick out, and because buildable land is scarce along its shores, the town of Guerrero Negro sits in a distinct, unusual position north of and above the bay. Just south, the Baja Highway cuts away from the Pacific to the Sea of Cortez. Guerrero Negro is a major ecotourist jumping-off point for whale watching and for the Vizcaino Desert Biosphere Reserve. Samuelson had passed through a dozen times in his twenties and a few since then with Kim, especially during the early, traveling years of their marriage.

Now I know exactly where I am, Samuelson thought, *and they don't know I do. I just need to figure out how to use that.*

The plane began a steep descent; the pilot said something over the loudspeaker, but Samuelson's tourist-Arabic from thirty years ago wasn't adequate to make out what.

They leveled off at low altitude, flying down a canyon toward the Gulf of California. They must be—

The hand on his shoulder made him jump. "Time to make your statement."

"That is impossible," he said. "I cannot betray—"

The man punched him, in the face, hard enough to numb

it. He hit Samuelson again, drew back his fist and looked into his eyes, waited for the vice president to realize what was happening.

He hit him again, much harder. "You must make your statement now."

"I will not," Samuelson said, "and you can't make me."

Those are the rules, where they come from. When anyone offers you anything, or asks for anything, refuse twice, accept on the third. Basic negotiation principle: Behave in a way that the other side is at home with.

He thought about that while they held him up and beat his ribs sore, leaving him coughing and unable to wipe the tears and mucus from his face.

When Samuelson had caught his breath, the man said, again, "Now, your statement."

"What must be in the statement?" Samuelson asked.

They dickered and haggled. Samuelson insisted that he did not want to read the official statement because it dishonored himself and his nation. He pleaded with them—couldn't he make his last words his own, and speak the way he always did to American audiences, wouldn't that be more believable? And could he please begin by saying farewell to his wife? Well, because a man can be in love, can't he?

One of his best negotiations in a life of negotiations. He had nothing to offer, and everything to gain, and the other side did not realize that he got everything he wanted.

When they had agreed, he was permitted a quick trip to the bathroom. Two guards watched him while he took a dump; did they expect him to hang himself in the toilet paper or pull a concealed machine gun from the electric shaver?

Face freshly washed. Calm. Ready.

The little light glowed on their camera. *Here goes.* "My fellow Americans, by the time most of you see this, I will be dead, because the men sitting just a few feet from me are planning to kill me, along with themselves. They demanded that I make a statement, which they are sending out in some kind of live webcast via cellular broadband, I'm afraid I don't understand the technical details, but apparently they fear that we may be fired on before they can transmit a recording. So, they tell me, I am speaking to you, right now, live, in streaming video, and this is going out over the web, and they've notified millions of media outlets and bloggers and so on to record it; I'm sure many of them will broadcast it.

"First let me just say, Kim—my wife, my one and only love ever—I love you as much as I did on our honeymoon in Guerrero Negro, when we hiked the canyons to the north and sailed up the Gulf of California, if—"

A rough hand grasped his hair. Someone shouted. He tried to jab his handcuffed hands upward into the crotch of the man holding him, but other hands pushed them down, so he tried to turn and bite the man's leg, but his head was held too tight. A knife pressed against his throat. *Well, I tried.*

The pressure slackened. His head was released. He saw that they were pointing the camera at the one who had been pressing the knife to his neck.

The man seemed to shake off the murderous rage as if it had never been, and handed the knife to one of his friends. The cameraman counted down, three, two, one, and the active-light went on. The man said, "We had hoped to present an honest—"

Samuelson screamed, "Bullshit! What's in those barrels? What's in those barrels?" as they yanked him around, trying to reach his mouth while he bucked and curled away from them.

He screamed, *Barrels on this plane!* twice more, and *Bullshit!* just as he got an elbow into someone's balls. One of them shoved a fist into his mouth.

He tried to bite the fist, hurting his jaw but getting no real grip, and then they forced something into his mouth; he was retching and couldn't breathe. He badly wanted to drift down into the darkness and pain, but he wanted more to see how all this came out.

ABOUT THE SAME TIME. YUMA, ARIZONA. 5:20 P.M. PST. MONDAY, OCTOBER 28.

Ysabel jumped when her phone rang. She grabbed it and said, "Yeah?"

"It's time. Do it." The connection went dead.

She couldn't quite place the accent but that was okay, too, she knew this was an international effort. It seemed strange that it wasn't a Spanish accent, though.

Oh, well. She jumped up, peed quickly, put her purse by the door, looked around to make sure there was nothing else for her to forget. She reminded herself again to drop the cheapie convenience-store cell phone in some place where it was likely to be stolen.

Then she sat down and worked the Stinger gadget. Really, this wasn't as hard as most video games. She tabbed over to the button that said, ARM ON LOCK, clicked on it, and typed the password—DAYBREAK, of course.

A red message flashed **Missile will arm when target acquired.**

She'd practiced acquiring the target all afternoon; she just slid the crosshairs across the television screen, using the little thumbwheel controls, till the red glow told her it had found the diesel exhaust (imagine the jackass nerve of those Border Patrol assholes, dumping diesel exhaust right out above a city, of all things!)

She pushed the key combination, and jumped at the roar of the Stinger's exhaust against the roof, a couple of feet above her ceiling. On the screen, the thread of smoke ended in a ball of fire under the aerostat.

ABOUT THE SAME TIME. WASHINGTON, DC. 8:30 P.M. EST. MONDAY, OCTOBER 28.

"That's not where we had our honeymoon," a soft voice said. Heather thought, *That must be Kim Samuelson, when did they bring—*

On the screen, John Samuelson's head was grabbed and a knife went to his throat; after a burst of shouting and a wildly swinging camera, the screen went dark.

Lenny Plekhanov, reading NSA feed, said, "We've got the cell-phone towers they relayed through—east coast of Baja—"

A young Asian woman said, "Confirmed, we have that tower's location, thanks, and an angle on them. North and east of Guerrero Negro, latitude—"

A message flashed up on Heather's screen; she looked down and said, loud enough so people could hear, "E-bomb attack on the Mexican Navy's Guerrero Negro station about forty minutes ago. Took out radio, cell phone, and the local landline station, along with the radars on the frigate and cutter in port, and at the airport. Several visual sightings of a big white plane."

The young Asian woman added, "Alerts out to ICE, Air Force, Air Guard, Navy, all the—shit. Yuma aerostat radar is out, and—Air Force says hostile action."

On the screen, one big green curve across the Gulf of California blanked out; the remaining green curves peeled back like the cross section of a bullet hole.

"Either that's the way they're coming, or that's the diversion," Garren said. "We'll—"

"They've killed him, you know. Or they will any minute. Shoot that plane down." Roger Pendano looked haggard and sad.

Did he even realize that he'd given the order for that almost an hour ago? Or that the operation isn't being commanded here anymore? Heather was afraid she might find out.

The silence went well beyond awkward before Garren said, "We are working on that, sir."

Pendano sank into his chair, hands on his head; he didn't move as everything else went on around him.

ABOUT TEN MINUTES LATER. CLAY SPUR, WYOMING. 6:45 P.M. MST. MONDAY, OCTOBER 28.

Jason's Goo-22 search had found an all-organic restaurant about an hour away, on a route that would take them back to I-25 eventually, so they headed east and south. "We'll miss being able to find places like this so easily," Jason said, as they pulled into the gravel parking lot, "but on the other hand, instead of having these little islands of spiritual meaning in an ocean of Big System, we'll all make meaning where we are, till the whole *world* will have spiritual meaning."

"Spiritual?"

Jason shrugged. "There's more to spirit than just God."

Once seated, with a big pot of coffee for the table to share, and a big meal ordered for each of them, Jason sighed. "It feels good not to be driving; thanks for giving me a ride clear back to Raton. The mountains are beautiful and the challenge is fun, but after a while, dude, it's all 'hand on the throttle, eye on the rail.' "

"Back to the spiritual already."

"A bunch of us at the commune like to play traditional stuff, and traditional includes gospel. No offense, but when I'm singing 'You Got to Walk with Your Lord Every Step,' it doesn't mean I believe what I'm singing."

Zach grinned. "You look way too much like one of the original disciples to be a current one."

Jason nearly shot the coffee through his nose, and said, "I thought Christian types were supposed to try to convert people and didn't have much of a sense of humor about it."

"That's another outfit. They get all the . . ." Zach froze, staring.

When Jason turned, the television over the bar showed flat Gothic letters, blue on yellow: ATTACK IN THE DESERT. SPECIAL REPORT.

One of the waitresses, braids and big skirt flying, ran to the TV and turned the volume all the way up.

"—joining us, again, the plane carrying Vice President Samuelson on a confidential diplomatic mission was seized earlier today, and government sources confirm that the streaming video webcast that appeared about forty minutes ago was *not* a hoax. Here's a clip of that webcast; we apologize for the poor quality of the video and remind you he was being held prisoner and threatened. You may want to take small children out of the room."

Samuelson's image appeared, too big, too grainy, and with the color uncorrected. They watched him speak the plane's position, the terrorists wrestling him, the knife at his neck, Samuelson dragged off camera. The network helpfully supplied subtitles so that they knew someone had shouted in Arabic not to kill Samuelson on camera, and "read our statement, read it now, we may have no time," over the sound of the vice president shouting *Bullshit!* and *Barrels on the plane!*, and that the thuds off camera must mean he was being beaten.

An announcer cut off Samuelson's scream of *Bullshit!* "We're taking you right away to live coverage from our San Diego affiliate where—excuse me, I'm not sure—" The man listened intently to his earpiece. "Should I?"

"That's some last words," Zach said.

Jason nodded. "How many vice presidents ever say anything *that* close to the truth?"

The announcer said, "We are going direct to live video from the traffic reporting plane from our network affiliate in San Diego. We have—"

A blink in the feed cut the anchor off; the picture stabilized into a military jet streaking across the blue sky, seen from beneath and behind.

"That's an A-10," Zach commented. "I built a model of that when I was a kid. Weird. It's a ground-attack plane, basically a tank-buster, not a fighter. Maybe something is going on on the ground?"

The camera angle widened to show four streaking contrails around the A-10, then rotated down to include the empty, ridge-scarred desert below. Sound resumed: "—believe are US Air Force A-10 attack planes en route to intercept a terrorist attack aimed somewhere in the greater Los Angeles area, which is apparently being delivered via the hijacked Air Force Two—the plane carrying Vice President John Samuelson. For those of you who just joined us—"

"Television is the medium for people who just got here," Jason said.

Zach nodded. "That's why children love it." The planes flew on, parallel white streaks in the blue sky, two of them big enough to show as glints of metal. The voice-over commentator began to go through it all again. Very softly, he added, "And why we need Daybreak."

ABOUT THE SAME TIME. YUMA, ARIZONA. 5:42 P.M. PST. MONDAY, OCTOBER 28.

Ysabel plunged down the stairs just slow enough to be silent; above her, she could hear Neil's high old voice, like an unhappy child, over and over, asking if anyone knew what that sound was, and didn't they smell smoke?

She popped through the ground-floor fire exit and walked quickly across the street, making herself not look back.

Stunned, exhilarated, scared, she held her cell phone to her ear and walked along the busy street, saying "unh-hunh, unh-hunh, yeah you're right." At the corner pay phone, she let herself look up and see the people staring over her head and behind her. *Just like acting class back at the community college, "acting is re-acting," nothing hard here.*

She turned and gawped like everyone else. The aerostat was sinking slowly, a tangle of junk hanging from it, but it didn't look like the diesel fuel had caught fire; good, less chance that anyone would be hurt. The Stinger had torn some big holes in the lower, air-filled part (to judge by the flapping bits of fabric) and small holes in the upper, helium-filled part (to judge by the way it was sinking).

Aaron had explained about the upper and lower parts, and it had been one of the few things he said about the aerostat that she could follow. She liked the way he tried so hard to be non-condescending and non-technical for her. That and his Latin-poet eyes.

Ysabel pictured *campesino* families, desperate for work, over the border in San Luis Rio Colorado. They would see the big balloon that had always been like a Yankee fist in their face sinking like a bad dream. She imagined them packing their few treasures from the old village and heading north tonight. Her face was aching for a chance to grin, but she kept it slack as she slumped heavily against the pay phone's metal hood and slid her phone onto the little metal shelf. Someone looking to make a pay-phone call would be happy to find a prepaid cell phone with no security on it.

The aerostat sank faster in the late-afternoon sun. More people stopped to stare, point, and yell. Time to go.

ABOUT TEN MINUTES LATER. WASHINGTON, DC. 8:50 P.M. EST. MONDAY, OCTOBER 28.

"How the *fuck* did a local TV station plane get that close without permission?" Garren demanded.

I think a man can be allowed an f-bomb under the circumstances, Heather thought.

The radar balloon shot down in Yuma had pulled a whole flock of Air Force and ANG fighters too far west, and they were now out of the chase. *Nonetheless, now we've got him.* A Global Hawk had picked up the 787 as it flew northward, hopping over ridges in the empty desert east of San Diego and just north of the border—an area slashed by ridges and draws with no more apparent pattern than the folds in a crumpled sheet of newspaper, striped and blobbed in green and brown brush. *Smart choice of approach,* she thought, *but we got you anyway.* In the last few minutes they'd been able to pull Fullbacks, the A-10 Warthogs, off point defenses south of LA and send them on interception courses.

The A-10s wouldn't have been as fast as the Dreamliner at high altitude in a straight-line chase, but the airliner was flying low and slow and zigzagging among the ridges, and they'd be able to dive on it. One of the Warthogs might well be first to the kill.

If Bad Dreamliner somehow dodged through the closing arc of A-10s, there were other chances. CVN 76 *Ronald Reagan,* just off North Island, had already catapulted two Super Hornets, which could overtake the 787 in a stern chase before it reached LA. Three Marine F-35s that had been returning to North Island had enough fuel to divert to intercept as well, and a flight of Utah ANG F-22s would be able to intercept just south of Long Beach, if Air Force Two somehow got that far.

Someone was going to shoot down that plane. She hoped Samuelson wasn't still alive.

"They've got an interception vector for an A-10," one of the DoD people announced. "First shot in about four minutes. Less than a minute after that we'll have a window for an F-18 to put an AMRAAM on his tail. If he's headed for somewhere around LA—and it looks like he is—we get at least five good tries to bring him down, plus three long shots."

Kim Samuelson was talking with President Pendano, their arms around each other as if they were already at the funeral.

Cam spoke beside her. "Do you have Jim Browder on the line, Heather? Urgent question for him."

"I've got him standing by on secure IM." She typed, **Phn me, encrypt #**.

Her phone rang; she docked it in her terminal, set it for Record, Transcribe, and Speakerphone, and said, "Jim. Mr. Nguyen-Peters of Homeland Security has a question for you. Cam, Jim is fully briefed per your instructions."

"Good. Dr. Browder, the vice president yelled 'barrels on the plane' three times. We're about to shoot it down over uninhabited desert, almost nothing human downwind for hundreds of miles. Is there anything that they could have put on it that will cause massive problems if we just blow the plane up? Anything that will be made worse if it burns?"

"Probably not in uninhabited desert," Browder said. "Planes burn hot. Fire should kill any weaponized germs or toxins we know about. Most nerve gases are destroyed by flame and heat, except maybe Novichok-5, which hasn't been seen since the 1990s and it's possible the formula is lost. Depending on which ex-Soviet scientist was telling you which self-serving mixture of lies and truth, that stuff might or might not have been heat resistant, but its chemical cousins are not. So I don't think you have to worry about anything chemical or biological."

"Nuclear? Radiological?"

"Nukes require very complex moving parts to work exactly right very, very fast. They're the last thing in the world that you could set off by just whacking them or burning them. So if it was gas, germs, or nukes, they were planning to pull the trigger or open the nozzle before crashing the plane, and shooting it down in the desert should take care of it."

"That leaves radiological."

"Yeah. If the drums contained flammable radiological material, of course, that doesn't stop being radioactive when it burns, and burning it might spread it around more. Either something like tritinated hydrocarbons or something like radiosodium might be kept in barrels. But I don't think it's likely; the physics is all wrong."

"Wrong how?"

"The flight time is too long," Browder explained. "The shorter the half-life, the stronger the radiation. If they used something with a short-enough half-life to be quickly, immediately deadly, that's going to be a half-life of hours rather than weeks or years. They've been on that plane for close to fifteen hours with it, and short-half-life radioactives are too energetic for any shielding less than tons of lead to deal with. They'd all be dead of radiation poisoning.

"That rules out things like sodium-24, which I thought of at first because it's the classic radiological weapon—real strong radioactivity and chemically super active, so it would burn its way right into the body and would catch fire easily and be hard to put out. That's why they store sodium in barrels, immersed in oil so it doesn't spontaneously combust from the air around it. But the reason sodium-24 has been talked about as a fallout enhancer is because you make it by putting ordinary sodium in a strong neutron flux, like around a hydrogen bomb or in a nuclear reactor. Even if they made it in a reactor the day before they seized Air Force Two, and loaded it right on, it would be mostly gone now—and would have killed them in the early hours of the flight.

"The other family of radiological weapons is long-half-life stuff that isn't very strong radioactively, and it could be on that plane—say tritinated methanol, methanol with superheavy hydrogen substituted for the ordinary hydrogen. If that burned it would put radioactive water into the air—but because it's comparatively feeble, it's purely a scare weapon, years or more likely decades before people would get sick from it, and you'd treat inhalation with lots of water and diuretics, it could be flushed out fast before it hurt most people. And on top of that, a long half-life means a small cross section of neutron absorption—"

Cam held his hands up in self-defense. "Whoa. I only got through one year of college physics."

Browder closed in for the kill. "The cross-section for neutron absorption is closely related to how easy it is to make something radioactive. The weak stuff, that would last a long time and wouldn't kill them while they flew here, is much more difficult and expensive to make than the strong stuff, which wouldn't last all the way here and would already have killed them. So, the only things they could deliver on a flight that long are pretty mild and expensive and difficult to make. If it was any of the really bad kill-you-right-now stuff, it would already have killed them. If they are using the weak stuff, it's mostly just a scare tactic, not something you really have to worry about; you need a good PR campaign, is all."

Heather rolled her eyes; leave it to the science guy to think that all you had to do was explain things calmly and rationally, and everything would be fine.

Browder added, "But in case there's something I didn't think of, definitely warn the pilots not to fly through any plume of smoke after the crash, and if you can bring it down without blowing it all over, that might be extra safe. You probably don't want the hero who saved us all to die of radiation poisoning next week."

Cameron nodded infinitesimally. "Excellent. We'll do that. Thank you, Dr. Browder, that's what I needed."

"Talk to you again soon, Jim." Heather undocked her phone. When Cameron finished relaying Browder's advice, she asked, "Wasn't that really more of a question for someone at the Department of Energy? I mean, they're the ones that build atom bombs and have all the physicists."

"I wish," Cameron said. "But there was no time—I'd've had to ask twenty of them and each one would have told me about one small detail. Your guy Browder used to be a science reporter, so he—"

"Fullback Fourteen will be on the target in thirty seconds," Marshall said. "Going to feed from the Pentagon's war room."

The big screen wavered a moment and then they were looking southward across the mountainous desert through the cameras on the A-10. A tiny white bird shape just showed in a corner of the screen. The room was so quiet that they could hear the static in the link.

ABOUT THE SAME TIME. THE DESERT BETWEEN SAN DIEGO AND ENGINEER SPRINGS. 5:57 P.M. PST. MONDAY, OCTOBER 28.

Greg Redmond didn't have spare time or attention to be surprised when he heard, "Fullback Fourteen, you've got first shot." His hands and feet mechanically did the necessary tasks as he listened. "Begin your attack immediately on sight. We have confirmed there are no civilian or military airliners anywhere in the vicinity. Investigative personnel have requested you bring it down with gunfire to preserve more evidence. Make one pass with the cannon, and if it's still flying afterward, send both Sidewinders after it."

"Roger."

"We have also been warned that any plume, smoke, or flame from the plane should be considered extremely dangerous, and you are not to fly into it."

"Roger. I have visual contact," Redmond said.

Far below, Bad Dreamliner was coasting between two

red-brown ridges spattered with deep green; in his head, Redmond was already solving the problem of coming in on it in a steep dive, figuring his pathway, and the old Hog was as familiar as his own body.

He banked, waited for his angle, and pushed the yoke forward to dive.

.   .   .

John Samuelson knew something was happening from the excited gabble. He'd been playing possum again, or just possibly he was actually dying because they had kicked his kidneys hard, over and over, and he might be hemorrhaging. Didn't matter. He was awake with a chance to see it play out.

He flung himself hard sideways, rolling onto his back, and opened his eyes. Two of his captors jumped at him. He screamed into his gag, and cocked his feet to kick at them.

A row of fist-sized holes appeared in the bulkhead above him. *We won. We did it.* He had been so afraid this was the beginning of the dive onto the target.

But the home team had pulled this one out.

The two men approaching Samuelson fell backward, and he seemed to be weightless. The plane was flipping—perhaps it had lost a wing?

Samuelson looked down to see a gushing stump instead of his foot. No matter, he had no more walking to do, anyway. He left the deck and felt as if he were flying, still trying to shout, "We won!" through the gag.

When he hit the forward bulkhead, the pain in the back of his head was nauseating, and his neck felt all wrong. Maybe that was just disorientation from the spinning plane? He wasn't sure where his tormentors had gone. He saw only carpet, a bolthead, and someone's cell phone sliding around.

He shut his eyes and tried to take a deep breath. He couldn't feel whether his lungs responded or not, so he just prayed. *God, please take care of things from here on out. Please accept me, forgive all my foolishness and pride, and make sure Kim knows I loved her.*

He gave up trying to breathe, and tried to smile, because he'd handed it off to higher authority, and it was all taken care of, but somehow his face wouldn't—

Shock, heat, darkness.

**ABOUT THREE MINUTES LATER. WASHINGTON, DC.
9:02 P.M. EST. MONDAY, OCTOBER 28.**

The image on the big screen was live from a camera on an
A-10 flying figure-8s upwind of the wreckage. Air Force Two
had shed a wing and rolled when the Warthog's big nose cannon, designed to pierce Russian tanks, had perforated a diago-
nal line across its body, down the wing root, and back across
one engine. The 787 Dreamliner had corkscrewed against
the mountainside like a missed football pass, breaking into a
cloud of parts and flame as it bounced uphill. The long streak
of blazing metal was now setting fire to the autumn-dry
brush; ammunition and fuel cooking off made more bursts
and explosions.

But there were also a half dozen hot yellow-white fires, as
bright as flares, pouring dense white-gray smoke into the air.
The heat of their burning punched wavery updrafts through
the red flame and black smoke pouring out of the wreckage.
As they watched, another one erupted, first with a burst of
orange fire and black smoke, but almost instantly becoming
another yellow-white flare pouring out the gray-white smoke.

"No need to repeat the order about staying out of the
plume," Lenny remarked, "if the pilots have half a brain."

"We've got a specialty hazmat chopper from North Island
on its way," one of the controllers said, "and there's a couple
teams in trucks on their way as well. We've already started
emergency evacuation of Engineer Springs—we were preparing that for the last twenty minutes, just in case. Not too much
wind today, so they'll have a half hour at least to clear people
out of Engineer Springs, and they're doing a reverse 911 to
the few people that live out in the desert itself, and trying to
backtrack everyone who's used a cell phone in those areas
in the last couple days in case of hikers or backpackers. We
shouldn't have too many people exposed to it."

"But," Cam said, *what the hell is it?*"

A voice said, "Oh, no," just as Heather looked back at the
screen and saw a non-military plane pass right through the
plume. It took her only a moment to realize that it had to be
that traffic plane from the TV station; during that moment,
the plane tumbled, then seemed to regain control. The little jet
descended rapidly, lowering his landing flaps, as if trying to

make an emergency landing—but there was nowhere good to land on a slope covered with desk-sized boulders and tangled brush. As it touched down, the plane flipped onto its back and burst into flames.

"Marshall, we need the last minute or so of that broadcast up," Cam said.

"Got it." The central screen flashed, scrambled, and re-congealed into a view of the burning remains of the 787 from much lower down. The audio feed came on with a feed-back squeal—"try for a closer look at this amazing tragedy from—"

The camera angle began to wobble, and the voice screamed "Oh, god, oh, my eyes. My eyes!" Another voice screamed—*the pilot,* Heather thought. The screams became hideous, barking coughs, the camera wobbled wildly, the plane stabilized. *He tried to land it,* Heather realized, *but he was blind and in horrible pain.*

On the screen, a confusion of rocks, sand, and brush slammed up at the camera, the sky rolled through the screen, and the signal went out.

"Did that go out live?" Cam asked.

"Yeah."

"Shit."

Heather had known him for fifteen years, and today was the first day she'd ever heard Cam use profanity. *I guess he was saving it for when it really applied.*

**ABOUT THE SAME TIME. CLAY SPUR, WYOMING.
7:08 P.M. MST. MONDAY, OCTOBER 28.**

Jason and Zach hurried across the dark, cold gravel of the parking lot like a couple of criminals. At least they weren't conspicuous; half the people in the restaurant were fleeing to their warm safe cars, down the highway, back to the family or the lover.

Zach started the car and, with more obsessive care than ground crew checking out an Orion for liftoff, ran over the lights and controls. "Is your laptop IBIS-capable?"

"Yeah. I was getting broadband Internet just fine till we turned off 90."

"Then let's go 90 to 25 all the way to Raton. I'm scared. I want to know my family's okay, because the country's under attack and I don't know what's going on." Zach sighed. "Now is *that* dumb, or what? I mean, *we're* attacking the United States, aren't we?"

"Well, the United States and the whole Big System," Jason said. "But I know what you mean. I feel it myself—damn foreigners have no right to attack America; only us Americans should attack America."

"Yeah." He put the car in gear and turned out of the parking lot. "That—uh, that whole thing with Air Force Two, that couldn't be—there was no way—"

"That *can't* be Daybreak," Jason said. "We all spent, like, forever talking collectively about what was in bounds and what wasn't, and I *saw* a bunch of ideas shot down for being too—you know, *terroristic.*"

"Yeah, except, why did it happen right on the exact day of Daybreak? Did all of Daybreak get conned?"

Jason balanced a hand. "Maybe. Or maybe somebody infiltrated us and piggybacked onto Daybreak. I can't imagine how it could all be coincidence."

"Makes me *sick.*"

"Me too. *God* I hope it has nothing to do with Daybreak."

On I-90, Jason unfolded his laptop and made the free connection to IBIS, the chain of wireless stations that ran down the median. "Good news," Jason said. "About every fifth or sixth wireless transceiver is down."

Zach raised a fist in ironic salute, and said, "What's the news?"

"I'll have it up in a sec. The first thing we need after starting Daybreak is Internet access. Seems like a great prank of God."

"Not God," Zach said, quietly. "Someone who is often mistaken for Him, I think."

ABOUT FIVE MINUTES LATER. WASHINGTON, DC.
9:15 P.M. EST. MONDAY, OCTOBER 28.

Something moved in Heather's peripheral vision; a message from Browder had popped up:

smoke of plane crash poss=Na2O, consistent w/eye&lung
injuries. check for radiation esp. beta & hard gamma & for
U or Pt. maybe i was wrong? maybe nuke on board?

Na: the chemical abbreviation for sodium. And Browder
thought the mystery plume looked like smoke from burning
sodium. She forwarded to Cameron right away, and a moment
later her headset was live. "Heather, I'm patching through to
Browder, and I've got four DoE guys and two hazmat people
from EPA kibitzing in."

"Right here and ready," Heather said.

"All right, for the record, we have Browder and O'Grainne
from Department of the Future; Caspar, Pellegrino, Mur-
chison, and Oe from Department of Energy; and Smith and
Svejk from EPA, and my iScribe is taking all this down. Very
quick briefing: We've got air samples from the plumes, both
the gray-white caustic one coming from the hot spots, and the
black smoke from the main body of the burning fuselage. The
gray-white caustic plume is almost pure disodium oxide dust,
and the spectroscopic analysis on the bright yellow-white fires
shows very bright lines for sodium and oxygen, so there's no
question that it's burning sodium.

"However the disodium oxide is not at all radioactive—
it's sodium-23 with a trace of other isotopes, not radioactive
sodium-24. This is consistent with Dr. Browder's speculation
that sodium was being carried on board as a radiological enhancer for a nuclear weapon, especially a fusion weapon, since
they produce enough neutron flux to transmute several tons of
sodium instantaneously. Any problems with my understanding
of the science so far?"

"Oe, DoE." It was an older man's voice with that flat,
clipped California-mall accent that all the stars used to have.
"We've always worried about sodium-24 more than any other
enhancer because of its chemical activity and extreme radioactivity, and because with the short half-life, the more eco-
conscious terrorists might feel better about using it, since the
radioactive component goes down from pure to less than a
part per million in about ten days."

"Caspar, DoE. Concur. The only reason to be carrying that
stuff was if they had a nuke on board they were planning to
use; metallic sodium is hard to handle and dangerous to work

with and there are much more effective ways to enhance a fire—powdered aluminum or magnesium would be way easier to handle and make ten times the mess, and besides, they were crashing an airliner, which is going to start a big fire anyway. So the only possible reason to go to all that expense, danger, and complexity was if they intended to convert it all to sodium-24 with a nuclear bomb."

"Thank you," Cam said. He sounded desperate. "And yet the other plume analysis shows no trace of any tritium or deuterium beyond ordinary background levels, no chemical traces of uranium or plutonium, and no unexpected radioactivity at all—the only radioactivity we're getting is a very slight trace of americium, which is almost certainly from the onboard smoke detectors. Any further speculation in light of that? I confess I'm baffled, but I'm not a physicist or chemist."

There was a long pause. "Browder, DoF. No uranium or plutonium means no fission trigger, as far as I know."

"Oe, DoE, that's correct."

"Svejk, EPA. Any trace of lithium or beryllium? We might as well check all the commonly known fusible nuclei that we can."

"A little bit, but the on-site assessor said that there's enough in half a dozen modern laptops and the plane's own computers to produce the quantity they are seeing."

"Browder, DoF. All the fusible nuclei you can check? I assume that means you can't check for helium?"

"Svejk, EPA. Not easily. But we can probably cross helium off the list because fusing helium-4 into carbon is so far beyond what can be done on Earth, and helium-3 is so scarce and hard to isolate.

"Caspar, DoE, concur. Also helium-3 is somewhat harder to work with than tritium or deuterium, to boot. If they were using helium-3, it would almost certainly be easier, cheaper, and more effective to use tritium."

"Nonetheless," Cam said, "I'm alerting the crews to watch out for a nuclear weapon in the wreckage. Anybody have anything they need to add before we end this call?"

On the screen, the burning sodium continued to light the site in eerie, dancing flames; network feed showed a swarm of talking heads, all trying to explain everything else to each other.

Heather messaged Browder: **thx, good job, stay online, wl b long night.**

He sent back: **^surest prediction DoF ever made.**

ABOUT THE SAME TIME. YUMA, ARIZONA. 6:23 P.M. PST. MONDAY, OCTOBER 28.

Ysabel took the Yuma city bus to the mall and picked up the pack she'd left at the door of Sam's Club that morning. The developmentally disabled guy at the service desk seemed to remember her, but maybe nobody would believe him, if anyone even thought to ask him anything.

She walked across the parking lot to the little tour company where she'd bought a pass for a cheapie three-day package that went down to a little bed-and-breakfast in Puerto Penasco. They promised you the fun of waking up "in a foreign country" the next morning.

She planned to set her clock and slip out of the bed-and-breakfast about an hour before dawn, when the third-class buses in the *zocalo* would be picking up hotel workers from the graveyard shift. She'd just get on whichever one was going the farthest south on Highway 2; from there, she could be lost among the peasants until Daybreak eliminated pursuit.

"Would you mind if I sit with you?"

Ysabel looked up to see the only other person under fifty on the bus. The girl had an awfully big backpack for a three-day trip; she wore baggy shorts and sandals with socks, and the super-retro WrapLens glasses that made you look like a giant insect, the early smart-lens glasses from back in the 'teens. She mumbled as she introduced herself, and Ysabel didn't really catch her name. *Oh, well, at least I remembered my alias is "Jane."*

The Bug-Faced Girl was off on her first vacation entirely on her own. "I've never crossed any border before, I've never gone anywhere by myself, and I've only really been to Kansas, Oklahoma, a ski resort in Colorado, and Urbana, Illinois, because my grandma lives there. So here I was with a real job, nobody I had to see or plan with, and I just decided I'd see some places I hadn't seen before. So I got a two-week pass on Greyhound, and went out to see the beach in San Diego, and now I'm doing this side trip so I can see another beach and sort of have been in another country. I must seem like the biggest dork in the world to you."

"Well, having seen more of the world, I know there are *way* bigger dorks."

Bug-Eyed Nerdchick took a second to get it, then laughed. "My mother is so freaked; but I left San Diego yesterday, and I was nowhere near where Air Force Two crashed."

"Where—?" Ysabel asked. *"Where what?"*

Miss High Adventure explained. Ysabel was flabbergasted—so *that* was why everyone had been piled around the TV set in the waiting area before they boarded the bus. Ysabel had figured it must be the stupid World Series; now she realized that she was fleeing across a border after shooting down a piece of military hardware, during a major terrorist attack.

It might be wise to be obviously buddies with someone conventional. And Nerdette herself was just saying she was "scared to death, even though I know this is about as safe as foreign travel gets."

So they chattered about everything in the world, with Ysabel changing just enough of her bio not to be too recognizable in case they were looking for her. She'd thought it was a pretty good joke to call herself Jane Llano—"plain Jane"—on her false passport—but now her head was filled with, *must remember, must remember, my name is Jane, Spanish major at UT-Austin, please don't let anyone ask about anything there because I've never been there—*

The border guard got on, and said, "Folks, they're asking me to scan all the passports and record them, because of what's happened, but it shouldn't take more than five minutes."

Ysabel thought she'd explode, but Nerd Chick actually put a hand on her back, and said, "Hey, relax, you're the old hand here. You know it's nothing to do with us."

"Yeah. I guess I'm having flashbacks. You travel down south of Mexico at all, into Nicaragua or Honduras, and sometimes border checkpoints are scary."

They scanned the fake passport without comment. The guard even smiled and said, "Have a good time, Jane." It would have been even better if the guy had happened to use SuperAmericanGirl's first name too.

As the bus rolled into Mexico, Miss Texas Nerdface of

2024 was telling an apparently endless story about some elaborate prank that her brother had played on her other brother, which involved hiding underwear. From there she progressed to talking about how exciting-but-scary the world was.

Honey, you've got no freakin' idea, Ysabel thought, between trying to think of more synonyms for *that's interesting* and *oh really?*

ABOUT THE SAME TIME. JUST WEST OF AVOCA, IOWA. 8:30 P.M. CST. MONDAY, OCTOBER 28.

Del Quintano was known as "Leprechaun" to his friends because, despite being solid Mexican as far back as the family knew, his bushy sideburns made him look more like the Notre Dame mascot than anyone had any right to. He'd made a virtue of it, growing his sideburns out and hanging the cab of his semi-tractor with little plastic leprechauns and decals, and he had to admit, his luck *did* seem to be pretty good.

He was listening to a talk station on IBIS radio, all the news about Air Force Two, shaking his head. Man, you never knew what was going to happen, except that when it did, every idiot in the world would call up every station in the world, and they'd all talk about it.

He had a mandatory sleep-layover coming up in Des Moines. A shower, a bed, and not being allowed to drive any farther until he'd had some sleep looked pretty nice to Del. Some of the old truckers complained about CELT, Continuous Electronic Load Tracking, because they couldn't skate around the rest-rules and take more work, but as far as Del was concerned, it meant nobody else could cut in on you while you followed the rules and worked a reasonable pace.

But even at a reasonable pace, that last hundred miles or so could get pretty tiring. Maybe he'd put on some music, something lively to stay awake to. "Radio, search, find coustajam," he said. He liked that new stuff.

The computer answered, "Searching, interruptions very frequent in IBIS, some *scrawk*." Then it fell dead quiet.

"Radio, acknowledge."

No sound.

"Radio, reboot."

"Rebooting and loading—" a harsh squeal, then silence.

"Computer, internal check."

A brief, rumbling hiss—then nothing.

Shit, he'd spent a fortune on a good voice-actuated system.

He pulled over at the next roadside rest. When he popped the cover, crusty gray-white stuff that looked like dried toothpaste fell out into his hand from the fuse box. He stared at the mess. It stung and burned where it had touched his fingers.

Del shook the mess off his hand into his litter bag, grabbed a wipe from his box, and swabbed his hands, looking in consternation at the tiny red dots that peppered his palms and fingers.

That gray-white stuff looked like battery corrosion. He took his flashlight around to take a look.

There were drifts and piles of that white crud everywhere, clustering and spilling around every little electronic gadget, engulfing every electric motor and encrusting every cable. The battery sat in a ball of crusty white goo the size of a beach ball.

"Holy shit," he muttered. He closed up the compartment, got in, prayed—not something he did often, and seldom this sincerely—and tried to start it again. There were clunks and thuds on the first try; fewer of them after he'd tried a few times and then nothing at all.

Furious, thinking about a late load and all that would cost him, and about the bed and shower waiting for him in Des Moines, he took out his cell phone to make the call to the dispatcher. The phone's screen was an unrecognizable scrawl of light and dark. Fighting panic, Del tried turning it off and on; it came on, wavered, and turned itself off. After that, it wouldn't come on at all.

On a hunch he didn't quite understand, he turned his phone over, pulled the battery, and tapped the phone in his hand; little gray-white crumbles fell out, stinging his hand again. The light in his cab went out, and wouldn't come back on.

ABOUT THE SAME TIME. I-90 EAST OF GILLETTE, WYOMING. 7:40 P.M. MST. MONDAY, OCTOBER 28.

It was warm without being stifling in Zach's Dadmobile. *He drives like my dad, too,* Jason thought. Dad always said it was his "precious cargo habit"—all those years of never looking away from the road because he couldn't stand to have one of his kids hurt. *Cool, actually, once you understand it.* "You must be dying to get home."

"Oh, yeah. Wrap up tight, down into the burrow with the cubs." Zach smiled. "I still want to take down the Big System—but not before the Big System gets me home and lets me find out that everything's basically okay. Speaking of that, I wonder why we haven't heard from the President yet?"

"That *is* weird, isn't it?" Jason said. "All I can find is recaps of what's already been in the news." His connection was still up and clear, and still tracking IBISNuStream Samuelson. In a fresh window he called up Goo-22. "We're not the only ones worrying. 'Pendano' is one of the five most searched words. But there's just one statement out of the White House—he won't be appearing at a fund-raiser in West Virginia in the morning. That's it."

"What do you suppose he's doing?"

Jason shrugged. "The media always made a big deal about what good buds Pendano and Samuelson were. Maybe he's crying."

"I never liked him, but I hope that's not true."

"Yeah. I liked him, but I know what you mean. Funny how it still matters even when we know it's all going away."

"What's all going away?"

"Dude. The Big System. I mean, Daybreak's here. Whoever grabbed Samuelson, why they did it, everything—it's all old stuff with no meaning, just history. This is just like a hangover or something. Once the Big System is down, we'll stop having all these emotional attachments to media figures."

"I don't know about that," Zach said. "I read history a lot. After Lincoln was assassinated, a few hundred thousand people dropped everything and went to Washington."

"I was kind of hoping Daybreak would mean going, you know, like all the way tribal, no government past the next hill."

"Oh, I don't know. I think it will turn out people still want to build some steam trains and sailing ships, and maybe even a few dirigibles or some telegraphs if they, you know, keep them clean and wrapped in antiseptic cloth all the time . . ."

"You mean if they practice safe machinery?"

"Exactly."

"I was kind of hoping to maybe get rid of the wheel."

"Wheels let you raise clean water from depth, and clean water means healthy babies," Zach said. "You can have my wheel when you pry it from my cold, dead fingers."

Jason liked to argue, and he was about to, but he felt that familiar, comforting internal hug, the reminder that you didn't quibble about Daybreak matters. Take down the Big System and then work out how it was supposed to be after. He felt a surge of warm friendship toward Zach, and it was a while before they talked again.

ABOUT HALF AN HOUR LATER. KENNEBEC, SOUTH DAKOTA. 8:56 P.M. CST. MONDAY, OCTOBER 28.

Marshalene was loving the drive across South Dakota. She'd pumped up some nice loops in a random feed so that the whole drive had been her favorite high points from her favorite songs, maybe two minutes of music over and over in random scramble. She wouldn't make it back to B-town tonight, but she'd keep going till she was sleepy, and if she was up till morning, that would be okay; someplace some hotel would take her money to let her sleep for a while.

She'd be over in fucking Iowa before she even had to think about refueling, pissing, and buying more munchies to keep her going till dawn or tired, whichever came first.

Then this unholy screaming, grinding noise scared the piss out of her, and the car tried, all by itself, to run off to the right. She pulled it back onto the road but it wasn't easy; in her remaining headlight (when had that other one gone out?) she saw a sign for an exit to County Road 19 and Kennebec. Kennebec reminded her of an East Coast name; it seemed like maybe there'd be someone there that got her when she talked.

The passenger-side rear motor had to be what it was, she realized, just like that hippie mechanic dude said. Damn, he'd been good, just not good enough to save what was obviously a dying POS car. Better go into a town and get some help. She took the exit.

Half a mile more, as that grinding noise built up, she was wondering if she'd reach Kennebec; it sounded like the *left* rear motor was going out too. She'd get it towed, first thing in the morning, from the motel parking lot, if she made it to a motel.

She sort of did. The engine had turned itself off but tried to come back on as the battery snapped and banged, and the number on the screen went up and down too fast to read—a bad short, for sure. The starter cranked twice, a funny, screeching noise, and died, but here she was at the driveway of a boarded-up gas station next to the COUNTRYSIDE INN MO-TEL VACANCY, so she coasted into it as far as she could, set the brake, and lugged her bag across the parking lot.

The mean old lady behind the counter had the TV turned way up, and clearly didn't want to talk to Marshalene, because the president or somebody, maybe the other guy, had been shot or was going to talk or something, but she got a room eventually, and when she got into it, it turned out her portable player was dead and all blobbed up with white stuff, so there was no music, and no gift shop to buy another player or any food within walking distance.

Really, some days you could just fucking cry.

ABOUT THE SAME TIME. WASHINGTON, DC. 10:15 P.M. EST. OCTOBER 28.

Heather convened the first meeting of Working Group Day-break about six hours later than she had been asked to head it up; things had simply been too much of a mess for anyone to have spare moments and mindspace during the pursuit and fiery death of Air Force Two, and none of the other working groups had been meeting either. But Arnie Yang had made the trip over and found his way through security, and to her pleasant surprise, Noel Crittenden, who was rarely willing to attend any meeting that might go after five, had dragged him-self away from his town house in Silver Spring and made the long trip in as well. "I might as well see some history since I've spent my life just knowing things about it," he explained.

Working Group Daybreak gathered around the conference table, almost everyone with coffee or tea because it seemed certain they'd be here all night.

Edwards and Reynolds sat next to each other, working up

a list of questions they wanted to ask; Heather fought down her paranoia and reminded herself that when she'd been in the FBI, she'd been trained to go into everything with a long list of questions, and anyway, the questions could hardly be anything but useful in the circumstances. Lenny Plekhanov and Nancy Telabanian were huddled over the document Arnie had just sent over, checking and rechecking graphs for his presentation, and messaging the analyst teams back at NSA, to make sure that Arnie's claims were fully supported by their data; no one at NSA would ever completely trust any analysis that didn't come from NSA, and worse yet, this analysis was just different enough from the math, semiotics, and cryptography they did in-house for them to distrust it. Firmly, Heather reminded herself that everyone preparing for the meeting was helping her, not spying on her.

The man from Deep Black, who had said to just call him Steve, was quietly reading from his phone. Orders? Reports? Enertainment? It might be his Bible; he walked and stood in a military way but he wore a black suit that looked like a Mormon missionary's or a small-town funeral director's. Deep Black Steve contrasted with Colonel Green, who, despite her uniform, slumped like a college student in a dull lecture, rubbing her face with tiredness; military people, even very senior ones, often pulled strange schedules, and perhaps she'd been up too long even before the crisis broke.

Arnie hurried in, the portfolio, briefcase, and papers hugged under one arm all on the verge of spilling and his laptop trailing a cord behind it.

Heather fought down a smile; she often suspected that one thing Allie found attractive about Arnie was that she was a natural organizer and Arnie was work for more than one lifetime.

As if to follow the thought, Allie herself came in after him, grabbing up some papers; if it hadn't been so comical, Heather would have been peeved, since Allie was distinctly not invited, but then Cam came in.

Allie said, "Heather, I'm taking the responsibility, Arnie found something vital, and we think Cam needs to hear about this right away. I'm sorry to rearrange your agenda when it's been so tough—"

Heather shrugged; *what can anyone do when the universe has its thumb on the MAX CHAOS switch?* "At least something important must be going on. Why don't we all sit and let Arnie spit it out? If you don't all know Dr. Arnold Yang, he's the resident genius at OFTA, and he's a statistical semiotician, which you could describe as doing what the pattern-recognition charlatans would be pretending to do if they were smart enough to understand it, except Arnie does it with math that would fry Einstein's brain, and he can not only find things he's not looking for, his methods can find things no one has ever seen before."

"That's a gross oversimplification—"

"Later, Arnie. What'd you find?"

"We've got the intersection between Daybreak and the attack on Air Force Two. Clear as a bell—no pun intended, the connection doesn't run through the Bell cell in Washington. Furthermore, we can be nearly sure it was deliberate right from the start, because on both the Daybreak side and il'Alb side, they did some pretty difficult, complex work to conceal the way they were coordinating with each other. That doesn't happen by accident, so it's no coincidence."

Edwards and Reynolds were leaning forward like leashed dogs smelling blood. *Small wonder, Arnie's offering them a chance to bust some butts and not feel helpless.*

"Here's the link." On the room's screen, he brought up a Saw diagram, the circle-and-arrow graph with contours that let an experienced professional read message traffic within an organization at once. "Heavy relaying made it hard to see at first. Many Daybreak messages worked like chain letters or spam, re-encrypting without decrypting, just proliferating till the message reached the right person with the right keys, and launched its own killer to eliminate all its copies from the net. Wasteful, messy, ultimately it gave our side a lot to work with, but it was fast and easy for Daybreak to use, and all the extra crap it generated meant it took us a long time to weed through all of it to see what was going on.

"Once we disentangled all that, we found eleven sources in il'Alb il-Jihado that were all messaging one Daybreaker in Guerrero Negro, who went by 'Aaron.' In turn, he led a very weird AG that didn't look like any other Daybreak AG—it was all individuals scattered physically within 200 miles of the flight path of Air Force Two over Baja and the Gulf. But they all seemed to believe he had a commune somewhere in the mountains above Guerrero Negro, and they were planning to flee there after carrying out missions.

"We've got five of Aaron's eight AG members identified. The first one, here, is Ysabel Roth—"

"She shot down the airborne radar, or someone did from her apartment," Reynolds interrupted. "Agents in Yuma got into there just about an hour ago. Can you give us—"

"She'll be fleeing toward Guerrero Negro, by some indirect route. Probably into Mexico and making things up after she gets there, she's fluent in Spanish and can pass for Mexican."

Reynolds nodded, and said, "Excuse me," then began ticking away on the keys of his laptop.

Arnie said, "Let me run through the rest of the identified and then we'll hit the non-identified. Peter Rapoch"—he brought up a slide—"released nanoswarm upwind of North Island NAS, so all those planes that were refueling or coming in and out of there are spreading the infection, and some of them may infect their home carriers when they return."

Colonel Green jumped to her computer to confirm that flights out of North Island were grounded.

It went that way for the rest of the list, and Reynolds was able to identify one of Arnie's unknowns with a suspect who had destroyed a microbiology lab at UCSD under the pretense that she was an animal-rights activist liberating the research monkeys. "But along with letting the monkeys out," Reynolds said, "she took a bat, wrench, and split cord to exactly the gear and computers needed to identify new bacteria and funguses in Southern California's coastal waters; she's delayed the lab work by weeks. Then on her way out, she 'accidentally' went through the political science department, and 'accidentally' ran into Professor Constantine Elwein-Gonzalez, who was there because he was on conference call for some of our anti-terror work, was 'startled,' and shot him. Elwein-Gonzalez happens to be the American who was probably most knowledgeable about il'Alb il-Jihado and had actually met and interviewed some of them; it was a classic setup of 'surprised an intruder,' and we know il'Alb likes that particular cover and uses it often—it's what they used when they murdered Pawhan. And the girl we're looking for—her name is Jasmine Chin—matches with everything you know about Aaron Group Suspect Seven."

"Let me take a second and relay all files to Agent Reynolds's computer," Arnie said, typing.

"So," Edwards said, "between Daybreak and il'Alb il-Jihado, we've got cooperation both ways. Daybreak operatives took down assets that we'd need for coping with the hijacking, and they were provided with information that let them carry out Daybreak-type sabotage because they knew our military would be highly active at certain bases."

"That's right," Arnie said. "Most Daybreakers didn't know that was going on, but then I suspect most il'Albis didn't either. The great majority of messages from Daybreakers still online are screaming that the whole Air Force Two business was completely contrary to the principles of Daybreak."

Edwards looked up. "Sorry that it's a world full of interruptions, but it is. Mr. Reynolds, I've got an e-mail from the Director; she has just authorized you to create a task force to round up the Aaron Group."

"Dr. Yang, will there be more about the Aaron Group?" Reynolds asked Arnie.

"You've got all I had. Good hunting, and let me know where to keep you posted."

Reynolds was out the door in a blur. *FBI Agent perspective: Nothing is really wrong as long as there's someone specific out there for me to bring in,* Heather thought.

She said, "Well, now that the people who needed to get moving are moving, Arnie, give it to us, short and sweet. I'll even let you say the words 'system artifact,' and hardly twitch at all—or now that you've got such a clear command structure in the analysis, is 'system artifact' even relevant?"

"Well," Arnie said, "the basic idea is that—"

Reynolds stuck his head in the door. "Here's an update: Ysabel Roth has been captured."

ABOUT THE SAME TIME. PUERTO PENASCO, MEXICO. 8:25 P.M. MDT. MONDAY, OCTOBER 28.

I am one shitty spy and an embarrassingly bad terrorist. Even if Ysabel allowed herself a couple points for having carried out the mission and getting out of Yuma before anyone really started looking for her, she was doing one shitty job now.

Because the bed-and-breakfast in Puerto Penasco was overbooked, they'd given her the "automatic overbook up-grade" and moved her into the Plaztatic Palace, as she mentally dubbed the Puerto Penasco Sheraton, and saddled her with a roommate—none other than Little Miss Scared Of Foreign Places.

At least they'd given her a coupon good for a meal, but she hadn't even thought of using that as an excuse to escape her unwanted roomie; instead, somehow, the earth-and-peasant-loving terrorist, scourge of the Big System, was now sitting over some bland noodle-veggie dish, trapped under the fake chandeliers in a plaztatic hotel restaurant, making polite conversation with Miss North Texas Loser Geek Girl.

If Ysabel had just thought of a good excuse to bring her bag down here, just act like it wasn't safe to leave my bag in the room, then fake one little interruption and scoot out the door with it, and I'd've been fine. So why didn't I have this thought forty minutes ago?

Back in the room exactly like the one you'd find in Cleveland or Tulsa, Ysabel said, "I saw more dirt in a day when I was three than this place sees in a year. Not exactly roughing it."

Nerd Chickie said, "I wish I had a tenth of your nerve, to just travel the way you do, and be right in there with the stuff. For me it's—even when it's just, like, Aspen, like, everywhere except home's an exhibit, behind a glass wall."

Oh, fuckin' gag me with a donkey dick, right now. "You need to get out more."

"Yeah, I guess I do." Completely unironically, Nerdette turned on the TV and voice-commanded it: "American news." She asked, "Were you going to do any of those organized activities tomorrow?"

Inspiration! Ysabel said, "I'm planning to be up early and go out into town; more fun than 'activities' with a bunch of people I could have stayed home and found at the Senior Center."

The girl laughed and shoved her horn-rimmed glasses up her freckly nose. "We do seem to be the youth in the crowd, don't we?"

If she looked any more wholesome and innocent, Ysabel thought, *I'd just sell her to a pimp for resale to a Japanese tourist with a rape-a-librarian fetish. Dammit, where's a good pimp when you need one?*

But she said, "Yeah. So I'm going to turn in now and get up at dawn. It won't be scary or dangerous or anything if you'd like to come along."

"That would be *so* awesome."

"Okay, so," Ysabel said, "why don't you grab first showers?"

"Eahh, I kind of want to catch the news. You can."

It would look too weird to insist, so Ysabel shrugged. Anyway, it might be her last shower ever with unlimited hot water. She'd dress and take off while Little Miss Forgettable was in the shower. Nothing easier.

Ysabel was just toweling off when she saw the doorknob start to turn slowly, soundlessly, most of the way around and then return to its normal position. She reached for the little lock button. The door slapped her arm back and the base of a lamp caught her under the jaw.

Room spinning. Skull screaming like a bad smoke detector. *What?* She was—

The girl jammed the lamp into Ysabel's naked belly, knocking the wind out of her, and let it crash to the floor, slamming Ysabel's foot. She grabbed Ysabel's long hair, wrapped it in a fist that pressed against her neck, and forced her head back and down, dragging her backward by the hair into the main room.

Ysabel's feet slid and wobbled till she lost her balance completely and fell sideways on her ass on the hotel-room carpet.

The girl punched her, hard, in the cheek. "Roll over."

She did. As she realized that the girl was tying her hands behind her back, she caught phrases from the American TV news: "believed to be," "wanted for questioning," and "Yuma."

Oh, crap, and because they were in this big American Plaztatic Tower of a hotel, there would be someone with good English at the front desk, who would take "I need the police right away" seriously.

The carpet ground against her face, everything hurt, and the girl said, "Hey, is *this* one of those adventures you're so patronizing about having had? You're right, they're *fun.*"

ABOUT TEN MINUTES LATER. WASHINGTON, DC. 10:36 P.M. EST. MONDAY, OCTOBER 28.

After all the excitement, Arnie was stuck, as ever, with giving his presentation at a time when it had to be an anticlimax. "Let's start with what I usually do, okay? So you'll see why it was I found what I found.

"Semiotics is the study of how signs mean—how one thing stands for another or how a message connects to its meaning. Like an oncoming car flashes its lights at you on the highway, what do you know? Something wrong ahead, cop or accident or animals on the road, so you slow down and pay attention. *Statistical* semiotics is about how *populations* of signs function as signs. Like it's close to night, or you're close to a tunnel, and in the other lane you see ten cars in a row with their lights on, so you know it's dark ahead, and you turn your lights on—and if other people do that, it becomes a message to other oncoming drivers."

"But they weren't sending a message," Heather said, playing the role to hurry Arnie to the point. "They just had their lights on, and you saw them."

"Many messages aren't sent by anyone," Arnie said, "even though they're perceived and received. A deer doesn't leave tracks or scent because it's trying to tell hunters or dogs where to find it. If there *is* an intention, that's expressed through yet more signs, which might or might not be important. So it doesn't matter that the other drivers weren't trying to say anything to you. And it doesn't matter that any one car had its lights on or off—one car could just be a forgetful person or one of those cars that doesn't give you a choice. But a *population* of signs formed a message. One swallow does not a summer make, but five thousand swallows and a million green buds on the trees and forty Memorial Day sales in the stores does.

"Those messages that no one intends to send, that are sent by a lot of different sources collectively, are called system artifacts. Like people doing the wave in a stadium; the wave isn't any one person, but it's visible to everyone. Like one color of scrunchy being reserved for the popular girls in a school; nobody makes it up, everyone just knows. Surprising numbers of fads and fashions have no originator for any practical purpose."

"So you guess at fads and trends like the pattern recognizers?" Colonel Green asked. "And you're studying how Daybreak is a fad?"

"No." Arnie had an expression that amused Heather every time she saw it; it was the same one she'd seen on an astronomer who had been asked to cast a horoscope. "The pattern recognizers and trendspotters just know a lot about fads in the past, and they watch the news and the social media and look for things that look like what happened before; it's all about their feeling and intuition."

"The sort of thing I do," Crittenden put in. "Highly believable and I like to think insightful, but nothing the historian at Charlemagne's court couldn't have done."

"At least it's entertaining," Arnie said, "but forgive my pointing out it's not science, and it can't tell you anything you don't already know on some level. What I do is describe in numbers the whole huge network of communications—everyone and everything, be it person, bot, book, web site, accident, whatever creates signs, and the signs they send, and everything that interprets the signs and the secondary signs that they send to each other about them. There are numbers and geometry to express all the ways the messages and their sources and targets are similar, different, parallel, whatever. That results in huge data structures, many terabytes even for the most elementary problems, which is why no one did this before supercomputers. Then, with a very fast computer, we use wavelet shrinkage—that's a statistical method for estimating fractals if you're up on your math—to find patterns that are persisting.

"Or to oversimplify and use an analogy—which is what Dr. Crittenden does, and why he's easier to understand than I am—the pattern recognizers look at the clouds, and say 'That's a horsie, I feel good about horsies, I guess it won't rain for the picnic.' I teach the computer to look at trillions of pictures of clouds and notice that puffy ones with flat bottoms are associated with lightning and hail—even if I've never seen a cloud before."

"Or a horsie," Green said, grinning. "I've got grandkids. I can relate to horsies."

"Or a horsie," Arnie said. "I don't find horsies, I find the pattern by which people learn to look for horsies—and

I also find some people talking to some other people are more likely to call them horsies, and under what circumstances, and maybe construct a relationship that associates with the prefix *grand-* in other relationships. And I can do that in languages I don't speak. So statistical semiotic analysis shows me brand-new patterns, things that haven't been perceived before relating in ways that people haven't named before; from there we can work out the tests and methods for detecting following those patterns if they're important and persistent.

"Usually these patterns that fall out of the math are just what we call an idea pump—a person or organization that just repeats a message and encourages interested people to repeat it—and those are intentional and single-minded. Like the pattern of beer commercials having pretty girls and occurring during football games in North America.

"Sometimes the math finds a complex system like Islam, 'Go Angels!', or model railroading, where there are central ideas that change little and repeat often, but generate a huge volume of secondary short-lived messages—like Catholicism, say, the pope says pretty much what every pope always said, but your Catholic mother says, 'What would Father McCarthy say if he found out you did that?', that's a secondary message reproducing and altering part of the primary message."

"You were going to explain system artifact, Arnie," Heather prompted.

Edwards cleared his throat. "I think I see where this is going from what Arnie's already said. So a system artifact is a pattern that carries a message and originates in the system, not from any one participant, but from everyone at once."

"Exactly," Arnie said.

"Like esprit de corps, or corporate culture?" Green said. "No one makes them up, and you can't order people to have them, they just sort of grow between people, but anyone who's been around them knows they're real."

Steve looked up, and said, "That's what you think Daybreak is. A group of ideas that . . . what, fused? Found a way to . . . ?"

"Evolved," Arnie said. "It started out as a huge, inchoate list of reasons people didn't like the modern world. As the people talked to each other, Daybreak lost all the reasons and justifications over time—I can trace out about the last half of that process—and converged on a basic idea: Working together, we can take down civilization, and we should. Within a few years, because Daybreak had acquired the priority of finding ways to propagate and to move out of virtual and into real events, it acquired skilled people, and got better at persuading them to join, and at giving up the aspects of their own ideas that separated them from other possible Daybreakers, and so on."

"How does it keep them in line?" Heather asked. *Good, good, mostly they're getting it, look at them nod. This is going better than I thought it would. Come on, Arnie, make it—*

"Well, that's something it copied from a lot of the New Thought and 'spiritual' parts of the web," Arnie said. "Made more extreme, of course. Most serious Daybreakers spend two to four hours a day staring into the computer screen while they play Daybreak messages that tell them to relax and feel calm and happy—and think about what they can do to take down the Big System. The messages reinforce negative associations for the Big System, so that the person automatically blames every small thing that goes wrong on plastic and electronics and corporations. They tie self-esteem to being Daybreak-oriented. And listening to the messages makes Daybreakers calm and happy.

"Then too, it spreads and infects other systems of ideas. About eighteen months ago Daybreak penetrated the coustajam movement in music, and that helped prepare a lot more people to drift into Daybreak; it's also invaded the Stewardship Christianity branch of fundamentalism, and the Japanese Middle Earth Liberation League, and the Sons of Boone and Applegate, and lots of other places. But no matter what door people come into Daybreak from, once they become self-aware that they're attracted to Daybreak, Daybreak will teach them to spend a lot of time repeating Daybreak messages to themselves, or playing them over and over from recorded media, in a deep suggestible state."

"Who writes the messages?"

"Lots of Daybreakers scattered all over. Then they send them to each other, and try them out to see how they work with prior Daybreak messages. And they all collectively select the ones to use in their meditation and the ones to discard. For people who have been in Daybreak for three years or so, Daybreak is as central as Jesus is for a serious Baptist or the Revolution is for a serious Communist, but much more systematic and internally consistent—optimized really. Daybreak doesn't need an enforcement system—no Inquisition, no thought police, no awareness of a friend who deviated and was shunned or arrested, because Daybreak is always a welcoming path that leads you deeper and deeper and makes you feel better at every step.

"So I think what we are seeing is the evolution of a new, much more powerful and effective kind of system artifact, and we have to understand it as such if we're going to—"

Cameron sighed, impatiently. "All that was interesting theory until you found the connection to il'Alb il-Jihado," he said. "But now as I see it you've got two possibilities. Wherever Daybreak might have come from and however people might practice it, it comes down to this: Either Daybreak found an enemy of the United States and allied with it, or the enemy found Daybreak and duped it. That means Daybreak has a leadership somewhere—leaders to be fooled or leaders to make the decision to be an ally—"

Shouting in the main room outside.

They all froze.

Cam muttered "Excuse me," and went through the door; by common consent, as they looked around, everyone seemed to agree to go see what the matter was. *Funny,* Heather thought, *none of us individually decided to drop Arnie's explanation and go out the door, but here we are, filing out. Have to ask him if that would be a system artifact.*

"I just think I should go with Kim!" President Roger Pendano's voice was wild, yelping, cracking with misery.

DoDDUSP Garren and half a dozen uniforms were all crowding around him, saying "Mr. President" in an urgent tone that meant *Listen!*

Cam headed for the little group by the door, trying to be there instantly while not looking like he was hurrying. Now Pendano's voice was too low to hear words, but the passionate, desperate, throat-mashing whine in the tone was painfully audible.

Lenny said, softly, "The president wants his dinner and his bed; look at the shoulders and the expression. Shit, shit, shit.

Maybe if Garren or Nguyen-Peters pulled a Patton on him, right now, and just slapped him?"

Heather shook her head. "I don't think the Secret Service would let Garren do that, and Cam's too gentle and has too much respect. Besides, it might just send Pendano right over the edge."

"He wasn't this way about the Federal Reserve bombing, or the attack on the *Franklin Roosevelt*."

Heather sighed and shrugged. "But those were 'routine terrorism'—nothing personal—it wasn't the enemy torturing one of his best friends, then blowing him to bits, let alone something he has to blame himself for."

Kim Samuelson departed like a lost little girl between three big Secret Service agents; Pendano slumped into a chair, face in his hands, with Garren squatting beside him and whispering, urgently.

"Breaks your heart, doesn't it?" Lenny said.

"Yeah." A thought struck Heather. "Might be something I can do. Back in a second." She walked directly over to Cameron, who held his hands up as if to fend off two generals and a Secret Service man. "Cameron, I have something urgent and relevant." She purposely stopped about twenty feet from him.

He held up an index finger to the group and walked over to her, whispering, "Thanks for the rescue, and what do you have?"

"Graham Weisbrod is good with former students in trouble. He's stuck *me* back together many times. Maybe if he can talk to the President—"

Cameron grunted as if he were deflating. "Anything that has the slightest chance of working, sure. Call Weisbrod. And thanks."

Heather turned around and nearly collided with Allie. Startled, she didn't speak until Allie said, "Sorry, I overheard. I was coming over to suggest the same thing."

Cameron smiled faintly. "Apparently Graham Weisbrod has some kind of amazing calming power on the minds of his former students. I don't mind telling you, if he can do that for you at a time like this, I wish he'd been my teacher too. Anyway, go get the guru and see if he can do anything for the president. If you've got a witch doctor on tap someplace, bring that one along too."

Chris Manckiewicz awoke, as he often did, to the vibration and the insistent, "Wake up, Chris, it's the phone," in his own voice, which came from the cell phone buttoned into the pocket of his soft cotton pajamas. He sat up in bed, put the phone to his ear, punched the "prep and stand by" button on the traveler's autocafé that he kept ready by his bed, and said, "Yeah?"

"Your guy Norcross is about to give a speech about the shootdown of Air Force Two," Cletus said. "Have you been asleep?"

"Yeah. Needed to catch up, Norcross's a baseball nut, I figured he wouldn't do much during a big game in the Series, my chance for a night's sleep."

Cletus chuckled sympathetically. "Oh, man, the fates really *are* after you, Chris. Brace yourself. Vice President Samuelson was on a secret peace mission when il'Alb kidnapped him and stole his plane, loaded it with some nasty-shit weapon, probably tried to crash it into Angel Stadium during the World Series, and his old best buddy and pal Prez Rog had to order it shot down. Air Force Two is burning like a fucking match head in the California desert right now, and the smoke from it is so deadly it's knocking planes out of the air. And Pendano hasn't been on the air with even one word about it, zip. Now that asshole Will Norcross is going to horn in and give a speech before the President does."

"Well," Chris said, trying not to sound pissed off, "you know, he *is* running for president."

"Yeah. That's what I meant. Cheap political stunt. Norcross just announced he'll be making a statement twelve minutes from now, in the front lobby of the Radisson Dubuque. You're in that hotel, right?"

"Right." Chris's practiced hand switched the autocafé on, and it gurgled as it began filling his carafe. "I'm on it. Live feed as it comes, and I'll pack you a wrapped-and-ready ASAP after that. Standard procedure."

"Hey, make sure it *is* standard procedure this time. This asshole is piling on our president at a real bad time. So do him no favors, you got it? Absolutely no fancy camerawork, plug in one camera, focus it on the podium, and just record the speech."

"I've got six remotes and the big one on the computer, Cletus. It doesn't cost any extra for me to use 'em, and you never know when the main cam will go out or something will pop. Using all the cams *is* standard—"

"Oh, horse shit. What was that last time, you got him at that church with all the screaming, weeping Jesus bitches practically busting out of their blouses, and that one-armed cowboy dude with that Navy thing on his hat and that big old tear in his eye—"

"He was a real vet, really was on *Roosevelt* when the suicide glider hit it, and he lost an arm fighting the fire—I verified that. And the tear was real. And my fucking story was real, Cletus."

"Oh, yeah, real. Real. So real we had to bring in two editors to fix it and grab all your unused feed so we could show just Norcross's face, which is what I fucking *told* you to shoot, just that and the empty corners of the room—"

"There weren't any empty corners. It was packed."

"Fuck you. If it wasn't for the fucking lawyers, I'd have trashed your whole file, but we have to keep that piece of shit on file now for twenty years in case we get sued. Asshole. Now, listen, I'm telling you. Don't stick us with more stuff we can't broadcast—you *know* that's what I mean. Now, one goddam camera, on Norcross, get his speech, *don't* get anything more."

"Cletus, what *do* you *have* against good video, anyway? You cut things like that hot girl losing it at the Save Our Nation rally—"

"Yes, I did. And I'll do it again, and I cut that damn stupid huge African-American family all waving and grinning, and the old lady doing the Pledge of Allegiance with her hand over her heart. We are not giving Norcross one more thing than the minimum. What do you want, an Emmy for covering some jackass who will destroy our industry? You think someone's going to thank you for that?"

"You keep shitcanning my best work," Chris said. He set his cell phone down, put it on speakerphone and full vid, then turned to dress so that as he swiftly whipped his pajamas down, the camera pickup would point straight at his anus. *Of course, this may be too subtle for Cletus.*

Chris snatched his working suit from the closet. With just one guy on the job, thanks to the wonders of tech, every so often he had to be the man talking in front of a building.

He listened while Cletus screamed at him; it was the same fight they had every other day. Chris only prayed that when the campaign ended, ten days from now, 247NN would re-assign him as far away from Cletus as possible, so he made sure these fights got plenty nasty.

After all, nothing else was at stake. Anyone could see that Pendano was gliding to reelection as smooth as if he had glass wheels.

Word was, even from Norcross's own people, that since the 'pubs knew it wasn't their year, with a popular Democrat running for reelection, they'd thrown the nomination to Mr. Jesus Guy just to hang the failure on that wing of the party.

Chris Manckiewicz knew all about how large organizations shaft enthusiastic people. One thing he *really* hated about this beat was that everyone who worked for Norcross knew that that they had no support, and, no matter how hard they worked, they'd been positioned to fail. *I hate having so much in common with them.*

Okay, maybe it *was* weird, even *scary*, that more than a third of the population was jumping up and down and wetting its Wal-Mart panties for a guy who wanted to add ten amendments to the Constitution to "make Jesus the Supreme Law," whatever that was supposed to mean. Chris wasn't going to vote for Norcross—but he wasn't going to hate him, either. All he really wanted to do was report him.

He hadn't said anything, being busy getting his tie on straight and running a fast suite-check on his gear, so Cletus felt ignored, and was screaming, "Listen to me, Manckiewicz!"

"I'm listening," Chris said. "That's why I'm not talking." If he could just show everything about the Norcross campaign, Norcross would be understood—and then for sure he wouldn't be elected. Did Cletus think the viewers were stupid, or what? Just last week he'd had some blond-maned teenage psycho-bitch for Jesus raving about *killing* all the gays, standing right in front of some weather-faced old farmer type, looked like a stock illo for "Farm country shot to hell," who was obviously checking out her butt. If they'd broadcast *that*—

"Manckiewicz, you just remember to do your job when I

tell you what it is. I need to deliver one thing to 247NN every day: twenty seconds per day of Norcross moving his mouth, to make things balanced. That's *all* I need to do."

"Well, you need to do that, *and* stay away from the bottle you're thinking about right now, and not think about your ex-wife with a mouthful of that football player's dick."

That drew a long scream, and Chris reached over and hung up the phone. Two true shots. *Okay, I'm a mean bastard. What's a guy got to do to get fired anyway? I've got all my clips for my good work, I can hustle a new job in zip flat, especially because that asshole won't talk about the things I say to him.*

Besides, one time recently, he'd provoked Cletus into falling off the wagon, and a story had gone out just the way Chris wanted. This might be the biggest story remaining in the campaign and Chris was all they had.

Bottoms up, Cletus, he thought. *Come on, after I was so rude to you, you deserve a drink, bucko. And then drunk dial your ex and violate that restraining order.*

He was down in the front lobby three minutes before official go time. The other six network guys weren't there yet, so Chris had his choice of spots. *Just this once, fuck Cletus, fuck 247NN, and do it right.*

Norcross actually waved at him, and said, "Hey, Chris," and he was alarmed at how much he enjoyed that. *Jeez, I wish I could just send them the story the way I want to, use it or have nothing. It would be so—*

Hunh. Only three reasons he didn't send out live stories just the way he wanted them, with everything locked. One, it made him nervous because live mix in the field was hard. Two, it was rare that they carried anything Norcross did or said live, even when they had him give them live feed. And three, because if he did it, he'd *definitely* be fired.

Hunh.

He set up the last of his six wireless remotes, scattering them widely; he was set up for some real reaction shots of the press corps, and some nice side angles that would really show emotions from the hastily-assembled audience—a few supporters who had been holding a post-rally party, about fifty people who had been at the bars or doing some late shopping, maybe another thirty businesspeople and traveling families who had been told history was happening and to come downstairs to see it, and a great number of hastily-dragooned hotel workers.

Three reasons why I can't do this right, the way I want to do it, Chris thought. *One, I'm not sure I'm good enough; two, it doesn't usually go out live; three, I don't want to be fired.*

Hunh. I'm good enough, it's going live tonight, and I'd enjoy *getting fired.*

He checked his remotes, checked his main camera, smiled when Norcross announced they'd have to start a few minutes late to accommodate the other networks. *All the time I need to be ready. Here we go, lock the structure, send only one camera at a time, lock the audio over the video I send . . .*

ABOUT THE SAME TIME. WASHINGTON, DC. 10:42 P.M. EST. MONDAY, OCTOBER 28.

Whack! Crash! "Uh, um, damn." *Thud, thud-thud.* Heather smiled, visualizing Graham's awkward, startled fumbling as the secured handset plunged to the end of its cord. "Heather. What's up?"

"I think your old student"—*I don't dare say the name or the office, but if anyone's listening in, they'll know, they just won't be able to prove it*—"may need your, um, *advice*—like the unofficial advice I've gotten from you a few times—and he might need it very, very badly. He's here at the, um, old hospital where I've been all afternoon. The guy I'm working with here is sending a car—"

"Yes, of course, of course, I'll be down front in about three minutes."

"You can go eight," Heather said, looking at her screen. "That's the earliest the limo will get there. Bring a spare shirt and a toothbrush. Oh, and the Arnie Show was less of a disaster than we expected—he deigned to speak English to the mere mortals. See you soon."

"Food's here!" Cameron's voice cut through the dense fog of chatter around her. "I'll have to ask you all to stay where you can see your screens and hear your alarms, and a few critical people including me will have to stay fully online, but otherwise I insist that you make this as much of a break as you can make it. We probably won't have any more major information coming in for the next half hour or more, so eat, relax, rest as much as you can, and take care of yourselves like the valuable people you are." Aides were wheeling in carts of food.

"Also," Cameron announced, "for those of you who care, the Commissioner of Baseball has ruled that since Game Seven of the World Series was tied at the end of the sixth inning when the evacuation began, by the agreement of both the Angels and Pirates management, we have the first tied Series in history; both teams will share the championship. America's bookies are in total despair. Now, eat, relax, and be ready."

"He takes care of his people," Lenny said, stirring wasabi into soy sauce.

"Yeah. One of many things he's good at," Heather said. She pried a piece of pizza loose and slipped it onto a napkin. "This is an embarrassing thing for anyone from the Department of the Future to say, but do *you* have any feeling for how this is going to come out?"

"For the country, no idea. For people like us, same as anything else, free food and overtime."

ABOUT THE SAME TIME. DUBUQUE, IOWA. 9:55 P.M. CST. MONDAY, OCTOBER 28.

Chris Manckiewicz ran through his cameras and mikes one more time. Clear tight view of the hastily-set-up rostrum. Nice wide angle of the area behind it, get Mrs. Norcross, the Secret Service, the local politicians, check. Clear view of the night cleaning staff and bellhops standing nervously in the back. Clear shot of the small group of press; camera preset to pan across a cluster of biz folks, a family with the dad and mom in sweats, young soldier in uniform with his arm around a dark-haired girl in a nice maroon dress. *Hell of an interruption for your leave, guy. Sorry about all the history breaking in.* Another camera preset to swing between the dignified black guy in a suit (the host for the coffee shop), the mixed-race-and-gender group of young people in scruffy clothes (bunch of art students from Loras, grabbed out of a bar), and the brown-skinned woman in a pale green uniform with a big ring of keys (the night building engineer). All remotes good, broadband to 247NN open and clear.

It didn't hurt that the crowd was pretty Frank Capra to begin with, but Chris thought he'd really set things to look all-American. And Lexy, Cletus's after-hours assistant and the only person who might hate Cletus even more than Chris did, had gleefully slipped the word to Chris: Cletus was drunk and passed out.

So here we go. Edited live and on the fly and direct to air. My personal masterpiece. The story I see, the way I see it, and fuck the network with a garden rake. Gonna be so worth it.

"So, Chris, here we are in another town for another speech." Norcross's raspy nasal tenor was instantly recognizable; Chris turned and smiled. The Republican candidate said, "I think you've listened to me more than my wife."

"I'm *sure* he has," Mrs. Norcross put in.

Chris smiled. "Break a leg, Senator. I'm ready when you are."

Norcross clapped Chris's shoulder and strode to the rostrum. *He looks exactly like he knows what he's doing.* People said Pendano was the guy Hollywood would cast as the president; Chris figured Norcross would be cast as the president's barber—the man usually looked like he had really expected to be out on the road selling vacuum cleaners today. *Nonetheless, I almost* like *the Jesus-spouting batshit-crazy son of a bitch.*

The room quieted instantly when Will Norcross said, "Soundcheck, one, two, three, soundcheck; are we good?"

Thumbs went up all along the media tables. Norcross drew a breath, glanced down—*probably praying,* Chris decided. *In his place, I sure would.*

ABOUT THE SAME TIME. WASHINGTON, DC. 10:59 P.M. EST. MONDAY, OCTOBER 28.

"Media alert," Marshall called over the speakers. "Will Norcross's statement is going in less than one."

"Main screen," Cameron said. The whole room turned silently toward the larger-than-life view from the Dubuque Radisson.

ABOUT THE SAME TIME. I-25, ABOUT FIFTY MILES NORTH OF BUFFALO, WYOMING. 9:01 P.M. MST. MONDAY, OCTOBER 28.

"Norcross?" Jason exclaimed. "We haven't heard from the President yet, and they're running *Norcross's* speech?"

Zach shrugged. "Well, Norcross *is* running for president, even if almost everyone is ignoring that fact."

"I don't want any damn *candidate.* The world's blowing up, and *I want my president!*"

"Funny remark for an anarchist."

"Hey, no anarchists in foxholes, or something like—" An emblem appeared on Jason's laptop screen. "Here we go."

ABOUT THE SAME TIME. DUBUQUE, IOWA. 10:03 P.M. CST. MONDAY, OCTOBER 28.

Norcross looked calm but worried; Chris zoomed to catch the firm-set jaw and little wrinkles around his eyes, like your favorite uncle about to break bad news. "Well, thank you all for coming out and listening to me when there's so much else happening. Let me begin by saying that all our prayers should be with the family of the late Vice President, John Samuelson; I suppose it's no secret that he and I disagreed about very nearly every possible subject almost all the time, but on the personal level, he was a man who could listen, and care, could hear your—"

Pull back wide to show the ragtag crowd, catch the feeling that everyone, Norcross included, was deciding what to think and feel as they went along.

"—ask all Americans to join me in praying for President Pendano and his team as well. Now, I have no desire to be a backseat driver—"

Apophasis, Chris thought; *saying you're not going to say something in order to say it. Nixon's favorite device, and Newt Gingrich's, and Karl Rove's—fine old Republican tradition.*

That's a beautiful girl with red hair in a Pendano T-shirt, great boobs, and that big cross around her neck helps show them off—cut there for a reaction. Wish she'd jump up and down—not that kind of speech.

"—go beyond politics, because our country comes first.

So I am speaking to urge all my friends and supporters, every one of you who rings doorbells and makes phone calls, every blessed one of you with a bumper sticker supporting me or Governor Milton or the Christian Bill of Rights—"

Wow, nice. Cut back to close in on Norcross, look at the firm way he's laying it down. Okay, next reaction is . . . that slightly bewildered young family in robes and pajamas . . . catch them right when Norcross hits his authority voice—yes! look at Daddy nodding solemnly, and taking Mommy's hand, perfect! *Gotcha!*

"—no backbiting, no second-guessing, no analysis of how this affects our chances—just get in there and *help.* There will be time enough for politics later. So this is my—"

Wow, he's already winding up. That was fast. Okay, throw in all the reactions I can:

Maid in uniform leaning on a dust mop, next to the obvious Washington guy, face careworn and exhausted, in the pricey perfect-fit suit.

Young black father holding a small girl.

White hair, DAV cap, wheelchair, *how come those guys always have a flag with them? Never mind, on to:*

Desk clerk in uniform, slumped against a pillar but smiling radiantly, as if she had just heard exactly what she wanted to hear, bowing her head in prayer.

Back to select, close up, focus, *hit it:*

Norcross's grin, like a boxer who is half a minute from going back into the ring; here was a guy who *believed.*

"—beyond liberal and conservative, beyond Christian and secular, beyond business as usual. It's about our country. So if you support me—support the president. Support our officials, support the nation, and pray for them and for all of us. Thank you and good night."

Stay on him . . . expression of a man sure he has just done the right thing.

Pull back to show the room. Pop cuts around to:

Stone-faced Secret Service.

Eager reporters clicking away at their computers.

The crowd: young, old, men, women, children, many races, uniforms, jeans, T-shirts, bathrobes, suits—all nodding, solemnly, seriously, as gazes caught, held, were acknowledged in one another's reactions.

He caught, over and over, that instant when fearful grimaces and stunned slack jaws became weary, determined smiles, like Norcross's, as they decided we are in it together, and we will get through it.

In the corner of his screen: **lexy: strike&go if no qns.** Norcross was already at the door, so Chris moved swiftly, automatically, shutting down remotes and slipping them into cases, locking the cases onto his cart.

Residual pride insisted that he avoid taking the phone call that fired him in front of other people. He zipped through shut down and pack up. No call.

Back in the hotel room, he set about the ritual mechanics of pretending to himself that he would relax—pouring a double of Myers's Dark Rum and RC Cola over cracked ice; taking a fast shower while thinking, *don't-ring-don't-ring-don't-ring, I don't want to be fired while I'm wet and naked* at the phone on the sink; settling the thick, soft robe around his shoulders.

The phone didn't ring.

He nerved himself and dared to look on BackChanL, the instant archive on demand; they had broadcast it just as he'd sent it. He watched right to the end. *Yep, my best work. Ever. And it went out to the public and look at all those hits, twenty times the nearest competition, my work defined that event for history! Worth getting fired for.*

Cletus still didn't call. Now, that was interesting.

Chris took a slow, welcome, savored sip of the rum and cola. Till it rang, life would be good. It might even be okay after.

ABOUT THE SAME TIME. I-25 SOUTH, ABOUT THIRTY MILES NORTH OF CASPER, WYOMING. 9:13 P.M. MST. MONDAY, OCTOBER 28.

The headlights swept out a long path as they descended the hill, and for a moment a fox's eyes shone back at them like tiny, starry mirrors from the pointed face; then the bushy tail flickered over the railing, and the fox was gone.

All the news feeds filled up with chattering commentators, and Jason said, "I think I can do better commentary than any of those guys. Sheesh. That's a way I've never seen Norcross.

Is that what everybody on your side talks about, that he's real different in person than he is through the media filter?"

"Well, I didn't see the screen, busy driving, but yeah, it sounded more like the two times I saw him in person and not like the usual chopped-up version on TV."

"I guess I can see why people vote for him."

After a little while, Zach said, "You know, I hope when everything settles out from Daybreak, and this, and all, we will still have a President. Having one is kind of comforting."

"Like Pendano *would* be, if he'd just talk."

"Yeah."

After a while, because no more news was coming in, and it didn't sound like the president would be making a statement soon, they put the laptop into news-warn mode and talked about family, and music, and how confusing and wonderful it was to deal with women. The lights reached out in the darkness, and Jason watched for more wildlife, but apparently that fox was going to be it for the night.

ABOUT TEN MINUTES LATER. WASHINGTON, DC. 11:25 P.M. EST. MONDAY, OCTOBER 28.

Graham Weisbrod arrived and went straight into a small conference room with Pendano. Though Weisbrod was twenty years his senior, the president hung on his arm. The silence in the ops room was even deeper and more awkward than it had been, until Cam said, "All right, everyone, break's over, noses to the screens, let's have some good options waiting when the President comes out." People got back to work, but much too quietly.

Cameron coughed politely behind her. "Heather, I'd like to borrow Arnold Yang for a couple of minutes, because I need a public-opinion expert, and you, because I need a Weisbrod expert."

"Better get Allison Sok Banh in on it too. She's good at keeping Arnie focused, and she's even more of a Weisbrod alum than I am."

A minute later, the four of them huddled in a conference room. "Dr. Yang," Cameron said, "I remember how useful you were with helping to prevent panic during Hurricane Gordon."

Arnie nodded. "I had actual data and could monitor it in real time, then—I don't know how useful I can be this time."

"Noted. I know I will have to go on guesses, but it's my guess that you will have a better guess than I will." Cam adjusted his glasses as if he might need to read some complex, subtle message from Arnie's face. "Here's how I see it. Will Norcross just finished making a public statement, and we still haven't heard from the President of the United States yet. And it's bedtime on the East Coast. People will be staying up to see how the crisis comes out. Individually, they're brave and reasonable. In small groups of neighbors, especially if they know each other well, and there's something they can do right away, they are often downright heroic. But as an audience, powerless to do anything but watch, people spread their anxiety and sense of defeat around the Internet like a bad cold. So we don't have a lot of time. Right?"

"That's consistent with my experience and everything I know," Arnie said. "And I have no idea what to do about it."

They nodded, not sure where Cam was going. He turned his intense gaze on Heather and Allie. "Heather. Ms. Sok Banh. You're both Weisbrod—um, whatever you call the former students who . . ."

"Disciples, if you want," Allie offered.

"You won't offend us," Heather added.

"So Weisbrod is a good friend and a kind man and all that, but—what are the odds of having a reasonably confident, ready-to-make-hard-decisions, President of the United States come through that door in the next ten minutes?"

Heather sighed. "Pretty much zip."

Allie nodded. "Graham can work miracles with some people, but not fast. Graham's way is to get you to talk, then analyze, and wait for you to decide to buck up and do what needs to be done."

"Exactly," Heather said. "He saved my life after every divorce, but it takes *days*. And this is a *lot* bigger deal. And neither of us is Roger Pendano."

"You can't imagine how much I wish one of you were. So we have about twenty minutes to put the President on the air in a sane, coherent, grave-but-upbeat style. And probably we can't. Dr. Yang, how bad is the panic going to be?"

Arnie waggled his hand, balancing the issues. "For a real

answer, give me a week and a quarter million dollars. But my guess is free. I think it's not going to be as bad as things got in Pensacola during Gordon. People won't necessarily run outside and do anything at midnight on a cold fall night. And the Daybreak damage to the Internet and the phone system might work in our favor—people may be more scared individually, but it won't be nearly so easy to spread fear and rumors. One-way open-access broadcast media like television, radio, and satellite radio are doing better because"— Heather and Allie both gave him a look—"of reasons too lengthy to explain right now. I'd make an announcement, right away, about Daybreak, and give people things they can do to help. Try to make everyone who won't go to bed feel useful, have them buy into the recovery."

Cameron nodded. "And what *can* people do?"

"I'll call Jim Browder," Allison said, "and extract three or four ideas."

Heather nodded. "Get something from Edwards too. The FBI never misses a chance for favorable press. And it occurs to me that if citizens are watching for them, we could bust a lot of Daybreakers right now, while their behavior is still unusual and before people's memories fade."

"Good thoughts. All right, Ms. Sok Banh, get whatever Dr. Browder can give you. I'll contact Edwards and Director Bly. Now I've got to run; based on what you tell me about our situation with Weisbrod and Pendano, I guess I have to think about a Twenty-fifth Amendment situation, and I'm the NCCC. Thanks for the quick answers."

"Hope they were right," Arnie said.

"Me too." Cam was out the door like a flash of lightning.

Allie was already phoning Browder, so Arnie asked Heather, "Am I admitting to too much ignorance if I ask you, what's the NCCC?"

"My god," Heather said, "I didn't realize what he'd said. Shit, it's really that bad."

"Now I'm really lost."

"Being the NCCC is Cameron Nguyen-Peters's other job, the one he never wants to think about, and nobody else does either. National Constitutional Continuity Coordinator. Which is defined as the person with the authority to give orders and run the government—briefly—in the event of a break in the national chain of command. 'Break' is the euphemism for 'everyone in the line of succession is dead, disabled, captured, or crazy.' So if things are that bad, Cam runs the government, as a temporary dictator, until the real government can be put back together. His job is to do whatever it takes to keep the country alive and free, and make the succession work out, or establish a new government if it can't. He might have to locate the President's successor, or direct the Army and Air Force to repel armed invaders, order the Coast Guard to search for survivors in DC, send the Marines to rescue the surviving cabinet from a hostage situation in the Capitol. So *if* everything goes totally, completely into the soup—Cam's our emergency dictator. And he sure as hell doesn't want to have to do that job—I know he thought about turning down being Chief of Staff at DHS exactly because that would put him in line to be the NCCC—so if he's thinking about doing it, things really *are* that bad."

ABOUT THE SAME TIME. DUBUQUE, IOWA. 10:32 P.M. CST. MONDAY, OCTOBER 28.

Chris had just finished savoring the iced cola and the Myers's Dark Rum, and was deciding between porn, sports, or an old movie, when the phone finally rang; a glance at caller ID showed it was Cletus (as expected), with Anne the producer (as sort of expected) and a bunch of "somewhere up the chain of command" names he vaguely recognized (hunh).

Considering just how far off his instructions he'd gone, maybe that wasn't a big surprise either. Probably the corporate counsel had said they all needed to be in on firing him.

This was definitely the way to do it. One huge satisfying act of defiance, like every American journalist since John Peter Zenger dreamed of. Besides, if they fired you out in the field, they gave you some expense money to get home with. Chris could rent a car, spend a few pleasant days driving home and enjoying the fine fall in the plains, the Rockies, and the desert, and be in a good frame of mind to start looking for his next job.

He took his last sip of his rum and cola, then picked up the call a split second before it would have gone to voice mail. "Yes, Cletus."

"Two things," Cletus said. "First. I fucking hate your guts. Pendano *still* has not gone on the air, you made Norcross look like Winston fucking Churchill as filmed by Frank fucking Capra, and the lightning polls are saying that *four* states that were safe for Pendano are now up for grabs. That was one brilliant piece of propaganda, you fucking goddam evil Christ-y-boy Republican wingnut."

"I was just trying to catch what it was like in the—"

"Fuck you. It's not 'like' *anything*, anywhere, at any time, till *we decide* what it's like, and *you* were the one who decided to turn Norcross into presidential material when he couldn't have done it for himself with a blender and a saw. So fuck you, asshole."

"Am I fired?" Maybe Chris would have another rum and cola, and just get up whenever he felt like it, before starting his cross-country drive. Blow a little severance on getting a convertible, go more southerly, enjoy some sun. Since Cletus had mentioned Frank Capra, perhaps he'd watch an old Capra film tonight, toasting the master and celebrating.

The other side of the line was strangely quiet. A choking sound? *Cletus . . . crying?* "No, *you're* not fired. *I'm* fired. They made me call you up to apologize, but I'm not apologizing, and they can't make me—"

The line was dead just long enough for Chris to check to see if anyone was still on it; it looked like only Cletus had dropped.

Anne said, "Well, thank God *that's* over with, Chris. Do you have any idea how *good* your work was tonight? *We* don't think it could have happened by accident."

Hunh. Funny, me either.

"Till this happened to go out live, and Cletus threw a hissy fit, we hadn't realized just how much of your superb work he'd been sitting on, but once we hit the archive files and saw it— well, my dear god, Chris, why didn't you just *murder* Cletus, and figure any jury that saw your work would acquit? I mean oh my *god*. You know?

"We want you to stay out there and cover the Norcross campaign the way *you* want to cover it, and then, after that, we were thinking that if you'd like, after the election, we could do a documentary. Call it *The Norcross Factor,* just as a working title, and maybe you could take all your short pieces that Cletus spiked, and put them together with some longer interviews with key players, and it might make a nice ninety minutes, like serious journalism we could all be proud of. Serious stuff. You know?"

Chris took a deep breath. "This sounds like, um, you are asking me to make a network documentary. After giving me free rein with the coverage on the campaign. Is that right?"

"That's right, and no, you are not hallucinating." The smile in her voice was evident. Why hadn't Chris ever noticed before what a pleasant person Anne could be? "Look," she said, "this is only *partly* politics, all right? If you'd been doing routine, ordinary work, it wouldn't have mattered. The thing is, oh my dear god, a lot of what you've been shooting is great, *really* great, video. You are *so* going places. Okay?"

"Totally okay." *Sounds like Anne just barely managed to throw Cletus under the bus fast enough. Well, it couldn't possibly have happened to a more deserving little turd with feet.* "I was always kind of hoping you'd take a more active hand."

"Exactly. Oh my dear god, we're going to do good work together, you know?"

"Yeah." *Mmm,* Chris thought. *Ass. I love ass. Kiss it when you're in a good position, and you'll never be in a bad one.*

"Cool," Anne said. "Well, then, this was productive, but it's late; any questions before I let you go?"

"Just keep my paycheck coming, and we're good."

"You got it, Chris!" Brilliantly decisive. Completely committed to him. "Till I hire a new editor, just send direct to me. Stay on it, and good night!"

"Thanks, Anne. Looking forward to it—good night!" Click off. *Hope I sounded like a brilliant guy giving his brilliant boss her props.*

Chris stretched, considered another rum and cola to celebrate, and decided to just go straight to bed; no predicting what he'd have to do tomorrow or how soon it would start. Might as well be ready. In this weird world, you never knew what might be your lucky day.

ABOUT THE SAME TIME. WASHINGTON, DC. 11:32 P.M. EST. MONDAY, OCTOBER 28.

To Heather, Bambi Castro sounded nervous on the phone. "Arnie's friend Reynolds at FBI just called. The FBI office in San Diego expects delivery of Ysabel Roth from AFI—"

"AFI?"

"Mexican Federal police, the *federales* you hear about in movies. Good outfit. They'll hand her over at the border tomorrow by ten, sooner if they can, and the FBI will take her straight to their office in San Diego. Reynolds was calling because he thought we ought to have someone there, but I guess he's not in a position to issue the invitation, but if we asked—"

"Ask. Right away." Heather's biggest problem with Bambi Castro—and it wasn't much of one—was that her chief field investigator, who seemed to have no fear and complete control in the field, was afraid of every minor bureaucratic hassle.

"Well, I could go out, and I think it would be a good idea," Bambi said, "I know the budget is tight but—"

"Ha. It'll never be *that* tight. We need someone at the interrogation. Take that next flight, and I'll make sure we pay, and they expect you. Be there when they interrogate Roth."

"On my way, thanks." Bambi hung up, and Heather let herself have a moment of pure envy; maybe when Bambi flew back, she'd have a couple good stories. *I can listen to them over tea while I adjust my shawl.* Heather turned back to her work.

"Do you always look so mournful when you have to spend emergency budget?" Lenny asked, from beside her.

"Mourning my lost youth," she said. "Biggest crisis since I was born, and I've got an office job."

ABOUT THE SAME TIME. MARANA, ARIZONA. 9:35 P.M. MST. MONDAY, OCTOBER 28.

Kai-Anne had wanted to live a long way from the base if she could, and Greg had been his usual agreeable self, even though all the extra driving fell on him. She'd sometimes worried that it was one more of her eccentricities that might mark him as a dead-ender for promotions, but he'd just laughed at her and said that compared to wanting to fly a Hog in the first place, living far from the base and marrying a tattooed lady was nothing.

Still, this was one night when she wished she'd thought about how long the drive was before locating the family; it hadn't been easy to find an emergency sitter, when she found out he was coming home that night, and she'd owe Mrs. Grawirth a lot of favors. And it had been a long haul down to Davis-Monthan, and now it had been a long haul back.

She knew what he'd been referring to when, just out of the base, he'd said, "Hon, the A-10 that did the job was me. Maybe talk about it later?" So it had been no surprise that he'd slumped in the passenger seat beside her, not asleep but not really there, just resting his eyes on the distant hills.

Kai-Anne had known something about this; she'd seen residual bits of it when he'd come back from Pakistan, from Iran, from Eritrea. She'd just never seen it so fresh and raw before. After driving about three miles, she'd asked, as gently as she could, "Want to hear about the kids and my day and all that?"

"Yeah."

So she'd told him, more or less as if dictating an e-mail into her iScribe, the way she did every day when he was overseas, so that he could have the news but not necessarily the catch in her throat or the tears in her eyes; she felt that dealing with her loneliness and missing him should be at his option.

Nearly always he'd call after he finished the letter, and they'd talk, and it would be company, but now and then after a bad day, or pulling extra duty, he'd drop her a note that said only, *Sorry, can't tonight.*

She finished the kids' adventures of the day as they approached the Marana city limit. "What would you like to do when we get home?" she asked. "The kids'll be asleep."

"Truth is, after something like this, I like to sit out and look at the stars. I was thinking I'd drag the chase lounge away from the pool and out into the back yard."

"Would you like company? We've got another chaise."

"Okay, you take the *shezz* and I'll take the *chase*." His favorite joke about the only thing she remembered from two years of French. "As long as you promise to try to sleep, young lady. I usually don't till really late. Somewhere around dawn I'll want to take a shower and go to bed." He stretched, and said, "And thanks for going along with my weirdness. I don't usually get to do this after combat missions." He sighed. "Then again, I don't shoot down and kill the vice president every day, either."

They didn't say anything else while they set up the chaise longues to sleep on; she left a window open in Chloe's room, and the boys', so she could hear if she was needed, and when she returned from making sure everything was all right inside, Greg was already focused on the stars, as if he might fall right into the sky. But he whispered, "I love you," as she pulled the covers over herself, and she said it back.

ABOUT THE SAME TIME. WASHINGTON, DC. 11:40 P.M. EST. MONDAY, OCTOBER 28.

"All right," Cameron said, looking around from the center of the room. "Marshall, up on the screen please."

The big screen displayed:

> The United States and other countries have been attacked by an international conspiracy called Daybreak, which is working together with il'Alb il-Jihado, the organization that killed the Vice President. Federal authorities have identified many members of the conspiracy and are rounding them up, but they have released large amounts of dangerous nanoswarm and biotes, which are microscopic, self-replicating devices and organisms, and we need the help of all citizens to cope with the emergency. We ask that all citizens do the following:
>
> 1) Watch out for grayish or whitish crumbs around electrical/electronic devices. They may grow in less than an hour, so recheck frequently if the device is operating. If you find them:
>
>   a) Scrape sample into glass jar w/metal lid.
>   b) Wipe down with lye, ammonia, borax, or baking soda.
>   c) Rinse carefully with water.
>   d) Wait for instructions about where to turn in sample.

2) Check under your car's hood for white crystals before driving and at least every fifty miles. If you find any, clean with lye, ammonia, borax, or baking-soda solution followed by clean water, making sure to remove all visible traces of the white crystals.

3) Watch out for strange smells, particularly like baking bread, mildew, mold, spoiling milk, or rotting meat, around plastic, rubber, or synthetic fibers. If plastic containers smell like they are spoiling, promptly move contents to metal or glass containers; save a sample of the spoiling plastic or rubber for government scientists if you have a clean, airtight glass or metal container you can spare for it.

4) Smell your tires before driving. If they smell like rotten eggs or ripe garbage, do not drive!

5) Keep gasoline, kerosene, lamp fuel, etc. tightly sealed in clean containers; try to use a whole container at once when you open one. If fuel smells like bread, fruit, vinegar, or beer, discard it at once—NOT down a drain—and do not use that container for fuel again.

6) Disinfect plastic you want to keep with alcohol, hydrogen peroxide, or bleach; be careful not to use strong chemicals on materials that cannot stand up to them. Do not try to disinfect gasoline or other fuels.

7) Watch for neighbors, particularly people with passionately Green politics or members of extreme environmental organizations, who came and went at unusual times on October 27, 28, or 29.

8) Watch for neighbors who have been unusually active in computer activities, particularly if they are not regularly employed in the industry.

9) Watch for neighbors who have taken up hobby biohacking in the past three years.

10) If you suspect neighbors may have been involved in Daybreak, consider them dangerous. Do not approach them yourself but do contact the nearest law enforcement agency.

"Anyone have any ideas about what else needs to be in the announcement?"

"If they can't put the fuel down the drain, how do they discard it?" a woman asked from the far corner.

"Working on that, but we may have no answer," a man scribbling on a pad next to Cam said.

"Tell them to take the precautions they would if they were going to lose power or other utilities in the next few days," Edwards suggested.

"Tell them to take special care if they have family members with electronic or plastic artificial parts," Lenny said. "Keep plastic surfaces and electrical contacts clean, and don't unnecessarily expose them to outside air."

There were a half dozen more suggestions before Cam said, "All right, that's it, that will go out on every channel as—"

From the hallway next to the big screen, Roger Pendano came in, standing tall, his eyes dry. He'd combed his hair and straightened his clothes. *He still looks like hell,* Heather thought.

Graham Weisbrod moved quietly into the room behind him, standing against the wall, with his hands behind his back.

"Mr. Nguyen-Peters, I have something for you," Pendano said, "that may or may not be helpful, but I think is necessary." His voice was flat, dull, and emotionless. He held out a piece of paper. "Here."

Cameron reached out as if he were being handed a live cobra or electric wire. He read. "Mr. President, are you *sure* that this is what you want to do?"

"No, but I'm quite sure it's the best thing for the country." For the first time, Pendano seemed to see the hundred other people in the main ops room. "It's very simple. I've invoked Section Three of Amendment Twenty-five; I'm declaring myself temporarily incapable. I need to get out of the way and let someone who can focus solve the problem. I'm going to go out the back way and return to the White House, and put myself in the care of a doctor. Then, I suppose, we shall see. Thank you all for your patience."

He shook Cameron's hand. "Just do your duty; don't second-guess yourself too much." To Graham he added, "Dr.

Weisbrod, I'm sorry that I'm not quite up to the job you always thought I had the ability for. I thought so, too, but I guess we were both wrong."

"Roger, please don't—"

"We'll talk, some day when there's time." He looked around at them as if memorizing their faces. "Everything else can wait. Get this country a President, and then . . . and then . . ."

To Heather's horror, he began to cry, first just sobbing with tears trickling down his face, still standing upright, trying to wipe his eyes with his sleeve, but then bending forward and breaking down completely, great wracking howls and cries, like a tantruming child, or a wounded ape. Weisbrod and Cam rushed to his side. The Secret Service had him out the door in another moment, but not one of the hundred people in the room could un-see what they had just seen, no matter how much they might wish it.

FOR TWENTY MINUTES AFTER. AROUND THE UNITED STATES (11:45 P.M. EST THROUGH 6:45 P.M. HAWAIIAN STANDARD TIME, MONDAY, OCTOBER 28; IT IS ALREADY 4:45 A.M. GMT (LONDON) AND 1:35 P.M. IN JAYAPURA, OCTOBER 29.)

Del had walked toward the lights of the distant town. With his flashlight also dead, he'd been unable to find his sneakers in the dark truck cab, and he'd had to walk there in his cowboy boots. He found a cop waiting by the main road, and before he'd gotten half his story out, the policeman had introduced him to a chemistry teacher from the local high school, and they were on their way back, in the police cruiser, to take samples from Del's truck. *At least I have one hell of a good excuse,* he thought. *Also, that hippie asshole that tricked me into taking that black egg? I don't mind describing him three thousand times if it means they catch his stupid butt. I'm just sorry they can't hang him.*

■ ■ ■

One particular Daybreaker in Boston had hated noise and rude people and hurry, and so he'd taken the job at Logan

International; he'd had a chance to brush biote solution on hundreds of airplane tires that day. The first one happened in Tucson; the tire sensors told the pilot he couldn't very well land on all flat tires, so after some discussion with the ground, they brought the airliner in on Ford Lake in Lakeside Park; it was a mess, but everyone survived what had to be the shallowest water landing in airline history, and at least there were plenty of cabs and buses there to pick them up in the city.

The next one had also picked up nanoswarm, and had to ditch in the Mississippi near St. Louis, unable to radio to explain what he intended; it would have been all right if he hadn't collided with a police rescue boat, but still, there were only six deaths.

Then at LAX, the tire sensors were gone and another flight tried to land on the landing gear, not knowing that the tires were rotted and the hydraulic fluid was leaking; there were over fifty deaths. From there on, it became worse; there was still enough television and Internet to make sure everyone heard about it and began to look suspiciously at their neighbors.

. . .

Almost half of the Lookout Pass truck train, which hit a patch of failed IBIS on a downgrade, went off a cliff, and that was the most spectacular loss of its kind. But the worst was actually in western Kansas, near Hays, when over four hundred trucks cyber-linked in a train, including seven gasoline trucks, a truckload of liquid ammonia, and a double trailer of liquid oxygen, had picked up enough biotes to weaken most of the tires. When deer wandered onto the highway in front of the lead truck, the four hundred trucks were moving at almost one hundred miles per hour, and the IBIS station nearest the front truck relayed correct braking instructions as the first driver hit his brakes. The third truck, however, lost eleven tires and rolled; forty trucks piled into it, and a failed IBIS station didn't allow for quick-enough braking for the next hundred or so trucks. An oxygen-gasoline mixture in the tangled wreckage ignited, setting off an explosion from the ammonia-gasoline mix behind it, and the flame front swept down the line and caught the rest of the gasoline trucks. Two more failed IBIS stations and uncountable burst tires completed the process; all but the last nine trucks were caught up in the vast wreck before anyone had time to react.

Power had already begun to fail in the small towns in that area, so there was nothing to hide the brilliant flames towering up into the sky. The best guess was that about 350 truckers died, along with about twenty State Troopers, firefighters from Hays and Goodland, and citizen volunteers trying to rescue people from the wreckage. It was never really possible to determine an exact number; in some areas near the center of the wreck, steel and aluminum ran and puddled onto the pavement.

A local reporter with video of the event, unable to access the Internet, tried to drive to Wichita with his video; at four A.M., walking away from his no-longer-running car on his rapidly decaying tennis shoes, he was run over by a headlightless van that was trying to get home before anything else stopped working.

． ． ．

Across the United States, the first incidents were scattered and few, and local people took care of it. The fear and anger over the Samuelson hijacking/murder found an outlet in bringing in motorists stranded as their engines stopped running or their tires exploded; in making up lists of canned goods to buy the next day; in putting together groups to go relieve the hard-hit towns. The last night in which nearly every broadcast station was up, and nearly everyone had a working receiver, was a time of hope and of heartwarming stories of people pulling together; many of those still awake at midnight only needed to hear that the people in charge were on the job and that everyone would be pulling together to sleep soundly.

ABOUT THE SAME TIME. WASHINGTON, DC. MIDNIGHT, EST. OCTOBER 28/29.

As the head of Working Group Daybreak, Heather was on the list for a brief caucus with Peter Shaunsen, before or after the swearing in, so she and the others, plus Mark Garren, had to wait patiently in the small video studio in the St. Elizabeth's complex. Everyone had assumed that when Pendano declared himself unfit, the Speaker of the House would become the Acting President, but Kowalski had firmly reminded them that his parents had not yet been U.S. citizens when he was born, and he'd been born in Gdansk. Kowalski was likeable, smart, knew his way around, and had been mayor of Knoxville and Tennessee Attorney General before running for the House; he'd have been fine. Instead, since the Succession Act of 1947 barred Acting Presidents who were not eligible to be President, and the Constitution barred naturalized foreign-born citizens from the presidency, there was nothing for it; the next one in line was Senate President Pro Tempore Shaunsen.

Because Vice President Samuelson had spent so much of his time managing the President's agenda for his party in the Senate, it had not mattered that Peter Shaunsen was a querulous, almost-senile old party hack who had first arrived in Congress in the Ford Administration, entitled to his position by seniority but nothing else. *Nobody wanted to quarrel with the mean old fool, so they let him stay in.*

She knew it might be indiscreet, but Heather quietly asked, "You couldn't do anything?"

Cam shook his head. "I'm afraid not. I did point out that he could decline and let Secretary of State Randolph take the job. He shook his finger at me and said I was very clever, but he wasn't giving up the greatest opportunity of his career."

"Couldn't the Senate convene and elect another President Pro Tempore?"

"Already checked, and the 1947 Act specifically prohibits that. We're not allowed to adjust the line of succession once it's invoked—that's to prevent a coup." Cameron shook his head, sadly. "I admit I'm less than crazy about a guy who talks about opportunity—and not duty or responsibility—in the middle of a mess like this. But like it or not, he's who we've got."

"You're the NCCC; aren't you supposed to find us a *good* president? I mean, if he was eating imaginary bugs and insisted that he was actually Carmen Miranda—"

"Directive 51 says I'm to locate the qualified and competent person highest in the line of succession," Cam said. "If Shaunsen were obviously mad, in a coma, or in jail in Beijing, or maybe even just hopelessly drunk all the time, it would be my job to pass over him and go to the first competent person in the line of succession. But the job of the NCCC is to hand over the White House to the correct President or Acting President, and then get out of the way, and 'correct' doesn't mean 'the one I'd prefer,' as I understand it; it means 'the first one in line who conceivably could do the job,' and I think I have to define 'conceivably' in a pretty broad, liberal way. Anyway, the Cabinet will be here in a few minutes—I've got Secretary Weisbrod and Secretary Ferein up there to greet them and bring them down as they come in; the Chief Justice should be here any minute, she's scaring the hell out of everyone by driving herself like she always does; and Shaunsen will be along as soon as the barber shaves him and he figures out what suit he's wearing. It was harder to find a barber on such short notice than it was to get the Secretary of Defense or the Chief Justice of the Supreme Court, by the way."

"Must be a pretty fine shave. I didn't even know that we swore in Acting Presidents. Isn't the Vice President the Acting President whenever the President has surgery with anesthesia? Have they all been taking oaths all these years?"

"We've never done it before," Cameron admitted. "But I had to promise it to Shaunsen so he'd come down here and go on the air."

"Shit."

"Unofficially, that's my opinion too. But we've had an oath ready for decades, in case there was a need for swearing in. It's the Presidential oath except that there's a bit about handing the job back when he's told to, and it has 'temporary' and 'acting' all through it. And it's not all downside; sure, it's stroking Shaunsen's oversized ego, and that's probably just going to make a bad situation worse, but the PR consultants do seem to think that it will help reassure Americans, now that they've been completely freaked by not hearing from their president all night."

"I never thought I'd say this," Heather said, "but this almost makes me wish Norcross was in office."

Cam smirked, just a little. "After today, who knows? He might be. But this isn't the way I wanted it to happen."

"No—"

Chief Justice Lopez came in, her motorcycle helmet still under her arm, with her two "wingmen," the Secret Service who rode with her. They discreetly steered her to Cam, who handed her a copy of the Acting President's Oath of Office. She pulled out a pen and began marking changes.

"That was vetted by the Attorney General," Cam said.

"Unhhunh. He knows the law. I decide if he's right. There's three spots in here that Shaunsen could use to stay in power when he ought to go, and I'm fixing those. Plus two misspellings and I guess they just don't teach them how to use semi-colons in law school anymore. We'll have it ready before I have to swear in His Nibs, and you know as well as I do that he won't look at it first—that would involve work." She bent to her task, unzipping her leather jacket and shrugging it off. "And don't sweat the clothes, I've got a spare robe from my saddlebag—one of your interns is pressing it right now. Another lost skill. Thank god you have some back-country girls working here."

As they drifted away from Lopez, Heather said, "There's never been any idea of putting the Chief Justice in the line of succession, has there?"

"No, not really. And it would have been a mixed bag. Taft had *been* president, Earl Warren or John Marshall would have been fine, Roger Taney would've been a disaster. Besides, it sort of violates the separation of powers."

"Doesn't bringing a president over from Congress do that?"

"Shh. One of a lot of problems with the '47 Act. In a better situation, I might have asked Lopez for a ruling about it. But I think we've got to have a President, any president, inside the next hour, so . . . let's hope he grows."

Graham Weisbrod brought in Secretary of State Randolph, who looked very tired and old—he'd already been planning to go back to Oxford, Mississippi, as soon as Pendano was re-elected. Weisbrod got him coffee and squatted to chat with him in a friendly way.

"Your old teacher and boss is definitely a people person," Cam observed.

"Yeah. Hey, am I keeping you from anything you should be doing?"

"Getting everyone to this room is what I should be doing as NCCC, and that's obviously something I delegate. Other than that, there's just not that much left of either of my jobs. Most of the emergency operations upstairs are closing down;

the disaster relief for stuff like the truck pileups and plane crashes is over at FEMA, catching Daybreakers is up to the FBI domestically, and the military are gearing up to go get as much of il'Alb as they can find, which won't be much—it never has been. The temp team upstairs has been great, but it's time for most of them to go back to their regular jobs. I'm going to shut most of it down and send as many of you home as I can. I might even sleep some tonight if I'm lucky."

Dwight Ferein, Cam's boss (*and a prize stuffed shirt if ever there was one,* Heather thought), brought in the Secretary of Defense and the Attorney General, settling them into chairs next to Randolph.

Peter Shaunsen came in. Cameron hurried over to meet him. Shaunsen looked around, and said, "What do we need to do?"

"You'll probably want a briefing on the emergency, and you might want a quick meeting with the Cabinet; we'd like you to go on the air with a stock speech we have to reassure the public; and of course we need to do your swearing-in."

Shaunsen said, "I'll meet the Cabinet right now, but just to say hello. I don't need to know details about the emergency, time enough for that tomorrow. Then let's look at the speech you want me to give. Then swear me in, and I'll give the speech and go home. Let's get it done."

In the small conference room, Shaunsen's voice quavered. "Only five Cabinet secretaries, and one of them is from Department of the Future?"

"The rest are on their way, sir," Cameron Nguyen-Peters said, his voice carefully neutral. "I'm sure more will arrive while we—"

"Let's see that speech." Silently, Cam handed him the text.

Shaunsen read. "Okay, after the third sentence, add, 'And I can promise that there will be many opportunities for our many different American communities as the situation develops.' And then . . . 'I'll be reporting on those in a public address, and submitting a proposal to Congress, just as soon as our experts work out the details.' Then we need to find a way to tell them that if they vote for Pendano, since it's too late to think about changing the ballots, we'll get them a good Democrat to take the job by the time the Electoral College meets."

Weisbrod glanced at the Secretaries of State, Defense, and

Homeland Security, and at the Attorney General. None of them met his gaze, so he said, "Uh, Mr. Acting President—"

"It's 'Mr. President,' according to the protocol," Shaunsen said, firmly. "I looked up the protocol on my way over here."

"Mr. President, then, sorry. Mr. President, I think in a national-security emergency like this—we've been attacked, massively, by at least two different enemies in coordination, *and* the country is in the grip of a disaster, *and* there's no guarantee that more and worse isn't coming . . . um, I think campaign rhetoric would be out of place."

"Will Fucking Norcross didn't think so, did that little Jesus-weasel? Telling everyone he was going to be above politics. Can't get more election-hustling than that, can you?"

"You have a point, Mr. President," Weisbrod said. "But you know much better than I do, when someone high-roads you, pre-emptively, that way, the only way to beat it is to go even higher road. If he campaigned above politics, all you can do is campaign even *further* above politics."

Shaunsen peered at Weisbrod with a keen expression that gave Cam a feeling, for the first time since his arrival, that the man was all the way here. "I suggest that when you leave your department, you think pretty seriously about running for county commissioner or maybe state senator someplace. You've got the instinct. All right, *just* the changes I made then; put them in the TelePrompTer, and let's go."

The Secretary of Transportation and the Secretary of Peace arrived during set-up, and the Secretary of the Treasury rushed in just as Shaunsen was in final read-through. Shaunsen looked over his eight Cabinet secretaries with a sour expression that made Weisbrod think, *When I was an assistant prof one year out of grad school, if a dean had looked me over like that, I'd've quit on the spot; good jobs make cowards of us all.*

At last Shaunsen said, "I guess it'll be okay if you bunch them close together and keep the camera in tight focus. Secretary Randolph, make sure you stand in close, and you too, Secretary Karathuri."

Weisbrod took a moment to realize that wasn't because State and Treasury were especially important; it was because those were the two visibly-minority people present. *So it's all a photo op. Well, at least that'll leave me out of it.*

Shaunsen looked around once more. "And you say it would be half an hour before we had everyone?"

"Yes, sir," Cameron said.

"Just doesn't seem as special as it should. Well, let's get it over with, an old man like me should be home in bed."

Moments later, the lights winked green on the cameras, the tech director gestured *rolling*, and Chief Justice Lopez held out the Bible. Shaunsen seemed to gain three inches of height and lose three decades in that instant, looking solemn and serious, and his delivery of the TelePrompTer speech was flawless as pure performance, though it annoyed the hell out of Cameron: When it came to the messages that Homeland Security had written, asking people to be understanding about the needs of defense and law enforcement, but not to wait for authority if there was something they could do right now, Shaunsen delivered it in a pro forma rush. But when it came to the words he had added, *all those promises that the crisis will generate plenty of pork,* he slowed down to put a grin and almost-wink into it. *Shit, shit, shit I wish Kowalski had been eligible—or Shaunsen had fallen down the stairs and broken his neck getting here.*

Afterward, Shaunsen extracted a handshake and congratulation from all the Cabinet officials, including the slightly-too-late Secretaries of Education and the Interior, and told Dwight Ferein, "I know your guy here"—he pointed at Cam—"wanted to give me some kind of briefing or something about the whole situation, but I'm not that kind of micromanager, everybody should just keep doing the good job they're doing, and I'll get caught up sometime this week on it. Meanwhile, I'm tired, and can you believe it, I've been in Washington all these years, and it's my first time sleeping in the White House? I've got to go before I fall over. You just tell your people to take care of it, and I've got total faith in them." Three minutes later, he had climbed into a White House limo and rolled away.

Ferein said, "Mr. Nguyen-Peters, I presume you heard the president."

"Yes, sir."

"Then I just want to apologize for him. Because someone should. I suppose I should see about turning the rest of the Cabinet around and sending them home with as many feathers smoothed down as I can, eh?"

"That would be very helpful," Cam said.

"I can see myself out," Weisbrod said, "and I'm relatively featherless."

Ferein had been a CEO of two different companies, an Army Reserve major, a state attorney general, and a one-term senator. He said, "If the job had fallen on me, I would not have felt up to it. I know perfectly well that I achieved adequate performance in several well-paid soft jobs, and a couple of very well-paid hard ones. But unfortunately, I think our Acting President believes himself fully up to it. I am not sure how to disabuse him of this notion, but if you have any ideas, I'll help in any way I can. Thanks for being my Chief of Staff, Cam, and my colleague, Graham. Now and then I need someone I can make an indiscreet remark in front of; it prevents my exploding."

"Part of my job, sir," Cam said. "I should go upstairs and send the team home. Graham, let's walk together."

In the elevator, Cam said, "I suppose the White House Chief of Staff will figure out a way to shuffle Pendano out, and Shaunsen in, gently and with proper care for everyone's dignity."

"Most chiefs of staff can do that sort of thing," Weisbrod said, smiling slightly.

"Yeah," Cameron said. "Speaking as a chief of staff myself, what I actually meant to say was, I don't envy the poor woman her job—especially since for all we know Pendano will wake up tomorrow morning and say, 'What the hell have I done?'"

"From your mouth to God's ears."

"No kidding." He stuck his hand out and shook Weisbrod's. "Just between you and me, Mr. Secretary, my whole job is really all human contact, all I really am is a big smart Rolodex that knows where to go for help. And thank you for adding yourself to my list of people I can count on, tonight."

"Fair enough. Honestly, I was just hanging around because there's not much for me at home other than too much reading and not enough company, and it felt nice to be at least a little useful."

"You were more than a *little* useful," Cameron said. "Especially thanks for talking him out of turning the emergency speech into the opener for Shaunsen for President."

"I'm just sorry that I couldn't figure out a way to keep him from putting in that silly pork-for-everyone stuff."

"At least you tried, and you did something. Four other Cabinet secretaries, including my boss, stood there like lumps. And Dwight Ferein called it on the nose, even if he was right about being no more than adequate; we have too many people who are adequate administrators for ordinary times, and who have attended too many seminars telling them that they're leaders with vision, and too many of them have believed it." Cameron nodded at Graham. "All that's my long way of saying, I will call on you again, I'm sure, because I think you can make it up as you go, and most of these guys can't."

"I'll try to live up to your faith," Weisbrod said. "And hope it's never tested."

"Was that phrase of yours, 'From your mouth to God's ears'?"

"Perfect on the first try. You sound just like my mother."

PART 2

TEN DAYS

MIDNIGHT INVADES

Most of the time, Americans live together like a colony of clams, growing and feeding by tapping into each other's resources, with nothing much going on beyond the individual level. The whole grows and flourishes because its members grow and flourish. It's efficient but purposeless unless you regard growth itself as a purpose—which nearly all Americans do.

Cooperation for a common purpose is about as American as sacrificing virgins to the Corn God; Americans have heard of it, but as something long ago and far away, not something they do themselves. When the force of circumstances does drive Americans to common action, usually it looks like a herd of cattle, either milling about until they calm down, or briefly stampeding. An especially urgent need or clear vision can make Americans form up more like a flock of geese, with a few out front pretending to know where they are going, and everyone else honking to keep the temporary, efficient formation together.

At midnight on October 29th, Americans were more like a wolf pack in which the alphas had just been shot: yapping, howling, growling, threatening, whimpering for comfort, barking defiance, and now and then, wheeling to maul each other.

WASHINGTON, DC. 12:14 A.M. EST. TUESDAY, OCTOBER 29.

At the curb, Heather asked Lenny, "Would you like to split a cab? We can talk while we ride. I had kind of a feeling that we were both having a lot more ideas than we wanted to put out in front of the high-level types in there."

"Heather, you *are* high-level—higher than Mark Garren, you're an assistant secretary and he's only a deputy under."

"Yeah, but he's got a few hundred employees and a budget of mumble-umpty-classified gazillions, and I have nineteen employees and a copy machine. We're equal according to the rules, but—"

"Ha. This town *runs* on rules. What do you call all that fretting about the Constitution?"

"A normal day for Cameron Nguyen-Peters."

"And a good thing, too. But if we're going to talk about that kind of stuff, let's do it securely." He pulled his AllVoice from the outside breast pocket of his jacket and requested a security-cleared limo. "It won't take any longer to get home, the driver'll handle my wheelchair better than a cabbie, and in the limo we can talk about anything in the world."

"Anything?"

Lenny waggled an eyebrow. "You were thinking of talking dirty?"

"*You* start!"

He snorted. "I may take you up on that. But entirely aside from your being an interesting human being and nearly identical to my idea of beautiful, you said some things I'd like to pick your brain about."

"Well," Heather said, "like Woody Allen said, my brain is my second favorite organ." She risked resting a hand on his shoulder.

He stretched and rolled his neck; he definitely seemed to like it. *Well, it has been a while, he's the only date that's been any fun in the last couple years, intelligence is sexy, and any guy that thinks I'm beautiful, that's a major plus right there.*

As she helped to move his wheelchair into the limo, he said, "You've done this before."

"My dad, for the last twenty years," Heather explained. "His spinal cord was severed when an idiot drunk kid broadsided his Harley. It was a blind curve, and between his bike and an all-death-metal musical diet, Dad couldn't have heard the drunk coming if he'd come with a brass band."

Lenny laughed. "My mom has a Pod Twenty-One with all the country music ever recorded on it. I guess we can never fix our parents, can we?"

"I'm not sure I'd want to, but you're right, we sure can't."

The limo pulled away from the curb. "Actually, I really want to give the old guy a call now that I've talked about him. It won't take long—do you mind?"

"I wish I could call my mother, but if I woke her up at midnight she'd put me in an orange crate and leave me at a foundlings' home."

"Aren't you a little old for that, Lenny?"

"No one's ever too old where their mother is involved."

"Pbbbt. You set me up for that one. Okay, I'll just be a minute."

Her father picked up on the first ring. "Hey, there, little cop-chick."

"Been following the news, Dad?"

"Naw, just worked my way up to Level Seventeen in DoomAge, been off in virtual ever since they canceled the Series. Can you believe they did that?"

"Actually, yeah, I *can* believe they did it. So you haven't heard about Daybreak?"

"I think you have to be Level Twenty for that."

"Seriously, Dad. Just for a sec." She explained it briefly, embarrassed, in front of Lenny, to have to explain it the way she would to a distractible nine-year-old, but that was sort of what her big fuzzy dad was in every way except the physical. "So clean out the motors and electrics on your wheelchair with ammonia, and plan to do that more than once a day, and disinfect your tires. Like they say, this is not a drill."

"Fuckin' towelheads. And hippies."

She refrained from pointing out that her father wore his hair down to his floating ribs with a beard that went beyond it and looked like he had dressed by rolling in a bin of denim and leather scraps. His comeback was inevitably that he'd voted for every Republican since Reagan, so whatever he was, it wasn't a hippie.

"Just take care, okay, Dad? And if the chair starts to act up, take it down to the VA before it goes dead on you. I don't want you stranded."

"Okay, your old man will look after himself, Ms. Cop-chickie. Job going okay otherwise?"

"Yep."

"Gonna bust the assholes that did it?"

"Working on it."

"That's my girl."

She rung off and shook her head. "I hope that's enough to keep him out of trouble. He's not really all that old, but you know what guys like him tend to say, it's not the years, it's the mileage, and he's really piled it on."

"Where's he live?"

"San Diego. He's about five blocks from a VA facility, and they supply and support his power chair, so as long as they have parts and power, he can keep rolling. As long as he doesn't get all stubborn and think he can fix it himself."

"Well, at least he doesn't have to worry about the heat going out," Lenny pointed out.

"Yeah. Hey, you know, we've been out more times than I can count—"

"Seven. Good thing you're the street cop and I'm the analyst."

"Pbbt. I was about to say, 'And I don't know much about your family.' That was going to be an invitation to talk about yourself. Serve you right if I only talked business."

"Oh, no, you're not getting out of it that easily." Lenny told her about how, once he was on his own, Mom Plekhanov had gone back to school to become a special-needs teacher; then Lenny heard about life as a six-foot red-haired girl on the suburban edge of East LA. Then she discovered Lenny could be very funny on the subject of having been a Two-Million-Dollar Baby, despite the obvious fact that he had spent his first eight years of life in constant pain. Then he pointed out, "Whoops. We're about two blocks from your place and we haven't talked one bit of business yet. What would the taxpayers say?"

She barely thought for an instant. "I don't know if it's practical for you, but you could come up to my place, I've got a fridge full of leftovers we can eat while we talk, if you want, and then I can give you a ride home—there's a lift on my car for when Dad visits, it'd be easy—or if it's too late, you can crash out in my guest bedroom like a gentleman."

"Assuming I am one."

"Or trying to fool me into thinking you are." *I'm smiling too much. But then so is he.*

"Works for me," he said. "Definitely works for me."

The limo driver had no apparent reaction to the change

of destinations. *Not reacting is probably a job requirement,* Heather decided.

At her apartment, she introduced the cats: "The Siamese is Fuss. He'll periodically yowl like death on steroids about nothing, and now and then he'll get the rips and run all over the apartment, for reasons that probably make sense to *him.* He's hardly ever affectionate with strangers, but once—"

Fuss sniffed at Lenny's foot with cross-eyed concentration for a moment, leaped into his lap, curled up, and purred like an unmuffled lawn mower.

"Except, of course, I can always be wrong about him. The big lazy wad of fur that waddled in over there is a crossbred Persian and dust bunny, and I call him Feathers. He moves whenever he imagines there's a possibility of something to eat. The only reason he appears to be alive is that he has a vivid imagination."

"That's funny," Lenny said, "based on the things you always say about your social life, I was expecting about *thirty* cats."

"That's for after I retire. I'm working my way up gradually. Now, how do you prefer to transfer from wheelchair to couch, assuming Fuss ever lets go of you?"

"I'm comfortable in the wheelchair."

"Yeah, but if I'm going to sit next to you and put the moves on you, I need you on the couch."

"Oh, well, in that case, if we can just move the coffee table to give me a clear space, and perhaps persuade His Nibs here to relocate—"

"We'll start with the easy one," Heather said, scooping the ReadPod, Converse hi-tops, pizza box, and Nestle's Wine-4-1 box off the coffee table and in one swoop to the kitchen. *Classy way to make a good impression,* she thought. *Oh, well, at least I didn't have a bra lying on it like I did all last week.* She lifted the coffee table over the back of the couch and set it behind.

Lenny rolled forward. Fuss yowled as if his tail were on fire, shot at least five vertical feet, and vanished into Heather's bedroom in a single gray-brown streak. "Well, that was easy," Lenny said. "I didn't know they could levitate."

"I have to keep the windows closed so he doesn't fly to the

moon every time the neighbors turn on their blender. Can I interest you in a beer?"

"I bet you can."

As she returned from the kitchen, a cold Corona in each hand, she saw that Lenny had transferred himself to the left end of the couch. *Giving me the choice of next to him or at the other end. Maybe this guy's a little too much of a gentleman.*

To avoid towering over him, which she knew annoyed the hell out of her father, she slid onto the couch next to him. As she handed him the beer she brushed her head against his shoulder.

He slipped an arm around her. She kissed him, warmly, slowly, without tongue, or gripping and pulling, or any of the big-production ways of saying, *Dude, you are so in.*

Though you so are. I just don't want to send you that message. Yet. She was just hoping that a plain old *I like you* kiss was what he was in the mood for.

Christ, I bet he's thinking something just as complicated. This is what happens when you spend your whole life monitoring communications.

After the kiss, he said, "Well, that took care of most of my worries about misreading each other's intentions. Um, is this the place where I tell you that although we have to be careful about my left arm and my right foot is hypersensitive, most of me moves, and the parts that—"

"We can skip all that till the issue comes up, Lenny."

"We can?"

She grinned. "Well, if I put you through the full explanation of the mechanics before we got going, I'd have to admit that I did that to you to my dad, and then he'd beat me. And I'd *deserve* it. He gets so tired of having to do all that talking just to explain to whoever his latest is that he's capable of having sex and it feels good. Look, I know that no sane man who was incapable would humiliate himself by starting a fire he couldn't put out."

"What if I'm not sane?"

"I've run into that a few times. Married it once, too. I recognize it when I see it, and you're *not* crazy that way. So . . ." she kissed him again slowly, "as I said, we can discuss any special issues when they come up. Or when anything else comes up.

Now relax, forget whatever happened with other women, and give me a chance to misunderstand you for myself."

This time he kissed back, and she thought the question was settled until he said, "I'm hoping to break whole new territory in miscommunication before you decide you never want to see me again."

"Are you this smooth with all the girls?"

"Only with the ones who are way too hot and interesting to be in my league."

"Flattery may not get you everywhere, but it'll probably get you more than far enough."

He finally gave her the kiss she'd been trying for, definitely as the guy in charge this time. "And how would you know what my idea of 'enough' is?"

"Research," she said, "starting now."

NINETY MINUTES LATER. OFF THE CALIFORNIA COAST.
12:15 A.M. PST. TUESDAY, OCTOBER 29.

"How are we doing for collision avoidance? We're outside the shipping lanes now, right?" Tracy asked.

She always worried like this, quite unnecessarily, when they were both below and trusting to automated systems, but Grady knew it was no use arguing. "Roll off me, fire us up some more herb, and I'll see what the satellite says. Have to admit I'm going to miss this." Grady gave one of Tracy's fine, firm breasts an extra squeeze—he liked being crass with her because, despite her protests, it turned her on.

She got up—he liked how sticky her thighs were as they brushed over his—and padded over to the table to reload the bong.

Grady sat up, pulled the laptop over, and dialed up his GoogleNavRealTime, setting it for CENTERHERE, 150 KM, and ALLBANDS so that anything registering infrared, visible light, or radar from any public satellite overhead, anywhere within 150 kilometers, would show up in the composite picture it generated; projected current position was shown in bright green, with the actual positions back along the track shown in progressively paler green as they came from longer ago.

"No danger of collision, no weather to worry about, still

good," he said, "and autowarning is active and working fine. We can sleep whenever you want to."

"In that case," she said, "how about I have the oven make us a fresh pizza, with lots of extra cheese, and we switch to a nice mellow red wine and some Gatorade so we don't get dehydrated, and we start drifting off to sleep? I'm excited about Daybreak too, but it's been a long day."

Grady had been thinking about one more good blow job from his pretty wife, but sleeping without having to set a watch was a pleasure that would be gone soon; might as well enjoy it while they could. He stretched and yawned. "We'll go with your plan. It was still warm last time I checked; want to go up on the deck and look at the stars?"

In sweaters and caps, they held hands, sipped warm green Gatorade from nice heavy china mugs, and savored the taste of the sweet/salty fluid and the cool, moist sea air. They admired the bright lights in the sky, picked out constellations, and even allowed the satellites to be sort of pretty too, before the automatic gizmo down in the galley summoned them to go back below for pizza.

"I won't miss a lot of things," Grady said, holding out his glass for her to refill, and pulling over another piece of pizza, "but sailing like this, with the machines to keep us safe and take care of us . . . well, even that. Yeah. Even that."

"Even that what?" Tracy got all weird and puzzled sometimes like he wasn't speaking English.

He let that go. "Even that will be better after Daybreak, 'cause we'll be able to afford a crew, and they'll be *family*— like your nanny or the maid was family when you were a kid. And, and, you know, like, it won't be like the machines, because they'll actually *care* about us. Besides, right now any schmuck with money can have the machines, and too many schmucks have too much money, so it's like, it's not special. Like it will be special when we've got crew that's like family."

"So pro fucking *found*, baby."

"Daybreak is like Christmas, you know? You know you can't really but wouldn't it be great to have it every day?"

"Not if Daybreak was on Christmas. We'd miss the big dinner with my family."

"Silly girl."

At last they curled up like little animals in a burrow. The

automated system was silent all night; the few ships in the area had people on watch and collision-avoidance systems of their own.

ABOUT THE SAME TIME. PUERTO PENASCO, MEXICO. SOMETIME AFTER 1:00 A.M. PST. TUESDAY, OCTOBER 29.

Ysabel's coverall, plainly worn by many people before her, felt dirty, but not as soiled as she felt knowing that she was guilty as shit of helping to assassinate the vice president. She'd even *liked* Samuelson.

She'd been more a part of Aaron's infiltration than of Daybreak itself; she'd been totally duped and she was totally bogus, and she hadn't really been acting for the planet and for the peasants and for her real values; she'd just been a tool for goddam Aaron. If his name *was* Aaron. Probably that was as phony as his commune and the sympathy she thought she'd seen in his big soft Latin-poet eyes.

She'd fired that missile and risked all this so that Aaron and the other phony Daybreakers could kill one of the most sympathetic, decent politicians the pathetic old US had managed to produce. *And* it would be blamed on Daybreak.

She felt dirty, but she felt more like a fool. For the first time in her life, her fluent Spanish was a drawback; the *federales* had already interrogated her. One of them had big kind eyes, and nodded like he understood her, and gently explained about the diversion and Vice President Samuelson being killed in a cloud of dirty chemicals that were smearing all over beautiful desert right now; she could feel how sad that made him.

She'd wanted the kind-smiling, warm-eyed guy to understand that she wasn't like this, that she'd made an awful mistake, contaminated herself with evil power-people armed-struggle hater macho games. And trying to help him to understand, she'd told the kind-eyed *federale* more than she meant to.

I swear, if I ever get out of this horrible mess, I will never look a man in the eyes again. I'll get a big dog with big dark eyes and long, shaggy facial hair, and talk to him all day long. Please God, that's a serious offer.

She couldn't back out of the things she'd already admitted. Furthermore, she knew she'd be asked a lot more, soon, because they were just waiting for a truck convoy to take her to Tijuana, where she'd be handed over to the US authorities at the border.

She could see through the cell door to where her pack was sitting; if she just had that, and was on the outside for just a few minutes, she'd so get away.

Unfortunately, not even a body length away from her so-close pack, she could also see the local cop and his gun. Her efforts to engage him in a conversation in Spanish had been met with a curt *Callate, fleje.* Not a lot of negotiating you could do with that.

She didn't know where she'd find it in herself to say, *Dad, it just seemed like I ought to fire this Stinger missile at that blimp—I mean aerostat.* Or maybe Aaron lied about that too and it really was a plain old blimp.

ABOUT AN HOUR LATER. RATON, NEW MEXICO. 3:30 A.M. MST. TUESDAY, OCTOBER 29.

At four o'clock in the morning, not much moved in Raton, New Mexico; a few lighted signs had been on through the night, and the first few of the morning were just coming on as sleepy workers flipped the switches inside on their way to warm up grills, lay out sales charts, work through the night's e-mail, or set up chairs.

Jason, sitting in the cold dark in Zach's passenger seat, lonely, scared, and determined not to show it, watched the first guy at the Greyhound station enter by the orange glow of the all-night lights. The man immediately flipped on the old fluorescents, lighting up the plate-glass window with cold glare; a moment later, the little neon-tube lights that said BREAKFAST SPECIAL, HOT FRESH DONUTS THIS MORNING SO GOOD!, and FRESH COFFEE all flickered to life. The man began loading a coffee urn.

"I guess that's my cue," Jason said.

"Wait till he turns on the OPEN sign," Zach said. "He looks like the mean type that'd leave you to freeze your butt off on the sidewalk till he was good and ready. And besides, the coffee's not ready, and you're going to need that. Might as well sit in here till they're ready to serve your breakfast."

"Thanks."

"Hey, it's been one long crazy twenty-four hours, you know? We're somewhere between bonded and crazy-glued." Zach sighed. "This was not how I pictured Daybreak."

"Me either. You think they'll catch us? All of the Daybreak people, I mean, or most of us?"

Zach leaned back and considered. Jason liked that gesture, as if something he'd said was valuable. "I think they'll try. More than we planned on. We figured by the time anyone knew about Daybreak, the Big System would be dead, and they'd have no way to find us or put out the word.

"Now people are going to find a lot more of us than they would have if whoever it was hadn't murdered the vice president. How did that slip through our filters? Why didn't the peers stop *that*? I mean, I personally quashed at least ten stupid, cruel ideas."

Jason nodded. "I saw a bunch of notes from one guy who thought modern medicine was the biggest, evil-est part of the Big System, and he was trying to find people to help him wreck hospitals. Everyone I knew hug-mobbed the guy to chill him, focus him on acting for living things—but then he drifted away. What if he just found another AG to join, where they were even crazier? Are we gonna hear tomorrow that someone poison-gassed a whole hospital?"

"Peer guidance was supposed to prevent that."

"Yeah, but every AG got to *pick* their own peers." Jason slugged his fist into his palm. "We had the same problem my stupid-ass brother and father did, putting all our faith in procedures and organizations and our own good intentions, which is how Dad and Clayt end up supporting every stupid war and seeing the positive side of every ecocide. Yuck. I thought we were supposed to be *different*, you know?"

"Yeah. 'Put not your trust in princes, nor in the son of man, in whom there is no help. His breath goeth forth, he returneth to his earth; in that very day his thoughts perish.'"

"I'm guessing that's your guy Jesus."

"No, Psalm 146. Big one for Stewardship Christians. But what I meant it to say was, hey, haven't we all said, all along, we're animals like the other animals? I wouldn't expect the dog to do everything perfect, either."

"Yeah." Jason thought. "But the real question is still, are they going to catch us?"

Zach said, "Yeah. I know. I was avoiding the question too."

A bakery truck pulled up, and the man carried two racks into the bus station.

"Just now I bet the doughnuts are warm," Jason pointed out, "and the guy in there is pouring himself coffee."

"Yeah, you're right, it's time, and I should be getting home to Trish anyway, she'll be worried silly. Got my number in case of trouble?"

"Yeah, but I'll be fine. Thanks for the ride, and the company." He reached for the door handle.

Zach said, "Just one thought, Jason. Don't stop at home, grab your girlfriend and just take off—*don't* stick around to see what your gun-crazy survivalist neighbors do. I have a *bad* feeling."

"Yeah. You take care too. Happy Daybreak."

"Happy Daybreak yourself," Zach said, not sure why he felt so afraid to drive the three miles to his house.

To Jason, the fluorescent lights on the linoleum and Formica looked cold, but it was a lot colder out here in the dark. To the far, cold stars, he thought, *soon, soon.* After all, what was more natural than things getting dark and cold, just before Daybreak?

ABOUT AN HOUR LATER. JUST SOUTH OF EXIT 19 ON I-75, BETWEEN DAYTON AND CINCINNATI, OHIO. BEGINNING ABOUT 7:00 A.M. EST. TUESDAY, OCTOBER 29.

Many of the far-bedroom commuters, who lived twenty or even thirty miles from downtown Cincinnati, in towns like West Chester, Jericho, Bethany, Gano, and Tylersville, liked to leave work early, to return to the big house with a view of a golf course or a jogging trail, in time to go to the kids' after-school stuff. For most office workers, leaving work at three thirty required starting at seven thirty, so by seven in the morning, southbound traffic on I-75, even here, well north of the city, ran heavy: a mix of sturdy family-friendly minivans, first-good-job new subcompacts, and I've-settled beaters. A few bright stars remained, and low in the sky, a crescent moon bowed to the east, pointing to the sun that was still an hour away. The horizon was a line of blue-black, and the trees along the highway, mostly stripped of leaves in late fall, broke the dim twilit sky to the east into myriad panels, slices, and wedges.

Traffic roared by at the speed limit. Trooper Davis appreciated the peaceful order of it all. He waited in a median pullout, not eagerly, for the first aggressive speeder to zip by. His days usually contained many moments worse than this.

He was thinking about the coffee in his thermos when the minivan in the southbound left lane had a messy blowout—the tire totally grenaded, dropping the minivan onto the rim at that corner, and he held his breath while the driver fought it across the right lane; luckily the red Camaro in the right lane behind it was alert and the pavement was dry, so the minivan made it over onto the shoulder—

Shit. Looks like the Camaro blew a tire, too, in the hard braking. The guy behind him, less alert, missed the Camaro by a hair, and only by swinging into the left lane. That sudden change triggered a wave of brake lights. Davis flipped on his bubble and siren and turned up onto the left shoulder to go sort all this out. At least his lights would make people slow down and wake up.

Passing the now-forming traffic jam, he saw half a dozen more blowouts. *Crap. That Daybreak stuff they were warning us about at the shift briefing.*

Closer to the front of the jam, he found a couple of fender benders. Davis called it in; didn't look like anyone was hurt, and no air bags had fired, spacing had been good, speeds not excessive, and pavement dry. Nonetheless, this was going to be a major mess. Just behind the original blowout situation, three collided cars in a rough Z stretched most of the way across both lanes; everything in front of them had either made it to a shoulder or was finding a way through and rolling on.

Davis decided that would do for a starting point. He braked, left the flashing lights on to tell drivers behind him that there was an officer on the scene, and walked up to the Z-form collision.

The drivers were two lady office workers in sensible little

hybrids, and a sad, frustrated-looking sales type in a cheap washable suit and an obvious by-the-weeker used Kia. Their paperwork was all in order, even the salesguy's insurance; the bar code on his license authorized a breathalyzer, but Davis didn't see any reason to do that. They all had grenaded, torn-off flats; Sales Loser's tire had blown after his car had stopped.

They agreed to move their cars over to the left, so Davis pulled the patrol car across the lane to block traffic for them, and set up a choke point to keep things slow as he worked out the jam.

He grabbed his electronic pad and headed up the snarl of traffic on foot, talking to dispatch on handset as he went.

At least a third of the cars in the jam had flat tires. An odd stench, not like cow or pig or chicken, but definitely like some kind of manure, hung in the air. *Yeah, this has to be that Daybreak thing.* From a low rise he saw that he already had a two-mile jam, at least, on his hands, and called in to the dispatcher, asking for another couple of cars "and a Daybreak specialist if there is such a thing."

With a sigh, he got back to work, moving everyone with a burst tire to one shoulder or the other, clearing a lane for the trapped but functional cars. He flagged down a couple frantic idiots who were trying to zigzag between shoulder and lane to get past, and gave them their well-earned tickets. He noted a plate number on one asshole who shot him the finger and zipped on by, calling it in for an intercept up the road.

The farther along he went, the more tires were blown, at least twenty so far in this quarter mile of stopped cars. He sent up a prayer of thanks; if this had been an icy morning, he'd be looking at real wrecks, deployed air bags, injuries, maybe even some deaths and fires, instead of merely the worst fall day he'd ever had.

He saw the shreds of tire on the front driver side of the next car and leaned over the window. "When this guy right in front of you pulls forward, you can pull forward into the space he's in, and then left, over there, onto the shoulder. It's that Daybreak thing from the news last night. The best thing for everyone to do is sit tight, off the road, till we get whatever it is cleaned off."

"Sure thing, Officer." The fiftyish woman wore a plain

cloth coat and slacks; she looked like an office worker, probably taking the two grandkids in the back to day care. *While
her daughter works a shift at 7-Eleven or McDonald's, bet
you anything, and not a man in sight anywhere around the
place. Oh, well, not my business.*

The car ahead pulled forward. Nice Office Lady turned
to go left onto the shoulder. With a sound like somebody'd
fired a 9mm inside a trash can, something stung his lower leg.
He looked down to see the remains of the other passenger-
side tire from her sedan, smeared across the pavement and
wrapped partly around his leg.

"Oh, no," she said quietly. "I only have one spare."

Davis flexed his ankle; it had stung but apparently done
no other harm. "Yeah. I don't know how soon they'll be able
to get help out here and it might just be to evacuate; I'd pack
anything you don't want to leave in your car, if you can."

"My god," she said, "What's that awful smell?"

He bent to shine his flashlight at the damp mess of her tire.
It looked wet or greasy, as if it had been splashed with black oil
or partly melted. The reek of raw shit nearly knocked him out.
"The Daybreak bug," he told her. "Be real careful pulling over."

Her other rear tire blew as she parked it; they exchanged
helpless shrugs.

As Davis walked on up the line the thuds and bangs
sounded like a distant war starting; with a loud report, one
tire just behind him flung goop-covered shards across his
calves, and he jumped. *I wonder if it's getting worse because
it's warming up.* The stench of rotting tires was like putting
your head up a sick goat's ass.

The smell grew stronger, the bangs and thuds more frequent, and some of the drivers were angrier with him, and
some more resigned. When the sun came up at eight, and the
temperature started to rise rapidly, the remaining tires started
to blow in great volleys, and the reek became strong enough
so that many of the stranded motorists were throwing up on
the roadside.

He had a moment of hope when the dispatcher called to tell
him a Daybreak specialist was coming out, but then the rest
of the explanation came: "He's a microbiologist from Wright
State. He's walking out to you—it's about six miles—and
he'll be taking samples of the rotting tires."

"Is there anything he can do?"

"As far as we know, he'll just take samples and start walking back. Might be a day or more before he even gets to his lab, and the power just went off up there, so he might not even be able to study the Daybreak bugs when he gets them there."

"Great. Well, there aren't too many cars that can move anymore, so I guess it doesn't matter if you get me traffic-control backups, or not."

"They're all stranded with flat tires. Right now we're trying to find some way of evacuating, but tell anyone who can walk home they should start, and not waste daylight. Nobody's going to come into the city today from the north—all those routes are under quarantine. The microbiologist will look for you by your car, so be there in an hour or so."

It was in perfect keeping with Trooper Davis's day that when he returned to his cruiser, it rested on four soggy, stinking piles of black goo. *Can't cry in front of the civilians,* he reminded himself, and leaned against the cruiser, drinking the coffee from his thermos while it was still hot. All he had left, emotionally, was a small shrug, and an unvoiced *Well, shit.*

Feeling better for the coffee, and unable to remain passive for long, he started his long walk up the highway, looking for anyone in trouble he might be able to help. He found plenty of people in trouble.

ABOUT THE SAME TIME. ON US 64, JUST WEST OF UTE PARK, NEW MEXICO. JUST AFTER 5:00 A.M. MST. TUESDAY, OCTOBER 29.

Jason had been walking along 64 for about forty minutes, ever since the bus's front tires both burst while the guy was trying to slow on a downgrade, and he'd slid sideways into a disabled semi in a runaway lane. That had scared the piss out of Jason, the three old Indian ladies, and the two servicemen on leave—all the passengers on the bus—but it had not been at all as bad as it seemed; the bus had not rolled, and the bump against the semi trailer had been at less than ten miles an hour, just a sort of steel-to-steel kiss really. So after all the fear, there they were, off the road, bus upright, able to take their stuff off, and the bus driver had had a working phone, so he'd called for someone to come and pick everyone up with a van from Taos, not far away.

Except he'd conspicuously not mentioned Jason, and the moment he'd gotten off the phone he'd said, "So you, get lost. You're not riding with us."

"What?" Jason couldn't believe this. "I paid for my ticket like anyone else."

"Yeah, but you got long hair and a beard and you look like a fuckin' hippie, kid. And everything was fine all the way from Lubbock, till you got on my bus, and now my tires are gone and they smell like moldy cheese. That might be a co-incidence and it might not. So I'm splitting the difference. They said to be alert for Daybreakers, and maybe you are and maybe you ain't. You look like a hippie and you got on the bus at one weird time. But I'm not turning you in—unless you decide to act like a shithead—but I'm not giving you no ride, either. Argue and go talk to the sheriff, or start walkin'— don't be around here when the van gets here."

One of the servicemen, an Army sergeant, had tried to intervene on Jason's behalf, but Jason could see that all this was going to do was strand two of them, or maybe three if his buddy backed him, so Jason said it didn't matter, he wasn't going to ride with people who treated him like shit, and walked off with his pack on his shoulder.

64 was usually pretty empty but tonight it was really-o truly-o empty, like a walk through a pine-scented void with brilliant stars. The crescent moon shed just enough light to silver the east-facing rock cliffs of the mountains and reveal the rest as dark lumpy shadows. It was cold and quiet, a perfect chance to think and reflect, if he'd had enough energy to form an actual thought. He kept putting one foot in front of the other; no sense freezing or giving up when it was mostly downhill anyway.

When he finally heard a truck behind him, Jason didn't believe it at first, but as the headlights flashed around the bends up the mountain from him, he stuck out his thumb. A second miracle happened; the truck slowed and pulled over into a turnout. Jason ran to the passenger side.

The truck driver, a plump, balding man with aviator glasses, did not look friendly or welcoming.

"How'd you end up out here tonight?"

Jason answered without thinking, "The bus got two flats, and the driver threw me off for looking like a hippie."

"Hunh. I saw the bus back there a ways. You've been walking a while."

"Yeah." Jason thought for a second. "I don't know how to prove I'm not a Daybreaker except, you know, I'm carrying a laptop computer, and they're supposed to be all anti-tech."

"That's a start. What were you traveling for?"

"Following a bunch of coustajam concerts." It was lame but the only thing he could think of offhand. "I had this idea that I'd pick up enough advertising money by covering them on the net."

"How'd it work out?"

"Complete flop. I'm living on money my dad sends, and I was planning to go home to Connecticut after the last three big concerts, work for him to pay off all the money he sent, and then go back to college and finish it."

The man was smiling slightly. "So you're actually just a classic spoiled rich kid and not a crazy hippie asshole who tried to destroy our country?"

"That's about it."

"Well, come on aboard. You and me are gonna wipe down all my tires with hospital disinfectant, which is what the truck is loaded with, and we'll do that once an hour till you get to—where you going?"

"Tres Piedras. It's not far."

"Well, you can help me wipe here, and then just before I let you off, and keep me awake in between."

Sloshing and scrubbing with the foul-smelling disinfectant, on the dark road, trying to keep up with the speed the driver was working, it occurred to Jason that he'd had worse times. When they climbed into the cab, there was even coffee from the autocafé and the pleasure of sun coming up behind them with the high mountains all around.

I'm really not a bad spy. Jason and the driver traded the little stories that strangers do to stay awake; his cover story gave him a chance to talk about his family. He was surprised that he worried about them and missed them, and hardly had to do any acting at all.

ABOUT THE SAME TIME. DUBUQUE, IOWA. 6:44 A.M. CST. TUESDAY, OCTOBER 29.

On the first ring, Chris Manckiewicz rolled out of bed, grabbed his phone from the nightstand, saw it was Norcross's campaign, and achieved enough coherence to accept the call. Press conference in ten minutes, meeting room downstairs, blah blah blah, could he be there?

Also, probably in less than an hour they'd be clearing for a flight to DC—total change of plans—if Chris could come to the press conference with his bags packed, would he like to do an exclusive in the air?

"I'm packed." He never went to bed without having packed his whole grip and laid out clothes for the next day. "And I'll be in the press room before your candidate is."

He even had time to comb his hair, brush his teeth, and message 247NN to open a channel.

ABOUT HALF AN HOUR LATER. PALO ALTO, CALIFORNIA. 5:15 A.M. PST. TUESDAY, OCTOBER 29.

"Okay, the Internet connection cannot possibly be down here at SRI," Cicolina said into the phone. "We created the Internet right here back in 1969. We had Internet when it had two terminals worldwide. And we built it to never go down, ever."

"I know that, sir, I'm sorry, I'm just reporting—" There was a squawk and a hiss, and when Cicolina tried to call back, there was no dial tone.

He turned to face the room of engineers and scientists, many of them in sweatpants, raggy T-shirts, and other night clothing; it looked like none of them had combed their hair, ever, but then they *always* looked that way. Not a pretty sight, but it was probably the best collection of brains on the planet, and considering Weisbrod had only called him an hour and a half ago, this was pretty damned good. *The things we do for our old teachers.*

Cicolina said, "All right, this is going to be tougher than we thought. Let's see what we can do; we always knew we might have to save the world."

They applauded. He thought, *Hey, as a motivational speaker,*

I guess I'm better than I thought I was. Then the lights went out.

By the time they made it up the staircase to ground level, by the emergency light, the mood was shot; everyone wanted to go home to family and friends.

He thought he'd lost them till they discovered all the flat tires in the parking lot, and that a good third of their cars wouldn't start, with great wads of nasty white stuff under the hood. For some reason, that pissed them all off, and they started dividing into teams to work on the problem of how to do a "cold start" on advanced civilization.

As he looked at the swarm of men and women bent in little knots around whiteboards and notepads, hastily relocated to the sunny second floor on the south side of the building, Cicolina said, "Reminds me of what the old-timers, back when I was just starting project management, said the Manhattan Project had been like."

"Yeah," Roseann, his assistant, said. "Except, you know, they had electricity and phones for the Manhattan Project."

ABOUT THE SAME TIME. WASHINGTON, DC. 8:25 A.M. EST. TUESDAY, OCTOBER 29.

Heather was so much bigger than Lenny that it had been easy for her to position an arm and a thigh to support his different, asymmetric body, and to sleep with his slight weight resting partly on her. When she woke to the soft chime of her phone, she moved Lenny to a more convenient position, careful not to bend anything that didn't seem like it should bend. He mumbled, and she squeezed his shoulder affectionately.

She made sure the phone was definitely *not* on video, and whispered, "Yeah, Arnie?"

"Norcross is going on the air any second. Considering the impact he had last night, and the way the media have been running excerpts from that speech all night long, I thought you'd want to tune in."

Lenny, beside her, was stretching and using his good hand to rub some of his back muscles. "I'm awake," he said.

She said "Voice identify and open," and an image of her computer desktop appeared on the room's ceiling. "Find Nor cross press conference today not yesterday soon not past," she said.

"On forty-six channels." Icons appeared on her ceiling.

"Select Spanfeed."

"Hey, we're both Spanfeed people. We're even more compatible." Lenny turned to put his head on her shoulder; she reached over him, her hands exploring his back, working muscles that were tight, and he sighed like Fuss did when she found the right places.

The image on the ceiling was almost life-size, as if they were looking through a glass wall into the meeting room at the Dubuque Radisson; Norcross appeared to emerge prone from a door about forty feet above Heather's ceiling and walk down the wall to the podium. "At least he's not walking in over the swimming pool."

Heather snorted. "Laugh while you can. One more speech like the one last night, and Mr. Jesus is probably the President of the United States."

Norcross announced his campaign would be aiming to win the presidency by the "shortest possible route," because it was now his duty to win the election and put matters right, and so he had calculated a pathway of appearances that would take him through the set of states he judged himself most likely to win—all the traditionally solid Republican states plus Ohio, Pennsylvania, Illinois, Missouri, Maryland, and Colorado. He admitted how hard it might be, but he added, "We need a President. I am qualified and ready to be one. The other side is not offering that, and we *have* to have it."

Simple as Norcross's message was as a text, the subtext was even simpler: I am religious, not a nut; I would not have done anything so stupid, and stupidity must be punished; I realize that you don't care for my policies, but I am your alternative, so I will be moderate domestically if you'll let a grown-up take over national security.

"Phew. He's the next president, all right," Heather said, as the network logo popped up with a picture of the Dubuque Radisson and the caption *Decision in Dubuque*.

"Yeah. Can the Democrats even replace Pendano on the ticket?"

"The ballot slot technically belongs to the party, not the person, in all the states, ever since that Caroline Kennedy uproar. Theoretically, the DNC *could* just tell everyone 'a vote for Pendano is really a vote for this other person.' But who do they have who could possibly win?"

Lenny Plekhanov said, "President Norcross. We'll have to get used to—"

Her phone beeped, and an ID appeared on the screen on the ceiling. "Confirm no video."

"Confirmed."

"Pick up phone."

"On line."

"Hey, Cameron," she said.

"I'm glad you got a chance to sleep," he said. "We're having a meeting of everyone working on the Daybreak problem, with Secretary Ferein and several other bigwigs, at one o'clock this afternoon. The meeting before the meeting will be lunch at eleven, and here's the address. Can you pass that on to Lenny Plekhanov? He's invited to both meetings."

"I'll be there," Lenny said.

Heather snorted. "You know, *some* people would *object* to your tracking our whereabouts? I mean just hypothetically and all. Thought I'd mention that."

Cam said, "Sorry about the intrusion—"

"I was yanking your chain, Cam, I really shouldn't do that."

"You might as well, everyone else does."

She grinned and rolled her eyes at Lenny; Cameron Nguyen-Peters had been known to everyone at the FBI Academy as "Eeyore." "Unofficially, how is the *real* president this morning?" she asked.

"Sedated. Graham Weisbrod had to talk him into that, too. As for the *Acting* President, and by god *that's* a good term, he'll be at the one o'clock meeting—along with President-Damn-Near-Certain-To-Be-Elect Norcross."

"Oh, you saw that speech too," she said, smiling. "Okay, Cam, see you at eleven."

"Well," Lenny said, working through the complicated, awkward process to move from bed to wheelchair, "it sounds like you and Cameron have a history."

Smiling, she came around and knelt beside him so he could use her as a stabilizing rail. With his fused hand braced on her shoulder, and his good hand on the armrest, he easily slipped back into the chair. She said, "Let me make a guess. Does *your* history happen to include being dumped a lot?"

"Can't be dumped *a lot* if you aren't picked up much," he pointed out, sullenly.

"Yeah. True. Okay, well, if my love life was a bridge, it would have holes in the deck, towers leaning every which way, and no one in their right mind would venture onto it. Mixture of poor construction and too much traffic, you know? So . . . I was Cameron Nguyen-Peters's one and only friend at the FBI Academy because, well, Christ, somebody had to be. A couple weeks before graduation, on the strength of its having been a while, my appreciation for his loyalty, and a few tons of plain old desperation, I went out with him. Once. He made the most gentlemanly and discreet pass I've ever seen in my life; the pass was an incomplete, because the receiver was by then not the least bit interested; he did not attempt a punt, end run, or field goal; and the game was called on account of he doesn't have a damned clue about human beings, and I've known warmer snowmen.

"Ever since, whenever we've worked together, he has been cordial, friendly, and a good old friend, and he sometimes asks my opinion about things because for reasons not totally clear to me he values my judgment just as if I had any. Oh, and now and then, when he's doing something really buttheaded, I tell him so." Still kneeling, she was below Lenny's eye level, and she leaned forward. "Now kiss me, dammit."

He did, and seemed to relax. She decided it wouldn't hurt to drive the point home. "Since that date, which I point out was around thirteen years ago, when he was merely a knee-jerk conservative, Cameron Nguyen-Peters has become a complete right-wing nut of the type that thinks this country is about the flag, God, and the Army, and so I wouldn't be able to listen to him talk politics for three minutes without strangling him. He is a cold fish emotionally and admits, himself, that he needs massive coaching in order to express the feelings he probably doesn't have. He is so irritating that every time he swims in the ocean, he causes pearls to grow in oysters a thousand miles away. He has several good qualities, such as being a pretty good sport about being teased, being an Angels fan, regular flossing, and the way he keeps his shoes shined. I've honestly dated worse, though not twice."

Lenny was laughing by that time, and said, "Is it really so terribly obvious how insecure I am?"

"They're detecting it with obsolete barometers in Maine, dude."

He kissed her again. *Well, at least he kisses like the question is settled.*

ABOUT THE SAME TIME. MARANA, ARIZONA. 6:45 A.M. MST. TUESDAY, OCTOBER 29.

Kai-Anne hadn't slept very much that night; the back yard was warm enough with her sweatsuit and blankets, but she'd kept waking up to find Greg still gazing up at the sky. Then she'd rub his neck and shoulders, he'd say he loved her, she'd kiss his forehead like she was tucking Bryan in, and then he'd tell her to go back to sleep. She wasn't sure how many times she did that before dawn; three or four maybe.

Just as the sun was coming up, he turned, hugged her, and said, "I think I can sleep now. Let's go inside."

"What do you think about while you're watching the sky?" she asked, as they dragged their blankets and pillows back into the house.

"Same as always. That the stars are far away and don't seem to be interested in us. That there's got to be a better way than killing people. And that I'm glad I've got you and Harris, Chloe, and Bryan. Sometime after the sun comes up, it always makes enough sense for me to sleep."

"Yeah. I guess I can see how that would work."

They didn't bother making the bed; they just stretched out and dragged the blankets, still damp from the yard, over themselves, and kept warm by holding each other.

ABOUT THE SAME TIME. ON US 64, A LITTLE EAST OF TRES PIEDRAS, NEW MEXICO. 6:50 A.M. MST. TUESDAY, OCTOBER 29.

The trucker had been working his satellite two-way connections, and Jason had been checking the Internet, and all the news was bad. "Buddy," the trucker said, "I hate to tell a man what to do but if I was you I'd get a haircut and shave *real* soon."

"Planning on it," Jason said.

All over the country there were reports of vigilante actions; people discovered their cars were dead, their kitchens were not working, the food in their refrigerators was spoiling—in short, that everything was going wrong—and remembered the long-haired guy down the street who nagged them about recycling, or the girl in the long skirt at the coffeehouse who always gave them a little lecture about using sugar instead of organic honey in their morning latte. People like to have someone to be angry with when there are too many small annoyances in life, and the first day of Daybreak comprised myriad small annoyances for which the Daybreakers really *were* responsible. Most of the people they were catching were not Daybreakers, but punching out the sanctimonious Green neighbor, or humiliating the preachy coworker, were pleasures not to be missed on a day so full of irritation.

"Hey," the trucker said, and turned up the volume.

The news from Tres Piedras was that the local people had thought they had found a nest of Daybreakers outside town, and the sheriff had declared that he didn't have the resources to deal with the situation. There weren't many details but a trucker driving through town had said he'd seen a mob with guns heading up the hill.

Jason knew he must look sick, but he hoped it would look like he was shocked at the news of violence rather than terrified for his friends and Beth. Kindly, the trucker said, "Buddy, if you want, you can stay in the truck—I'm going right through and we'll go all the way to Phoenix if the tires hold. Or if you really have to be there, maybe we should let you out someplace where you can walk?"

"I know a trailhead on the highway near town," Jason said, feeling his mouth moving as if it belonged to someone else. "You can drop me there, and I can walk in, no prob, there's a trail right to the public park." *But I'll take the one that goes uphill. Five and a half miles and it's kind of a climb to the commune, but maybe I won't be too late.*

**ABOUT HALF AN HOUR LATER. RATON, NEW MEXICO.
7:20 A.M. MST. TUESDAY, OCTOBER 29.**

Tiff was shaking him. "Honey, you gotta wake up, I'm sorry, it's Teddy."

Zach sat up in bed. "What's wrong?"

"His asthma's worse than I've ever heard it, and the inhaler—" She held it out to him; the plastic cartridge had ruptured; it stank like sour milk. "All our crates of them, they're all bursting and they all smell wrong—"

"That biote wasn't one of mine," he said, stupidly, feeling like *Lord, Lord, if it can just not be my fault . . .* He started getting dressed. "The Walgreens we have the prescription at is twenty-four-hour, phone them and—"

"No phone. Our landline is down, and on the cell the store's line just comes back with a busy—"

Louder gasping from Teddy's room. Tiff rushed back to him; Zach grabbed his wallet and keys.

In the freezing early mountain morning he thought, *Please start, please please start, please still have your tires—*

He blessed the old thing a thousand times in his head as it started on the first try, and drove carefully, not sure what might happen if he pushed it. At Walgreens, he bought five inhalers—the legal maximum—and they all looked all right. On his way home, he used the cell to tell Tiff to scour the medicine cabinet with Drano and rubbing alcohol.

Harold Cheiron, Zach's across-the-street neighbor, was waiting in the driveway for him, not letting him pull in—and holding a deer rifle. Something moved in his rearview—Cheiron's wife with a shotgun.

Then he saw that on either side of him were that couple from down the street—what were their names?—he with a bat, she with a pistol, all of them looking ready to use them.

Cheiron gestured for Zach to roll down the window. "So where are you coming back from?"

"My—my son Teddy, I had to go out and get asthma medicine for him, what's this about? I have the medicine here—" He held up the Walgreens bag.

Cheiron advanced to the car window and looked at it. "I'll give this to your wife. You wait here."

Harold returned and brought Tiff, who was holding Teddy

(breathing easily now), and leading Noah by the hand; he was fresh from sleep, dragging his stuffed dog with him.

"She was scrubbing down her medicine cabinet," Harold said, "like trying to get rid of some kind of germs or something, and inside, they have boxes and boxes of inhalers, which have all rotted, and he's got a neat little workshop down there where he was building some kind of electronic gadget, it looks like, probably a lot of them, to judge by all the parts he had and the little jigs and marked breadboards. *And* he came in at about four thirty yesterday morning. *And* their walls are practically papered with The Earth Is The Lord's posters. Now, on *Good Morning America*, they said the things to watch out for were people who came and went at unusual hours yesterday, people whose hobbies seemed to include home laboratories, Green types, and people who seemed to be having troubles with weird germs. I vote that this family ought to go talk to the sheriff; any other votes?"

It was unanimous; Zach and Tiff didn't get votes. Shortly they were all piled into the back of Cheiron's panel truck, rolling slowly through the street. Cheiron's wife drove; Cheiron sat, the shotgun held across his chest, in back with Zach and his family. "You're lucky we like you around here, and you have kids we'd rather not hurt," Cheiron said to them, apropos of nothing. "They're asking people to go to the cops with suspected Daybreakers but there's all kinds of stories about people taking the law into their own hands. Naturally since it's mainstream media reporting, they're worrying more about vigilantes getting out of hand than about what you Daybreak bastards have already done."

"Harold," Mrs. Cheiron said. "Their boys are right here."

"Sorry. Daybreak jerks. Anyway, if you're guilty, we don't want you to get away, and if you're innocent, the sheriff will be a lot more protection than your house was. Don't bother telling me one way or the other. Once we hand you off to the sheriff, you're all *his* problem. If they let you go, I guess I'll owe you an apology."

Teddy gasped and Tiff got the inhaler into his mouth again; before she pocketed it again, she wiped it with a Diapie-Wipe. Zach watched her dully, trying to pretend he didn't understand; Harold Cheiron stared at them, face to face and back again, like a cougar deciding which sheep to jump on; probably he was just trying to remember everything he saw them do for the sheriff.

TWENTY MINUTES LATER. WARSAW, INDIANA.
9:30 A.M. EST. TUESDAY, OCTOBER 29.

Back when Robert Cheranko was a kid who didn't talk much because, really, words were kind of a nuisance, his classmates had nicknamed him Silent Bob, after some dumb movie that was already old then. Exactly one guy had ever asked him if he preferred Bob or something else, and he'd immediately said, "Robert," which Karl Parsoni remembered from then on. As a result, Robert had never even thought about applying to be promoted and getting a truck of his own; he was an assistant lineman for high-tension wires, and he hadn't done anything more about qualifying or promoting since—at Karl's urging—he'd gotten his certificate for live-line operations.

Every day, he and Karl cruised back and forth, starting and finishing in the same office in Warsaw, in Kosciusko County, sometimes getting as far as the Ohio or Illinois state lines, now and then getting clear up to the lake or down to the river, just answering calls. Karl would do about ninety percent of the talking, which suited them both, because Robert thought Karl was the most interesting guy he'd ever listened to, and Karl agreed with him. Mostly, Karl, an amateur naturalist, talked about the birds he'd seen along a stream, or habitat for this kind of fish or that kind of shrew, or where the elderberries would be good this year; high-tension lines run through what Karl called "a fair-enough bit of rough-enough country," which Karl liked to see on a regular basis.

Today, the orders had been "short and smart," as Karl said, pointing at the paper as he peered at Robert over his reading glasses. In his red Bean chamois shirt, suspenders, and immense white beard, he looked like a slightly and harmlessly mad Santa Claus. "Robert, they haven't said where, but they just want me to investigate some high-tension lines close to home. There are big increases in line resistance around here and they want us to see what we can find, leaving it up to us to decide where to find it. There's some lines where if the truck dies it won't be more than a mile and a half walk from my hunting cabin, but that's a good fifteen miles out of town. Is there anything in the world that you'd hate to be without for a couple of weeks or so, say back at your apartment? We might be stuck out there that long if things really take a bad turn, but I'd rather be stuck someplace with wood heat and kerosene lamps."

Robert considered. "Family pictures—my sister and folks are gone, I'd like to have those pictures around. And if I'm going to stay at a hunting cabin, I should get some more warm clothes. Plus I eat the same stuff over and over, and there's plenty of it 'cause I buy in bulk, might as well bring the can and box stuff along."

They grabbed the pictures, clothes, and food, and at Karl's insistence, they brought along Robert's banjo. "I'm not very good," he pointed out.

"Yeah, there might be a lot of time to practice. If you've got extra strings, bring them too."

Karl drove slowly down the narrow, cracked blacktop between the cornfields, chattering on, as always, about the way the crows were flocking, about the absence of other traffic, about the way the streams might change if there weren't so many pumps around to keep pushing the water back onto the land.

Robert savored the hot coffee from the thermos; he knew it all came from overseas, and in case there wasn't any for a long time, he wanted to make sure he appreciated it. They stopped at the cabin and unloaded the supplies from the truck, then followed the dirt road to where the power lines crossed.

Robert saw it first. "Look at those things hanging from the lines—the bright shiny things."

·With binoculars, they could see threads and strings hanging down from the power lines themselves, some of them as long as two or three feet.

Karl scratched thoughtfully under the huge beard. "Whatever those are, they're made out of something, and my guess is it's the power line; they're stripping metal off it. Either it's going to break, or they'll reach the ground and short it out or maybe start a fire. We want to take a couple of those aluminum strings, in a sample bottle, back to look at, and call that good."

"Sounds right to me," Robert said. "We could put a jar on

the end of a live-line pole and maybe shake one of the nearest ones in, from the tower, if you think it'd be safe."

"Except the tower probably has some too, that would get on our boots and get loose in the truck."

Robert scanned to the top of the tower; sure enough, bright strings of metal hung from it as well. "Well, they're easy enough to reach," he said. "And I don't know how they got them up there but they aren't on the lower parts of the towers, so my guess is they're still working their way down. They said lye kills 'em?"

"Yeah, and I've got some industrial lye in the lockbox."

"So I put on the spare gloves and apron and booties, go up to the strut below the first string we can see from the ground, and I use the live-line pole and jar to see if I can just take one off. When I do, I bring it down, cap it, and scrub the jar off with lye. We leave the spare gear here, take the jar back, and figure we've been about as safe as we can be."

Forty feet above the ground, Robert spotted a small string he could reach and stopped to take stock for a moment. That was when he realized how *quiet* it was today; no noise from Indiana 25, though it was less than a mile away; no tractors out turning under the last of the corn and soybean fields; no cars moving, and just a few people walking, in the little cross-roads town of Palestine off to the west. He could hear dogs barking, distant cattle, mobs of birds, and the wind. Nothing else.

The cabin had no landline, and their cell phones were dead, so they chanced a trip into Palestine and phoned from the pay phone at the gas station. Karl was on the phone for a long time; when he finished, he said, "Well, I'm supposed to put the jar in the mail to Indy, try turning my cell phone on once a day to check for messages, and if not, they'll send us out notice by mail, to the hunting cabin. I want to take a little snip of the string for my own interest."

He got another jar from the car, and working gingerly with tweezers, broke the aluminum string and dropped one end into the new jar. It took a while at the post office to buy a shipping box and send the sample through the mail—the clerk there thought it might qualify as hazardous material—but the truck still made it all the way from town to the cabin.

Karl went in to put the aluminum string under the microscope, and Robert said he wanted to look the truck over first. He washed off the tires, moved it to a dry spot, and decided to take a look underneath.

A good dozen metal threads hung from the undercarriage, anywhere where an aluminum surface was heated by the engine. Robert sat and thought for a time.

When he went inside, Karl said, "Look what I have here." He pointed to the microscope.

In the circle of bright light, the surface of the string showed as a pitted moonscape; as Robert watched, small square bodies crept along the surface, coming and going to the end, where a spiderlike cluster of squares sat like a nest. "They're sort of like ants," Karl explained. "The little square things carve trails in the aluminum as they go along, loading it onto themselves; then when they're full, they crawl backwards along their trails to find the breeding ball."

"Breeding ball?"

"That's what I'm going to call it. It's a huge knot of square things, maybe a few thousand of them, that dark dot at the end of the aluminum thread, and it appears to be making more square things out of aluminum and, I don't know, carbon and oxygen from the air, maybe. It keeps making more of them and sending more of them out. Whenever they come back, they deposit the aluminum between the breeding ball and the main piece of aluminum. Then they go out and mine more. Somehow they know not to touch aluminum that was laid down by other square things. So over time they keep building up aluminum under the breeding ball, and that becomes the thread we see, and gradually the aluminum gets turned into square things. I'm betting if you take a square thing and put it on aluminum by itself, it will start a breeding ball, and then start sending out more square things to feed it—"

"Karl," Robert said. "It's all right. I know."

The old guy looked like a flabbergasted Santa Claus.

"I was only at the car five minutes," Robert said. "You couldn't possibly have learned that much by looking at them under a microscope in that short a time. And every 'guess' you made this morning was dead right. And somehow, when you split the sample to send to Indy, you knew to keep the breeding ball for your side of the sample, and probably what you sent them is just a piece of crumbly aluminum wire, right? By the way, the underside of the truck is being eaten by your square things—you've got a couple foot-long threads on the muffler—so I'm guessing it won't be more than a couple days before the nanoswarm gnaw through to something important."

Karl smiled ever so slightly, as if he were just about to share the punchline of the best joke in the world. "I guess I'm like everyone else. I underestimate you because you don't chatter much."

"Probably. So . . . how'd you get into Daybreak, Karl?"

"Depends on why you want to know. You going to turn me in?"

Robert hadn't thought that far. He shrugged and looked around at the cabin; cast-iron, wood-fired, basically 1850s technology, and stocked for a long haul. "You like it quiet too," he said.

"Well, except for the sound of my own voice. And I like music now and then, acoustic and live. Part of why I recruited a banjo player."

Robert thought for a few long moments, hard. Back in town he had some clothes, some old porn he hardly bothered with anymore, and some household stuff.

Out here, there was a reasonably comfortable life in the woods—and more quiet than he'd ever encountered before.

"I'm just sad," Robert told Karl, "that you didn't invite me in on it. Did you make those little square things yourself?"

"Me, and a couple grad students at Purdue, and one old hobby programmer down in Kentucky, but yeah, they were my idea, sort of; got the idea from a real old poem, by Stephen Vincent Benet."

"It would've been fun to work on them with you. But I think we'll have a pretty good time out here, anyway. I like quiet."

Karl stuck out his hand, and Robert shook it, and that was all the more either of them ever said about Daybreak again.

TWENTY MINUTES LATER. SAN DIEGO. ABOUT 7:00 A.M. PST.
TUESDAY, OCTOBER 29.

Bambi Castro slept well on the plane, as she always did, and woke just as the plane descended over San Diego's gorgeous harbor, crowded with warships, with the pleasure craft of the rich, with cruise ships giving the middle class a taste of luxury, the occasional freighter, the swarm of commercial fishing boats . . . she'd been away too long, hell, it was always too long. Any excuse to go almost anywhere on the coast south of LA was always welcome, but Bambi had grown up in a big house on the hills, within sight of the harbor, and besides being beautiful, San Diego was home.

The fates were on her side, and she sailed through the rental-car process and was on the highway, heading north, in no time. Locally, the FBI was in an office park up on the mesa to the north. The road rose through the sort of craggy rock, distant sea, and scattered palm, sage, and pine landscape that makes visitors say, *Now, this is California.* She had her iScribe talking through the car's sound system, reading her all the stuff Arnie Yang and his team had put together overnight.

A message from David Carlucci, the local FBI chief, said that Ysabel Roth had arrived in Tijuana in a Mexican Army APC—the last running vehicle from the convoy she'd started out in, the others having succumbed to brown and green saline gunk, tentatively identified as soluble chlorides, around their wiring and electronics. A helicopter—carefully wiped down and sprayed with oil internally—had been dispatched to pick Roth up, and would bring her into Montgomery Airfield, near the FBI office, within an hour and a half.

Bambi's rental car was a nice little Chrysler sedan that handled well on the big, swooping curves of the California four-lane that Bambi had thought must be the best driving in the world when she had learned on it. Since then she had driven on four continents, and now she *knew* it was the best driving in the world.

No one else out on Aero Drive, perfect weather, beautiful day, and an immensely important case in front of her; it was enough to make her heart sing over the drone of Arnie talking about the affinity group structure resembling New Age book discussions and political activist "flash demo" response nets. She *should* be more serious, but . . . *well. Look at this morning!* For the pure pleasure of it, she swooped across the empty lanes, over to the right-hand lane, and downshifted to swing back.

The car pulled hard to the right, toward the rocky wall

beyond the shoulder; she heard the harsh scream of a wheel motor loaded far beyond capacity. She fought the wheel, trying to pull the nose back to the left, into her lane.

A loud boom shook the car; she spun out, broadside to the lanes. The four motors de-synched, and the rear passenger-side motor went out completely; she fought for control as the electronic differential tried to counterspin so hard that she thought the car might roll. It bucked and jolted, and the engine clamped and died as the generator failed to disengage.

Unfortunately, there was still plenty of power in the batteries and capacitors. The car slid backward into the oncoming lane.

Bambi jammed on the brakes to regain control; the ABS shuddered and the car vibrated with the regeneration moans in the remaining motors. The little Chrysler finally stopped sideways on the wrong side of the road, and then leaped about fifteen feet backward, impelled by the front motors, as some electronic control fired too late or at random. The rear bumper slammed into the guardrail so hard that the trunk flew open. She yanked the key to cut the power, slammed on the parking brake, and jumped out, afraid that the car might head over the brink and down the steep slope.

The car held still, but there were arcs and sputters—the quick-acceleration capacitors must be breaching. She clicked the key control, and the hood flipped open. The heavy emergency discharge cable, like a fat black rubber snake, with two thick insulated handles at its neck, flopped onto the pavement. Carefully, she took it by the handles and looked around for a ground post.

God bless California's damn-the-expense safety-crazed legislature, she thought. *However much Daddy rumbles and grumbles about taxes.* The guardrail was a modern one, with grounding posts every hundred feet or so; she dragged the cable to the rail, pumped the buttons to open the locking slot, fitted it over the metal edge, and checked to make sure she had continuity. She clamped onto the rail, walked a few steps up the road, made sure she wasn't touching the rail or any conductor that touched it, and pushed the connect button on the hand control.

A flurry of bangs like rifle shots. Flashes under the hood like welding arcs. Reek of ozone. Up the road, a seagull sitting on a guardrail post squalled and flapped into the air. *Sorry, fella, glad I didn't roast you.*

Bambi looked down at her hand control; the small screen said FULLY DISCHARGED.

Very gingerly, she reached into the ruptured trunk and dragged her suit carrier through the broken opening, then re-claimed her laptop and iScribe from the passenger seat. The car's front end was a foot inside the shoulder, so it was no longer in traffic, and it sure wasn't going anywhere. Bambi looked out over the steep hillside, between the high hills, down to the Pacific on the horizon. "Shit, shit, shit."

She popped the hood. Wads of something that looked like spiky snow around the battery, the generator, the ca-pacitors, the front wheel motors, and the cyberrack. With her phone, she shot and narrated a couple minutes of video and sent it to Jim Browder's mail; he'd know where to for-ward it.

She phoned Dave Carlucci, the local agent in charge.

He said, "Don't worry about anything. You're only a mile and a half away right now, and I'll just drive out and retrieve you myself; we've got a biohazard car with a sealed engine compartment that I'll be using all morning to retrieve stranded people. You're not only not late, you'll be one of the first ones here. And we won't be starting even close to on time. The he-licopter on its way to pick up Roth was forced down."

"Nanoswarm?"

"Probably the tailored decay bacteria. The crew reported that the engine oil had turned into something that looked like lime Jell-O, smelled like fermented maple syrup, and func-tioned more like glue than oil; gave them a very dramatic en-gine seize-up. So the *federales* are just going to drive Roth up here themselves, since they've got one car that seems to be immune to everything for the moment, knock on wood. Everything's going to start late and it's all going to be a mess; welcome to the brave new world."

Carlucci suggested that she walk up the road to an over-look point where there were benches and a drinking fountain, since it might take him a while. She dug out her walking shoes from her suit carrier—normally she favored something with more drama, which she liked to think was all that remained of the spectacularly spoiled wealthy teenage airhead she had once been. With her feet strapped into all-too-practical shoes, the walk was almost nice, too; she waved off a couple of cars that pulled over to offer rides.

While walking, she called up the rental car place and told them the car was probably totaled.

"No surprise," the rental car guy said. "I hope this was the government's money and not yours."

"It is, but it's my ass that has to get home eventually."

"I understand. We'll try to come up with some way to help you out with that, though it might not turn out to be a car. I'll call you as soon as I know."

"Unless the phones die."

"Yeah. Hadn't even thought about that yet. You have any-where to go if you're stranded?"

"If I had to, I could walk from here to my dad's house." *Which is an ugly extravagant fortress that you probably see every day, now that he's built it and moved in.* "Hope you're okay too."

"Well, except for probably not having a job. Jeez. I used to party with these eco-hippie dudes who'd get all mystical talk-ing about how someday there would be Daybreak and things would be great. I'd like to punch a few of them, I think."

"Officially, citizens should not take vigilante action."

"And unofficially?"

"Break something that they'd need a modern high-tech prosthetic for." She appreciated his laugh. "Thanks for trying."

She'd had a drink of cool water, found a bench with just enough shade, and done more meditative breathing than she'd done in years by the time Carlucci turned up in the biohazard truck.

Bambi asked, "So what's the deal with Ysabel Roth?"

"She's just crossed the border. The Bureau people in Washington have authorized me to offer immunity from pros-ecution, as long as she's willing to turn over the bigger fish."

They turned into the parking lot. Bambi said, "Our number one expert, Dr. Yang, thinks there's no such thing as higher-ups, leadership, or any of that in Daybreak. It's a brave new pond, and all the fish are equal."

"Well, then Roth is real, real screwed—but then, so are we."

ABOUT HALF AN HOUR LATER. WASHINGTON, DC.
11:00 A.M. EST. TUESDAY, OCTOBER 29.

In the private party room of an Italian sub shop about two blocks from St. Elizabeth's, Heather cleared a chair and Lenny rolled into the space; she sat next to him. Cam was huddled up at the end of the table with Graham Weisbrod, Arnie, Allie, and Jim Browder; unofficially, he'd told all the DoF people, earlier, that although as a conservative Republican he had thought the Department of the Future was a boondoggle, now he couldn't live without it. Graham Weisbrod had cheerfully pointed out that they were just doing for the government as a whole what Mark Garren did for the Pentagon—and no secretary of defense in living memory would have tried to function without someone like the DoDDUSP.

"The conspiracy theorists must be up on their roofs and howling at the moon. Washington is one of the few cities where all the cars are running, and most of the tinfoil hat brigade can't get online to scare each other about that," Heather observed.

Arnie turned away from the little group at the top of the table and grinned at her. "The few who can get online are making up in creativity what they lack in numbers. New paranoid Daybreak craziness is breeding with old paranoid conspiracy craziness like muskrats downstream from a Viagra plant."

"You spent a while working on that metaphor," Lenny commented.

"Guilty," Arnie said. "Amusing myself in the shower this morning."

Cameron was nodding, and the others were taking seats; apparently his "meeting before the meeting before the meeting" had concluded successfully. Cam said, "It's not just lunatics that are having crazy thoughts today—and the crazy thoughts aren't necessarily wrong." The prearranged food came then, and as everyone ate, Cam reminded them to take any leftovers home and eat them soon—"No telling how much longer your kitchen will function."

That the warning was given so casually—with everyone just nodding and continuing to eat—told Heather more than anything else how much things were slipping.

They ate quickly. Cam stood. "All right, everyone, thanks

for coming. I just wanted to have a quick talk before we present the findings-and-recs this afternoon to the Acting President and the Republican candidate, because that discussion could go off track, so I want to make sure we all stick close to the message."

Besides the senior people from DoF and OFTA, and Lenny from NSA, Edwards was there from FBI, and Colonel Green from Cyber Command, along with the usual handful of quiet people in uniforms or black suits.

"The quick outline is this," Cam said. "We have a vital issue that we need to explain briefly to the top-level people, which is potentially extremely distracting, and we must not allow them to be distracted. So with all the speed I can muster, and in language as much like English as Dr. Yang can muster"—even Arnie and Allison laughed—"we're going to tell you what the issue is, what the sides are, why it doesn't matter right now, and what we need to focus on. Then everyone will pull together this afternoon to keep focus where it needs to be. Clear?"

Everyone was nodding vigorously, and Cam said, "All right, first what I think, then what Arnie thinks, then Dr. Weisbrod will tell you why it doesn't matter who's right. As for me, here's what I see from the extensive Daybreak decrypts, especially once we found the messages of the il'Alb cell in eastern Afghanistan that ran the Bell group in DC, the rebel raid on Sentani airport, and the seizure of Air Force Two. I see elaborate and sophisticated development of communications, information sharing, and so forth between the global Daybreak organization and il'Alb; at the least, the cell that put together the Air Force Two attack knew when Daybreak would be. To me it just looks too big and complex to be run by anything smaller than a national government. We also have clear-cut interpenetration between il'Alb and ISI, which implicates at least a part of the Pakistani government, and some overlaps with Saudi and Syrian intelligence.

"As I interpret this, we have been attacked by at least one foreign power—probably Pakistan, possibly Saudi Arabia—with a direct assault on the highest levels of our government, and widespread general sabotage carried out by a few fifth columnists and many dupes. Therefore, we are in the opening stages of a military-terror campaign aimed to bring down the United States and probably the West in general. The attack on Air Force Two was supported by domestic saboteurs, not unlike the way an invasion might be supported by rebels or a resistance movement. We are at war with a single, coherent enemy who has hit us with a carefully planned and executed deliberate military attack. We just don't know who it is, yet.

"And with that, Arnie is going to spin out one of the wildest stories I have ever heard in my life, but I do believe you all have the right to hear it before you reject it."

Arnie Yang nodded. "I feel handicapped by not being able to whip out the charts and graphs and give you all homework, so let me just explain it this way. Cameron's interpretation of the material was only possible because he was able to pick out a few hundred needles in a haystack that had, oh, around six billion strands of hay. And the reason he could pick them out was because he was looking for them, and because he had search algorithms that were provided by my methods. So, in effect, he found his conclusion by looking through my telescope. I just want to tell you what my telescope has to say.

"If the whole thing had been coordinated, led, put together by some single guiding intelligence, there are at least fifty different indices and measures that would show an idea pump in the system—and they don't."

"Review 'idea pump' for us new people?" Colonel Green asked.

"Something that just repeats itself over and over, pumping an idea out into the conversation. Like a TV commercial, or a sacred text, or a politician staying on message, or a spambot. If there's an idea pump in a communication system, it's highly detectable, by lots of methods: If we trace chains of repeated ideas backward, they all go back to a small group of places; the same ideas keep coming back as if no discussion had happened; the same ideas come disproportionately out of one small part of the system; whenever conflicting ideas run into each other, the one from the idea pump wins by sheer volume of repetition. There're lots of ways to measure and count all that.

"Well, not only is there *no* idea pump in Daybreak, Daybreak has an elaborate, localized system of ideas that first paralyzes idea pumps and then takes them over. Daybreak captures whatever gets near it; for example, I can show you a few thousand small businesses that thought the Daybreak network was going to be their channel into the green market, and instead they became suppliers and safe houses for Daybreakers, often going broke while doing Daybreak stuff that didn't make them any money. One reason why coustajam stalled out in the last couple years and didn't take over pop music, like a lot of people thought it would, is that so many of their most talented composers, performers, and bands were putting all their time and effort into Daybreak.

"So I think *if* an outside force like il'Alb *were* exerting central control over Daybreak, there'd be at least some evidence that there *was* a center or some control. I think Daybreak itself was a giant system artifact, a message that doesn't originate in any one place in the system but is produced by the system as a whole. And I think it was one with a genius for recruiting and suborning other ideas and organizations it ran into."

"Uh, hold it, a message that recruits and takes things over?"

Arnie shrugged. "Ever had a friend go through a religious conversion? Or develop an addiction? Or get hired into an organization with a tight, obsessive culture? It's still your friend but don't you feel, sometimes, that you're not really arguing with him, but with his Catholicism? Or 'that's not really her, that's her alcoholism'? Or 'I miss my friend, I wish IBM-guy would shut up and let him talk'? Complex ideas contain instructions on what to do for contingencies—like computer games. Ever notice that the game seemed to be playing against you, or leading you in some direction? Ever known anyone to be led into a new life by Jesus, or have his life changed by a book? Ideas do things all the time; we try to pretend they don't because when they do, they make us nervous.

"I know Cam thinks a thought requires a thinker, but that's just wrong. The really big, complex thoughts—like, oh, say, a movie, or a religion, or a philosophy—are much too big to fit into one head, and yet they are thought all the time. In fact I'd say nothing big enough to be important comes from an individual; nobody ever made up a worldview all by himself on a desert island. Important ideas all grow and form in thousands or millions of heads, often over more than one lifetime.

"But you don't have to go that far with me to see what happened with Daybreak.

"Daybreak was more or less like a cluster of obsessive self-reinforcing thoughts that kept recopying and refining and becoming sharper and clearer while getting more detached from reality, in much the same way that, oh, for example, some of you might be unable to stop wondering whether a co-worker doesn't like you, or a persistent high-school memory might come back to you over and over. That can happen just as easily—maybe more easily—in a group in conversation, as it can in a mind in private thought. Haven't we all been in a conversation that turned into an idée fixe, where no matter what you tried to change the subject to, everyone ended up talking about the same thing?"

"Marijuana helps induce that effect," Edwards pointed out.

"It does, to some extent; so does ecstasy, either the drug or the religious experience. There's a great play where a lunatic came to think he was God because he realized every time he prayed, he was talking to himself. After a while the voice of the conversation can sound like the meaning of the universe. As long as it's only for a few hours after midnight in a dorm room or a bar, it didn't matter very much.

"But the modern world improved everything, or at least made it more effective. Internet came along and made it possible for a conversation to go on like that 24-7-365, with thousands instead of a dozen participants, and a lot of the meditation and hypnosis and biofeedback tactics for focusing attention found their way out of Eastern philosophy, and a lot of the tactics for making an idea compelling found their way out of Western advertising, and one bright day, you had a great big idea that was running on so many brains and computers all the time that it was beginning to think itself. Unfortunately, it was an idea that's been around since Rousseau or earlier—'civilized self-hatred.' The modern world created a perfect environment for the growth and flourishing of a general feeling that the modern world had to go."

"Are you saying that it was . . . like a suicidal obsession?" Lenny said. "Depressive thinking that got out of hand?"

"Cam asked me the same question," Arnie said. "Yeah. I always come to the same answer: I think Daybreak was like an immense death wish of, by, and for our whole global civilization. Furthermore, it has succeeded. It self-cured the same way a lot of suicidal obsessions do—it actually pulled the trigger and killed the system it was running on. But that's just a step on the way to seeing what happened to il'Alb."

Lenny asked, "Is the idea you're driving toward that it wasn't a case of the terror groups infiltrating Daybreak, and turning it to their own purposes, but that Daybreak took over il'Alb?"

Arnie nodded. "Yeah, I'm avoiding saying that because I know it'll kind of freak people, and you're right, I need to face up to it. Here's the thing. One reason Daybreak grew so fast and effectively was its fierce immune response to ideology; it strongly discouraged anyone from talking about *why* to take down the Big System; the idea was to only to take it down. That let it grow very fast—it never had to fight with most of people's pre-existing beliefs. Most Daybreak AGs started as separate organizations—little chapters of Earth First or small anarchist parties or Stewardship Christian prayer groups. After a while in touch with Daybreak, they still might have *said* they believed the same old weird stuff they always had, but their commitments and priorities were aligned to make them operating tools of Daybreak.

"You know how they used to say that the Internet experienced censorship as damage, and just wired around it? Well, what I'm saying is, Daybreak experienced il'Alb as just one more affinity group that wanted to hit part of the Big System, and it subverted them the same way it did any other group, then directed them to the target that best suited Daybreak's purpose on a given date."

"And you think this because—"

"Because at every point where I've got data, and the processing algorithms to look for patterns, the communications look like that is what is happening—and I don't see *anything* that looks like there's any internal dictator, or any orders coming in from outside. I've got ten thousand ducks quacking and waddling, with one deluded chicken that thinks it's a duck in the middle. I think it's a flock of ducks; Cam thinks it's a malign conspiracy of chickens."

After a long silence, Graham Weisbrod said, "So there you have it. Either we are being attacked by a foreign power using an absolutely brilliant new strategy—I call that the Covert Hitler interpretation—or what has just happened is more like a disastrous storm in the noosphere—call it the Hurricane

Daybreak interpretation. And at first glance it would seem that the thing we have to do is figure out which it is. But Cam and Arnie asked me to be the neutral party explaining why we need to be aware of the question, try to answer it, all of that— but we don't want to get into it today.

"Here's the deal. Several very large Daybreak affinity groups announced to the rest of Daybreak that they were prepared—but they never activated. And around those groups there were a lot of messages with a single theme—that you can kill a man by giving him a poison that kills all the cells in his body, or by whacking him on the head, but the way to be sure is to do both. That message was all over the Aaron Group, for example. So looking at the situation, we're reeling from Daybreak and from the Air Force Two attack—two different kinds of massive damage—and those affinity groups seemed to be working on places where it would be more effective to hit us later, when we don't have the tools to mitigate the attack or defend ourselves."

"Such as?" Edwards asked.

Cameron shrugged. "Well, right now we could probably still evacuate a big city if we had to. Enough working phones, radios, and vehicles, especially in the so-far-lightly-hit places like DC and Miami. So right now a nerve gas attack in a downtown would be copable-with. But in a week or two, when no one has a radio, a phone, or a car?"

Dead silence in the room.

Weisbrod looked around. "So it doesn't matter today, or probably even this month, whether it's Covert Hitler or Hurricane Daybreak that has just walloped us. Whether it's a foreign enemy or a ghost in the system, it is probably going to strike at us again in the next few days, hard, at least a few more times.

"Strike us hard with *what*?" Colonel Green said. "Isn't that the real question?"

Cam nodded, taking the command of the meeting back from Weisbrod. "Yes, it is. And if Jim Browder here is right, we think we may know what they've got aimed at us. So the job for today's meeting is to make sure that the president— whichever of them is going to be the president—does not get caught up in my suspicions and paranoia, or in Dr. Yang's charts and equations, but focuses on the scary thing Dr.

Browder will be presenting. That's the message you'll all be pushing as hard as you can—'it doesn't matter, let's talk about pure fusion bombs.'"

"You want our group to be an idea pump for that," Edwards said.

"Bingo." Weisbrod, Cam, and Arnie spoke simultaneously, and everyone laughed.

**ABOUT THE SAME TIME. OVER EASTERN OHIO.
11:30 A.M. EST. TUESDAY, OCTOBER 29.**

It was being a morning for superlatives. As he'd ridden in the candidate caravan to the Dubuque airport, Chris Manckie-wicz had received a text from Anne telling him he was getting Cletus's old title and the biggest raise of his career. *Plus* he'd just finished an exclusive with the now-probable winner one week before the election. Of course, it did happen on board the *Low on Taxes, High on Jesus Express*, the dumbest name ever come up with for a campaign plane.

Norcross urged him to "ask the tough ones, Chris. My polling people tell me thirty million people will vote for me on election day and hate themselves for it a month later— and hate me twice as much. I have to make them feel okay about this, because it's their country too, and just their bad luck that they're getting me for a president. If you don't hit me with hard questions now, and give me a chance to say the right things, they're never going to have a chance to give *me* a chance."

So Chris had asked about the Christian Bill of Rights. Norcross had said, "Yes, it is my belief that the Christian religion has a special place in American culture and we should codify that, but that is not what people are going to elect me to do, so I won't act on it while our country is in danger, nor try to slip it in without adequate debate while the country is busy trying to survive."

He was equally blunt about everything else. Tax cuts? "Of course I want to do that. Everyone in office does. But just now we have no clue what shape the economy will be in or what actions the government will need to take; we'll just have to see."

Obscenity? "Well, I'm not for it, but when I'm worried about how nearly four hundred million people are going to make it through the winter, I'd be pretty silly to think the biggest thing we had to cope with was naked ladies. When everyone is warm, has a job, and can eat, then yes, there are spiritual issues I want to address."

At the end of it, Chris thought, *My camera, my editing: the first draft of how a president formed out of an obscure nutcase senator.*

He worked quickly and well, slapping camera cuts into place, cutting stammers, nervous laughter, and trail-offs. *Someday, people will point at my work and say, that's why he became President.*

Norcross's media people had given him access via his wireless to the plane's satellite and roving land links. The box on the screen said it took a full minute, and 81 tries, for the whole transmission to go all the way through and receive an acknowledgment from 247NN.

A moment later Anne appeared in a corner of his screen. "Chris," she said, "you have one of the best communication platforms still running in North America. We'd use our own planes, but they're grounded with burst tires and shot electronics." A burst of scrambled sound, and the picture broke up.

"Didn't get that."

"Sorry. Okay, quickly, e-mail from me has addresses of everyone who can receive finished product at all our affiliates. Send that interview direct to them. I've e-mailed them all to expect it. We don't want them to miss it but I don't know if we can"—another burst—"from here with our"—a shriek and a black screen for a long moment before the picture came back, much grainier. "Did you get—?"

He saw that her e-mail had come in, copied the list from it, and immediately sent out the finished interview again, as she had requested. This time it took 94 seconds and 139 tries, but it still went through. It took his e-mail, a simple short text telling her it had been accomplished, nine tries.

Abruptly, Chris laughed. Norcross, sitting on the other side of the lounge reading his Bible, looked up over his reading glasses. "Someone send you something funny?"

"Not exactly *funny*. I've just done my best interview ever

and I got a big raise this morning, and probably the network will be gone before my next paycheck."

Norcross nodded, turned, and called, "Robbie? We need a plan to deal with the disappearance of electronic money in the next forty-eight hours."

Robbie, his economic advisor, sitting up from a nap, rubbed his face. "Right. Of course. So you need a plan in forty-eight—"

"No, I mean all electronic money will disappear for good in forty-eight hours. That's what, ninety percent of the economy?"

"Old figure. Nowadays, more like ninety-seven percent."

"We're an hour from Reagan National. Have a plan when we land."

Robbie groaned, but he sat down and unfolded his laptop. A moment later he looked up, and said, "I'm getting 'Try again later,' from all the Internet connections—which is about thirty line-of-sight stations. Better make that 'our plan for what to do with the money already gone,' I guess."

ABOUT THE SAME TIME. NORTHEAST OF TRES PIEDRAS, NEW MEXICO. 9:45 A.M. MST. TUESDAY, OCTOBER 29.

Jason stayed low on the ridgeline and watched. He didn't know why he was so stupid that he had to see what had happened to the commune.

Beth, he thought. *Just couldn't run out on you, babe, not while there was a chance you were still alive.*

The main house had been burned to a hollow black shell. There were bodies in the farmyard, but without binoculars, he wasn't sure who. He was pretty sure the one hanged from the barn pulley was Elton. Two men with rifles guarded the farmyard, so he couldn't go down to look for clues.

A very soft voice said, "Hey."

He turned. Beth had streaks of soot on her face and looked pretty sick. She sat down beside him. "We should get away from here. Then can you tie up my wrist?"

"Sure." They moved cautiously back down from the ridge line, and he found a couple of thick pine sticks and, with some junk line from his pack, lashed together a sort of splint.

"Needs a real doctor," he whispered, apologetically.

"You'll do." She kissed his cheek. "We better walk while I can. If you can find us somewhere warm for the night, that'll help; I think I'm a risk for shock."

They crept along the ridge trail, back into the state park. On the broad, well-marked trail, he asked, "How'd you know I'd be there?"

"It's where you used to take me for sex, hon. About the only place where we could watch the commune to make sure no one was coming and still have some privacy. And if you'd went any place else, they'd'a catch you."

They filled his water bottle and shared long drinks at the first public pump. "I think they'll be looking along the roads," he said, "but we can take this trail over to the camping area in the next drainage; won't be a lot of hikers out and nobody's gonna think of it as transportation just yet. Gonna be a long day, baby."

She shrugged, and winced at how that pulled her wrist. "Then we better get going."

They walked. After some time he ventured, "Uh, how'd you get away?"

"I fucked the three guys that took me off to kill me, and then cried, and promised no one wouldn't ever know if they let me go. They didn't really wanna kill me, I guess. Probably it was like their first lynching, and they weren't real good at it, you know?"

"How did you feel about—"

"Like I feel about taking a big old painful crap when I really have to. Better'n not having done it. Prolly I'll have bad dreams and stuff later."

The sun was still high in the sky when they topped the ridge; Beth looked sick, but she seemed to be bearing up, and after he added a couple more sticks to the makeshift splint, she seemed to do better.

Somewhere, he figured, *there's a place we can blend in and not be looked for. I just hope we don't have to join a mob and kill any Daybreak people, because I think if she had to, to live, Beth could do that. And I'm not sure I could.*

**ABOUT THE SAME TIME. SAN DIEGO. 9:00 A.M. PST.
TUESDAY, OCTOBER 29.**

Almost everywhere in the world, the first thing a cop does,
when bringing a visiting cop into his territory, is to offer coffee, and any visiting cop to whom it is not allergenic death or
spiritual anathema had better accept. "So," Carlucci said, "I
didn't even know we *had* any future cops. What do you do,
arrest crooks before they're born?"

Bambi ignored the joke she'd heard too often. "I'm one of
five DoF employees that have the power to make an arrest.
Congress in their wisdom realized it was always possible we
might stumble across some present-day crime. You're lucky
all of us didn't come. This is the first real case we've ever
had."

"I guess that—" Carlucci's phone rang, and he picked up.
"Carlucci. Yeah, I—right. On my way. I'll bring as much
backup as I have. See if you can reach anyone en route and
re-route them to give us some more backup. I'm on my way."
He asked Bambi, "You reasonable on the G-54?"

"Fully qualified."

"Great. Follow me." A few steps down the hall, he leaned
into a room where two men sat on desks facing each other.
"Terry Bolton, Larry Mensche, this is Bambi Castro, she's
badged with OFTA and coming along; gear up, and set Castro up with a Glock. Now, because we need to be rolling ten
minutes ago."

Bolton pulled on holster, coat, and all in one fluid motion;
Mensche arose from a pile of papers, tucking away reading
glasses as he went, and was halfway into his coat by the time
Bolton was opening the arms locker on the wall. "Can you tell
us what it's about?"

"That number one high-priority suspect we were expecting? She, a couple AFIs, and a few Mexican Army GAFEs are
all trapped in a DN-7 with collapsed tires on Imperial Avenue.
Big mob that wants them to hand her over for a lynching."
Carlucci sounded no more excited than if he were talking
about picking up muffins for a church breakfast.

Bolton handed Bambi the holster, three clips, and the
G-54. She checked it out; perfectly maintained, of course.
Carlucci was explaining, "—local patriots got wind and bar-

ricaded the 805 around exit 12A, which wasn't too complicated since practically no cars are able to move, so they just
dragged a bunch of stuck cars together to form a line across
the freeway."

In the bright sun, they all flipped on shades automatically;
Bolton took shotgun in the hazmat Hummer, leaving Bambi
next to Mensche.

Carlucci pulled out fast. "Mensche, best route? We need to
get onto Imperial south and west of exit 12A, with—"

"Fifteen down to El Cajon, over to 54th Street, south to
Imperial, hang a right," the agent said quietly. "You don't
think there's going to be anybody blocking alternate routes?"

"Sounds like they're improvising. They didn't actually ambush the DN-7—the Mexican commander got a tip-off from
a traffic cam and had already end-run the crowd, he'd have
gotten away clean but they lost five out of six tires in one big
spinout. The mob up on the 805 saw that and ran down and
surrounded them." Carlucci's eyes never left the road, a good
thing at the speed he was driving.

"Anyway," he added, "the mob can't really get at them—
they've got twenty-millimeters on robot turrets, so by way
of explaining 'stand back,' they shredded a couple of parked
cars—but we've got to go get them out. Just now, Mexican
troops in uniform are having a hard time talking to Americans, especially Americans who think they're bringing in
Ysabel Roth to personally lead the looting and burning."

They hurtled down the empty freeway, dodging between
wrecks and abandoned cars. "This thing has a tank of antiseptic and sprays a mist of it on the tires as we go," Carlucci
explained, "just in case anyone is wondering if I'm trying to
kill us all. Siren and light, you think?"

Bolton said, "If they're going to shoot at us, they'll do it
with or without the sirens, eh? Give 'em a fair shot at doing
the right thing."

Carlucci turned on the noisemakers. Approaching the
crowd at a sedate twenty miles per hour or so, they allowed
everyone plenty of time to consider.

"We got this," Mensche said. "Lot of folks doing the old
slow fade, they want to be at the back of the crowd when we
tell them to clear out."

A space opened around the armored personnel carrier as

people drifted back into alleys, or behind cars, a mob that all wanted to be bystanders—out of the situation but not so far they couldn't see it.

The DN-7 looked like most APCs since World War II; the triple autoturrets on top, only ten centimeters high, were remote-controlled, so that the operator watched through cameras and aimed and fired without being exposed to enemy fire. Fly-eye bubbles in the center of the roof and on all the corners meant there would be no blind spots, and the turrets were far enough out to sweep anywhere from next to the wheels to dead overhead. The black and brown glop on the road showed where the DN-7's foam-cored tires, invulnerable to bullets, had succumbed to the biotes.

"Bold Hammer One, this is Bold Hammer Four, I have you visually and I'm approaching behind the crowd surrounding you," Carlucci said. *I guess we're Operation Bold Hammer,* Bambi thought.

"Bold Hammer Four, this is Bold Hammer One, I copy." The accent was slight; *federales* in Sinaloa worked so often with their American counterparts that most were fluently bilingual.

"How you doing in there, Lieutenant?" Carlucci asked.

"Not bad. No injuries. If we could move we'd be fine."

"What's the situation with Bold Hammer Two and Three?"

"Could be an hour till they get here."

"Does the passenger understand that if she tries to run in any direction except into our vehicle, that mob will kill her?"

"Yes, Bold Hammer Four, she understands that. She's terrified. Let me see if she's willing to try the transfer." During the long pause, Carlucci worked the loudspeaker, telling people to go home, explaining that he was the FBI, that they were going to take the prisoner into custody, that it was vital for her to be captured alive and unharmed for interrogation. He reminded everyone that Mexico had been hit hard by Daybreak, too, and that "on this issue we are allies and shoulder to shoulder; this is no way to treat a friend and an ally." Over and over, he urged everyone to head for home.

The DN-7 had armored extensions around its main troop door that could reach out to the Hummer, but Murphy's Law dictated that the door would be on the far side. Making a virtue out of necessity, Carlucci drove the Hummer in a slow circle around the DN-7, twice, as if just trying to clear the crowd; more of them faded away, leaving the street almost empty except for a few stragglers.

"Not much of a mob, now," Bolton observed. "Back to being pain-in-the-ass civilians."

"That's the way I prefer them," Mensche said.

As he finished the second circuit, Carlucci said, "Mensche, I'm going to match your door up to their troop door; the extensions will slam out at you, then you open. Drag Roth in if she isn't moving fast enough. Castro, try to look friendly and welcoming—as freaked as Roth must be by now, she might bolt in the direction of a woman who looks sympathetic."

As the armored extensions thudded against the body of the Hummer, Mensche flung the doors outward, and the troop door retracted vertically. Two masked GAFEs in uniform threw a small woman in a baggy green coverall forward; Mensche caught her and turned in his seat, dragging her across his lap. Bambi pulled her the rest of the way in by the shoulders; Mensche slammed the door and shouted "Go!"

They had covered four blocks when the left front tire blew; Carlucci said, "Sniper, hardware store—" before a hole appeared in the windshield and he barked as a slug hit him on the Kevlar vest. He crouched low and zagged into a side street to the left; Bolton and Mensche had lowered their windows and returned fire; Bambi was lying across Roth to protect her.

Another shot clanged harshly off the rear fender.

"Just one shooter I think," Bolton reported, "and he's running. Give it a block and hope the rims hold out."

"They're supposed to."

In a residential street, they stopped and Bolton and Bambi jumped out to look at the situation.

The spare was dripping off its rim; it looked like lumpy chocolate pudding. "It was exposed to the biotes and it wasn't being sprayed with antiseptic."

"Yeah, the spray for the tires was so the car wouldn't spread germs—not because anyone ever thought anything would eat it." Bolton folded out a spray gadget from the roof, sprayed the pavement, stood on it, and wetted himself all over.

Bambi followed his example. "I'd just like someone to know that I'm probably destroying the last good Italian suit I'm ever going to wear."

Bolton snorted. "I started out in fire and bombs, where you buy the cheapest suit you can 'cause you're always buying new ones. This thing's all poly; it'll probably rot off me by nightfall."

Every tire on the cars on the street was rotted and flat, but knocking on doors, Bambi found an older lady willing to donate the apparently unharmed spare from a pickup parked in her garage.

They finally returned to the FBI office on Aero Drive four hours after setting out; the Mexican troops got there almost immediately after, having walked the whole way. Only two more of the ten expected observers for the interrogation had arrived; both were local.

Carlucci said, "I vote for showers and food all around; there's lunchmeat and bread in the fridge, and we might as well eat it since god knows how long the power will stay on. Ms. Roth?"

The girl looked up, dazed; she had said nothing other than that she wasn't in pain and didn't need water, on the whole trip in. "Yeah," she said. "Yeah."

"What I wanted to ask," he said gently, "is if you'd like to clean up. I understand you're a vegetarian; I'm afraid all we have is a tub of coleslaw and some bottled water, and every shop I've seen on the trip had a sign saying 'No more food.' But you might feel better if you ate something. You do realize you're safer here than you would be anywhere else?"

"Yeah." She drew a deep breath. "Look, I . . ." She appeared to be trying to pull her mind together. "Um. Okay, here's the thing. I know this will sound like I'm trying to fake insanity or something, you know? I'm sure it will. But . . . I feel like I just woke up from some weird, godawful dream, and I remember doing it but I can't believe it. It just doesn't make any sense to me, 'kay?" She looked around "I'm just think—" Roth went limp. Bambi barely caught her before she hit the floor, and lowered her gently.

Roth's muscles were cramping hard enough to be visible through her clothing, and her breath was irregular and violent It was plainly some kind of seizure, but not one Bambi had ever seen, or heard about in any first aid class.

ABOUT FORTY MINUTES LATER. WASHINGTON, DC.
1:00 P.M. EST. TUESDAY, OCTOBER 29.

Norcross was on time, though just barely—one small advantage of Daybreak was that media were having a hard time communicating with home offices, so the spectacular almost-crash-landing at Reagan National had not created a media barricade to force his way through. For the moment, cars continued to run in Washington, and his limo got right through to St. Elizabeth's, though the blown tires on the *Low on Taxes, High on Jesus Express*—despite an immediate scouring of the runway with steam and acid—had probably brought the tire-destroying biotes to the city, if they hadn't already arrived with someone sneaking past the military checkpoints via back roads.

Norcross immediately set about learning everyone's name and position, and freely admitted it when he didn't know what a Deputy Assistant Secretary for Information Technology did. *This guy not only wants the job, he's determined to do it,* Heather thought. *I guess I wish I didn't feel like I'd have to take a shower after voting for him.* She glanced sideways at Lenny, who looked like he wasn't quite sure what was wrong with a bite of pickle.

"Definitely knows how to work a room," she whispered.

"Shhh. I'm trying hard not to like him."

Shaunsen arrived fifteen minutes late, cheerfully apologizing. He told them all he had a couple of vital meetings on the Hill, so they would still have to finish on time.

Dwight Ferein, the Secretary for Homeland Security, did everything he was supposed to do: He was dignified, concerned, warm, and very brief. "He wears a suit well," Lenny muttered.

"Cam wears his better."

"Yeah, but he doesn't have huge silver hair and a red tie. Who's gonna trust a skinny young Asian guy when there's a photogenic old white poop available?" Lenny added, very softly, "Hey, one benefit coming up. Won't matter anymore how people look on TV. We could elect Abe Lincoln again."

Cameron cleared his throat; the muttering in the room died; and Cam raced through the foreign-enemy versus system-artifact issue. Shaunsen asked no questions; Norcross made up for it with focused, did-his-homework probes for details, systematically setting appointments between DHS and Norcross staff. That didn't take much time.

That brought them to Jim Browder's side of the presentation. "Cameron flatters me that I'm good at pulling the basic science together for this; I'd like to thank Dr. Tyson, Dr. Puller, Dr. Chin, and Dr. Kayan for explaining it to me and for sitting here waiting to pounce on my first error." Nervous laughter died quickly.

"We had a mystery from Air Force Two, about the plumes of smoke right after the explosion and crash." His bulldog glare stabbed out between his thick single brow and the reading glasses that perched on his nose like a doll's glasses on a bear. "They were carrying about twelve tons of pure sodium. There are far better chemical weapons and incendiaries than that and we know they had access to most of the modern arsenal. The only conceivable use for so much sodium was if they were trying to enhance the fallout from a thermonuclear weapon.

"Furthermore, we did find traces of deuterium—heavy hydrogen, the raw material for hydrogen bombs. But instead of the tritium that is usually used to enhance and catalyze the fusion reaction, we found traces of helium-3; a preliminary model shows they might have had as much as a kilogram of helium-3 on that plane, which is superficially insane—any college senior in physics can make tritium with some standard industrial equipment, but helium-3 is hard to extract, hard to work with, much more expensive and scarce—"

Shaunsen nodded. "I know helium-3 is fusible, and I've looked at projects to get it from deep ocean vents or the moon's surface. I'm guessing that if it's worth going to the moon for, they don't sell it at the corner store."

Norcross nodded and said, "Tell us what's interesting about this."

"Well," Browder said, "it's nonradioactive, so it would be hard to detect, and it's so scarce and expensive we don't look for it at all. And a helium-3/deuterium H-bomb would put out a lot of energy and a lot of neutrons, the neutrons would have transmuted the sodium-23 into sodium-24, and you'd have had a real horror weapon there. But normally a hydrogen bomb needs a regular fission bomb, with uranium or plutonium, as its trigger, and there should have been a lot of fissionable material in the smoke plume or the wreckage or both."

Norcross nodded. "So your mystery is, why would they use the most difficult to obtain, expensive stuff? And then neglect to have a trigger?"

"Exactly what we're saying, Mr. Norcross. We think the enemy has a helium-3 source somewhere—a deep ocean vent, a gas well that happens to be rich in it, or maybe a volcano, or just possibly the Iranian-Chinese moon expedition last year did some unannounced experiments with lunar regolith and extracted some helium-3. As for why it looks like they built a pretty good little hydrogen bomb, and then forgot to put a trigger on it, the pieces we found look like they may have at least believed they had a working 'pure fusion' bomb."

"Didn't we have a treaty to deal with those?" Shaunsen demanded.

"An executive agreement because they didn't think they could get it through the Senate. The Obama Administration halted our research, and most of the world's governments agreed not to work on it, because from a peace and weapons-control standpoint a pure fusion bomb is about as bad as it gets: made out of common or nonradioactive materials, so it's hard to detect; most of what's in it is off-the-rack industrial stuff. Can be made arbitrarily small—I don't mean the space one fits into, though that might be very small, I mean that unlike a regular atom bomb, it doesn't have a minimum blast equivalent to a thousand tons or more of TNT; theoretically they could miniaturize it and use it as freely as gunpowder, but the temperature it creates, right where it goes off, would still be hotter than the face of the sun. So it would erase the line between nuclear and conventional. And it doesn't require any testing that anyone could detect—you could do little tabletop lab experiments to find out most of what you had to, with no big flashes visible from orbit, or seismograph signatures or messy craters to inform anyone what you were up to. And not least, a lot of little pure fusion bombs would be much more effective at setting a big city on fire than one big ordinary H-bomb. From the standpoint of keeping atomic energy away from human skin, the pure fusion bomb is a complete nightmare—undetectable, mostly made of cheap stuff, scalable, didn't require testing, probably more effective, what's *not* to be afraid of?"

"That was a good agreement," Shaunsen said. "Too bad the Republicans kept us from making it a treaty, and now we're stuck with these gadgets."

"Well, here's our concern for right now. The only thing that kept pure fusion bombs from making the whole world worse was that we didn't have the right mix of knowledge and materials till recently. And with Daybreak, we probably won't have the materials for much longer. But if they managed to build one at all—and with determination and enough computing capacity, it's just conceivable that they did—there's no reason to think that Daybreak, or il'Alb, or whoever would have built just one. I've been over what we know about the technical skills and resources of the cells and AGs that still have not done their thing, and seven of them might have pure fusion—"

Shaunsen rose. "I just looked at the time. I've got a major reconstruction bill to review at the Senate; the country needs to get moving and fixing things. I leave the defense decisions in your capable hands."

The Secret Service closed ranks around him, and he was gone.

"Well," Will Norcross said, "*I'm* free."

THE EASTERN PACIFIC, SOUTHWEST OF LOS ANGELES. ABOUT 11:00 A.M. PST. TUESDAY, OCTOBER 29.

When Grady and Tracy finally arose, they carefully removed one of their shortwave radios from its sealed glass jar. The few news broadcasts they could find all told the same story. Grady snarled, "Fuckers. They're hunting us down." A whole commune had been massacred near Santa Fe.

"Then we want to be at sea for as long as we can," Tracy said. "Southwest for the next few weeks; there'll be somewhere in the South Pacific for us." They crowded on sail in the fresh breeze and turned their backs on North America. "We'll come back when it's on sale again," she said. "We're full up on supplies; let's not go home and be hanged from a phone pole."

They were still idly talking about the cool new world to come when a phone rang, and they both jumped. Grady went below and found it, ringing away just as if the Big System were not gone. Apparently there was less nanoswarm down here than up on the deck.

Caller ID just showed that it was coming in from an overhead satellite; of course the nanoswarm couldn't get at the satellites and not all the ground stations would be out yet. Could be anyone with direct satellite on any of the worldnets, even just a wrong number or a solicitation call from a charity. Curiosity overpowered Grady—*what if it's the last phone call I ever receive?* "Hello?"

"Hello, Mr. Barbour. This is Nautical Specialties."

The name was familiar, but Grady couldn't remember from where.

"Uh, is this a sales call?"

"Customer service. We are calling you to ask about the specialty work you had us do in the hull of your vessel, the *Mad Caprice*. We wanted to make sure that the secret vault in the false hull is still satisfactory."

"Uh, yeah, I looked there just before we left on this, uh, vacation, and it was, you know, cool. Everything was dry and everything was there that was supposed to be." Like hell was he going to talk about that half ton of gold on the phone.

"And just to make sure, you remember the sealed part of the vault, that was to be accessed by our technicians only— you remember that it contains our patented moisture-control equipment, and that it would void the warranty if you were to enter that sealed area?"

"We haven't touched it, really."

"We had sort of hoped to inspect it when you came in to Los Angeles in a few days, if you remember—"

"We won't be—" What the hell? This guy seemed to know too much. Tracy would be all over his case if he told them anything about where he was going, but it couldn't hurt to tell them where they weren't. "Uh, look, we changed our minds, sorry, but we're not going to LA, so if—"

"Well, in that case, we just have one more question and then we'll be done with you."

"Oh, okay, sure."

"Does your snotty, stupid wife still have big tits, and do you still have a tiny brain to match your tiny dick?"

"I—hey, what the—"

During Grady Barbour's last instant of existence, his brain

was signaling his mouth to form the word *fuck*, but the signal never arrived. *Mad Caprice*, Grady, Tracy, and several million liters of water vanished in a ball of solar-temperature plasma; across the next few minutes, the fireball rose and cooled, the steam condensed, and the mushroom cloud formed.

ABOUT THE SAME TIME. A CAVE IN EASTERN AFGHANISTAN. 12:05 A.M. LOCAL TIME. WEDNESDAY, OCTOBER 30.

The men watched the screen in some amazement; even from low orbit, a smallish nuclear detonation is still impressive. "The last bit was just at the behest of the Daybreak AG that built the gold vault for him," the man who had been on the phone explained, in English; the five men at the table had nineteen languages among them, but English was the only one they all had fluently. "The carpenter must've guessed something of what I had given him to install behind the vault, and he asked me to give him that message just before I 'used that thing,' as he put it. Since the test shot on Air Force Two didn't happen, we had to use this as an alternate test, so I had to contact them by direct satellite phone to run down their position and buy the time on an orbital camera to watch the test. I had to talk to them anyway, so it didn't hurt me to do a favor for a friend."

"Did she really have big tits?" one of the men asked.

"I saw surveillance films," another man said. "They were okay."

"I wish we could have blown off the weapon on Air Force Two; it wouldn't have occurred to anyone that *that* was a test shot. As it is, we have to hope that the blast wasn't noticed."

"There *is* all of Daybreak going on, so we had to do it before any critical component died, and they were less than forty kilometers off Los Angeles. They may think it was an attack on that city."

"True. And regret is useless, as the shot has been fired. If there are no more matters for discussion, it's almost midnight and you have a long way to go in the dark."

**FOUR MINUTES LATER. CHEYENNE MOUNTAIN, COLORADO.
12:15 P.M. MST. TUESDAY, OCTOBER 29.**

"What the fuck?"

That is not standard military protocol for a man watching a computer screen, so the captain moved over to administer a reprimand and find out what he was seeing. "Spy satellite just saw this. About 40 klicks southwest of LA. We've been copying on any shot bought on a commercial camera just to see what other people were looking at. Someone pointed the camera right at this. See, this little sailboat, it looks like, just minding its own business, then it gets a phone call—they pick up the side lobes from him talking to an overhead satellite—and then—"

The flash was brilliant; from its post far away, the satellite watched the mushroom cloud form.

"I jumped in on the military satellites and we're getting more of a look, and *Reagan* isn't far away from them and is bouncing up a recon."

The captain decided no reprimand was warranted.

**ABOUT TWENTY MINUTES LATER. WASHINGTON, DC.
2:45 P.M. EST. TUESDAY, OCTOBER 29.**

Heather hated to admit it but she was beginning to really like Will Norcross's game spirit. For forty minutes he'd questioned, probed, and listened—especially listened—as he tried to absorb the whole complex mess of Daybreak, its relation to il'Alb, and why recovery was apt to be so time-consuming and difficult.

The door popped open and an assistant burst in. "Mr. Nguyen-Peters!" She held out a sheet of paper; Cam took it and read.

"Congratulations, Dr. Browder," he said.

Jim looked like he'd received an electric shock. "For what?"

"Somebody just fired a nuke off about twenty-five miles southwest of LA. Luckily we got the flash on a random recording from a Deep Black satellite and were able to get it to a team with working gear to analyze the recording. No uranium, no plutonium, in fact for some unimaginable reason the only significant heavy element in the spectrography of the flash was gold, but there was a huge amount of that. *Reagan* was less than 100 kilometers away and scrambled a drone; they got a sample from the mushroom cloud itself. Unusual amounts of helium-3. Lots of tritium and sodium-24, which is what you get when you blow off the helium-3/deuterium reaction in seawater. No trace of polonium or any other hard alpha emitter, and only as much beryllium as you'd expect from batteries and capacitors on the ship's electrical system, plus what's in the seawater. Some excess lithium and deuterium, consistent again with a fusion bomb. You were right—they've got a pure fusion bomb."

"Weird," Browder said. "Very weird. Why would someone waste a bomb on empty ocean? It wasn't by any chance an enhanced-fallout weapon?"

"Dead on again," Cameron said. "Preliminary measurements show the plume is hot as hell with induced radioactivity, and the center of it is heading dead on for Los Angeles. We've got people scrambling to try to tell everyone to get out of the way, but it's pretty much hopeless; we're going to lose the city unless the wind shifts."

"What'd they jacket it with?" Browder asked. "Sodium, cobalt, potassium?"

"That's the weird part," Cam said, shaking his head. "What's in that cloud, besides the sodium-24 and the tritium from the salt water, is all the hot isotopes of gold."

"I guess it works," Browder said.

"Only about as well as cobalt would have. They make their atom bombs with helium-3, and jacket them in gold . . . I just wonder if we're facing a bunch of compulsive nuts who have to do everything the hardest, most expensive way they can think of."

Will Norcross stood. "I'm told there are other briefings I need to get to," he said. "What I just heard was this: We have established that our enemy, whatever it may be, has pure fusion weapons, which we also know is one of the worst possible things for any enemy to have. Is there anything else I can do here, besides be in your way?"

Heads were shaking all over the room. Norcross gave them that cocky grin that so many liberals found unbearable. "Then do what needs to be done; make the country proud of you." He nodded and exited.

"Now *that* was a curtain line," Lenny said, under his breath.

"I'm scared that the phrase 'President Norcross' is starting to sound sort of comforting," Heather agreed.

Cameron Nguyen-Peters glanced around. "Defense, security, intelligence people, they're going to want you in your home departments. Law enforcement and everyone in charge of catching Daybreakers, now we know it's not over yet, we've got to round up as many of them as we can, as fast as we can, and you'll want to go too. Department of the Future, Department of Energy, Department of Peace—all you analysts, brain trusters, think tankers, all you idea people, plus all the liaisons to civil agencies, if you can, *go home*. If you're not tracking bombs or tracking Daybreakers, get out of here for now. And . . ." Cam was obviously trying to find a way to say it gently. ". . . look, we're in the national capital here, and we're facing an enemy with nuclear weapons; I don't know why we still exist, in fact. So . . . if you can find a way for your families and loved ones to be out of town—do it. Move your family somewhere safe. Clear? I'm not dismissing anyone, we need everyone here, and you took an oath—but your spouses and kids didn't, so get them out of the danger zones, and free your mind to concentrate on the mess we have here."

Heather asked, "How long till the plumes hit the coast?"

"About an hour," the guy from NOAA said. "Call anybody you have out there and tell them to run if they can get over the mountains, or find someplace to dig in for a couple weeks and hope we can get rescue people out there in that time. But it would be better to run."

On her way out, she saw that Lenny was scribbling something on his pad; she looked down to see he'd written, *If yr cats okay, my place 2night. U lucky sexy bitch.*

Night in with my guy. While the power's still on. Yeah, he's right, I'm a lucky bitch. Hope he doesn't expect me to be as sexy as I am lucky.

**ABOUT TWENTY MINUTES LATER. WASHINGTON, DC.
3:30 P.M. EST. TUESDAY, OCTOBER 29.**

*Must've been kind of an interesting building back when you
could see something besides just the dome,* Chris Manckiewicz thought. He'd been inside the concrete and steel barricades around the Capitol many times, but he was thinking
of the newsreels from the thirties and forties, when the vast
flight of steps had been unimpeded by all the hardware.

Norcross had been summoned to some secret briefing, and
Shaunsen was going to hold some big press event in a couple
days, but meanwhile Chris had little to do except wipe his
gear with lye and rubbing alcohol; if anything "historic" happened, Chris was to shoot it and try to send it, and if it got
there, Anne said she'd "probably find a way to use it, and if we
do, definitely find a way to pay you."

So here he was, idly wandering among the historic buildings on the Mall, like any tourist with time to kill.

"You look like a reporter." The tall woman, her gray hair
dyed a fairly natural shade of red, was dressed in knee-high
boots and a real old-school jacket/straight skirt/string tie suit,
as 1970s as if she'd just walked out of his grandparents' class
pictures. She had a pleasant flat expression. "Am I right?"

"Uh, yeah, how did you know?"

"Because you're Chris Manckiewicz," she said. "I'm Rusty
Parlotta—I used to work for the *Washington Times* back
there were still paper papers."

"You were the city editor," Chris said. "Some people said
you were the last of the greats at that."

She smiled, this time for real. "Actually, what I wanted
to talk to you about is, I plan to be the *next* of the greats,"
she said. "You're looking at the new editor and owner of the
Washington Advertiser-Gazette. I've got a buddy who col-
lects and restores old printing machinery. Between what he
can make work and what he can build because he understands
it, he's promised me we can put out a paper. Maybe not with
photos, even, but a paper. Have you ever written?"

"I write my stories and keep a blog. Yeah, I can turn out
a sentence."

"And are they still paying you?"

"I've got cash, if anyone will still take it." He'd extracted

$750, the legal limit, from the one working ATM he'd found, and he had the two grand in hundreds that were all the branch of his bank would give him. Shaunsen had frozen prices, so his money should last a week or so—if the hotel didn't close its doors, the way most businesses had in the last big price freeze a few years ago. *Didn't even think about needing black-market barter, but it's gonna be 2017 all over again, bet on it.*

"I thought you might need a job that pays in food and rent."

"I was just thinking that."

"Well, the *Washington Advertiser-Gazette* is putting out its first edition tomorrow, while a lot of the higher-tech gear still works. I've even got newsboys I'm paying in food for their families, because I grew up Mormon and I have a few months of canned goods and dried beans in my basement. My news staff will be the first eight people to take me up on the offer of a room in my big old wreck of a house—inherited from my folks, and I'm sentimental—plus meals. We'll go to real money pay as soon as there is real money to pay you with, and you first eight eventually get shares of the biz. Tomorrow morning, there's going to be kids out on the streets yelling 'Read all about it in the *Advertiser-Gazette!*' Want in?"

Chris laughed.

"Is my offer that funny?"

He thought for a moment. "No, it's great, and I'm taking it. I'm just thinking, forty-eight hours ago I was so fed up with the network that I was looking for an excuse to quit and drive back from Iowa to California. I told myself that with my resumé, I'd have a great deal from someone else in a *day*. And I was *right*."

"Well, of course you'll keep your TV job as long as you have an uplink, and they'll keep sending you money, for whatever that's worth. But your main job will be turning out words for me. And unlike 247NN, I have fresh cabbage, a cellar full of potatoes, and *tons* of canned organic tomatoes," she said. "It was a real good year."

"It just keeps getting better. How many more staff do you need?"

"Three more staff, but one more trip around the Mall and I should have them—it's crawling with lost reporters whose gear isn't working, who don't know what to do. Or maybe we should

look into the Capitol. You're more current than I am, you'll recognize people. Look for anyone you know is good."

"I saw CNN's military affairs specialist go in a few minutes ago—"

"Perfect, let's go," she said. "Walk with me."

He hurried after her. *My god, I watched her covering Bill
Clinton on TV when I was a snot-nosed middle-schooler, and
she still moves like a missile.*

He knew the answer, but he asked, "And am I working
tonight?"

"You'd better be or the deal's off. You're the national affairs editor. I'd've given you police beat or sports, but the guy
who wanted both is not only already signed up, he's an experienced organic gardener himself, and he brought a couple tons
of food into the deal."

"Well, I sure can't compete with that," Chris agreed. "National Affairs it is. Are we a Democratic or a Republican paper?"

"Yes, some of the time."

"I like the way you think, ma'am."

"Call me 'ma'am' again and you'll be out in traffic yelling
'Read all about it.' If there's traffic."

The halls of the Capitol were deserted, and Rusty Parlotta
shot through them like the ghost of Gloria Steinem, intent on
finding her last three staff. Chris, still carrying his TV gear,
panted after. *Wow, I'm going to like carrying just a notepad
a lot better. Wonder if I can buy a fedora somewhere in this
town, and if there'll be a place in the hatband for the press
card?*

**ABOUT FOUR HOURS LATER. WASHINGTON, DC.
ABOUT 9:00 P.M. EST. TUESDAY, OCTOBER 29.**

Everything was still working at Lenny's apartment, so Heather
took the chance to make her calls. At FBI headquarters in San
Diego, Bambi listened sympathetically. "I'll call him in half
an hour to give you some time to talk to him," she said, "but
this big old town *sprawls*, you know. He's at least nine miles
away from me. However . . . you know about *my* father?"

"What about him?"

"He was one of the early leaders of the Castle movement,

back when some of the crazier survivalists thought the Democrats were going to take their guns away and put them in concentration camps. And he was one of the ones rich enough to build his Castle. Plenty of room there—"

"Oh, dear Jesus, your dad is *Harrison* Castro?"

"Now hiring vassals," Bambi said, "and there's always room for a few more, I would guess. I'll give your dad the password."

"I don't know if I want to sell my father into serfdom."

"Well, it'll be safe and definitely beat being dead, and I may not be unbiased, but I sort of think my father isn't such a bad guy."

Heather half-chuckled. "Okay, truth is, I'm dreading talking my fuzzy biker dad into it, but he's also patriotic as all get-out and hates hippies."

"See, they're made for each other. I promise, Heather, give me your dad's number, I'll call him and set him up with my father, and he'll be fine. Dad'll probably send guards out to help bring him in."

"The world's getting pretty weird, Bambi."

"Tell me about it. Any word from Edwards's psychologist buddies about Roth's seizure?"

"They said it can be a stress reaction in people who are trying to act contrary to a hypnotic suggestion, especially a longstanding deep one. They also said that goes with an increased risk of suicide and alcoholism. Have fun with the dear tyke."

"I'll pass the word along to the FBI here, in case it hasn't gotten through their channels. Good luck, and if this is the last time the phone works, try not to worry."

"Same to you, Bambi. Thanks for being on the job."

It only took about ten minutes to persuade her father to accept a berth in Castle Castro; she had a horrible, sinking feeling that her father kind of liked the idea. *Well, at least Bambi won't have too much opposition to cope with.*

While she was talking to her father, the lights went out briefly, and then Lenny's extensive battery and generator backup kicked in. He wheeled swiftly through his place, turning things off to stretch the emergency systems, but just as Heather hung up with an "I love you, Dad, and you take care of your dumb butt, that's an order," the building power unexpectedly returned.

Lenny said, "Hey, it's a Power Return. Important tradition. Always celebrate Power Returns with sex."

Afterward, Heather said, "Hey, weren't they saying power might go on and off three to six times a day for a while?"

"That's why it's so important to follow the Return of the Power tradition.".

"And where did this tradition come from?"

"Well, technically, it won't be a tradition till the next time we do it."

For a while they just lay together, listening to the reassuring hum of the refrigerator. "You've really got strong arms." She ran a finger along Lenny's right triceps and smiled. "Good thing too, since you have a thing for women my size."

"If by *thing* you mean *insane obsessive fetish*, I guess you're right. Mind if I nuzzle that neck?"

"Mind? I insist." She rubbed his back and arms while he pressed his face to her skin; amused at his deep breathing, she asked, "Are you memorizing my scent, Lenny? Would you like a couple of my old towels to help you track me through the swamp later on?"

"You'll think I'm silly."

"Only if you are."

"Right." His strong arms wrapped her, his right hand caressing her back gently and his fused left hand touching as light as a feather on her arm.

She leaned forward and kissed it along the ridge of knuckles. "Is this hand sensitive?"

"On the palm." He turned it over and she kissed the solid flesh there, brushing with her lips. "Feels nice." He took another breath of her scent.

"Um, do you just really like the way I smell? You said it was silly . . ."

"And sad. I thought of it when you said that about my arms."

"Your arms make you think of my smell?"

"I get the arms from lifting weights, and I haven't missed a workout in years. My wheelchair recharges by plugging into the wall; if the power goes out for good and I lose my generator, I've got three manual wheelchairs handy—a track-racing model, a mountain-racer, and a nice big comfy general-purpose one. But none of them will do me any good if I don't keep my arms and hands in shape, so that's why there's a weight room back that way," he explained, nodding down the hall.

"And exactly what does that have to do with the way I smell?"

He curled against her; she felt dampness and realized his eyes might be tearing, so she just held him and waited.

Finally he raised his head. "Look, um . . . here's the thing—"

"Oh, my god, you've found another gigantic Amazon woman, but you don't think you can lift us both at the same time."

He laughed, but then he said, "Heather, if worse comes to worst, we might only have a week—and I'll treasure every second of it and try not to be sad—but look, Beautiful, I'm dependent on a lot more gadgets besides the wheelchair. Some of them are implanted and they have surface contacts."

"I know, babe, I've stroked a few of them."

"Jesus, yeah, you can't imagine how amazing it is to be rubbed around that little circular plastic spot over my kidneys, the place where my skin grows up to it itches all the time—"

"Well, say so." She pressed around it.

"I just did. And that feels good—yeah, right where the skin merges into the plastic." He sighed happily, but then he went on. "See, Heather—if one of my plastic parts starts to decay, or if nanoswarm gets into my body, I won't last very long. My immune system is pretty fucked up anyway, actually, that's what destroyed some of the natural equipment, and I don't think I'm going to develop immunity to any of Daybreak's little pranks."

"I'll wipe you down as much as you need with antiseptic, peroxide, whatever we need. I hope my cats weren't—"

"Naw. Clean as people, basically, or cleaner. I love cats and as long as the Daybreak biotes don't breach my seals, I'm fine. And if I have to give up being touched by people to stay alive, I'm taking the next outbound to the other side."

She shuddered. "You sound way too serious."

"Well, look, my point is, if I have to leave the party too early, I want to remember how good you smell, because . . . well, look . . . this is going to sound ridiculous, I mean we've really only been together forty-eight hours—"

"If you're about to tell me you're in love with me, you'd better hurry up before I beat you to it." She disentangled him for just a moment, adjusted her position, and pulled him back to her so that they were face-to-face. "The whole situation makes me feel so dumb. I enjoyed all the times we went out in the last few months, and all those other times we just talked for the hell of it. I kept thinking I should drop you the big hint about sex. I liked that you called after every date, I liked catching you for coffee now and then, I liked the way every so often you'd e-mail me something that made me smile or just phone and we'd talk for an hour and a half, and . . . crap, Lenny, I just thought we had a lot of time. So if we only have a week, yeah, we should probably get around to saying—"

"I love you." He smiled. "I wanted to get that in before the world ends."

"Hey, I love you too. The end of the world can make a person think that maybe there need to be a few less nights eating out of the fridge and talking to the cats. And you've made me nervous. Teach me how to clean you, 'kay?"

Heather had just finished rubbing Lenny down with sanitizing wipes, when her phone chimed. The screen said it was Arnie.

"Hey, lovebirds," Arnie said. "I think Cam was scared to call you again."

"We were just doing a few specially vile, filthy acts, hoping he'd call," Heather said. "What's up?"

"The Acting President is about to go on all channels and apparently give a speech that Cameron Nguyen-Peters, and Secretary Weisbrod, and as far as I can tell everybody, have just spent two hours begging him not to give. Nguyen-Peters called me to tell me he'd like all of 'the extended team'— that's what he's calling us—to catch it and send any observations or thoughts we might have to him, pronto. He asked me to call you, and, yeah, I think he's afraid of violating your privacy."

"And you aren't."

"Hell, boss, if I wasn't afraid my car would turn to green smelly Jell-O halfway there, I'd come over, sit on Lenny's couch, eat Doritos, and comment on the action." A shriek from the background told Heather that Allison was somewhere around too.

"That won't be necessary tonight, but we'll keep you on the list in case we ever sell tickets. Thanks for the heads-up, Arnie." To Lenny, she said, "The end of the world is *not* going to leave us alone."

ABOUT THE SAME TIME. WASHINGTON, DC. 9:30 P.M. EST. TUESDAY, OCTOBER 29.

Chris Manckiewicz wasn't sure how he felt about being the only electronic media with functioning gear at the White House. He had to wonder how many people would ever see it, considering the problems between the availability of working transmitters, televisions, routers, links, and generators.

He stayed simple, keeping the center camera in focus and occasionally cutting to the left or right plan angle camera for visual variety. Since his computer was still working and the battery was still up, having gotten a recharge at Rusty's house from her windmill-driven charger, he could do the little bit of editing, and the occasional small shifts of focus, with his left hand and a tenth of his mind.

His other hand was scrawling in a steno pad, against the imminent inevitable death of his computer and iScribe. He honestly didn't see how the old-time guys did this by hand with no electronic backup.

He had always liked making up ledes that were too truthful to run, and he had a great one for this speech:

> *In a speech that resembled nothing so much as your creepy uncle trying to lure you down to the basement with toys and ice cream for a special game of "keeping secrets," Acting President Shaunsen today attempted to bribe the public while revealing he had no idea what is going on.*

Shaunsen's emergency plan suspiciously resembled the budget bill last year that Pendano had killed with arm-twisting in the Senate and threats of veto, calling it "a thousand too many giveaways." Every big plum was introduced with, "and for all you good people in . . ." Chris began counting them in his steno pad; at least thirty cities and counties were mentioned in a speech that clocked at less than an hour. He drew an arrow to remind himself that this would be somewhere in his story for the *Advertiser-Gazette*.

It creeped Chris out. Shaunsen didn't appear to realize that there was any danger. The Vice President was ash and bone, the President was rumored to be mad, and the Acting President was giving everyone a happy-days-are-here-again, Republican's-nightmare version of the New Deal. Shaunsen finished out by assuring everyone that a vote for Pendano would result in "getting you the good Democratic president you all deserve. So as the young people say, no biggie, just chill."

Christ, that was out-of-date when I was in grade school— but then, so was Shaunsen.

The net was up enough for him to file the video; Anne replied that it would be showing immediately on six stations between the Atlantic and the Ohio River, and they'd be able to relay it to a few others in the next few days.

Chris dropped the rags soaked in household ammonia into his gear bag, shouldered it up, and set out for dinner and bed as his counterpart might have in Jefferson's day—on foot. A three-mile walk would just about give him time to settle on an angle and a lede.

ABOUT THE SAME TIME. ON US 285, IN COLORADO, JUST NORTH OF THE NEW MEXICO STATE LINE. SHORTLY AFTER 8:00 P.M. MST. TUESDAY, OCTOBER 29.

Jason thought, *That was one long day.* Beth seemed to be better; they'd found a spring pump and some apparently un-infected plastic bottles at the BLM trailhead after crossing to this side of the mountains, and risked an afternoon nap a little way up a slope of sun-warmed scree, out of sight of the trail. Sleep and water helped both of them; they made good time on the little county road west to the crossroads with US 285.

They headed north, away from the Tres Piedras country, *keep moving, one foot in front of the other, just cover ground.*

285 was an asphalt incision bisecting the magnificent emptiness of the San Luis Valley, shadowed by the immense Sangre de Cristos, winding over a series of rises, visible all

the way to the horizon in each direction. The sky's vivid unmarked blue might have gone on forever.

They walked for hours as the sun went down, and it seemed only time passed; the road was the road, with nothing on it, and that was all.

In the high mountain valleys in the fall, even if the day is warm and summery, the temperature falls well below freezing at night. Jason figured they had to keep moving until they found somewhere warm to sleep, and so far nothing had presented itself; exhausted as he was, he thought he could probably walk all night by the dim starlight, but he was worried about Beth, who might stumble and fall on her broken wrist.

At first he wasn't sure what the black silhouette against the dim gray glow of the distant mountains was. Closer, and they saw a faint rectangle of red light going ceaselessly on and off. They were almost on it when he realized it was a huge car, one of those monsters his father called "full-sized," so old it had to be a just-gasoline model; they hadn't made anything that big in ten years at least. A single red LED slowly flashing on and off had illuminated the back window, creating the red rectangle, dim as the starlight. *Wow, it is dark out here.*

They had been approaching from upwind, and in the darkness the car was just a silhouette, so he was almost on top of it by the time he smelled the stinking, spoiled tires. The car was stopped on top of the dimly glowing dashes of the centerline; Jason peered inside. The man lay with his seat tilted far back and his head lolling to the side of the headrest, lighted by the slow-blinking red glow from the dash. Jason tapped, knocked, yelled—no response. Finally, he tried the door.

It was unlocked. The dome light came on, and by its light Jason saw the man was dead, his hands still clutching at his chest. The blinking light's label was ONSTAR ALERTED. Probably the car had pulled itself over—there was a reason they called that a "dead man circuit"—and been calling for help all this time.

Gently, Jason lifted the corpse and reached under the Western State sweatshirt. He found external pacemaker pads on the sternum and behind the left scapula, both thoroughly rusted with nanoswarm. *Oh, buddy, I hope those aren't the ones that I was spreading. I didn't want to kill anyone anyway, and you're so about to save our asses.*

He dragged the corpse out of the car and over to the side of the road. *Now I know why they call it* dead weight. *But we can't bury—*

"Oh, Jason, come look!"

In the back seat, Beth had found a case of Mountain Dew, a couple of sweaters, and a heavy winter coat, along with a ditty bag of medicines and a gym bag containing a sweat suit. When Jason popped the trunk, they found a bonanza—it looked like the old man had gone to a Wal-Mart to load up on cheap groceries. The bagged frozen vegetables were squishy but still cold, and they had helped to preserve the milk, bread, and lunchmeat—and to keep the beer and pop cold.

"Let's try something," Jason said. He turned the keys in the ignition and was rewarded with the creaky grind of the starter, and then the warm purr of the big engine. On the rims, they drove away, making a noise like the metal shop of the damned, putting about a mile between themselves and the body before Jason pulled far over into a slow-vehicle turnout.

"Almost a full tank of gas, too," he said.

"But no tires, and it sounds like you've already wrecked the wheels."

"Yeah, but now we're far enough away from the body to not have to meet Mr. Bear or a pack of coyotes tonight. And we wanted the car, even though it's never going to move again. This thing has a 'keep-warm' setting."

"Keeping warm sounds real good. What's it do?"

"My dad had one of these old gas-only cars when we lived in Vermont. Some of them for high altitude and cold climates could be set to idle from time to time just to keep the battery charged and the water in the radiator warm, for parking on the street when it was twenty below outside, with a detector for monoxide in case you mistakenly left it on in the garage. So we set it to keep warm, turn on the heater full blast, and every time the battery gets low or the radiator water cools off, it'l idle a few minutes and warm us up. One long comfy warm night with food."

"But . . . Jeez, Jason, aren't we burning a lot of gasoline polluting, you know, all that stuff?"

"One car would have a hell of a time polluting the San Lui Valley in one night. The gas is just going to turn into goo in a couple days anyway. And the car is going to die as th nanoswarm eat it, Beth, but for right now enough is working to keep us warm, and there's more than we can possibly eat in the trunk. I vote we eat ourselves silly and sleep till the sun wakes us up."

She shrugged. "Well, the way you say, it makes sense and all. I just feel all weird and stuff about sitting burning gasoline and going nowhere in the last running Cadillac. Feels like something my dad would've done."

Beth was vegan, and Jason had always felt a little guilty that he wasn't, and, of course, both of them were philosophically opposed to plaztatic food, but lunchmeat sandwiches with salsa from a jar, Doritos, Pringles, irradiated chili in a plastic tub, and partly melted ice cream—all washed down with milk, Orange Fanta, and Budweiser—made the most wonderful dinner date they'd ever had, with the big heater keeping the old Cadillac toasty and the brilliant stars shining in through the dark windshield.

Beth switched on the radio; the scan button ran through four hundred channels without finding a signal, but "it's probably not seeing a working cell tower anywhere, and that cliff behind us is probably blocking the satellites. So—" She leaned forward, peering at the old-fashioned physical buttons by the light of the screen. "Hey, this thing is so old it still has FM and AM besides cell." She flipped the toggle; there was nothing on FM, but on AM the voice leaped out at them: "—think officially at the moment we are a 130,000-watt station but it might be more if Ernie can find a way. The reason we're doing this, of course, is that nearly every other station is off the air, but we have working generators, we've been able to keep one studio and our transmitter running, and we have a functioning fiber line to Washington; we just have to hope enough of you out there have radios that can pull in our signal.

"Once again, anyone with working recording and broadcasting or net-connected equipment is requested to record this broadcast and pass it on in any form possible, to as many people as you can reach with it; the Acting President has authorized compensation for your time and trouble.

"For those of you who just found this station, you're listening to Radio KP-1, Pittsburgh, Pennsylvania, USA, broadcasting at 1020 on the AM band, which is actually KDKA's transmission facility linked by a fiber-optic line to WQED-

TV's broadcast studio, using partly hand-built tube electronics from Westinghouse Labs. Mark this spot on your dial as we think we're likely to remain on the air permanently, thanks to technical support from Westinghouse and PPG.

"In a moment, Radio KP-1 will be carrying a live broadcast from Washington of a speech by Acting President Peter Shaunsen, who will be addressing the nation to explain current plans for dealing with the Daybreak emergency. While we are waiting, here are some other announcements that the Department of Homeland—one moment please—yes, the President's speech is about to begin, so we now take you to the Oval Office, where the President's speech will be reported by Chris Manckiewicz of The 24/7 News Network."

Jason took a deep draft of Mountain Dew, and settled in to listen; he didn't think he'd ever paid this much attention to someone talking before. Beside him, Beth was stone-still and alert.

The engine purred away on idle from time to time; otherwise the night was silent. When the Acting President's speech was over, and the station had gone back to broadcasting orders (mostly to preserve valuable resources) and requests (mostly to report where useful material was) from Homeland Security, Jason turned the radio off.

"Don't," Beth said. "We can leave it on real soft, but don't turn it off, please."

"Sure." He turned it back on. Something about her tone made him reach out to touch Beth, and he found her face wet.

"You okay?"

"No. Yeah. Kind of. I—I *liked* hearing the president on the radio. And hearing the radio. It was like, the world's gonna go on, that was what it was like. Like there's still an America and everything. And I know he was just like making a lot of promises to win an election—"

"Which he won't."

"Which he won't—but you heard him, Jason, he was like reaching out to the whole country, here's what we're going to build and do and make, let's get going, let's get to work—and it was just kind of . . . beautiful. I mean I know it's all a fake and a lie but I was real glad that Chris Whatsisface didn't start *telling* us all about how it was all bullshit and all. I just . . . I wanted to know someone was doing something, I wanted to know the government was trying, and I wanted to hear the radio and know we weren't the only people left on Earth."

"Truth?"

"Sure."

Jason took another delicious sip of Mountain Dew, thought about how long it might be before he had more of it, looked at the night sky swarming with stars around the dim reflection of the radio's glow. "I wish I'd never fucking heard of Daybreak, and neither had anyone else."

Beth started to cry, harder, and he reached for her to see if she was okay. She said, "Me too, but I wasn't gonna say nothing to you."

He felt queasy and sick from what they'd been saying, and Beth looked like she was in more pain, so he said, "We'd better sack out."

They fell asleep with the radio still going, under piles of clothes and coats, Beth in the front seat, Jason in the back, to give her most of the heat. The seat leather smelled good and the warmth of the heater and the soft engine turning over every few minutes were comforting; the last thing he remembered before falling asleep was the little insect voice of the announcer reading a complicated post from DHS, asking anyone who had any antique steel puddling tools, and any iron sculptors, blacksmiths, and heritage craft ironworkers to gather at Homestead, Pennsylvania, in three months' time.

Somewhere well past midnight, the engine suddenly seized and died. Beth cried out and woke up; Jason sat up, breathing hard. Not willing to let cold air into the car, he crawled forward and tried to restart it; the starter cranked without success. He left the heater fan running on battery power, recirculating the warm air from inside the car, to extract the last heat from the radiator. KP-1 was still on the air, reporting that they'd gotten ten-hour-old Internet voice mail from Banff, Alberta, and were passing on a request for the government in Ottawa, dissolving provincial governments till further notice, and asking that local governments report ASAP.

Beth curled up and went back to sleep. Jason eventually did too, but for a while he kept waking from dreams about Elton's body dangling from the barn's pulley. Something about the radio creeped him out, as if the old plaztatic world was lunging to get him, and the stars were too far away to save him.

"Hey, am I crazy, or is there a *newsboy* down on the street?" Lenny asked.

"Those are not mutually exclusive questions." Heather rushed to the window beside him. On the sidewalk below, a boy of about ten waved a paper over his head, shouting, "Read all about it!"

"Might as well see if we're both hallucinating," she said, strapping on sneakers.

In the street, she asked "How much?"

The boy smiled. "One paper for five dollars paper money or one can or box of food, has to be edible by itself, no fridge stuff, and I don't make change on food," proud that he'd remembered the whole spiel.

Heather traded a ten for a five and took the paper upstairs. It felt strangely like the local newspaper she could remember from when she'd been in college and had occasionally read one out of boredom; it was even about as thick as the *Costaguana Weekly Courier*, and had the same smeary, slightly greasy feel to it.

The front page had a little box:

For stores, restaurants, and warehouses known to be empty of food, see pages 4–6.

Three full pages listed all the stores both individually and by chain, noting the few of them that were still open to sell toiletries, cleaning supplies, and so forth. "Probably I can get some deals on disinfectant," Heather said, "if I hustle over to the Safeway three blocks over."

"Also check Rite Aid," Lenny suggested. "Especially home hair-dye kits."

"Are we going in disguise?"

"They have goopy extra-strength peroxide. We can use it

to scrub around the seals on the windows, the air intake for the generator engine, stuff like that. Wonder if the gasoline would be safer if we could add antibiotics to it? Or if that would just spoil it?"

"We could—shit. I was about to say maybe we could Goo-22 *antibiotics* and *gasoline*. How the hell did people find things out before the net?"

"Think about when we were kids. Phone books, dictionaries, paper encyclopedias—"

"Well, yeah, when I was a *little* kid. Mostly I remember the heap of them in the Dumpster when the school got a grant. How long since anything like that's been produced? 2015?"

"Yeah. I can't imagine anyone ever thought about gasoline spoiling anyway." Lenny sighed and ran through the auto-checks on the control screen of his wheelchair, which was becoming a nervous habit. "Well, it was a nice thought. I have fuel enough for about a week, but it'll be infected well before then."

"And there's food in the fridge and freezer for about that long. It won't benefit us at all if it spoils. So we'd better have breakfast today and read the paper to each other like more or less normal people."

They skipped reading the text of Shaunsen's speech and agreed that they liked Rusty Parlotta's editorials calling for everyone to admit that the system was down and act more like a grown-up about it. Lenny thought Chris Manckiewicz's reporting was biased too liberal, and Heather that it was just liberal enough. "I wonder if they'll have comics, and sports pages, like old-time papers?" Lenny said, as they were eating the last of the mixed, chopped fresh fruit. "I'd like that."

"Me too. My dad used to read me *Rose is Rose* and *Heart of the City*, and we always went over the stats on the Lakers every Sunday in the *Times*." The classified ads were mostly people looking to barter expensive cars and computers for canned food and guns. There were black smears on her hands, just below the little fingers. "On the other hand, the web was never quite this grubby. There couldn't be *lead* in the ink, could there?"

"That little story about 'local printer-hobbyist finds new occupation' said he didn't use lead-based inks, but it doesn't hurt for either of us to be washing hands constantly, considering."

While she was scrubbing, the phone rang; she heard him talking for a minute before he wheeled into the bathroom. "Cameron Nguyen-Peters wants us to attend a meeting of DRET at DHS."

"What's DRET?"

"Daybreak Research and Evaluation Team; it means 'Cam's bunch of smart people that help him figure stuff out.' They've got a biowar-rigged Hummer that sprays its own tires with disinfectant and has an extensive air filter system, coming to pick you up in about half an hour."

"For me? You said he wanted—"

"I think I'd better not go outside any more than I have to; in here, I've got it mostly sealed and as disinfected as I can get it, but out there, I could come down with nanoswarm or biotes, and be just as dead as any transistor radio. I'll have to work mostly by letter and phone from now until there's a better solution."

"I don't like the idea of leaving you here by yourself."

She could hear him trying not to snap at her. "And I don't like being confined to the house, but I think I'll have to live with it. Meanwhile, I'm moderately well-armed, the place has power on to support me, I can fix most of what will break in here, it's a lot safer from contamination, and we both have work to do. I'll be here, you'll be there, we'll be fine. I'll set out a dish basin with some disinfectant at the door; when you come back, be sure you dip your shoes and scour everything else."

ABOUT AN HOUR LATER. MARANA, ARIZONA. 8:30 A.M. MST. WEDNESDAY, OCTOBER 30.

When Kai-Anne pulled the curtain aside to see what the noise was about, she jumped back; a man with a bat stood in their driveway. She looked again and saw that there were perhaps twenty people with bats and guns. She didn't know what it was about but she knew she wanted a cop. She checked the landline; no luck. The cell phone was dead too.

"What's going on, hon?"

Greg's voice was low, trying not to wake the kids.

"Bunch of people outside with guns and bats," she said, trying not to sound nearly as scared as she felt.

"Shit. We're dealing with excessive citizen initiative here; remind me to thank the Acting President and the Moron Stream Media. Answer, but don't open the door if they get up the nerve to knock. I gotta dress. Don't go out there yet."

What's he mean, yet? He can't mean he's going to—

They were shouting at each other out there, arguing about something or maybe nerving each other up. *Please let that be an argument.* The only person she could distinctly understand was the guy outside the door with the bat; he was yelling at people to *calm down, we just gotta ask some questions, just some questions, let's not guess till we asked our questions.*

Greg came out in uniform; he could always be dressed in less than a minute. "My guess is they saw that hippie chick that nobody knows very well going in and out in the middle of the night, and decided there's a terrorist here. I just need to have a little talk with them." He looked her up and down for a moment and said, "You're perfect."

"I am?"

"Nobody's going to believe you're a terrorist in a Winnie the Pooh sweat suit with baby-puke stains. You'll see. Come on."

When he opened the door and stepped out, holding her hand, she saw one old guy in the back pointing the rifle, and thought, *No, don't, please listen—*

Greg looked over the crowd. "Let me introduce myself. Captain Greg Redmond, U.S. Air Force. I fly an A-10 out of Davis-Monthan. Anybody here want to take a look at my service ID?"

The guy with the rifle lowered it; the crowd didn't seem to know what to do.

"Anybody?"

Mr. Loud Baseball Bat set the bat down, looked at Greg's ID carefully, and said, "It's Air Force, and it's him."

"All right," Greg said, "So we've established who I am. This is my wife, Kai-Anne, and the mother of our three children, who some of you have probably seen around the neighborhood. Most of you know it's not easy being an Air Force wife, I guess, with all the moving and me being away a lot, and even harder being a mother of some little ones.

"Now, I'm just guessing, but I think you might be standing out on my lawn because somebody on the television, or the Internet, or something, said to watch out for people who were coming and going in the middle of the night before last, when our country was attacked. So I thought I'd just tell you all that Kai-Anne was picking me up from the base, because they let me come home for the night, after I was out flying all day because of that whole situation with Air Force Two. And because we're all pretty worried about our country today, you were concerned that she might have been involved with this Daybreak thing, or maybe with the murder of our Vice President and you came here about that."

By now all the bats were drooping, the handguns were holstered, and the rifles and shotguns pointed safely at the ground.

Greg nodded politely. "Well, what you have found is one tired Air Force pilot who wants some more sleep, and one Air Force wife with too much to do, who happens to have dreads and a couple tattoos. By the way, her husband likes all those. And three little kids sleeping. That's all.

"If you'd called the police, they could have come out and looked and made sure it was okay, without all this disturbance for everyone. So I'm betting you'll hear of other houses where people came and went late last night, because there's always people that need medicine in the middle of the night, or people who pull a night shift, or even I guess guys sneaking back in after an affair."

"How would you feel about *that*, Kai-Anne?" a voice called from the crowd.

"Anything I wanted done to him, I'd do myself," she said.

There was a nervous, stuttering laugh, and people began to drift away. In a few minutes, the crowd was gone; a couple of older men came forward to thank Greg for his service and assure him they "didn't mean nothing."

"Did you recognize any of them?" Greg asked, when they were standing alone on the porch. "Remind me why we moved here."

"You wanted to be somewhere safe for the kids, and I wanted to be someplace quiet, away from the base, where nobody would bother us or pay attention to how we lived."

He started to laugh, and hugged her. Maybe life wasn't all that bad, anyway.

ABOUT 45 MINUTES LATER. WASHINGTON, DC.
11:45 A.M. EST. WEDNESDAY, OCTOBER 30.

For the moment, DRET turned out to be Heather's Daybreak Working Group, including Arnie and Steve from Deep Black, plus Graham, minus Lenny and Agent Reynolds, plus a promised staff of as many as they needed as fast as they could hire them. They were all queuing up for lunch as Heather arrived. "The crew at your checkpoints looks pretty nervous," Heather said to Cameron. "Have you had incidents?"

"I woke up once during the night when a drunk got obstreperous at a guard post outside, because he wanted to know why we had lights and he didn't, and he'd apparently never heard of a Coleman lantern."

"So you're sleeping here now?"

"As much as I can persuade people, *everyone* will be soon," Cam said. "You and Lenny would be very welcome, Graham moved in this afternoon, Crittenden and his wife will be here before tonight, and I think I've got Arnie and Allison talked into it. Jim Browder is insisting on hanging on to his big house way out past the Beltway for three reasons— one, he can't get over the fact that it's the house he always dreamed of; two, his wife would never leave it; and three, he's an idiot."

"No kidding. But we all are. I think Lenny will want to stay in his apartment until the power fails. And I won't leave till he does. It's not easy to adjust to the new conditions, is it?"

"I guess not. I'll be a lot happier if this facility can serve as a dorm for the emergency management team. There's a lot of unused space at St. Elizabeth's right now, with the offices that have left and DHS not yet fully moved in, so we have the room. And it's relatively easy to protect the grounds."

"You're expecting trouble?"

"Should I stop expecting trouble right now, when so much of it just arrived?" Cam permitted himself one of his little, tight-lipped smiles. "Every time we did a simulation or a game-out of any widespread, multiple-path emergency, the Red team always hit us with an assassination, or a kidnapping, or general bad stuff happening to the critical personnel in Blue. And when Red didn't do that, the refs did—'the physicist you need is trapped on a collapsing bridge,' that kind of thing.

"I don't want to lose anybody. So if you can, see if you can talk your guy into moving down here; I wish we could give him accommodations as good as he has up in Chevy Chase, but he's going to be losing those within a week anyway no matter what, and we might as well move him while we're still fairly sure of having some motor vehicles running."

"Makes sense. I just don't want to think about trying to persuade Lenny to accept being dependent at all—he'll hate that so much."

"Don't we all?" Cameron asked. "All the—"

His phone rang; he spoke for just a moment and then said, "More mess. The meeting will start late because I've got to run to another one; I'll be back with you in twenty minutes. Meanwhile, enjoy lunch and have brilliant thoughts that solve all our problems." He trotted away.

Since she was last in line, Heather sweet-talked the lady and got two sandwiches to take home for Lenny.

ABOUT THREE MINUTES LATER. WASHINGTON, DC. 11:55 A.M. EST. WEDNESDAY, OCTOBER 30.

Cameron Nguyen-Peters slipped into the small room and said, "I have just a few minutes but I'm told this is urgent?"

"We think so," the tall man with narrow shoulders and thick glasses said. "I'm Dan Tyrel, your NOAA liaison. Weather forecasting. This just came in from Navy radiofax; they've been loaning us computers and satellite links from the Atlantic fleet, so we can still do some weather forecasting."

He held up a piece of paper; Cameron looked and saw an immense white pinwheel in the Gulf of Alaska. "Big storm, that's all I see there."

"That's the first major winter storm. We've been in Indian summer the last couple weeks. When that comes across it will bring high winds, blowing snow, the works," Tyrel, the NOAA liaison, said. "A little early this year but not unusually so."

"We've put an alert out on KP-1 and Radio Blue and Gold," the short black man beside him said. "I'm Waters, your Agriculture liaison, and I bet you didn't know you needed one."

Cam nodded. "Well, now that you mention it, it's obvious

How bad a storm are we looking at here, and what will it do to us?"

Tyrel said, "Snow in the Rockies and maybe the Great Plains, freezing rain in the Great Plains and the Upper Midwest, and cold and very wet wherever the main track exits the continent, on the average that's the Chesapeake Bay area, but it could exit as far north as Maine or as far south as Georgia."

Waters jumped in. "With snow over frozen ground, and the farm machinery not running, winter wheat will be a problem; some of it won't get planted even though we have seed, unless we can maybe get some of the urban refugees out there planting with pointed sticks in the next thaw. The feedlots are so dense that pigs and cattle can probably keep each other alive just from body heat, if they can find enough food for them. Poultry factory systems have to be heated in cold weather, so we're losing a lot of chickens and turkeys in the Midwest in another day or two. We can put word out for pre-emptive slaughter but they may not have workers to do it, and we don't have the facilities to can or preserve most of the meat.

"The biggest impact is on range cattle, and that's huge, because the ranchers in the Mountain States were one of our best hopes of feeding everyone in the next few years. A mild wet winter, that would have helped immensely. As it is—well, there's just not time to bring all the cattle and sheep in. No way. And we're going to lose some ranchers, besides some cattle; some of them will get caught out in that, trying to save their stock, and when they do, we lose a skill and knowledge base that took decades to build."

"How many more storms like this, this year?" Cameron asked.

"Maybe as few as three, maybe as many as nine, winter storms come in on that track every year," Tyrel said. "Some that just give everyone a cold, snowy day, some that are bad like this, now and then one as bad as the Blizzard of '86."

"I don't even remember that one."

"1886," Waters said. "Destroyed the cattle industry for a decade afterward, put an end to the cowboy era. We lived through the one in 1978 because we had helicopters and snowmobiles."

"What are the odds of anything that bad?"

"This storm, not at all." Tyrel shrugged. "Not even close for size. The next one or the one after that, god alone knows."

Cameron stared into space. *From now on, I'm going to appreciate every bite of every steak.* "And we don't have anything that can help?"

Waters said, "The carriers don't have hay and the planes don't dare touch down on land, so we can see how bad it is but not help."

"How long before this hits?"

"Idaho and Montana by Friday," Tyrel said. "The East Coast, maybe as soon as Sunday, maybe as late as Wednesday. You'll need to have everyone indoors by then."

Cam shook his head. "I don't know if we could do *that* if we had three to five *months*. Is there anything about this that's positive?"

"It's almost certain that no storm after this will kill nearly as many cattle, or sheep, or ranchers for that matter," Waters said. "But that's because you can only kill something once."

ABOUT THE SAME TIME. ON US 285, SOUTH OF ANTONITO, COLORADO. 10:15 A.M. MST. WEDNESDAY, OCTOBER 30.

The sun through the windows of the old Cadillac was warm and pleasant, and Jason and Beth awoke slowly, stretching and yawning, pushing the piled coats and sweaters off themselves. Jason said, "Good thing we slept long as we did—it's actually warm in here. Look at that, the sun's halfway up the sky, must be ten o'clock."

"Well, babe, I was totally tired. A gang rape and a twenty mile walk is like, exhausting." She glanced at him, and said, "Hey. Don't *you* start being all sensitive about it."

"I just figure you're in some weird kind of denial about things. They also killed all our friends."

"And broke my wrist," she said. "I was hanging on to the shed door trying to keep them from dragging me out, and one of them whacked it with a rock. So you think I should just sit down and cry?"

"Just seems . . . I don't know, weird . . . I mean—"

"Jason, babe, I promise that as soon as I stop needing to be on top of shit, I will break down all *over* the fucking place. I fact I pretty much guarantee it. In *fact* right now I am doing my fucking level best to not just lose everything and cry the rest of the day curled up in this old car. *In fact* you're *not* helping me get through this shit, and *in fucking fact* I wish you'd play along and help me out. *'Kay* babe?"

"Totally," Jason said. "Sorry if I—"

"Apology accepted. Now, as my asshole Uncle Billy always said, open an extra large can of shut the fuck up. What's for breakfast?"

"Let's see if I can improv us something hot," he said. "If I can build a fire quick, there's aluminum foil in our friend's groceries, and we could just dump some veggies and meat into packages of that and cook 'em Boy Scout style."

"Okay, you *gotta* make that happen," she said. "Because my mouth just started watering, thinking about it."

Jason was proud of himself; he was able to solve the problem in about ten minutes all told. He began by pulling a respectable heap of deadwood out of the dry wash about fifty yards away from the pullout. Then he went back into the guy's emergency kit, and sure enough, there was a gas siphon and a set of pull flares. He siphoned about a cup of gasoline into an empty Bud can and sprinkled that over his heap of dry wood; then he pulled the tab on a flare and shoved it into the pile. The dry wood, aided by the gasoline, caught at once.

While the fire burned down to a bed of coals, he dumped the formerly frozen vegetables in heaps on a long strip of the aluminum foil, added three slices of lunchmeat and some flaztatic petroleum cheese-like substance onto each heap, ran down the whole line with ketchup, mustard, pepper, and a dribbling can of beer (all the seasonings there were), and finally tore and folded the foil to enclose each heap and form a cookable package. The packages went directly onto the fire.

"That's three times what we can eat," Beth said.

"But I figure we eat a third and take the rest with us," Jason said. "Even if I have to do it in a cardboard box on my shoulder. And if we don't open the packets till we're ready to eat 'em, they should keep pretty good."

When Jason fished the packets out with a stick, and used the work gloves from the emergency kit to open two of them, they discovered how hungry they were; of the ten aluminum-foil-wrapped balls of food, they ate five there and then, gobbling down the impromptu gullion with their fingers as soon as it was cool enough to touch, washing it down with plenty of Mountain Dew and Coors. A bottle of Windex and a roll of toilet paper got their faces and hands tolerably clean afterward.

Though it was warm enough at the moment, the big, heavy sweaters from the back seat seemed like something they shouldn't leave behind, so Jason tied them into fanny packs. Each sweater held two liters of Mountain Dew, plus snack chips, packages of cooked gullion, and a couple of lunchmeat sandwiches, enough to make it to Antonito, they hoped, which a sign said was seventeen miles away.

For a long time they just walked, and now and then Beth would reach out and take his hand with her good right hand. They stopped only once, when the Mountain Dew bottle in Jason's sweater pack abruptly exploded, giving him a little bit of a bruise on the ass, soaking his back, drenching the sweater and crushing some of the food. The bottle smelled like spoiling milk; so did the bottle from Beth's pack, so they opened that and drank as much as they could; the liquid would do more good inside them than in the spoiling bottle. The warm fall sun dried his back fairly quickly, but the sweater still hung wet and cold against his ass, and the food in it was probably a soggy mess. *Maybe, if we don't make Antonito by dusk, I build a fire and recook my packets to dry them out. Don't know what I can do for the sandwiches; maybe wrap them the used foil and bake them too?*

They topped a long rise and looked down to where the road bent between two rock outcrops; there was a group of people down there, and a horse and wagon. Beth's breath caught for moment, and she asked, "Should we run?"

"They've already seen us and—hah. I think we're fine."

The little figure running lickety-split toward them was girl of about ten, grinning and waving at them like a maniac.

Beth laughed with relief. "Yeah. Hostile people don't send their children out to meet strangers."

"Betcha they thought of that too."

The girl rushed up and said, "Hi, I'm Gretchen Bashon and I'm here to welcome you to Antonito, Colorado. Do you have any other people in your party or were you forced leave any injured or disabled people behind?"

"There's just us," Jason said, smiling, "and we're glad to see you."

"Okay, are there any injuries in your party?"

"My left wrist is broken but I can walk," Beth said.

"No other members in party, lady—uh—"

"Beth."

"Lady named Beth has a broken wrist but can walk. Okay. Okay. Uh, material you are bringing in?"

"Just our clothes and a little food."

"Okay, and the last one is skills you have?"

"We're hard workers, good cooks, we can both do some fix-it stuff, and we can do organic gardening and raise chickens. Wilderness survival for me, and my name is Jason, and Beth can quilt, crochet, and sew, at least once her wrist heals."

Gretchen repeated it back twice, and then said, "'Kay, back soon!" and rushed away. They were still more than a mile from the little cluster of people. "Might as well keep walking toward them," Beth said. "We don't want them to think we're lazy."

Shortly, the wagon, pulled by a big brown horse, came clopping up the road to them. Gretchen sat shotgun; the driver was a little, bearded gnome of a man who looked like he had been born to play a Western sidekick.

"Jason, Beth," Gretchen said, carefully formal, "this is my dad, Dr. Jerry Bashore. He teaches art at Adams State College in Alamosa."

"Or I did till four days ago," Bashore said, tipping his straw cowboy hat to them as if he'd walked right out of the movies. His accent was much more Staten Island than Gabby Hayes, Jason thought. "Decided I'd better come out and pick you up; I know you can walk, but if your wrist is hurting, that'll make you tired. I was just about to take a fresh batch of folks into town, anyway. Gretchen, give Beth a hand getting into the wagon bed."

In the wagon, they discovered bales of straw, and Jason laughed. "You usually give hayrides in this thing!"

"Yep. Students loved 'em, extra money in tourist season, and it helped my two oat-burning buddies earn their keep. I'd already gotten the straw in for Halloween."

There were four others waiting for their rides into town, which Bashore—"call me Doc, everyone does"—told them would be about four miles, an hour's drive, "but you don't have to work, the horses do. And they know the way better than I do."

"So this thing is all made out of metal and wood?" Jason asked.

"Yeah, but I nearly had it seize up earlier today. The silicone grease turned to watery, sticky stuff, more like Elmer's Glue than anything else. We had to take the hubs apart and re-grease 'em with fat from the Dinner Bell Café's grease can. Also, I had a prairie schooner top for this, which would come in handy, except it was made of nylon with plastic tube ribs, and it turned into brown snot overnight. But there's nothing electric, and no plastic fittings, on any of the parts that make it go. And I guess we can make another cover for it. Giddup, there, fellas, we have people to deliver."

As far as Jason could tell, the horses moved no differently; *probably that's just for effect,* he thought. *That's okay. Right now I'd take a masked man on a white horse followed by a whole troop of cavalry.*

Something was shaking beside him; he turned and saw Beth crying, big wracking sobs, her whole body trembling. He put his arm around her and she buried her face in his shoulder, resting her injured wrist on his thigh. He stroked her, made soothing noises, and looked up at the blue sky, just now being invaded by high cirrus in the late afternoon—a sign that the warm chinook was about to be over and the first big storm of the winter was on its way.

ABOUT THE SAME TIME. WASHINGTON, DC. 12:30 P.M. EST. WEDNESDAY, OCTOBER 30.

"That's the story," Cam said, "a big, cold wet storm, crossing the northern US or possibly veering south, within a few days. Bad enough to cause death from exposure. What should we prepare for? Anyone got something to say about the impact of that?"

Steve from Deep Black nodded and pushed his glasses up onto the bridge of his nose. "We're still getting pretty decent data from reconnaissance drones flying off carriers—not as detailed as we would like because they have to stay high up to avoid catching nanoswarm and taking it back to the carriers. But what we see looks semi-okay. The impromptu evacuation of the cities in the Northeast is going faster than we hoped—lots of people are just walking out, with whatever they can carry in shopping carts and wheelbarrows. Private motor traffic seems to have stopped completely; we think there are probably almost no tires left, and so many biotes around that the few tires there are don't last long.

"We see high densities of people walking out of the big cities on highways. The flow started early this morning, right after the regular trucks didn't come in and the grocery stores ran out of a lot of staples. Still a lot of people staying put and hoping it will get better right now, of course, but as they see people streaming out, they'll probably start to move, themselves.

"That's the good news. The bad news is, we're not seeing any evidence that they're turning off the road and getting indoors much of anywhere; it's warm enough today for them to keep walking. Most of them have been moving for less than twenty-four hours, so to some extent they may still have scruples, and to some extent the people they're meeting are in the same situation they are—there's big parts of the Northeast Corridor where you can't really walk to a real evacuation area in less than a week—"

"Just for my information," Graham Weisbrod said, "by 'real evacuation area' you mean . . . ?"

"A place it makes sense to evacuate them to, rather than just the same bad situation farther up the road. If there's no food, no heat, hardly any shelter, then traveling there isn't really evacuation—at best it just gets them closer to the real evacuation point later. From well north of Boston to down past Richmond, we've got a band of highly populated areas that are about a week's walk from real evacuation areas."

"So to live they'll have to walk for a week without food or a warm place to sleep?"

Cam said, "That's right. They'll start to improvise tonight and tomorrow night, when it gets cold and they're hungry. They'll start knocking on doors, and then knocking *down* doors; there's going to be some violence, and a lot of people will be building fires out of whatever they can find, and wherever there's something to loot, there'll be looting.

"Then each successive wave coming out of the deep population centers is going to be worse; by the time the last ones make it out, they're going to be really dangerous and not especially sane, and that's what people will be out there as the storm hits. Which means a lot of them will die and solve the problem of themselves for us, but while they're doing it they'll tear up the areas they manage to reach pretty badly."

Steve fidgeted. "I saw some of the pictures a couple hours ago. Take I-80 across New Jersey and into eastern Pennsylvania—we got some photos from there—pictures from the air show literally hundreds of miles of highways covered with people walking. The highways run through huge suburban areas of single-family housing; once it gets dark, and especially when the cold and the rain hit the refugees, those little suburban houses will be obvious targets, and basically you'll have a . . . I mean, I don't want to sound . . . but that crowd on the highways, hungry, cold, nobody there to tell them what to do—"

"They're going to hit that suburban tract housing like a ravening barbarian horde," Graham Weisbrod said. "Which they'll be." His face was drawn and tight as if he were watching it happen already. "Not because they're bad or even because they're angry, but because . . . well, hell, I think about my kids when they were little and helpless, I imagine them hungry, crying, and cold, and yeah, I'd break down a man's door and maybe kill him just for a can of beans for the kids, especially if I'd had all day to stew and think about the fact that no one was coming to help and how I needed it more than the guy who still had a house, until I rationalized it all. It might be hard to talk myself into that the first time, but by the second time on the third day, it would be business as usual."

ABOUT THREE HOURS LATER. WASHINGTON AND CLEVELAND PARK, DC, AND CHEVY CHASE, MARYLAND. 4:15 P.M. EST. WEDNESDAY, OCTOBER 30.

Heather was the last drop-off for the biohazard Hummer, and he invited her to move up to the front seat "for two more eyes and one more gun." He left the scanner running; no signal on any emergency bands. KP-1 was holding on, broadcasting government announcements from Pittsburgh. The midshipmen at Annapolis had hand-built a radio station they were calling Radio Blue and Gold; a young-sounding kid was reading the morning's *Advertiser Gazette* over the air. A faint, sputtering station that claimed to be coming from RPI's physics lab came in for a second, then faded.

I left a mountain of chow on the floor for Fuss and Feathers, and set out five litter pans; they'll be all right for a week, which is more than you can say for us.

The driver said, "I don't want to try to go all the way to this address in Chevy Chase. Last reports, an hour ago, there was a lot of bad stuff going down. The minute I drop you off, I'm swinging over west, picking up my family, and heading out, as far and fast as I can. Listening to all the nice people I've been driving, I've heard about the two-hundred-mile dying zones around the cities, there ain't gonna be any United States in another week, it seems to me, and I've got one of the few vehicles that can keep running, at least for a while, and if I take it right now to haul my family, maybe they can live."

Heather thought about her sidearm in its shoulder holster; this was a deserter who was stealing a vital piece of government property. Lenny was alone and his apartment block was an obvious target; they could set the building on fire, or just break in from too many sides at once, or maybe just plug an exhaust pipe on his generator. Getting to him was the first priority.

"Look," she said, "I probably can't stop you anyway, and I guess in your place I'd be thinking of the same thing, but how far up Connecticut Avenue can you take me? I've got a friend who might be trying to hold his place against god knows what; that's the Chevy Chase address you have. It's more than twenty miles to his place, so I'd never make it before dark. Take me as close as you feel okay with, please? A few hours, and being there before dark, might be life and death."

"You got it, lady. But the first time I hear a shot or see a mob, you're out, and I'm running, clear?"

"Clear," she said.

They had turned off Connecticut, less than a mile from Lenny's place, when a big crowd spilled onto the street three blocks ahead. The driver whipped a U-turn and stopped for an instant. "Here's where you get out, ma'am. Thanks for understanding."

Heather jumped out, her bag already on her back, and slammed the Hummer door. She zagged left and put a mailbox between her and the crowd in the street.

She'd only really seen looting in training films; it just wasn't something that likely for her to encounter in her areas of law enforcement, security, or intel. *They always told us to go around (how far off a main street? How much delay?) or go past (what's all the running and yelling about there, anyway? But I don't see any guns).* As she cautiously approached, she saw that the people running in and out were teenagers and younger, and the crowd in the street was overwhelmingly mothers and grandmothers. By the front door, a stack of empty coolers with a HELP YOURSELF sign showed how the manager had gotten rid of the frozen foods the day before.

Now the doors lay thrown down on the sidewalk, and the kids were bringing out the few overlooked items for inspection. Heather saw a couple jars of pickled jalapenos, some store-brand canned sauerkraut, and a few boxes of Hamburger Helper presented to the waiting crowd of women; there were few takers, except one lady filling a backpack. "You are all crazy, you can eat this stuff, and I'm takin' all I can carry. They don't have no big pile of steak and Cheerios hid back or nothing."

Around the corner, Heather found a Rite Aid with its doors wide open; a tall, thin man in a store apron was painting

NO MORE FOOD, HELP YOURSELF, PLEASE NO FI

on the window.

"Is there any disinfectant in there?" Heather asked him.

"Lady came by and got most of the rubbing alcohol and I think the hydrogen peroxide, another lady got the bleach," the man said.

"Got hair-dye kits?"

He laughed. "Oh, man, now there's a woman's vanity. You want to stay a redhead while the world ends? Aisle Four D."

Tearing open the hair-dye kits, dropping the soft bottles of peroxide into her pack, she thought, *I must be a good person. I could shoot him and no one would ever know or care. Or maybe I just want to save ammunition.*

Still room in the pack. She put a shoulder to the door of

the pharmacy section, and grabbed three large jars of pills whose labeled names ended in -cillin.

She went out the emergency door, wishing that ALARM WILL SOUND had not been a lie, and ran past the row of cars with rotting, stinking tires, and a sour odor that she figured was probably gasoline going to vinegar. *Okay, Lenny, now I'd sure appreciate it if it turns out you've been having the dullest afternoon of your life.* She took the last few blocks at a trot.

The door of Lenny's building was propped open. The doorman's body lay behind his desk. The exit wound in his back was huge—shotgun blast, from the front, high up by the neck.

Staying drawn and ready, she closed the building door. No sense attracting more scum into the place. Heather ran up the stairs toward Lenny's apartment, trying not to think about what she might find.

Loud voices through the fire door, but they didn't sound close.

She pushed it gently, opened it far enough to slide into the empty hall. She crept along the wall toward the turn that led to Lenny's front door.

Beside her, a broken door gaped; Heather saw a child's bare, motionless leg sticking from under a sofa. The sight froze her; she had seen violent death, but this was a kid for god's sake—

She heard a door open, down the hall, and slipped into the apartment. She reached out to touch the child's leg, hoping—

"He's dead," a soft voice said beside her. A young woman, perhaps twenty years old. "My boyfriend's son. They killed him and his dad. I hid in a closet. I feel bad."

The voices in the hallway rose to a crescendo, and Heather made a shhh gesture and listened. Somebody named James was loudly welcomed by the group, and the leader, if that was the word, was explaining that "—from a neighbor bitch, she told us so we let her go after we done with her, there's a cripple guy in there with like a generator and a frigerator and all that good shit, man, we could party the biggest bestest party anybody ever partied."

"Burn 'im out."

"Then what happens to all that good shit we goin' in for, know what I'm sayin'?"

"Then just break the door down."

"You see that little square in the door, there, just down from that peephole? That's how Michael got shot, trying to take it down with his shoulder, and that cripple guy, he just pop that little square open, bang, shot Michael dead, man. He was our friend and everything and that cripple guy killed him."

"See, if it was me, in there I mean, I'd just like spray down the whole hallway, and all y'all'd be dead, you know?"

"Maybe he's low on ammo."

"He shot back soon as we tried shooting through that door, so he ain't all that low."

I wish they'd all talk, Heather thought, *because I'd sure like to know how many of them there are. But things won't get better for waiting, that's for sure.* She turned to the young woman beside her and handed her a table lamp lying on the floor. "Was it those assholes that killed your friends?"

"Yeah." The young woman's voice was full of tears.

"'Kay. When my butt disappears through that door, start counting. At fifty, throw the lamp into the hall and scream—loud and a lot."

"Fifty, throw the lamp, scream."

"Right." Heather scrambled through the door and down the hall to wait about three feet short of the turn that led to Lenny's apartment, silently counting—

The lamp crashed into the hallway and the young woman screamed and wailed fit to fetch the dead. Heather held her pistol in both hands, chest high, drew a breath—

Blur around the corner. She squeezed the trigger, and the body fell sideways. Another man tripped and fell across him, and Heather shot him in the back of the head, then jumped across the hall for a view farther down the corridor. A man stood staring at the bodies of his two friends and Heather shot him in the chest; two more men, yelling "Don't," backed up in the hallway.

There was a brief, stuttering burst from behind them; Heather ducked sideways. *It would really upset Lenny if he accidentally shot me.* After the burst, Heather peeked, and saw the two men trying to drag themselves forward, their backs a bloody mess. She stepped into the short hall and shot each of the struggling men on the floor in the head; no point in their suffering, but no way to bring in a prisoner. She verified that the other men were also dead.

"All clear," she called.

Lenny's door opened; he was in his mountain racing wheelchair. She hadn't realized how neatly the side bracket would hold a machine pistol.

"Glad you got here when you did," he said. "They'd brought in the intellectual in the group, and he'd've figured something out."

"I had some help—let me get her," Heather said. She went back to the apartment, where the young woman still sat, stroking the leg of the dead boy.

"We never got along," she said. "He was jealous about the time his dad spent with me. I wanted us to get along, but . . ." She was watching something a thousand miles away. "I guess we'll never get along now."

"I've got to talk my boyfriend into going to a safe place with me," Heather said. "He'll argue, but I'll win. You should come with us. I think they'll have room for you there too, and even if they don't, you'll still be somewhere safer than this building. Please come along?"

"I'd just be a drag on you."

"You were a big help, setting off my diversion."

"Because I could tell you were going to kill those guys and I wanted to help." In the gathering gloom, Heather couldn't really see the young woman's face, just the shadow of her shape. "I was in the closet and I heard them kill Stan and Dennis. I heard Stan begging for Dennis's life. They killed him anyway."

"You helped me kill them all."

"Didn't bring Stan back. Or Dennis. Look, you guys just go. Please. I'll just sit here till I think of something." She turned and curled away.

The sun was going down fast. Heather said, "Just let me make the offer one more time—"

"No."

Hope I have more luck with Lenny. She turned to go; Lenny was rolling into the apartment. "Stay with us tonight and see what you think in the morning."

The girl looked up. "You're the guy they were trying to kill."

"Yeah. I'm sorry Stan didn't come over to my place and bring you and Dennis. I asked him to."

"I know. He said you can't live in fear."

"So here's my thought. Heather and I can't make it to any-where safe before nightfall, so we're stuck here for the night. At least do us the favor of not being out here where we might have to hear someone killing you. Come morning, you can come with us or not."

"I really don't like the idea of staying the night here," Heather said. "I know you've got the generator, and your in-dependence, and everything, but—"

"I hate to leave," Lenny said. "But I like living. Now—come on—I think Stan said your name was Sherry?"

"Yeah." The young woman stood up, kissed her hand, and pressed it to the dead boy's leg, and led the way out into the hall.

"I thought you'd argue with me," Heather said.

"If it was just me, I might, but I keep noticing more and more people risking their lives to accommodate me. We've all got to get through this with whatever we've got, and I know that everyone will have to help and be helped, but I don't want to cost anyone anything more than I have to." He rolled ahead of her and Heather followed him around to the door; she'd wondered how he'd gotten through a hallway blocked with bodies. The answer turned out to be that a mountain racing wheelchair rolls over a corpse as easily as a log. "We'll want to wipe your wheels when we're inside," she said. "You've probably picked up some nanoswarm or biotes."

"Now, there's my practical girlfriend."

"I still wish we were moving tonight."

"Me too, actually. But realistically, it's over twenty miles to St. Elizabeth's. And except for the White House, no one's got a secure car they can risk at night to come up here, and I wouldn't bet on Shaunsen deciding to rescue us. So I'm guessing we'll end up going under our own power tomor-row. Better to go at dawn, when the predators are sleeping off looting the liquor stores; we can be most of the way there before anyone notices us."

He unlocked the door and let them in. When he was on the mat with the door closed behind him, he said, "Bleach and rags under the kitchen sink; could you help me clean the blood off my wheels? I know it's silly, since I'm leaving so soon, but I hate the thought of staining my carpet."

**ABOUT THE SAME TIME. SAN DIEGO, CALIFORNIA.
3:30 P.M. PST. WEDNESDAY, OCTOBER 30.**

Last night, Carlucci had declared Roth to be a cooperative witness, which meant she could have food, water, and sleep at will. No one had asked her about it; she'd still been passed out from her seizure.

Roth had seemed all right but subdued that morning, so Carlucci had tried a low-key interrogation at ten A.M.; by noon, when they broke for lunch, Roth had repeated, many times, that she wanted to cooperate but she didn't know much and it felt like something was wrong with her mind.

Hoping a younger woman would have better rapport, they'd sent Bambi Castro in from 1:30 to 3:30, but though Roth was less guarded with her, she really hadn't extracted any more information. Now, it was Larry Mensche's turn. Maybe his warm and fatherly personal style would work out differently, but Bambi doubted it. She went to treat herself to fresh coffee; she wondered how long it would be before supplies of that ran out.

In the break room, Carlucci was just filling his cup. "Weird, isn't it? She keeps saying she wants to help, but did you get anything out of her?"

"No, and it was time to give up. I needed some coffee, because I'm getting tired, and I promised I'd bring back a cup of herbal tea for Roth, because she's been cooperative. I tried to kid with her and told her it wasn't *real* herbal organic, just a plaztatic copy, and she started to cry and said a lot of people around the world *need* plaztatic copies of real stuff, and she never understood that before, and she's *so sorry*. But then after that for fifteen minutes she was like, aphasic. Like after a stroke. It's like she's dying of guilt and I would swear to god she *wants* to confess and spill her guts, but when she tries she goes into brainlock." Bambi swallowed a deep, warming slug of coffee. "I'm wondering if Daybreak protects itself by not letting them talk?"

"I agree. I can't tell if she's lying, too out of it to have a clue, or being blocked from talking. Maybe Mensche'll be—"

"Trouble!" Bolton yelled from the front door; Bambi and Carlucci ran to see.

About 150 people, looking a little like a parade, a little

like a charity walkathon, and a lot like a mob, in jeans and sweatsuits and T-shirts, were coming up the road toward them. "The light's behind them, so they probably can't see us through the windows," Bolton pointed out. "Good thing, too. I count four rifles and three shotguns being waved around; handguns would be anyone's guess." He handed his binoculars to Carlucci.

"Hunh. KILL THE BITCH NOW. MEXICANS GET FOOD, CITIZENS GET SCREWED. BREAK DAYBREAK. And TERRORISTS SHOULDN'T GET SHOWERS WHEN TAXPAYERS HAVE NO POWER. At least that last one is sort of clever."

"Can we stand them off?" Bolton asked.

"Yeah. Most of those guns they have won't work—some wouldn't have even before Daybreak. A lot of people don't clean or maintain their weapons. And they're not that well-organized. Figure it that half the crowd thinks it's going to a school board meeting and the other half thinks they're going to storm the Bastille. But I'd rather not shoot American citizens for being outspoken and stupid—it's kind of what the country's all about, you know?"

Bolton nodded. "If we run them off, how long before more come back?"

"Well, these guys must have been brought here by word of mouth, so they're just the first wave . . . and I'd hate to have to try to hold this place at night . . ."

"What if we move the prisoner?" Bambi asked.

"Where and how?"

"We take the biohazard Hummer out the back garage exit. My father is Harrison Castro, and I—"

"Wait a sec, the guy they call the Mad Baron is your father? Billionaire, built himself a Castle overlooking the harbor maybe five years ago?"

"Yep. Survivalist nut like Grandpa and Great-grandpa before him. He could hold that place against an army. He'll take in anyone I tell him to, no prob. He's got a protected way down to his private pier, he owns too many sailboats to remember all their names, and I've been sailing since I could stand up. We take Roth there, rest up, maybe he's got radio and if he doesn't he's building it, we call in to DC for instructions, and we can either keep Roth in the Mad Baron's Castle, or I can run her up the coast, or for that matter, Dave, trust me on this, I was raised in boats and I could sail her around the Horn to Washington if I had to."

"Oh, I believe it." Carlucci raised his binoculars again; the crowd was still climbing the long slow slope of the hill, but they would be there in less than ten minutes. "Bolton, you drive. Take the two meanest-looking GAFEs with you. Wedge Roth between them in the back seat; Castro will bring her to you in a second." Bolton was gone in an instant. Carlucci said, "Castro, get moving. I'm officially remanding the prisoner to the Department of the Future, as of this second."

"Thanks. If you need somewhere to be, Dad's got room for hundreds. Bring your families. Even if I'm gone, he'll let you in if I tell him to."

"I couldn't—"

"You sure could. Your family too, 'kay? If you don't bring them, Dad will make you go get them anyway. Food, a roof, a safe bed, and plenty of people working to keep it that way. You won't get any better offer, trust me. Now you go stall, and I'll go get our terrorist, and I'll see you at Castle Castro." Bambi raced down the hall to the interrogation room. "Mensche, sorry to interrupt, but we've got to relocate the prisoner, mob on the way, and they're close, get details from Carlucci." She grabbed Ysabel by the hand, saying, "This way, now."

At the Hummer, she pushed the girl into the arms of one GAFE; the second one jumped in immediately, so that they had the prisoner wedged and seated. Bambi hopped into the front seat. She hadn't had time to grab her bag, but there were probably ten "just in case Bambi comes to visit" closets at Castle Castro.

Bolton said, *"No levante su cabeza, por favor."* Ysabel Roth gulped, nodded, and leaned forward so that she was completely below the level of the windows; one GAFE beside her tossed a couple of blankets and a towel in a disorderly heap on top of her. "All right, I hope you know the fastest way," Bolton said.

"I know the best. Just keep this thing on the road and don't outrun the sprayers on the tires. We have enough antiseptic juice to make it there?"

"Yep, I filled up when we got back."

Mensche burst into the garage, waving his arm in a rapid roll: *go, go, go, go, go!*

Bolton started the Hummer, and they rolled forward; Mensche ran ahead of them and yanked down on the manual chain to raise the door.

They lurched into the drive behind the office park, away from the main public parking area, and Bolton gunned it, turning away from Aero Drive. "It's near the Harbor," Bambi said.

"Yeah, I know, I'll turn back by going another way I know, but I'm hoping we won't be—"

Something made a clank and a thud; everyone jumped. "That's a bullet being stopped by the Kevlar curtains under the body panels," Bolton said. He threw the Hummer in a tight turn around a couple of dead cars and was on a main road, running flat out; another *clang-thud!* from the rear door announced a second shot.

"Hang on," Bolton said, and threw the Hummer hard around another turn, down a ramp into a different office-building parking lot; he circled three-quarters of the way around the building, climbed a ramp on the other side, and shot around a long, arcing road. "We were probably out of range, but why take chances? Now I'm going to double us back onto Aero, a nice safe mile and a half from the office, and with a couple rises in the road between us and them. If the tires and the luck hold, we'll be down to the Harbor in less than fifteen minutes. Castro, can you explain that to our two soldiers? The only Spanish I know is for making arrests."

She snorted. "Dad has pretenses of Old Californianess. He was too proud of his heritage as a descendant of the conquistadors to let his daughter learn Spanish. I don't suppose either of them knows French, Russian, or German."

A muffled voice said, "My Spanish is fine. Can I sit up? It's hot under here."

"Wait till we're on Aero," Bambi said, "but please explain now for the soldiers. They must be confused as hell."

Ysabel Roth spoke for a short while and answered a couple of questions. Then one GAFE spoke to her for a couple of minutes, and she translated, "Hey, they say that being in the GAFEs means always being as confused as hell."

"Our kind of outfit." Bolton slowed as they approached the Harbor; more and more wrecks and junk lay in the road. "Ms. Roth, get down and stay down; we're going slow enough to be a good target, and it's always possible that someone had a working CB or something and we might be ambushed."

Once, as they passed an apartment block, people ran out toward the Hummer from the driver's side, but the GAFE on that side lowered his window and showed them his weapon, and they stepped back. "Just need food for the baby," one of the men yelled. "Just need some help."

They kept rolling, and Bambi tried to think of anything else they could have done. She couldn't seem to come up with anything.

Harrison Castro had been careful about not letting anything important about Castle Castro leak into the media, despite a whirlwind of attention while it was being built. The outer surfaces were thin brick-and-concrete facades that looked fake-medieval, with far too much glass to be defensible; inside that relatively fragile box there were what amounted to concrete bunkers, with recessed steel shutters to cover the windows as needed. *If anyone tries to shoot the place up,* he had often explained to her, *all that Hollywood-movie-castle crap will be blown into a heap of rubble, but behind it there's bunkers you'd need tanks to take. And that's the point where the ass-hole taxers, regulators, interferers, and Democrats find out that I'm an arrogant, practical, effective, energetic bastard disguising himself as an arrogant, pretentious, effete bastard.*

Brush had been planted to conceal the turnoff, but Bambi had no trouble guiding Bolton into it. They bumped and rumbled up the apparent temporary dirt road to the first checkpoint. The guard was all business until Bolton lowered the window to talk to him, and Bambi said, "Hi, Mr. Duck!"

The guard was beaming. "Glad to see you home, and hope you're staying. Are these friends of yours?"

"Terry Bolton here is, and I'd appreciate if you gave him an all-areas pass, and let him come and go as he needs. The rest are a case of bringing my work home with me."

"You remember the way to the Secure Garage?"

"Yep."

"I'll let the house know you're comin'. Mr. Castro will want to come down and say hi."

"You still have a working radio or something?"

He grinned and shook his head, then pulled two flags from the holster at his side. "Mr. Castro always thought the world could end, and he made us all learn semaphore. Got a mirror for flashing Morse, too, but we're being careful not to be conspicuous."

On the way up the road, Bolton said, "Uh, his name is really Mr. Duck?"

"He was the only guy named Donald around when I was little, and I couldn't pronounce Przeworski-Abdulkashian, but my father was not about to have me calling an adult by his first name, so I couldn't call him Donald either. Hence . . ."

"Mr. Duck. He seemed to like it."

"I was an awful kid but he thought I was cute."

Bambi directed the biohazard Hummer through a complex, circuitous approach to the house along more than three miles of winding dirt roads. "What are all those branch roads, anyway?" Bolton asked. "Guest houses?"

"Some of them. Some are strongpoints, and some are both. And a lot are dead ends that are easy to cover from the house."

"This place *is* a castle, isn't it?"

"Yeah. Did I mention my father is a bit eccentric?"

When they came around the last curve into the parking area in front of the Secure Garage, Harrison Castro was already there waiting for them, his shock of white hair billowing over his high forehead, bandito mustache curled up by his immense toothy grin, and in his around-the-Castle clothes— loose blue tunic and pantaloons, black boots, and an open cowled red robe that made him look like he had escaped from the set of *Star Wars for the Color-blind.*

"'Scuse my having a warm family-values moment while you stop giggling," Bambi told Bolton, popping her door and running to her father.

After a long hug, the older Castro said, "Well, I know why you didn't call ahead. You'd better introduce me to everyone else."

Bambi explained quickly, and Castro shook everyone's hand, even Ysabel Roth's. "Bambi says you've come over to our side, and you're trying to help with information?"

"Yes, sir, I don't know what—I mean, I sort of—uh, I have been trying to—"

The girl looked as if she'd been punched in the gut, her face pale and sick, and abruptly she fell down in the parking lot. Bambi and Bolton rolled her over. Her pupils were dilated but the same size; her breathing was harsh, deep, and irregular; there were flecks of foam around her mouth, and little twitches in the muscles of her face, but her arms and legs lay still and limp.

"Well, that's twice," Bambi said.

"And both times when a stranger said something to her about defecting," Bolton pointed out. "Maybe Daybreak really does have a mind-control virus or something."

Harrison Castro turned back from where he'd been giving orders to a servant. "We've got four doctors sheltering with us, and I think one of them is a neurologist. And we have a clinic inside. We'll patch her up."

"Is there anything you don't already have here, Dad?"

"No lawyers. Figured I won't need them. A baron makes his own law." He had his same old sly smile. It made Bambi edgy; Dad spoke too much truth in jest.

THE NEXT DAY. CHEVY CHASE, MARYLAND. 4:30 A.M. EST. THURSDAY, OCTOBER 31.

"About two hours to dawn," Lenny said, waking Heather. "Time to get moving."

They made last use of the generator-driven pumps and auxiliary propane system, taking hot showers and fixing a big, hot breakfast. Sherry ate with them, saying nothing, but when they had finished, she said, "I'll go with you, if one of you will go with me to get my hiking boots from Stan's closet."

Heather went with her, and because it seemed to make sense, she kept her hand on Sherry's shoulder the whole time, as the young woman stepped around both the bodies and found boots, socks, and a big warm sweater. "Christmas last year," she whispered, as she pulled it on.

With a half-sob, half-cry, Sherry turned back for a moment and grabbed two pictures from Stan's desk, slipping them into the big pockets of the sweater. Heather held her for a moment till her sobs subsided, and they went out, not looking at the bodies.

Lenny had packed bags for Heather and himself, and after a last visit to "what's probably the last working toilet in Chevy Chase, you can say you were here before they put up the plaque," as Lenny explained it, they folded Lenny's mountain racing wheelchair.

Down the stairs, Heather carried Lenny—he weighed less than a hundred pounds—and Sherry managed the folded wheelchair. They trotted back upstairs for the packs as Lenny sat in the dark lobby behind the front desk, with a path of retreat through three doorways, and the machine pistol in his hand.

"How'd you find him?" Sherry asked.

"Through work. We're not in the same office but now and then we had to talk to each other."

"He's very cool. You're so lucky."

Oh, Christ, I'm no good at this social stuff. Do I ask her about Stan? "Thank you," she said.

"You both work for the government, for like, the army and stuff, or you're spies or something?" Sherry grabbed up her own pack and Lenny's, leaving Heather the single large one she was planning to take.

Heather pulled it on. "Yeah, I guess it shows."

"Kind of. Not too many people have all those pictures of Republicans on their walls, or quite so many guns, or a big poster of a tank in the front room."

"Actually it's an armored fighting vehicle."

"And *very* few women—even if they're Lenny's girlfriend—would know that difference," Sherry added, smiling. "I'm glad to have you guys to walk out with, really. Didn't mean to sound critical. I was just leading up to a question. If you know, and if it's okay to tell me, you know? Did somebody do this to us, or did it just, like, happen?"

Heather checked one more time; Lenny had accidentally acquired a perfect weapon, a rebuilt M4 with the plastic parts replaced with good wood and metal, and all surfaces plated or anodized, about as Daybreak-resistant a gun as anyone could have made. Of course, there would be trouble later on as so much ammunition was reported to be deteriorating, but at least yesterday Lenny's H&K had been working just fine.

She just hoped she would turn out, if necessary, to be as good a gunfighter as this was a fighting gun.

"We should get going," she said. "The answer to your question is we don't know if it was an enemy action yet, or something that just sort of happened to happen, but whatever it was, the thing to do is get the country back to functioning."

"Good enough."

They went down the stairs quickly and quietly. "Nothing's moved out on the street since you left," Lenny said. "I vote for going as quick as we can, all the way south in one fast trip."

"Makes sense to me," Heather said.

"I'm just along for the trip," Sherry said. "You know, you're the first people I've ever seen who just *have* guns—not like showing them off the way the gangsta wannabes do, just like, it's a tool is all. Right now, I wish I was that way."

"There're three spares in my pack," Lenny said, "all loaded and ready. That's why it was so heavy. Heather, when we're going through open spots, in daylight, maybe you can give Sherry a fast course."

" 'The Complete Idiot's Guide to Shooting People,' " Sherry said. "Sounds good to me."

For the hour before the sun came up, they hurried south along Connecticut Avenue, occasionally having to dodge around clusters of abandoned cars but mostly able to just proceed quickly.

"Aren't you worried about snipers?" Sherry said, after a while.

"Very," Lenny said. "But I'm more afraid of getting into something hand to hand. Tip me over and I'm fucked; at gunfire distances, it's at least even, maybe better. And I can always shoot to make them keep their heads down while Heather closes in to rip their heads off with her bare hands."

"Pbbbbt."

"Hey, you and I know we're a couple of scared desk jockeys. Sherry thinks you're Daniel Boone and I'm Q. This way at least one of us has some confidence."

The sun found them near a pocket park with good views in all directions; Heather gave Sherry a fast course in using the pistol, finishing by telling her, "Look, it's really nothing more than this: You point it at people you intend to shoot. Don't point it at anyone you don't. Put your finger inside the trigger guard only if you plan to shoot someone. Once they've seen you point it at them, they're going to be pissed, so shoot. If you decide to stick around after this, then we'll go into exciting subjects like cleaning and maintenance. For one long day in the street like we're doing here, it's a magic stick for blowing holes in people, so only point it at people who need holes in them, but if they do, put a hole in them quick. 'Kay?"

" 'Kay. And thanks."

When they had all had a rest, a long drink of water, a sandwich, and a well-guarded trip behind the bushes, Lenny said, "Time to get rolling again, I guess," and they were back at it.

It was about ten A.M., and they were looking for a good place for their next rest stop, when they saw another living human being—an old man in tattered clothes pushing a grocery cart. He waved at them in a friendly way, hollered "They ain't got nothing at Rescue, I'm tryin' Salvation Army," and kept going.

"How much of all this do you suppose he's noticed?" Heather asked.

"Everything or nothing," Sherry said, "that's what most of them are like. Some of them are at the public library all day and are better informed than most congressmen, even if their take on things veers into weird; and some of them, if ten-legged aliens landed at noon, they'd have forgotten it by the time they started looking for their afternoon bottle."

"You sound like you know your way around."

"I used to be in social services. Went down into bad places with just my cell phone. Plus, of course, all the police in DC to get my middle-class ass out of there if anything went south. So I spent some time around bums."

"Aren't you supposed to call them the homeless?"

"Different beat from mine. I was dealing with the crazy guys that bother pedestrians; mostly the homeless are people and families that are managing in shelters, or relatives' basements, or cheap hotels. My guys were bums—harder to help but more entertaining, that's how Stan used to put it."

She wasn't crying, and seemed to be all right. Lenny glanced at Heather, then tried, "I didn't know Stan very well, but we used to visit now and then. He had me teach Dennis some gun safety, because he said there were always guns around and Stan didn't want Denny to be afraid of them, the way he was."

Sherry nodded. "That was Stan. Never sure when to be idealistic and when to be practical. I'm going to miss him. I'm glad you guys took me out of there. If there's a life to come and all that shit, if I'd just stayed there and mourned until someone killed me, Stan'd've been so *pissed* at me."

"Practical," Lenny agreed. "We should get rolling."

They saw children who didn't seem to have anyone to be with, a young mother with a baby who wouldn't come close enough to them to talk, and some small groups of armed people who kept their distance.

"Wonder how many of those are out looting and robbing, and how many are preventing it?" Heather said, after a group of three men with pistols and bats had traded waves with them.

"And how many start out to do one and end up doing the other?" Lenny said.

Just after eleven A.M., a biohazard Hummer turned a corner in front of them and came to a stop. A man in a black suit with well-shined shoes got out. "Cameron Nguyen-Peters sent me out to fetch you," he said. "And to tell you you could at least have tried a pay phone, or flashing Morse code, or something."

Those last few minutes were surreal; suddenly the trip that should have taken the rest of the day took less than ten minutes. The air was just the right temperature, there was cool clean water for all of them, and on their way along the parkway, shots were fired at them twice.

"That didn't happen while we were walking," Heather said.

The driver shrugged. "When you were walking, you looked like people; now you look like the Man."

ABOUT HALF AN HOUR LATER. PALE BLUFF, ILLINOIS. 10:30 A.M. CST. THURSDAY, OCTOBER 31.

Carol May Kloster wondered if anyone had even thought, yet, about what they'd do for record keeping when they ran out of pencils, since as far as anyone could tell, every single ballpoint pen in Pale Bluff, Illinois, had turned to goo in the last week.

She also wondered if there was really any point in taking down the report from the Food Committee tonight; surely their own records should suffice, without her taking dictation? Especially when George Auvergne had such a knack for going on.

So far the news was that there were enough apples stored,

and they probably would not need to commandeer more basements. They were lucky that Pale Bluff had been an orchard town for a hundred years, and luckier still that forty boxcars of just-harvested apples had been waiting on the siding, not yet off to the national market.

According to Linda Beckham, the town's one dietician, there were calories enough in all those apples, enough vitamin pills had been salvaged from plastic bottles thanks to a smart pharmacist, and the local hunters and fishermen could bring in enough deer, pheasants, and small game with rifles from the local black-powder club for enough protein; they'd make it through without starvation or significant malnutrition. If the winter was cold, ice fishermen could help out, and they were talking to a Hutterite community up the road about trading apples for cheese.

As the only person in town who still knew Gregg shorthand, and therefore could take accurate minutes (*take that, iScribe!* she thought), Carol May had job security but she was probably doomed to be the only person who listened all the way through each meeting. She wondered whether what she had done in a previous life had been good or bad.

The Community Kitchen Committee was figuring they could keep everyone fed until June, when early beets and radishes would start coming in. The Planting Committee had located enough seed potatoes and corn. The Poultry Committee reported that there'd be eggs enough around July, and at least some chickens for the table by fall next year. They had a plan for seeing if they could capture and pen wild ducks as well.

The last committee to report was Amusements. Mrs. Martinez pointed out that the candy for the Pale Bluff Community Halloween Party was already on hand, and some children already had costumes; "I was thinking, it's Halloween tonight, why don't we just let the kids have a last rampage at the candy? There won't be any more for a long time, and it wouldn't be bad to put a little extra fat on the kids for the winter—"

Reverend Walters got up and started yelling about how Halloween and Satan were behind Daybreak. After a moment, Carol May decided to just note down "Reverend Walters objected." It looked like she'd be eating lunch on the second shift again.

**ABOUT 45 MINUTES LATER. ST. ELIZABETH'S FACILITY,
WASHINGTON, DC. 2:15 P.M. EST. THURSDAY, OCTOBER 31.**

"Mr. Nguyen-Peters," Mason's voice said, over the intercom, "the President's limo is pulling into the driveway."

Cam's lips tightened, and he nodded slightly. Heather thought, *If I were Cam, I'd be thinking, "There's about two hundred phones left that work in the whole government, and we have two of them, and Shaunsen can't call us first?"* It seemed of a piece with using the limo; tires survived about a day without peroxide wipedowns, and maybe three days with, yet the Acting President drove everywhere in Washington. He said it was to improve his visibility; *to mobs and snipers, I hope.*

Well, this is why Cam has his job. With no more than that momentary wince, he stood up, slipped his jacket back on, tightened his tie, and was ready.

Graham Weisbrod looked up and said, "In case we don't resume soon, are we're agreed that it's a priority to get any captured Daybreakers into a secure interview situation with Arnie?"

"Absolutely," Cameron said. "You're right that we can't settle whether Daybreak was a system artifact or a foreign enemy until we can look inside it. Definitely we need to understand Daybreak more than—"

The door flew open. Secret Service and Marine guards moved in, stepping to the side. Then two men in black uniforms with red berets entered, shouting, "Ladies and gentlemen, the President of the United States!"

So these were the National Unity Guard that Shaunsen had put together from young Democratic Party staffers and members of some community groups; *nice muscles and tats, but they sure look slobby standing next to Marines and Secret Service,* Heather thought. As far as anyone could tell, it was a patronage job; presidential cheerleaders, mostly job-needing sons of important supporters. Somehow he'd found the time to do that in the middle of the country blowing to hell. *Now that's time management.*

The National Unity Guards turned to flank the doorway and clapped rhythmically as Shaunsen came in. Well, at least the routine didn't finish up with "Yay, go Prez!"

Shaunsen all but bounded into the room. "Sorry I didn't call in advance but I was already down at this end of town, and I just happened to have an idea I wanted to run by you all. I think we need to create a new Cabinet secretary post—the Department of Information."

The silence among the little group of men and women would have devastated a man who was paying attention.

"I just saw the hatchet job that little shit Manckiewicz did on the exclusive interview I gave him, and it seems to me that with media down to the *Advertiser-Gazette*, Radio Blue and Gold, and KP-1, what we have here is a near monopoly that needs some administration and regulation. Rusty Parlotta was a whiny, complaining, out-of-control hippie when I was first in Congress, and she hasn't improved one bit since. And Manckiewicz is a fucking Republican, you can tell it. Now if there's one thing we depend on in the present emergency, it's the flow of accurate government information to—"

"Mr. President," Cameron said, quietly, with just enough force to stop Shaunsen. "Radio Blue and Gold is a government outlet, the *Advertiser-Gazette* is printing every announcement we ask them to even though they don't have the ad revenue to remotely cover the added printing, and KP-1 runs our announcements constantly. And the First Amendment—"

"Of course we'll have full First Amendment rights for every licensed media outlet," Shaunsen said, nodding. "You're right, that's very important."

"What I'm saying, sir, is that Constitutionally—"

"That's what I have a Solicitor General for. He's figuring out what I can and can't do, and if I've been breaking the rules, he'll get back to me in a few weeks. Now, here's the other big issue I'm worried about. I'm getting concerned about how much power the military is accumulating. Over one of your ham radio links just today, the governor of Alabama, can you imagine that, actually asking for Federal troops to take over Birmingham—"

"Satellite photos show a double row of barricades zigzagging across the city, and bodies lying unburied between them, Mr. President. The governor can't move the Alabama Guard anywhere even if he could call them out. He was probably just hoping that you could give him some options—"

"Oh, the Pentagon would just *love* to hear that. They've always really wanted to run the country—"

"Nonsense, sir." Cam, Heather, and everyone else in the room turned to stare at Weisbrod. "DoD like being big. They like expensive toys. They like being busy. They want to feel that they're the most important thing going. They tend to think everyone and everything else is secondary or unnecessary. But as for running the country, they clearly don't *want* the job. In that regard, they're no different from the Department of Education."

"Or the Department of the Future?" Shaunsen plainly intended that as a shot.

"Well, except we've never been big."

"But your new buddy here"—Shaunsen pointed at Cameron as if he were a bad dog—"is fixing that, isn't he?"

Cam said, "Sir, the Department of the Future has been exceptionally helpful and done an exemplary job, so yes, I've tended to use them. We've got a situation that is way too big, right now. Anyone who can help, helps, and like everybody else, where the armed forces have been able to help, they've been great but hopelessly inadequate—just like the post office or anyone else in what's left of the Federal government."

"You know," Shaunsen said, "I had the impression that the job of the NCCC is to hand over the White House to the correct President or Acting President, then get out of the way. That's what Directive 51 says. And it's a presidential directive; I don't need Congress, I can issue a new one any time. I wonder if you haven't been using a lot of your NCCC powers even though now we have an Acting President."

Cam stood as stiffly as if he'd been given an electric shock. "I assure you, Mr. President, everything I am doing—*everything*—is in my role as chief of staff to DHS, and with the full authorization and knowledge of Secretary Ferein."

"Good. Then let *me* assure *you*, I have lawyers, and we'll make sure it all *stays* Constitutional." He looked like he was trying to fix Cameron with a stern, warning glare, but Cameron just stood there, not responding at all, and after a moment it was Shaunsen who turned away. "So Cameron, Graham—and the rest of you—give some serious thought to what the responsibilities for our new Secretary of Information ought to be, and what we need to do to de-involve the military in the post-Daybreak emergency." He turned to go.

Weisbrod said, "Mr. President, may I ask a major favor? I haven't been able to look in on Roger Pendano since his illness. If you could give me a lift to the White House, we could talk more about your ideas, and I'd have time to pay my old friend a visit, and still walk back here before dark."

"Well, I've got quite a bit of work to do in the car, of course, but I'll try to make some time to talk." Shaunsen went out first, to the rhythmic clapping of the National Unity Guard; Graham followed with the Secret Service and Marines, who closed the door behind the party.

"Has anyone told him he's the Acting President, not the acting emperor?" Heather asked.

Cam winced. "Don't make my job harder. You know Weisbrod; what do you suppose your boss was up to?"

"Improvising and seeing if he can improve matters, plus he really is worried sick about Pendano."

"Well, I wish him luck. When he comes back, if you see him before I do, send him to me; I'd like to hear what's going on in the White House." He sighed and looked around the room. "For the record, I am acting as the Chief of Staff for the Department of Homeland Security, and I have not—since Acting President Shaunsen took office—exercised any power as NCCC. If in any of your opinions that isn't true—either now or in the future—tell me at once. In front of others if you feel it's necessary, and don't forget to copy KP-1 and the *Advertiser-Gazette* on that. We are going to come through this process with our Constitution intact, and so far we have bent it less than Andrew Jackson, Abraham Lincoln, or Franklin Roosevelt did, and I regret even as much as we've had to do. The Constitution stands. End of message, reply not expected, that's all folks."

Heather thought she'd never seen a harsher message greeted with more smiles. *Still, this would probably be a bad time to tell Cam he'd make a good dictator.*

ABOUT THE SAME TIME. CASTLE CASTRO. (SAN DIEGO, CALIFORNIA.) 12:04 P.M. PST. THURSDAY, OCTOBER 31.

The guard at the main gate was nice and polite even before he saw *David Carlucci and Family*, and *Larry Mensche and Family*, on the guest list that Bambi had submitted. "You'll be glad to know," he said, "that Mr. Bolton's family joined us earlier, and of course we're glad to have all of you—let me just get full names and relationships for everyone—"

Carlucci nodded. "David Ignatius and Arlene Mather Carlucci, we're married, and these are our son Track Palin Carlucci, and daughter Ann Coulter Carlucci." The two teenagers looked embarrassed; the boy said, "My friends call me Paley," and the guard added *(Paley)* after the entry.

"And they call me Acey," Ann said, "like the initials but A-C-E-Y."

"They do not, you made that up, you just *want* them to—"

"Here at Castle Castro, we will call you Acey," the guard said, firmly, "since you want us to. And Mr. Mensche, is there just you?"

"Lorenzo Isaac Mensche," Mensche said. "And call me Larry. Just me, my ex is someplace in Nevada and our grown daughter is up in Oregon. And—uh, excuse my asking, but what the hell do you suppose that is?"

The grinding and squealing sounds from the wheelchair itself were only part of the effect; the tires had been replaced with what looked like a wrapping of old socks, and behind it, a bicycle kid-trailer, with more sock-wrapped wheels, held bottles of beer and cans of Spam piled in a jumble on top of a sleeping bag. Both the wheelchair and trailer sported jaunty American flags, and the man in the wheelchair looked about as much as one can look like a biblical patriarch with a samurai sword on his lap and a shotgun hanging from a strap.

"Hi." His grin was immense. "My name's Patrick Lamont O'Grainne, and I believe I have a reservation."

The guard glanced down, and said, "Another Bambi Castro guest. Of course. Even when she was in high school, Ms. Castro always brought in the most interesting people." He drew his semaphore flags and began sending to the next station up the hill. "We're very glad to have you all here."

ABOUT THE SAME TIME. WASHINGTON, DC. 3:08 P.M. EST. THURSDAY, OCTOBER 31.

"I really appreciate the ride, and the chance to talk with you privately," Graham Weisbrod said, pushing his glasses up his nose and peering intently at Shaunsen.

"Well, there's so much to get done," Shaunsen said. "We've got a crisis here, and if we play it right, it'll be the New Deal all over again, with a Democratic majority for the next—"

"Mr. President, I'm as loyal a Democrat as you are, sir, and we are *not* going to win this election—"

Shaunsen shook his head. "Crises come and crises go, Secretary Weisbrod, but Americans always want hope, and we are the party of hope. That's one of the problems with your whole Department of the Future; it's unnecessary and trivial. Everything that really matters goes on forever. When things get smashed up, the country rebuilds, and the Democrats lead it. Sure, it's bad right now. It was bad when the Depression hit, and after Pearl Harbor, and after the Federal Reserve bombings. But times like this are when we show the voters we can make the money move and get things done."

All right, I'm going to hate myself if I don't try, so here goes. "Mr. President, do you realize that we can't reliably deliver mail from here to Richmond, there are now fifteen states from which we have only had satellite photos in the last twenty-four hours, all communication is down with Ottawa and Mexico City, let alone Europe or Asia . . . and we have people going hungry ten blocks from the White House because *there isn't any food*—"

"If Congress acts fast, we'll have the money—"

"You can create the money, but they can't eat it." *Good God alive, I feel like his reality therapist. If the National Unity Guards there weren't giving me the fish-eye I'd slap the son of a bitch, I swear to god I would.* "No one in the Northeast urban strip from Boston to Richmond can reach adequate shelter or food in time. Within a week, the first bad storm is going to kill tens of millions of Americans at a minimum. Right now, the best hope we've got is that there are little towns all over the country managing to organize things within a few miles of themselves, and we're only hearing about them from ham radio operators who are just barely managing to keep their stations on the air—"

"Every one of those little towns will see a nice big grant, I guarantee it, for all the good work they're doing." Shaunsen reached out and touched his knee. "Graham, you are such a sad *worrier*, and the public always wants a happy *warrior*. We'll make it all work, and the economy is going to take off like a rocket once we get these programs running. You'll see. I've always said, you think about the future so much, you don't see the long run."

The limo zigged and zagged past the wrecks on the street; no one came out to look at it, perhaps intimidated by the Secret Service, perhaps just not caring about it anymore.

40 MINUTES LATER. THE WHITE HOUSE, WASHINGTON, DC. ABOUT 4:00 P.M. EST. THURSDAY, OCTOBER 31.

Forty minutes since Weisbrod arrived at the White House, and he'd spent all of it sitting in the Secret Service break room while the people dithered about allowing him in to see Roger Pendano. The Secret Service people were pleasant, polite, and much less formal than he'd ever seen them, but his thoughts were mostly on his old student. *What if he's so far gone in madness, he can't recognize anyone? What if—*

One of the Secret Service returned to the room and said, "Secretary Weisbrod, I'm supposed to take you to see President Pendano now. The doctor wants you to know he's not in the best shape. He said you should go as soon as the president starts to look tired or sick, because his health is precarious. Okay?"

"You've got it. He was my friend a long time before he was president, I won't do anything to endanger or hurt him."

"Just passing it along because the doctor told me to, sir. Right this way."

Two years ago Pendano had said he did not want to live in rooms where the First Lady had spent her last few months dying, and that any living space more than a comfortable minimum made him feel like he was "rattling around with no place to be." He had moved up from the traditional Second Floor to the Third, into a bedroom with space for clothes and bed, with an adjoining sitting room for reading and watching television. They had put in a small kitchen so he could have food without bothering people, and a connecting door to a tiny guest bedroom for rare visits from his grown daughter. The mostly unoccupied floor below him gave him the quiet he craved.

The Secret Service agent escorting him upstairs had told Weisbrod that Shaunsen was already living in the traditional Presidential Quarters on the second floor, taking measurements and sketching. Weisbrod didn't think he'd ever before heard a sarcastic tone from a Secret Service agent.

Weisbrod had been here a few times before Daybreak. Every so often, during the last couple of years, the president had invited Weisbrod; Peggy Albarado, the Secretary of Peace; Laura Pressman, the Secretary of Education; and Vice President Samuelson up to his sitting room to talk about "ideas and the long run and where everything really ought to go" while they killed a couple of bottles of good bourbon. He had called them his "Liquor Cabinet."

The Secret Service man led Weisbrod to the door, nodded politely, and said, "Help him if you can, sir. We all want him to get better."

"Thanks." Weisbrod knocked. He interpreted the vague grunt from inside as "come in."

The man who sat on the couch looked more like the mummified remains of Roger Pendano than anything else. *God, on Monday he was fine, and it's only Thursday!*

"Roger?" Weisbrod sat next to him, and turned on the lamp.

The president's skin was a sick tone of gray, the lines of his face seemed to have deepened by a good ten years, and his eyes were half-closed; he hadn't really even looked up to see that it was Weisbrod. Tentatively, Graham reached out and rubbed a shoulder; slowly, Pendano turned, and then jumped.

"You think I just appeared."

"Yeah, yeah, I . . . Graham?"

"It's me, Mr. President."

"Am I . . ." Pendano looked deeply frustrated. "I'm supposed to make sure about my pills. I think that's after you go. And I took the ones for when you're here." His eyes looked desperate.

Weisbrod stood, taking the president's hand. He led him over to the pill bottles and pointed. The president nodded, and pointed to the bottle of little red pills. "Just had those a little bit ago." He pointed to the big white ones. "All the time, and supposed to take one right after you go." He was panting, and sweat beaded on his forehead from the effort of walking to the table.

Weisbrod pulled out his personal notepad and pen, and wrote:

> They are giving you very large doses of barbiturates.
> They just gave you speed to wake you up.
> Dangerous for you?????
> →

The president nodded his head vigorously. Next to Graham's arrow he scribbled, *Last EKG worse thn we told press, kidney failure 2 . . .*

He stopped to catch his breath; sweat was actually dripping from his forehead. Weisbrod put a hand on his back and helped him stand straighter; bringing the pad along, he walked the president to the couch. Weisbrod cleaned Pendano's face with a wet cloth from the bathroom, and loosened his belt and tie.

"I feel better," Pendano said, softly, writing, *They started drugs rt after Shaunsen came.*

Need to get off them? Weisbrod wrote.

Can palm/spit out. Somthn 4 DTs?

"I'm glad you're feeling so much better. I'm pretty sure we can do something to help you get well; I'll try to stop by more often." He pointed at the note about DTs and nodded vigorously; Pendano extended his hand, and they shook.

They passed more notes, but Pendano was already exhausted. Weisbrod got him to drink as much water as he could hold. *So much crap to wash out of him, I don't know what else we can do.*

He made sure all the notes and the pad they'd been written on were in his pockets before he left, after scribbling one more. Firmly, he told Roger, "I'll be back, tomorrow if I can, but at least every other day and as often as I can. We're going to get you well, Roger." He wrapped Roger up in his arms, pressed his mouth to the man's ear, and barely breathed, "You were my best. You were always my best. We need you again, Roger, do this for us."

There were tears in the president's eyes, but he nodded vigorously and his handshake was surprisingly firm.

On his way out, Weisbrod showed the Secret Service man a note folded to leave the top line visible: ABOUT GETTING THE PRESIDENT WELL.

The man took the note and it vanished; Weisbrod just had to hope he had picked the right guy to pass it to. *Christ, Christ it's more like Imperial Rome than I could have imagined.*

At the door, they issued him a .38 police revolver, and made sure he knew how to use it. *Pity I didn't have this, riding over with Shaunsen; I could have done the best thing ever did for the United States.* He checked his watch and the sun; if he pushed himself and if his sneakers didn't fall apart on the way (he had a spare pair of leather shoes, not as comfortable but more durable in the new world, in his bag), he might make it back to St. Elizabeth's with daylight left; the worst would be crossing on the Capitol Street bridge, with nowhere to run if he were ambushed.

As he hurried past the Capitol, he saw a familiar figure from many dinner parties and interviews in a long public life. He waved and shouted, "Hi, Rusty! I like the paper!"

"Hey, Secretary Weisbrod! I see you're using Washington public transit like we all are. I'll be sure to report the gesture." He had thought she was walking dogs, but saw she had three goats with her. Seeing his start, she said, "I live close, and laugh all you want, this is a fair bit of cheese right here." She grinned. "Say something quotable."

He gestured at the Capitol building. "What better place find a bunch of old goats supplying the press with cheese?"

"Dammit, you're the fourth guy who said something like that."

"We can't afford just any old future!"

"That's the Weisbrod I remember. Have a good night!"

He hurried on into the dark canyons between the office buildings, staying in the middle of the street and away from the abandoned cars where someone might jump out, and thought, *Goats on the National Mall.*

The only lights visible as he crossed the Capitol Street

bridge in the dusk, looking up and down the Anacostia, were the Coleman lanterns of the sentries in the Navy Yard and at Fort McNair.

I guess it's a good night at that. The gun I have to carry in my pocket while on official duties probably works. A bad night would be one when I needed it to and it didn't.

I wonder if Romulus Augustulus had a futurologist, and what it was like for him to trot through the dark, deserted streets of Rome.

ABOUT THE SAME TIME. THE WHITE HOUSE, WASHINGTON, DC. 6:30 P.M. EST. THURSDAY, OCTOBER 31.

Roger Pendano looked down at the collection of meds in front of him and thought, *All right, last week, I was taking two a day of the green one, for blood pressure. Now there are four of the green one, three times a day, plus two big whites. So that'll be one green down the hatch, and the rest down the toilet.*

He was starting to feel sweaty and sick, and he probably would not sleep tonight. So what? It would make it easier to act groggy and out of it tomorrow, and *anyway, I have it coming.*

THE NEXT DAY. WASHINGTON, DC. (DRET/ST. ELIZABETH'S.) 7:00 A.M. EST. FRIDAY, NOVEMBER 1.

For a former conference room with a bed from a nearby hotel dragged into it, and a coat of black paint on the interior window for privacy, it wasn't nearly as bad as it might have been. With no water to spare for showers—there was barely enough for drinking, cooking, and periodic toilet flushes—Cam had lined up enough hydrogen peroxide and baby wipes so that she could thoroughly bathe Lenny and have enough left over to at least wipe herself down. "Cam said not to spare the wipes on yourself," Lenny reminded her.

"One date fifteen years ago, and the man thinks he can tell me how I smell."

"Actually, he said—"

"Yeah, I know, babe. It makes sense. I have to stay clean because you're going to be touching me. I was making a joke." She ostentatiously took one more wipe from the glass cookie jar and scrubbed herself carefully.

"What was so fascinating about that jar?"

"Oh, just thinking it's like the ones in a little coffeehouse in Myrtle Beach, where I like to stop when I'm driving south—and realizing I might never travel that far again."

"I think you're clean enough down there, and I don't have any plastic parts that are going to get close to it."

"Hah. Only because you haven't seen some of my favorite tricks."

"Well, whose fault is that?"

She liked his smile a lot, so it seemed like a good time to bring the big subject up. "I'm going to suggest something so stupid that I can't believe I'm proposing it, so don't laugh at me. It involves you and me being in love."

"Then tell me. You know I won't laugh."

"I want to give up birth control."

"You do remember I might die of plastic rot next week?"

"I can't forget it. Or that I'm turning forty next year and a whole lot of things they used to be able to do so that a person could be a mother late in life are going to be impossible. Or that I've had one lover in my life whose genes I'd be happy to carry."

He gestured across his whole body.

"Lenny, you told me—I know it's not genetic."

"They don't *think*. You want to bet on some *doctor's* opinion?"

"Shit, yes, and absolutely, Lenny. *Now*—while the knowledge is still current and you're alive. You said all the tests show you have normal DNA. If you live—and I want you to, so bad, you know—well, you and I will raise a kid. If you don't—over the last few thousand years, how many people got started because a soldier had only one more night at home? Or a gunfighter, or a matador, or anyone in any dangerous occupation? Dad tells me his grandma was a coal miner's wife, and she never missed a chance with her husband, figuring it could always be the last." She looked at him a little sideways. "Uh, given how much care you've had to take of your health, just to ask—have you ever had the experience unprotected?"

"No, actually. Never had a relationship last long enough—"

"Well, this relationship is going to last the rest of your life, which ought to be long enough."

"The rest of my life?"

"Three days or forty years, I'm the one that's going to be there. And you really ought to experience skin-to-skin, more than once, and I'm getting old to start a family but, honestly, Lenny, what the hell? Now watch close, because I happen to love the way you look at me when I'm naked." She ran her hands up her sides, delighted that he was too distracted to continue arguing.

ABOUT AN HOUR LATER. ST. PAUL, MINNESOTA.
7:30 A.M. CST. FRIDAY, NOVEMBER 1.

Strong winds, running thousands of miles ahead of the storm front that was still crossing British Columbia, blew across the Midwest that morning.

St. Paul died of bad luck. A gasoline truck, its contents not yet turned to vinegar or sewage by biotes, had lost its tires and been stranded in front of a T-shirt shop on Snelling Avenue. The owner of the shop, who had not been making any money for at least a year anyway, had departed around noon the day before, slinging up a pack to walk south toward Rochester, where his sister lived. He had left the door unlocked in the back to let people come in out of the cold.

One family had found that unlocked door; that morning, with no breakfast and the water not running, the mother had smoked her last cigarette down to the filter, pinched it out, and thrown it into the wastebasket, where it had smoldered among damp paper towels, old advertising, and some near-empty cans of fabric paint.

The towels nearest the butt dried, and began to burn. The battery smoke detector, not yet eaten by nanoswarm, wailed for a while, and went out. The burning paper towel spread to an old catalog; the old catalog set off some of the fumes from the fabric paint, and the scraps and paper in the basket acted as wicks for the rest.

Anyone in the shop could have put the three-foot-high flames out by pouring a couple of glasses of water into the wastebasket, but there was no one. Sparks from the waste-basket spread to the hanging T-shirts; hanging fabric is very highly flammable, with its enormous exposure of surface area to available oxygen, but the T-shirts were packed so tightly that only the top surfaces caught, and smoldered slowly in the inadequate airflow. Even now, if anyone had walked in, they would have smelled the smoke, pulled the shirts out of the rack, and stomped them out.

No one came; the streets outside were empty, the work-ers not at work, the mobile residents long since headed out of the city to find somewhere with food and heat, leaving only those who could not move easily—families with young children, the disabled, the old, the mad, the fatally stubborn.

The fire in the wastebasket had died out by the time that the top of one T-shirt burned through, so that the shirt dropped from its hanger, its fall fanning it to flames that licked at the bottoms of the shirts surrounding the gap it had left in the rack; that formed a small chimney, which enlarged as flames raced up the hanging surfaces.

In less than a minute the rack was ablaze. Flames roared up against the ceiling and along the acoustic tile. The metal block in the sprinkler overhead melted, as it was supposed to do, but only the bare dribble of water left in the pipe came out—not nearly enough.

The flames leaped from rack to rack, now, a new rack ev-ery few seconds, till the whole shop was hotter than a pizza oven. It grew hot enough to soften the cheap metal fittings, then hot enough to ignite the posters on the walls by radiative heat. Finally it was hot enough to crack the big front window and let out a jet of the white-hot carbon monoxide and partly burned hydrocarbons extracted from the T-shirts and carpets by anoxic roasting.

That hot gas mixed with the outside air and exploded; the explosion shattered the window. Hot gas and air mixed and exploded. Flames roared three stories high. The back door blew wide open hard enough to rip it from its hinges.

Now air could flow from front to back, and in the after-math of the gas explosion, it rushed in to fill the vacuum. The draft through the shop, with all the fuel well above kindling and waiting only for the oxygen, worked like a blowtorch White-hot flame poured over and around the abandonec gasoline truck. In minutes, the heat brought the gasoline to a boil, pressurizing the truck with flammable vapors; the hull of the tank grew hotter and hotter until finally the vapor flashed over, and the explosion sprayed just over thirty tons of gasoline into the air and ignited it; every building for two blocks around began to burn.

The fire watch on the steeple of the big old Presbyterian Church on Ayd Mill saw the explosion and flames, and as ordered, she rang the bell and shouted down to the two boys who were her runners. Neither of the fire stations they reached could help; one had no working fire truck, and the other discovered that the hoses they would need to pull water from the little creek and pond half a mile away were rotted. The boys ran back and forth so that the fire chief with the working truck would know to head for the fire station with the unrotted hose.

By the time both fire crews were loading the clean hose onto the hastily-wiped-down truck, the wall of flame whipping westward from Snelling was four blocks long and widening, and advancing at about a block every ten minutes. One truck pumping water from half a mile away wouldn't have been able to make much of a difference when the fire started; now the whole idea was ludicrous. They evacuated the equipment from the path of the fire; only the haphazard firebreaks formed by freeways and big parking lots stood between the conflagration and downtown St. Paul, and as the wind rose steadily that afternoon, tens of millions of sparks were drifting across them, and some were finding new, flammable homes on the other side.

ABOUT SEVEN HOURS LATER. CASTLE CASTRO. (SAN DIEGO, CALIFORNIA.) 2:09 P.M. PST. FRIDAY, NOVEMBER 1.

"So that's the story," Bambi said, very quietly to Carlucci, Bolton, and Mensche. "There's one radio room here, and it's Dad's, and he decides what signals go out. And I know from long, long experience what he's figuring out at the moment—how far can he push before the Feds push back. Once he has that analyzed, then he'll either be gentle as a kitten, or look the hell out."

"It sounds like your father has been preparing for Daybreak his whole life," Carlucci said.

"Yeah. He's anything but a Daybreaker—more of an old-fashioned Ayn Rand type than anything else, with a mixture of Robert A. Heinlein and probably Sir Walter Scott too—but you could say Daybreak is fulfilling pretty much every dream he ever had. In five years people will be addressing him as 'Baron' or something like it, at his insistence. It's what he's really always wanted.

"So, here's the thing. He'll create law and order all around Castle Castro, and probably extend it up and down the coast—I doubt he'll worry about where the border is, let alone the county line. People in his sphere will eat and have somewhere safe to sleep. I don't for a moment suggest that anyone else ought to take over. But . . . Roth is the only Daybreaker we've captured so far. She's a priceless source of information. Do we want the Federal government to have to go through my crazy Baron Dad to access the most important witness it has?"

"So what did you have in mind?" Carlucci asked.

"Is there a covert, hidden-inside-the-message code you can send to the Bureau in Washington? Something to tell them that you need to be ordered to move Roth to somewhere else? Because I've got a place, and it's one Dad will accept. Quattro Larsen, who freeholds Castle Larsen up by Jenner, will pretty much do whatever I tell him—no snickering and giggling about why! Dad will be delighted if I'm ordered to go up there because he's been trying to set me up with Quattro since I was thirteen, and Quattro and I have had a covert code since we were teenagers, so I can set that up with him too."

"Well, put that way, of course," Carlucci said. "Hell yes. How will we get her there?"

"It's going to be a one-way trip, so it probably isn't we," she said. "You don't want to leave your family here, and the same consideration rules out Terry. So it should be Larry and me."

"Where's Jenner?" Larry asked.

"Near the mouth of the Russian River, north of San Fran. Plenty of time to explain once we're on our way."

Mensche looked thoughtful. "My daughter, Debbie, is a screwed-up drug addict who has never finished any schooling or held a job, and she's doing three-strikes time at Coffee Creek."

"Oregon?" *How to spot a Fed,* Bambi thought. *We know all the big state pens.*

"Yeah. Up till this week, she didn't write or call and didn't want me to. Her mom would go over from Nevada a couple times a year to see her and send me short notes about her, mostly just that she's healthy, and not getting out anytime soon. I—well, I'm worried, because I just hope someone remembered to do something for the prisoners when things started to crash, even if it was just to leave doors unlocked. I worry about that. I want to know she's okay—"

Bambi nodded. "And I'll get you almost halfway to Coffee Creek. And Quattro can give you a lot of help too, and he will if I ask him." She reached out and touched his shoulder. "We'll find out what's happening with Debbie and make sure she's okay." She glanced back at Carlucci. "Well, there you have it. Roth goes because she belongs to the Feds, and we can't leave her here with a Baron of San Diego who intends to be the Duke of California someday. Larry goes because it's a one-way trip, and it gets him closer to his family."

"Why are *you* going?" Carlucci demanded. "And how?"

She smiled at him, focusing her warm Miss Used to Do Beauty Contests Beam into his eyes. "Well, I had enough trouble with the old tyrant when I was just his daughter; I'm not sticking around to find out what it's like to be his heir and vassal. And somebody's gotta sail the boat."

THE NEXT DAY. WASHINGTON, DC. ABOUT 2:00 A.M. EST. SATURDAY, NOVEMBER 2.

Despite what the rest of the country knows in its bones, *some* of the people in Washington are responsible sorts who are capable of forethought; they began to leave when the electricity stopped coming back up, while some cars and trucks were still running. Their disappearance made things inconvenient and difficult for the less foresighted, who, seeing things deteriorate quickly, left soon after, making things still worse for the remaining people with even shorter time horizons.

Around midnight, a tipping point was passed. National leaders and government personnel had withdrawn into safe places like the DRET compound at St. Elizabeth's. Ordinary citizens had fled, if possible, knowing what was coming.

At two A.M. the people left were the completely immobile, the stupid, the stubborn, and people without foresight or impulse control.

Crowds in the street were hungry and looking for excitement. The remaining inventories of booze and bling in stores and warehouses were unguarded. Nearly all police had deserted; hardly any of the unlucky people left in ordinary residences were capable of defending them. Some of the boldest and most impetuous of the street crowds broke shop windows; no one stopped them from carrying off liquor and jewelry (white crusts and foul odors around the electronics kept them mostly untouched). Bartenders and bouncers died; doors and windows broke; the cornered innocent died with nowhere to run; recalcitrant defenders burned in their refuges; and authority did not show up.

When the remaining population in the streets fully understood this, like a hot room flashing over when a window breaks, like an auction stampede when the last lot is up, destruction and violence spread through the city.

Washington was still the capital. Federal law-enforcement people and military units moved in and backed up the few surviving city forces; units of the Maryland and Virginia Guard joined them, and not long after dawn, the rioters had been swept into a few large holding areas, fire lanes cleared to isolate the big fires, and a sort of order restored, especially in the area close to the National Mall.

Tens of thousands of bodies lay in the wreckage, or unburied in the streets. Some blocks burned for days, unattended. Countless old people, children, bedridden patients, people whose powered wheelchairs had stopped running, and the few brave people who would not desert them, died buried in rubble, smothered in smoke, or roasted alive. Great scars of tumbled buildings, toppled poles and posts, and broken concrete slashed into the heart of the great city. And in a few large auditoriums, stadiums, and office buildings, tens of thousands of people who had formed the mob, or fled one mob and been caught up in another, or just gone out to see what was happening, were held there by the guns of the guards, waiting in hunger and despair for whatever might come. The horror was: nothing did.

Midmorning of the next day, when he was briefed on the situation, Peter Shaunsen, Acting President of the United States, asked three questions: Was anyone interested in being on the rebuilding commission? Could some of the fire lanes be cleared and paved into boulevards or malls to beautify the city? And what was being done to ensure that everyone who was not dead was able to vote?

A Secret Service man who was at the meeting skipped his next shift to walk over to see Chris Manckiewicz at the *Washington Advertiser-Gazette*. He expected to be fired when he returned, but no one even asked about his absence, so he just picked up his gear and went to his post.

SIXTEEN HOURS LATER. OFF THE CALIFORNIA COAST, ABOUT TWENTY MILES WEST OF THE MOUTH OF THE RUSSIAN RIVER. 2:30 P.M. PST. SATURDAY, NOVEMBER 2.

Ysabel was "not what you could call a natural sailor," Bambi said, not for the first time, to Mensche. The Pacific is choppy in the fall, but nonetheless, most people got some kind of sea legs after a day on the sea.

Bambi had adjusted to the constant retching noises from the girl hanging over the railing. As they had worked their way north, the waves got a little bigger, heralding a storm forming far up toward Alaska, but the prisoner seemed no worse, or at least she had no more to expel.

"At least she's not a flight risk right now," Larry Mensche pointed out. He *had* turned out to be a natural sailor; she'd taught him to hold a course by the compass, allowing her to get long naps all along the way, so that she was in much better shape than she had expected to be.

"I can see why people like this," he observed. "But I'm guessing this is perfect weather, right?"

"About as perfect as it gets in the fall, yeah."

A strange urking noise from the rail made Mensche scuttle forward and slap Ysabel's back a couple of times, clearing something that hadn't quite come out right, then wipe her face with a damp cloth, surprisingly gently. When he returned, Bambi said, "Considering how much of a pain in the ass to the whole world she's been, you're pretty nice to her."

"She looks a lot like Debbie," Mensche said. "So . . . even if it doesn't make any sense—"

"Naw, it makes all the sense in the world." Bambi squeezed his arm, and he nodded, appreciating the support. *One more point for the man, he can tell the difference between the pretty chick being his buddy and copping a feel.* "Hey, chances are that if your daughter needs the help, someone's taking care of her. Remember that's half the stories on KP-1—people looking after each other, communities banding together to make it through, all that. She's probably swinging a shovel on a road crew and getting one big bowl of soup a day, but she's got somewhere warm to sleep and she's safe, bet you anything." It sounded lame to Bambi even as she spoke it; she had to think, *If the guards just locked them down and walked away, how long before—*

"Yeah," Mensche said, "but I can't help worrying. Anyway, so how'd this guy end up with a name like 'Quattro,' and how'd your dad decide he was the man for you?"

She shrugged. "Our parents knew each other, very well, actually. When I was a lonely teenage girl, and he was a miserably lonely geek of an engineering student, we corresponded all the time, inventing codes to keep the old man baffled. It was years before I realized how much I'd *encouraged* the old bastard, since he thought Quattro and me must be hiding our love affair. Quattro was my lifeline; I needed someone to agree with me when I said that all the kids in my high school were stupid and worthless and superficial, especially because I was pretty and popular and a brat and a half, so I didn't have the loser support network that so many alienated kids do. Dad's plan for me to fall in love with the dashing older man and unite two Castles and two Castle-movement families, however, foundered on the fact that I'd sooner have married one of my pet llamas at the time.

"Quattro's not attractive? Nice guy but no spark?"

"Nowadays he's a damn handsome Howard Hughes type, he's only seven years older than I am, and I occasionally think about seeing whether any sparks might happen. But back then, give me a break, he was *old*, not to mention a weird geek, despite being my best friend ever—which wasn't hard back in those days, all you had to do was *like* having me for a friend. Hardly anyone else did.

"Anyway, so about his name. Quattro's parents were chronic jokers. They noticed that a lot of dumbasses didn't know that Mercedes was a girl's name and that the car was named after a major investor's daughter. That particular ignorance led, later on, to people naming their kids P-o-r-s-c-h-e instead of P-o-r-t-i-a, and even lamer baby names like Lexus and Avante, because the same dumbasses thought it was all classy and shit to name their daughter after an expensive car.

"So apparently the Larsens, being even more eccentric than my father, and maybe slightly richer, decided to sarcastically name their children after cars, figuring that all the friends they wanted to keep would get the irony. Hence Quattro. He says it was a compromise between Prius and Thunderbird.

"Anyway, Quattro was raised as one of those heroin-in-vending-machines libertarians, and they gave him his own Castle for his twenty-first birthday. I guess a Ferrari would have been too humdrum. So now he has a fortress outside Jenner that's damned near as elaborate as Dad's. You'll like him, he's pretty much post-political, good heart, nice guy . . . hunh. I *might* have to check the spark thing."

"I really appreciate your taking me along—I know you didn't have much choice, but I guess I'm glad it's me. I don't think the Federal government will last much longer."

"Dad would agree with you."

"Yeah, but he's working on it, I'm just assessing. Anyway, if they dismiss me . . . well. Just a few hundred miles to walk to Coffee Creek and see what happened to Deb, or if I can't find out there, maybe I can walk over to Reno and see if my ex knows anything. Something to do, you know?"

As they sailed on, clouds gathered to the north, and the sea rose a little every hour. Late that afternoon, the sea breeze started to blow inland. She headed the boat in toward the coast. "How exactly will you find where we're going?" Mensche asked. "Without GPS I mean? I'm assuming that weird telescope and the windup clock have something to do with it."

"I don't really need to know longitude, because we've been sticking close to the coast. Latitude is a piece of cake with an accurate clock—like the chronometer from Dad's collection, here—and this little gadget that you call the weird telescope is used to measure the angle between the sun and the horizon, or where the horizon would be if the water would hold still—that's what the level on the side here is for. So I'm sailing along a line about five seconds of latitude south of the mouth of the Russian River. That should bring me in someplace along the state beach; once I spot land, I just sail north till I see the mouth of the Russian, and in we go—Quattro's Castle is just west of Jenner, on the river, so it'll be the first Castle on our left."

"It's weird how fast people got used to 'Castles' in America."

"The Castle movement didn't start till some of the fringier rich people freaked out that Obama was president, so yeah, it's less than twenty years. Though really the house I grew up in, before Dad built the big one above the Harbor, was a Castle in all but name. Some rich guys have always built fortified big houses in isolated spots; Dad's is only noticeable because he decided to build it so close to a big city."

The weather held, and they enjoyed the last of the sandwiches and apples before they saw the coast, savoring the warmth of the sun and the crispness of the air. The late-fall-afternoon sun was still painting the coast in rich golds and deep blues as they turned north; it was not quite sunset on the river when Mensche said, "So, I guess this is where I say, 'Castle, ho!'?"

"Not advisable to call me a ho, but otherwise, yeah."

The man who met them at the pier looked like he was trying to dress as something between the Crocodile Hunter and the Veteran Surfer: khaki safari shirt, baggy knee-length shorts with too many pockets, old-style leather boots. He wore an immense hogleg of a revolver on one hip and a huge belt knife on the other. The effect was somewhat spoiled by his camo strap cap held together with a piece of shoelace where the plastic strap had been, and by a straggly brown-and-gray ponytail that would have been more in keeping with an old-school software developer or a trustafarian venture capitalist.

"Right when I thought you'd be," Quattro said, smiling. "How was the trip, Bambi?"

"Not too different from the usual except for having to dust

off a tiny bit of my celestial navigation skills. This is Special Agent Larry Mensche; and this is Quattro Larsen. And this is our prisoner, Ysabel Roth."

"Kind of a harsh introduction, isn't it? Young lady, can we parole you while you're on the grounds here? Will you give your word and keep it that you won't run away?"

Ysabel gasped, "Promise me that the world will stop bucking and rolling, and I'll do whatever you say."

As they walked up the pathway to the big house, Bambi noted dugouts, trenches, and walls to cover troops moving out from the house; two garden sheds that would make good blockhouses; and a wide-walled patio with a loopholed wall that would allow small artillery to cover the mouth of the Russian River. "You're a lot less public about your Castle than Dad is about his."

"Remember the silly commercials when we were kids? He's a PC, I'm a Mac. His fortress looks like a fortress and it's all built around its fortress-ness. My fortress just works."

Larry stopped dead and whistled. "Is that your airfield?"

"Yeah. Cool, hey?"

"I *loved* classic planes when I was a kid. Pre-jets, I mean. So, yeah, I built models of several of those. But aren't they falling apart just like everything else?"

"Parts of them are, and avgas is going to be a problem. But the really old birds are less electrical and less plastic than present-day airplanes, and their engines were built for unreliable cruddy fuel. I've had that DC-3's engines up and running on biodiesel, even long before Daybreak, because I thought regular fuel sources might be cut off. And the only thing electrical in that engine is the ignition, and I think I'll be able to replace the plastic and rubber with wood, glass, and metal. Back before there was vulcanized rubber, when they needed airtightness, they used different kinds of shellacs and oils on silk and linen, and there was the stuff called goldbeater's fabric that was basically treated gut. And as of last night, when *Arcadia* made it back here safely, I've got a couple materials scientists from Cal Poly, who are very glad to have their families safely out of the chaos, working on what we can make tires out of. I really want it for the planes, but I'm not opposed to the idea that being the re-creator of the pneumatic tire might make me richer than God."

"I can see the viewpoint," Larry said. "I don't suppose, while we're here—"

Quattro grinned. "Hey, my inner teenage geek always needs other guys's inner teenage geeks to hang out with. First chance, you and me are doing the extensive hangar tour—starting with that DC-3, and I've got about almost all of a Lockheed Electra 10, most of the guts in boxes. That one's kind of iffy for getting to fly again. I'll probably never have the shops and tech to refit my P-51 from the Dominican Air Force for post-Daybreak, and I'm not sure how much I can knock together from one fairly complete DC-6, three spare engines, and one DC-6 airframe. The real thing I've got my hopes pinned on is that I have—brace yourself . . . ta-da! Most of three Stearman Kaydets, one of them that I actually had flying before Daybreak."

"I think our inner ten-year-olds are going to be best buddies," Mensche said, "especially if yours likes to hear mine say, 'Wow.' "

THE NEXT DAY. CAMBRIDGE, MASSACHUSETTS. SHORTLY AFTER MIDNIGHT EST. SUNDAY, NOVEMBER 3.

Building a radio station out of things you could find in the kitchen or the hardware store, plus scrap parts from everywhere, was the sort of interesting problem that MIT students enjoyed; it was a way to take their minds off the mess that surrounded them. Digging through the old paper library was fun in a nostalgic way, the trip out to off-campus storage with ROTC armed guards was a romantic adventure, and when finally they had a voltage controlled oscillator, built around five tubes that had been hand-built into test tubes and pickle jars, up and running, it felt like a major victory.

The crystal receivers for AM radio had been pulling in stories from KP-1 and Blue and Gold for a couple of days, so they had plenty of material for rebroadcast, and a couple of student reporters from the Tufts newspaper had managed to put together a local news report as well. FM radios that hadn' been turned on or plugged in typically had not attracted many nanoswarm, and as word went from neighbor to neighbor people dug out batteries and long-unused radios, wiped them with Drano and hydrogen peroxide, and heard the first news in several days.

So a surprising number of people were tuned in at two A.M. on Sunday, listening to the rereading of the day's news, when the west wind began to rise. The hand-built anemometer at the improvised weather station on top of MacGregor jammed when nanoswarm from its bicycle-generator sensor penetrated the main bearing; two engineering students who climbed up to the roof to wipe and lubricate the anemometer looked southwest and saw the flames in Brookline.

The student announcer at WMBR broadcast the news immediately; within an hour, citizen volunteers were clearing fire lanes along Fisher Avenue and Lee Street, dragging wrecked cars out of the space, wetting down storefronts with water from the reservoirs, dousing the sparks that crossed the line, and helping fleeing residents find shelter.

Dawn came and the volunteers worked on in greater and greater numbers; at midmorning it began to snow, and the fire retreated.

By noon, the fire lanes were secure. Most people drifted away, but many lingered because of a rumor that they might all be paid, in food, or perhaps in a bus ride to a better location, or in an allocation of an abandoned house that had a woodstove—with *something*, at least, for their hours spent saving the city, sweating and hungry in the icy dark. Someone said that since the radio station at MIT had spread the word, probably the people who would pay them were there, and although most people didn't want to walk that far, a few hundred made the trip, all the way across Harvard Bridge, marching in the thick snow, gaining determination to demand payment as they went.

The fighting may have started with nervous or overzealous ROTC guards, or perhaps the crowd, by the time it got there at around four in the afternoon, was simply too far gone into its desire to smash something. But by the time the so-called Battle of MIT was done, a dozen buildings were wrecked, much of the library had been carried off for fuel or burned in bonfires, and the radio station was off the air for good. When the National Guard arrived in the early hours of Monday morning, the campus was deserted, and there wasn't much to do except catalog the damage.

LATER THAT EVENING. WASHINGTON, DC, PITTSBURGH, PENNSYLVANIA, AND MOST OF THE UNITED STATES. 7:00 P.M. EST. SUNDAY, NOVEMBER 3.

Chris Manckiewicz's introduction for the radio presidential debate stressed that despite everything, voting would still take place on Tuesday, and added, "Because our Republic is stronger even than this." He went on to explain Vote Where You Are, the system Shaunsen had worked out for people to vote on a simple honor system: find any State, Federal, or local official on election day, no matter where you were, give them your address and as many preferences as you could, and the votes would be passed up the chain, exchanged around among the states, until every vote came home to its proper roost.

"It's the only thing about him that doesn't make me gnash my teeth. It's sort of weirdly magnificent," Lenny said. "Shaunsen is a corrupt old idiot, but he's so much a politician that he can't imagine canceling an election. *Heroic* lack of imagination."

"Shh," Heather said, adjusting to hold him closer. "Shut up so I can hear the history getting made."

His good hand ran gently down her flank, and she thought *Well, there's something even more distracting.* But she focused her attention and waited to hear the two candidates sharing a moment with the rest of the country.

KP-1's *Tech Tips* had broadcast directions on making workable crystal radios using Christmas LED bulbs as the crystal, which allowed you to add amplifying power from a battery, so it was hoped that a majority of surviving Americans would find a way to hear this broadcast; after all, it wasn't as if there was a lot of competing entertainment.

Norcross spoke first, and surprised them by not mentioning religious faith at all; he simply said that he wanted the job of putting the country back on its feet, and he knew what a big job it would be.

Shaunsen repeated his long list of something for everyone, suggested that Norcross was apt to impose religious tyranny, and *gay-ron-teed!* that everything would be back to normal in two years; he reminded everyone to simply hand whatever public official they could find on election day, "Yo name, your address, and the big bold words STRAIGHT DEMOCRAT!"

Manckiewicz asked about several subjects; the answer from Shaunsen was always a list of where they were spending money, and "Be sure to vote STRAIGHT DEMOCRAT!" After the third such conclusion, Lenny muttered, "Wonder how many gay Democrat votes he's losing?"

"About like everyone else, straight, gay, male, female, black, white. Everyone with a brain who hears him," Heather said.

"And same question, Mr. Norcross?"

Norcross said, "Well, it just seems to me that we can be balanced about this. No, the experts really don't agree yet on whether we were attacked by what they call a 'system artifact,' meaning sort of a mind-virus that just kind of grew in the Internet like termites in the baseboards, or whether it was an actual act of war by some nation or terrorist outfit. But common sense says a reconstructed nation can fight better, and a secure nation can reconstruct better."

"Isn't it amazing what having a big, important job does to some people?" Lenny said. "Norcross went from Jesus nut to almost-statesman; Shaunsen went from third-rate to tenth-rate."

"Yeah, I almost feel good about voting for Norcross. Where did he get all that system artifact stuff?"

"Oh, Cam told both of them about it at a briefing; Norcross listened, I guess. Or maybe Shaunsen listened but didn't care; probably he just figured that whether we're being attacked by self-aware malware, or an international terror network, or for that matter Satan or freakin' Monaco, why worry which? Shaunsen's solution will always be to spend money."

THE NEXT DAY. WASHINGTON, DC. JUST BEFORE 7:00 A.M. EST. MONDAY, NOVEMBER 4.

That morning, the price for a copy of the *Advertiser-Gazette* had gone up to "thirty-two ounces of canned food or forty-eight of dry," according to the masthead, but Heather had still had to struggle through the crowd around the newsboy for a copy; the kid looked like he was standing in a food-drive donation bin. Back at St. Elizabeth's, where the power was on temporarily, she paged through it quickly under an ultraviolet spotlight, and then rolled it up, ran it through a degausser, and finally let them put it under a salvaged dental X-ray machine for about ten times the dose a human being should take in a year. That was the new procedure for documents that had been exposed outside, since yesterday they'd lost a satellite uplink to biotes that had probably come in on some paper maps from USGS.

It was worth it all, though, for the experience of being able to have powdered eggs, instant mashed potatoes, and freeze-dried coffee in their little makeshift bedroom, especially since, with the power on again in this wing for the moment, they had light enough to read to each other. Heather took a turn reading the rightmost column on the front page, which carried the basic information about the Vote Where You Are program.

While Heather ate, Lenny read the roundup story on the post-Daybreak disasters around the country: the big fires in St. Paul and Boston, the rioting and looting in DC, the weather disasters unfolding across the northern states.

They switched again for Lenny to have his toast while it was warm. Heather read Chris Manckiewicz's editorial about the already-appearing corruption of many reconstruction projects, Shaunsen's non-answers and attempted demagoguing during the debate on KP-1, the creation of the unneeded and threatening National Unity Guard without Congressional authorization, and finally the symbolism of the limo issue: that Washington's scarce and vital supply of tires and gasoline had been depleted "so that the Acting President may wander around glad-handing and trying to persuade people that he is fit for office. We call on the voters to elect Norcross, and because the country cannot afford more of Shaunsen, we believe that we cannot wait for Norcross to take office in January. We urge the House to impeach Acting President Shaunsen and the Senate to remove him.' You know, I am getting to like Chris Manckiewicz and Rusty Parlotta more than—"

There was a knock at the door. "Heather O'Grainne, please report immediately to Mr. Nguyen-Peters in his office, and he requests that you bring a day bag and a firearm."

"On my way." She bolted the last of her eggs and pota

toes, gulped the last of her coffee, and kissed Lenny tenderly; nowadays she kept a packed day bag, including a weapon, by the door.

IMMEDIATELY AFTER. WASHINGTON, DC. 8:15 A.M. EST. MONDAY, NOVEMBER 4.

Cam looked up from his desk as she came in; he looked stressed-out, overworked, and relieved to see her.

"What would you say," he said, "if I reminded you that you have taken an oath—several times—to 'support and defend the Constitution of the United States against all enemies, foreign or domestic'?"

"I'd say 'well, duh, Cam,' and ask if I was being accused of treason."

"Good. Would you say that a President—or an Acting President—who deputizes members of his staff, arms them, and sends them out to arrest someone is acting Constitutionally?"

"I think that would be a job for the Supreme Court to decide. What's that idiot done?"

"Doing. We have about three hours. He's sending his National Unity Guard to go arrest the whole staff of the *Advertiser-Gazette* at their morning meeting. We've got it straight from a Secret Service informant, confirmed by another inside source."

"Christ. How can he arrest them? On what charge?"

"He just plans to hold them through the election. Supposedly he's preventing unfair private interference in a Federal election."

"Well, at that point he's raped the shit out of the First Amendment, and he's violated that oath he insisted on taking, Cam. You want me to go stop him?"

"I want you to arrest all the National Unity Guard he sends. There's an excellent argument that he can't appoint law enforcement officers on his own hook and all by himself, which we'll find some good lawyer to argue for the Supreme Court. But what I really want is to catch people *acting upon his orders, subverting the Constitution, arresting without warrant or charge*, and several other good phrases that come right from Madison and the Federalist Papers as grounds for impeachment. Per Speaker Kowalski's request I'm assembling a file to use in impeaching our Acting-Out President. Incidentally, how do you feel about the theory that the NCCC is responsible for making sure we have a *qualified* Acting President during an emergency, and that when an Acting President disqualifies himself during an emergency, the NCCC can take it back and give it to the next choice in line?"

"Wow. Ask me again if you ever have to do that. I figured you'd just impeach Shaunsen."

"I'd rather do it by impeachment, but if Kowalski can't find the votes to impeach, or the Senate won't remove, we still have to have a functioning president, ASAP. So this latest little escapade looks like one more length of rope to hang him with, and I want someone I trust to handle it. If you make it to Rusty Parlotta's place, before the Acting Presidential Bozo Brigade shows up at eleven, and bust their asses—ideally if you can swear that you saw them try to make the arrest— will appreciate the hell out of it, Speaker Kowalski will make great use of it, and the country will be a lot better off."

"Not to mention we'll both have kept our oaths."

"I like that part too."

"So why did you send for me?"

"Because in all of DRET, you're the only person with Fed eral power to arrest who I'm willing to have improvise."

**ABOUT TWO HOURS LATER. WASHINGTON, DC.
ABOUT 11:00 A.M. EST. MONDAY, NOVEMBER 4.**

"All right, that's got to be them," Heather said, watching from the window. Two young women and two young men in th black uniforms with red berets, walking like they were audi tioning (unsuccessfully) for the role of the determined sherif in a community theatre. *God, it looks like "when Guardia Angels go bad."* "Rusty, Chris, are you sure you want to d this? Let me remind you, once again, I could just meet ther at the door."

"You're asking us to throw away the best story we've ha yet, Ms. O'Grainne," Rusty said. "Not to mention that M

Nguyen-Peters is absolutely right. If they actually say they're arresting us on the Acting President's orders—with Betsi inside here taking notes, so we'll have their exact words—then we can get that asshole out and a real president in. So what the hell."

"Uh, what the boss said," Chris said, grinning.

"All right, then, go on out, and move away from the door quick in case I need to come through fast."

Rusty went through first, then Chris, and they moved down the front porch to the left, clearing a path for Heather immediately. She rested the door on her hand, ready to fling it open.

"Can we help you?" Rusty asked.

One of the young women stepped forward, nervously brushed her hair away from her face, and began to read from a card. "By order of the Acting President of the United States, this company is to cease publication immediately and all staff present on the premises are to come with us. You are also to turn over all materials, supplies, and equipment to us; you may petition to have them returned when the present emergency—"

"On what charges?" Rusty asked. "And do you have a warrant?"

"We don't need a warrant, we're not cops, we're here from the President," the taller and more muscular of the two young men said. "And it's a National Security Emergency. And you're under arrest."

"Read your Constitution. You don't come onto this porch without a warrant, and if you're going to arrest me, you have to tell me what the charges against me are—"

"Fucking Republican, it's not *your* fucking Constitution," the man said, and drew his gun.

Heather burst through the door, crouching into firing position and shouting, "Freeze, Federal police!" in one swift motion.

The young man may have just started and accidentally pulled the trigger; he may have intended to shoot Rusty Parlotta all along; for whatever reason, his gun barked, and Heather shot his head—*practically textbook combat handgun,* she thought, as she bellowed, "Throw down your weapons! I am a Federal agent, and you are all under arrest *now*. Throw down your weapons!"

Stunned, bewildered, the two young women and the surviving young man dropped their guns; Heather ran forward, bellowing, "Lie down, lie down on your faces, hands behind your backs," and was putting the ties on the second one as she recited, "You have the right to remain silent . . ."

It was only as she tied the third one that she realized someone else had been shouting, and she turned to see Chris bending over Rusty, cradling her in his arms in a sort of *Pieta* as he tried to hold her so that she could breathe. Beside Chris, ineffectually, a man tried to stop the still-flowing, bubbling chest wound. Heather rushed to join them, but even as she did, the blood flow from the gushing wound diminished, and the dim recognition left Rusty Parlotta's eyes; they kept trying to revive her while a runner fetched a doctor, but they all knew she was dead long before it was official.

THE NEXT DAY. BOSTON, MASSACHUSETTS. BEGINNING AT 7:00 A.M. EST. TUESDAY, NOVEMBER 5.

Election day wasn't anything anyone had expected: It was surprisingly smooth and dull.

In the burned-out areas of Boston, soldiers walked down the street with notebooks and megaphones, asking people to come out and vote. Many of the people who came out were disappointed to find out that it wasn't about food, or about rides out of the area, or heated shelters. But once they understood what it was about, they almost all wanted to vote. Since the printed ballots had been mostly destroyed, the soldiers hand-copied the correct spellings of the names and parties from the blackboard at headquarters, then each carried a clipboard with that sheet on it, so that voters would have something to copy correct spellings from.

ABOUT THE SAME TIME. PALE BLUFF, ILLINOIS. 6:00 A.M. CST. TUESDAY, NOVEMBER 5.

An hour behind Boston, in Pale Bluff, they all voted right on the dot of six in the morning, in the interest of giving Freddie Pranger the maximum daylight for the trip to Springfield. An old mimeograph had been found, along with a still-sealed package of mimeo sheets. A long-retired schoolteacher had figured out how to make it all work, using a turpentine/ethanol mix for fluid. They had printed up a set of ballots, and everyone promised not to peek; in the same community hall where they had all listened to a radio pulled from a sealed box and switched on just before the debate, 681 adult inhabitants and 104 adult refugees cast their ballots, sitting next to each other, filling them out all at once, careful to keep their eyes on their own ballots.

The township clerk shuffled them in a big cardboard box and started counting. An hour later, a landslide for Will Norcross was announced, and the results for local elections were written up on a whiteboard and recopied onto a sheet of lined notebook paper. While they waited, they'd all had a pancake breakfast.

Then Freddie Pranger, who had been in the Special Forces and was still a good shot, packed the results total in a small bag. He figured he'd make Springfield in three days, and depending on what he found, might be back in a week. He also carried a letter from the mayor of Pale Bluff offering to secure the roads and operate a postal service within ten miles of the town; that offer had been ratified by unanimous voice vote just before Freddie left.

They stood in the street, waving good-bye to Freddie; then people returned to their homes and jobs, with plenty to do, and nothing more about elections for the next two years.

ABOUT AN HOUR LATER. ANTONITO, COLORADO.
ABOUT 10:00 A.M. MST. TUESDAY, NOVEMBER 5.

An hour behind Pale Bluff, election day in Antonito was sort of a half-holiday by common consent, with everyone taking either the morning or the afternoon off to vote, and incidentally just to enjoy having time to themselves, or to chat with the neighbors.

Voting was by secret ballot at the town council secretary's office. She had a big sign out front:

COME ON IN AND VOTE,
REGULAR TOWNIE OR REFUGEE,
WE'LL MAKE SOMETHING WORK FOR YOU!
PUBLIC SERVICE IS WHAT I DO!

The older lady behind the desk, whose nameplate said she was SUZEE B., wore a gray beehive and glasses that made her look like she had escaped from *The Far Side*. She looked gray and sick, and the empty ashtray beside her probably explained it. The tobacco supply had run out, and many of the local folks were going through withdrawal.

"Here to vote?"

"Uh, yes, and we had a question—"

"Just ask when it comes up. Let's start with your names."

When it got down to address, Beth and Jason couldn't very well use the commune's old address, not knowing whether any of their old neighbors might someday come this way. Jason said, "Um, we're refugees and the last we saw of our home—it's not going to be there if we ever go back."

Suzee B. looked up, nodding in sympathy, her mouth skewed a little to one side. "That sucks, don't it?"

"Yeah," Beth said, and her voice was choking with tears. Jason never knew when that would happen to her; most of the time she insisted on pretending nothing much had happened, but every now and then, some little kindness or attention from anyone—Jason or a stranger, it didn't seem to matter—would completely undo her.

The lady looked at Beth, glanced at Jason, and said, "Bad getting here?"

"Bad starting out." That was as honest as seemed safe. "Uh, what we wanted to ask was, we just rented a garage from Dave Wilson, over on Third Street? And could that be our address? So our votes count here where we're going to make our home, instead of back where we—"

"We don't never want to see it no more," Beth said, wiping her eyes.

"Honey, you're making sense to me, and I'm as much authority as there is. Dave's at 442 Third Street, there ain't no 444 or 446, and you're closer to Dave than you are to the laundrymat at 448. So your garage is now officially 444. Are you a Mister and Missus yet?"

"Not yet," Jason said, "though the thought has crossed my mind, and we've talked about it."

"We been kinda busy," Beth volunteered.

"I know how that goes. But look, just now, the whole government record system is me, so while you're here, want to get married? I've got the registry right here."

It seemed like a good time to do it, so they voted, married, and were put on the list for jury duty. "You could be caught in the draft, too, Jason," Suzee warned. "There's some idiots around here talking about the town needing a militia."

"And there probably won't be enough paper to make a card for me to burn," Jason said.

She laughed. "Glad to have two more liberals in town," she said. "That makes three of us."

THREE HOURS LATER. CASTLE CASTRO. (SAN DIEGO, CALIFORNIA.) 12:00 P.M. PST. TUESDAY, NOVEMBER 5.

Harrison Castro looked over the assembled population of his Castle, everyone except the sentries who had voted earlier. He drew a deep breath, reminded himself that he had no mike and had to *project*, and began. "We have formed a bond, you and I. I am feeding and housing you; you live by my protection; you have brought your families in here to live, and I am the freeholder of our Castle here. In the last forty-eight hours you have all helped me turn away mobs who would have destroyed everything. By now we all understand—we are in this together. We are engaged in a titanic struggle to make a new civilization. I hope that a fully Constitutional, free, and sovereign America will be part of it, but I know for certain that a strong and free Castle Castro will be, because together, you and I will *make* it be."

Loud cheers broke the silence; Castro noted that his four selected claques had all hit their cue perfectly, and almost everyone else had followed. He was not particularly displeased that Special Agents Bolton and Carlucci were among the few not cheering wildly; that was their privilege, and owing to their occupation, they were thoughtful men, not easily swayed and very inclined to consider things for a long time. Besides, many things would be easier if the Feds departed sometime before spring; they were handy men with weapons, and good counselors, but next summer would be easier without Federal eyes watching.

"So," he said, "as the freeholder of Castle Castro, I would prefer that you vote in the following way . . ." He read off his list of intended votes, beginning of course with Norcross for president. "But again, it *is* your ballot. Let me offer you two options: Vote your way, if it disagrees with mine. Keep your ballot secret, if you wish. Place completed ballots in the red box to my left, and I swear upon my loyalty to my country and my family that I will report your votes faithfully and accurately to the California Secretary of State in Sacramento.

"Or, I would take it as a personal favor if you do this: Sign your name to your ballot but do not mark on it otherwise, and place it in the blue box to my right. In other words, acknowledge that because you have freely taken my protection and given your loyalty, you owe me your political allegiance, and you give over your political power to me for my use, just as you give me your bodies to use in fighting to defend Castle Castro and doing the work that must be done to house and feed us all.

"If you choose to give me your unmarked ballot, with your name on it, I will fill out your ballot for you and report it, with the others. *And* I will enter you into a list of people I will give preference to in any appointments or openings that may come up, because loyalty should be rewarded. All right—" He saw Carlucci trying to get his attention; the man might decide to be difficult, so Castro hurried somewhat at the last, spoiling some of the effect. *Damn Carlucci anyway.* "All right, all right then, now everybody *vote!*"

Later, as he sifted through the blue box, he discovered that Carlucci and Bolton had each signed their names, and rather than put an unmarked ballot in for him to mark, they had voted exactly opposite his desires on everything. Carlucci had added, "I do not think you understand what it is to be an American, sir, and I will leave your protection tomorrow, grateful for your help but unwilling to further give you mine."

A man of honor. Good. And not sticking around. Even better. I'll miss his gun. Oh well.

Bambi was charmed when, for the uncountable time, Quattro asked, "Do you think setting out the food and all is too much?"

She looked into his eyes and rested a hand on each of his triceps, dragging downward with her fingertips, willing his tense shoulders to descend. "Jenner is a tiny town, and it's all laid out to be accessible to the road, the beaches, and the hills; nobody would ever have given any thought to defending it, it's a place meant to *welcome* people. So they know that they depend on you in case of real trouble. You've shown them where they'll bunk, trained their militia and armed it. It's your canned fruit and tomatoes that'll bring them through the winter without scurvy. They've gratefully accepted all of that; why would they think you were trying to buy their votes with a few sandwiches?"

"Okay. I'll try to stop worrying. I just hope they'll like what I could set out. I wish I could throw a real all-you-can-eat, too, you know, 'cause I'm pretty sure a lot of them are going hungry."

Larry Mensche smiled. "Hey, truth here, Quattro? Relax and let people enjoy what you've done."

"Yeah. People are just so difficult for me."

"Just think of us as really fallible machines," Mensche said. "Can I ask one strange question? Should we let Ysabel vote?"

"Well," Bambi said, "she's never been convicted of anything, she's an American citizen, and her one vote isn't going to change anything."

Mensche nodded. "That's what I think. Quattro?"

"Dude, she's *your* prisoner."

"But it's your Castle."

Quattro shrugged. "After all my years of wanting to be the freeholder of my own Castle, I found out I'd rather be an American citizen. Let's let everyone vote today."

**FIVE HOURS LATER. LINCOLN, NEBRASKA. ABOUT
9:00 P.M. CST. TUESDAY, NOVEMBER 5.**

In Lincoln, the governor sat down with her secretary of state and poured a glass of whiskey for each of them. "We won't have the ballot results from the back corners of the state for at least a week, will we?"

"If we're lucky. If there's another big storm, could be two weeks before people on foot carry all the reports in."

"But the only ones that need immediate reporting are the ones for the presidential race, right?"

"Yes, ma'am." The Nebraska Secretary of State was a quiet man who generally let people arrive at their own conclusions, but he feared his governor's nerve might fail her. He said, gently, "Nebraskans are not crazy—it's going to come in massively for Norcross."

"But if it takes weeks to report—"

"Well, exactly." He drew out a sheet of typewritten paper, and said, "We got a radio link working, thanks to the physics kids at the university, but they're having a hard time keeping it from crusting up, and they think they only have a couple hours in the battery they built before that goes, too. So it's now or never. As it happens, what I have here is a copy, from a paper almanac, of the numbers from when Reagan carried this state, adjusted upward by either five percent or ten percent per county, re-proportioned to the last census. And if we report it, the only difference is everything that needs to happen can happen a couple of weeks early."

She played with the pencil in front of her, pushed her glasses up her nose, and finally said, "You know, I don't believe any of the eight states that have already reported had it any easier retrieving ballots than we did."

"Rhode Island's pretty small," he pointed out.

"They had results half an hour after the polls closed. Do you think anyone can even cross Providence in less than half a day, right now?" The governor stared at him; her old-fashioned black horn-rimmed glasses glinted. "What do you want me to say?"

"Nothing," he said. "I want you to say nothing. I suppose I've been around long enough to want to be able to say truth-

fully that I'd told you, and you'd said nothing. I'll radio these
in right now."

**ABOUT ONE HOUR LATER. WASHINGTON, DC. 11:30 P.M. EST.
TUESDAY, NOVEMBER 5.**

"The poor old West Coast isn't going to matter any more after Daybreak than it did before." Manckiewicz looked at the
whiteboard on which one of the reporters had sketched an
awkward map of the United States that afternoon. They had
the generator running so there was light, and in an abandoned
drugstore someone had found a few calculators whose pack-
aging had not yet rotted.

The signal chimed; he pulled on his headset. "Okay, KP-1,
this is Chris, and count me in."

The engineer in Pittsburgh said, "Five, four"—Chris drew
a deep breath—"one, go."

Chris began. "Hello, this is Chris Manckiewicz, of the
Washington Advertiser-Gazette, with a special report for
KP-1 News. Latest figures indicate an unprecedented landslide for Norcross. We're ready to call Ohio and Missouri,
again for Norcross, which means he needs only a dozen more
electoral votes to become—"

The note in front of him had been sitting there for a while,
and he knew what was on it, but he thought a population too
long trained to drama would like it better this way. "Wait
just a moment, I've just been handed a note—all right, then.
It's . . . *all . . . over!" (Corny, sure, but corn lifts spirits, and
now's the time for it, if ever.)* "Illinois, Nebraska, and Colorado have all tipped over for Norcross. Will Norcross is the
next president of the United States."

He recapped the whole story from the beginning, then
signed off and turned to the staff. "Vern, are we preset with
the 'Norcross Wins' headline?"

"Have been since yesterday. And I've been setting in the
numbers as they came. Do we do an extra for tonight, or just
go with a full story tomorrow? You never did settle on that."

Chris leaned back. *God, I wish Rusty could have seen this.*
"You know," he said, "there probably hasn't been an extra at

any American paper in, I don't know, twenty years? There haven't been very many paper papers since the big bust in 2012. And an extra just sounds kind of . . . I don't know, romantic. Besides, if we wait till morning, Shaunsen's goons may be back here to smash our press. And there're a few thousand people milling around on the Mall; I don't know whether all of them will have canned goods, but there are quite a few living out of their backpacks. If we do half a print run on the extra, how soon can we get it out?"

"Forty minutes, if you've got any newsies to carry it."

"We have five of them pretending to sleep downstairs right this minute, remember? So what the hell. It's romantic, Rusty would have *loved* it, and I'll be damned if we're going to give those bastards a chance to stop our reporting. Be sure to re-run all the stuff about Rusty's murder in there, too, and all the Shaunsen corruption stories. Let's make it hot for the son of a bitch."

THE NEXT DAY. WASHINGTON, DC. 6:50 A.M. EST. WEDNESDAY, NOVEMBER 6.

The breakfast meeting for that day was set an hour earlier, to give everyone a chance to eat before whatever might come. There had been no word from the White House after the election had been called for Norcross the night before; not even when Manckiewicz had walked up to the White House gates at three A.M. and asked if a concession speech was forthcoming.

The phone from the White House rang. Cameron looked at the clock. "Five minutes early. This won't be good." He signaled the transcriptionist standing by to get on the other headset, and picked it up. "Yes, Mr. President."

"What kind of a stunt do you call that?"

Cameron kept his voice even. "I beg your pardon?"

"More than half those radio links to state Secretary of State offices were military," Shaunsen said. "And a bunch of the ones that weren't military were Republican. And nobody reported on any congressional or Senate races, just on the presidential race. And more than that, they've been telling me for days that they can't get a message anywhere faster than man can go on foot, yet somehow they all had counts within hours of when the polls closed. This is the biggest voter fraud and stolen election there's ever been. This makes W Chimpface Shrub look like an amateur. And I don't know any way they could do this without your being in on it. And who the fucking cunting hell's idea was it to route everything direct to the news media?"

"If you mean the *Advertiser-Gazette*, sir, and KP-1, the election results were broadcast in clear—per your instructions—and they just listened in like anyone else could do and put the numbers together."

"Eat shit."

"Sir, have you been drinking?"

"That's none of your business!" The phone slammed down. Cameron looked over at Weisbrod. "Did you get that?"

"I could hear him through your head," Weisbrod said. "The question is, does he realize we've got him beaten, or does he drag it out even further?"

"He wouldn't be able to drag it out if we could just take some Twenty-fifth Amendment action. What's the situation with the Secretary of State?"

Weisbrod shook his head. "I have all but three Cabinet votes lined up your way, but Randolph is not one of them, and without him, there's no Twenty-fifth Amendment case. He won't budge. He doesn't want to make history, he doesn't want to be part of a coup. He doesn't want to do anything, actually, other than try to get home to Mississippi. He's worried about his family."

It had stymied them for more than a day. The problem was that the Twenty-fifth Amendment requires *both* the Vice President and a majority of the Cabinet to certify that the President is unfit. Their little cabal of responsible people at St. Elizabeth's was already on shaky ground, for there was no actual Vice President and Congress had never provided for the position of Acting Vice President; the Secretary of State was the next eligible person in the line of succession, which might or might not count as the same thing as "the Vice President," depending on what Chief Justice Lopez thought.

"Maybe if the Secretary of State resigns," Weisbrod said. "And if—"

The presidential line rang again, and Nguyen-Peters ges-

tured to the transcriptionist, who slipped on his phones and
bent to his work.

The gist of the tirade was that Cameron Nguyen-Peters
had been fired, both as Chief of Staff for the Department of
Homeland Security and as NCCC. As Shaunsen ran down
Cameron said, very quietly, "Sir, that is not a lawful order."

"I'm the damn *president*!"

"*Acting* President, sir. You can order my boss to fire me,
though he won't. You can fire him and *try* to make his suc-
cessors fire me; they won't. You *can't* call me up and dismiss
me directly.

"Furthermore, as NCCC, it is my job to ensure that the
acting presidency is in competent and legally qualified hands,
and I don't feel I can say that with you in office; to leave now
would be to desert my post during a crisis, and the President
can't lawfully order a Federal official to neglect or act contrary to his duty. So I'm *not* fired, sir. Thank you." And he
hung up. He turned to Weisbrod. "Graham, if you have one
good idea right now, you are my hero."

"Don't let your toast get cold, and let's talk through this
thing one more time."

"That's *two* good ideas. Got any more?"

"Well, President Pendano . . . when I talked to him on the
phone on Sunday, because I was worried they'd move him
with the rioting going on—he sounded *much* better than he
did when I visited on Friday and on Saturday. I think he's off
the barbiturates and through the withdrawal, but I couldn't
chance asking when there might be some National Unity
Goon listening in. So suppose he's better. What if he were
to transmit a letter to Congress certifying that he's ready to
resume his duties?"

"Could he do that? I mean—I know, Amendment Twenty-
five, Section Three, he can always send the letter, but could
he *be* president?"

"That's not what I have in mind, Cameron. No, I don't
think Roger Pendano could be president again. I don't think
he's even going to live very long, or if he does, it will be as a
wreck in a nursing home. If he were going to rise to the need
he'd've done it the first night. But he might be able, for a very
short time, to be a figurehead. And I think he'll do that if we
ask him. If we got Kowalski on it for the House and whoever

it's going to be for the Senate, and Roger Pendano were to appoint a Vice President and then resign—"

"I see what you're saying, it scares me, and I don't like it."

Weisbrod pressed on. "Twenty-fifth Amendment, Section 3, he resumes his duties if he sends a letter that says he's fit and a majority of the Cabinet agrees. No agreement from the VP required. If we all vote that he's fit, and the Senate and House confirm as soon as Shaunsen protests, then Roger is the President again. Between DRET and the Cabinet, we could take care of everything, just have him read announcements and maybe wave from stands. It'll be easier to hide than Roosevelt's wheelchair or Wilson's stroke were. And if he appoints a successor right away, and the House and Senate confirm immediately, we won't have to keep the act going for much time at all."

Cameron nodded. "Who did you have in mind for the successor?"

Weisbrod smiled. "Frankly, I was thinking you."

"God no. I have zero charisma and I'm unknown outside policy circles and it would look like a coup. Same reason we can't use any generals. But I do have a thought, which I'm swiping from all the stuff I've been reviewing about irregular successions and possible irregular successions in the past."

"There's a precedent for this?"

"There's definitely a precedent, even if it's 108 years old. Back in 1916, just before he was re-elected, Woodrow Wilson thought the country might reject him, and elect Charles Evans Hughes. The main issue of the campaign was Wilson's policies about the war going on in Europe. If Wilson lost, especially back in those days when a new president was sworn in on March 4th, it would have been five months till the new policies came in, at a time when there were decisions to make every day. Wilson thought that was way too long for the country to stay with a foreign policy it had rejected, so he planned that if Hughes won, Wilson would appoint him Secretary of State, the Senate would confirm, and then Wilson and Vice President Marshall would resign, making Hughes the President under the 1886 Succession Act, the rules at the time.

"So I suggest that Roger Pendano pick Senator Will Norcross as his Vice President. The country voted for Norcross, so he has immediate legitimacy. And we don't have to go through a whole additional succession on January 20; we can put Norcross in, in a perfectly Constitutional, regular way."

"And Norcross at least grasps that the situation is desperate, and he'll act rather than weasel around it," Weisbrod said. "I see the logic. But Will Norcross still scares me. Do you think he understands that if we do this for him, he owes us a more middle-of-the-road, national-unity sort of administration than he campaigned for?"

"I think that you and the Cabinet should put that question to him directly, in your first meeting with him after President Pendano reassumes office." Cameron was nodding now, liking the thought more as he considered it. "*Yes*, extract promises from Norcross that he's not going to treat this as a mandate for the Christian Right—by all means. Insist that he say it in public, not just to you. Please. Because we need the country to pull together. Now—you're the guy to talk to Pendano, and you know it—do you think he'll be okay with it?"

Graham sat still for a long, long moment. "I think it's what Roger would prefer, if he can be coaxed into it. But we've both got to be clear about what the deal is. So, here's what I think we're agreeing to: Pendano can never function again as President—but he has the power to eliminate Acting President Shaunsen, and the country needs that. If Will Norcross commits to being a national-unity president for all the country, and leave his religious views to his re-election campaign if he has one, then he's the best man for the job. Therefore, we are doing this because the country needs a functioning, full-time, national-unity president, right now. Have I forgotten anything?"

"Not a thing," Cameron said. "Ditto, as some of my colleagues on the right used to say." He extended a hand and the two men shook. "And I'm glad we're friends."

"Ditto," Graham said. "All right, well, nothing will be improved by delay. I'm going to grab Heather O'Grainne and head over to the White House."

"Excellent. I don't think we can count on Shaunsen to give up without a fight, when push comes to shove, and I mean that pretty literally. Bringing a big man, especially military or security, into the White House would look suspicious; Heather's a good, inoffensive alternative."

"You know, that may be the first time she's ever been called *that*."

ABOUT AN HOUR LATER. WASHINGTON, DC. 10:00 A.M. EST. WEDNESDAY, NOVEMBER 6.

"All right," Chris said, opening the morning meeting, "what do we have for prospects for tomorrow's paper? What's everyone working on?"

"Got a roundup," Hayley said. "Hunger riots all up and down the East Coast."

George Parwin looked up, and added, "Bad news in all the major cities—roundup or bunch of shorties, no details on any of them. According to a ham in New Hampshire, thousands of people died of exposure after walking out of the Boston metro area looking for food, when a freezing rainstorm caught them. Confirmed for sure, two days ago half of Chicago burned because there was no way to put it out—must've gone not long after St. Paul, actually. My DoD-intel source let me look at aerial photos of street barricades and armed men splitting the black and white neighborhoods in St. Louis."

Brown said, "Food story—satellite pictures show that early blizzard might've killed a quarter of the cattle in Montana."

"Okay," Chris said. "And of course, metro and local, Shaunsen is pledging good government jobs for everybody, and plans to sue to get results thrown out in some states where he lost, because of the 'unfair advantage' Norcross—"

"Hey!" The shout was from Don Parmenter, up in the cupola, where they tried to maintain a watch with binoculars. "Troops moving out of Fort McNair and Fort Myer."

"Where are they going?"

"This way. Too soon to tell otherwise, but they're definitely *not* heading out of town."

"Right," Chris said. "Okay, everyone, the story ideas sound fine; George, write them up as separate shorties, we can always stick them all back together if we need the space for anything else. Brown, yeah, go with that, on the Montana story. And I better run, because odds are those troops mean something's going on." He shouted. "Hey, Don, want to come and see if we can get caught in a battle?"

"You know that's why I took the job," Parmenter said, hurrying down the stairs. "Let's not miss it."

ABOUT AN HOUR LATER. THE WHITE HOUSE, WASHINGTON, DC. 11:00 A.M. EST. WEDNESDAY, NOVEMBER 6.

The Secret Service ERT at the plywood barrier in front of the White House entrance had his machine pistol wrapped in a plastic garbage bag. He looked exhausted, but smiled when he saw who it was.

"Hey, Dr. Weisbrod. Gonna make the future better?"

"Doing what I can. They only deliver it one day at a time. Heather, Karl; Karl, Heather."

Heather asked, "Isn't that garbage bag going to rot like all the other plastic?"

"That's the idea. When it starts to, I know the gun oil and the bullets are suspect, and I turn it in to the armorer; he tears it down, degreases it, sterilizes all the surfaces, reloads with ammo from sealed boxes, and puts it in another bag. It will work till we run out of sealed boxes, I guess."

"How soon is that?" Heather asked.

"Everyone I know is scared to ask. Don't tell me if you find out." Karl looked the bagged weapon over, apparently seeing no signs of slime, fuzz, melting, or rupture. "Can't believe how heavy these all-metal-and-wood things are—makes me respect the old-timers from when I first joined." He turned and waved a distinctive signal to the man inside the doorway. "Just letting him know you don't have me at gunpoint. Go on through."

They were passed from guard to guard up to the third floor. The Secret Service smiled at them; the NUG-thugs didn't.

To Heather, Roger Pendano looked like he'd aged twenty years, developed anorexia, and taken a bad beating that morning, but at least the president's eyes had a little light and fire in them.

They sat down in the cluster of leather armchairs surrounding a low table, and Pendano launched at once into a rambling monolog about college days that made Heather's heart sink, especially since he seemed to be drawing on a pad, until he flipped the pad over and showed them:

Been flushing my pills per G's sugg'n. Depr'n worse ↓↓↓ / feel like self↑↑↑. Playing dead 4 doc. Hate life, want 2 die, BUT und'st'd ↑↑↑. Heard Shaunsen tell doc keep me dosed no matter what, 2 imp't 2 USA. Who won elec'n?

Heather withdrew a jelly jar from her bag and put on rubber gloves from a sealed bag; she unscrewed the top of the jar and took out a BugSweepR, turned it on, and took a tour of the room while Pendano and Weisbrod talked about how good the tollhouse cookies used to be across the street from campus. Following the "warmer/colder" indicator and the point indicator, she discovered two bugs (under the table and behind the headboard of the bed), a TV remote (behind a bookcase), and an old digital watch (under one couch).

The remote or the watch, of course, could also be a disguised bug, so she put them all in a screw-top metal can half-full of nanospawn crystals, shook them vigorously, and tied the can to the faucet in the bathroom with bare copper wire. A scan with the BugSweepR revealed no signal coming from any of them. She emerged from the bathroom and nodded at the men.

Graham began to explain. "Mr. President, Norcross won; the country is starving, freezing, and burning; and Shaunsen seems to be groping his way into some kind of bass-ackwards coup. The number of impeachable offenses he's committed this week alone is beyond counting."

"I've been painfully aware about those," Pendano said. "Scott Jevons, one of the Secret Service men, has been smuggling me the *Washington Advertiser-Gazette*, but he wasn't on duty this morning, so I hadn't seen the election results. I can't say I'm surprised."

Heather tilted chairs against the doorknobs of both entrances to the main room, then dragged a couch around to provide some cover between the men and the doors. *Best improvisation I've got.* She crouched behind the couch. *Come on, Graham, get to—*

"Roger." Graham's voice was soft, gentle—and as intense as Heather had ever heard. "Roger, I wish I didn't have to ask, but we've got to get rid of Shaunsen, and—"

"I thought that might be what you were here for. Amendment Twenty-five, Section Three; I figured Randolph was too much of a wuss and too old to do anything." Pendano groaned, shaking his head as if he'd been punched. "I don't know what will happen if I try to resume my office. I . . . I'm not the man I was a couple weeks ago. I'm not sure at all who I am, now."

"It would only have to be a for a few days," Graham said. He explained quickly.

Heather said, "We probably have five minutes before they react to the bugs being dead," she said. "Let's get moving."

"So we put Norcross in early and he's promised to act presidential?" Pendano stood. "That solves the problem, all right. But you get me out of office *fast*; I'm ashamed enough of what I've become without having it paraded in public." Pendano moved to his private correspondence desk, pulled out a sheet of paper, and scrawled:

November 6, 2024

To Speaker Kowalski and the President Pro Tem—

"Who did Shaunsen put in as Pres Pro Tem at the Senate?"

"He refused to do that, and he hasn't resigned his seat, either, even though the Twenty-fifth Amendment says he has to," Weisbrod explained.

"Great. Crap, Graham, I'm sorry I cracked up on you all. All right, then." Anger seemed to straighten and steady him, and he bent to write, quickly and in a surprisingly firm hand:

November 6, 2024

Dear Speaker Kowalski and President Pro Tem Shaunsen or his successor,

In accordance with Sect. 3 / 25th Amendment / US Constitution, this is my written declaration that I am now able to resume the discharge of the Constitutional powers and duties of the office of the President of the United States. With the transmittal of this letter, I am resuming those powers and duties effective immediately.

Sincerely,
Roger L. Pendano
cc: Chief Justice Lopez, SCOTUS
     All Cabinet Secretaries
     Mr. Cameron Nguyen-Peters, NCCC

"That last one is giving Cam the power to straighten this mess out if necessary," Pendano explained. "He may be a crazed right-wing nut and the coldest man in Washington, but if Shaunsen does any more damage to the Constitution, it will be over Cam's dead body, and I don't think that'll be easy to achieve. One of my best appointments, I think."

"Absolutely," Weisbrod said.

"The lawyer in me says we'd better have both of you witness it," Pendano said, extending the pen. Graham signed, WITNESSED NOVEMBER 6, 2024 and his name; below that Heather signed, her eyes never leaving the doors.

Weisbrod said, "Heather, just in case, I'd feel better to have you carrying this."

She folded it and placed it carefully, thinking, *Not everybody gets to have the fate of the nation stuffed into her bra.* "Now I'll just put the dead bugs back and—"

Pendano shook his head. "We'd better just run for it." Unselfconsciously, Pendano shucked off his robe, turned to his closet, and pulled out an old white shirt and a pair of jeans. "Please forgive the lounging-around clothes, they're all I have right now."

"I don't quite follow—" Graham said.

"I do." Heather felt sick. "This letter has to be officially received by Kowalski and Shaunsen, and they have to admit they got it, or receive it in front of witnesses. If President Pendano were to die before it's delivered—"

"Shaunsen would succeed in his own right," Pendano said, "and then you'd be good and well shit up the crick, as one of my favorite voters used to say. And there'd be a lot of stories they could tell to explain my death—I'm in poor health, I'm insane and died struggling against restraints, I could be found with a big load of sedatives in my belly—given the moral character of our Attorney General, I could be found with an ax in my head, and he'd rule it suicide. I need to put myself out of their reach, *now*, or make them damn well get my blood on their hands in public."

He had dressed while he was talking, and now he slipped his feet into loafers. "Secret Service outside—black man, shaved head, short and solid, mustache?"

"Right."

"Good, that's Scott Jevons. Ask him to come in."

Pendano explained the situation in a few swift, brutal sentences, not hesitating to say that Shaunsen was in the process of a coup and would murder him if he could. "I know it's a lot to ask of you to make the decision."

Jevons shrugged. "The President and a Cabinet Secretary have just told me that the President is healthy and taking back over. The President looks good to me. My job is to protect the President. That's how *my* outfit will see it." He pulled a cell phone from his jacket pocket, untied the condom in which it was bagged, and dialed. "Big Fox, this is Bravo. President Pendano has just signed a letter, witnessed by the Secretary of the Future and the Assistant Secretary for . . . uh . . ."

"Future Threats."

". . . Future Threats. The letter says he's well again, and he looks like it to me. He believes some people here in the White House may pose a threat to his safety. In the, um, present circumstances I recommend we move him to DRET at St. Elizabeth's, with a stop at the Capitol to present the letter to Speaker Kowalski. Standing by for—"

The door crashed open; Jevons shot first, hitting the NUG in the head. Heather got the one who came in after him. Gunshots rang in the hallways below; Heather and Scott Jevons moved to cover the elevator and stairs.

Scott had been shouting into the phone; he looked up from it, his face streaked with tears. "Mr. President, the Secret Service are being killed, the NUGs jumped us—"

Graham clapped Heather on the shoulder. "Can you climb down from the balcony behind us?"

"I probably—"

"Yes or no."

"Yes, or whatever else—"

"Deliver that letter to Kowalski. Now. It's effective as long as neither of you knows that Roger is dead—so go before you see anything."

Heather dropped hand over hand down a fire access ladder and plunged down a folding fire escape onto the South Lawn. Gunfire was rising to a crescendo inside; Shaunsen's forces were probably rushing the last few Secret Service holdouts and getting ready to storm the Third Floor. *When I last saw Roger Pendano,* she reminded herself, preparing to be a good witness, *he was alive and totally sane.*

As Heather burst through the open, unguarded gate, she still heard a few gunshots behind her, but she put all her effort into the race along the Mall toward the Capitol. On morning runs, she'd sometimes gone this way. *This would be one great time for a personal best.* She ran.

ABOUT TEN MINUTES LATER. THE WHITE HOUSE, WASHINGTON, DC. 11:26 A.M. EST. WEDNESDAY, NOVEMBER 6.

The only sound was Pendano's labored breathing, and Graham Weisbrod saying, "Easy, easy, easy," as he sat on the floor, cross-legged, holding his old student's head in his hands. Scott Jevons cut Pendano's shirt and pants away, finding the small wound in the front and the big one in the back, trying to find a way to stop the terrible flow of blood.

"Prof?"

"Yes, Roger."

"I don't feel good."

"You're hurt. We're taking care of you."

"It hurts." Pendano's body went limp.

The old professor and the young Secret Service agent were still sitting silently with the dead man when a voice from downstairs proclaimed, "This is Major Block, commanding the National Unity Guard. Surrender the former president or—"

"He's dead," Graham said loudly. "One of those rounds you were firing up through the floor got him. We won't shoot if you come up."

The National Unity Guard did not look military or even at all professional, to Graham's eye, but there were certainly a lot of them; probably Shaunsen had promised them all good pay and fast promotions. *Probably hired more of them from the crowd they swept up during the riots—that would be Shaunsen, all over.*

After a while, Shaunsen came in, squeezing through his guards, with several young aides in tow. The Acting President looked hard, once, at the body.

Then he told the NUG behind him, "Get the Chief Justice over here, right now. And Kowalski, too. And a doctor to confirm the death."

Weisbrod said, "Sir, this is a crime scene. We don't even know officially who fired the shot, or on whose orders, or—"

"That'll be enough, Weisbrod. I'm going to fire you right after the swearing-in. Meanwhile, you might as well come along and be in your last Cabinet picture. Make any trouble, though, and you're going straight to jail."

They hauled Weisbrod to his feet. His shoes, socks, and trouser legs were soaked with the dead president's blood, and he could still feel the warmth of Roger Pendano's head where he had cradled it on his thigh.

Shaunsen was bellowing orders to go get the Chief Justice, go get the Speaker, wasn't there a lawyer in the house who could swear him in, or did it have to be a judge? No matter, get him a damn judge this minute.

Weisbrod let them cuff him and hustle him awkwardly down the stairs and into a chair in the Secret Service break room, with a dozen or so captured Secret Service. They weren't allowed to talk. He lost himself in trying to trace the patterns in the carpet.

He heard a great deal of running and whispering in the corridors, and occasional shouting, but he didn't bother to sort out any words. Eventually six NUGs came in and let the Secret Service and Weisbrod have some water, and uncuffed each in turn long enough to go to the bathroom; the light from the windows suggested it was late afternoon, and his growling stomach agreed. *This is probably not the time to ask for a sandwich, all the same*. Weisbrod thought about how many reasons Shaunsen might have to keep him alive and came up with zero. *Probably they'll wait till dark, but maybe not even that long*.

ABOUT THREE HOURS LATER. THE WHITE HOUSE, WASHINGTON, DC. 4:47 P.M. EST. WEDNESDAY, NOVEMBER 6.

Weisbrod started awake. He had no idea how he had fallen asleep. The NUG who had kicked his leg to wake him also gave him a drink and uncuffed him to piss, then recuffed him and led him down the hall and into the Oval Office. The Secretaries of State, Defense, and Treasury were bunched together in the corner, all looking embarrassed. The Attorney General stood apart from the others not meeting anyone's eye.

Chief Justice Lopez was quarreling loudly with three presidential aides, and it wasn't clear whether she was a guest or a prisoner, but it was *very* clear that she thought she had been tricked into being there. There were more National Unity Guards than he could easily count.

Shaunsen looked around the room with a satisfied smile. "Now," he said, "first of all, let's establish that the President of the United States is dead. Dr. Brunner?"

The woman who stepped forward was small and square-built, with white hair and deep lines on her face. She shrugged as she read a statement out loud that she had examined the body, determined that it was Roger Pendano, and determined that he was indeed dead, the cause of death being a gunshot wound through the lower abdomen which had, among other things, torn the abdominal aorta, leading to an uncontrollable hemorrhage and death from loss of blood.

"Good," Shaunsen said, "Now according to Amendment Twenty-five, U.S. Constitution, as well as Article II, and the Succession Act of 1947—"

"Everybody down."

Graham knew instantly by the authority in the voice. Handcuffed, all he could do was fall over on his side. He caught a glimpse of a man leaping over him. The White House echoed with gunfire and low whumps and thuds that Weisbrod assumed must be some other weapon; from Weisbrod's perspective, the Oval Office filled up with the boots and camo pant legs of a swarm of soldiers.

Whatever was going on in the rest of the White House, it sounded like it was happening pretty fast. *The National Unity Guard were mostly street-kid activists and Democratic Party organizers deputized and given guns, probably their most seasoned fighters were some old gangbangers. It took more than a hundred of them to overrun about twenty Secret Service,* Weisbrod calculated, *and they had surprise and the Acting President on their side. They're no match for these professionals—wonder where we got them?*

"Your attention please," a voice said. Everyone turned and stared at Speaker Kowalski, who stood in the doorway with Will Norcross. As Kowalski and Norcross came in, Heather O'Grainne popped out to flank them on one side and Cameron Nguyen-Peters on the other.

"As of 3:38 P.M. today," Kowalski said, "Acting President Peter Shaunsen is under impeachment by a unanimous vote of the House of Representatives. I have a copy of the bill of impeachment with me to present to Chief Justice Lopez. And since both law and the Constitution prohibit anyone under impeachment from succeeding to the office of the President, he is not and cannot be the President."

Will Norcross looked more like a confused junior clerk than ever; his voice was soft but firm. "Furthermore, as of 4:12 P.M. this afternoon, I have been elected President Pro Tempore of the Senate, and at the request and direction of the NCCC, acting under Directive 51 to locate and emplace the succeeding president of the United States—"

"If I have to," Shaunsen said, "I will tie the whole government in knots for the next hundred years. I was not under impeachment at the time of the President's death, I was still Acting President and had not resigned my position as Senate President Pro Tempore—"

Lopez cleared her throat. Her expression was surprisingly gentle but left no room for questioning, like a mother saying *absolutely not* to a recalcitrant child. "If I have anything to do with it, every case you bring will be dismissed out of hand and at once. As for grounds, you may refer to such doctrines as paramount national survival and the phrases 'If the President is suspected' to be found in Madison's notes on impeachment. Less officially, the game is over."

In ten minutes, Norcross was sworn in, and Heather had had the distinct pleasure of being the arresting officer for a former president (or acting president, at least). Shaunsen, demanding to speak to "the unbiased national media," was taken to an FBI holding area; they uncuffed Graham and found him a chair, a cup of hot coffee, and a sandwich in a kitchen alcove. "Never mind feeding me," he said to Heather and Cameron. "I can't eat right now anyway. *That* was a photo finish. Where'd you get the troops from, and how'd you get them here so fast?"

"It's the Old Guard," Cameron said. "First Battalion, Third Infantry Regiment. The same outfit President Washington would have called for if he'd had a riot or a coup attempt to cope with. The battalion has a company at Fort McNair and the rest at Fort Myer. As soon as you and Heather started for the White House—since nowadays that's a two-hour trip—I had our signalers sending to the semaphore station on top of the Pentagon, and they relayed to both McNair and Myer. Just a precaution at that point, because I thought we might need them, and it takes a while to start four companies of infantry moving, and even longer for them to walk as far as they did today.

"Meanwhile, like every really paranoid or crazed president we've had since World War II, Shaunsen had the White House bugged everywhere, as much as he could with the nanoswarm and biotes eating the bugs. Lenny had brought in some talent to hack the White House listening system, so we knew when you went in to see Pendano, and we heard Scott's call to the Secret Service, and this guy Block, the National Unity Goon in Chief, yelling 'Plan J *now*!' "

"What's Plan J?" Heather asked.

"The National Unity Guard code message for 'kill or capture all the Secret Service you see, and then go upstairs and kill President Pendano.' "

Heather shuddered. "That's why the Secret Service got clobbered—they walked out into the halls to secure them and probably most of their deaths were in the first half minute, and by then they were down to a few guys trapped in rooms."

"Surprise wins a lot of things," Cameron said. "It did for us too. The National Unity Guard didn't set much of a watch. I think they were all busy figuring out which ones of them would be getting which patronage plums for having been such good little thugs. We pretty much just walked openly to our assembly point on the GWU campus, put the intel we had together, sent a runner over to Congress, and we were ready to go as soon as Kowalski and Norcross were ready. All standard Army doctrine: pre-position overwhelming force and grab the whole show all at once."

"So we have a functioning president again. Is it bone stupid or what that Kowalski couldn't have been the president all along?"

Cam shrugged. "The Constitution was intended to be hard to change—and we've still done things as stupid as Prohibition. When it only rains every hundred years, it's a miracle that any hole in the roof ever gets fixed. There's at least twenty little bombs waiting to go off buried in our Constitution, and if

I ran Congress, I'd appoint the equivalent of a bylaws committee, put through a Cleanup Amendment, and stump the states for it like a madman. But that's my weird perspective; it's my job to worry about all those little Constitutional bombs, and it's the nature of things that they hardly ever go off. But since you asked, that's what I'd do if it were up to me."

"If anything *more* goes wrong," Weisbrod pointed out, "it *might* be up to you."

Cameron grimaced. "Don't even *speak* of it. The NCCC office has just been as important as it ever needs to be, and Directive 51 is now safely back in the attic of history. They can dust it off sometime after 2200, if they're too stupid to fix the Constitution before then."

Graham nodded. "This is like watching the magician show you the trick bottom and saw slot in the box. I take it there was no problem explaining the matter to Kowalski."

"In that briefcase he was actually carrying two sets of papers—one for if Pendano was alive and the other for if Pendano was dead. We had a runner ready to go back to the Senate; they were sitting there waiting to vote for cloture, and then convict Shaunsen without debate. We had him. It looked scary but nobody was getting sawed in half."

Graham Weisbrod cupped his hands around his coffee and savored the warmth, the smell, and the last wonderful sips. "Nobody *vital*, you mean. You'd have gotten Norcross in and Shaunsen out, somehow, pretty soon. But speaking as the guy in the box . . . well, I still think that was a little close."

ABOUT AN HOUR LATER. THE CAPITOL STREET BRIDGE, WASHINGTON, DC. 6:30 P.M. EST. WEDNESDAY, NOVEMBER 6.

Alpha Company was walking back to McNair that evening, which would be most of the way back to St. Elizabeth's, so Heather, Graham, and Cameron traveled with them. At the Capitol Street bridge, five men volunteered to escort them the rest of the way.

On the bridge, looking out into the dark city with just a few flaring lights here and there, and the many campfires in the distance, Heather asked, "Graham, did you really think they'd kill you? I mean, I know they killed Roger Pendano, but that was a stray round—"

"Well. Um, well. Uh, for the last few days I've been thinking a lot about early Imperial Rome. Isn't that just like an old prof? But I have been. Just consider this: If you figure Roger Pendano was effectively President again as soon as he signed that note for you to take to Kowalski, then so far, today, we've had four presidents—Shaunsen, Pendano, Shaunsen again, and now Norcross."

"That's pretty Roman," Cam agreed.

"Well," Weisbrod said, "what used to happen to the people close to the emperors, during the power struggles?"

Cameron said, "Hunh. Yes, I see your point. And look right here and now. In the capital city that supposedly governs the continent, three of the key powers behind the throne—who just put the fourth leader of the day on the throne, I like that touch, Graham—can't walk home at night without an escort of armed men."

"Interesting," Graham said. "I had that Roman thought, the first time I can remember having it, right here on this bridge. And look around you. Doesn't it *look* like the Dark Ages?"

The wind picked up, and the handful of little flames in the darkness all danced and bobbed. They were glad to get off the bridge, and back to St. Elizabeth's, but all of them lay awake that night.

THE NEXT DAY. WASHINGTON, DC. (DRET/ST. ELIZABETH'S.) 1:00 A.M. EST. THURSDAY, NOVEMBER 7.

Norcross had set the meeting for 11:00 A.M. and specifically ordered them all not to schedule anything before it. He'd said he'd make sure civilization didn't fall apart while they caught up on sleep. It seemed like a very unfortunate phrasing.

Norcross arrived at St. Elizabeth's in a well-scrubbed biohazard Hummer, not a limo, and in a suit without a tie, "like a guy who is here to work," Heather commented to Lenny.

The room was buzzing; when he smiled at them and said, "Thank you all for being here," people applauded reflexively.

"Here's my first news for you all. I've spent a couple of hours reviewing this operation. Plainly you're the key to everything we're doing. I know I said some ambiguous things about the Department of the Future on the campaign trail, but honestly, I can't see any reason to break up a winning team at this point. By the same token, Homeland Security's task force here has done exceptional work, and the many liaisons from other Federal departments have as well. So first off, good job, and I want you to keep doing what you're doing.

"But there's one big change I do have to make. I have become uncomfortably aware that there is a real possibility of a new and different kind of nuclear weapon, one we probably could not have detected even before Daybreak, which we are completely powerless to detect now, and which might be pre-emplaced anywhere the enemy could reach—the pure fusion bomb. Of course, if they do have pure fusion bombs, Washington would be Daybreak's first and foremost likely target and I can only guess why they have not yet hit us with it.

"Therefore, I am scattering all critical Federal operations away from Washington, to secure areas where it is less likely that there are pre-emplaced nuclear weapons, and where there are enough local resources to support the relocated Federal offices. All of that is bureaucratese for *everybody's going to military bases in the boondocks.*

"I'm ordering you to move immediately—and by immediately, I mean the people who've been bunking here or can gather up their families fast enough will move this afternoon—to Fort Benning, Georgia. For those of you who don't know, because the people at Benning were on their toes and worked ceaselessly, they've managed to keep a few transport planes running. Right now ground crews are burning scrap wood on the runways at Reagan National, and following up with caustic soda, and a boiling-water rinse; hopefully it will be as biote-free as they can make it just at the time the planes land, turn around, pick all of you up, and take off again—*that fast,* if we can do it, to minimize exposure time on the ground.

"I want all of you in a place that is unlikely to be destroyed; we can't lose one of our most useful nerve centers. And the odds of our enemy—if there is one—having sneaked a weapon onto the home base of several of our elite units is much smaller than their chances of having concealed one in an open civilian city like Washington."

He waited out the chaotic upsurge of chatter.

"Make sure you take every scrap of paper with anything important on it, and all your paper books and maps and so on. Those communication gadgets you've jury-rigged too, of course.

"Priority for personnel is this: First regular Federal personnel without families in the area. Then the volunteer assistants, who've been doing such great work here, the ones without local family first. Then families of Federal personnel from the area; then families of assistants from the area. Everyone boards at Reagan National in five hours, at four thirty. We expect most of you to walk so that the biohazard-capable vehicles can be used to move books and papers."

"Sir?" Graham Weisbrod asked.

"Dr. Weisbrod. I don't know if I told you officially that I de-fired you this morning, but if you're asking, then, yes, I want you to go on this."

"That wasn't my question, sir. I was just going to ask why we're not relocating the whole Federal government to secure bases. I can understand why you might send us in the first wave, but it doesn't sound like you're going to move yourself."

"Excellent question." Norcross sat down on the desk behind him and looked around. "This is an issue on which I've overridden many of my advisors. Here's why I'm staying put, and so is Congress, at least for the foreseeable future.

"One, we need to have plenty of people near one of our most precious resources—the paper archive of the Library of Congress. We've got no way to move it before next spring at the earliest, it's essential that we not lose all that knowledge, and it's essential that we don't just preserve it but use it. You realize that somewhere in there, on paper, is how to make pretty much every gadget and chemical that civilization needs? Including the ones that can be biote-resistant and nanoswarm-resistant? I've already got a dozen guys on their way here from JPL who will be sifting through early rocketry material, because we'll need to be able to get things into orbit again sometime in the next few years; my science advisor tells me that it will be a lot easier to harden tube electronics against nanoswarm, and there are literally *miles* of shelves about tube electronics in there.

"Aside from that, you realize we could potentially have thousands of books about all of the useful arts that we can reprint and distribute? How to navigate by the stars, how they used to survey for rail lines and canals before lasers and computers, all sorts of skills we'll need for the next century, because, ladies and gentlemen, if nobody's told you yet or you haven't figured it out, undoing Daybreak will be a work of generations. Knowledge is power, and that power is *here*, and while it is, we need to be here.

"Then there's the psychological side. Much as I've always criticized relying on Washington to solve our problems, the fact is, when things get really bad, *we do*. It should *not* look like the Federal government is running away.

"And the risks may be smaller than they appear. Pure fusion bombs require fast computers and high-powered lasers. Maybe the reason no bombs went off in Washington is that the nanoswarm ate them.

"For all those reasons, I'm willing to take the chance, and take my stand right here. You might say I'm betting my life on it.

"And no, you are not going to argue with me about this one today. You can argue with me sometime next spring, when I will visit Fort Benning. Meanwhile, I have nine other stops to make today, and you need to get packing." He nodded and smiled as they applauded, and was out the door before anyone could raise any further dissent.

"Well," Lenny said, "at least we get one more airplane ride before the end of the world."

ABOUT FIVE HOURS LATER. WASHINGTON, DC. 4:30 P.M. EST. THURSDAY, NOVEMBER 7.

Chris Manckiewicz saw the plane taking off from Reagan National late in the afternoon and trotted over to the White House. In Norcross's open administration, all he had to do was ask: DRET had gone to Fort Benning.

That night, at dinner, after people read their stories aloud and everyone voted and argued about what should go in at what length, just at the dessert course when people tended to miss Rusty the most, he said, "All right, new business—*big* new business. Let me lay this out for you. Our new president has sent one Cabinet Secretary, the NCCC, and his most consulted, most-used, working-on-the-most-important-stuff group of advisors to one of the best-functioning surviving military bases. Does anyone besides me see what this probably implies?"

"Favors for his strong constituency down South," George Parwin said, in his usual tone of dismissal.

"Not the way I read it, George. Will Norcross is not purely venal and he's smart enough to know he can't afford to be perceived that way. So I don't believe he'd severely inconvenience himself by moving his key advisors out of easy range just to rake in graft or pick up votes in elections that might never be held. I think what he's doing is sending a continuity team outside the city."

"You mean he thinks he might lose *Washington*?"

"Put it together. He's sending one guy in the line of presidential succession, the guy whose job would be to make sure that the succession goes in an orderly way, and the team of advisors behind our present policy—to one of the best-defended sites on the continent."

"You read a lot of stuff into things," Hayley said. "My turn for dishes, and my vote is we don't change anything we're doing." She stood and gathered plates.

Man, I miss Rusty. I'd've made her see sense and she'd've made them see it, I just know that. "Here's what I was thinking. I think some of us should go down to that area to establish a new paper there. One linked to the *Advertiser-Gazette*, of course, and sharing stories, but I think they've just made Columbus, Georgia, an important city—"

"Where's that?"

"It's where Fort Benning is," Chris said, trying not to think *you idiot* loudly enough to be heard, "and we need a bureau there, and that bureau should be self-supporting—meaning it puts out its own paper. So I was wondering if anyone wanted to volunteer?"

The stares at him were blank. "We're barely weeks old, Chris," Don Parmenter said. "We're just getting people to read papers again. That just sounds to me like spreading ourselves too thin."

Okay, Plan B. "What if I were to turn my interest in the paper over to you all—we can figure out who gets what shares—and keep maybe five percent, not enough for control or to matter much, and then go set up my own paper down in Georgia? With some kind of guarantee that you'd pay me for any stories I sent you, that you used, and I could buy content from you?"

"I think you're re-inventing the AP."

"Well, it's gone, and we're a newspaper. Shortly to be two newspapers, with more to follow. We *need* an AP. It makes some sense, you know?"

"It does," George conceded. "What worries me is that you'll get a hundred miles south, realize how crazy you were and come home and want your paper back."

"Word of honor, I won't do that. If I get a major attack of regret, I'm going to want to keep moving toward Georgia anyway, because I'm sure not going to want to come back here and face you guys. You're not the nice types who would give me my newspaper back and never say anything about it, you know?"

"You *bet* we're not."

That night's production work was combined with a sort of farewell party. Chris had more to drink than he intended and gently fended off a couple of friendly offers from staffers who thought they might not mind a good-bye tumble with the ex-boss. He shook Parwin's hand, and they drafted documents that everyone witnessed, and the next morning, for the first and only time, he was privileged to be the last one up; most of them were already out on assignment by the time he arose.

ABOUT THE SAME TIME. REAGAN NATIONAL AIRPORT, WASHINGTON, DC. 4:30 P.M. EST. THURSDAY, NOVEMBER 7.

Because she was with Lenny, Heather was able to hook a ride on a biohazard Hummer to Reagan National, and they had more time to go through the antiseptic scrubs and degaussing, and for Lenny and the technicians to figure out how they could kill any nanoswarm that might be on him without destroying internal electronics that kept him alive. Eventually Heather claimed a bench inside the transport, next to where Lenny tied down his wheelchair, and they napped and cuddled, holding hands and occasionally muttering "I love you," or "I'm glad you're here" at each other.

"Wake up, sleepyheads."

Heather sat up; Arnie and Allie were there, with Graham, and Sherry, who was practically beaming. "Hey, you're not getting rid of me that easily. You're who I want to be when I grow up."

"Oh, god, I don't even know who *I'm* going to be when I grow up. So did they get all the volunteers and assistants onto the planes?"

"Yep," Graham said. "And all the families for everyone. Tight squeeze, but we're all making it. It'll probably smell way too much like us by the time the flight is done, but we'll all be there, and apparently the commanding general at Benning, Norm McIntyre, is some kind of old buddies with Cameron and going out of his way to make us welcome."

Lenny stretched and yawned, then put his hand on Heather's arm. "To tell you the truth, I'm probably a coward or something, but I'll be just as glad to get away from DC. It does feel like living in a bull's-eye, and I'm not convinced the serious rioting is over with."

"Not to mention Benning has occasional electricity and better access to hot water," Allie said. "And compared to DC, a lot less freezing our asses off this winter."

They set their newly decontaminated gear down and packed in close, making room for the many other little knots and balls of coworkers, families, and whatever other ways people had assorted themselves for the trip.

Flying through the early night, they all took turns at looking out the window to see America by night, from the air, with only candle, bonfire, and lamp light. Probably fewer than a thousand people had ever seen such a thing; and very likely, not many more would, perhaps ever.

PART 3

ONE HUNDRED
DAYS

BLASTULA

*Every new life begins with division: the fertilized cell splits,
and the split parts split, and the split parts split again, until
there is a ball of identical cells, the blastula. In the beginning
there is division.*

The new world grew and divided and divided again. In
the next two weeks, the electric power system collapsed completely as the nanoswarm destroyed components for the control systems; biotes ate insulation and shelter; and wrecked
transportation, bandits, and riots kept anyone from reaching
substations and power lines. As late as November 15th, perhaps one in twelve homes had electricity; nearly everyone
listened to President Norcross's Thanksgiving prayer broadcast on an unpowered crystal set, or using carefully hoarded
batteries, by candle or lamplight.

By the last week in November, Detroit, Louisville, Buffalo,
Kansas City, Jacksonville, Chattanooga, and Sacramento
had all suffered catastrophic fires like the first ones in St.
Paul, Boston, and Chicago, spreading for many blocks, with
firefighters powerless. No one knew how many died; no one
looked for bodies in the rubble.

On November 11th, nanoswarm infected the nuclear aircraft carrier Ronald Reagan; by November 14th it was clear
that even whole-crew round-the-clock efforts could not erad-
icate them. On November 17th, 18th, and 19th the ship made
one last fast pass northward along the California coast.
The helicopters judged to be still safe flew back and forth,
off-loading crew onto any wide, flat spot near enough to a
town; when the helicopters went bad, the last few hundred
of the crew departed in boats. Finally a skeleton crew took
her northward, hoping to keep her running long enough to
scram her reactors and scuttle her in the Queen Charlotte

Trench, eventually to be run over and buried several miles deep by North America itself. If the reactors did not breach in the next few decades, the ship would be under a hundred feet of bottom mud before any radioactive materials leaked. Nobody had heard from Ronald Reagan since; probably there wasn't a working radio on board, but they had hoped that the captain and residual crew would have been able to reach shore in a small boat by now and find an operating ham or other way to call in.

The Sixth Fleet, after losing two support ships and about forty planes to airborne nanoswarm, had made the risky run through Gibraltar, and joined the Second Fleet, out in the Atlantic. The Navy ships didn't have much of anywhere to hide; near the American Atlantic coast, prevailing winds carried nanoswarm and biotes eastward, and the Gulf Stream flowed out of extremely human-and-technology-infested waters.

To conserve precious oil, the nuclear ships towed the others, as much as possible. They spent several days on the Grand Banks because the fishing was good, and there were many thousands of mouths to feed, but those waters are rough in November, and they had to flee southward at the first signs of storms.

Satellite and cautious air reconnaissance revealed all but complete collapse in Africa, without even apparent local order; India appeared to be holding together with a couple of sizable rebellions under control and immense planting efforts under way. South America was in flux, with some local military commanders carving out chunks of territory and threatening to seize capitals, but the analysts thought i would stabilize into something like its old map, with a few cities and provinces either becoming independent or switching nations; Europe was breaking down in something that looked distressingly like warlordism, and famine was worst there Streams of refugees poured up the Rhine Valley and across the German plain from the Low Countries; without power machinery for the pumps, the sea was creeping in, and everyone knew that in a bad storm, there would be no rescues Russia was collapsing into the hands of dozens of petty kings each with his own transmitter, manifesto, and mission to save the world, but at least it looked like a fair amount of winter *wheat was being planted; if roads to the west, especially rail lines, were re-opened soon enough, next year might be better.*

After a rocky few weeks, central Mexico was regaining control of the rest of the country, and the Mexican government was in regular touch with Washington and Ottawa; there was talk of a unified continental policy, and of joint action to stabilize the Caribbean, where drug lords, local military, religious cults, criminal gangs, and American filibusteros were re-creating the Pirate's Main of four hundred years before.

The American Midwest and East were freezing and starving; surely not all of the reports of cannibalism were true, but it seemed likely before spring. Death tolls from exposure and hunger-related diseases were high but nothing like those in Asia or Europe. The South was under "soft martial law"—local military bases providing government services—and doing fairly well, with little chafing at the lost rights so far. Mountain West city and county governments seemed to be holding together.

More than sixty different theocracies had been proclaimed in California alone, which was turning into another general pool of anarchy.

For Federal, State, and local governments, the libertarian/survivalist Castles were rapidly becoming more of an asset than a liability. President Norcross turned back a request from Harrison Castro and forty other freeholders to grant them an official status, but he did permit Federal agencies to acknowledge Castles both as locations and as local governments in his reports. "Just a matter of reality," he assured his staff. "Yes, we'll need to remind them that they're large local businesses, not feudal fiefs, sometime. But for right now, most of 'em do what we need 'em to do, so don't let's pick any fights we can't afford."

The divisions went on, everything everywhere splitting into more pieces; and as the pieces began to make their own way in the world, they began to take different pathways.

Differentiation is the way a blastula becomes, eventually, a whole new person in its own right; no longer a blob, its cells become bone and muscle, hair and blood, and then arm bone and leg muscle, eyebrows and scalp hair, a pumping heart, a seeing eye; and three weeks after Daybreak, differentiation was proceeding.

CASTLE LARSEN. (JENNER, CALIFORNIA.) 11:00 A.M. PST. WEDNESDAY, NOVEMBER 27.

"Maybe we should stop for today and start again on Friday," Larry Mensche said, "I'd still like to ask about a few things, but you've already had two seizures and you look exhausted." *Funny thing,* he thought, *with this one, you don't do tough-cop nice-cop, you do "the nice cop who is pleased" and "the nice cop who is disappointed." Going by what I'm seeing of her personality here and now,* this *little girl shouldn't have been able to be a* shoplifter, *let alone a terrorist—she was only ever any kind of rebel because she didn't want to disappoint her parents.* While he waited for her answer, he filled a glass with cold water from the pitcher and handed it to her.

She drank gratefully. "Why not tomorrow?"

"It's Thanksgiving," he said, "and I guess Quattro Larsen has sort of a big day planned. He's—"

Ysabel's face crumpled and she grabbed for a fresh handkerchief from the pile beside her.

He sat beside her on the couch and asked, "Missing your family?"

"Yeah. Used to be Dad and Mom called from wherever in the world they were, no matter the cost or the inconvenience. They never had anything to talk with me about . . . or we'd have a really brief cold awkward conversation . . . or we'd argue. But it was something that happened every Christmas and Thanksgiving. But they were in backcountry Tanzania so . . ." she seemed to grope for some conclusion, and settled on, "now they can't call."

She wiped her eyes furiously, adding, "And considering I've just helped a few hundred million people starve to death, I have a lot of fucking nerve getting upset about having my Thanksgiving spoiled."

"You feel what you feel."

"Thank you. You're very nice to me."

"You know things I want to know, Ysabel. And you tell me I stay nice because you stay cooperative."

She looked up at him with a sadly twisted little smile. "So if I ever stop talking, you're going to get out your Taser?"

"No," he said, "and Bambi wouldn't either. We'd just turn you over to someone else who would."

"That's how things work, really, isn't it? Daybreak used me to get you, you'll use me to get Daybreak."

"Would you like food, or do you just want a nap?"

"I feel like a piece of wrung-out shit, but seizures make me hungry, I guess they burn a lot of energy. If there's any of that bread left from breakfast? With maybe some of the veggie butter? The sugar rush'll probably knock me out."

Mensche left her in her room, with the outside lock thrown; Larsen had put bars on the windows, but Mensche'd never seen anyone who was less of an escape risk. He found Bambi and Quattro sitting in the kitchen, drinking some of "the possibly last stash of coffee for a hundred miles," as Quattro called it, and going over a map, trying to figure out whether the best way east would be to sail to Tehuantepec and try to cross Mexico there; walk on I-70; or wait for one of the steam trains that the railroad nuts were working on getting running.

"Of all the precious resources," Bambi said, "who'd've thought our railroad nuts would be so invaluable? If we can just get the coal to them, we have at least a hundred good, operable steam locomotives, if we can believe KP-1."

"Now that the mainstream media is basically one radio station," Quattro said. "and we don't have any way to check up on them, everyone believes them again."

Mensche sliced three thick pieces of Quattro's whole-grain concrete, which he privately thought of as "political-extremist bread"—only right-wing survivalists and left-wing granolas could possibly pretend it tasted good. He smeared it with veggie butter, more political-extremist food. "Roth's pretty wiped. The questions that Arnie Yang has been sending all seem to hit her like electric shocks, but after she comes out of the seizure, she spills her guts. I don't know how he does it, but he's some kind of genius."

"At DoF, we *called* him the House Genius," Bambi Castro said. "Need someone to watch your back while you set it down for her?"

"I'm more likely to be attacked by a dishrag. This little chick is *beaten*."

. . .

He lunged for the bolt, dropping the tray, and flung the door open before he was even conscious of hearing the strange, throttled noise. She had tied one corner of her sheet around the motor of the ceiling fan; she held the other end over her head, fighting the loop she had tied as if it were trying to fasten itself around her neck. Though her eyes bulged from her deep red face, only her own straining muscles constricted her throat; she held the sheet back from herself as if it were an anaconda trying to put a loop around her neck.

Mensche couldn't break her grip, but he could hold the loop away from her head. *What the hell can it be like inside her head?* He remembered something Arnie had suggested. "Ysabel, your parents love you very much, and they want to see you again someday."

Her face seemed to fall into itself like a ball of burning newspaper, she let go of the sheet and fell to the floor; a great gasp of air howled painfully into her throat. Mensche sat down next to her on the floor and pulled her over so that she could hang on to him; Bambi burst in, but Mensche just shook his head and gestured *shhh*.

Bambi whispered, "Hey, your daughter?"

"Yeah?"

"She had a great dad, you know."

"Thanks." Mensche didn't see any reason to explain about the endless fights and screaming when Deb was a teenager, about being played against Deb's mother into hapless veering between excessive bribes and excessive punishment, about believing Deb when she lied and doubting her when she needed his belief, about any of those awful years of too much hope mixed with too little a decade ago. *Any damn idiot can look like a good dad if he only has to deal with* one *kind of trouble and his whole life isn't at stake.*

ONE DAY LATER. ANTONITO, COLORADO. 7:15 P.M. MST. THANKSGIVING DAY, NOVEMBER 28.

Thanksgiving Day was unseasonably warm. Jason got a day's work from the town on the north approach crew, takin a long walk up US 285 to help bring refugees in; whenever the weather lifted enough, desperate refugees from the Front Range would leave their improvised shelter and start trickling into Antonito along 285 again, some thrown out, some because walking south had become a habit after they'd escaped the linear deathtrap of the I-25 corridor from the Springs to Fort Collins.

They had ridden out in Doc Bashore's wagon and set up base six miles north of town at dawn. After that it had been a long day of taking his turn walking out, sometimes as much as two miles, to meet the little clusters of refugees, figuring out their immediate needs, and then flagging for a nurse, or for Doc and the wagon, or just walking them back in.

"It was great of Doc to come all the way out on 17 and give us all a ride in. That wagon's no faster than walking, but if we stay here, I want to get one, and the horse to pull it," Jason said. "I *love* the part where the horse does all the work."

"Till you get home. Doc's prolly *still* rubbing that horse down. He says you gotta always take care of the horse before you take care of yourself. How come you had to end up way over on 17?"

"Bobby Kronstadt ran into some hostiles, and we all ran like mad to back him up—now *that's* exercise. Four big angry men, and one very shrill woman, looking for a town that'd want them to run it, and mad as all *shit* that it wasn't us. Told em we didn't care where they went, but they weren't getting any closer to our town. Bobby and I tracked them all the way cross-country till they headed west on 17. Cap figured we were the youngest and healthiest, with the best shoes. That'll teach me to let you make moccasins."

"Aw, bullshit, baby. The other guys prolly think you're lucky 'cause I'm hot, but they *know* you're lucky about them shoes."

He grinned at her. "You know I think about how nice it is to have the mocs every day on the trail." He stepped closer to her. "All day long I think, can't wait to get home to that gal o'mine, and see if there are any new shoes . . ." His fingers traced delicately down the sides of her neck, stroking the dragon tattoo.

"The soup's pretty hot, now, but I think them potatoes'll prolly need to cook some more."

"Then let 'em. Our first Thanksgiving here should be a good one."

When they were happy and satisfied and just cuddling on the bed, she asked, "So is this Thanksgiving being good so far?"

"Oh, yeah, I'm about as thankful as I can get."

"Let me get dressed and see about the soup, and maybe I can get you thankfuller."

Beth's fringe benefit for helping with the mass dressing-out of mule deer and pronghorns at the community kitchen had been a generous pail of trimmings. For their Thanksgiving soup, she had boiled that with some potatoes, a share of leftover cooked rice from the community kitchen, a can of tomatoes, a handful of thawed-but-probably-not-yet-spoiled frozen brussels sprouts, and a couple of old, stringy carrots. They promised themselves that by next Thanksgiving they'd have turkey, or at least chicken.

For now, compared to Thanksgiving with his family or at the commune, this was, hands down, the best he'd had: no football, no tofu, no sermons about making something of himself, no dark little hints about Beth having grown up in a doublewide, no sermons about not oppressing people.

"For two refugees, this place is a palace," Jason said.

"You're right, I really am even more thankful."

"Yeah, baby, we're *so* lucky. And I listen to that wind and I just think, the place is warm and toasty and all ours." She pulled out a potato on a long-handled fork, cut it in half, and tried a bite. "That's about as done as it's getting."

Later on, when the warmth, safety, privacy, and full bellies pulled them toward bed, they banked the fire, put the soup-pot into the cold corner of the room to keep it fresh longer, and washed with warm water from the iron bucket that Beth kept by the stove. Holding Beth, on a box spring and mattress with real sheets, up on a platform Jason had made from some old crates and boards, he thought, *This is living.*

ONE DAY LATER. FORT BENNING, GEORGIA. (DRET COMPOUND, NEAR THE COLUMBUS SIDE OF THE BASE.) A LITTLE AFTER 1:00 P.M. EST. FRIDAY, NOVEMBER 29.

Heather had made the appointment with Cameron specifically, rather than Graham, because *stupid me, I thought if Cam just understood the other side, that would solve the problem. Now I see that's what was causing it.*

He was giving her his usual small, polite, meaningless smile, and he'd been nodding more and more as he listened to her. Finally, he said, "Heather, that's just politics. The real world is complicated and contradictory, but policies have to be clear and monovalent to be carried out. If Graham wins the argument—and he might, he and Norcross talk a lot and get along well—then I will shrug, carry out the policy, and pray that Graham is right. You know it's not personal with me and Graham. I *like* the man. I know he's sincere, and respect his judgment. *And* Arnie is the cleverest guy in the world *and* absolutely indispensable, but every so often, his extreme cleverness overpowers his common sense, he starts sniffing up his own butt, he falls in, and he disappears up his own ass like a star falling into a black hole. And when that happens, I have to *not* follow Arnie up his own ass. So I say—"

There was a knock at the door, and before Cameron could say, "Come in," Sherry stuck her head in. "Heather, note from Lenny—he said it was urgent—meet him over at the infirmary."

"Go," Cam said.

Heather hurried through the gray fall mist, her heart sinking.

It wasn't fair.

They'd made the dangerous trip down here, lived through the constant danger of exposure in Washington, she'd carried him in her bare hands down through corridors and stairwells that must have been crawling with biotes, and she'd been so careful to scrub and clean him everywhere, brushing every bit of exposed plastic with alcohol and . . .

She knew it couldn't make any difference, but she ran, anyway. *Maybe he has something else, maybe it's serious but it's not that, maybe—*

At the door to the infirmary, she made herself slow to a

walk. *If this is it, I'm going to do it right.* Inside, they'd been watching for her, and she was guided down the corridor to the room where Lenny waited.

Give Army doctors credit, they don't run off and let people face their troubles alone, Heather thought. The lady who stood there waiting for her was tall and dark, with close-cropped hair; she was as dignified, and implacable, as a mountain. "Ms. O'Grainne. I'm Dr. Lee. Dr. Plekhanov wanted you to be present while we discuss something very serious."

"I came as quick as I could." She was crouched beside Lenny; *he hates to look up, don't make him do that,* she wanted to say to Dr. Lee, but then she saw that the doctor had squatted down on Lenny's other side.

Lenny said, "Heather, babe. This is it. Dr. Lee just scraped four millimeters of decayed plastic goo off my kidney drain—"

"But—Lenny, there was nothing this morning—"

"Of course there wasn't," Lenny said.

Dr. Lee added, "We'll never know how it got to him, and it wouldn't help us if we did. It could have been floating on the air this morning while he was getting dressed. The stuff grows so fast, faster than yeast in bread dough or a virus in your sinuses, Ms. O'Grainne."

"I just . . . he was *safe* when I left this morning."

Lenny's strong good hand reached out and took her by the back of the neck, turning her face to him, catching her eyes. "*I* was safe. Time enough to talk about me like I'm not here when I'm not."

She let him hold her while she cried, not for long, but enough to find her heart again. Wiping her eyes, she said, "Dr. Lee. You said there was a difficult decision to make."

"Well, I've drilled out as much plastic as I dare, and refilled with surgical cement from a clean tube. Maybe I got all. Maybe nothing will happen. The next few hours, a day at most, and we'll know.

"In a way, the sensible, conservative thing to do would be to replace his kidney drain with one of the clean spare drains we sealed into glass jars right after Daybreak. None of those has any visible signs of decay. The problem with surgery that we have nothing we can use inside the human body that reliably kills nanoswarm, and we might let that in, where would destroy Dr. Plekhanov's pacemaker, or his artificial kidney or spleen, or attack his aortal booster pumps. Between all of those he has six running electric motors, four micro-computers, and eight motion-driven generators in his body. Losing any of those could be fatal, and internal nanoswarm excreting strong acid would be a painful way to go.

"But I can tell you still think surgery and a replacement drain would be better. "

"Even if I got the whole infection today, I'm not sure that my surgical cement plug will hold together. Dr. Plekhanov has to remove the accumulated fluid about every ten days, and I'm afraid my fix on that plug will break when he does; there were no specs to tell me if that surgical cement would work in that application, but it was all I had."

"So that's the choice," Heather said numbly. "Replace the drain now, while the biotes are in check, and hope the nano-warm don't kill him; or wait and see if the drain starts to spoil again, and run the risk of an emergency surgery with even more danger."

"That's it," Lenny agreed.

"Not much of a choice."

"Oh, it's a big choice. There's just not much selection." Lenny put his hand on her cheek; she pressed against it. *His fingers are so strong, right now he's still so healthy—* "Dr. Lee says we can figure that surgical cement plug won't last either; something will contaminate it even if it went in clean, and sooner or later it will start to decay. The new drain, if they put that in, will come down with decay sooner or later too; maybe in a week, maybe in ten years, but eventually. The longest they could keep me alive would probably be in an almost-sterile environment, where you could visit me and we could touch if every time you go through the kind of scrub that they gave us coming into Benning.

"And yet I'd still be doomed, Heather, we *both* know that. I'm a little chunk of the Big System, and Daybreak is going to kill the Big System. But here's the thing. We don't know if my brain getting infected was a once-in-ten-years fluke, or if it's something that is bound to happen every three months. But we do know that drain has already been infected once, and despite Dr. Lee's best efforts, it might not be clean now. And we do know that surgical cement isn't going to be as durable as the original plastic. So I figure, if everything is perfect with the repair job she just did on me—I've got less than a year. Just too many things that are too close to certain to go wrong.

"But if I go in right away for the surgery . . . well, there are three possibilities. Opening me up is always dangerous; too many parts are broken already. Or I might get nanoswarm. Or—and I think it's the most likely—they'll get me back to where I was a day or so ago. And at that point . . . maybe getting a plastic infection is something that will happen every few weeks, and that's all the life extension I'll get. But maybe this really was a freak case, maybe it won't happen again for ten or fifteen years. I might even live long enough for them to redevelop all the stuff that's needed to keep me alive.

"So, basically, if I don't go in for the surgery, it's a near certainty I'll die this year. If I do go in for surgery, odds are I'll just die this year anyway, *and* there's maybe an increased chance of dying tomorrow, but there's a tiny little chance of living with you for years and years. So . . . hey." He brushed her tears away with his hand again. "Do you need some time to get it back together?"

"Yeah, but I can spend the rest of my life doing that." She sighed. "I see the point. I really do." She wiped her eyes. "Lenny. You're not doing anything to me that I'm not also doing to you. You know I'm not going to sit this whole thing out behind a desk; any time, Cam or the president might send me where I could come down with a bad case of shot or stabbed. Even if *you're* here for ten more years, there's no guarantee I will be. So I think you better take your chance to really live."

Lenny nodded. "I told Dr. Lee you'd say that. There's one thing you can do that would be great."

"Name it."

"They can't open me up and get to work till midday tomorrow. I can't safely go back to our place, so I'm in the hospital for tonight, but if you're willing to let them do a full scrub on you, we could be in the same bed."

"A full scrub is like the one we had on arrival, where they shave my head and exfoliate me?"

"That's the one."

"I'm glad you like your girls bald and bright pink."

"I like my girls *you*. Bald and bright pink is just a side benefit."

SIX HOURS LATER. FORT BENNING, GEORGIA. 7:30 P.M. EST. FRIDAY, NOVEMBER 29.

Her skin was rubbed raw, and Lenny suggested that next time she ask them to use finer-grain sandpaper, but they forgot it all in the pleasures of one more night with each other. "I'm glad you're good at in-the-moment and for-right-now," Lenny said, "because I sure needed you to be tonight." His powerful hands were gently pulling and tugging at her scalp muscles, enough to force them to relax, and the release of tension was wonderful. "Does this feel good?"

"Mmm. The best."

"I'm kind of liking it myself." He rubbed and tugged firmly, and she let herself get lost in the sensations, being just here, just now. "Got the energy for another round, or is it time to sleep?"

"I'm not sure I want to sleep at all, tonight." She moved him gently into a better position and kissed him.

Coming up briefly for air, he said, "Well, they're going to knock me out for a lot of hours tomorrow; why sleep now?"

THE NEXT MORNING. FORT BENNING, GEORGIA. 6:48 A.M. EST. SATURDAY, NOVEMBER 30.

The next morning, they were turning toward each other, cuddling and touching, not sure whether to be awake yet, when Heather smelled a combination of rotten cheese and flyblown meat.

Lenny saw her expression and sniffed. "Fuck. Oh, shit. Where do I have it?"

The new piece in his plastic kidney drain, which Dr. Lee had sculpted so carefully from surgical cement, had brownish ooze around its edges. Heather kissed him once more, and said, "They'll be rushing you through everything from here on. You make it through and come back, 'kay?"

"I will if any of it is up to me. Whether I do or not, I love you."

"And I love you." She pushed the call button that would start the chaos, and dressed all but instantly in the scrubs they'd given her; Lenny asked her to help him into the awk-

ward hospital wheelchair, and she was just making sure
was comfortable, even if it was only for the short trip dov
the hall, when the nursing team arrived.

**ABOUT FOUR HOURS LATER. FORT BENNING, GEORGIA.
11:15 A.M. EST. SATURDAY, NOVEMBER 30.**

They had put her at some distance from the operating roo
Dr. Lee had said, "I don't want your instincts kicking in
there's some running and yelling."

Heather admitted it made sense, but still, she wished s
were close enough to be sure of knowing whatever was goi
on. She knew they'd be taking a lot of extra time, worki
with extra-sterilized instruments and giving everything mu
more than the usual scrubbing, double-checklisting ever
thing to make sure that nothing was contaminated inside; ca
tion would take time, and so would working as systematical
as they would have to.

She was bored after a while, sitting in the waiting area,
when she saw Sherry passing by, she flagged her down ar
had the dullest and most tedious paperwork files brought ov
and sterilized; she sat with her legs up on the bench, scri
bling out each new document, accumulating a tidy heap.

They offered her lunch just before the hospital kitch
closed to start fixing dinner; she couldn't have told anyor
afterward, what it was. *Pretty typical hospital experienc
that's what I'll tell Lenny, because he'll scold me for han
ing around here and fretting.* She kept working because it w
easy to put a few words down on a form, stare off into space f
a few minutes, then put a few more words down on the form

Late that afternoon, Dr. Lee came in, sat beside her, ar
put an arm around her; she was already weeping when t
doctor finally said, "His heart just stopped—even with t
pacemaker going—and nothing would restart it. We do
know if it was a toxin from the infection, or something wro
in his artificial systems, or it was just time; but he just stoppe
and we couldn't start him again."

They sat together for a long time, but neither of the
seemed to have anything to say.

That night, back in their quarters, she packed Lenny

things, because she didn't expect to sleep, and if she didn't do it then, she might not for a year. His clothes went into a box for decontamination and distribution; his books and papers would go to his colleagues to look through, to try to pick up the threads of his work; the few mementos he had carried in his pack from his apartment to across DC, when he'd made the trek with Heather and Sherry, went into her own keepsake box. *Maybe someday I'll meet his family, and they can explain the ones that I don't know about. I wish I'd thought to ask. I guess people always think there will be time.*

TWO DAYS LATER. FORT BENNING, GEORGIA. 11:00 A.M. EST. MONDAY, DECEMBER 2.

Heather remembered every detail of Lenny's funeral; for safety's sake, he was cremated. She remembered blubbering something briefly about how much he'd meant to her; it hadn't been exactly what was on the little typed sheet she'd written, because she couldn't read through the tears. She remembered more about the other speakers—Arnie, warm and fond, helping everyone smile with gratitude that Lenny had been in their lives; Graham, brief, stiff, too dignified; Cam, reading a short message from President Norcross, and then adding his own few sentences.

"Taps" had always torn her heart out even before now; there were no firearm salutes because guns that definitely fired were still too scarce. Norcross had requested that Lenny's ashes be stored on the base until it was practical to inter them at Arlington.

Afterward, Allie walked Heather back to her now-too-lonely quarters "just to make sure you get to bed okay tonight." She hung around, giving Heather orders—"Now into your pj's, now turn the covers back—"

"Are you going to read me a story?"

"If I have to. What I'm not going to do is leave you here sitting up for days, or wandering around, till you're sick and exhausted."

"You're a good friend."

"I'm a good staffer. Strict orders from Graham and Cam both: Make sure she's okay."

"You're also a good friend."

"Yeah. Get into the bed; I'll turn the light off on my way out."

Heather stretched out and shut her eyes. *Not sure about sleeping, but I'm certainly tired.* "Thank Arnie for me. His eulogy was . . . well, it was Arnie that made me remember *Lenny.*"

"Sometimes he has a pretty human touch," Allie said.

That seemed odd but Heather was sleepy. "Okay, you can go. Really. Turn out the light. I'll try to sleep."

"'Night, Heather. I'll check in on you tomorrow."

She didn't even hear the door close.

**THE NEXT DAY. NEWBERRY, SOUTH CAROLINA.
7:30 A.M. EST. TUESDAY, DECEMBER 3.**

Manckiewicz had originally thought he would follow the interstates and skirt Atlanta as he had done Richmond, on his way down to Fort Benning. But he'd found that away from the big concrete ribbons, people were friendlier and barriers easier to pass, so he'd gone higher than and west of his original plan. Whenever he met a traveler headed back to Washington, he gave the traveler a hand copy of his writing so far on the trip, and told them to present it to George Parwin for a bath, bed, and meals. The endless hand-copying seemed to improve his style. *I sure skip the clichés when I know I'll be hand-copying them four or five times.*

In Spartanburg, he'd heard that the refugee pulse from Atlanta had been far larger and more violent than anything he'd encountered before, probably because it was the biggest city he'd passed so far and its position next to the mountains narrowed the way out. He heard the fires to his west had been worse as well, so he had decided to go south through the space between Columbia and Augusta; both towns were apparently keeping it together, so there shouldn't be more than occasional bandits—or the petty fortified houses that their right wing-nut owners called Castles, which could make you just as dead if you walked into their territory before you knew where you were. Once he was well south of Atlanta, he'd cut west toward Fort Benning again.

He'd been pretty tired and his pack had been almost empty three days ago when he found work, helping to build a solar-hot-water setup for a businessman in Newberry, South Carolina. The guy was rigging up an abandoned hotel that had had water-radiator heating and cooling, not for travelers since there weren't many yet, but figuring he'd be able to offer comfortable shelter once his water-driven machine shop was up and running, and that would be how he'd secure employees. "Sort of a company dorm," he explained. "Got a guy talking with me about maybe building a little coal-gas or Brown-gas project to supply that hotel kitchen. I got a lot of belt-driven stuff out of two old closed factories, and I'm planning on waterwheels for small hydro."

Newberry, Chris had written in his diary the night before, *is one of a thousand small towns aiming to become one of the industrial centers for a new America. Collum Duquesne does not look at what is lost, but at what can be gained. He wants Newberry to have a newspaper because it would increase its influence in the region, and wants to help me find financing. Reluctantly, I told him I had decided to push on to Fort Benning; I'd rather be the paper, or at least a paper, for the capital of the United States.*

Yet the spirit of the smaller cities that are seeing their chance . . .

When he had finished his entry, he'd carefully made three hand copies of it in case he ran into a traveler headed in the right direction. He'd been gratified, in North Carolina, when he'd found a week-old *Advertiser-Gazette* with his story about his passage around Richmond. He'd fantasized that when he arrived at Fort Benning, they'd have a complete run of the *A-G*, and he'd find all his stories there, along with a letter addressed to him demanding more.

Then he'd laughed at himself, packed what he had, including a big load of tradable canned food, blown out the candle, and gone to sleep. Now he was on his way out of Newberry, on the road to Fort Benning, aiming to cross the Savannah on the Thurmond Dam.

Houses and shops were getting fewer and meaner when something caught his eye on a side street. Weeds had already grown up around it, and the door hanging at a broken angle from the store was hardly unusual, but something—he approached more closely and saw what should have been impossible, unopened cans strewn around.

He trotted up the street and solved the mystery: the cans were labeled only in an alphabet that he thought must be Hangul. If the store was too far away from any Korean community, probably the people who looted it had only taken cans labeled in English, or with pictures of what they contained. He set to work stacking cans by matching characters; when each pile had a few of each different kind, he opened a can in each pile. The lychees were wonderfully refreshing, more for their liquid than the fruit itself; the second pile turned out to be a ferocious kimchi that he could only take one bite of before needing more lychees. The third held small, tightly-packed meat and vegetable rolls that were pretty palatable. When he was sure he understood what all the cans contained, he decided to take all the lychees, half the tinned fish, and some of those rolls; now his pack was well and truly topped up.

He was just crouching down to make sure his bag was properly balanced before tying it up, when a brilliant double flash of light, as if lightning had hit in the street just outside, froze him. He ran outside to look.

One giant sun rose in the north-northeast, and another in the northwest. Two great blinding balls of light, five times the width of the full moon, climbed up from the horizon. They were too bright to look at, and Chris covered his eyes belatedly, but though the fireballs had left his vision temporarily a red blur, he could tell as he blinked and the view of his palms slowly came back that he had been blessed, by being far enough away not to be blinded. The sense of heat from the fireball was like a very hot sunlamp, but things were not bursting into flames, and his skin felt warmed, not burned.

Belatedly, through the fog of shock, his training from his days as a cam jock in Iran asserted itself. *Nuke. Get away from windows and people.* Slowed by his pack, he had covered four blocks when something slammed against his feet and made him stumble to his hands and knees; he'd lived in California long enough to think *earthquake,* and then to realize it was a big wave moving through the ground. Less than ten seconds later, another shock wave rolled under his feet. He was surrounded by cracking and crumbling sounds as walls broke, chimneys fell, window glass snapped in distorting frames, and utility poles tipped, cracked, and leaned crazily.

He turned and looked back. Where the fireballs had been there were now distinct mushroom clouds; *I was right, it was two nukes. Wow, this is like video from Iran in 2018.* The mushroom clouds looked funny, though, cut off at the tops, as if some god of the sky had simply dragged an eraser in a straight line over the tops of the clouds. *Let's see, the rule they gave me, the shock waves in the ground should travel at about ten miles every three seconds, so . . . but that makes no sense. It was at least three minutes, that would put the bombs . . . six hundred miles away. I shouldn't be able to see the mushroom clouds or the light, let alone feel the shock waves in my feet! There are no bombs that big!*

He'd been told, not for attribution, that Daybreak or il'Alb might have a new kind of nuke, but he'd had the impression it might be smaller, not bigger.

He had still not heard the sound. Sound travels at five seconds per mile; every Boy Scout learns to count one, Mississippi, two Mississippi, and divide by five to find out how far away the sound is. Figure three or four minutes had gone by and he had yet to hear the sound; and the sound should carry farther but slower than the ground shock, he thought, so he could not have missed it. Say four minutes. That was around fifty miles. More than fifty miles away . . . six hundred miles? That should take three thousand seconds, which would be fifty minutes, most of an hour. Well, if he heard a really big boom around forty-five minutes from now, he'd *have* to believe it. He looked down at the windup watch he'd found in a jewelry store and made a mental note.

The mushroom clouds looked odder still, distorting and stretching out to the east in a shape like a bucket-topped boot, with the toe sliding eastward. *Normally they stay in the troposphere,* he thought, *where winds aren't much more than a hundred miles an hour at most, but in the stratosphere and higher . . .*

He bent, opened his pack, and pulled out his big map of the United States. Assume that he was only seeing the top parts of the mushroom clouds. Assume the bomb was so big you could feel the ground wave six hundred miles away. Orient the map with the compass . . .

Washington. And Chicago. I'm almost at the apex of an isosceles triangle of them.

Hit with bombs so big that the top of each mushroom cloud flew right into space.

By the time he had refolded the map, the morning sky was streaked, everywhere, with millions of shooting stars, bits of the mushroom cloud re-entering. Some of those shooting stars were still falling later on, when he had put a couple of miles behind him, stopped to enjoy a can of lychees and listen, and finally heard, right on schedule, the two terrible booms.

Whoever my readers are going to be, how the hell am I going to explain even the idea *of bombs that big to them?* He chewed that over as his feet put him on the road that would lead through McKinley and Lincolnsburg tomorrow; he preferred betting that the concrete-pier bridge would still be standing, rather than take his chances on a dam after shock waves like that. By the time he camped that night, in an east-facing clearing, he had several good analogies and was seeing diagrams in his head. *Gotta find a printer, a graphic artist, and the capital of the United States,* he added to his mental do-list, as he fell asleep in the cool, wet forest, a light rain just spattering on his tent. *Nothing to it, really, if I just keep moving.*

BEFORE, DURING, AND AFTER. EARTH. 12:30 P.M. GMT. TUESDAY, DECEMBER 3.

Each of the five flashes would have appeared as a tiny round dot—not a point, but a circle—to the naked eye of an observer standing on the moon, and though the flashes on the night side of the Earth, darker than it had been in more than a century, would have been more dramatic, the circular flares would have been visible even on Washington and Chicago, both in bright daylight.

From low Earth orbit, where the weather satellites orbited, the five mushroom clouds would have looked far more impressive; they were the five biggest nuclear bombs ever set off on Earth, each of them five times the power of the gigantic Russian test shot that had terrified the world sixty years before. The tops dispersed strangely, for they were literally in space—more than a hundred kilometers high. From orbit one could see the boundary where the particles of debris and smoke ceased to billow and separated into trillions of lines of fire, outlining a parabolic funnel like the top of a vase, cooling into invisible grit and pebbles that re-entered as bright streaks in all directions around the pillar of fire. Out to about 150 miles altitude, weather and communication satellites ran into the debris and were pounded apart by their own high velocity.

The maintenance vehicle shed for the East Potomac Golf Course, far down in the southwest corner, had long been superseded by a newer one on the north edge of the course, and so it had been unused for a long time; months before Daybreak, a succession of semi trailers, all with papers perfectly in order, had arrived and delivered a large number of crates into the unused shed. If anyone had looked at the papers seriously, they might have muttered, "Hunh, guess they're finally doing something with that old tractor and truck shed."

A few days later, an apparent group of joggers had noted a signal from a man with binoculars down a long fairway from themselves. Abruptly they had turned as one and sprinted through the side door on the shed, where the padlock had been cut and reattached so that it locked nothing. The "joggers" had not emerged for eight days, and when they did, they had slipped out at about six in the morning, running back the way they had come as if just finishing a morning run. Inside the shed, painted matte black to blend into the dark interior, a sphere nine meters in diameter sat with its top between the rafters of the old shed.

Beneath the black paint was steel three centimeters thick, covered on its inner surface with a tungsten-thorium foil, a special order made by a Chinese firm that didn't ask what it was for (tungsten-thorium alloys are common in, among other things, jet engines and expensive specialty light bulbs; obviously someone wanted a super-dense conductor that was strong in thin sheets at high temperatures. *Must be some new product, maybe we'll see some of them in the store next year,* the factory manager had thought).

Inside the steel sphere, resting on dozens of steel legs, there was a second sphere of thin plastic; no Daybreak biotes had penetrated because the outer sphere had no openings. The space between the two spheres was about a half meter, and in that space were 131 pure fusion devices, each identical to the device that had been destroyed in Air Force Two, and that had detonated inside *Mad Caprice*, weeks before. They were just about a meter apart, from center to center, and each one talked to its six nearest neighbors via a laser relay; the messages they sent each other were simply comparing their clocks, keeping each of them synchronized to the tenth of a nanosecond, such a small interval of time that each bomb, in its quiet every-second calculation, had to measure and compensate for the travel time of the light from all its neighbors a meter away.

Inside the thin plastic sphere was about 220 tons of lithium deuteride, the basic fuel for the H-bomb.

The programmed moment arrived. The sphere of 131 small fusion bombs—each only a twentieth of a kiloton—detonated, so nearly simultaneously that if anyone had been able to observe the gamma rays from each bomb, they would have been seen to meet at the centers of all the equilateral triangles between the bombs.

Radiation exerts pressure; the gamma rays from the fusion, moving at the speed of light, squeezed the lithium deuteride sphere to the density at the core of the sun. Arriving an instant later, the relativistic protons—hydrogen nuclei moving at close to the speed of light—held the immense ball of fusion fuel together, and compressed it even further.

Meanwhile, the protons that had not gone into the fusible mass collided with the tungsten-thorium foil, releasing a shower of hard X-rays, which further compressed the lithium deuteride at its center.

Technically, the material was now so compressed that it was no longer lithium deuteride but a dense soup of lithium and deuterium nuclei, pushed into each other by the terrible force; in a microsecond, a small fraction of the most-compressed fused into beryllium and released enormous energy; the ball of nuclei was further heated by that energy, yet held together by the incoming radiation. The added heat caused more fusion, releasing more heat and bringing on still more fusion.

An instant later, less than the time it would take for light to reach your eyes from a stoplight a mile away, the balance changed; the outward force from the fusion-heating of the sphere was greater than the inward force from the radiation.

The energy released.

The 250-megaton blast scooped out a crater 350 feet deep and nearly four miles across. The fireball was almost twenty-five miles across, and extended into the stratosphere in the first millisecond. President Norcross, his Cabinet, the Congress, the Supreme Court, and every living thing in the city had no time even to sense that anything was amiss; a signal could not cross a single synapse in their brains before they just ceased to be. Washington's vaporized remains boiled upward so violently that when the cloud of plasma cooled enough for molecules to form again, much of it fell as glassy artificial meteors ranging in size from peaches to BBs, the farthest-flying ones landing in Iceland. The immense ground shock wave in the melted rock created concentric ridges every hundred yards or so for ten miles beyond the crater rim.

The heat radiated by the fireball was effectively far greater than that in a familiar fission-triggered bomb, because the fireball lasted much longer; it charred skin 100 miles away, and set dry treetops on fire as far as 150. The most remote fires it triggered, in the suburbs of Philadelphia, in office towers in Richmond, and on some east-facing hillsides in Charleston, West Virginia, burned uncontrolled. Weeks after Daybreak, almost nothing and no one was left to fight them; fires spread across that whole vast area.

Blast effects were less than they might have been with an old-school H-Bomb of the same megatonnage, but still, the blast wave toppled office buildings at twenty miles and knocked down houses at sixty.

Every pure fusion weapon is innately a neutron bomb, creating deadly levels of fast neutrons at distances where people under cover can survive the flash and blast—sixty miles away, anyone sheltered from the terrible burning light and the flying rubble received a payment-due from Death, to be collected at leisure after days or weeks of diarrhea, vomiting, hemorrhage, and lesions.

. . .

The bomb that burst in a Chicago warehouse at the same moment did many of the same things; the famous skyline was gone. A four-story-high wall of boiling water rolled north on Lake Michigan, and over the next three hours the towns on the shore drowned, and the big wave still had energy enough to cause flooding around Huron and Superior as well. Immediate deaths were fewer, for the great fires in Chicago and Milwaukee had emptied those cities; most of those vaporized, buried, burned, and irradiated were already corpses. Still, the immense plume of neutron-bathed water, silicon, nitrogen, and carbon rained down across the northeastern United States, fell into the ocean even a hundred miles out, and commingled with the ashes of Washington on the Atlantic floor, and for the first few days, it was intensely radioactive, and many humans and many more creatures, especially the mammals and birds, received the dose that would kill them in the coming weeks.

* * *

On October 31st, as the world slipped into chaos, a ship had anchored in the North Sea, four long, strong cables securing it to the bottom, at a point carefully located with the GPS systems that were still working at the time, on a line between London and Antwerp. Now, in the early hours of the evening, the black sphere in the abandoned ship detonated; the mass of water it vaporized and converted into a superheated shock wave was about one-quarter the volume of Lake Erie.

London, Dover, Lille, Calais, and the cities of the southern Netherlands burst into widespread flames, great conflagrations that were to burn on for days. Some fires, where particularly flammable objects were facing the fireball, broke out as far away as York, Amsterdam, and Paris, and the mighty artificial tsunami from the blast topped and breached dikes all along the Dutch coast and carried mountains of debris into all the channels of the Rhine; in that instant every chart became obsolete and for decades the river would be finding new courses.

Because the bomb had detonated in seawater, across the next forty-eight hours, deadly radiosodium and tritium fell in dust-gray salty snow as far east as Moscow. Europe had been freezing, starving, and disintegrating before; radiation poisoning killed millions, and before the spring, millions more, their immune systems weakened by the radiation, died of tuberculosis, cholera, typhus, flu, plague, and every old returning enemy of humanity.

* * *

The bomb in Jerusalem took most of the inhabited parts of Israel, the West Bank, Gaza, Jordan, and southern Syria. Detonated on land, like the Chicago bomb but with even less water, it caused a rain of radioactive tektites, some falling as far away as India; in centuries to come, the Monist faith would declare those bits of glass, in which the only remaining relics of several peoples and of shrines sacred to three great faiths were intermingled eternally, to be sacred. There were more than enough so that, no matter how big the Monist Confession grew to be, all Monists could have as many sacred tektites as they wanted.

. . .

Shanghai, Nanjing, and Hangzhou formed an equilateral triangle; at the center, the fifth great explosion worked its same monstrous results.

Though it was one of the Earth's largest cities, with a huge population to feed and care for, the combination of discipline and cooperation, plus the sizable fishing fleet and better-than-average food reserves, had been working in Shanghai, and while there was misery enough for everyone, there had been relatively few deaths, and the civil order, if far from perfect, was functioning. In the last ten days, emissaries from Shanghai had been out to negotiate with the smaller cities that could be reached on foot or on the new oiled-linen-tire bicycles that one entrepreneur had created. Boats had begun to go south along the coast to the other commercial cities, and there had been talk of a Next China, of which Shanghai would be the leading city.

That was over in the blast and flame that smashed the western side of the city and set much of it on fire. The Shanghai city government staggered on for most of a week until deaths from neutron-induced radiation poisoning finally brought everything to a halt; the fires that had been almost controlled by hand pumping and bucket brigades broke out anew, and finished the city off in the next few days.

. . .

Buenos Aires, perhaps the assemblers had been less careful, or the biotes had been luckier. The sixth black sphere had been breached, the enclosing plastic sphere had turned to slime, and the lithium deuteride lay in a heap in its botto asymmetric with respect to the nanoswarm-encrusted sph of 131 pure fusion charges. Less than twenty of them fir They vaporized the lithium deuteride, fused a very small of it, and mostly just scattered it around, creating a de cloud of poisonous, corrosive gas that drifted into the har and out into the great mouth of the Rio Plata, where it kil so many fish that the sea wind stank all that following su mer. The blast itself, not much more than a kiloton, leve ten city blocks around the harbor, killed over two thousa people, broke countless windows, and scared the hell out everyone, but by morning the next day, as news trickled from the rest of the world, Argentines thought of themsel as the luckiest people on Earth.

ABOUT THE SAME TIME. FORT BENNING, GEORGIA. (DRET COMPOUND.) 7:30 A.M. EST. TUESDAY, DECEMBER 3.

Graham had insistently told her, after the funeral, that he v rising at 5:30 most mornings and it would be all right to kno on his door at any time after 5:45, especially if she nee company. Heather had awakened at 5:35, having slept for most twelve hours, unable to go back to sleep, lonely, and s Annoyed at herself, she had knocked on Graham's door.

He'd welcomed her in to eggs, toast, and bacon, and l to be talked out of using up his last reserve of instant coff Instead, after cups of hot chicory milk, he'd put the kettle and made tea to put in sip-cups (hers with powdered milk brown sugar, the way she liked it). "You and I are going a walk."

If there is any form of recreation that an Army base usu offers, it is room for people to walk long distances. The was dawning slow and gray, the sun unable to fight throt the thick cover to find the color in the grassy hills; it wo only grudgingly brush the pines. They walked in silence, G ham clearly just letting her decide whether there would conversation or not.

"I guess I'm being dumb about this," she said.

"Are you saying that because you really think that, or cause you feel you're expected to say it?"

"I guess because I feel I'm expected to say it. I was only with the guy, really, for about a month, but it feels like he was the love of my life."

"Maybe he was. I haven't heard there's a time limit or a legal waiting period on that."

"Yeah."

"Love does weird things that don't always fit in with our self-interest. That was one reason why I told students I'd advise them about everything else, but never their love lives."

"Probably sensible of you."

"Or cold-hearted. Take your pick."

From the crest of the ridge, the evergreen forest in front of them was shrouded in fog; beyond, the few lights in the dark and still town dimly illuminated long tendrils of rising woodsmoke. A distant creak-and-squeak told them the cable-car rig was beginning to run for the day. It was dark from the overcast, and when distant lightning flashed, Heather said, "Maybe we should head back; that looks like it could storm."

They turned and headed back the way they had come. After a couple of minutes, she said, "It might be a while before I know what to do with myself."

"If you don't have any use for yourself, your country does," Weisbrod pointed out, "and eventually you—what's that?"

Heather knew the way a native Angeleno does. "Earthquake." There was a second shock moments later. "I didn't know we even had those around here."

"I don't know," Graham said, "maybe the New Madrid fault? That's actually supposed to be the biggest one in the country but it's up in Missouri or Tennessee, I remember, so if we're feeling that here, St. Louis must be rubble. We'd better hurry back."

ABOUT AN HOUR AND A HALF LATER. FORT BENNING, GEORGIA. (DRET COMPOUND.) 9:00 A.M. EST. TUESDAY, DECEMBER 3.

The lecture hall was packed to the walls. Senior personnel like Heather and Arnie were wedged in uncomfortably down front; Larry and the other "gofers-general," as Allie had dubbed them, were jammed shoulder to shoulder up in the back rows.

Not at all like his usual entrance, in which he'd stop to tal[k] with or encourage a few people along the way, Cam strode i[n] swiftly, surrounded by uniforms, straight to the podium.

He nodded at Graham and gestured for him to come dow[n] and join him.

The room had fallen terribly silent.

"I must begin by confirming some very bad news," Ca[m] began. "About an hour and a half ago, nuclear weapons o[f] unprecedented power destroyed Washington, DC, and Chi[i]-cago. Spectrographic data and some airborne sampling ha[ve] now confirmed that these were pure fusion devices, as fir[st] identified by Jim Browder, who many of you knew as [a] friend and colleague.

"I am making inquiries into the possible location of anyo[ne] in the chain of succession who may have been outside Was[h]-ington, but I do not think it is likely that I will find anyone; a[ll] evidence is that the President and the entire line of successio[n] except for Dr. Weisbrod, have perished in the attack."

Heather sat stunned; *maybe I've cried so much lately th[at] I don't have any more in me now.* Around her, she could he[ar] small gasps and sobs.

"Satellite photos, seismographs, and other reconnai[s]-sance," Cameron added, "show similar detonations have o[c]-curred in the North Sea, near Shanghai, and in Israel. A so[-far] unverified military shortwave message, purporting to be fr[om] the Argentine Navy, claims that there was an abortive atta[ck] on Buenos Aires as well, but it sounds as if either the bom[b] fizzled or it was a different type of weapon.

"The weapons are estimated at between 225 and 4[00] megatons. There is no experience with anything remotely t[hat] size, so we must expect very large, surprising effects ab[out] which at the moment we know nothing. A reporter for K[P] in Pittsburgh has reached us via a ham operator's backup [rig] for example, and reported that when KP-1 was knocked o[ff] the air, its main antenna literally vaporized; overhead wi[res] all over Pittsburgh are burning or melting; and in some ca[ses] water pipes, railings, and railroad tracks became hot enou[gh] to burn unprotected flesh. Dr. Solomon, our specialist for [nu]-clear weapons physics, says she thinks it may be that a burs[t] that size, even at surface level, either puts out enough X-r[ays] to reach the ionosphere and cause an EMP, or that possi[bly] the fireball is so hot, and so long-lasting, that it is still emitting X-rays or gamma rays even as it rises to altitudes of fifty miles or more.

"Observers everywhere are also reporting an apparent meteor shower, dwarfing anything ever seen before, in broad daylight, which we are guessing is a hitherto-unknown form of space-transiting fallout.

"Most of you will already have urgent business on your desks; the rest of you can expect to have something vital to do within a short time. I only ask that you show even more of the dedication you have shown as we cope with this latest enemy attack; I don't for a minute believe we will go down, but if we must, let us go down fighting. Better yet, let us win."

TEN MINUTES LATER. FORT BENNING, GEORGIA. 9:15 A.M. EST. TUESDAY, DECEMBER 3.

Graham Weisbrod and Cameron Nguyen-Peters had become not so much close friends as close comrades, and Weisbrod knew something was up from Cam's careful politeness. He didn't know General McIntyre or General Phat well, *but one way or another, I guess I am going to.*

After they had gathered in a small room, and Cameron had offered them all water and coffee, Graham Weisbrod said, "Cameron, you have thoughts you haven't shared with me. There's some reason you didn't just rush into swearing me in and getting the NCCC monkey off your back. Is there a cabinet officer out there who might be alive?"

The younger man looked down at the floor, and then up to Graham's eyes. "We sort of established, during the whole horrible Shaunsen Acting Presidency, that the NCCC is not only responsible for locating the presidential successor and getting him sworn in, but also sort of for . . . well, the quality of the successor."

"I'm not mad or brain-damaged, I haven't been kidnapped, and no one is holding any of my loved ones hostage."

"But you're the very last in line; there is no legitimate successor after you, at least not till you appoint a Vice President, and a new Congress—which there is no provision for seating—confirms him. So I need to think; if we swear you in, you're the President, period, from then on, with no ability to take it back." Cameron sighed. "Shaunsen was a bad precedent."

"Cam, plainly you think that I'm not fully competent to be President. I'm liberal and you're conservative, but that isn't the reason, unless you're much more petty-political than I've always taken you for. Look, pretend we're just having a beer and talking pure theory. So . . . why should I not be president?"

Cameron looked straight into Weisbrod's eyes. "I made a terrible mistake before when I made Shaunsen president. And a more terrible mistake in not removing him promptly. And you would be the President, not the Acting President, so I could not Constitutionally remove you. I know you're not Peter Shaunsen, and you would not turn the whole thing into a corrupt bonanza."

"I understand that. When the President of the United States died in my arms, it made an impression. That's not the answer to my question. I understand that *if* I am a terrible mistake you will have no way to undo it, and that makes you hesitate. But you still haven't told me why you think that making me President might be a terrible mistake."

"Because as far as I can see, we are in a war—a war for national survival—and I *must* have a president who will seriously prosecute that war, all the way to victory."

Weisbrod considered. "General McIntyre, General Phat, I'm assuming you are here as witnesses?"

"Actually," Phat said, "I wasn't told why we'd be gathering and I'm not altogether sure that the Army should be playing a role in choosing the commander in chief. It feels too much like Bolivia."

McIntyre nodded slowly. "I suppose Cam wanted to make absolutely certain that we knew why he hadn't sworn you in, because if I thought the rightful President under the Constitution was being prevented from taking office . . . well, I'd have to take action. I took an oath, and I meant that oath."

Cameron nodded. "It seemed best that no matter what we decided, the military leadership should at least know what was going on."

Phat said, "I guess I'm stuck with asking the question, then. I've spent most of my time making sure our troops have some mobility and that our units are holding together

I purposely haven't followed the policy debates. So . . . Dr. Weisbrod, if you wouldn't mind . . . I understand that Mr. Nguyen-Peters thinks there is a war, and based on the events of the past few months—and particularly today—it sure looks like a war to me. Maybe you can explain why you think it's not a war? If that *is* what you think."

"That may be the politest way I've ever been asked to prove I'm not crazy." Weisbrod relaxed, and sketched out the basic ideas and evidence from Arnie's work in a few minutes. "The problem is that most of the analysis we would use to locate the enemy, formulate strategy, and fight the war would be coming from Arnie's analyses—but those same analyses show that there's no enemy, no war, just a self-extinguished system artifact that left behind an undetermined number of booby traps."

"Well," McIntyre said, "it seems . . . it's an odd idea. So it's a system artifact that grew out of people sharing their self-hatred with each other—through the net . . . wallowing in it, really, I guess . . . and it took over and called all these forces into being, including planting the sleeper bombs . . . and now it's gone, except for whatever traps it left behind, and here we are in the ruins. I hope you'll pardon me when I point out that even if it's true, an old soldier like me would probably rather believe in a real bombable, shootable enemy."

Weisbrod smiled. "I guess I'd understand that."

Phat was picking at his fingers nervously; he looked up, and asked, "So suppose Dr. Weisbrod is unfit to be president? I guess not believing in the existence of the enemy, in war-time, *would* qualify as unfit—unless there really *isn't* a war or an enemy, I mean. But suppose you declare him unfit, Mr. Nguyen-Peters. What would you do then?"

"In a general way, I'd ask our military and our intelligence agencies to find the people, organizations, nations, whatever, responsible for these terrible attacks; defeat and subjugate them; bring them to justice and to unconditional surrender so that they can never do it again. Then rebuild the country, and ways around all the Daybreak roadblocks to technology; suppose it's a hundred or thousand year program."

"And Dr. Weisbrod? If you are made president?"

"It's surprisingly similar in many ways. I'd start from the idea that the enemy is gone and was never exactly a person or people anyway, though for public morale we should haul some of Daybreak's minions in front of a judge. Because I wouldn't spend years chasing an enemy that doesn't exist, we'd still have more of our nuclear ships, operating aircraft, all the tools to make the job of reconstruction easier and faster. If we try to fight a war, no matter how careful we are with the little bit of remaining high-tech hardware we have, it will be gone before we realize that there never was any war, and it's all been a tragic error. I just don't think there's a war, and therefore I think there's better, more urgent use for resources that we'll be losing very soon anyway, the way we lost the USS *Reagan*, or the way the reconnaissance planes are going now."

The silence stretched.

Cameron said, "I've never had a duty this painful before. Graham, I am going to hold you incommunicado, and announce that in view of our wartime situation, although you are the president, you have been moved to a confidential location for security reasons; I'll have to issue orders over your name, I suppose, and I'm sorry for that as well. Gentlemen, I'll need a few chosen troops to help carry out this decision, and they are to be absolutely discreet—and as gentle and kind about this business as it is possible to be. We need to accomplish this before Graham leaves this room." He visibly forced himself to look directly at Graham. "I'm sorry."

"I'm sorrier for your broken oath than I am for me being locked up," Graham said quietly.

"I think I'm keeping my oath. It's my heart that's breaking." Cam turned to the two generals, who were standing frozen, numb, unsure what to do. "General McIntyre, I'm making that officially an order; please detain Graham Weisbrod incommunicado, with all the reasonable comfort—"

"Sir, no. With all due respect, I cannot obey that order, in light of my oath."

"General Phat, please relieve General McIntyre and carry out my orders."

Weisbrod watched, numbly, as it all happened; it wasn't until he and McIntyre were being led between armed guards to their new home that he thought of something to say. "General, do you play chess?"

"Not as well as I should."

"Me either. Perhaps we'll get better with all the practice."

· · ·

"Mr. Nguyen-Peters," General Phat said, "may I have a word with you?"

"Of course."

"I don't much care for this situation. I am thinking strongly of following McIntyre into arrest. You would probably find Grayson, the next officer in line, to be a much more cooperative person."

"I see. I had thought that too; I had also thought that if General Grayson takes over the Army, the Army is very likely to take over everything. But I don't think I can safely try to remove him at the moment."

"Which is one reason why I will stay in, at least until we get Grayson shunted somewhere harmless. Instead, it occurs to me that as NCCC you can do pretty much anything you want, is that right?"

"I'm supposed to restore Constitutional government as soon as it's feasible and I have qualified people to do it with."

"Well, then. So as long as you pursue that goal, you can do whatever you like?"

"Subject to my personal sense of honor."

Phat nodded. "I see you have one; I see it eating you alive. All right, here are my conditions for not resigning. First of all, move the temporary government off this base. The United States should be run from a civilian capital city, not an Army base. Second, full elections in '26. Give us a Congress and President, put together a Supreme Court, do whatever it takes, but I want to see a civilian Constitutional government—and not one where you get to decide who it is or who's elected. Third, the minute it takes power, resign."

Cam asked, "You realize that you're imposing more difficulty on the government during a wartime crisis?"

"If some difficulty, as you call it, is going to stop us from following and having our Constitution, sir . . . well, then it's not much of a Constitution, our oaths don't mean much, and it's all just a game, eh? Congress made me an officer, Directive 51 made you the dictator, and none of that would exist without that Constitution. It created us; we owe it some loyalty, even in the face of 'difficulties.' "

"So I'm not going to bargain you into any easier arrangement, am I?"

"Not a chance, sir. I'm a good general and a poor negotiator, and I'll only do the thing I'm good at. And if you agree, I will expect you to keep your word."

Cameron sat down, and said, "How long before I have to move to a civilian capital?"

"I'll give you a month."

"And . . . well, there's already an existing plan, it's in one of the classified annexes to Directive 51. I'm sure we can elect a House twenty months from now, which is actually on schedule. We can stagger the Senate terms the way they did back in 1788, elect a third of them to six-year terms, a third to four years, and a third to two. We could elect a president for two years, to get back on the original four-year cycle that started in 1788, but I'd rather put one in for four years and just start from a slightly different beginning date. Probably have him appoint a three-man Supreme Court, next guy takes it to five, next guy takes it to seven, and so on; that's more or less what they did by accident back at the start. We have rules for creating provisional states if need be, out of areas where there's no government, but I'd rather just leave some states present and-not-voting . . . those are details, I think about those too much . . . yeah, it can be done. I'd rather take ten years about it, but I *can* do it in two."

"Then—if you want my support, and frankly, sir, you will need it—remember what they used to say on *Star Trek*—make it so." Phat was not tall, or physically prepossessing at all, but his salute and the way he strode away plainly declared a deal that Cameron had better keep.

TWO DAYS LATER. FORT BENNING, GEORGIA. 11:15 P.M. EST. THURSDAY, DECEMBER 5.

Heather was working on catching up on Bambi's and Larry Mensche's reports from Castle Larsen. Cameron had wanted more extensive report because he was trying to figure out some kind of dragnet to catch more former Daybreakers, in hopes of eventually locating the ringleaders, along with the foreign and terrorist-organization connections that he was sure were there

Well, her job was just to report what was coming in; they could make whatever use of it they liked. As Ysabel Roth recovered, Bambi and Mensche were beginning to worry about suicide—

A knock at the door.

"Come in."

It was Arnie; he looked tired and ill. "I was kind of hoping for an unofficial chat," he said.

"My favorite kind," Heather said. "Do we need enough privacy to take a walk?"

"Maybe. I don't know. I've been kind of turning a bunch of ideas over and having trouble sleeping."

"Well, I can always carry you home on my shoulder," she said. "Let's just take the trail up the ridge, and you talk whenever you feel like talking."

On the gentle slope in the strong winter scent of the evergreens—the cold of the mornings seemed to cling to the shadows even though the afternoon was warm—Arnie said, "I know sometimes I'm an irritating bastard."

"You're also a brain we depend on, Arn. And if something's disturbing that brain, spill it."

"There's an idea I've been hoping to run by Graham, privately, but I guess he's not coming back anytime soon?"

"Basically he's stashed till the war is won. Cam is convinced that Graham is target number one. My guess is that they found some way to take him out to an aircraft carrier."

"That's what I'm having a problem with."

They walked on for a while, Arnie kicking occasional stones from the trail; he must be trying to think of the least offensive way to say it. That, all by itself, was out of character. "Look," he said, "I don't want to sound like a sore loser about the system artifact idea. But just consider where Daybreak used its big bombs. It looks to me like Daybreak wasn't able to change its plans. Chicago, Milwaukee, Gary, the whole industrial southern end of Lake Michigan, had been a burned-out wasteland for most of a month. Its factories and facilities, labs and resources, canals, roads, and rails were already useless. And yet they hit it.

"At the same time, Fort Benning and a dozen other vital centers went untouched. It looks to me like Daybreak intended to destroy several of the places where technically advanced civilization is most likely to regrow: the northeast United States; northwest Europe; the industrial heart of modern China; Israel, Jordan, and Palestine. Add in LA and south California if that bomb in the Pacific was just a case of the delivery crew screwing up. Add Buenos Aires for that matter. All of those were places with good concentrations of resources nearby, plenty of people with technical educations, and some kind of entrepreneurial tradition.

"So it looks to me like they may have been targeting the places where they *guessed* civilization would re-grow and they had to make their guesses *before Daybreak*."

"What difference does it make whether they picked the targets before or after Daybreak? Weren't the guesses *obvious*? Didn't their plan *work*?"

"*Some* of it worked brilliantly. Shanghai was a great guess and so was Buenos Aires. The Palestine bomb looks like someone using a bomb to pay off a score or settle a debt, or maybe just to make sure the Israelis didn't inherit the Earth, but things were collapsing there and they didn't really need to do it—for Daybreak's purposes it would have been more effective on Mumbai. Los Angeles was *weird*."

"It sure was, wasn't it?"

"Okay, I guess the whole idea is stupid." He lurched on up the trail ahead of her.

"Arnie, wait." She swallowed hard and said, "It was a really dumb joke and especially considering everyone there was killed with that radiation bomb it was extra dumb and totally heartless and I'm sorry. You're making me nervous about where this is going, and I don't know if I want to hear it, but I guess I have to listen to you anyway, because you sound like you might be right."

He stopped, very quietly, and said, "Why hit Los Angeles with *two* bombs? They'd already have hit Anaheim, if their plans had worked, and besides, we still don't have any idea why they used radiological enhancement instead of a super bomb there, let alone why they used gold instead of cobalt. If they had any way at all to monitor what had happened in the month after the nanoswarm and biotes were released, and target accordingly, there were fifty better targets than Los Angeles or Chicago or even Washington—Pittsburgh, Savannah, Fort Lewis, or here for that matter. Especially the Nort

Sea, Washington, and Chicago bombs mostly just re-scattered rubble, re-ignited debris, and killed people who were going to die anyway." He ticked it off on his fingers. "That looks to me like something that can't change its mind—a dead hand, not a live enemy."

"So you think if this were really a war—"

"The enemy would have shifted to target Fort Benning, San Diego, Denver, or Pittsburgh, not Chicago. But Chicago was a good guess before Daybreak."

"But you yourself said Shanghai was a good target."

"On that one, they got lucky. No law requires all of their luck to be bad."

They walked on for a while.

When they stopped to look down on Columbus, at all the plumes from the chimneys and the streets crowded with wagons, workers, soldiers, and families, Heather said, "So I see what you're thinking. And all the explosions being ground-bursts suggests they were pre-positioned too. But maybe they just had to do that anyway. They planted them where they expected it to work, and set timers, because they knew they couldn't count on having a working plane or missile by now. Not because they aren't still around, but because the only way to use the bombs was in places they had chosen before they started the war."

"That could be," Arnie said. "And I thought of it; that's why I can't go to Cam, and say, 'Look, it *has* to be a system artifact.' All I can tell him is 'It's not as strong a proof that we're at war as you think it is.' I don't deal well with uncertainty."

"That's a weird thing for a statistical guy to say," she said, taking his arm and steering him back down the hill. *Don't go into a depression on me, Arn, I've got to keep myself glued together, and that's hard enough.*

"Even so," Arnie said, "my gut isn't uncertain at all. I realize they probably just buried the bombs and put them on a timer to go off five weeks after Daybreak. It was one more try to put another stake through the heart of civilization, to make sure the Big System doesn't rise up again—but they didn't have any way to aim. But it was the kind of thing a system artifact does. It doesn't feel as confusing and weird and malicious as something a human being would do."

A thought struck Heather. "Arnie, how are *you* doing on the human side?"

He shrugged; transparently he didn't want to volunteer but was desperate to talk about it.

Heather put a hand on his shoulder. "Come on, guy. Your brain is a national resource. I can't let anything disturb it without filling out forms in triplicate."

"Well, it's Allie. This'll sound stupid. I just get . . . it bothers me that she's so obsessed with finding out Graham's secure location. I mean, okay, he's one of her closest, oldest friends, okay, she really liked being his chief of staff, okay, all that, okay—"

Heather hugged him. "You know, two of my ex-husbands were really jealous of Graham, and after every divorce he was the first guy I ran to. It sort of goes with being his former student."

"Did your exes have any *reason* to be jealous?"

"I don't know. Graham never made a move. But his wife was still alive back then, and he was pretty crazy about her and about his kids. Anyway, all I mean, Arnie, is that if you think your jealousy is irrational, it probably is."

"I didn't even want to think it was jealousy." He turned and beat his hands on a dead tree, not hard, but as if trying to wake something up. "I feel so stupid and schoolboyish. It's just . . . see, it's really a New Asian thing, you know, the big deal they started making about it a few years ago when they realized that Asian-Americans were . . . um . . . well, not exactly taking over, but because . . . um."

"I'm not one of the Euros who thinks you're a menace, Arnie. And I read the news too, and we're the same generation. I'm used to the idea that in most offices I've worked in there's been way more dark straight hair than frizzy red like mine."

"Wavy," Arnie said. "Lenny always insisted it was wavy. You don't get to change that. Even though at the moment"—he reached out and brushed her scalp—"it's more fuzzy than anything."

The mention of Lenny had brought tears to her eyes, and Arnie looked away awkwardly. "Anyway," he said, "anyway, um . . . okay, so it's like, why the deal with Allie is a New Asian thing, at least to me. See, there were two stereotypes. Nerdy genius people and stylish brilliant people. And for guy like me—nerdy genius—the idea of someone as styl-ish and brilliant as Allison Sok Banh wanting me for a boy-friend . . . jeez, I don't know if I can explain what it meant. It made me feel, I don't know, different about myself, less like a freak, more like . . . um . . ."

"More like a genius, which you still are," Heather said, firmly. "And you're attached to someone who besides being brilliant and stylish, is also ambitious, and is used to climb-ing on the coattails of her mentor, who has just disappeared. Relax, Arn, the part of you that's saying to just chill is right. Concentrate on the issue you just brought up, and thank you for making me pay attention. You're right to be worried. If it's really a war, we're losing, and if it's not we've got to stop fighting before we do something stupid."

FOUR DAYS LATER. ATHENS, GEORGIA. 2:35 P.M. EST. MONDAY, DECEMBER 9.

"I'm looking for graphite lubricant," Chris Manckiewicz said, "the pure stuff that's used for a Linotype machine. I'll trade cans of tomatoes for it."

The old man behind the counter said, "You're about two weeks too late. Guy came in here and bought me out of it just before Thanksgiving. Also got a box of matrices and I think some escapements from a torn-down Linotype."

"Humm. Think he was getting them to sell or getting them for his own Linotype?"

"Oh, he was a hobby printer, easy to tell that, trying to set himself up as a real printer. I guess he'd got ahold of an old Linotype that had a gas heater for the metal pot or some-thing, real old, World War One or so, in one of the little towns near here, and he had most of a couple more recent ones, and was trying to figure out how to cannibalize everything all to-gether. Took every Linotype supply part I had. He's local, and I've got his card because he wanted me to tag up with him if anything else for a Linotype came in. You want to get in touch with him and see if the two of you can do some kind of deal?"

Chris nodded. "Oh, yes, sir. Maybe he's sorted out what he's keeping by now; I'll probably want anything he didn't end up using. Hope he likes tomatoes."

A few minutes later, Chris was walking south, in the middle of Lumpkin Street, hands well in sight, no weapons visible, all the things you did in a peaceable, functioning town nowadays. A beat cop stopped him for a minute to get his name and business—that happened to everyone all the time these days, and Chris reminded himself to comment about that in some story soon—and seemed pleased that a newsman was looking for a local printer, and even more pleased to find out who it was. "Abel Marx is a good guy," the cop said, "you'll get along. And he's no writer or reporter, he won't be wanting to compete with you—he'll be happy printing your paper. He'll be glad to have a steady job to do with his printing stuff, he loves that, but even though he opened up his shop just a couple days after Daybreak, he hasn't had much work yet, just the flyers for the town government."

Reporters and policemen learn to keep a conversation going because you never know what bit of information might be useful, so Chris and the cop had a nice chat there in the street. The cop learned a great deal about conditions east and north of town. Chris learned that Athens, Georgia, hadn't suffered terribly because so many of the students had fled homeward immediately, leaving the town with food reserves for a much bigger population; the remaining students, being young, strong, healthy, and willing to work, had been the labor force needed to deal with the many crises that Athens, like every other functioning town, had faced daily.

"And of course the real critical thing we did, we were able to throw out a line of militia all over to the west of town, so the refugee wave out of Atlanta were turned aside, or went back, or at least calmed down before we let 'em in. We really only had to hold about a half dozen crossroads," the cop explained, "and from Atlanta to here is one *long* walk for hungry, desperate people, so they didn't arrive in too good of a shape.

"Once we sorted the dangerous ones out, we could take a lot of decent folks, put 'em in the dorms and hotels and all. The bad actors showed up early, and there was some bad fighting over by Bogart that I was in, but once we chased off the worst, we could be pretty Christian with the rest. I felt pretty good about that."

Chris wrote down the officer's name—John Longstreet—and station, thinking, FIGHTING AT BOGART—*there's a good lo article to put together for some issue soon. VETERANS SHARE MEMORIES OF FIGHTING THAT SAVED OUR CITY. HEROIC LOCAL MILITIA KEEPS ATHENS SAFE. MILITIA VETERANS RECALL BATTLE OF BOGART. Something like that. Create local pride and tie it in to support for the paper.*

"So how do you feel about Athens being declared the new capital?" Chris asked. "I was over in Lincolnton, on my way to Fort Benning, when I heard. So now I'll just let the government come to me. Want to be my first man on the street?"

"Can you spell 'this is gonna be a pain in the ass for us cops'?"

"Yep. And I can spell anonymous."

"Then we have a deal. Abel ought to be in his shop, still, if you hurry."

As he neared the university, he could see the scramble of preparations for the Temporary National Government that was supposed to at least try to be here before Christmas. Nothing could really have prepared a classic state-college town for abruptly becoming the capital of the United States, but at least the University of Georgia had enough big buildings with big rooms for meetings, smaller rooms for offices, and the remains of a library close at hand, as workers carried the paper books, journals, and so forth back from storage, scrounged for shelves, and dragged out most of the lounge furniture that had been put in when the library had gone electronic.

Chris collected man-in-the-streets from a crew of the workers at a bar called Dawgz Inn; they were pretty happy about having work and getting paid in meals and sleeping quarters, and they all said the idea of a newspaper in town just seemed to fit in with being the capital.

He didn't hurry, figuring he could always find Abel Marx the next day or the day after, and he stopped several more people for his man-in-the-streets, figuring they'd talk about it and the rumor mill would be running in his favor by the time the first issue came out. No doubt, for some in the town the arrival of the Federal government was just one more disaster—their reasonably orderly lives turned upside-down by an infestation of pushy strangers. For others, of course, it was going to be a gold mine, and probably a lot of them were praying their thanks regularly.

The shop was where he'd been told; a cardboard sign in the window proclaimed

ABEL MARX, PRINTER
POSTERS, FLYERS, PUBLICITY
BOOKS AND MAGAZINES
NO JOB TOO BIG OR TOO SMALL

The man behind the counter was huge, with immense, dark, sensitive eyes, deep brown skin, and a south coast Georgia accent as thick and slow-moving as a swamp creek. He listened to Chris for a while, and then gave him a slow, broad smile. "So you got no capital to launch on?"

"Depends on whether you think of canned tuna, tomatoes, and chicken soup as capital."

Marx laughed. "Guess it does. What I was thinking about, though, is this. This town needs a paper. I need work. You need to get a paper out there. That sounds like a good bet to me. So instead of worrying about the bill, how about, you put it together, I print it, and I'm say forty-percent owner of the paper?"

"Deal." *I'd've given him forty-nine if he asked.*

"You happen to have a place you're staying?"

"Not yet, I'm here with what I walked into town with."

Marx grinned at him. "My mother owns this building There's an office next door that could make a good newspaper office, I guess, get a few desks in there, and we have at leas four up in storage, you and me could move them down there *And* there's a little one-bedroom apartment up there tha might work for a man who doesn't have too much, you know specially since they got city water coming back on in a week or two they think, and water's included. Got a old woodstove we can drag up there, you could heat a couple big pots o water on it and have yourself a bath now and then."

"Mr. Marx—"

"Call me Abel."

"Abel, then. And I'm Chris. Uh, what field were you i before Daybreak? I mean, you said you liked printing becaus your father and grandfather were printers, you didn't say yo were one before now, so, I was just wondering—"

Abel grinned at him. "Up till Halloween, I was a car sales man. Best in the city, four years running."

They both laughed. "All right," Chris said. "No sense fighting it when I can see how it's going to go. How much was your mom thinking of asking for rent on that office space plus that apartment?"

"Well, now, the apartment will be furnished—"

"Abel, how much?"

"Well, cash or canned goods, might be more than you can carry, but if Mom could invest in your paper . . . say, for the office and the living space, both furnished . . . twelve percent?"

"Hmm. That would give you controlling interest."

"If you think I can control my Moms, you got some learning to do."

"Nonetheless, what if I offered her six percent? Six percent of what is going to be the most influential paper in America?"

"Who reads newspapers anymore? And it ain't like America is really, you know, America, anymore, not as we knew it, you know . . ."

"But your descendants will be major stakeholders in the country's next big media empire."

"Maybe you have a point. I'd come down to eleven. But you know, we're fronting everything but the content, and yeah, we need content, but—"

"Now here's a thought. Maybe I could come up to seven for this. Every paper in the world makes most of its money on advertising, you know. And I can write decent ad copy"—Chris hoped that was true, not having tried yet—"but I don't know about selling ads to local businesses, that takes a salesman and someone who knows local people—"

"And in between printing, you think . . . hmm. What's a normal commission on an ad?"

"Ten on the little ones, twenty on the quarter page or bigger—"

"Call it fifteen and thirty and Mom's share could go down to nine—I think I could talk her into that."

"So fifty-one, forty, and nine, and you get fifteen and thirty in commissions?"

Marx nodded.

"Done," Chris said, sticking his hand out.

After a meal of canned tuna and beans, smeared onto fresh homemade bread, they began shifting the furniture around, as Abel filled Chris in on what his improvised press could and couldn't do (*actually I bet eventually it can do whatever he really wants it to,* Chris thought) and Chris explained the news business (*based on my two months in print journalism—but then, I've at least written most of a paper, and he hasn't printed one yet. We'll make it work. And I'm gonna have hot baths!*)

ONE DAY LATER. CASTLE LARSEN. (JENNER, CALIFORNIA.) 3:18 P.M. PST. TUESDAY, DECEMBER 10.

Bambi had been trying the old tack of deliberately getting off the topic and talking about something the subject liked to talk about, to distract the subject with her own interests, get her to really enjoy talking and having the interrogator's attention, and then see what she might blurt out.

Ysabel seemed to have the same problem as she'd had on the day of her capture; consciously she wanted to spill everything, but whenever she tried, her nervous system went into spasm. So Bambi had steered Ysabel into talking about the year her parents had worked with creating community-based businesses in a fishing village in Chile. It sounded kind of stupid to Bambi—her parents had put a year of their lives into trying to organize small, occasionally profitable fishing operations, where the boat owner made all the decisions and made all the money, into something where many people participated in the decision and making money was only one consideration. "It doesn't sound like all that voting and all those meetings would produce much in the way of profits, or fish," Bambi said, trying to get Ysabel lathered up about defending it.

Ysabel surprised her and laughed. "I was a rebellious fourteen-year-old at the time and I said that to my mother constantly. She about had a fit. For her the fishing business wasn't about business and wasn't about fishing, it was . . ."

She froze.

Oh, crap, how could this *trigger a seizure? I didn't even say the word—*

But Ysabel's tense muscles and mad stare were not a seizure, or at least not yet. She swallowed hard and barked, "*Daybreak.* Daybreak! Fucking *Daybreak.* Daybreak was *ju* like that. Daybreak didn't care *what* happened to people, it just wanted to be *right*, like my damn stupid parents who were so busy being *right*—like the fishing! The fishing village . . . you know what Daybreak destroyed in that village, you know what's gone now?"

Well, at least it's not a seizure, but I have no idea what she's so worked up about. "Uh, I guess you'll have to tell me—"

"Three things—radio, outboard motors, and nylon fishing nets! No weather forecasts to keep them off the sea when bad crap is blowing in, and no way for a boat that hits a big school to help anyone else find it! And without a motor, a fishing boat spends hours and hours just getting in and out of harbor—so they get less hours to fish! And nets that rot—that's a day or two every week just to keep pulling out the rotten strings and putting in fresh hemp or jute! Probably a lot of villages don't even have anyone who knows how to make a net by hand anymore! Oh, Christ, what did Daybreak do? What was I thinking?"

Bambi saw a couple of small muscle twitches, but it looked like Ysabel was going to remain conscious. "Tell me more."

"Don't you get it? More fishermen drown in storms, more days with no fish because they don't find a school, if the wind's not right it could be three hours to get out in the morning and three hours to get in at night and no fishing in all that time, and maybe a third of their days on shore hand-fixing a hemp net that rots, because their nylon one fell apart—that's if anyone even *remembers* how to make the hemp net. More work for less fish! They're gonna *starve*, Bambi, that's what me and Daybreak did to them, those fishermen are gonna starve!"

Ysabel's sobs were terrible, wracking sounds, as if she were being punched in the gut on each one, but, Bambi thought, as she rubbed the girl's back, there was something strangely healthy there, like the bursting of a boil.

After many long minutes, not looking up, Ysabel said, "When Daybreak had my head, I couldn't see that that was what it was *about*."

"About what?" Bambi asked.

"Daybreak was about *killing* the fishermen. It wasn't an accident at all, it was deliberate. Daybreak was about killing the fishermen and their families to punish them for liking what they liked and wanting what they wanted. I wanted to *force* those fucking fisherman bastards to stop having time to sit around and watch old American soap operas and drink German beer, like they wanted to, and not to send their kids to school to become all engineers and lawyers and shit, because that was like a plaztatic life, and they were supposed to reject it and hate it, like I did. It was their, like, *job*, they were *peasants*, they *owed* it to me to be peasants, all close to the Earth and in harmony and everything, not . . . not . . . I needed them to be *real*."

Ysabel's fists were sunk deep and knotted in the couch cushions. She was breathing shallowly and fast, pupils dilated, and then she sagged, all at once. She sat with her head down in her hands. After a few seconds' pause, she said, "Right there, did you hear that, I slid right over into being all Daybreak again. It just grabbed me. Now, here with you, isolated from it, I came right out of it, but back when I had Internet, I'd've plugged in, and the Daybreak newsfeed would've fed me like fifty stories that hit me right where I most hated the Big System, and all my friends would've been there yelling, yeah, that rocks, and I'd've been moving deeper into it, thinking more about how the Big System had to come down and death to the plaztatic people, and telling myself it was because I loved the peasants so much. See? That's what hits me when I have the seizures, only it hits so hard and fast I can't tell you about it . . . but I guess I just did."

She looked drained and exhausted, and Bambi said, " should write this up and send it to Arnie Yang; are you okay?"

"Okay? Yeah. Maybe for the first time in a few years. gotta sleep, though, I really do."

Bambi left Roth tucked in, with a nurse/guard from tow watching, and went to talk things over with Larry Mensche She was going to miss the FBI agent—he'd be headed nort to the Coffee Creek prison, to try to find his daughter, Deb bie, and make sure that she was all right. That was his rea mission, as far as Bambi, Larry, and Quattro were concerned officially, he'd be gathering intel about the Castles betwee here and Canada, how they actually leaned politically, how much they had taken over their regions, whether they wer still just well-prepared rich nuts, or a base for the temporar national government to organize from, or a nascent enemy to be suppressed.

Between his official and his unofficial duties, she wanted his thoughts about Ysabel. He'd said he loved backpacking in the old days because it gave him time to think things over; perhaps a week of walking north would give him time enough to see into this riddle, and maybe he'd find a way to send her the answer.

THE NEXT MORNING. FORT BENNING, GEORGIA. (DRET COMPOUND.) 8:09 A.M. EST. WEDNESDAY, DECEMBER 11.

Bambi's report on Roth's interrogation was on Heather's desk when she came in. *Oh, man, this is going to be another report where Roth's interrogation turns up results not consistent with anything except a system artifact, Cam isn't going to like that, he's going to think Bambi's leading her into that instead of pursuing the information about the enemy*—trying to head off trouble, she scribbled a note that it looked like even a medium-high-level member of the conspiracy like Roth must have been carefully kept away from any knowledge about who she was actually working for.

· Yeah, that ought to keep Cam off her case; she didn't need another fight with him. Cam said he talked to Graham daily, *so I bet he's getting an earful. Wish I could be there, but I understand, if Cam's afraid that there will be a nuclear attack again, he's got to keep the President hidden.*

She tossed her hand-scribbled memo into the out basket, grimacing at her childish scrawl. It still beat the manual typewriter they'd assigned her, despite the bottle of Lock-Ease she'd applied to the ancient contraption.

Okay, what else *have I not done in weeks? Maybe on my calendar*—

Well, there. She hadn't torn off a calendar page; she had never really used a paper calendar before Daybreak, but when she and Lenny had started talking about having a child, she'd tried to start tracking her cycle. And then they'd realized that from a fertility standpoint, *there's no benefit to knowing the fertile days if you have sex every day anyway, so*—

Hold it.

The calendar was still reading November 11, the date she'd taken it from its box, here in her new office, and hung it. She tore back through the pages to make sure—

Hunh. Her heart leaped up.

They hadn't had long to try, but she and Lenny had *really* tried. (The memories made her smile so much.) And since her teen years, Heather had always gotten her period right on time, bang, set your watch by it. But in the frantic environment of DRET, with so much going on all the time, she'd lost track. She'd been overdue by ten days on the day Lenny died . . . *and I'm about to be overdue for the next one.*

She thought about running to the infirmary but wasn't sure whether you were allowed to run in . . . *"my condition."*

She walked, briskly, to the infirmary.

ABOUT AN HOUR LATER. FORT BENNING, GEORGIA.
9:45 A.M. EST. WEDNESDAY, DECEMBER 11.

The first non-medical person to hear the news, besides Heather, was Sherry, which just seemed right; this particular infirmary liked her as a gofer, so she was frequently their runner and gradually picking up nursing, record keeping, and all the other things that might make her useful, to add to her old social-work skills. When Heather saw her rocketing by the door, she just stopped her and told her.

Sherry grinned. "Wow. And you didn't know?"

"I didn't get morning sickness, but I now know that a lot of people don't. And I'm a big girl, as you may have noticed; Lenny was small because of his condition but he said his whole family was short and skinny, so it's probably not a real big baby, and even if it is, there's plenty of room anyway. I might not even start to show for another few weeks, the doctor says. But he had enough working gadgets to be able to tell me, yep, I've got a healthy little person inside me."

The younger woman hugged her. "Heather, I know for you it's probably a pain in the ass—"

"Or somewhere around there. Eventually."

"Pbbt. You are walking proof that the world is going to go on, and the human race isn't beat yet, and that's how I'm

going to look at it. Listen, I've been seeing a nice guy named
Everett, he's a civilian contractor guy, used to be part of base
security, and him and me just got quarters together—we were
thinking of throwing a housewarming—can we throw you
a little party? Just something to celebrate, because there's
something to celebrate? Here it is two weeks before Christmas; why don't we let a little happiness into the world? Say
yes or I'll keep talking till you do."

Heather said yes. On the way back to her office, she noticed that Benning was kind of pretty, this time of year, when
the sun was shining.

**TWO DAYS LATER. COLUMBUS, GEORGIA. 7:15 P.M. EST.
FRIDAY, DECEMBER 13.**

"Car bearings work okay with corn oil, especially if you
never go faster'n twenty," the driver explained, "and it turned
out that the historical-re-creation guys had a guy who knew
wheelwrighting. So he put the wheels on this old school bus—
scuse me—" He reached up with the long pole and lifted the
grapple off the tow rope; momentum carried the old school
bus forward, and he set the grapple down on the next east-
bound cable. "And took off the cab roof so I could use this
here pole, and the only steering we need to do is to not hit the
posts and not hit the other buggies. And the old thing rolls
along like a kid's quacky duck."

Heather watched idly as the operator kept the cable buggy
moving; he'd become good at a craft that hadn't existed two
months ago and wouldn't have existed if an engineer who volunteered at a museum hadn't happened to be the main restorer
on an old steam thresher, and realized it had an engine big
enough to drive the cable system. Allie and Arnie were chattering away, talking and pointing at things, in the seat behind
her; at least it looked like they were happy with each other
again. *Could be the problem was all in Arnie's mind.*

I feel pretty good myself. Their first trip out of the DRET
compound since getting here, and it was for a party.

The party itself was pleasantly, predictably dull; everyone
congratulated Heather and looked for a nice way to say that it
was a shame Lenny couldn't be here for this. She was asked

if she was hoping to have a boy or a girl ("Yes," she would say, "it would be so much easier than having a monkey or a platypus"); if she had thought about names ("Leonardo if it's a boy—that was Lenny's full name—and Riley if it's a girl—that was my mother's name"), and if she felt well ("Strong as a moose, let's not start pretending I'm a blushing flower now!")

Most of the conversation, though, was about the upcoming move to Athens. The state of Georgia was donating the new TNG District, and the campus of the University of Georgia would be the capital buildings for the foreseeable future. The move was already under way now that the Corps of Engineers, under the hasty tutelage of Georgia's dozens of old railroad buffs, had pieced together a viable pathway for the three operating steam locomotives that they'd managed to find. Conveniently, the line that hauled coal to the U of Georgia power plant was still in business, so there would be access directly to the campus/government buildings.

They were using the lines through Atlanta, because they needed only minor repairs for the moment. Given that Atlanta might not be re-inhabited for generations, the Corps was planning to rehab the connection from Bishop to Madison because rail traffic between Benning and Athens, a major military base and the new national capital, with a war on, was anticipated to be very heavy.

There were two other good reasons for doing the project, according to one pleasantly drunk young engineer that Heather found herself talking to—it cut a hundred or so miles out of the trip, and whereas Atlanta was dead and couldn't possibly do any legislators any favors to get the rail traffic Macon was functioning pretty well.

Everett's bread and hummus were delicious, and a French chiropractor did talk Heather into the single glass of red wine "for the iron, to be sure, it's just for the iron, and you don't have to enjoy it even one little bit, if you are too American for that!"

She's probably right, but how will I ever explain it to Lenny if I give birth to a Frenchman?

Much of the time she felt like she was trying to remember the whole party so she could tell Lenny about it afterward, but it felt good rather than sad. *Lenny, I am going to bore our child stiff with reminiscences about you, guy.*

On her way back from the outhouse, Arnie took her arm and guided her into the darkness of the side yard. "Allie's bringing Everett around to here. You know what his security company guards?"

"I don't know, nukes?"

"Some of those. Mostly, though, for some years they've had the contract to run and guard the special facility where they keep the politically awkward cases."

"Which are what?"

"Well, originally . . . School of the Americas was here— the place where America trained right-wing dictators and their secret police, and sometimes helped them plan coups. There was also a research arm, where DIA and some other agencies interrogated Soviet or Cuban agents that we knew the coms wouldn't want back. And now and then, the facility held American radicals, usually ones who had been 'disappeared' while overseas. Basically the Department of Never Seen Again."

She shuddered. "I thought those days were over, but since there's a war on—"

Arnie held up a finger. Allie and Everett joined them in the dark. Sherry's boyfriend was a very dark-skinned African-American, tall and fit, with close-cropped hair and beard. He didn't bother with formalities. "Okay, you didn't hear this from me. But it's true. The secret holding facility has a couple new guests—one of them is General McIntyre, who used to be the base commander. He's there because he wouldn't arrest and hold the other one—"

"Graham Weisbrod," Heather breathed. "Is he all right?"

"Except that he's rightfully the President of the United States, and he's in jail, he's just fine." Everett glanced around them. "Look, I don't know what it's about, and I ain't a lawyer, but I don't think the Continuity Coordinator gets to pick the president, or decide when the Constitution applies. That sounds all backward to me. And I took an oath back when I was in the service myself, to support and defend the Constitution—not to work for any old guy who said he might give us our Constitution back sometime. You understand? just . . . it's not right. So here's the other thing you didn't hear from me. General Phat, I guess, doesn't want to have McIntyre and Weisbrod in his secret stockade, so they're going to move them up to someplace outside Athens. Seems to me that what with passing through a lot of empty country . . ." He shrugged.

"If we wanted to do something, would you help us?" Heather asked.

"I'd sure want to be a guy that you could ask."

"We're asking," Allie said.

"Then I guess I'll try to help. Enough for tonight, see you in a day or so when I have an excuse to bump into one of you. I'll let you know through Sherry." He vanished into the crowd; Heather went the other way. Arnie and Allie were about to have a quarrel, she could tell, and she preferred to be well away from them before it started. *Well, I suppose Arnie has a point. Being volunteered for a coup, or a countercoup, without being asked first,* is *outside the usual boyfriendly duties.*

FOUR DAYS LATER. IN THE RUINS OF ATLANTA, GEORGIA. 1:15 P.M. EST. TUESDAY, DECEMBER 17.

"I feel like I'm in a damned costume," Heather complained to Arnie.

"We all are," he said, pulling his hat lower and making sure the bandana was still up around his face.

Sergeant Rogers chuckled. "That's good, a costume. I guess it is." He too wore jeans; a big flannel shirt (to hide the body armor, just unwrapped that morning and not yet deteriorating); the broadest hat he could find, low over his face and a bandana covering his nose and mouth. "I guess we look like the James gang or something." That little chuckle of his was beginning to creep Heather out. "I just want to thank you for letting me be in on this." He and nine Rangers from Third Battalion were the nucleus of the force; Everett, who had once been a Ranger himself, hadn't had much choice about whom he could recruit on four days' notice.

Heather had persuaded them to let her come in as an added gun. She hadn't mentioned that she was pregnant. Everett hadn't ratted her out about that either, or else the Rangers had figured if she didn't care, why should they? Whatever the reason, she was grateful; she didn't think she could have stood to be on the sidelines for this.

Everett sat now, quiet and staring into space; *everyone waits for action their own way,* Heather thought. *Bambi wants to chatter like a mad sorority girl, I get cross and whiny, and as far as I can tell, Rogers thinks everything is slightly funny and there for his amusement.*

"Checklist, Plan B," Everett said, looking around at the five Rangers who were present. "It's still possible that somebody's been turned or caught, or something big came up at the last minute. The steam train from Columbus is supposed to be flying two American flags on the front and back cars, with two red flags on the front of the locomotive. One of our guys is in charge of those flags, and his backup is one of ours, too. Check?"

"Check," they chorused.

"So if it's one American flag down, Rogers?"

"Package is not on the train but everything else is fine, so we pull down the block from the track, let them roll by, and if it's safe there'll be a note dropped from the last car."

"Two American flags down, Machado?"

The short skinny man did not move from the crate where he sat with legs spraddled, but his voice was loud and clear. "Package is not on the train, we're blown, run for it."

"Extra American flag, Diem?"

"Package is on the train, proceed with operation, expect surprises or difficulties."

"Extra red flag on the front, everybody?"

"Come in prepared to shoot, sir."

Everett had them recite, more times than Heather could count, "Two American two red, go by plan. One down, let it pass. Two down, run. Three up, make it up. Three red, fight."

Everett had rolled off two trains ago, reset a switch, and hung a flag; hours later, Heather and the main team had dropped out of a boxcar and hurried under cover while everybody up front was busy dealing with backing the train out of the siding it should not have gone into. Since the engineer had already been hitting the brakes after seeing the flag, and there was literally at that point not another train for miles, there was no danger, just a loss of time; since Heather and the rest of the team were not officially on the train, they were not missed when it rolled again.

Now they waited at the chosen interception point, where

an observer—Sherry, taking her turn up there—in a high window could see the train far off, but the oncoming train wouldn't see the barricade of semi trailers across the tracks too soon. The objective was to have them come to a dead halt so that the locomotive, and the five cars carrying security forces and the prisoners, stood just opposite this warehouse.

"Train," Sherry sang out. Everyone stood up, stretched, reached for gear, and froze when Sherry added, "Three American flags and three red flags."

They've got Graham, things have changed, expect to fight.

Heather felt the pit of her stomach roll over. *Hey, Leonardo,* (she didn't know why but she was sure he was a boy), *hang on, kid.*

The time before they heard the steam train's whistle screaming, and the grinding of wheels on rails as the brakes tried to take hold, was long; the time before the train came to a halt, where they had planned, longer still. They had moved forward into their positions by the doors; three Rangers had darted across the tracks to take up their places behind Dumpsters and wrecked cars. Rogers barked, "Go!"

Heather was with Everett and the slim man named Machado; they were tasked with rushing the second car, where Weisbrod and McIntyre were supposed to be, if their informant was right and if no plans had changed in the interim. Heather was just putting her hand on the door handle when it slid open. Kim, the Ranger on the train in charge of securing the car, had opened it. "In," he said, and they dashed in.

There was a dead soldier propped in one corner. Heather had a nasty moment when she saw Graham and General McIntyre lying face down on the floor, but Weisbrod said, "We're all right, Sergeant Kim is just making sure we stay that way."

Kim gestured at the dead man. "He said he was sent to secure the prisoners, and I told him they weren't his prisoners anymore, but he was mine. So he went for his weapon. Bad move. I think he was Georgia Guard. So I made our special guests lie down flat, locked the doors, and waited for you. There was some shooting up forward, but my orders were to just hold this car."

"Dearmond, or someone, changed the flags," Everett explained.

There was a knock on the internal door toward the

locomotive—thud THUD thud THUD THUD thud, the agreed signal. Machado moved to the door and slid it open, cautiously.

Rogers stepped through. "Dearmond and Crespin just learned to drive the choo-choo," he said. "The engineer jumped for it, letting the dead man switch stop the train. Dearmond was supposed to be the guard in the locomotive cabin, and Crespin was supposed to detain six Georgia Guard in the next car. They got the Guard under control—just a couple injuries, they'll all be okay—but they had to figure out how to be an engineer and a fireman for about a quarter mile there."

"Hell," Dearmond said, "it's pretty simple. You don't even have to steer or navigate."

"So what's in the car behind us?"

"That would've been Taggart's job."

"Well, we can't move our main package till we've secured the next car." They directed Weisbrod and McIntyre to crawl out of the line of fire. Then, cautiously, Rogers moved to the far side of the car, and made a flurry of hand gestures out the open boxcar door.

Crashing and shouting in the car behind them; a shot, and then what sounded like a volley.

"All clear, sir, but we've lost Taggart," a voice called.

"Dammit." Rogers dropped from the car and ran to the one behind it.

There had only been three Georgia Guard in that car, but they had been clever or lucky, and when Taggart seized control, one of them had shot him. They had lain in wait, hoping to ambush whoever was attacking the train; they had not anticipated how fast things would happen with three Rangers entering from two doors and a window simultaneously. Only one of the Guard had fired, and he had been killed instantly by the returned fire.

"This really sucks," Rogers said. "Taggart was just transferred here from the Second Battalion, which is based up in Washington State, and his family's all up there. He might've been home for Christmas, and . . . well, shit. Guess we'll have to let the Third Battalion bury him, too, and hope they won't let the politicians make an example of him. But I don't see any way we can take his body with us."

They laid him out carefully on one of the benches. "You Georgia Guard need to attend to *your* dead. We can't leave you here completely unarmed," Everett explained to the exhausted, frightened young men. "But we also can't let you interfere with what we're doing. Now, I am going to tell you this once, and I hope you will believe me. First of all, this is Graham Weisbrod, the sole surviving member of the Cabinet and that means he's President, and as soon as we can we're gonna put him in front of a Federal judge to take the oath. We were rescuing him because he was being held illegally. Your duty as loyal soldiers under oath is to help us, and I am sorry that there was no way to explain that to your brave comrade before the shooting started.

"But whether or not you believe me, I think it's advisable for me to confiscate your weapons and move them on up the tracks to those semi trailers. I'll leave two men with your weapons; if any of you comes out of this car while they are there, they will shoot, and they are expert snipers. Just before they depart, they'll wave a white flag at you. I suggest you take your time about retrieving your weapons, and especially do not even think about trying to run to them and fire upon my rearguard. By way of incentive, the weapons will also be partly disassembled.

"Once you have re-secured your weapons, I suggest you immediately send a man up the track in one direction, and down the track in the other, with a red flag to stop the next train. Any questions?"

There were none. The rescue party and the freed prisoner moved out quickly, walking up the tracks until they were out of sight of the train, and then veering sharply to the west.

"I don't suppose you'd mind telling us where we're going," General McIntyre said after a while. "I think the risk of recapture is small, and I'd really like to know what is going on. It sounds like some of you are serious about supporting and defending the Constitution."

"We like to think so," Heather said. "The bandanas are kind of hot and hard to breathe in, too, and I don't feel like dressing like a Wild West train robber anymore, anyway." She took hers off. "We have about an hour to walk, but we do have water in our packs. We have a stretcher if either of you is injured, but you look—"

"The water would be good, but I can walk fine," Weisbrod said.

"Same here. Now where are we going?" the general asked.

"Peachtree; used to be one of the big general-aviation airports for Atlanta."

"You've got a functioning airplane?" Weisbrod was incredulous.

"Well, for certain values of 'airplane' and 'functioning,' yes," Arnie said.

ABOUT AN HOUR LATER. PEACHTREE AIRPORT, ATLANTA, GEORGIA. 3:15 P.M. EST. TUESDAY, DECEMBER 17.

Heather breathed a sigh of relief when they arrived at Peachtree; there was a clear runway. They'd had only three aerial and six satellite photos, all days apart, and it had always been possible that someone or something had made the field unusable.

Arnie began rigging up the transmitter, though he warned, "This'll be tricky—I might or might not be able to reach the plane before it leaves St. Louis."

Graham found a notepad and a pencil in the abandoned doublewide office of a construction contractor. "Too many years as an academic," Graham said. "I can't think if I don't take notes. All right, Heather, I've been locked up for two weeks, there's a lot I need to know. First tell me what's up with the Castle movement. How many of them are there and what exactly are they doing that you know about?"

He grilled everyone in turn, even the Rangers, scribbling as if his life depended on it. "General McIntyre," he said, "any new observations about what we've just heard?"

"Uh, I'm not sure whether I'm sad or glad that I was never one of your students."

Sherry was running toward them. "The Ugliest Airplane in the World is coming in to land!" she shouted.

"That's ours," Heather said.

That was one of Bambi's nicknames for Quattro Larsen's cherished baby. The other was the Checker Cab of the Air. It was his rebuilt DC-3, now equipped with greased-linen tires and a homebuilt gadget that sprayed a stream of hot lye solu-

tion from a charcoal-heated pot over the generator and battery, sweeping off and killing the nanoswarm. Its top spee
wasn't even the original 150 mph, it had to stay below 10,00
feet and not fly in freezing weather because the spray coul
ice the engine—but it was an airplane, and it flew, and it ha
made it all the way here from Castle Larsen more or less c
schedule.

It was bright yellow all over, except for Quattro Larsen
personal insignia, the black-and-white-checkerboard patterr
around the nose and on the tail. The rebuilt old-style radi
engines ran on his homebrewed biodiesel. The blue-blac
streak across the wing behind each engine attested to th
miserable fuel quality, and according to Bambi, the lubrican
were mostly lard; she'd said she had dubbed it the Check
Cab of the Air to avoid having it called the Flying Frier, base
on its odor.

On touchdown, the plane whumped like a pillow hitting
bed; the tires weren't as full as they should be, and the no
dipped for an instant, but Quattro wrestled it into taxiing
a stop.

Climbing down, he said, "The whole back of the plane
full of cans of biodiesel, which is why my airplane smells li
a bad fire at KFC. I plan to take a nap; all of you are going
fuel the plane, under the direction of my lovely copilot."

Bambi was grinning at them, jaunty in a striped stoc
ing cap that tied under her jaw, carpenter's safety goggles
probably-cashmere sweater, and bib overalls. "Come on," s
said. "He needs the sleep, and I know what to do."

As Heather was waiting, with her five-gallon metal can
biodiesel, for Graham to finish pouring his into the fuel ta
he said, "This is reminding me of *Lost Horizon*. The sc
where they refuel the plane in the middle of nowhere."

"Lost Horizon?"

"Great movie from the 1930s . . . you'll have to see it so
time . . ." He gazed at something far away. "Shit. It pro
bly existed online, and maybe on obsolete media like C.
DVDs, and plastic-based film, so . . . shit. I guess it's gor
He shook out the last drops of the can into the funnel, a
said, "I don't know why, with so much else that was so m
more important gone, the idea that 125 years of movies
gone should bother me so much, but I feel like crying."

ook the can over to the stack of empties; Heather uncapped
er can of biodiesel and began to pour. *Probably we'll all feel
ike crying, often, for the rest of our lives.*

HE NEXT DAY. OVER SOUTHERN ILLINOIS. 8:17 A.M. CST.
EDNESDAY, DECEMBER 18.

I can see why you wanted to rest up before flying this thing
gain," Heather said to Quattro Larsen, raising her voice to
e heard. "Also why you didn't want to go till the sun was
ll up."

"I was nervous about that too." Larsen's eyes always looked
orward and outward; they had been blessed with a warm day,
oove freezing even a mile and a half above the Illinois prai-
e, but that only meant a greater potential for abrupt changes
the always-unpredictable Midwestern weather. "I'll be glad
touch down in Belleville instead of St. Louis."

"What's in Belleville?"

"A politically secure airfield. In St. Louis, there was fight-
g along the neighborhood boundaries and I had to negoti-
e a truce from Denver, via radio. Now that your old buddy
guyen-Peters has been on KP-1 telling people not to harbor
, and that the President is a lunatic, and so on, I'm guessing
e areas north and west of Lambert Field will line up with
am's government, and we won't get a ceasefire again. On the
ner hand, I think we've got friends at Belleville—"

"We do," Arnie said. He was hunched over the tube ra-
o, 1950s vintage and military, but some souvenir company
d rebuilt it into an oak box stamped with stars and bronze
gs. "They've cleared a runway and they can get us clean
el within a day from our friends in St. Louis." He fiddled
a moment, and said, "I'm getting . . . shit." He spoke into
e microphone. "Yankee One, this is the DC-3 you are hail-
. If necessary we will comply with your order to land. Are
u aware of who is aboard here and why?" Covering the mic
th his hand, Arnie said, "It's an F-35, off one of the carriers.
's gotta be working at the outer limits of his range, but he's
finitely got us; if he fires, we're dead."

"Let me see what I can do." General McIntyre came for-
rd and took the headset. "This is General Norman Mc-

Intyre, temporary commander of the armed forces, appointe
by President Graham Weisbrod. If you are acting on order
originating with the NCCC, please be advised that he ha
been removed from his position as of this morning."

He listened intently for a moment, then interrupte
"Patch me through to your CO if you can. Better yet, if *h*
CO is Shorty Phat—that would be General Phat to yo
Lieutenant—put me through to *him.* Just put me as far u
the chain of command as you can—you've caught us, you di
your duty, we'll play ball, but we need to talk to your highe
ups." A bare three seconds later he asked, "Have you con
municated my request to your—"

**THE SAME TIME. 95 MILES ABOVE PITTSBURGH,
PENNSYLVANIA. 9:24 A.M. EST. WEDNESDAY, DECEMBER 18.**

The lumpy bundle of fused rock was roughly cylindric:
about five feet in diameter and ten feet long. It had been fa
ing from the moon toward the bright radio source for thr
days now, correcting as it went with little jets of steam.

The air so high above the ground is thin, almost a vacuu
but the rock was moving at 25,000 miles per hour, seven mi
per second. High spots on its surface were beginning to gl
cherry red, and a streak of heated, glowing air was formi
behind it, more than enough to activate its temperature a
pressure sensors. The timer began its countdown.

One second later, the surface went from glowing red
glowing white, and the layer of water inside began to boil; ▪
rock was 88 miles high.

Two seconds. If the rock had had an eye or camera to s
most of one side of the Earth would still spread out bef
it. An envelope of white-hot air enclosed it; at night it wo
have been brighter than a full moon. 83 miles high.

Three seconds. Observers on the Plains and in the Ro
ies, looking from the west toward the east, saw it as a wl
streak in the sky. The ice inside liquefied. 79 miles high.

Four seconds. The internal temperature and pressure s
sors signaled charges in the pins holding the hollow r
together; the pins ruptured, and the back of the rock blew
ward on a plume of steam, to fall wherever it happened to. ⸀

·ock, shaped like an inverted drinking glass, righted itself
vith its broad curved bottom pointed down and its Shriner's-
·at top surrounded and held in place by the slipstream.

The device, about as big as a large armchair, had been
made on the moon, by the painstaking efforts of many thou-
ands of robots, themselves also made on the moon. Its job
vas to reach this point, 75 miles above the Earth, directly
·ver the loudest radio source the scanner on the moon had
detected—KP-1. It squatted there on its rock perch like a trap-
door spider waiting for prey.

Three more seconds elapsed. At 65 miles above the Earth's
urface, the device—an entirely helium-3 fusion device—
·etonated. Its explosive power, about one megaton, so far
·om anything, caused an irrelevant stirring and heating of
·mpty air.

What mattered was not the blast. From about thirty to
·bout sixty miles up, varying by latitude and season, the
·arth's atmosphere is electrically charged—it is called the
·nosphere because a charged atom is an ion. Normally little
·ectric current flows there, despite the gigantic potentials.
·ut if something creates enough free electrons in that part
·· the atmosphere to carry current, mighty arcs—effectively
·ghtning strokes many miles across and thousands of miles
·ng—abruptly appear in the ionosphere, and those gigantic
·irrents cause the EMP below.

The helium-3 pure fusion warhead was the best EMP
·mb ever devised. First the soft gamma, a sizable part of its
·ergy release, irradiated the ionosphere within a thousand-
·ile radius, knocking electrons off the unimaginably many,
·any atoms in a thousand miles of even very thin air. Less
·an a microsecond behind, the relativistic protons released
· the explosion, with their own charge and enormous veloc-
·, raced through, ripping electrons from the atoms as they
·ssed, hitting nuclei so hard that they left their electrons be-
·nd like the dishes on a swiftly snatched tablecloth, and in
·neral breaking everything in their path; one proton, at such
·gh speeds, had to collide violently with more than 30,000
·ms to lose its force.

In a microsecond, a disk of the ionosphere, two thousand
·les across and more than thirty miles thick, became as con-
·ctive as the inside of a fluorescent tube. Vast currents, with

far more energy than the bomb that had freed them, surge
back and forth in the atmosphere.

And as everyone learns in high-school physics, a chang
ing electric field induces a changing magnetic field, and vic
versa; that is how radio propagates in a vacuum, electric fiel
change inducing magnetic field change that induces anothe
electric field change and so forth, world without end, un
til there is an antenna somewhere to drain off the movin;
energy.

The great current surge high overhead induced an ex
traordinarily strong and rapidly changing magnetic field a
the earth's surface, which induced a current in every con
ductor. The effect was strongest around Pittsburgh. Stil
standing power lines and barbed-wire fences flashed int
vapor; highway guardrails and aluminum rain gutters elec
trocuted birds sitting on them; coathangers in abandone
closets crackled and sparked violently, causing fires th
no one came to extinguish. Currents formed in the wirir
of battery lanterns, leaped the OFF switch, burned out th
filament of the bulb, and exploded the batteries; the electr
generators at Westinghouse, rotating at terrifying spee
abruptly melted and flung themselves as molten met
around their housings.

And at KP-1, a mighty current roared down the just-rebu
antenna, destroying all the station's equipment and killing
dozen scientists and engineers instantly; no one heard th
over the radio, for anyone listening on a crystal set close t
was electrocuted, and those farther away were suddenly, de
perately trying to put out the flames.

The surge weakened with distance, but still, at St. Lou
the Gateway Arch rattled and sparked with artificial thunde
in New York Harbor, the skeleton of Miss Liberty sizzled w
blue glows; everywhere, instantly, far too much electricity.

Dying off with distance, the surging, whirling, swi
changing electromagnetic fields were still strong enough
create shocks and sparks around every conductor they cross
in Kansas City, Winnipeg, Halifax, and Raleigh.

THE SAME TIME. OVER SOUTHERN ILLINOIS, A FEW MILES FROM PALE BLUFF. 8:22 A.M. CST. WEDNESDAY, DECEMBER 18.

Inside the oak cabinet something went off like a flashbulb; a moment later, Heather realized that the plane had stopped shaking. Larsen slapped at the panel of dials and tried throwing switches.

"Come in, Yankee One," McIntyre was saying.

Arnie had already leaned across him, turned the casing around, and was prying off the back. "No good, sir," Arnie said. "All these tubes are burned black and that smoke smell is roasted insulation."

Quattro stopped flipping toggles. "All our electric stuff is fried. I'll have to glide us down onto the highway. At least it's empty. Was that some kind of secret weapon?"

McIntyre said, "That F-35 might've popped us with an e-bomb, one of those missiles that sets off a baby EMP."

"I doubt it," Quattro said, pointing ahead of them to the F-35 spiraling downward, leaving a thin trail of smoke behind itself. "Those are fly-by-wire with no hydraulic or mechanical backups for the electronic controls, so when it takes an EMP hit, it's done. And I doubt he used any weapon that would get him too."

There was a flash of flame and a burst of smoke from the Navy jet and a dot shot away from it, then blossomed into a parachute. The dead F-35 plummeted onward.

"He must've been angling generally down at us when his controls locked, and it sent him into that tailspin," Larsen said. "The Daybreakers might have had a point about relying too much on too-high tech; this old thing is controlled by hydraulics that are not as complicated as the brakes on a modern car, and it's built to glide pretty well because the original engines it was built for were kind of pathetic. So I think I can glide us down on I-64 and just hope we don't run into an abandoned car. Landing in about one minute, and I suggest you all get belted in and tied down *right now*."

Already, the land was coming up to meet them, and everyone was strapping in; McIntyre was last, muttering about always having hated to fly anyway.

At the last moment, Larsen had to pull the stick back to

pass over a deer on the road, so the DC-3 came in higher and harder than intended, but though they were soft, the linen and oil tires held, and though the tail rose alarmingly, the nose didn't touch, the landing gear didn't buckle, and when the tail wheel slammed back down, the plane shuddered but didn't bend. They were shaken through almost eighty degrees, and Heather vomited as the old airliner came to a rest, but that was the worst of it. Quattro was leaping out the door with a fire extinguisher, and Bambi followed him with another, shouting for everyone to get off the plane *now*. After they had stood for a couple of minutes, a hundred yards back, watching Quattro and Bambi circle the DC-3, nothing had happened. Bambi and Quattro set their extinguishers down and came over to explain.

"Mostly empty tanks can slosh," Quattro said, "especially an older design like that, and if you shake the plane hard enough, some fuel can slop through the pressure reliefs. Between two hot engines, the heaters for the sterilizing spray and god knows how many little sparks the EMP might have caused, I didn't want to take any chances; something weird might happen."

Heather looked over the Checker Cab of the Air and the little crowd of Army Rangers, ex-Feds, current geeks, one general, and one president, and then back to the slightly mad ex-millionaire—and freeholder of Castle Larsen—in his bulky farmer coveralls and vintage leather flying helmet. "That's a reasonable concern," Heather said. "It is always possible that something weird might happen."

FIFTEEN MINUTES LATER. ATHENS, TEMPORARY NATIONAL GOVERNMENT (TNG) DISTRICT. (FORMERLY ATHENS, GEORGIA.) 9:40 A.M. EST. WEDNESDAY, DECEMBER 18.

"So that's as much as we can get from the instruments," the physicist was saying. "And the Navy's data were invaluable. I'm afraid we lost at least six aircraft, including the—uh—"

"The one chasing Weisbrod's plane," Nguyen-Peters said. "What's your estimate on the extent of the damage?"

"So far nobody has called in at all for three hundred miles around Pittsburgh, but it's awfully soon. I'm sure they're all fighting fires, and probably any equipment they wrapped up

nd put by arced over and died, so even if they have the time
hey probably don't have the radio. Outside that radius, it gets
etter, until in the outermost ring it's just small fires in the runs and current surges burning out stuff the nanoswarm would
ave eaten eventually anyway."

Cam smiled with grim satisfaction. "Well, I'm glad Arnie
ang and Graham Weisbrod are alive and in good shape, be-
ause the next time I see either of them, I *so* get to say *I told
ou so*. Look what we have. A direct hit with an EMP right
bove Pittsburgh, knocking out KP-1, the Westinghouse and
PG labs, and all that stuff at Pitt and CMU. Just about the
orst blow we could have taken, obviously aimed, perfectly
med to disrupt our attempt to recapture Weisbrod, leaving
s more disorganized. That meets Arnie's criteria if anything
oes. No question anymore—it's a war, because we have an
emy."

"I'm glad we have that settled, sir," General Phat said.
May I have a moment of your time? General Grayson will
me with us if you don't mind."

In the privacy of the office, Cameron said, "Something is
rious."

Phat handed him a short, signed, typewritten note. "My
signation. I had very grave doubts about this whole situation
om the beginning. We now have a legitimate President of
e United States who will take the oath anytime now, if he
sn't taken it already. I don't see any way I can go any further
th you, so here's my resignation, and good luck to you and
eneral Grayson."

Cam blinked at the small, harsh-featured man in front of
m, one of that generation of military heroes that had come
t of the Iran campaigns. He and Grayson both towered over
at, and yet Cam felt small to the pit of his soul. *This is
ere a charismatic guy like Pendano would know just what
say, to win him back.* All Cameron could think of was,
ell, but . . . I turned out to be right. I think the evidence is
erwhelming that we're under attack."

"That's true, sir. But the evidence is also overwhelming
t under the Constitution, we have a president, to whom I
e my loyalty. And I didn't take an oath to back whoever
d the right analysis. I took an oath to support and defend
e Constitution. Were you ever in the service, or an officer?"

"No."

"Then you wouldn't get it. But then Grayson doesn't either do you?"

"You can stop harassing me now that you're not my supe rior officer."

"I also have that privilege as your prisoner. Do you want t call an MP or shall I go find one?"

ABOUT TWO HOURS LATER. SOUTHEAST OF PALE BLUFF, ILLINOIS. 12:15 P.M. CST. WEDNESDAY, DECEMBER 18.

"Sir," Rogers said, lowering his binoculars, "after due inspec tion and observation, I believe the person approaching us i Davy Crockett."

McIntyre gave him a sour glare. "You're enjoying the al sence of a proper chain of command more than you shoul Rogers. Let me have a look."

To the naked eye, the figure that had just come over a lo rise in the road was no more than a dot. McIntyre looke through the binoculars. "Well, that looks like a black-powd rifle, that's definitely a coonskin cap, and there's fringe on h jacket. But he's wearing leather dress shoes, and I don't thir Davy Crockett's jacket had a zipper, either. Perhaps yo Ranger training at observation is failing you."

"Could be, sir. Maybe he's hunting? The dog looks like i doing more than just hanging around and keeping compan and the sheath knife is too short to be much in a fight but ju right for field dressing something."

"I missed the knife, so we're even." McIntyre handed t binoculars to Heather, saying, "Well, let's see how a Fed do with this."

She saw everything they'd pointed out, and then laughe "You guys missed something a law-enforcement pers wouldn't. There's a badge on that silly hat, and I'm guessi that white armband means something too. He's some kind cop."

When they had closed the distance, they saw he w young, maybe not even thirty yet, deeply tanned, and thin the point of scrawny. He kept his black-powder rifle, whi Machado whispered looked like a percussion cap/paper c ridge model, carefully pointed at the sky, and when the dog ran forward to meet them, he said, firmly, "Skip. Back here." Skip trotted back behind him, as if saying, *Okay, boss, we'll play by the rules, but they smell okay to me.*

"I'm Freddie Pranger," the man said. "Long Range Patrolling Constable for the village of Pale Bluff, Illinois."

"General Norm McIntyre, U.S. Army, and—"

"Then this is the party I'm looking for," Pranger said. "I'm assuming you are Graham Weisbrod, the former Secretary of the Future?"

Graham nodded. "And current President of the United States."

"That's what folks want to discuss back at Pale Bluff," Constable Pranger said. "I'm betting most of those M4s still work, so I'm not going to try to make you come along, but I was sent out to invite you in. We can give you beds and food for the night, and have a little discussion. Our governor up in Springfield has sent us word over the semaphore chain that you're to be detained and turned over to the state, but quite a few people in the village don't hold with our governor, being as he's actually the secretary of state, and the wrong party too—the real gov and his lieutenant were up by Chicago when the big bomb went off.

"So the folks in town voted that I was to walk up this road and make you the offer of shelter and a chance to talk. There're people around Alton who could find you a train west, we passed the word to them, which I guess we'll do if you win the vote."

"What happens if we just walk on by?"

"Nothing—from us. Don't know what any other town up the line might do. Probably'd depend on how *they* voted." He took off the coonskin cap and rubbed his damp hair. "What I can offer you is, Pale Bluff is close, we have a lot of apple pies baking because some of our people are out to impress the president, and you'll get a hearing at the Town Meeting; our mayor doesn't allow people to act out much."

"Roof, bed, pie, and a fair hearing," Weisbrod said. "A pretty good deal."

"Well, that, and we're mostly Democrats here. Next few towns are iffy."

"Then I think we have a deal, Constable Pranger."

ABOUT THREE HOURS LATER. PALE BLUFF, ILLINOIS.
4:30 P.M. CST. WEDNESDAY, DECEMBER 18.

It was even easier than they had expected. A few older men,
and one young woman with a big cross on her neck, made a
fuss about Weisbrod's being wanted by the armed forces and
the police, but the testimony of a general—particularly one
who talked as eloquently about the Constitution as McIntyre
did—seemed to quiet them.

Asked to make a final statement before the vote, Graham
Weisbrod said, "Let me just say that it is the essence of living
under a government of laws and not of men that we have to let
the laws go against us, sometimes, when it's our turn. Right
now, I don't know what they've figured out about this EMP
down in Athens, because they haven't released their official
statement, but the news from Radio Pullman, which wasn't
knocked out, says that the physics guys at WSU think it was
centered over Pittsburgh, which, as we all know, is where KP-
is. We all hope they'll get back on the air soon. I expect when
they do we'll hear some more bad news from Pittsburgh itself
and from Youngstown, Wheeling, Erie, Johnstown, and so on

"If that was where the blow fell, then depending where the
Atlantic Fleet was, they may have taken some damage too.
hope you'll remember them in your prayers.

"And please, everyone, keep looking for the pilot of the
Navy fighter. He ejected and his chute opened, we all saw
that, but he might have come down as much as ten miles away
from where we did. If he hasn't found a nice town like this, o
a friendly farm, he might be pretty cold and hungry right now
and of course he might've been hurt by the fire in his plane, o
in the ejection. Please keep looking out for him."

Not bad for a guy who's no politician, Graham, Heather
thought. *Some of the vets-first crowd is nodding like you re
ally pleased them.*

"Anyway, let me point out an irony here: if the Pittsburgh
EMP turns out to have been a clear-cut act of war, then the
political difference between me and the NCCC will be *zero.*
None, zip, *nada.* If it really is a war, we'll go win that war.
And we'll do it without abrogating or mauling our Constitution. I understand that Mr. Nguyen-Peters acted in good faith
feeling that in time of war the country must have a preside

who is committed to that war—but that's *not* what it says in our Constitution.

"The Constitution makes the President the Commander in Chief, so it gives him the duty to repel foreign attacks. But it doesn't require him to see them when they aren't there. He owes you his judgment and perception as much as he owes you his loyal, energetic service.

"Up till today, I saw no war. Once I become more acquainted with the evidence—and I will be getting more of it soon, I believe, from many sources—then if indeed we are under attack and at war, I will contact Mr. Nguyen-Peters, offer him an apology, and reconcile; I will not want to lose a man of his abilities when our needs are so great.

"On the other hand, should the evidence prove—as I believe—that Daybreak and the terrorist attacks associated with it were the result of a now-extinguished system artifact, a terrible self-organization of the malicious and wilful destructive side of all of us, manifested through a technology we did not fully understand—if the evidence shows it—then I call on Mr. Nguyen-Peters, his supporters, and whatever civil governments and military units may have aligned with him, to join with us in reconciliation, without any penalty or prejudice. It is the holiday season; it is appropriate for there to be peace among men of good will, and deep though our differences are, bound though I am by the Constitution, I extend my hand, and hope to find it clasped by another man of good will."

The vote on "Resolved: That the Village of Pale Bluff recognizes Graham Weisbrod as President of the United States of America and so will offer all needed assistance within our power," was 289 for, 36 against.

There was one more item of business on the agenda; Quattro Larsen asked for volunteers to help him walk back to the DC-3 and see if it could be rehabbed. "I'm guessing," he explained, "that it's a matter of replacing some wires and fuses, and probably rebuilding the spark coil, and I guess I'll have to figure out what to do about the deflated tires, so far away from any source of compressed air. But it seems like a shame to lose one of the few remaining airplanes, and honestly, it's kind of my baby; I've worked on it so long that I guess whether I get volunteer help here or not, I'll be walking back there tomorrow to work on it again."

He had half a dozen volunteers immediately.

After the meeting, as they were shown to their rooms in the community center's emergency shelter (four large bedrooms with six cots each, usually used for when flooding or fire left a family homeless), a small woman with narrow glasses, gray hair, and a too-lumpy-to-be anything-but-home-knitted poinsettia-patterned sweater approached. "President Weisbrod? I'm Carol May Kloster. I'm the Secretary for the Town Meeting."

"Pleased to meet you—I was a secretary till recently myself!"

The woman flushed deeply. "I, uh, I took down your remarks in shorthand; I was wondering . . . would you mind signing them, and maybe dating them? Because I think I might have just seen the most history I'll ever see, up close. I'm sorry all I have for you to sign with is the pencil I took the notes in."

Weisbrod smiled broadly. "Carol May Kloster, I was hoping there'd be notes, because I'm not sure I remember what all I said—I was speaking from the back of a parking-ticket envelope I scribbled about twenty words on." He signed and dated with a flourish.

As he turned to go to his room, Allison Sok Banh was standing in front of him. "Graham," she said softly, "what have you done?"

"I did something wrong?"

"You pledged to give up the presidency that it's already cost us our safety and security—and a couple of men their lives—to give to you. What if it turns out that the EMP is the proof that we really are in a war?"

"It might be ironic, but it would simplify things," Weisbrod said. "And I wouldn't give up being President; the legitimate succession is too valuable. I'd just tell Cameron I was willing to stooge for him, take the oath, and do and say whatever he told me to; as soon as he had a Congress available, I'd appoint whoever he picked as VP, and resign immediately after confirmation. If he does turn out to be right, what else can I decently do?"

She was standing very close and glaring into his eyes; her intense anger startled him. "*You're* the president. If it turns out we're in a war, you're supposed to lead us, as best you can—not find someone else to do it, not take instructions, but *lead*. Having been wrong once doesn't excuse you from doing your duty." She seemed to force herself to stop before saying more than she wanted to, and finished with, "The Constitution and the Congress made you the president. Be the president."

"Well, at the moment," Weisbrod said, "my presidential priorities are identifying a place for the president to sleep tonight." He meant it as a light joke to deflect the subject; but he saw in her face what she had thought for a moment, and that it was a welcome thought. Awkwardly, he said good night; looking down, he realized he was holding her hands.

When he looked up again, she was smiling. She squeezed his hands and said, "Sleep well," and was gone around the corner to sleep with the other women tonight.

THE NEXT DAY. ATHENS, TNG DISTRICT. (ATHENS, GEORGIA.) 10:15 A.M. EST. THURSDAY, DECEMBER 19.

You are going to be in deep shit for this," Abel said, leaning over Chris's shoulder, "and I am not so sure that I will not be in deep shit for setting it and printing it."

Chris looked up and said, "Now you're a critic."

"I ain't a critic, but if I got to be I'll sure as shit be a censor. You are going to embarrass the crap out of the NCCC, and he's not going to take it well, because just now he's dealing with the fact that he's *sort of* the president, and Graham Weisbrod's *sort of* the president, and that's one more than people are used to, so everyone's good and nervous to begin with. Then on top of that, there's the fact that good old Cam, it turns out, was keeping his good old buddy Graham all wrapped up tight in secret jail, and all the time giving out that they was still friends and Graham was calling the shots, which means NCCC-Cam's now established for a big fat liar, *and* he's got his escaped other president, *and* if that story about him taking the oath in that little town in Illinois from a city traffic judge is true, it's a sworn-in and taking-control kind of president. Last time anything like this happened around here, a guy named Sherman burned the damn state down."

"He also freed your ancestors."

"Yeah. Everybody's got some good points and some times you got to take the bitter with the sweet. But now that I'm free—and like you say, right now I'm America's leading publisher and the founder of a media dynasty— I don't want Georgia burned down anymore. It's like once you *own*, instead of *rent*, you care about the property more, you know? No more Shermans, that's what I say. And when you got two governments in one nation, that kind of thing can happen."

Abel's goofing around, of course, but he's got a more than-real point. Chris considered for a moment. "How many people would you guess feel like you do?"

"All of 'em, if they have any brains. Look, go out in the street and interview the man in it, and tell me we ain't worrying about a new Civil War. Talk to some of the army guys and see if they ain't worried stiff that they're gonna have to shoot some of their own. Ask a guy who just got a roof over his family's head again, and something for his kids to eat, if he wants it bombed. And then ask any of them if they think it's a good thing to have two governments, and one trying to arrest the other one. It's like two cops gone bad, both playing for different gangs, and the whole damn country is stuck in the crossfire."

"Well," Chris said, rising from his chair and pulling on his hat. "Yeah, I think you're right, I'd better get out and do some man-in-the-streets, and talk to some people up at the campus and see if I can put together something about this."

"I was trying to talk you out of it entirely. I'm telling you you're embarrassing the government, and that is not something a government forgives."

"It's Cam Nguyen-Peters, Abel. I know him. I've interviewed him over beer and pizza, you know? And there isn't a guy in the whole blessed Republic with more of a commitment to the Constitution, which includes the First Amendment. I'm telling you, he is *not* going to jail a newspaper editor."

Abel sat on the desk, resting his large, strong hands his massive thighs, looking like an imminent human avalanche. "And I am telling you, you're embarrassing a man with power, and two-thirds of his power is the respect he gets. And as for the Constitution, yeah, he loves it—and he's trying his damnedest to put it back—because *we ain't under right now.* And weren't we just talking about him locking up a buddy? But I can't stop you, so I guess I'm just gonna wait for my chance to say. *I told you so.*"

"I guess we'll have to go for a third printing," Chris said, though his arms ached and he was thinking *They must call his job the printer's devil because you work like hell.* "That's the sixth newsboy to come in empty and needing more. We can set out the sandwich trays for them and have papers in their hands in an hour, if we hustle."

Abel looked with satisfaction at the mountain of cans and jars, and the box stuffed with TNG scrip. "Definitely our most profitable day," he said, "I got to give you that."

They turned back to the press; it didn't like to work this long without wipe-downs and general cleaning, as the lye they used to keep the nanoswarm off the electric motors tended to turn all the lubricants into soft brown soap that burned into black gunk in the bearings. *Have to tear the old girl down for a day after this run is over,* Chris thought. *Glad we're not a daily yet.* He glanced down at the marked-up sample sheet. *Now,* this *headline will be part of history:*

> SEC'Y WEISBROD FLEES,
> TAKES OATH AS 49TH PRES'T,
> CITIZENS DREAD CIVIL WAR II

"Hey, Mr. Big Editor, quit daydreaming so Mr. Lowly Scum Printer's Devil can get to work."

"Caught!" Chris said, and started to move one of the big rolls of paper into the ready rack.

"Mr. Manckiewicz?" a voice said.

He turned to see a man who wore a blue suit, white shirt, and red tie, and might as well have worn a sign around his neck: COP. The man held out a piece of paper and said, "I have a warrant; you need to come with me."

"Am I being arrested? What are the charges?"

The man shrugged. "You're to come with me. I'm authorized to use force if you won't come peaceably. So are you coming with me?"

Chris looked around. Abel. Abel's building and business. Newsboys eating and depending on him for their meals and work. And though Chris was in much better physical condition than he was a few months ago, this guy looked young and strong and probably had a gun.

"I'm coming," he said. "Let me just get someone to help with the printing—"

"You won't have to do that," the man said, "because I have an order here that says no more of this edition is to be printed and the paper is not to bring out any more editions till further notice."

As they walked toward the campus, the man said nothing, despite Chris's urgent questions. *I guess it's not the accused that has the right to remain silent anymore,* he thought, and then *Hunh, an America where they don't read you your rights.* That made it real to Chris; for the first time, ever, he felt *America is gone.*

THE NEXT DAY. ATHENS, TNG DISTRICT. (ATHENS, GEORGIA.) 10:30 A.M. EST. FRIDAY, DECEMBER 20.

Cameron Nguyen-Peters looked around the room. *Problem of balance in a democracy,* he thought. *You had to keep everyone loyal and on the same page in times of troubles, but you also had to give them the feeling that what they thought and felt, individually, mattered.* Democracy was the greatest system ever invented for producing buy-in, but it constantly risked turning everything into a debate.

"Well," he said, "I think the first thing to say is that the results of the investigation at least indicate we were not crazy. There is no evidence that any of the conspirators had any involvement with any foreign power, or with any domestic Daybreak terrorist organization. Absolutely none. So one reason we didn't see it coming was that they genuinely acted on their own—but that also means we haven't just been hit by another attack from the actual enemy, we're just suffering from disorder in our own ranks."

The rest of the meeting ran like clockwork and the or

people who talked were the ones making reports. Vaguely, at the end, Cameron thought, *I do miss the Weisbrod group; they had so many interesting ideas. But one thing to say for this team, they'll never make me late for lunch.*

THREE DAYS LATER. DENVER, COLORADO. 11:30 A.M. MST. MONDAY, DECEMBER 23.

"Where did they all come from?" Graham asked, looking out at the vast, swarming throng on the south side of Denver's Union Station.

"Well, a lot of the population of Denver starved, or moved away, or was killed in the big fire a few weeks ago," the mayor said, "but luckily for us the Front Range urban strip was narrow, so anyone who could walk either east or west was only a day or two from shelter and food. Some of them have been coming back as trade gets going again, and the state capital was always here, so a lot of the agencies we needed were too, and well, we just managed to get it going again, sort of, at least right here around the downtown. So some people have returned, maybe more than in other big cities. And then you brought in visitors from everywhere south to Trinidad and north to Laramie. People just want to see that they have a president again, I guess."

Graham looked over the crowd and nodded toward the signs that said ONCE A DEMOCRAT, ALWAYS A TRAITOR and WHY WASN'T HE IN WASH DC THAT DAY? GOT TRUTH? "Looks like some people aren't all that happy with what they're seeing, but then that's the 'normal' we're trying to get back to. Well, I guess it's time."

The fourth attempt to build a working amp had failed earlier that morning, after a promising start, when insulation had rotted off a wire and the resulting short had fried an irreplaceable capacitor. For the moment, they were stuck with the technology that would have been familiar to Abe Lincoln: the mayor shouted for everyone to shut up. The crowd leaned in to listen, and fell silent, and except for the occasional chuff of escaping steam from a locomotive that had recently been rescued from the Denver Railway Museum, people seemed to be able to hear.

. . .
_____

For reasons obscure even to herself, Heather had chosen to be
out among the crowd. She'd told Graham, "it's so I can shou
'louder' if you start to mumble like a dotty old college professor," but she just had a feeling that she should be out among
the crowd.

The Federal District Court judge who swore Graham Weis
brod in used a family Bible to do it, which he would be taking
home as a souvenir; as Graham said, it was more dignifie
than tipping him a hundred. They weren't sure whether th
oath administered by the traffic court judge of Pale Bluff wa
enough, so to make sure, they were re-doing it with the firs
available Federal judge. After that, with the whole Suprem
Court dead in DC three weeks ago, this would have to do.

They had managed to put together enough musicians pro
ficient on band instruments for a respectable rendition c
"The Star-Spangled Banner," and found a local singer wit
the range; Graham had told her, "Make this the plainest on
you've ever done; hit every pitch and every emotion, but don
make a show out of it." She had glared at him, but she com
plied, and everyone cheered at the end.

Weisbrod's inaugural address was as brief as he coul
make it, which meant it was "still six times as long as Lin
coln's Second Inaugural," as Weisbrod himself pointed ou
"It's a garrulous, bureaucratic age, you know." He called f
provisional elections in 2026, leading to a "restart" in 2027,
be modeled on the 1788/9 startup of the Federal governmer
thus de facto agreeing to Cameron's publicly announced pla
he called for "immediate and thorough investigation to dete
mine whether the recent tragedies suffered by our nation, o
planet, and our species were the acts of deliberate enemie
and to find a course of action."

For most of the speech, he outlined a plan for ongoing r
construction and redevelopment, including research into c
ing, reversing, or neutralizing the effects of the nanoswa
and biotes. Arnie had pleaded with him to include a line abc
just learning to live with them, because, Arnie said, the od
were overwhelming that that would be what they would ha
to do, for decades or centuries. Graham had said he did
think anyone was ready for that thought yet.

There was a carefully drafted paragraph that the judge and General McIntyre had worked over, in which Graham unambiguously claimed his Constitutional role as commander in chief, but thanked Cameron for his prior execution of his duties as NCCC, and stipulated that troops who had obeyed their commanding officers had committed no offenses. As Graham said, it was difficult to express the idea of amnesty, pardon, and complete forgiveness without using any of those words, but they had managed to do it, and that was what the country needed.

The speech ended with a rousing closing about enduring the tough days ahead and emerging as a great nation.

The woman standing beside Heather in the crowd said, "Oh, well, I suppose he has a lot on his mind."

Something in the woman's tone of disappointment made Heather take a closer look. The woman was tall, only an inch or two shorter than Heather; slim, rangy, and muscular; perhaps thirty years old; with the sort of sharply etched, squared-off features that Heather's father had always described as "skipped the pretty stage and went straight to handsome." Her companion was a short, powerfully built man of around fifty, in baggy, worn clothes that suggested he'd lost some weight lately; he wore a thick wool jacket over a couple of shirts and sweaters, thick steel-framed glasses, and a ski band around his ears that exposed the pink and peeling skin of his bald scalp. Both of them had on well-worn leather boots resoled with thick rawhide, and looked so tired and discouraged that Heather blurted out, "What did you think Weisbrod missed, or should have talked about?"

The woman assessed Heather with an expression that held no expectations; just a simple *Who are you and how do you fit into my life?* The short man said, "Well, Leslie and I—uh, I'm James—uh, we walked all the way from Pueblo to get here, they don't have a train running yet, and we thought since it's one of the biggest government dealies in Colorado, you know, the president might have at least mentioned us, or invited us to write to him, or something, so we'd know what he wanted and needed from us."

"I—uh, I work for him," Heather said, "and the Federal government is . . . well, even now it's huge, and of course he was only the head of a small department till recently, so he's not necessarily up on everything . . ." She was afraid that she might be talking to a couple of petty bureaucrats administering a program that was gone forever, worried about their pensions and perks; she didn't want to fend off inquiries from the Federal Poultry Inspection Corps or the Regional Authorized Paper Rearrangement Facility, and she especially didn't want to make any promises to them. "How far was it from Pueblo?" she asked, lamely, and feeling how lame that was.

Leslie, the tall, rangy woman, said, "It's about 135 miles. It wasn't really bad because we could break the trip at Fort Carson in Colorado Springs, where they let us stay a night, and the town of Castle Rock is in okay shape now, so we could get some food and shelter there. So we only actually had to camp every other day."

Heather was wracking her brains; *what's in Pueblo? Anything? Or are these two postal clerks with delusions of grandeur?*

She could tell they were about to turn away. She imagined them walking back, defeated, for the long week or so it might take, and perhaps getting stuck in a blizzard; she couldn't stand it. "I can't remember what Federal facility is in Pueblo," she finally admitted. "I used to be in law enforcement so I know it's not a prison or an agency regional office."

James surprised her by clapping his hands together and laughing. "Leslie, what did I say to everyone about it not being like the old days?"

She rolled her eyes and looked like she'd eaten something sour. "Great, now he's been right about something and I'll have to hear about it the whole walk back. Well, we're the people you *used* to hear about on television, as in 'Pueblo, Colorado, 81009.' The Government Printing Office and the Federal Consumer Information Center. For the past couple decades we mostly maintained a homepage that gave access to around two hundred thousand Federal web sites, so that if people wanted HUD's information about removing lead paint or the Department of Agriculture's procedure for collecting soybean subsidies, they could find it online. But we're still the Government *Printing* Office and we have a few billion pamphlets, books, maps, everything that the Feds put together that consumers might want, including a lot of stuff on paper

that goes back a few decades, everything from home gardening and canning to building your own pottery kiln to safe field
sanitation, and especially with the Library of Congress gone,
and the damage they say that the big libraries in the East have
been taking, with us having all this practical stuff, we just
thought—"

"Especially," the short, heavy man put in, "because we do
still have a lot of the old printing machinery, I don't know
which parts can be put back in service but some of the people
who used to run it retired to Pueblo—"

Heather felt like she might just stare for an hour, but *oh
my dear god don't let them get away!* "You mean, we've got a
whole library of all those practical skills—"

James's head was pumping up and down violently. "And
lots of impractical too. 'Greek Word Roots Used in Scientific Vocabulary.' 'Chemistry Sets for School Instruction from
Materials Purchased in Drug, Hardware, and Feed Stores.'
'Fundamentals of Amateur Astronomy.' Stuff going back
ninety years to the 1930s and before." For the guy in the cynic
role, he wasn't doing much of a job. "I mean, we don't know
what will be useful, but it's all there in the warehouses, and
Pueblo's kind of lucky; Fort Carson held down the Springs
and blocked the main road from Denver, so we didn't have
much of a refugee problem or a civil disorder problem, and
we still have plenty of food and clean water, and we do have
those presses, so, really, if the president is serious about getting civilization restarted, and if he meant that line about 're-
learning all the old arts of peace'—"

"Oh, he meant it," Heather said. She stuck out her hand.
"My name is Heather O'Grainne. I can walk you straight to
President Weisbrod. Might even be able to get you a meal or
two, and some supplies for your trip home. And there's a couple people—Dr. Arnold Yang, maybe General McIntyre—
that I want you to meet too. In fact, I think maybe we should
have you talk to Arnie, *then* to the president. Can you come
along now? And where were you staying?"

"We're in the bedroll crowd at the Oxford," Leslie admitted, looking a little embarrassed. "The GPO didn't exactly
have a budget for us to do this, so—"

"Then you're staying in the same hotel with the president
anyway," Heather said, enjoying the irony. "And I've just

shared a major national security secret with you. Hope you don't mind climbing stairs."

But on the top floor, Arnie and McIntyre were "the two most unavailable people you could have asked for," Allie explained to Heather.

"Do you know what it's about?"

Allie glanced at Leslie and James, and Heather said, "They're Federal employees I just found, and they're the guardians of something we really want to keep."

"How about we feed them while I tell you the classified stuff?"

"Deal," Heather said, and steered the GPO employees down the hall. To the Oxford cooks, she said, "These are Federal employees, part of the party till I tell you different, and feed them, okay? They've come here over a hard road."

In a room alone with Allie, she asked, "All right, what is it?"

"Radiogram from Cam. There's been another EMP, this time over the South China Sea. Nailed the Canton/Macau/ Hong Kong area, Manila, most of Taiwan, and the Western Pacific Fleet. They're going to have to scuttle one carrier and two subs—all the reactor control stuff fried and the reactors failsafed into shutdown—and they're towing all of them, hoping to get them into a deep trench like they did the *Reagan*. And just like before, no identified launch site."

"So what's the huddle about?"

"Cam's radiogram was making the point that we're getting hit with targeted attacks, don't we see there's a war on? That area was the best-equipped remaining base for rebuilding civilization in Asia, plus they also destroyed the protection and resources that area was borrowing from us; they could hardly have hit the human race harder. I don't know if Cam knows yet about those stupid things Graham said in Pale Bluff, but he's acting as if he did—practically inviting Graham to just hand over the presidency. Makes me furious!"

"Well, it definitely looks like a targeted attack."

"It looks like an attack targeted by a robot, not by a living thinking being. Arnie's already pointed out that so far the pattern is that the EMP weapon hits the brightest radio source. He wants to do some serious study before anyone goes into a decision blind."

"I thought you usually didn't like it when Arnie wanted to study everything to death."

"If one of Arnie's studies can keep Graham Weisbrod from kicking away everything he ought to claim, then as far as I'm concerned, Arnie can study everything and everybody till doomsday. His idea for a test is really simple: He just wants everyone worldwide to go dead on the radio as much as possible, or at least keep signals to very low energy, and he wants to do some kind of experiment, I don't get what, to see if whatever it is knows what it's shooting at, or just shoots at the brightest radio signal.

"Meanwhile, McIntyre just wants his old job back so he can be put in charge of knocking out the launch site, assuming we ever manage to find it. And Graham keeps scribbling on his damned pad and muttering 'Hmmm,' and he's just not speaking up and asserting himself, which is what he needs to do!" Allison Sok Banh was normally one of those reserved women who must endure the ice-princess label, but that didn't seem to be her problem today. "Anyway," she said, calming a little, "they told me to brief you, so I decided I'd just save time and tell you the truth."

"Shit. You want to be careful with that stuff, people get hurt playing with it. Before we go into any more detail, I've got two people who walked six days to get here, with access to a resource that might help save the whole country across the next century, and it sounds like I won't be able to set them up with anyone to talk to."

"Well," Allie said, "there's me. How about I go out there, make all sorts of nice apologies for everyone, turn on the charm, and generally win them over to the cause?"

"Well, you can certainly do it—I've seen you—"

"I'm pretty sure I can speak for Graham and make it sound convincing. And if they need a presidential decision on something, I'll sweet-talk Graham to go along with whatever deal I need to cut or arrangement I need to make. He listens to me a lot these days." Something about Allie's smile bothered Heather, and she hoped she didn't know what it was. "Better fill me in on what your two new friends do and why you think this vital; we want them to feel valued, and nothing creates the impression of neglect like being asked the same questions over and over."

**THE NEXT DAY. EAST OF GRAND JUNCTION, COLORADO.
1:45 P.M. MST. TUESDAY, DECEMBER 24.**

Heather and Allie sat at a newly-bolted-in picnic table in the observation car that was attached ahead of Amtrak One, as the presidential car was being called, much to Graham's annoyance. Spectacular scenery rolled by; they had time to review Allie's notes about what was available at Pueblo.

"I can't believe how many obsolete-tech people came out of the woodwork," Heather said, after a while. "Steam railroad buffs. Hobby printers. Guys who build their own tubes for tube amps. Steam car collectors, and that guy with all those nineteenth-century machine guns, and of course guys like Quattro with his old airplanes. I suppose it's not that shocking that there's a whole nest of them with printing presses and warehouses full of pamphlets down in Pueblo."

Allie shrugged. "People spent their working lives learning a technology, and that's a pretty deep commitment. That nice lady in Pale Bluff was a Gregg shorthand expert, probably one of the youngest and last I would guess."

"Steam trains, though? Too far in the past; no one nowadays grew up around them."

"Oh, well, as far as I can tell, steam trains are a *religion.* We think that the United States might have as many as two hundred working steam locomotives, eighty-four of them narrow-gauge. Anyway, the bottom line is this: If James and Leslie are giving me an accurate picture, in their warehouse they have all, or almost all, the information we need to get people at least back to a 1940s or 1950s level of comfort—much of it on reserve printing plates, which means with some materials and training, enough to paper the country with GPO is a huge repository of how to do everything, and we just need to get a train running down to them, find them the paper and ink and maybe some spare parts, and feed them regularly."

Heather smiled, thinking how happy Leslie and James must have been after their meeting with Allie. "So I did good putting them in touch with you? This is about as excited I've seen you get about anything since Daybreak."

"You did brilliantly. And of course I'm jacked about the Heather, if I'd been smart enough I'd've been praying

Pueblo or something like it to turn up—they have so much potential for knitting the country together. Back when distances were bigger and travel wasn't common, that used to be one of the things that reminded people they were Americans, not just Nebraskans or whatever—that little pamphlet from the Federal government about how to keep milk from spoiling, or how to build a tower for your windmill. Hah, now there's a view!"

The land fell away to the south and west as they descended the long curve, and below them a deep lake, surrounded by redrock, reflected the sky back. "I've driven through here but never seen what it looked like—my eyes were always on the road ahead, too much to worry about," Heather said. "Speaking of which . . . you think we'll find a way to bring Cam and Graham back together?"

"I think Graham still hopes so, but as for me—"

"We're coming up on Glenwood Springs," Sherry said, sticking her head up from the stairway below. "Nobody's told me if that's Colorado or Utah."

"Colorado," Heather said. "Two more stops before Utah. I should splash some water on my face; it's my turn to be standing near Graham, looking attentive and visibly holding a gun."

As Heather heard the speech for the fourth time and ostentatiously looked over the crowd, hoping to seem intimidating, Allie was standing pretty close to Graham Weisbrod and shining Nancy-Reagan-style adoration at him.

Crap. Innocent or not, this is gonna weird out Arnie, and I need him not crazy. And I don't really think it's innocent.

Furthermore . . . Graham had been a media darling for a long time and knew how to work a crowd. But had he always enjoyed it quite this much? Maybe we need a politician for this job, but I'm not sure I wanted the politician to be Graham. This is the guy who used to tell me that I knew better; I wonder, nowadays, if he does?

THE NEXT DAY. ATHENS, TNG DISTRICT. (ATHENS, GEORGIA.) 9:30 A.M. EST. WEDNESDAY, DECEMBER 25.

wasn't the worst prison in the world; they fed him the same they did the guards, and he was allowed notebooks and paper, and the time to sit and write.

When the summons came, the guard said, "While you're meeting with the NCCC, we're supposed to pack all your things. He said to ask you if the notebooks go in a special order, and if you'd rather have them any particular place in this."

The man held up a canvas/steel rucksack that was probably an antique, since there was no whiff of rotting plastic or nylon about it.

"If this one goes in this outside pocket," Chris said, "with a few pens, so I can whip it out and write fast, that would be great. The older ones over there on the bench should all go in on top of my spare boots and clothes, so they won't get damp from just setting the pack down, but not too close to the top in case rain leaks in."

"Kind of bury them in the middle? Got it. He also wanted us to see if you wanted one or two more spare blank notebooks to take with you, but he thought you'd be able to forage for them on your way, too."

"Maybe one spare would be nice, so I don't have to forage too soon. Where am I going?"

"Beats me, Mr. Manckiewicz, I'm supposed to take you to the Natcon, and get your pack ready while you're in with him. Maybe he'll tell you."

Cameron Nguyen-Peters was thinner than ever, and whatever traces of a smile had ever been around his mouth had vanished. He still had his pliers-like handshake and disconcerting way of looking directly at you. "Chris," he said, "you are a problem, and there are only three things that can be done with a problem—ignore it, solve it, or make it someone else's problem. Have a seat, and we'll discuss the situation and the options."

"Um," Chris said. "I kind of thought I was being held for sedition or some such."

"Well, that's the problem. I have a war to run, and the war may go on for decades. From a winning-the-war perspective, which is the only perspective I can really allow myself, free press has a lousy track record. Yes, I know"—Cameron waved a quick dismissal—"there have been many journalists who did great things for the war effort in past wars, and many ethical journalists who at least did no harm, and so on. But even the best journalists in the wars where they did the best jobs sometimes leaked vital information. As of this moment we're beaten, Chris, badly beaten, and I think we're more likely than not to lose—*don't quote that,* anywhere, ever. But I think there's still a chance to win—if we get it all together and fight seriously. The next year or so will tell the tale, and if we win, then in 2026 we'll hold those elections, and in 2027 I will set the entire Constitutional apparatus back up. I suppose after that I'll retire to a farm or something, or maybe hire you to ghostwrite my memoirs. If we lose it won't matter. But for right now, the Constitution is suspended—to preserve the possibility that someday I will set it back up."

"I don't imagine you're asking for my opinion."

"Not at all. But here's the rest of the situation. There can be no point in getting into a civil war, and frankly, almost all of the country's remaining military strength is down here in the South—actually pretty much in a belt across the bottom of the country from the Carolinas to Arizona. The upper-left-hand corner of the country that went over to Weisbrod, which we might call the Goofy Quadrant, are no danger to us. None. They have historically low rates of military enlistment, they're not very disciplined in any other way, they're just not going to put together an army for a civil war, and if they try it will take them years. And they can't possibly be an invasion route for the other side—whoever that is—because we control most of the warships still moving. So the Goofy Quadrant can't help us much in the war, and they can't hurt us much, and common sense says to let them go.

"Which brings me to my solution to the problem of you. I'm giving you the gear you need, and a space-a pass that you should be able to ride out to somewhere on the Plains or maybe down to the Canal Zone, telling you to have fun and to do what you do, and sending you over to Graham Weisbrod. As a public official, I can't ignore you; as an American, I can't stand to do anything that would solve you; but luckily, I can make you someone else's problem. Good luck, Chris, and Merry Christmas! I'll watch for your byline."

Chris thought, *Well, Cameron Nguyen-Peters has given up smiling for the duration, I guess, but I've seldom seen him so cheerful.*

FOUR DAYS LATER. SOUTHEAST OF PALE BLUFF, ILLINOIS. 11:00 A.M. CST. SUNDAY, DECEMBER 29.

Chris had struck I-64 the day before, and thanks to his old TV days and his time at KP-1, he hadn't had to sleep outside or go hungry so far; people here remembered him, and when he said he was going to Olympia to start a new paper there, mostly people seemed to be happy to help.

He'd risen with a couple nice old-farmer types before dawn. They'd given him a large breakfast, filled both his canteens, and sent him on his way. Good weather was holding, so far. *There're a lot of worse walks in the world.*

He topped the rise and decided that he was either having the best luck or the worst hallucination of his career. Right there in front of him was what could only be the DC-3 that had brought Weisbrod to Pale Bluff, Illinois. That meant two things: a chance to look at a piece of history, and that Pale Bluff was nearby, which meant a hundred good interviews in all probability.

He was about a hundred feet from the plane when he realized that there was a man inside, talking to himself and swearing. He crept closer and discovered a man in a pair of coveralls, seated on the floor of the plane, and busily wrapping pieces of copper wire with flannel and Elmer's Glue. It looked like the maddest craft project he'd ever seen.

The man said, "I don't have any money or food and I'm not leaving soon."

"I wasn't going to rob you or jack you. Are you, by any chance, Quattro Larsen, freeholder of Castle Larsen?"

"I am. I am also Quattro Larsen, man bored out of his skull as he wraps miles of wire and hand-rebuilds fuses. The barometer is falling, the hygrometer is rising, and the clouds tell me I've got a storm coming; I've a day at best to get this idiot thing fixed so I can fly south, dodge the storm, and get home. And I'm a fumble-fingered idiot. Plus I won't be able to work after dark; I don't have any artificial light, and I'll have to walk back to the village in the dark. So I am getting very scared and very sorry for myself."

"Mind if I climb up and join you?"

"Help yourself."

"Suppose you show me how to wrap wire. My name

Chris Manckiewicz, I'm a reporter, and I'd be very happy to be your assistant. And it so happens I have a small oil lamp."

"I used to hear you on the radio."

"So you know you can trust me."

"Wrap some wire and let's see."

THREE HOURS LATER. PALE BLUFF, ILLINOIS. 2:00 P.M. CST. SUNDAY, DECEMBER 29.

Chris explained who he was quickly; Carol May Kloster said, "Well, I'd sort of like to hang on to the original document. Can you read shorthand?"

"Not a blessed bit. They didn't even teach it anymore in -school."

"Well, of course, I'm flattered and honored that you want a copy of this, but I've only had time in the last couple of weeks o make four copies in decent handwriting; my niece Pauline has made about twenty in shorthand, practicing her Gregg, so I vas going to give you one of those instead. But that's all right; kind of like the idea that my work is going to be published in he country's biggest newspaper."

"Actually if you wanted to send me news reports or even ust letters from this part of the country, I need a Lower Ohio Valley Correspondent."

"You have no idea how long-winded I am."

"You have no idea how short on copy, and reporters, I'm oing to be, especially if I'm trying to cover the country. My uess is that if you wait a couple of weeks and then address it o *Chris Manckiewicz, the Newspaper, Olympia*, and give it o anyone going that way to be passed on to the next person oing that way, it'll find me. Sort of like Internet by hand."

He looked down at the copy of Weisbrod's speech, and his yes were pulled into the paper; before he knew it he'd read he whole thing. "Hey, this is a great speech, and yes, you get ll the credit for transcribing it. Here's your first assigned gig: rite me an account of your impressions of the speech, how e said it, how people reacted, everything."

"Really? You want me to write something like that for you?"

"No, just make something up and I'll throw it in the astebasket."

She swatted him playfully, they grinned at each other, and Chris figured *I've got no paper and it's breaking my heart, but I've got a stringer, and that's a start.* Carol May said "Pauline should be back any time; she was going to round up a few teenagers who don't have enough to do to go out and help you all with getting the plane ready. You're just lucky the harvest is in, and we all like Mr. Larsen, so we can spare him some time and effort to keep him flying. Especially since he was so good as to put us on the map and has been such a pleasant man to have around these past few days."

"He thinks he's not good with people," Chris said, grinning. "Can't be persuaded otherwise."

"Pooh. All he needed to do was ask for help; I'm glad you came along to do it for him!" Carol May Kloster looked at the sky. "If you all hurry, he can take off sometime before the storm hits, and I'm sure that would be a good thing."

FOUR DAYS LATER. SACRAMENTO, CALIFORNIA.
2:30 P.M. PST. THURSDAY, JANUARY 2.

Heather and Bambi were working the crowd in front of the platform, looking for anyone with a weapon, when Bambi whooped. Grinning like a maniac, Quattro Larsen stepped forward. They embraced, laughing just as though it had been years instead of weeks. *Another thing we all have to get used to,* Heather thought. *Nowadays a thousand miles is a long way.*

"I take it your giant mechanical bumblebee is working again?" Heather said.

"Giant—I'll have you know, if there's ever a National Museum again, that's the one plane that for sure'll be in it. At least after there's another operating plane on the continent besides my other one."

"The Stearman's flying?"

"That's how Chris and I—Chris!"

Chris Manckiewicz turned from where he'd been taking notes on an intense conversation. "My entire history of the period," he said, mournfully, "which is all future historians will ever know of our age, will be filled with the phrase, 'But then Quattro shouted for me, and we had to go.'"

"We met at the *Washington Advertiser-Gazette*, a long
me ago," Heather said, sticking out her hand.

"I remember you, Ms. O'Grainne, and thanks for all your
elp on that day."

"I had no idea at the time you were a pilot. And how did
ou get out here?"

If Manckiewicz could do anything, it was tell a story,
nd after a few minutes he'd made Heather laugh more than
he had in weeks, describing the adventures of "a guy who
ought the props must be the fake parts of the plane," on his
rst trip as "assistant mechanic, copilot intern, master chef,
d chief wailer-in-terror." "But," he added, "by the time
e landed at Castle Larsen, I was approaching competence,
ough I am told I never attained the kind of copilothood that
as first achieved by the one, the only, the Amelia Earhart of
r generation—"

Bambi made a fart noise with her tongue.

"Which is one-third of the mission here," Quattro said,
noothly. "I was kind of hoping your interrogation of Ysabel
oth is not complete, that Bambi Castro is still essential to it,
d that you'd see the wisdom of leaving them both at Castle
arsen, actually."

Heather grinned at him. "And you didn't even mention se-
ring the enduring loyalty of a critical Castle on the Califor-
a coast."

"Seemed rude and unnecessary."

"Well, as for Roth, I don't think we'll get more cooperation
t of her in another location, and we don't have to guard her
ere she is. And we don't have any way to hold employees
inst their will, nor—"

"Larry!" Bambi shouted and waved.

Heather turned around and found herself facing a guy
o seemed to have been sent from Central Casting as "old
rdough"—baggy wool pants, rope suspenders, immense
nnel shirt, floppy broad-brimmed hat, and bushy beard. *All
needs is an arrow through that silly hat.*

He grinned. "Do you have any idea how great life is when
n't have to fit the FBI dress code?" He stuck out his hand.

Heather looked down at her current outfit—a heavily
ned men's safari shirt (you could never have too many
kets), black-powder carbine on a sling, combat knife in

an arm holster, camo pants, and calf-high moccaboots she
traded a case of pre-Daybreak Coors for in Limon, Colorado-
and said, "Well, I have to admit, I could get through quite
few more years without ever putting on black pumps, jacke
skirt, and a blouse. Biz outfits used to make me look like
giant poodle."

"Me too," Mensche said. "I don't care *what* Hoov
thought, speaking as an FBI agent, the pumps always *kill*
my back."

"Did you find Debbie?" Bambi asked.

"No luck yet. But she was alive when that bunch of wom
left Coffee Creek, and she was among the leaders, and at lea
I've established that no one ran into them around the mou
of the Columbia or on the south shore of Puget Sound. It w
while I was up there that I persuaded the governor to inv
you all to move the Federal government there, and now
seems to think that it was his idea and I was his brilliant
sistant, so he thinks he owes me some favors. I'm plann
to cash in on them by having him put out sort of a perman
APB for Deb. Meanwhile, I'm thinking maybe Deb's gr
out of Coffee Creek headed east for some reason, gonna try
pick up the trail that way."

"So are you leaving the FBI for good?" Quattro asked.

"Soon as they open an office, I plan to transfer to the
Marshals. I'm not looking to be Eliot Ness anymore.
thinking more Wyatt Earp."

"Or Gabby Hayes," Bambi suggested.

**TWO DAYS LATER. THE COW CREEK COUNTRY, NORTH OF
GRANT'S PASS, OREGON. NOON PST. SATURDAY, JANUARY 4.**

Word from farther up the line was that coal was getting h
to locate, so they were towing six coal cars in addition to A
trak One and the supporting staff and troop cars, which m
for a slow climb; they had crossed into southern Oregon a
hours ago, and stopped for the obligatory speech in Gra
Pass, which seemed, like many smaller cities that had alw
been somewhat isolated, to be doing relatively well.
crowd had been enthusiastic, putting Graham in what Hea
was beginning to think of as a too-good mood.

We'd have been in Olympia three days ago if it weren't for [al]l the whistle stops, she thought. *It's like he's practicing run[n]ing for president—and I guess with there being an election [n]ext year (again, dammit!) and his being the president, he [m]ight decide to run for re-election. Now there's a . . . scary? [c]heerful? ironic? well, it's a thought, anyway.*

After Grant's Pass, the rail line swung wide of I-5 and the [m]odern roads, winding up through the Cow Creek country, [th]reading between pine-covered, fog-shrouded mountains, [tu]rning back and forth in great swooping bends. *We started [la]te, too, out of Ashland. For a daring escape, this has sure [tu]rned into a parade.*

She was just checking whether there was any tea left— [th]ey had run out of coffee two days ago and she was still [he]adachy from caffeine withdrawal—when the train's brakes [sh]rieked. Everyone and everything fell or slid forward. Chris [M]anckiewicz, in the corner and working as ever in one of his [no]tebooks, grunted sharply in frustration.

Heather staggered to her feet and headed forward. *Oh [cr]ap, having to start on an up slope, and towing all this coal, [i]s going to take forever to get going again.*

Strange sound—familiar and yet not familiar—and then [sh]e realized.

She shouted, "Helicopters!" and dropped to her knees to [pe]er over the edge of the window.

Here, where the rails made a wide 180-degree turn, there [wa]s a broad spot on the road to their right, and the creek was to [the]ir left, far down the hill; a Marine helicopter was skimming [jus]t above the road, dropping men in battle armor as it went, [an]d they were rolling and diving into the brush between the [roa]d and the train, moving forward in a rapid buddy rush, each [ma]n advancing a few paces ahead of the man covering him, [sto]pping, and covering the man behind him who ran forward [in t]urn, a swift leapfrog to close the distance.

Shots cracked from the Ranger car; Heather rolled onto the [flo]or as windows shattered from the Marines returning fire. *[Th]eir stuff has been sealed on shipboard all this time and [the]y've still got modern smokeless powder and automatic. At [lea]st twenty of them to our nine Rangers and three Feds.*

[M]anckiewicz rolled, punched the door, and darted into the [Ra]nger car. Heather considered following—*get the guns to-*

gether, better organized defense—no, I can probably do mo
good here, between the Rangers in the lead car and the pres
dent's car, at least slow them up if they try to come throug
here, keep them from having this car to work from.

She rolled and came up beside a shattered window. *The*
want him alive, otherwise they'd've bombed the train (
shredded it with the helicopter's guns. So—

She drew her 9mm and fired at a hand reaching over th
sill of the window beside her; it was a relief that the gu
worked at least once; she'd cleaned it just that morning, b
the ammunition had been smelling strange for weeks, and sh
was using Crisco because they had no unspoiled gun oil.

Scrambling sounds outside the car. A burst of automat
fire from the Rangers' car; apparently maniacal maintenan
had kept a few of their modern weapons working.

One of the Marines outside poked a stick over the si
careful not to waste a round, Heather didn't go for that, b
positioned herself carefully to see where the next try wou
come, watching both sides because it occurred to her that o
of them might try crawling under the cars.

Another flurry of automatic-weapons fire, mixed w
some deeper bangs from black-powder guns, from the (
ahead. Then some bangs from far back on the train; Rog
and Machado, if she remembered right, had been takin;
turn as snipers in the caboose, and either they had a shot
the attackers, or more likely the attackers were trying to fla
them on that side.

The stick came in again, still on the road side of the tra
but a moment later on the creek side, a stealthy hand reach
up and tried the window; Heather aimed and squeezed
trigger, but it didn't fire. She ejected the bad round as she cr
closer; then there were two hands.

Heather took the least risky alternative and smashed acr
both hands with the pistol butt. The man shouted. Look
into his eyes, she jammed the gun toward his face, wonder
what she could do with a prisoner in the circumstances but
wanting to kill him. As he leaned back away from her gun,
Marine's injured hands lost their grip. He fell backward do
the gravel-covered embankment, rolling toward the creek
below. She ducked back down; a shot hit the ceiling ab
her head.

Yes, they're definitely trying to take Graham alive, and they probably don't want to kill any of the rest of us if they don't have to. I don't really want to kill any of them either.

Another Marine was halfway through the window behind her, leveling his weapon, as she rolled sideways; he fired, not aiming, and she came up, aimed, fired, and heard him shriek in pain; at a guess, she'd broken a bone in his arm, and he was unable to stop himself from sliding back out of the window.

Another sound penetrated her consciousness, a raspy buzzing with a sort of whining overtone; *some other aircraft? They must've sent everything they have.* A last couple of gunshots sounded in the Ranger car ahead; now it sounded like a bar brawl in there.

The door from the Ranger car slid open.

A Marine moved in. Heather tried firing her 9mm and came up with another dead round; the Marine kicked it out of her hand and presented her with a view straight into the muzzle of his own weapon. She raised her hands—

The thundering boom outside took both her and the Marine by surprise as the railroad car shook. For a moment they stared wide-eyed at each other, aware he could have been startled into killing her; then he stepped back, to give himself more distance, and looked out the window. "Fuck," he said. He could tell he still had her in his peripheral vision, so she didn't move, but she said, very softly, "What?"

"Don't know. Did you all have air cover?"

"I don't think so," she said.

"Because our chopper just blew up. I don't know what hit but it sounds like a lawn mower engine up in the sky."

Heather listened and heard the same rattling buzz she'd heard before; she turned cautiously to look and saw a biplane.

"The fuck?" he said, looking at it around her.

"Cropduster with an antitank rocket?" she said. "Nobody told me we had anything that would fly except the Gooney." *If we win it won't matter and if they win I don't want them to be looking for Quattro Larsen.* "Even *that* wasn't working this morning."

"Fuck," the Marine said. "So we've got your train and you've got us; it's a standoff unless—"

Heather heard another, more familiar, sound, the stutter-

ing, coughing roar that had to be the Checker Cab of the Sky
She held her breath, then made herself relax.

"That's another plane," he said. "Must be one of yours
can't be one of ours."

"If I keep my hands where you can see them, can I pu
them down?"

"Yeah." He pointed his rifle away from her but kept it or
his hip where he could swing it back; she put her hands dow
on the back of the seat in front of her. "Escalera, USMC, I'r
a corporal."

"O'Grainne, OFTA, I run it."

"Never heard of it."

"Sometimes I wish I hadn't."

"I bet." There was another, smaller explosion outside
"God, that chopper is burning like mad, someone really h
it with something."

"Did you have friends on there?"

"Shit, we've been at sea forever, a carrier's like a sma
town, after a while you know everyone."

Heather waited with her captor; after a time they hear
the rumble and thud of the DC-3 landing. "Smart enough
land out of sight and range," the Marine said, with grudgir
approval.

"While they figure out which side is in charge," Heath
said, "don't lose track of this: I clubbed one of your gu
pretty hard and he rolled down the slope into the ravine. Mai
sure they find him; he's probably still alive but he might n
be in great shape."

"Okay, thanks."

More time went by; Heather figured that to land on t
road, out of sight of the train, they must have come down
mile or more away, so this was going to take time. She ju
hoped there were enough—

They must have had that bullhorn in a clean box, Heath
thought, missing the words because of the strangeness
hearing amplified speech again. "—Alpha Company, Seco
Ranger Battalion. Your aircraft has been destroyed, and v
have you surrounded. We have functioning automatic wea
ons, and there is no escape route; we have both ends of t
train under observation and can fire on any point around t
train. Please release the president and his party unharm

You will be treated in accord with the Geneva Conventions, and we intend to release you as soon as possible."

"Shit," Escalera said. "We've been out in the world so long now, with what's gotta be growing on us, they won't let us back on the ship till we've been *boiled*."

TWO HOURS LATER. THE COW CREEK COUNTRY, NORTH OF GRANT'S PASS, OREGON. 2:30 P.M. PST. SATURDAY, JANUARY 4.

Sorting everything out seemed interminably long to Heather. Everett, in the car ahead of her, had been wounded, and would probably limp the rest of his days, but the medic seemed to think he'd be able to keep and use the leg. Rogers and Machado had been killed by Marine snipers; the Marines had had their ambush in place since the night before.

"How did *you* know we were here, and in trouble?" Heather asked.

Quattro perched on a rock beside her while they watched all the people with authority argue with each other. "This morning, Bambi and I were flying the Stearman, and this gadget, up to Olympia, to catch the big party, you know? And we were following the tracks because we thought we might see you. When what to our wondering eyes should appear, I guess you'd say, but a Marine helicopter on one side of the mountain, and a pile of logs on the tracks on the other, which we didn't think was a good thing.

"I guess we were high enough, and it's always so overcast, and they just weren't listening so they didn't hear us over the noise of their chopper's blades—they were rotating when we passed over. So we continued on up to Olympia, I hopped over to Fort Lewis—where they still had some real avgas, can you imagine that—great stuff!

"I did some fast talking and the Second Ranger Battalion either decided they were loyal to the president or they wanted an excuse to go fight Marines. Now, the Stearman was a trainer, the trainee seat is normally the front, and it's an open cockpit. So we put one Ranger that was supposed to be a crack shot with a shoulder-fired missile in the front seat. It turned out he was."

"That was four men killed instantly," Heather said, an-

noyed by a feeling that Quattro was in this whole thing because it was the kind of adventure he'd imagined having when
he was fourteen. "Your sharpshooter must've hit right on a
fuel tank or maybe set off some ordnance."

"That would be my guess. It was one sweet shot." So much
for compassion. "But yeah, Bambi and the sergeant kind of
thought there might be a lot of negative feelings around, so
they just headed back to Fort Lewis. No reason to rub anyone's
nose in it, you know. And I kind of think she wanted to go
someplace else anyway. I don't think she's real used to the idea
of killing anyone—let alone burning several men to death."

"I hope she doesn't ever get used to that," Heather said.

"That's very reasonable," Quattro admitted. "Want to give
me a hand cleaning scunge out of the DC-3 while they make
up their minds who's riding in it? I'm one of two people that
has a guaranteed seat, so I don't need to be involved in that
discussion."

They scrubbed with rags and sticks—"jeez, I wish we had
toothbrushes, except if we did, I'd want to keep them for my
teeth," Quattro said.

Heather bent to her scrubbing. "Quattro, let me ask you a
dangerous question—what do *you* think? Is it a war or a system artifact that we're up against?"

"I think in a couple years I can be selling canned fish
into the middle of the country, before people get iodine
deficiencies. And that's *all* I think. I used to think I cared
about political issues. Now that I'm the freeholder of Castle
Larsen, I think about feeding people, building shit, making shit work, all the people that count on me, and shit that
won't get done without me. Basically it's down to people
and shit. I prefer it that way." He took another rag, put one
end in the bleach, pulled it up and shook it, and wiped along
an already-shining surface near the spark coil. "And I don't
envy you your job, Heather, but I sure as hell am glad someone is doing it."

"I'm not so sure I'm glad it's me."

"Well, *I'm* glad it's you. You at least kind of seem to have
your head on straight." He glanced around, and lowered his
voice. "Is it just me, or does it look like our president is becoming excessively presidential? I mean, when we picked him
up, he was just a little guy trying to do a big job; now I think

ne's becoming a very big guy who feels entitled to a very big
ob. The way he was with the California legislature? Like
ucking Mussolini or something. And lately when he speaks
o a crowd, like in Sacramento . . . he's not quite the guy that
saw in Pale Bluff."

It was very much what Heather had been saying to herself,
and she wanted to argue, but it just seemed . . . true. "It used
o be he was right about so much, and no one listened. Now
hey—"

A Ranger sergeant from Fort Lewis was trotting toward
hem, carrying a clipboard, and Chris Manckiewicz was run-
ing beside him, comical as only a middle-aged former fat
uy trying to keep up with a young athlete can be. "Looks like
here've been some decisions," Heather said.

The sergeant said, "Mr. Larsen, we've finally got a mani-
est together, sort of, with who's going where. Ms. O'Grainne,
ou're on, along with Mr. Manckiewicz here—"

Heather was annoyed. "So apparently the new president is
o far gone into playing president that he has to have media
overage—"

"Uh," Chris said, "I think that—"

"I don't blame you for wanting to be with the president,
hris, but—"

"Actually," Chris said, "it's more of a—"

"But I'm getting *seriously* pissed off and worried about the
ay that he's coming down with Shaunsen's disease, and—"

"Heather." Quattro's voice was soft but very firm, and she
opped. "Chris gets a seat because he's sitting next to me;
's the copilot."

"Oh," Heather said, flushing.

"So I'll be busy on the flight," Chris said, "but I do think
ou've got some interesting things to say. How about an inter-
ew once we're in Olympia?"

OUT TWO WEEKS LATER. OLYMPIA, NEW DISTRICT
  COLUMBIA. (OLYMPIA, WASHINGTON.) 1:00 P.M. PST.
ONDAY, JANUARY 20.

's hard to put together much of a band when all the plastic
es," Ramirez was saying, apologetically, to Heather. "Some

of the more expensive wooden clarinets with felt pads, a few all-metal brass instruments, a couple of drums where the skins are really skins, that's about all we could do. Too many little plastic rings and gaskets in modern instruments, so that even the ones that were mostly metal or mostly wood have pads and fittings, here and there, that are gone and can't be replaced right away." Ramirez was the senior bandmaster from Fort Lewis, where four units had bands and three National Guard bands came for practice. He'd rounded up players and instruments from the Army, the National Guard, several different fife and drum corps, a couple of conservatories, and local high schools, and managed to get them all together to rehearse on just three weeks' notice. He didn't even seem to think it had been hard, saying only that "band standards tend to be patriotic numbers, anyway, we just had to work out what version of what we were playing."

Heather had been put in charge of this silly little parade which was officially the Inauguration of the Fiftieth President. *By counting Shaunsen, the boss gets a significant looking number—and he wanted that. I don't know if he becoming more presidential, but his marketing instincts are getting sharper. Maybe that is becoming more presidential.*

Ramirez would be leading and conducting the New National Band, and the only evidence he had that all his hard work mattered was Heather's interest—*which I'm faking as hard as I can, so I sure hope it works.* All she knew about music was that it came out of funny-looking machines, and you didn't want to marry the people who made it.

They decided without much fuss that the band would play whatever songs popped into Ramirez's head along the two mile route of the march, "America the Beautiful" as they passed the reviewing stand, "Hail to the Chief" when Graham went up to the rostrum, and "The Star-Spangled Banner" just after the Pledge of Allegiance.

"Remind everyone of the word change on that one," Heather said.

"One indivisible nation under God," he said. "We've been practicing. Nobody's told us why."

"Because Graham Weisbrod is a fussy old professor, and grammatically that's closer to right, and there are a large number of people, some with guns, out there, who have oubts about whether we are really one indivisible nation, so e're supposed to say we are. And Graham says that 'under od' was wedged in there in the first place, decades after the ledge was written, because a lot of Rebs who wouldn't admit ey'd lost the war wanted to separate the ideas of 'indivisible' d 'nation.'"

Ramirez glanced around first, and kept his voice low. 'ou've known President Weisbrod a long time?"

"Twenty-one years. More than half my life."

"Do you think he's up to the job?"

"I think he'll do his absolute best to do it," *except of course en he's reveling in having his ego massaged—and what- er else Allie is massaging for him.*

Meow, she self-critiqued. She knew that wasn't completely r, and hell, a few months ago, if Graham had found a unger, intelligent girlfriend like Allie . . . *Well, but I have clean up the mess that this made of Arnie to keep our Ge- s in Chief functioning, and deal with Allie's complete de- ion to Graham's career; used to be he had a chief of staff o would tell him when he was being an idiot, not encour- e it. It seems dumb in an egotistical way, Graham, I just nt to say that to you and have you listen, I just want you consider it.*

"I guess that's all we can really ask of anyone," the dleader said.

His words fit her thought so well that it took her a moment retrace the conversation. "I wish I knew for sure that Gra- n Weisbrod's best would be as much as we need. I wasn't lly trying to evade your question, or not much, anyway. It's t that there's three questions behind it. Will Graham do best? He always has, as long as I've known him." *Crossed ers.* "Will his best be good enough for the job? I wish I w." *Crossed till the knuckles bleed.* "And could *anyone's* t be good enough to do the job, or is it just impossible? ly God knows that." *And You'd better be crossing Your fin- s, too.*

The man nodded. "Well, tell him we all pray for him to ceed."

"He knows, but I'll tell him again."

Comparatively, arranging the Rangers was easy; they w how to march, they all knew where they were going,

they'd march there. "I don't think we can get lost," Capta
Parmenter said, grinning. "We know we're between the ba
and the screaming junkpile."

She grinned back. "Thanks for giving me a one-minu
break between people with difficulties. Congratulations o
the unit honor and I'm going to applaud my brains out whe
you receive it."

Her next stop was at the "screaming junkpile"—the e
perimental coal-dust turbine car from Evergreen State th
was going to be carrying the mayor, the governor, and t
base commander from Lewis. Its best feature was also
worst; the experiment with putting a damped hydraulic ir
a double-bowed axle, so that the whole thing could run
steel-rimmed wheels, seemed to be working, but with or
a greased axle for a bearing, it made a horrendous grindi
squeal. At least it would keep people from noticing any m
takes by the band. *Actually it could easily keep people fre
noticing a fire engine, an air raid, and Rainier erupting.*

The two engineering professors in charge of it were war
ing it up, so it was hard to hear each other over the whoc
and howl of its exhaust, but she figured they knew that th
were supposed to follow the Rangers and not drop back wh
their foul blue exhaust might annoy the president, who wo
be riding with General McIntyre, the new Secretary of
Armed Forces, in a ceremonial coach, pulled from a museu
in which an early governor of Washington had once ridder

*And if Allie is in there with them, I'm going to rip her h
off to use for wadding when I ram her puny tits down
throat. The least he could do is make a First Lady of h
they should be thinking about how it looks to have the C
of Staff be the presidential skank. Whoa, that thought cc
naturally. Guess I'll have to keep working on those pro
sionalism and civility issues. Maybe HR will offer a semi
or something.*

Behind Graham Weisbrod and Norm McIntyre, th
would be a wagon with the rest of the Cabinet-To-Be, mo
politicians with a scattering of professors and businesspeo
all from Washington and Oregon.

Heather made sure the new Cabinet were all there, re
to "walk and wave." Heather told them that as far as she
concerned, it would be fine if Commerce and Future I

nds during the parade; made sure Education's backup
heelchair would stay within easy reach; and reassured Trea-
ry and Foreign Relations that this wasn't too much like a
rcus coming to town. *Not too much. Actually I'm afraid it
1y not be enough.*

*Wonder if anyone will even notice that Graham Weisbrod
organized and renamed half the jobs in the Cabinet? Let
one that he should have waited for Congress to do that, that
s their prerogative.*

After the Cabinet, there was the agglomeration of volun-
r organizations and units whose positions Heather had al-
ated by rolling dice, which she privately thought of as the
partment of Everything Else: everyone who just wanted to
in the first inaugural parade ever held in the new national
ital. There were Boy Scout troops, fragmentary high-
ool bands, and the GLBT Small Apple Growers (it had
ome clearer once she realized that it was the farm, not
apple, that was small); several unions, veterans' associa-
1s, and the Daughters of the World Wars; antique machin-
buffs driving steam combines and highwheels, a diving
vage company that was pledging to be the "first back in
water," and the "Portland to Reno Reconstituted Pony
press, Orphans Preferred." She wasn't sure she wanted to
culate about how you reconstituted a pony.

The parade took a surprisingly long time, for many rea-
s. Some of the marching units were made up of the el-
ly, some of the rolling units broke down, and the Secret
nd Master of the Parade appeared to be Murphy, but mi-
ulously, though it was chilly, it wasn't painfully cold. The
ther was astonishingly good; Rainier gleamed magnifi-
tly in the distance, the sky was a deep cloudless blue, and
winter sunshine was almost warm. Graham Weisbrod and
m McIntyre seemed to be perfectly happy to just stand
wave from their platform in front of the Winged Victory
ue, as an hour went by getting the last unit into the West
le between the Capitol and the Governor's Mansion.

When, finally, everyone was in place, and it was estab-
ed that the hand-built tube amp was working for the mo-
t, the ceremonies began. Graham took the oath of office
n, this time from an Appeals Court judge. *If he wants to
ny higher he'll have to appoint some Supremes.* They all

said the new, modified pledge to the old, unmodified fifty-s
flag—Graham's position was that there was no other gover
ment, just a somewhat-uppity temporary regional milita
command; that no other states had aligned with it, just sor
were reporting to that temporary office as a matter of conv
nience; and that the eleven states in the Northeast that ma
people were calling the Lost Quarter were going to call in a
minute now. Graham had General McIntyre confer the n
title of the President's Own Rangers on the Second Ran;
Battalion, which was authorized to expand into a regim
with all deliberate speed.

Finally, Graham began his Inaugural Address. It mi;
have earned an A on a creative writing prof's assignment
"write your inaugural address," Heather thought. Weisb
pledged that everyone would work hard, thanked everyone
coming, announced the Cabinet lineup officially, and ur;
every state that was able to do so to elect or appoint repla
ment Senators and Representatives and have them here
February 1st. He commended the offer from the Governo
Washington, who had prepared a list of citizens of other st;
who were known to be in Washington and willing to be
pointed if getting someone here before February 1st woulc
too difficult.

He swung into his vision statement with enthusiasm,
to judge by the cheering, the crowd was eating it up. "We
forced to meet here, and not in what had been our capita
234 years, because we failed to see that the powerful engi
of our collective dreams had been possessed by the wil
self-destruction. We stand in the rubble of our earlier ci
zation, with the way back barred to us, with some unkn
number of other barriers ready to spring up if we try to
that road. We must therefore rebuild with caution, with
awareness that some roads will close as we try to take th
that time after time we may have to turn back before g
forward again, that our situation demands a patience and
mility that we lacked the first time—but we shall rebuild

Corny, Heather thought. But after all, things were goir
be improvisational and low-rent here for a long time. M;
the country needed more corn. Maybe she was just getting
old and cynical.

Maybe the Graham Weisbrod who might have tske

w overdone this was would not have been as effective a
:sident as the one she was watching now. *Is that possible?
'his really for the best?*

He wound up with ". . . with a vision that we will again be
a position to choose a future, and we will choose wisely,
1 build that future—because this is America, which has
vays been the land of the future!"

Walking back from the ceremony to her quarters in the old
:rgreen dorms, she watched the sun go down over the lake,
1 as she so often did these days, rested her hand on her belly
1 thought, *Kid, I don't know how we're going to do it, but
've got to find somewhere better for you to grow up.*

She felt a presence moving up from her side, and glanced,
f-hoping for some pathetic would-be mugger she could
)ck down or dismiss with a glare.

Nothing so appealing. Chris Manckiewicz.

She asked, "How's the fish-wrapper business?"

"The *Olympia Observer*, at this point, has five staff mem-
s locally, nine stringers nationally, and a promising line
a printing plant. Which I needed anyway because I keep
ing to revise the resumé. The 24/7 News Network, the
shington Advertiser-Gazette, the Athens Free Ticket to the
' . . ."

She chuckled, though it wasn't very funny, just to show she
e no ill will. "Chris, I know you want to interview me be-
se I'm having differences with Graham Weisbrod and I'm
altogether happy with the direction the new government
king. Honestly, I understand that, and I understand that
e I've been his close friend for so long, now that he's presi-
, it's news. I'm not begrudging you that. But I'd rather try
ring him around in private conversation—not by arguing
him in the press."

I'm also working on the definitive history of our era—"

Catch me when I'm retired. But I'm saving the hot stuff
ny memoirs." She gave him a little wiggle-finger wave and
ed off toward her quarters, the former commons room of
onors dorm, which gave her the privilege of a fireplace.
erday's soup was going to taste wonderful; she'd put it in
)anked coals, and with luck enough fire would have stayed
: to keep it warm.

**FIVE DAYS LATER. OLYMPIA, NEW DISTRICT OF COLUMBIA.
(OLYMPIA, WASHINGTON.) 7:15 A.M. PST. SATURDAY,
JANUARY 25.**

Chris Manckiewicz held it in his hands, turned it over, look
at the perfection of its plain gray cloth cover.

"That was the fabric that was cheap, but we worked
some wax and a little linseed oil, and it'll at least shed wa
while it's new," Rob Cartland, the printer, was saying. "T
and all that went on with a big linoleum block stamp. Use
smaller stamp for the spine. Thud, thud. Twenty-two hund
times each way. You can thank my son Ephraim that it ca
out so neat; he's the one that thought of that frame gadge
the stamp always hit in the same place. I know it ain't l
they do it in a real printing plant—"

"You *are* the real printing plant," Chris said. He turned
book back over and read the India-ink linoleum-cut cove
himself: *A Battle of Articles: how our Constitution made
struggle between Olympia and Athens inevitable, and w
citizens can do about it, by Chris Manckiewicz, publi.
and editor, the* Olympia Observer. "And we're ready to g
setting up and printing issue one, right?" he asked, very
necessarily. "Because I'm sure depending on the book to
me some subscriptions."

"Ready to go, and your credit's still good with me," C
land said. "I just wish my old man was here to see this.
those years being his assistant on his silly projects, tr
to make things come out just the way they did in 1880,
swearing I'd never look at a piece of paper after I got a
from the son of a bitch, and . . . well, here I am. A livin;
me and probably for Ephraim, too."

"I've been a printer's assistant," Chris pointed out, "th
only for a month. But that was enough time for me to say,
be *good* to Ephraim."

"He's a smart kid, and so's Cassie. And this is my ch
to leave a successful business to both of them, and they'r
enough and serious enough kids that I think they appre
that—so many kids are so much older and more serious,
just these few months."

"Gone hungry, been homeless in a world without ho
seen friends and family die," Chris said. "I imagine that

them pretty fast." He turned the book over in his hands again. "Of course, if you'd like to write something up about that—maybe a feature, parents noticing how much more mature the kids are? Or an editorial about whether or not it's a good thing? I'll always be looking for material."

"I doubt I will, but I'll pass the idea on to Cassie. She's always writing letters to friends—all the people she used to text with—the ones where she knows their street address or can find it. Mostly just trying to find out if they're still alive, I guess. She just heard back from two of them this week. She might have some things she could tell you about."

"Sounds like it. And there's a whole generation of possible customers that doesn't remember newspapers at all; I need some writers from that generation if I'm going to get the habit restarted."

"If you could sell newspapers with coffee as a single package," Cartland said, "I'd be your slave forever. My dad used to read the paper and have coffee, every morning. For me, it was Twitter and a Red Bull, and for my kids it wasn't even *that* organized. But I remember he used to look like the most relaxed creature in the universe, feet up on a spare chair, big mug of coffee by his hand, looking for something to read out loud to all of us. God, I thought he looked like a *moron*. Now my definition of luxury would be to start every day off like that."

"Well, we'll have the newspaper, weekly at first; the coffee's kind of a problem, of course, but at least we're on this coast, and among my first stories in the biz section, there's a woman here in town who bartered for five sailing yachts with a warehouse full of liquor, and had enough booze left over to hire crews; she's billing those as the 'coffee fleet' and I guess they'll be running over to Hawaii, down to Mexico, wherever, to bring in the beans. My guess is she's going to own the West Coast in a few years."

"Lisa Fanchion. Yeah. My guess too."

"I have an interview with her in the notepad already," Chris said, smiling. "Closest I can get to coffee till some of her ships come back. I was teasing her that when the coffee fleet comes back, I'll be trading full-page ads to get some, and she just shrugged and said she figured the boats coming in would be news, which I'd have to cover for free, and once that's in the paper, she'll have all the buyers she'll need. She thought it might be twenty years before she needs to advertise. She really doesn't miss a trick."

Cartland laughed. "Well, one thing you can say for Daybreak, it's a great opportunity for smart ruthless bastards, ne?"

"Like everything else that ever happened," Chris agreed. The two picked up their wheelbarrows, aiming to be in the market at first light, since they'd be mostly paid in barter goods that would be better when fresh.

EIGHT HOURS LATER. OLYMPIA, NEW DISTRICT OF COLUMBIA. (OLYMPIA, WASHINGTON.) 3:00 P.M. PST. SATURDAY, JANUARY 25.

At mid-afternoon, they were getting used to the rhythm of things. One of them would push a wheelbarrow into the market, full of copies of *Battle of Articles*; the other would then depart from their slot with the other barrow, laden down with produce, jewelry, paper cash, and pre-Daybreak canned goods, moving it into their lockup in the print shop. The one who had just arrived would take over the head of the line where so many people waited for a copy. Apparently the idea of a book about something that had happened since Daybreak appealed to people.

They would be back to press, and for the moment they would have to work the newspaper in around printing the book. *Though if the newspaper is as big a hit as the book,* Chris thought happily, *we might have to find more printers someplace. Wonder if anything survived up toward Tacoma?* That was a bad fire but some areas didn't burn.

He sold the last book and handed the Ping-Pong paddle to the man at the front of the line; they'd hit on that as a system to preserve "firstness" and reduce anxiety; now all Chris would have to do was shout "stand behind the man holding up the Ping-Pong paddle!" until Cartland came back with the next load of books.

"Mr. Manckiewicz?" a man said at his elbow.

"If you want to buy a book, get into the line; I'm not going to help anyone jump it, I'd be lynched."

"Not what I had in mind," the man said. "Do you have a moment for a possible scoop?"

"Tell me what it is and I'll tell you if it's a scoop." He glanced sideways; the man was in T-shirt, jeans, and a leather jacket, holding out a file folder.

"Read," the man said. "Make notes. Make a copy if you can find the time to type that much, photograph it if anyone you know has a working camera. Use any of it you want in your paper. But don't tell anyone where you got it, and I wouldn't publish while you still have it. You'll see why not. When you're done—and make that within one week—move the potted plant in the *Observer*'s window to the other window, and leave this folder, with all the documents in it, out on your fire escape by your window at noon. Bye." He dropped the folder at Chris's feet; Chris picked it up, looked again, and the man was gone.

Well, either the guy is very paranoid and watches a lot of old movies, or the guy is very paranoid and I've got a scoop. He looked around and didn't see Cartland coming yet; the man with the paddle was being good about yelling "This is the line for the book about the two governments! Line up behind this paddle!" so Chris didn't have much to do. *Either this barrowload or one more, and we're sold out. This is going so well.*

Curiosity overpowered him and he peeked into the folder. The document was new, and had been typewritten rather than printed; there were several XXXed out mistakes on the first page, which was a letter addressed from "General Norman McIntyre, Sec. Armed Forces" to "Dr. Graham Weisbrod, POTUS." *When I was working for 247NN, they'd have given a fortune to get any document from this level, but I suppose nowadays getting hold of a high-level national document isn't much harder than stealing a proposed zoning plan from a small-town planning commission used to be.*

At the bottom of the first page was scrawled, "Recommended, further discussion suggested."

Still no sign of Cartland. The line was still quiet, patiently waiting for their chance to buy a book. *I hope that guy way back there with the live lamb gets to the head before we're out of books; Cartland's kids would love that as a pet.*

He flipped the letter to the back of the stack and looked at the title page. OVERALL PLAN FOR SPRING OFFENSIVE.

He froze. On the next page was a map of the Dakotas,

with arrows running along rail lines and roads, and junctions marked with D+2, D+9, and so forth, all the way to Minnesota. The next page was a table of West Coast and Rocky Mountain Castles that had declared for Nguyen-Peters, with columns for "troop strength," "probable arms," "allies," "estimated food stocks"—

"Mr. Manckiewicz?"

"Yes, I can't accept this, it's—"

It wasn't the same man; it was four of the President's Own Rangers. "Sir, we have to ask you to come with us, and we were told to secure all documents in your possession."

"Yes," Chris said, "you definitely need to secure this. The man who gave it to me—"

"You can explain that later, sir."

It wasn't until they cuffed him that he realized what was happening. *Wonder if they're registering trademarks anywhere yet? Maybe I'll start a whole* chain *of papers called* Free Trip to the Pen.

FIVE HOURS LATER. OLYMPIA, NEW DISTRICT OF COLUMBIA. (OLYMPIA, WASHINGTON.) 8:45 P.M. PST. SATURDAY, JANUARY 25.

At first Captain Wallace, Army Counterintelligence, seemed pretty nice; he explained that he had once been a Seattle police detective, working fraud, ID theft, and cash-hacks, and he was still more used to civilian investigations. He hoped Chris would cooperate.

Chris told him exactly what had happened and described the man as well as he could remember; Wallace was oddly uninterested, as if he already knew who had done it (*Perhaps the spy was already busted?* Chris thought). He established that Chris had looked at the documents but had no intention of disclosing their contents.

"I hate the idea of a civil war," Chris explained, "but if there is one, I'm on the side of this government, and I don't want to do anything to jeopardize victory."

"Is that a matter of revenge? You were jailed by the Athens government before being sent here—"

"Well, it didn't make me especially like them, of course

but my real problem is that the Southeast is turning into one big Army base, gearing up to attack some squatty little patch of dirt that had nothing to do with Daybreak. And while they're getting ready, they're wiping out most of the traditional liberties."

"Such as freedom of the press?"

"Well, I'm pretty attached to that one. Look, I had just realized what I'd been given when the Rangers came and busted me. I hadn't had time or opportunity to turn it in—jeez, I guess your office would have been the right place, I didn't even know *that*."

"Yes, actually, my office would have been the right place."

"Off the record, did you catch the guy?"

"You might say that. Off the record entirely, though." Wallace sat down, so close to Chris that their knees almost touched. "So let me make sure of a few things. No one else saw the documents but yourself. How would you describe what you saw?"

"It looked like the first stages of a military offensive against the Athens government—securing our communications through Montana and the Dakotas to the New State of Superior, and cleaning out Castles that might act as enemy bases in our rear."

"I can see you've done some military reporting before."

"Second Iranian War; I was embedded with Tenth Mountain for three months, and almost all that was at headquarters."

"Ah. And your record there?"

"Flawless on security issues, Captain Wallace. Not that anyone can prove anything with all the computers down."

"True, but good to know." The captain sat down and gazed straight into his eyes. "And you would not have divulged or published because—?"

"Because I'm a loyal citizen of this government. I'd be interested as all hell of course and I might have written a book *after* the war—probably would have—but I wasn't going to let anything I publish harm us in the struggle, if it comes down to a war between a military-intel-administrative dictatorship and the actual Constitutional government."

"You wouldn't let anything you publish harm our side?"

"No, I would not. No matter what they show in the movies, not every reporter—"

The captain grabbed Chris by the lapels and shouted into his face, a long wailing scream, hot breath pouring in through Chris's gaping mouth and flooding his throat, spittle spraying into his staring eyes. With his nose almost on Chris's, he bellowed, "And yet you go and publish, and sell it in the marketplace, a book jammed full of *lies*, that slanders our president and our entire leadership, explains in detail the illegal position of the junta in Athens, directly says the Constitution is at fault, and cannot be called anything but treasonous slander! You run that ridiculous speech that you invented for the president to have given in Pale Bluff, promising to hand over power to the junta! *In your own words*, this book is exactly intended to harm us in this struggle! What do you have to say for yourself, you lying sack of shit? *How much did they pay you to do this, in Athens?*"

Captain Wallace shook Chris, yanking him back and forth, and repeated the accusations, over and over, screaming and scattering spit over Chris's face. When he ran out of air he threw Chris back in the chair. "Now, if you *really* meant that about supporting the legitimate government, you'll sign these documents!"

"What if I don't sign?"

"What if you don't sign?" The captain grabbed him by the hair, tilted his face back, and slapped him. "Didn't you say you were *supporting* our side? Didn't you *say* that?"

Chris knew he was going to be here for a long time.

FOUR DAYS LATER. OLYMPIA, NEW DISTRICT OF COLUMBIA. (OLYMPIA, WASHINGTON.) 9:11 A.M. PST. WEDNESDAY, JANUARY 29.

"So," Arnie said, turning the page over on the old flip chart, "big windmill with generator here, supplies power to this rotary-quenched spark gap, the high tech of 1915 here today. It's a big piece of equipment, with a huge capacitance and a high voltage, so we'll want to keep people far from it. Then we hook it to this oval of old high-tension lines, which will be our antenna. And the result is that we've got the biggest, loudest radio transmitter on Earth, by far.

"Now, in a warehouse, we found four hundred toy tele

scopes, all metal and glass, which we set up in arrays of fifty, spaced and angled to be looking at space above the antenna. Dark construction paper over the eyepieces like so. We use old surveying transits, sextants, and the almanac to get them aimed perfectly—"

"Let me guess. It's a religious ritual," Graham Weisbrod said. Several Cabinet members chuckled, which made Heather add a few points to their Sycophancy Index, a statistic she'd been making up for some time; Allie, sitting at his elbow, laughed and rubbed Graham's arm.

Arnie flushed, and Heather beamed a thought at him: *Come on, don't let the bitch fluster you, she's trying to fluster you. You'll have a bucket of beer, and the kid and I will have some milk, and we will joke around about the Sycophancy Index over dinner, and it won't matter.* Arnie seemed to gather himself as if he could hear her. "So this will attract one of the EMP gadgets—whatever they are. From a robot's-ear view, I'll be the biggest and most obvious target this side of Jupiter. The toy telescopes that happen to catch the flash will burn holes in their construction paper, so the array will tell us about where the bomb went off, and the recording windup clock here can be coordinated with it."

"If you have the telescopes, why do you need the clock?" McIntyre asked.

"We coordinate them. The EMP will be a huge, unmistakable mark on the disk, but in the few seconds before it, we'll also be recording the echoes of the radio waves off the object, and with ten accurate chronometers scattered over a few thousand miles, we'll be able—using graph paper and a lot of hand calculations—to put together what amounts to one good radar image. We'll have its trajectory, and we'll be able to solve that trajectory backward and know where it came from.

"And here's the kicker. The AM modulator will work off a mechanical-disk recording device—"

"A record player, Arnie," Heather said. Even she couldn't help grinning at that one.

"Well, yes, it works just like an old-fashioned phonograph, and we'll be broadcasting that we are using this gadget to identify the source of the EMPs, over and over, and nothing else."

McIntyre nodded. "So if it's a real thinking enemy, or even

a medium-good artificial intelligence, it won't target our big transmitter—it'll hit something with more value, or hold its fire."

"Exactly," Arnie said. "But if it's just a machine, no smarter than a bug, as we think it is—well, then it'll go for the brightest light on the porch. And if it's just a machine, with no enemy in control of it anymore, then basically there's no war and we're just dealing with a leftover mine. No war."

Graham nodded. "Thank you for your clarity. So if your experiment works, we're facing a system artifact, not an enemy nation or organization—"

"Well, the experiment works either way. The result will either be consistent with a system artifact *or* with enemy action—"

Allie said, "We already *know* it's a system artifact, Arnie your research on that was *brilliant* and you did it back when you had real computers to work with. What we need is an experiment that *proves* it."

"Proving it is impossible," Arnie said. "All we can do is marshall more and better evidence. Even if results are completely consistent with a system artifact, it could be an enemy laying low by pretending to be a system artifact. And for that matter something that looks like conscious enemy action might be a system artifact getting lucky. So—"

"And you want to launch a project this big, and involve the illegal junta in it, when it doesn't prove anything?" Allie asked. She was sitting very close to Graham, who was looking down at the table. Heather thought, *I hope that means he's at least a little ashamed.*

Heather had tried to steer Graham into approving it without seeing the politics behind it, but that wasn't going to happen, so she waded in. "What Arnie is proposing is that we try an experiment, predict the results, and see what happens—and because the EMP will happen where we'll be watching we'll see more. It's not expensive, it mostly uses resources that were just going to crumble in the next few years anyway and besides if the government in Athens goes in on it with us and sends observers and scientists, then whether or not we get anything scientifically out of it, it ought to kind of get the ball rolling toward reconciliation."

"There's already been too many gestures of reconcili

tion," Allie put in. "If you ask me. Especially with Manck-iewicz publishing that so-called Pale Bluff Address that—"

"That you and I both heard Graham actually say," Heather said. "Don't forget that detail. Are you going to put *me* in jail for remembering it? Whether you approve of it or not, he said it, and it was a door to reconciliation, which—"

"Door to *surrender,*" Allie said, looking at McIntyre.

Weisbrod made a tent with his hands and stared into space. *God, I hope that means you're actually thinking and not trying to impress your aggressive little minion with what a thinker you are,* Heather thought, *and I wish I didn't have to worry about that. It just seems so unfair. I never had to worry about that before.*

"Well," he said, "if you could float the idea past Cameron Nguyen-Peters, through a back channel, then I'd say we wouldn't want to be the side that said no."

"But we're not quite saying we're going to do it, for sure."

"No, I guess we're not."

"Then what if they say the same thing?"

Weisbrod shrugged. "We'll consider that situation if it comes up. Right now we can just probe each other about it. My guess is that they won't want to run the risk of an experiment that is apt to bolster the system-artifact hypothesis." He smiled at her, and it was a moment where she saw the old Graham. "So I'm saying go ahead because I think we'll get some cheap propaganda points, and if they agree, we'll get some slightly more expensive propaganda points. Either way, we come out ahead, and I don't really think there's any risk of our being embarrassed." He glanced around the room and said, "Any dissent?"

He's not including Allie's pouting expression as dissent, Heather thought, *that's something.*

SIX DAYS LATER. OLYMPIA, NEW DISTRICT OF COLUMBIA. (OLYMPIA, WASHINGTON.) 7:15 P.M. PST. TUESDAY, FEBRUARY 4.

Because they did not dare use radio anymore, the fastest secure communication these days was via the Bubble Drop: letters written in pencil and wetted with disinfectant were sealed

in a glass jar with a nail tied to a piece of copper wire. The jar
was degaussed in the Big Ripper, as the Evergreen State physicist who had devised it had dubbed it—a generator-magnet-
coil system, driven by a weight descending on a line from a
six-story building. Whatever was inside the coil received
enough strong, shifting electric and magnetic fields to kill
most nanoswarm, and if any of them survived, the field and
current surges were enough to cause them to start breeding at
the junction of copper and iron. So if an hour after degaussing,
no white fuzz was growing where the nail joined the wire, the
bottle was pronounced sterile.

Then Bambi Castro, taking the Stearman on the down-
coast mail run to the nine Castles that were aligned with
Olympia, would fly the jar a hundred miles or so out into the
Pacific, loft a brightly colored paper kite on a five-hundred-
foot cotton kite string, and work downward until the plane
was just skimming the waves. At that point, she'd toss the jar
tied to the kite string, over the side, where it would drop into
the water and act as a sea-anchor to the kite.

The Stearman would head for land, and a Pacific Fleet
Navy helicopter, which had been watching from a safe distance upwind, would swing in at low speed and, using a
grapnel on a long rope, grab the kite and begin hauling up,
eventually bringing the jar to within a hundred feet of the
helicopter, where it would hang until it could be set down
on a ship's deck—not one of the precious nuclear vessels, of
course, but one of their still-functioning oil-fueled escorts.

On shipboard, they'd dip the jar in boiling water and
pass it to the carrier in a zipline package. From the carrier
it went into a parachute package in an F-35, to be dropped
on the golf course at Athens; the F-35 would go on to land
on a carrier with the Atlantic Fleet. The whole process was
awkward, but it emitted no radio waves, included a reconnaissance of the country, and posed relatively little risk of
contaminating the Navy's precious few remaining ships,
planes, and helicopters.

The return process involved a jar launched on a hot-air
balloon from the Georgia coast, snagged by a helicopter, and
walked through the same process, with one package of mail
eventually being dropped by parachute onto Gray Field at
Fort Lewis.

"And that's what's amazing about this," Arnie explained. "Cam must have written back within an hour or two of getting the message, which means he must have put everything together in that time. He's gotta be pretty serious about this."

Hello, everyone,

After discussion with the scientific staff, we've agreed that the experimental attempt to attract and study an EMP weapon (which we believe to be directed enemy fire, and you believe to be a sort of massive leftover Daybreak booby trap) would be thoroughly worthwhile. Given the damage certain to be sustained by remaining electrical systems in any location where this happens, we propose the former NREL experimental wind turbine development area at Mota Eliptica, about 150 miles east of Lubbock, would be a relatively harmless site that has adequate power generation and high-tension-line capacity; the construction and observation could be supervised from a main office in Pueblo, Colorado, where, as you note, there is already appropriate Federal office space, and it can be another joint activity under the Federal Reconstruction Information Service (or whatever we end up calling it) that we have already agreed to share.

Hopefully in the process we'll be able to locate and attract some surviving engineers and scientists from the many pre-Daybreak Rocky Mountain defense and scientific facilities.

We'll go halves with you on project cost and equipment; we're assembling a team of half a dozen scientists and engineers who will take the train overland to Pueblo as soon as we know you're coming as well. We'll be glad to have Dr. Arnold Yang as project leader; I trust his integrity completely.

Naturally we understand that you believe that the experiment will turn up evidence indicating that the device producing EMPs is wholly robotic. Obviously, we think something different will be the result. It seems to me that would be all the more reason to run the experiment.

A target date of June 30 for starting up the attraction device would give everyone time to install as much anti-

EMP protection as we reasonably can and to alert the
Castles and the independent cities.

We actually already have constructed a few crude
recording-radar sets (ones that make a paper record) very
similar to what Dr. Yang proposes, and we will dedicate
as many of them as we can spare to this project. I sincerely hope we will be able to cooperate on this issue, and
on many other issues in the future.

Warm regards,
Cameron Nguyen-Peters
Coordinator, Temporary National Government

"We know it has to be a trick," Allie said, glancing at Gra
ham, "so the question is what kind of trick. It looks to me li
they're turning it into military intelligence gathering, whic
means implicitly we're agreeing to get involved in their w
against the Unfindable Enemy. I don't know how we'll ba
out of this—"

Arnie said, "This is exactly what we wanted, and I do
see why we don't just accept it."

The room felt freezing cold, despite the big fire bu
against the February damp.

Softly, Heather said, "Graham, you said you didn't want
be the one who said no."

"And I don't," he said. "And I won't be. Make it happe
Arnie, you're the project leader—you'll be in the field; you
report to Heather, since she was already going to set up t
reconstruction research offices in Pueblo. Allie, this is o
where I'm not taking your advice. General McIntyre, fine
smart intelligence officer to send along so that whatever th
learn by working with us, we know that they learned it. Do
stop them and for god's sake don't sabotage the project, I
I want to know what they're getting out of this." He look
around the room with the face of a man who not only ca
please everyone, but can't please anyone. "That's a decisi
people; make it happen or show me why it's wrong."

When he left, a couple of minutes later, he was talking
tently with McIntyre; Allie was on his arm, *working it pre
hard,* Heather thought. *Meow,* she reminded herself. *But
glad to see her lose one, and if I'm a cat, she's still a bitch*

She felt something flutter as she stood, and instinctively
reached down to touch her belly.

"Kick?" Arnie asked.

"Big one."

"He's trying to tell us," Arnie said, "to get things in order
before he gets here."

She gave Arnie the raspberry, and the two of them went to
gossipy lunch; at least he seemed to be recovering from the
whole Allie mess nowadays, and a year or two down in Texas
playing with the physicists would probably mend whatever
was left of the crack in his heart.

But walking home, trying to get her mind on the little bit
of packing she needed to do, she couldn't help thinking that
Arnie had a point about putting things in order. The little
kicker gave her another feathery touch, and she thought, *Kid,
Mommy had better move you someplace before I get too big
and off-balance for the running, jumping, and fighting end of
things. Hang on tight; I think this ride might get a little wild.*

THE NEXT DAY. OLYMPIA, NEW DISTRICT OF COLUMBIA.
(OLYMPIA, WASHINGTON.) ABOUT 8:00 P.M. PST.
WEDNESDAY, FEBRUARY 5.

Graham Weisbrod looked tired and old in the flaring light
of the oil lamp; a Renaissance painter might have loved the
way the gold-yellow light flickered and played on his face, but
Heather was saddened by every wrinkle and sag. *This job is
eating him alive.*

Graham smiled as if it took an effort, but he seemed to
mean it. "Heather. God, thanks for coming. I need someone
to tell me I'm full of shit."

"At least *some* things haven't changed."

"Like a beer?"

"Um, I know I'm not showing yet, but—"

"Not showing and not European, either," he said. "How
about pineapple juice in a can?"

"Oh, that's better anyway."

"I know—I'm hoarding it—that's why I offered you beer
first!" He grinned, handed her a can from a cooler beside him,
and poured himself a glass of beer.

*Maybe he's his old self again. Maybe he called me here
talk about getting his act together.*

The pineapple juice was wonderful; she hadn't tasted a
in months and really hadn't expected to taste any ever agai
Graham looked pretty blissed at the taste of cold beer, as we
Finally, he said, "All right, I'm being a coward here, Heath
I have something difficult and painful to discuss, and I see
to have acquired several roomfuls of sycophants, not least th
First-Lady-To-Be."

"You're marrying her?"

His nod was curt and challenging.

"Congratulations." It seemed the best thing to say. "You'
been alone way too long."

He relaxed and extended his beer glass; she clinked it w
the canned juice, and they toasted something or other: frien
ship, or his marriage, or her avoiding the fight. Graham sa
"Somehow I never internalized the plain old truth that it :
ally *is* lonely at the top." He half smiled. "I need a real frie
to help me think straight about this thing in front of me."

Heather savored the last sip of pineapple juice, a cover
buy time to think. Maybe Graham was coming to the re
ization that he'd succumbed to the temptations of pomp a
power. She felt the baby kick. *Hey, kid, don't be cynical, le*
that to people who've been born.

Weisbrod ran his hand over the top of his head, mak
all the little white wisps stand up, in exactly the way the n
dia handlers used to take him to task about when he had f
come to DoF. "Well, it won't get any easier. Look, I'm gett
very worried about Arnie Yang. He came up with this exp
ment idea, which was fine as far as it went, and I though
might put some pressure on Athens, so of course I said to l
into it. Then they came back with a way to put some press
on me, fair enough, but it makes me wonder about Arnie–
he really . . . loyal?"

"Well, yes, he is."

"I just think, as we go into this next year and a half, we
got to be very careful not to give too much to the other side

Heather said, sharply, "And you think they're the ot
side."

"Well, we don't exactly agree on who's the government

"Yes we do—or we will if you and Cam both keep y

pid eyes on the prize. You're both caretakers. Your job is to
ep things together till the real government arrives. And the
al government of the United States isn't going to be elected
l twenty months from now, or take power until three months
ter that. You and the other caretaker are having coordina-
n problems. It's not a civil war unless the two of you decide
have one—and if you do, now *that* is disloyalty." She sur-
ised herself with her tone; *maybe I just don't like the idea
at I can be bought for a couple reminiscences about college
d a can of pineapple juice.*

"Have *you* changed your mind? Have you decided that Di-
tive 51 trumps the Constitution, too?"

*He isn't pulling off the et-tu-Brute/must you betray me with
iss act nearly as well as he thinks he is. Crap, now he's little
l lost King Lear asking me to prove I love him the most.*

She forced her voice to stay low and even. "Graham, we
ew Shaunsen *out* for suppressing a journalist. Now you've
ne it—the same one that Cam jailed—and you've all had
excellent reason that the country needed to be secure,
the leader needed to be secure, and after all this was just
ng to be temporary, and all that. I'm still in the intel loop.
now you're slowly moving troops forward, a station at a
e, along the transcontinental rail lines, and Cam's doing
same thing from the other side; you're both deliberately
ning the risk of having American troops killing other
erican troops to establish who gets control of Jesus Junc-
, South Dakota. We've already had a skirmish between
Army and the Marines. Cam is turning the Southeast
o one big Army base—"

"And I've sent letters of protest—"

'And you're turning the Northwest into one big social ser-
es bureau or maybe high school. You're both trying to nail
vn your pet things before the new government can make
decisions, sending every signal that they'll have to abide
the decisions you've pre-made for them. But *they'll be
ted*, unlike either of you, and *they* should make the deci-
s. That's how it works. The people are going to pick them
o what the people think should be done—not to carry out
er of your sets of expert professional *plans*. That is, *if you*
Cam even *permit* the elections, and I'm seriously doubt-
either of you will."

Graham looked like he'd been shoved backward agai[n]
the wall and was trying to breathe. *Well, good. Maybe I c[an]
hang out with Chris Manckiewicz in his cell.*

After a moment, Weisbrod took off his glasses and clean[ed]
them with a little glass atomizer and flannel rag from [his]
desktop. "I suppose that I can see how it can look that way [to]
you. From where I sit—"

"You're sitting in the most comfortable—not to ment[ion]
ego-stroking—job you've ever sat in. That gives you a gr[eat]
number of things, but perspective won't be one of them."

He set his freshly cleaned glasses down, blinking at h[er;]
it was one of his old manipulate-the-student tricks, and [she]
wondered if he'd forgotten that he'd admitted to her th[at]
since he wore bifocals, when he did that he did not see [the]
other person more clearly but only as a blur. Finally, sof[tly,]
he said, "Suppose that I were to try—fallible as I am, a[nd]
subject to my own opinion and judgment—but *suppos[e* I]
were to just *try* to achieve a regularly elected, fully emp[ow]-
ered government twenty-three months from now. Imagin[e]
that is my goal, what do you think I should do about A[llie]
Yang's constant backdoor communication with the . . . w[ith]
the other caretaker's part of the government? What do [you]
think I should do about the polarization and sense of stru[ggle]
that is building daily?

"You *don't* want me to try to bring Athens under our c[on]-
trol. You don't seem to be advocating that we surrende[r to]
them. And although 'unite in favor of the elected governm[ent]
that will replace you both' is a very nice sentiment in the l[ong]
run, I don't see that it tells me what to do this week. So le[t me]
put it squarely in your court. What should I do about the p[res]-
ent circumstances?"

"Start with what you're doing. Send Arnie and m[e to]
Pueblo, and give wholehearted support to the experim[ent,]
and if Cam is letting you have all those home-built rad[ios,]
thank him and ask him for all the data he gets." She le[aned]
forward. "Expand my mission to the GPO in Pueblo, ca[ll it]
something like the Reconstruction Information Developm[ent]
Center, some broad title that lets us throw our weight be[hind]
everything that can re-unite the country, and put us in ch[arge]
of getting every kind of information the country needs [and]
getting it to everyone who needs it by every means we [can]

Support us as much as you can and challenge the boys in Athens to give us even more support, but let us have our independence from both of you."

She had been surprised about her anger at Graham before, but she was double-surprised by her enthusiasm for an idea she had only thought of that moment.

He put his glasses on again, and said, "More beer for me. Do you want more juice? Pineapple again? Or I'm saving a couple small bottles of orange."

"Whichever you'd rather give me. I take it we're going to talk about the possibility of setting up what I have in mind for Pueblo rather than you pressing a button and bringing in people to straitjacket me and take me out the back way."

"Yes we are." He handed her another can of pineapple juice, opened a beer for himself, and said, "You're behind the times, by the way. If I wanted you arrested and taken out privately, there's no bell-and-buzzer system for me to use—too hard to maintain it. I've got a concealed string to a bell downstairs under my desk."

She held the can of juice up in salute. "Modern times."

"Modern times. May we get back to good old soulless technology as soon as we can." They both drank reverently, savoring the remnants of the old civilization. "Actually I like what you're proposing, but the name's got to change—that acronym would pronounce like *ridick*, which would be an invitation for puns on *ridiculous*. We'll call it the RRC, the Reconstruction Research Center—now there's a golden expression, that'll let you do anything. Anyway, a third power in the middle of the continent—one that has people's loyalty but not an army—could be an honest broker we could call in for misunderstandings, and not only do a lot of good, but do it in a way that caused people to attribute it to the federal government—basically build up a reserve of good will for that elected government in 2027. It would tend to keep Athens honest, and I'm sure they'd say it will help to keep Olympia honest. Maybe in the long run, it would be easier for both this government, and the Athens government, to gradually cede influence to it. I see many advantages. Futurologically—"

"Now that's an awful word."

"It was inevitable once we let *futurology* be coined." The

oil lamp was suddenly leaping high, casting bright flashes of red and yellow on his pale skin, and as he leaned forward and dimmed it, the swift-falling shadows cut deeply into his face until he seemed a million years old. She wondered whether any part of the effect was deliberate. "Look, here's the thing. Given a real choice, the human race *will* rebuild technological civilization; the knowledge is widely distributed and people know they want it. But the way Daybreak has hit us, very likely there won't be anyone left alive who really remembers our world by the time they're anywhere near being able to make it over again. And besides the biotes are alive and the nanoswarm might as well be; we can't exterminate them any more than we ever could cockroaches or rats. The new world will live with them all the time, one way or another.

"So the new world will have to have the idea that there can be a future, different from today, and that it can be better. A future that will be built more consciously, not because people are smarter or better, of course, but just because they're aware. So we're going to inject you—and a little band of ex-futurologists—into one of the early, nurturing streams of information where the new civilization will be taking root and growing. You'll . . . I don't know, *suffuse* it with the future-oriented perspective. I think that in the long run I will cast a longer, better shadow on history through that than I am apt to do through anything I do here—not that I intend to stop trying here." His smile was as warm, wry, and welcoming as she remembered. "Or in short, Heather, I'm going to play you the dirtiest trick of all. I'm going to give you exactly what you just asked for, and more."

"More?"

"You're right that the President of the United States has simply no damned business at all arresting and holding a journalist without trial, which is exactly what I've done with Chris Manckiewicz. Absolutely right about that, you know. But on the other hand, I can't let him run around loose in the capital, either. On the other hand, Pueblo is going to be the continental center for distributing information for at least the next few years; and we both know that the government ought not have a monopoly on information, eh? So I'm going to release Chris Manckiewicz into your custody . . ."

"Oh, crap," Heather said. "And he'll have the whole tra

trip to interview me." She clinked her juice can against his beer. "You're a treacherous old bastard, Prof."

"Let's just hope I'm an *effective* treacherous old bastard," he said, answering her toast.

They might have ended the conversation there, but they had drinks to finish, the lamp's glow was warm and friendly, and they were in more comfort and safety than they had been accustomed to, so they talked late into the night, almost none of it about business.

ONE MONTH LATER. ANTONITO, COLORADO. 8:30 P.M. MST. THURSDAY, MARCH 6.

Today had been an extra-long day; Jason had gotten up at the break of dawn for a day of assigned labor on the repair project for the rail line to Alamosa. When completed, it would give Antonito a connection through Walsenburg, over on the east side of the mountains, to the rest of the country. The newly organized Antonito and Northern Railroad (in which Jason proudly held nineteen shares of stock, one for each day he'd worked) should have restored the line so that a steam engine could run at speed over it by the end of the summer, and the enthusiasts up at the Railroad Museum in Golden thought there might be a locomotive they could use on it by then.

Meanwhile, filling and leveling a roadbed with picks and shovels was hard work, but it paid well, and Jason not only enjoyed the share-per-day program, he was thinking of trading five deer hides he'd cured for another two shares. *The price will go up a lot once the railroad is running, especially because by late summer the valley will be producing a lot more food than it eats, and the trains will have a good reason to come this way. Might as well buy stock while it's cheap; that's the time to do it.*

He imagined his brother, Clayt, laughing and clapping him on the back, and it felt good but sad; he wished his brother could be here to rag him about it.

Jason came home just as Beth arrived herself, fresh from a day of teaching textile crafts at Doc Bashore's school. Many adults wanted those classes, so they were offered late in the day, and Beth was rarely home before dark. They did their

usual hi-honey-I'm-home ironies as Jason lit the pre-laid large
fire in the woodstove; then he pumped three big kettles of water and set them on the back of the stove. "I've been working
on the railroad, all the live-long day," he said. "Hey, there's
a song idea. But while I'm thinking up the song, I want a hot
soak."

"Good plan. Soak some of that off and you might score
with a hot schoolteacher, especially if you let her take a quick
splash in the tub first, before it's half sweat from you." She
pulled down the pizza pan from the warming rack they'd built
over the stove; the dough had risen, and it would be ready
to bake as soon as the oven was hot, in about forty minutes.
Meanwhile, they each had a bottle of Coors—bottled beer
was fairly durable, especially in an unheated winter, and there
had been plenty of it in the area on the day of Daybreak—and
a slice of black bean bread with goat cheese. As the fire caught
and began to warm the small converted garage, they stripped
down to underwear for comfort, and Jason contemplated a
couple more beers; some elk, goat cheese, and home-canned
tomato pizza; and a hot bath, and thought, *Well, this is more
like what I had in mind for Daybreak. If I could ignore all the
corpses I guess I might feel all right about it.*

"Did you see the new *Weekly Pamphlet* down from Pueblo
today?"

"No, there's not a lot of reading time out there. Has someone come up with a way to make gopher meatballs taste
better?"

"The people in Pueblo are geniuses, Jason, but that would
take more than genius."

The Pueblo *Weekly Pamphlet* was widely mocked and de-
rided, and just as avidly read. Realizing that it might be a
long time before people could reliably write to request free information, and probably even longer before an old-fashioned
paper catalog could be prepared, the good scholars of Pueblo
looked for anything potentially useful in surplus in the warehouse, and once a week, sent out a pile of pamphlets in rough
proportion to the population of the towns that had subscribed.

The pamphlets were whatever happened to be possibly
useful in the America of today, and to take up too much room
in the warehouse of yesterday: how to hand-sew a shirt from
scratch without a pattern, how to maintain a compost heap

and so on. People had laughed when they received "Fun Indian Crafts for Boys and Girls 10–15" until they discovered it had directions on making moccasins. Some of the pamphlets must have been eighty years old—the one on laying out a victory garden probably was—and people laughed at the silly graphics and odd social assumptions of the past, but the pamphlets were read eagerly, passed from hand to hand, and their recipes and procedures recopied into notebooks; the interpretation of some of their directions could provide a whole evening of conversation nowadays. ("When they say to cull the runts in the baby rabbits, can we still eat them, just as long as we don't let them breed?"—Jason remembered two guys arguing about that for most of an afternoon while they dressed deer hides together.)

"This one's from the wrapper," Beth said. "So it's a bigger deal." Each bundle of pamphlets was tucked into the wrapper, a folded sheet of newsprint, on which were printed all the government announcements from both Athens and Olympia. They double-wrapped each package of pamphlets, since wrappers were printed front and back; the receiving towns posted the wrappers somewhere everyone went: the town hall if there was one, the general store for towns that had been able to maintain private commerce, the town dining hall for those which had not. People stood in line to read the wrapper with pencil and pad at hand; there might be any number of possible things, from a call-up of reservists for a particular year to the offer of a position of postmaster in a neighboring town. Decoding the wrapper was another source of conversation—did the search for former commodities investors mean that futures markets might re-open? Did the request for information about aircraft near Austin, Texas, mean enemy reconnaissance, an eccentric inventor, or an attempt to find a person maliciously spreading rumors? Did the request for desks and chairs in the Denver area mean some Federal offices would be opening there?

"So . . ." Jason said, "what's the news?"

"They want former Daybreakers to come to Pueblo and be studied. It says 'No one will be investigated, arrested, or punished.' They're looking for people who have turned against Daybreak and would like to help undo it."

"And that's us. If we want to do it."

"Yeah."

"How do you feel?"

"I love life here," Beth said. "I got friends, we got our own comfy place. And my wrist ain't all the way healed yet, and it's a long, hard, dangerous walk, and . . . but we said it, Jason, we said it ourselves, we said it all the time all winter, we said we wanted to undo Daybreak, it was all a big mistake."

He sighed. "Yeah. Well, for tonight it's hot fresh pizza and a hot bath."

"And a hot schoolteacher."

"You see what a lucky bastard I am. But, yeah, look how warm and comfortable we are. Life seems, I don't know, more meaningful, I mean, the work we do really matters to people we care about, and I kind of find myself thinking that maybe Daybreak was a good idea after all. Except for everyone we killed, of course. And all the sadness and physical misery and people dying too young."

"I can't even tell if you're being sarcastic."

"Me either. If the oven's hot enough, let's put the pizza in and open another beer. We're not going to decide tonight."

PART 4

ONE MONTH
AND TWO DAYS

pril has always been the month of danger in the Northern
emisphere; if you think of war, if you brood upon it all win-
r, if you are longing and thirsting to fight, then in April the
round is just dry enough to move upon, there has been just
1ough good weather to drill the troops, the danger of sudden
inter storms is low enough, the need for men for the spring
owing and planting has mostly passed.

In more recent centuries, late summer became dangerous,
:cause armies moved so swiftly that there was the hope to
1ish the fighting just as the snow fell and "send the boys
>me for Christmas."

But this year, almost nothing moved any faster than it had
1850, and as with so many things, the rhythm of war fever
Il back into its more ancient pattern.

From Pueblo, Heather and her team followed the bad news
at poured in from everywhere.

On April 1st, on the old Great Northern Line, a steam train
spatched by the Olympia government was intercepted on the
1g trestle east of Minot by pro-Athens partisans who were
least partly led by Air Force officers from the base. The
1in carried 250 newly-sworn-in Federal officials to be the
ison with the New State of Superior, which was supposed
combine the states of Wisconsin, Minnesota, and Michi-
n until they could resume their independent existences.
:e partisans' makeshift barricade derailed and destroyed
e precious steam locomotive, and in the brief confused
:lee after the wreck, about forty of the Olympian clerks and
ministrators were killed. Some witnesses reported injured
:n and women being shot where they were pinned in the
eckage. Three Olympians who had returned fire during the

brief fighting were hanged from the trestle. The rest were im
prisoned on the former air base.

Simultaneously, in Green Bay, the capital of Superior, th
Olympian temporary government was attacked by an arme
mob which purported to be defending the traditional right
of Michigan, Minnesota, and Wisconsin. Quick action by
company of Wisconsin Guard suppressed the mob. Amon
those captured were ten soldiers from Fort Bragg. Treate
as soldiers out of uniform on a sabotage mission, they wer
sentenced to death the next day, but the governor of Superic
suspended their sentences.

On April 4th, Alpha/2 of the President's Own Rangers a
rested the pro-Athens commanding officer and many of hi
officers at Mountain Home AFB, taking the survivors bac
to Olympia for a possible prisoner exchange—or a trial
necessary. The remaining personnel on the base were given
choice of "nine minutes to swear loyalty to Olympia, or ninet
days to walk to Utah."

On April 12th, forces from Fort Bragg, having come u
stream from Cairo, arrived in St. Louis and intervened in f
vor of the white-supremacist army to take control of St. Loui
thus severing the southern rail link between Olympia and t
New State of Wabash. Simultaneously, the Ranger Regime
(Reconstituted) from Fort Stewart took control of the thre
key independent cities in the mountains, which had refused
align with either national government: Chattanooga, Lexin
ton, and Louisville.

The white-supremacist triumph in St. Louis was sho
lived; once the city was firmly in Athenian hands, the wh
leadership was put on a sealed train and sent to firmly Olyi
pian Cedar Rapids. They were told to have all the fun th
wanted as long as they never came back; the mayor of C
dar Rapids jailed them, saying, "We'll think of a charge
it later."

On April 13th, in Lincoln, Nebraska, an Olympian po
master ordered the sorting room to pull mail addressed to
of the states that had declared for Athens out of the mailba
and leave it outside on the loading dock; on his own auth
ity he imprisoned two postal workers who refused to comp

On April 14th, Second Battalion, Third Infantry, a mec
nized unit converted to horse cavalry, was dropped off b

st steam train in Berthold, North Dakota, just after sunset.
t four in the morning they hit the compound on the former
inot AFB where the Olympian officials were held, rescu-
g all the prisoners, and leaving seven guards dead. On their
ay out, they torched two workshops and four experimental
anes under construction.

On the docks in Morgan City, Louisana, in early March,
avy officers loyal to Athens had attempted to commandeer
' *Polyxena*, a schooner from Monterey that had arrived caring forty tons of hand-canned orange pulp and fifteen tons
beets. The crew fought them, destroying the Navy's dinghy
d killing a lieutenant, and escaped with its cargo; the bank
Morgan City canceled payment. In Jamaica the citrus and
ets were bartered for marijuana, which was bartered in Ca-
as for beef jerky; *Polyxena* headed south, bound eventually
und the Horn. On April 16th, the Athenian government
ued a warrant for *Polyxena*'s crew for piracy and barratry;
Olympian government declared *Polyxena* to be under its
tection.

On April 17th, Radio Perth (Australia) was knocked off
air by an EMP; massive fusing systems in that city limited
damage, and fire crews were ready for the many small
s that sprang up around unused water pipes, electric ca-
s, guardrails, and wire fences.

On April 19th, Heather found herself facing two very un-
py factions of workers from the EMP Attraction Project.
er some jockeying and arguing, she identified the three
itical agents from Olympia and the two from Athens and
them onto the next available trains under guard. With each
ty, she sent a letter.

While the letters were on their way, on April 22nd, Cam-
sent a brief, coded radio message to the remaining car-
groups in the Pacific, ordering them to be prepared to
e Olympia; the Pueblo code room, which was now reading
sides' codes, decrypted it on the 24th. Heather hoped her
r might get to Cam within a day or two more.

She could tell that Olympia was reading Athens's code,
, because on the 23rd, according to a message which
hed Heather through the Reno pony express on the 25th,
ham Weisbrod authorized equipping four partially rebuilt
es, and twenty small boats with their experimental diesel

outboards, to carry two hundred pounds each of nanoswar
crystals packed in glass bottles. They sent a copy of the
der and photographs of the machinery being used to ma
nanoswarm—just a simple make-and-break electric coil, r
unlike an old-fashioned doorbell, powered by a windmill ge
erator—to Cameron Nguyen-Peters, via biplane to the neut
city of Hannibal, Missouri, where a fast train picked it up
delivery the next day.

On the 27th, Arnie told Heather that there was an immen
spike in communications traffic, including radio, to and fr
Olympia and Athens. "That's it," he said.

"How much time do we have?"

"At a guess, with the tech they use, and where I think
Navy carriers are, seventy-two hours before one side or
other jumps. But it could be less. They're racing each oth
the one that's ready to go all-out first probably wins."

Heather nodded. "Is your land line phone link up to
experiment? Could you send them something, and if you
dered them to broadcast it, could they do it?"

"Yeah, but you don't mean—"

"Can you power it up?"

"Yeah, but none of the instruments are in place yet and

"Well, then. All right. I'll build you another one, I pro
ise, with my bare hands, if big bad EMP cooks your exp
ment. But tell your scientists they can take any observati
they want as long as they get this sent *now*." She handed
a little folio of ten neatly typed sheets. "Can they record
the phone line?"

"That was always the intention, but they won't be ha
because this is all out of order."

"By which you mean—"

He shrugged, plainly unhappy himself. "We were go
to do a set of sequential tests, starting with raw noise
then ramping up until we were broadcasting outright a
Daybreak propaganda, and see at what point the EMP
Obviously if it's for random noise, it's a system artifact, ar
they won't hit us till we're screaming *Everybody kill a L
breaker and cut down a forest,* it's an enemy. This broad
if we were following the rules for the experiment, would
the *last*, not the first, one we would run, because it will d
fire for sure if anything can. But you know, we'll at least

et the observations that might let us figure out where the
ombs are coming from. And I hate to be practical and sen-
ble, but you're right. No point waiting to run better experi-
ents if we're about to lose civilization to an idiotic civil war
ght this minute anyway." Arnie looked down at the docu-
ent she'd drafted, leafed through, and whistled. "You're rely going for broke, here. Just to make sure, this is what you
tend?"

"Yep. Transmit at full power. Broadcast it in clear, then in
thens code, then in Olympia code, like a Rosetta stone, loop
e recording, and keep playing it till we get replies."

"All right, I'll phone Mota Elliptica and tell them to stand
, then wake up Manckiewicz—if he ever sleeps—and by
e time he's practiced, they'll be ready to record him. Just
e you asked. Probably we'll have it going out over the air
thin three hours."

"You still look pretty unhappy, Arn."

"I'll get over it." He let out a whew as if he'd run five miles
d barely made it in time, and Heather saw that he was re-
sing to tell her how big a sacrifice this really was—*which
ans he's convinced it is necessary too, and he's shutting up
avoid putting any pressure on me.* Arnie held his hands up,
lm out, in complete surrender. "Heather, it's the right thing
do. But we *are* throwing away an experimental protocol
t all my people worked very hard on, and I will have to
othe them about that, and of course this might not work."

"Sitting on our thumbs for sure won't work."

"Like I said, I hate being sensible and practical, especially
en it's the right thing to do. I better run; if we're doing it we
d to do it *now.*"

O DAYS LATER. PUEBLO, COLORADO. 2:58 P.M. MST.
NDAY, APRIL 29.

isbrod arrived first, in Quattro Larsen's DC-3. He looked
e the oldest man in the history of the world, exhausted and
, and for the first time she could remember, Heather saw
welcome in his eyes and no smile when she shook his hand.
here to?" he asked.

'By agreement, you each get a secretary, no guards, and

a side of the table in my office. You can rest and wait in a
adjoining room with a bed, bath, and food till Mr. Nguye
Peters arrives; we expect him this evening. I take it that t.
First Lady, here, is now your secretary?"

"You could be less sarcastic," Allie said.

"I could. You should hear me with Cameron."

Later that evening, Heather met the Black Express, the fa
unmarked steam train that carried Cameron Nguyen-Pete
to Pueblo.

She knew that both of them were men of honor; she h
not worried at all about the possibility of being seized or k
napped while meeting each of them.

The horse-drawn carriage, a replica stagecoach from so:
tourist spot, had been blacked out. When she, Cameron, a
the quiet young man who was to be his secretary were seat
Cam said, "This is very nearly blackmail and certainly tr:
ing on our old friendship."

"Graham Weisbrod said the same thing."

They rode quietly for a while. Cam peeked around
blind. "How are things out here?"

"Not bad. Rail lines are up and running to Austin and
buquerque, and even though there's not much Denver left,
connection's still there for east–west lines. Between that,
big post office, and the GPO, Pueblo will probably grow r
on trade."

"I can see why you would want peace."

"There's something selfish about preferring to be free
build and prosper?"

Cameron made a face. He bent forward, clenching him
as if he were in a straitjacket. "You always had a knack for
awkward question."

They said no more till at last the President and the Co
dinator sat across the table from each other in Heather's ir
office.

Heather said, "I appreciate your coming today. I kno
have traded on our past friendship, nearly blackmailed yo
and of course I have ensured that by broadcasting a Rose
stone version of your codes, if you weren't reading each o
before, you are now. So now I have you both at a table
don't care to be at. I'm just glad to see you here. And he
your special guest."

"Special—"

Chris Manckiewicz came in looking as if he were about to e hanged, except less comfortable.

Cameron leaped to his feet. "I didn't think it was necessary • say 'no press!' "

Graham rose almost as quickly, saying, "And neither did _"

Chris looked sicker than both of them put together. Heather has made me swear to absolute secrecy, and added at I can't publish until she gives permission or until twenty ears after both of you are dead."

"Nonetheless—" Cameron was packing his briefcase.

"I am not here as press," Chris said. "I may someday turn it to have been here as a historian, but that's not the point."

Weisbrod looked as if he'd been hit across the back with a t. He glared at Heather. "It does seem to me, looking back, at this is far from the first time you've manipulated me, and at my friendship for a lost, angry girl—"

"Is still appreciated more than anything in my life," eather said. "In so many ways, you are the man who taught e to think. Did you expect me to give it up?"

Chris said, "Perhaps if you explain what you have me here _—"

Heather said, "Sit down, both of you, and I will tell you at Chris is doing here."

Graham hesitated, shrugged, and sat, and Cameron has-ed to sit at the same time.

Heather smiled. "I should have realized I could depend on ur curiosity. Here we go. This is in the nature of an experi-nt, my dear friends. And I mean that. A day doesn't go by en I don't think about you sitting in your capitals, trying to :ide what you think is going to be right, worrying about the ilization that is resting in your hands, taking on a burden • big for anyone. A day doesn't go by when I don't worry •ut my old friends, and miss you both. Believe that or not, it's true."

Cameron's nod was barely perceptible; Graham's eyes re suspiciously damp, and he lowered his gaze to the table 'ront of him after whispering, "I believe you."

"So this is in the nature of a scientific experiment that I 1k has not ever really been tried, though philosophers have

been proposing it for thousands of years. Chris may or m
not ever be the historian of the moment; you might think
him as being more like your confessor here. He is here b
cause he tells stories well, and he asks questions well, and h
never been afraid of a follow-up; and because, in effect, h
not so much an expert witness as an expert at *being* a witne

"So . . . guys . . . I don't know if Chris will ever write t
history, but more than any leaders before ever have, this ev
ning you are standing before the bar of history. Chris is goi
to tell you some stories, ask for your reactions, and we w
do that for two hours—just two hours—and at the end of tl
time, you may talk to each other if you wish. And after tha
will give you the best meal we can manage in Pueblo and
you back on your way tomorrow."

"What sort of stories?" Cameron Nguyen-Peters asked.

"Why don't I just start?" Chris asked. "Coordina
Nguyen-Peters, President Weisbrod, let me explain that
my last few weeks, editing the *Pueblo Post-Times*, I've b
up quite a network of correspondent reporters, all over
country, and because I think it's important for people to
the habit of reading newspapers again, and truly nothing s
papers like good feature writing, I run a lot of features, stor
from my stringers about interesting people, places, situatic
I get many more than I can use, and I maintain a file of th
stories. So some of these will be familiar from the pape
you read it."

The significant pause stretched long enough for Grahar
say, reluctantly, "I read each issue as it reaches Olympia.
important to know what's influencing public opinion."

"I've read every word you've published, ads included," C
said. "Reading's always been what I do so I don't get lor
while I eat, or before bed."

"All right, then," Chris said. "So let me tell you about I
Bluff, Illinois. That's where Graham gave a speech on
way to Olympia that—no, Cam, you don't get to talk abou
Yes, I know you feel that he has not lived up to its princip
Just for the moment let's agree that it was a speech anc
gave it. Now let me tell you about something. Pale Blu
a divided town; a beautiful little town surrounded by ar
orchards, which local legend has it, quite incorrectly, v
founded by John Chapman—Johnny Appleseed. The

ноping to trade a few tons of apple butter and apple jam—
and maybe some apple wine—this fall to some other towns
nearby, for some things they need later on. Apples are sweet
food with a lot of vitamins and they keep well in cellars, so
they're something the country needs. And all the people in
Pale Bluff have all worked like absolute mules, you know, to
take in about seventy-five percent of their pre-Daybreak population in refugees, and find work and shelter for everyone.

"So today, it's not rich, and it's not an easy life, but there's
enough fish and game, and enough gardens, and lord knows
plenty of apples, with chickens and sheep and maybe goats
coming on line soon. There's a guy in town who's trying to
trap some live wild turkeys because the domestic ones need
too much care, and his idea is that if he can breed enough
live ones, there'll be something special for Thanksgiving and
Christmas, and everyone can at least have a few mouthfuls of
tradition, you know? Also, there's a little choir forming up,
too, because people miss music, and they've got some good
singers."

Graham sighed. "I remember all this. Carol May Kloster's
column is what I read for dessert, after I digest the hard
news stuff. I always enjoy her piece. May I ask, is this going
anywhere?"

"Just getting there. You see, when Quattro and his DC-3
landed on the highway there, it demonstrated that I-64 near
the village would make a good airfield. And with Pale Bluff
a center of operations, there's real potential for getting control of the whole lower Ohio Valley.

"And what I hear from Carol May is that there are quiet little meetings going on, people in Pale Bluff who favor Athens,
favor Olympia, getting together with like-minded citizens.
Right now they're talking about putting together political
parties for the elections in eighteen months. But you know,
if the war starts . . . my guess is you each have an agent or
two in those little clubs, and that in certain circumstances,
you would tell that agent to start some trouble, between all
those neighbors who have sweated and worked together all
that time; oh, say, think maybe of two workmates that went
through the whole hard winter arguing politics together . . .
and now you're putting it on course for one of them to murder
the other. And maybe you should think about their daugh-

ters being best friends, too, you know? But then after a few murders and some burnings, and a few hearts broken forever, well, one of you would get control of Pale Bluff. And the first thing you would do, to make it defensible, is to clear the cover around that village. That would be those orchards, you know. Regrettable of course, good-bye apples, but you have to do what you have to do.

"So that was my story, and here's my question. Exactly what can you gain in the war that would be worth a dozen or so murders and burnings in that little town, and cutting those orchards down, so that soldiers could come in and throw out the families and fortify the buildings? Cameron?"

"I see the point and it's a well-taken idea—"

"No, I wasn't looking for a review. Pale Bluff might be your key to controlling the lower Ohio Valley. Now just explain why you must control the lower Ohio Valley, eh? What's it for?"

Cameron looked down at the table. "I suppose if I don't answer it will look even worse."

"I have no opinion on how it will look. I'll probably write the story, and only the people in this room will see you. Though of course many of us are your old friends. I like think all of us are, actually."

Cameron Nguyen-Peters sighed. "All right. If we can gain the Ohio Valley this summer . . ." He shrugged. "All right this is your point, of course, it doesn't have much to do with apples or choirs or little girls who are friends."

"It's your call, Mr. Coordinator. But can't you draw the line? Aren't you willing to say that the benefits of a united country, when we're getting ready to fight the war for our survival, are just too important—that yes, it's sad that two kids can't be friends anymore because one of their daddies knifed the other one for the greater good?"

"If we're occupied and conquered—"

"Do you believe there's a force remaining on Earth that can come to this country and do that, right now? But let me ask that hard question in an even harder way—those people in Pale Bluff—how much of their orchards, which is what they depend on for food and prosperity, and how many of the houses they've labored to make work in this new world without gas or electricity, and how much of the society they constructed—how much of that should go down the toilet so that you can control the Ohio and parlay that into controlling the country?" Cameron started to answer, but Manckiewicz said, "Your question this time, Mr. Weisbrod."

Weisbrod said, "It's the old professor in me, or maybe Cameron is a better man than I. I can at least make myself say that as a matter of principle—as a matter of principle, I don't like having to answer that question. But I can see why you asked it. Apparently my principles are no stronger than Cam's; perhaps I am a better man than I thought."

Heather could see Allie was about to pop with rage, and moved to sit beside her. *I've arrested presidents in my day, clocking a First Lady would just be dessert.* The silence wore on as the two leaders sized each other up with new eyes, neither quite willing to be the man who said, *Yes, on my head be it.*

"In some dumb book I read as a kid," Chris said, "someone said that people who put principles before people are people who hate people. All right, another question: Did you happen to read Cassie Cartland's piece about the re-opening of the schools in Pueblo, and the way everyone turned out to see high-school kids running footraces? Now, you probably have never heard this, but Pueblo is a city of heroes. More Medals of Honor earned per capita than any other city in American history; if there's time tomorrow I could show you the monument, right across from where they had the finish line for the 0k. I have to say, you should have seen how seriously those kids run, how much it means to them to be in school, and that, you know, we think of ourselves as one of the places that is re-inventing civilization, and the honor of their school actually *means* something besides a fund-raising slogan. Cassie's at that school herself, and so's her boyfriend, by the way. Does either of you have a principle important enough to blow the legs off one of those boys, or blind one of those girls, or kill one of them by turning them into a mess that they couldn't be recognized by their mothers? You know—those women in the bleachers that Cassie was so funny and warm-hearted about? Got any principles so strong that you could justify having them all do that to each other?"

"Now, wait a minute," Graham said, taking off his glasses in his favorite dramatic gesture. "This is the classic move of

pitting ordinary private feelings of personal decency agains
serious and important ideas that apply to the general good of
the world as a whole—"

Chris was emphatically shaking his head. "Which is made
up, among other things, of kids and mothers. So if a few
mothers lose a child or two—or send a kid off to war and get
a murderer back—"

"That's just what I mean, a killing in war is not murder—"

Chris looked up at him with the mildest of expressions
and said, "You know, Roger Pendano died in a firefight over
principle, which, I seem to remember, was vitally important
And by that time he was an old broken man who really jus
wanted to die. And was it worth it to prevent Shaunsen from
ruining the nation?"

Cameron started from his thoughts. "I—well, yes, I d
think so. Pendano knew the risks, he was mature, he wa
ready to die . . . and we're talking about the whole future of
great country . . ."

"Mr. President, you knew him well, he was your frien
for thirty years. Was the country worth the cost of the man?

"I'd say . . . yes. Yes it was."

"Would it have been worth it when he was twenty-one?"

Weisbrod glared. "This is going to be a long two hours."

"Coordinator Nguyen-Peters was brave enough to try ar
answer. Are you?"

"Oh, Christ on the cross, how many times do I have to loc
at some life or other, some kid eating ice cream or a fath
holding a baby or somebody putting a roof on his house ar
say, over and over, 'Yes, I'd kill him for my ideals'? I get
I understand what you are driving at. I might even concede
Graham said, cleaning his glasses, "that, well, yes, all rigl
All the fuck right. You are right. It does *not* make me pro
of myself to say, 'This man has to lose his life, and his fami
has to go hungry, and that other family must be without t
shelter of the house they worked like hell to put together, ar
both families' sons must kill each other . . . and say that i
that has to happen just so we can establish that the Successi
Act of 1947 takes precedence over Presidential Directive :
And it would *suck* to be that man's little boy, and that kille
brother. There. Yes, I said it—"

"And did you mean it and believe it?"

"I—well, I guess—I said it. I can act like I mean it. And I have to think it's the right thing to do."

"What if you had to say that to that man's little boy?"

"Lincoln managed to write the letter to Mrs. Bixby."

"Dr. Weisbrod . . . are you Lincoln? And is the issue slavery?"

"The issue is a house divided."

"Which could come back together in just about two years—if there's not too much blood between the people by then," Heather said. Everyone stared at her. "Sorry, I'll shut up."

"It is indeed a day for miracles," Cameron said, quietly, and then Graham laughed, and even Chris did.

"Let me suggest something," Chris said. "When Heather suggested this to me . . . well, what reporter can resist asking the questions of history? And all right, we've determined that I can make you both very uncomfortable—"

"Because war is wrong," Cameron Nguyen-Peters said. He was no longer looking away, but at all of them, each individually. "Because like it or not you always end up making all those horrible decisions. Which you can always make . . . *always* . . ." He seemed to be finding anger somewhere deep within. "Decisions you can always make by just making them in words. The principle of proper Constitutional succession is important enough to send soldiers who are stressed out of their minds and literally driven mad into an area where no one is watching them, where they may catch a mother and her ten-year-old daughter, and rape them in front of each other and leave them with their throats cut for the family to find later.' And shit like that *happens* in civil wars; it's the kind of thing that happens with half-trained troops that get thrown into battle, see their friends killed, rebuild their whole minds around hate. If you just think in words you can say, 'Sorry, too bad for that little girl, must be hard on her mother to watch that, kind of tough on the soldiers to live with that afterward'—but when you start to think about, oh, that the little girl smiles like nobody else in the world ever did before or will again, or that she and her mother have a favorite joke that only the two of them know . . . Heather, this wasn't a *bad* idea, but I'm not sure the world is ready for it."

"Can't find out if the world is ready if we never try it," Heather said.

Graham laughed sadly, and said, "Twenty years after telling me, screaming at me really in my office, that it didn't make any sense, my favorite student adopts Gandhian futurism."

Cameron looked the question at Graham.

The old professor pushed his glasses up his nose and explained as if an undergrad had asked an obvious question. "Gandhi pointed out that one of the most important lessons of history is that many things happen that have never happened before. So just because something never happened or never worked or people weren't ready . . . well, next time could be different."

"Like Daybreak," Cameron said softly.

"We've only been talking half an hour," Chris said. "And I am looking at two guys who don't look to me like they want a war."

"We didn't, exactly, before," Graham said, sounding very unsure.

"Or we didn't want to face it," Cameron said. "If it's all right with you, Graham, I'd like Chris to read us more stories. And ask us more questions. If we really need to have a war . . . considering how terrible it will be for other people—shouldn't we be able to face an unpleasant hour and a half? I mean, actually, we should have to face a lot more, but—"

"Agreed. That we should have to face up to what we're doing, I mean. I don't think I'm eager for this. But I think you're right, we should."

In the next hour and a half, Chris introduced them to forty or so Americans, post-Daybreak, and Heather thought he'd never been better, not on television, or radio, or even in print. *He probably figures lives are depending on it. Must be good to work like lives are depending on you.* Chris drove on—how many victims in the crossfire would be worth it to make a given statement? how many burned libraries? how many men with hideous crimes in their memories for the next fifty years?

"The dogs of war," Graham said after a while. "Cry havoc and let slip the dogs of war. That's what Shakespear was talking about, that once you let them loose, they get . . . excited, they bark each other into a frenzy, they want to do more and more . . . they're only safe on a leash, never when turned loose. Not even when you *must* turn them loose, an of course, Cam, if there is a surviving Daybreak out there for us to fight, we *will* have to turn them loose. But whenever you do, the dogs of war will tear up whatever they can get—your enemy, sure, but everything else too . . .and to turn them loose on a friend, or a relative, or someone who is just trying to do the right thing by their own lights . . ."

They let the question hang while Chris pushed them again, making them think about how long it takes to put a railroad line together with hand tools, and how little time it takes to put a hole in it; then about what it must feel like to be on the road, walking away from the home where you had everything, where you'll never return, and with no idea where you're going to go. And they talked about the strange power of words—not just the little holes and gaps in the Constitution, but the slippery points in every principle and idea, in every story all people tell themselves—

The lights went out; everyone froze, and Heather walked to the window, leaned out, and said, "Power off everywhere, that I can see." She shouted to a runner downstairs.

A few minutes later, they had a radio that had been stored in a Faraday cage, and Heather was trying to raise Arnie at the research facility at Mota Elliptica.

The response came almost at once; he too had pulled out a bare radio from a shielded cage. "We *got* 'em," he said. "We *definitely* got 'em. We had a great big EMP here, and Cam's radars worked, we have a trajectory from just before it went off."

"And have you traced it back?"

"Well, that's the weird part," Arnie said. "Um."

There's no place so terrible that I won't be relieved to know it is where the enemy is. "Where did the bomb come from, Arnie?"

"It entered at escape velocity almost straight down, boss. So we don't exactly know where it came from—"

"Damn, can you narrow it down?"

"Well, that's what I'm trying not to say. We sure can. On that trajectory the one thing we know for sure is it didn't come from Earth."

Cam leaned forward. "Could it have come from the moon?"

"That would be my first guess," Arnie said. "But definitely not from Earth."

After they signed off, Chris said, "Well, your two hour expired, a while ago, but . . ."

"But we've established that whether it's an enemy or a left over booby trap, it doesn't want us to make peace, and we would like to," Cameron Nguyen-Peters said. "Shall we, Graham?"

"We shall." Graham Weisbrod seemed to sit straighter, and some of the age seemed to fall off him. "I don't know wha we're facing either, but whoever or whatever it is, I'd mak peace just to spite it."

Chris glanced up from the notes he was making. "And i that the only reason?"

"No, not at all," the two leaders said, in unison, an laughed like any two men sharing a coincidence.

TWO DAYS LATER. BEGINNING AT MIDNIGHT. WEDNESDAY, MAY 1 (KNOWN AS OPEN SIGNALS DAY EVER SINCE).

It was a world of crystal sets and home-built antennae, b now. Most people did not have radios, but nearly everyor had a friend who was an inveterate listener. The EMP on Ra dio Perth had put an end to high-power continuous broadcas ing, but stations slipped on and off the air in short burst and radio stations on sailing ships were beginning to mo out into the world's oceans. Radio Free Pacific broadcast tv or three hours of English or Japanese at irregular interval Mostly it broadcast stories from the *Pueblo Post-Times*, or few coastal papers in North America; now and then it broa cast grim eyewitness reports from the Asian coast. Once it ra an hour in Russian about a town in Kamchatka that seeme to be doing well.

The hobby radio listeners were people who couldn't slee or had to stay awake, or were blessed somehow with tir off. None of them could be sure when one or another stati would open up for an hour or two on some frequency or oth so there were listeners at all hours hoping to find some ne that would make the bearer the center of attention. The rest the people counted on the obsessive listeners to fill them knowing that if anything interesting came over the airwav Rosa down the road, or Ivan who lived over the bar, would delighted to tell them all about it at the first opportunity.

There were many stations, of course, that broadcast endless strings of numbers, or phrases from books, or several that broadcast strange, incomprehensible gibberish from some scrambler system. Those tended to be on the air even more briefly.

As midnight began on May 1st, several of the garbled stations began to broadcast in plain English. They gave passwords and authentications, and then, addressing agents and military units by code names (it had been decided that it would be neither fair nor desirable to use real names), they gave order after order to stand down, back away, undo the sabotage, release the prisoners, pull back to base, move back from the precipice. Radio TNG in Athens directly ordered the Pacific fleet to move out of striking range of Olympia. Radio Olympia ordered the destruction of the bottled nanoweapons and of the nanomakers. Hostile troops within short distances of each other were ordered to make contact under flag of truce and arrange for mutual peaceful policing of their areas; known political prisoners were ordered released.

As morning worked its way around the world, people were awakened by their radio-hobbyist neighbors, and as they heard the news, huge crowds formed around nearly every station and listener.

The *Pueblo Post-Times* brought out its first extra, and Chris dropped by Heather's office. "Not one confidential word divulged," he said, setting down a stack of copies. "No need for it. The headline and the story are too good to clutter up with unnecessary intrigue, anyway."

Heather looked down; a picture of Cam, from some official document somewhere, was juxtaposed with one of Weisbrod from the inauguration. Both were smiling, and by mirror-reversing Graham, Chris had made it appear they were smiling at each other. Above them the headline said only,

PEACE!

THE NEXT DAY. PUEBLO, COLORADO. 11:00 A.M. MST. THURSDAY, MAY 2.

"I've wanted all my life to begin a speech with 'I suppose you're wondering why I've called you all here,'" Heather said. "Let me explain who we are, and then who we really are, and let me tell Chris in front of all of you that in order to have a chance to hear this, he had to become one of us, and that means he is bound just as much by his oath as the rest."

She looked around the room, and said, "This is the first official meeting of the governors of the Reconstruction Research Center. Both the Temporary National Government in Athens and the Provisional Constitutional Government in Olympia want me to remind you that we are funded and supported by both governments. The official minutes will show that we sat down, talked about our jobs, had lunch, and adjourned. Please *read* the official minutes Sherry gives you because we all want to tell a consistent story.

"Unofficially, over here in reality-land, kids, this is the story." She looked around the room and smiled. "We're going to put our country back together. We're going to put civilization back on its upward track, in technology of course but also in decency, justice, and living together in peace and freedom—and in whatever it is we need to understand about the Daybreak event to ensure nothing of the kind happens again.

"Bambi Castro, Larry Mensche, Quattro Larsen—you're my senior field agents. I will say go find this out, go do this and you will. And I know it'll get done. We'll be recruiting what amounts to a small army of people to work for you; think about what kind of people you want, what they have to be able to do, and what you want them to know, because to the limit of my resources, they will be recruited and trained exactly you say.

"Leslie, James—you're my information people."

"Librarians," James said. "To be a librarian for this operation is to be at the heart of it, and I'm proud to have the title."

Leslie added, "I promise I won't start dressing frumpy it'll make you feel better."

Heather nodded. "You'll also have all the resources and people I can find for you; your job is twofold. One, preser

nd correlate everything the field agents, scientists, and who-
ver else learn about our strange new world; two, find out
hat the world needs to know and make it available. Neither
b will be easy—"

"But we will love both of those jobs," Leslie said.

"I'll hold you to that." Heather nodded to Chris Manckie-
icz. "You are not the first, nor will you be the last, suppos-
lly independent news source to be subverted. I will try to
e only truthful propaganda and to muscle the *Pueblo Post-
mes* around only as much as necessary and only for good
ds. We can be sure my success will be imperfect; your most
portant job may be to forgive me.

"That brings us to Dr. Arnold Yang, officially our direc-
of research, nominally the supervisor of Mota Eliptica,
d actually our specialist in Daybreak itself—what it was,
whether it still exists in some form, how to defeat it, how
build the counter-Daybreak if we need it. And he'll be as-
ted by Izzy Underhill, here." *Keep reminding myself not
call her Roth.* "Izzy's pretty quiet, but Arnie assures me
t most of the information we have about Daybreak traces
ectly to her."

"So that's what we're really doing. Any questions?"

"Do you think we'll undo Daybreak in our lifetime?"
rry asked.

"Undo it? If you mean, it will be like it never happened—
er. If you mean, get back to the same technical level, I
't know, but I know we'd better start."

Arnie asked, "You don't really believe that Graham and
m will keep their word perfectly, do you? I know we'll have
ple out in the field to watch them, but for right now, don't
think it's pretty likely that both of them are cheating just
tle, here and there, on an a-little-won't-hurt or technically-
-is-in-bounds basis?"

"I'm sure that's happening," she said. "Furthermore, both
hem will be having trouble getting some of the underlings
comply. And we'll be nagging them all the time about it.
d the next people in their positions will almost certainly
have the sort of scruples and be as sentimental as they
." *For example Allie would've stared Chris down with all
sympathetic expression of a rattlesnake, and gone right
ad. And it's not just her, there's fifty more of her at Olym-*

pia and fifty more at Athens, any time we want to see then
"But for right now, luckily, this country really doesn't want
civil war, and Graham and Cam don't have the heart to pu:
them into it. Give most of our people a world where they ca
comfortably make their own way, and not think too mu(
about abstractions, and a lot of people will find a way to k
happy. That is what we have to count on.

"No, we haven't removed the prospect of war, and v
haven't made real peace yet. But we've given people at leas
summer away from it, and then it won't be fit fighting weathe
and after that, well, the horse may talk. So I'm not going
despair because we haven't solved all the problems or ma
Right the Eternal Victor. As far as I'm concerned, we've ju
won a big victory for a lot of things I believe in, that I thi
most of our people believe in: good home cooking, com
clean houses, honest work you get paid for, making thin
easier for the kids than they were for us, letting your neight
go to the devil in his own way, and some time on the ba
porch to read the paper and drink beer and argue with r
neighbors."

Izzy cleared her throat. "You know, that's kind of a Di
break image."

She shrugged. "It's kind of a Daybreak world. I don't l
it, but they won, and we have to admit it. We're stuck
ing the Daybreak program for some decades or centuries;
might as well live it fat, prosperous, peaceful, and conter
She stood, enjoying once again the subtle shift that her b
ance had taken. "And speaking of fat and content, I'm ab
to go enjoy eating for two. Anybody want to come along ;
help celebrate peace? You too, Izzy, my treat till we regular
paying you."

The young woman was still quite shy, but she nodded ;
seemed pleased to be included, especially once she knew t
Bambi and Arnie would be coming along. The four of th
strolled out into the pleasant Rocky Mountain spring, mo
just enjoying a day with less fear than they had had in a l
time.

Heather heard the running feet behind her and the habit
a lifetime kicked in; she turned and crouched, ready to fig
The two young people running after them froze.

It was a couple in their early- to mid-twenties, a man v

mountain-man beard and long brownish hair, and a young woman with longish red hair, a pleasant, chunky Earth-mother figure, and large brown eyes. Each wore trousers and belted jacket that was probably copied from a karate gi, with thin underjacket and a heavy outer one—the coarse fabric was probably home-woven—and low moccasins. Scanning automatically for identifiers in case she ever needed them, Heather noted that the young man was deeply tanned—*he must work outside*—and the woman's left hand hung a little funny, as if she were wearing her wrist wrong.

"I'm sorry we startled you," the young man said. "Back your building they sent us running after you. My name's Jason, and this is Beth, and back at the office we were told to say we had a Code Fourteen Matter for you—"

Code Fourteen. Heather almost whooped; two heavily involved former Daybreakers for Ysabel and Arnie to study. Two more chances to see to the bottom of this.

"We were just going to lunch," Heather said, "and it's a special enough occasion that I feel like taking people to lunch, so why don't you come along. Have you seen the newspaper today?"

"Peace," Jason said. "Yeah. That's so great."

"Well," Heather said, "Dr. Yang, here, will be one of the main people you will be talking with, along with Ms. Underhill."

Ysabel smiled nicely. "Call me Izzy. Everyone does, or they will if I tell them."

Since "Code Fourteen Matters" could not be talked about in public, instead the group spent some time getting to know Jason and Beth, who, it turned out, had been living a carefully anonymous life in Antonito, until they had spotted the ad in the *Weekly Wrapper.* They seemed likeable enough, and after lunch, Arnie and Ysabel took them off for their first extended interview.

"Well, that's more progress," Heather said. "Surprising how much of that there's been lately. I almost feel like I'll be able to take my maternity leave with an easy conscience."

"Shh," Bambi said. "Murphy hears us."

"Oof. And so apparently does the kid who just kicked me. Hey, little person, don't be too eager to get out here; we're not going to be ready for you."

. . .

As they settled into the room where they'd be staying whi
Arnie and Izzy debriefed them, Beth observed, "I wasn't su
we were doing the right thing, and now I feel sure we are."

"Ha. You're just as tired as I am of manual labor."

"Well, yeah, a bed and meals just to be hypnotized, ar
talk and talk and talk—that's a pretty good deal," she admi
ted. "There's hot showers here you don't gotta chop no woo
for, baby. How freakin' cool is *that*?"

"I may never come out until I'm one big wrinkle."

"Let's take our showers together, then, so we share a
there is. I'll wash your back if you'll wash mine."

Later, after they had made love and cuddled up in t
strange bed, Beth said, "Even with peace, and being that w
found our way here, and everything, I'm still kinda scared."

"About what?"

"Just that it's different." She turned to press against h
more firmly, and said, "But I'll get used to it, baby, I'll get
brave. Besides, it's kind of cool that the big leader-lady he
what's her name, that big lady with the auburn crew cut—"

"Heather."

"Yeah, Heather, it's cool that she's totally pregnant. Mea
she thinks there's hope, don't you think?"

"Babe, of course there's hope. This is America."

AFTERWORD

residential Directive 51 is real, but despite what you may
:ad on the web, it is probably *not* anything to fear. The un-
assified part of Directive 51, like its predecessors, specifies
hat we will do in case of "decapitation"—sudden destruc-
n of the top echelons of the Federal government.

President Bush signed it into existence in 2007, replacing
e Clinton Administration's Directive 67 (1998), which re-
aced George H. W. Bush's Directive 69 (1992) and Directive
' (1990). The earliest continuity-of-government directive
1ose existence is public seems to be Reagan's Directive 55
982). It is believed that the first continuity-of-government
licy may have been issued as a classified executive order in
47 or 1948 by President Truman.

To his credit, George W. Bush was the first president to
ake any substantial part of a continuity-of-government di-
ctive public. All continuity-of-government directives prior
Directive 51 remain entirely classified. Much—we citi-
ns don't know *how* much—of Directive 51 itself is clas-
ied, on grounds that an enemy who knew our national
rvival plans prior to an attack would be in a position to do
1ch more harm.

By its nature, continuity-of-government planning violates
e separation of powers, which, you probably learned in high
1ool, is a cornerstone of Constitutional government. The
nstitution gives Congress the power to determine the suc-
:sion to the presidency, and puts the President or his subor-
1ates in charge of carrying out the will of Congress.

But Congress cannot know which of the president's officers

would survive a decapitation attack, what resources would b
available, or what the situation might be. Therefore Directiv
51, like every succession directive or executive order before i
provides that in case of an unprecedented disaster, a specifi
Federal official will become a temporary dictator, with near
unlimited power and a mission to restore Constitutional go
ernment as quickly as possible. The person on whom th
terrible responsibility might fall is to be called the Nation
Constitutional Continuity Coordinator, or NCCC. We do n
have an NCCC as I write this; the office exists *only* if th
worst has already happened, a practical precaution so that th
NCCC cannot take power arbitrarily.

Directive 51 designates the person in charge of assumi
power as NCCC after a disaster; at the moment I write thi
it is to be the Chief of Staff of the Department of Homela
Security. In normal times, this is the person who ensures th
DHS personnel are assigned to appropriate duties and coo
dinates things like high-level meetings and major long-te
projects. The reason for designating the DHS Chief of Sta
as the NCCC-in-waiting is that the job entails:

1) a very high security clearance

*2) extensive knowledge of security/military/police/
intelligence operations in progress, and*

3) no direct responsibilities during an attack.

Or in short, this is the person who knows the most wh
having the least to do; the best-informed person we can affo
to send out of Washington just before the nuke goes off or
gas is released. In all probability, the NCCC-in-waiting w
be the holder of some different office by the time you re
this—presidents change and there are innumerable reas
for designating one office or person rather than another—
the general principle of the best-prepared, least-essential p
son has been followed for at least a quarter century.

Like any imaginable continuity-of-government policy,
rective 51 gives the NCCC the power to decide and do whate
is necessary without check or balance. Our only protect
against the obvious potential for coup, corruption, suppress
of all our liberties, deliberate aggressive war, concealmen

igh crimes, and other abuse up to and including the abolition
f the Republic is the honor of the individual designated as
ie NCCC, the good faith of the surviving Federal officers,
nd the commitment of the American people to Constitutional
overnment.

ACHNOWLEDGMENTS

his book would have been much less fun to write without
ccasionally being able to run ideas past my small coterie of
rmchair strategists: John E. Johnston III, Trent Telenko, Tom
olsinger, John Ringo, Mike Robel, Kevin O'Donnell Jr., and
ck Greene. I would particularly like to thank Rick Willett
r an extraordinarily thorough and accurate rescue of the
xt, and Michelle Kasper for wonderful patience in allowing
m the time and space in which to do it. I also received much
lp from some other people who prefer, for a variety of good
asons that I must respect, not to be acknowledged by name.

JOHN BARNES is a multiple Hugo and Nebula award nominee and the author of *The Return* with Buzz Aldrin. He lives in Colorado.

Look for the new novel in the Daybreak series
by award-winning author

JOHN BARNES

DAYBREAK ZERO

*A year has passed since the catastrophic event
known as "Daybreak" began.*

- 9 months since Daybreak killed seven billion people

- 8 months since Daybreak vaporized Washington, DC

- 6 months since rival governments emerged in Athens,
  Georgia, and Olympia, Washington

- 4 months since the two governments of what was formerly the United States were on the brink of war

- 3 months since war was (barely) avoided

- 2 months since Athens and Olympia agreed to work
  together

- 1 month since the survivors discovered that Daybreak
  isn't over . . .

Praise for

DIRECTIVE 51

"The tension level is high, the big ideas will make
you think, and I was kept up all night."

—S. M. Stirling, *New York Times* bestselling author

An exciting debut novel
from author Joan Frances Turner

DUST

*What happens between death and life can change a girl.
Jessie is a zombie. And this is her story . . .*

"*Dust* is a thoughtful, poignant, and frightening book about the
dead. It is a truly original idea told from a viewpoint that will
surprise and horrify, and may make you change sides in the
next war between zombies and humans."
—Laurell K. Hamilton, #1 *New York Times* bestselling author of
the Anita Blake, Vampire Hunter novels

"*Dust* is spectacular. Not because it's about zombies and gross
as hell, not because it leaves the genre in its 'dust,' but because
it's such a great, unsettling portrait of raw hunger and hope.
What George Romero started with *Night of the Living Dead*,
Joan Frances Turner finishes with *Dust*, an undead romp among
American ruins."
—Jeff Long, *New York Times* bestselling author of
Deeper and *The Descent*

"*Dust* is an amazing novel! Joan Frances Turner has done
for zombies what Anne Rice did for vampires. With wit, fine
writing, and psychological nuance, she has created a compelling
alternative reality, populated with sympathetic characters, in a
gripping story that is guaranteed to interfere with your sleep."
—Douglas Preston, *New York Times* bestselling coauthor of
Gideon's Sword and *Fever Dream*

penguin.com